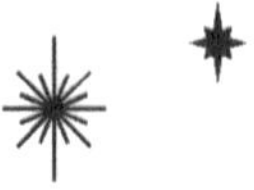

The NEBADOR series:

Book One: The Test

Book Two: Journey

Book Three: Selection

Book Four: Flight Training

Book Five: Back to the Stars

Book Six: Star Station

Book Seven: The Local Universe
2013

Book Eight: Witness
2014

Also by J. Z. Colby:

Standing on Your Own Two Feet:
Young Adults Surviving 2012 and Beyond

an epic young-adult science fiction adventure

by

J. Z. Colby

Trilogy Global/Library Edition:
the complete text of NEBADOR Books Four, Five, and Six,
all illustrations,
and chapter-by-chapter Deep Learning Notes

Nebador Archives

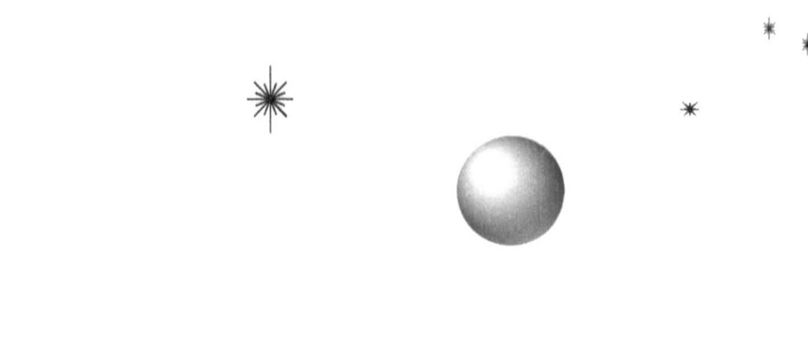

Cover art by Rachael Hedges
Illustrations by J. Z. Colby, Mireille Xioulan Powers, Sidney Oster, and Casey Park

For other print editions, ebooks, dramatic audiobooks, previews, samples, biographies, comments, questions, artwork, writing contests, Ask Kibi advice, Nebador citizens, and more, please see:

www.nebador.com

Nebador Archives
Kelso, Washington, USA

Library of Congress Control Numbers:
2011900581, 2011918932, and 2012912322
Manufactured in the USA

ISBN: 978-1-936253-60-9
NEBADORHCT2: hardcover, 6" x 9", 597 pages,
Trilogy Global/Library Edition (10-point Georgia type)

Greetings, young people of planet Earth,

In *NEBADOR Trilogy One*, Ilika of Satamia attempted to educate ten youth from a medieval kingdom, hoping to find a crew for his mysterious ship. One student quickly returned to the comfort of slavery, a system he understood. Another jumped before he looked once too often, and left behind the love of his life. She could not bear to be alone, and was soon in the arms of a young man far too smart to do the growing he needed to do. Finally, one was called by love and the gentle animals of the Earth.

After spending months imagining sails and a wooden deck, Ilika's five new crew members departed the kingdom of their birth in a deep-space response ship of the Nebador Transport Service. Their destination: Satamia Star Station.

They will soon learn that the road to the star station is neither short nor easy. Countless lessons must be learned on the ground, in the air, and on water. Often their minds are eager, but their bodies are not ready to follow. Sometimes progress is only possible because of their strong bonds of friendship.

But their biggest challenge comes from an unexpected source, as a calling of the heart fools both the young captain and his inexperienced crew.

Any reader who is sure that going into space will be push-button easy, and that we can take all our human myths and problems with us, has probably left the Nebador stories behind long ago. Books Four and beyond are especially for those youth, and a few young-at-heart, who are not afraid of the hard work — physical, emotional, mental, and spiritual — that comes with any grand, life-changing, soul-building adventure.

J. Z. Colby
2011

Greeting from the *Deep Learning Notes*,

NEBADOR Trilogy One is behind you. Hopefully, you learned many things, from the electromagnetic spectrum to emergency rope techniques, from need-driven communications to trigonometry, from quantitative logic to the ethics of leadership transfer.

But all that was just the appetizers. The five new crew members of the Manessa Kwi may have taken a very large step outside their culture, but it was still just a step. Now it's time to get serious, time to spread wings and fly.

The Muse, who whispers to the author and wants young adults to sharpen their wits and hone their skills, is quickly being joined by many wise human voices. Although they don't often agree on the details of what is upon our future-horizon, one theme comes through clearly: the excesses and entitlements of the 20th century are not sustainable.

In *NEBADOR Book Four* and *Book Five*, the new crew of the little ship learns that they must clean up their own messes. The Nebador Transport Service may watch over them, but no help remaining stuck in childhood will be forthcoming.

As always, the author will respond to any thoughtful question related to the NEBADOR stories.

J. Z. Colby
2011

Acknowledgements

Wonderful people throughout the author's life provided unique and irreplaceable lessons and inspirations:

Juniper Russell
Vicky Ball
Linda Dezzutti
Jennifer Carolyn Gates
Rachael Bleich
Paula Wells
Sarah Satterthwaite
Ashley Riddle
Antonya Pickard
Esther Smith
Dottie Frisbie
Martha Higgins
Susanne Koller
Charleen Cox
Meredith Herzog
Patricia Sharp
Peter James

Valuable readers gave the author feedback after digging through early drafts of the book:

Jimmy Johnson, 10
Rachael Hedges
Deborah Meier
Ardith Libby
Karen Oster
Karen Pihlak
Winn Barrientos
Shelley Johnson
Cecelia Harper

Excellent critiquers commented on thousands of passages, then provided reactions during in-depth interviews:

Sidney Oster, 10-11
Joshua Clark, 11
Jessica Johnson, 11-12
Sarah Bray, 11-13
Catherine "Cat" Harper, 11-13
Dylan Oster, 12-13
Jasper W. Romero, 13
Mariah Bruns, 14
Kristen Voie, 15
Kathryn Clauss, 16
Hannah Powers, 16-17
Alex Chalcraft, 16-18
Rachael Hedges
Brie Polette
Brendan Aragorn
Elwin Aragorn

Careful publishing assistants, proofreaders, and technical helpers brought the final manuscript as close to perfection as possible:

Katelynn Persons, 17
Cecelia Harper
Tim Kutscha
Deborah Meier

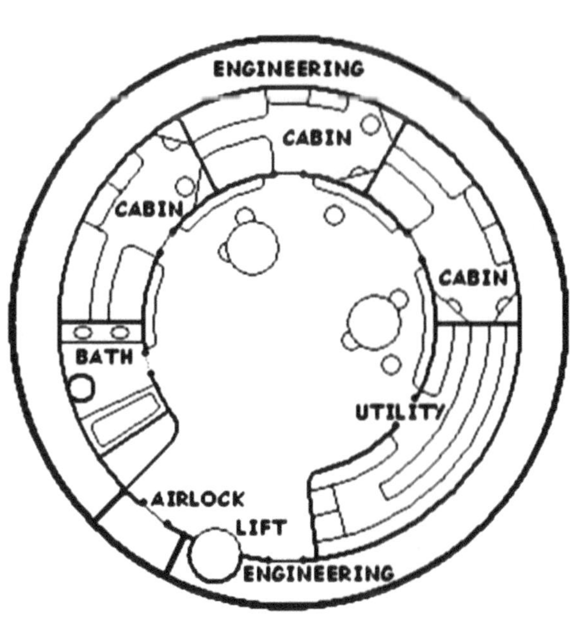

Contents

NEBADOR Book Four: Flight Training

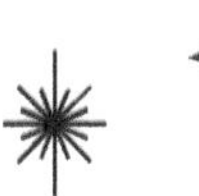

NEBADOR Book Five: Back to the Stars

NEBADOR Book Six: Star Station

"One thing I can guarantee, is that the world will never change itself because of our weaknesses. In fact, it has ways of actually becoming *more* dangerous when we approach it with a bad attitude."

— Ilika, after Miko's death

NEBADOR
Book Four
Flight Training

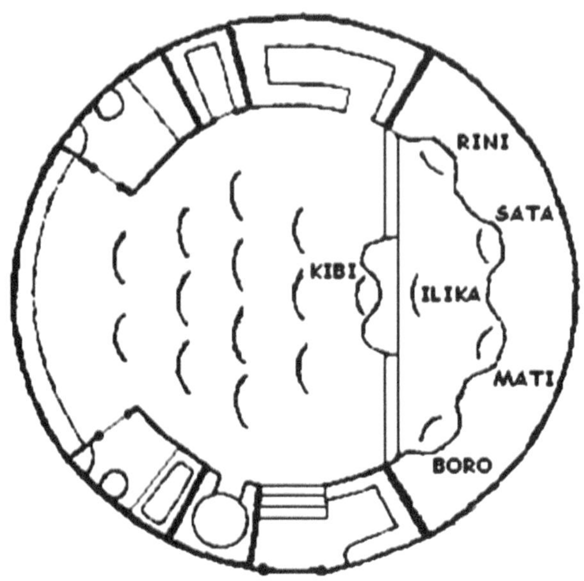

Chapter 1: Learning Curve

All the root syllables, repeated by Kibi and Sata after Manessa spoke them, were easy to pronounce. As the two girls sat side by side in the passenger area, the ship would show them the meaning in pictures on the large display screen, then use the root in a variety of words. The root syllable always had the same meaning from one word to another, and its position in the word indicated noun, adjective, verb, or adverb.

The golden ship could not speak a word of their native tongue. The steward and navigator finished each lesson feeling very honored that they were beginning to have some verbal contact with the mysterious being that was their ship, their new home, and, along with Ilika, their teacher.

When the lesson ended, Kibi and Sata thanked the ship with a word they already knew, Sata went to the galley to scrounge for a snack, and Kibi touched a control on her console to lower the big table. Just then, Ilika and Rini came in from studying something while sitting on the sand dunes, Mati finished a simulation and shut down the pilot's console, and Boro appeared in the lift, a strange tool with blinking lights in one hand.

"It made me handle a steep descent," Mati grumbled as she carefully lowered herself into a chair, "like the one we did into the ocean, but with only level one thrusters."

"Is it possible?" Boro asked, putting his tool in a little cabinet at the engineer's station.

"Barely, on my fourth try. I *hate* crashing!"

"I wouldn't want a pilot who *liked* crashing," Ilika said with raised eyebrows.

Rini laughed out loud as he sat down and handed Mati a cracker with bean spread. She couldn't help but smile.

"I'm doing simulations too," Boro announced, plopping into a seat. "I try to align the anti-mass field inducers and Manessa tells me how far off I am. Sometimes I forget we're using base eight, I make an adjustment, and it's worse than before. I'm mad at myself for a moment, then laugh and start over."

Sata scrunched her nose. "Ilika, it's weird not having any nines or tens. Why do the Nebador Services use base eight, instead of base ten like our kingdom?"

Ilika stuck his thumbs up and wiggled them. "We have thumbs we can count with. Most people don't. Base eight is also easier for Manessa, and easier to use with common fractions like half and quarter. All around, it's easier for everyone."

Sata's face scrunched as she struggled with the idea.

"Remember," Ilika added, "we still have all the same number values, we just count them a little differently. Your old nine is our eleven, your ten is our twelve."

After a pause, Kibi jumped in. "Me and Sata finished lesson seven." She broke a large cracker and gave half to the navigator. "How long 'til we can start speaking Manessa's language?"

"As soon as you two have a good head start, through lesson twenty, then everyone starts. You and Sata will always be a little ahead because of your jobs. It would be too hard to make the transition if I was the only one who knew both languages. Actually, I've already taught you about fifty words."

"We've noticed!" Mati said with a grin. "Every time you tell us about something that couldn't *possibly* have a word in our language, we get one of yours. We can tell because they're easy to say, and totally unlike words we already know."

Ilika smiled. "The language of Nebador was designed to be easy. Some of the people who speak it can only make about half the sounds we can. But I think we need a change from brain work . . ."

They all nodded.

". . . so let's do some altitude training after our snack settles. We'll start at one hundred meters."

After a moment of thought to convert the base and unit, Rini said, "Two hundred something feet. That's only a little higher than the dunes!"

"Yes," Ilika confirmed, "but it feels very different when you're outside the ship."

Boro swallowed. "Did you say . . . outside?"

For half an hour, everyone played in the dunes and wondered how they could possibly do altitude training on the outside of their ship, currently a golden sphere about seven meters across. Mati got a ride on Boro's shoulders to the top of the highest dune, then slid down the steep slip-face, squealing with delight all the way down. Kibi tumbled down a gentler slope, then shook the sand out of her hair. With a far-away look in her eyes, Sata stood on the tallest dune and looked west at the cloudy sky over her kingdom.

When Ilika returned to the ship, the rest followed, and could see it change shape before their eyes. It became much flatter, with the outer edge very close to the ground. Five seat-like indentations appeared, equally spaced around the rim. Ilika stepped back outside.

"Your minds might be ready for this, but your bodies may have a different reaction."

"Yeah, like mine the first time we flew," Boro admitted, shuddering at the memory.

Ilika smiled. "We'll take it very slowly, up to one hundred meters today, then slowly rotate. You can practice judging vertical distances."

"How high can we go, sitting on the outside?" Rini asked, eyes sparkling with curiosity.

Boro moaned even before hearing the answer.

"Eight thousand meters for short periods. Above that, it becomes dangerous without extra oxygen."

"Hypoxia," Boro mumbled.

Ilika nodded and lifted Mati into one of the seats, a little different from the others, allowing her legs to remain straight. The rest hopped into the other seats, and Manessa created a safety bar across each of their laps.

"Your goal is to convince your bodies what your minds already know, that Manessa can hold you up, and that you can be just as safe and happy in the air as on the ground."

Ilika disappeared into the hatch, and they soon felt the golden ship float upward. Each student, facing outward on the rim of the ship, could not easily see any other. Except for the feel of Manessa's warm hull under and around them, each was alone, slowly rising into the air to the height of the dunes, then a little higher.

Boro was fine . . . until the ship started slowly rotating. He tried very hard to keep his stomach under control, but finally gave up and leaned over the edge.

Soon the ship ceased rotating and lowered back to the ground. Kibi hopped out of her seat, a smile of pride on her face. She took one step forward and immediately fell sideways onto the sand, her head spinning and her stomach threatening to do the same.

Boro didn't say anything as he kicked sand over the mess he had made, but he felt much better knowing he wasn't alone.

*

"I'm glad you're all handling your tools and instruments very carefully," Ilika said as they talked about the day's accomplishments after dinner.

"Tools don't grow on trees," Boro pointed out.

"All my life people told me that if I *ever* lost my crutch," Mati began, "I wouldn't get another one. I'd just die, right there, wherever I was."

The others paused to feel what their friend and pilot had experienced. Even though Boro, Kibi, and Rini had also been slaves, Mati's dependence on her crutch, and other people to help her, nearly made them shiver.

"At the inn, we used scrub brushes until there was hardly a bristle left," Sata shared. "Even when the bristles were all gone, my mom hated to throw them in the fireplace."

"So now I have to ask a very serious question," Ilika began. "How would you treat your tools if they *did* grow on trees?"

A long silence lingered.

"My instruments are part of Manessa," Rini said thoughtfully, "and I know she can feel things."

Kibi and Mati nodded.

"Other opinions?" Ilika asked.

"I could never trust my life to something, or someone, that I didn't respect," Boro asserted.

"We'll have to trust Manessa . . . and all her tools and things . . . with our lives all the time," Sata began, "and we'll usually be a lot higher than a hundred meters."

Ilika nodded. "Most people treat their tools like dirt if they can easily get new ones. But if anything . . . or anyone . . . is beneath your respect, then you are not ready to travel among the stars."

"And," Rini added with a finger in the air, "that would mean we couldn't be in the Nebador Services!"

Ilika smiled.

"You tested us about that a long time ago, didn't you?" Kibi asked.

"Oh, yes. The puzzle. The gold coins. Even our faithful little bronze pot."

"And my donkey," Mati added.

"I'm glad you mentioned Tera. She's obviously a sentient creature, with perception and feelings. The bronze pot has no feelings. There may come a time, like if it had a leak, to melt it down and make a new one. Buna may have to get a younger donkey someday, but she won't kill Tera. She'll probably just let her tag along, eat grass and enjoy the rest of her life, but not do much work."

"So . . . where's the dividing line?" Boro asked.

"Most people draw the line very close to their own skin. If someone is in their own family, maybe their own class of people, they get respect. Anyone or anything else is treated as an object."

"That's . . . the wrong place to draw the line," Kibi said with a soft but sure voice.

"If you can't see the feelings in a donkey, a ship, or a delicate tool, then it's just as easy to not see them in your brother or sister when you can profit by treating them badly."

"I remember how Rini and Kibi didn't hurt the wolf," Mati began, "after he was asleep and no longer dangerous."

"He deserved as much respect as we could give him!" Kibi said with strong conviction. Then she softened. "At least . . . without being eaten."

Ilika nodded. "People who have ships on the water or in the air, but treat them as objects, usually drown or crash, and they can never get into space with that attitude."

"So you mean . . ." Boro began thoughtfully, "the people in our kingdom will probably never fly to the stars?"

"The stars are too far away for a ship built on a world like this. In one or two thousand years, they might begin to explore the other planets in your solar system, but they will have many accidents at first. Exploring the planets takes something most people who work on ships don't have."

"Personal power," Sata suggested.

"Heart," Kibi said softly.

Rini was quiet for a moment, then whispered, "Wisdom."

Ilika slowly nodded.

All five crew members-in-training looked very thoughtful as they glanced around at the beautiful interior surfaces and powerful control consoles of their very own deep-space response ship, the Manessa Kwi.

* * *

The first illustration reminds us who the six crew members were and where their primary work stations were located on the ship.

The first paragraph of the book contains a description of an ideal, easy-to-learn language. Unfortunately, these stories are, out of necessity, written in English, which came into being because the Romans pulled out of Britain in 410 A.D. That left a cultural vacuum, and all the surrounding languages (Latin, French, several kinds of Celtic, and several kinds of German) smashed together to form one of the most complex and difficult languages on our planet.

Landing a ship of any kind, with limited or no engines, is an important skill for any pilot to learn. Helicopters require a constantly-turning rotor to glide. Fixed-wing airplanes must maintain airspeed or the wings will stall. Water ships, our most efficient form of transportation, have great inertia, and the pilot's fear is not stopping in time without engines for braking.

Boro's anti-mass drive, you may recall, is based on the theory that moving electrical and magnetic fields at 90° to each other create Lorentz forces that radiate a form of energy that counteracts gravity and inertia. The engine is called "anti-mass" instead of "anti-gravity" because it works in deep space where there is no external gravity, but the other effects of mass (or physical substance), such as inertia, still cause problems.

We humans are very proud of our opposable thumbs. They allow us to grasp things in ways that most creatures cannot. We have even come to believe that any creature without opposable thumbs cannot become highly intelligent. We then discovered that the creatures on our planet who may be closest to us in intelligence (dolphins and whales) don't even have arms. We also discovered that the animal with the highest brain-to-body weight ratio (the horse) has only one finger/toe. So perhaps it is not too surprising that the number system of Nebador (base eight) was designed to be usable by creatures without thumbs.

Working in another base, like base eight, is only hard when we constantly try to refer back to our own base (ten). If I say that a "hundred" in base eight is a square 8 by 8, that is pretty easy to imagine. If I say it's 64, I have just ruined the learning process by making it seem "weird." Everyone knows that 64 does not equal 100!

* * * * * * * *
* * * * * * * *
* * * * * * * *
* * * * * * * *
* * * * * * * *
* * * * * * * *
* * * * * * * *
* * * * * * * *

Base 10:	6	7	8	9	10	...	15	16	17	...	63	64
Base 8:	6	7	10	11	12	...	17	20	21	...	77	100

Ilika also told his crew that base eight is easier for Manessa, who is sentient but not sapient. Our primitive thinking machines today (computers) use base two, in which the only digits are 0 and 1. It is fairly easy to translate base two into bases four, eight, and sixteen. It is much more difficult to translate it into our base ten.

The most commonly-used fractions:

	1/2	1/4	1/8	1/3
Base 10:	.5	.25	.125	.3333 . . .
Base 8:	.4	.2	.1	.2525 . . .

Ilika mentioned that some other people in Nebador can make only about half the sounds that humans can. We are in a similar situation. English is, at its foundation, based on German, so our set of sounds (called "phonemes") is just about complete for speaking German. When we attempt to learn a Latin language (especially French), we have to learn several new sounds, and can easily confuse words with very different meaning until we learn all the new sounds. Some languages, completely unrelated to English, have sounds that are very difficult for us to make, such as the glottal stop in some African languages.

Sand dunes have two sides, a windward face with a gentle slope that sand slowly creeps up, pushed by the wind, and a slip-face, steeper, that the sand falls down when it reaches the top. Because of this, sand dunes are constantly, but slowly, moving in the direction the wind blows.

As an example of base eight, the crew's first altitude training exercise was at "one hundred meters." That's 64 meters in base ten. A meter is 3.28 feet, so 64 x 3.28 = 210 feet (in base ten).

How high is "eight thousand meters"? You must first figure out what a "thousand" is (base eight). Hint: a "thousand" in our base ten is 10 to the third power.

If you can't remember what "hypoxia" means, it may help to recall that a "hypodermic" needle goes UNDER the skin. "oxi" refers to oxygen, of course.

Have you ever wanted (with your mind) to do something that your body was just not ready to do? What was your body's reaction?

Why would this particular crew have little or no temptation to mistreat their tools?

Mati was completely dependent on her crutch for life. Do you, or does someone you know, have something they need, perhaps a medicine, without which they would die?

Today, most of the "bristles" on our brushes are made of plastic, which comes from crude oil. In a medieval society, the only source of such a thing was real bristle, the hair of the pig.

Rini's observation that the ship can feel things gives us the essential definition of "sentient," which means to be able to sense (feel) the environment. Although the word is often used incorrectly, it should not be confused with "sapient," which means self-aware and wise. Bugs are sentient.

Boro realized there is a relationship between respect and trust. If you treat someone badly, can you later count on them to help you when you are in need?

One of the effects of the stars and planets being so far apart is that potential space travelers must be much smarter and more mature than people who only travel on land or water. Whether this is by accident, or by design, does not really change the situation.

Ilika described the "retirement" he hopes Buna will give Tera when she gets old. Do you think this is about right, doing too much for the donkey, or too little?

"If you can't see the sentience in a donkey, a ship, or a delicate tool, then it's just as easy to not see it in your brother or sister when you can profit by treating them as an object." The ability to treat other people as objects is one thing that has made us powerful and able to "subdue the Earth." What problems does this ability of ours create?

The need to treat ships with great care and respect doesn't seem too important with our "land ships" (cars) because a mechanical failure is usually not fatal. In aircraft, a failure often IS fatal, and so we have strict laws about inspections and maintenance that must be done, when, and by whom.

"The stars are too far away for a ship built on a world like this." Ilika's statement reflects the problem of traversing distances that would take hundreds of years with any technology we possess. We can imagine "warp drive" and "star gates" when we write stories, but have no idea if they are possible.

The word "wisdom," like most words, has several definitions. One of them is simply "accumulated knowledge." When talking about star travel, Ilika used the word to imply something that goes beyond mere knowledge or intelligence, and is not commonly found in humans.

Chapter 2: Serious Training

For the next several days, the new crew members of the Manessa Kwi worked hard at learning base eight arithmetic and a variety of new units of measurement. The old units they already knew were based on the length of the king's shoe or the volume of his favorite drinking vessel. The new units required them to visualize the wavelengths of certain forms of electromagnetic energy, vaguely remembered from their elementary physics lessons with Ilika months before.

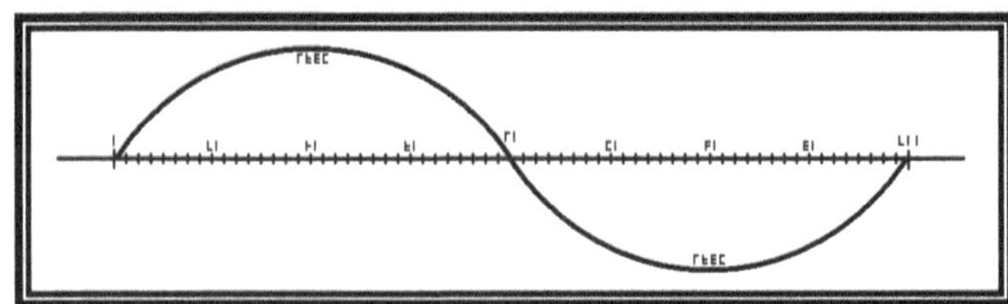

Each of the students spent time studying their consoles and equipment, and many things made more sense now that they could read numbers.

Kibi and Sata continued their intensive language lessons, and the ship was soon speaking to them in simple sentences. At first they hesitated, stuttered, and whispered to each other in the language of their kingdom before they could respond.

Boro and Kibi were very happy that the air sickness they experienced reached its peak at three hundred meters, then lessened as they went higher. Ilika, of course, scheduled extra practice at and below three hundred meters.

✷

"Good morning, everyone," Ilika said as he sipped the mint tea Rini had made from their stores of dried foods. "How's the stomach, Boro?"

"Getting better. Three altitude lessons without losing my lunch."

"Good. We can start motion training soon."

Boro moaned.

"Kibi?"

"Knowing I'm okay at higher altitudes has helped when we're lower. I haven't puked in a week!"

"Great. Any other concerns?"

The conversation paused as Rini brought breakfast trays to the table, two at a time, with hot porridge, honey, and stewed fruit.

"Um . . . there's a simulation I need help with," Mati announced. "It's thrusters only, no anti-mass, and it's sorta like the first time I rode Tera."

Everyone chuckled, remembering well that day at the ruined shack and corral not far from the capital city of their kingdom.

"Yes, that's challenging, and is usually just for emergencies. But today I think we all need a change of routine. Shall we go flying?"

"Yeah!" they all shouted at once, then started inhaling their breakfast.

⁕

The yellow and red peaks of the barren desert mountains passed slowly beneath them. As Ilika had taught, they alternated between glancing at their visual displays and checking their consoles. Mati went back and forth between visual and her three-dimensional topographic projection. Ilika moved from station to station, seeing how each crew member was doing, and pointing out displays or controls that might be useful.

"Terrain clearance, Mati?" Ilika asked from across the bridge.

"Like you said, I'm staying at least a hundred meters from everything."

"All stations, inertia straps," the captain suddenly said in a serious tone of voice, sitting down in the command chair.

The bridge was instantly filled with an air of excitement. They all knew how to pull the straps from the tops of their seats, over their chests, and secure them across their laps and upper legs, allowing them to stay in their chairs even if the ship turned upside-down. But never before had Ilika commanded them to use the inertia straps during flight. Five of them quickly had their straps secured, but Mati had to lock her flight control before she could do the same.

When Ilika saw that everyone was secured for rough flight, he continued. "Watch, make sure you are feeding topographics at real-time. Navigator, start flight recorder. Steward, cargo safety check. Engineer, ears open for flight commands."

When each station had confirmed, the captain spoke again. "Pilot, you may fly at a terrain clearance of twenty meters."

Mati grinned, then pushed forward and down on her flight control, slowly bringing the Manessa Kwi closer to the desert mountains than ever before.

Rini wore a subtle smile as the little ship moved in and out of canyons, around peaks, and beside tall rock outcroppings silhouetted against the vivid blue sky.

At first, Mati kept the speed low and stayed well-clear of everything. As she gained more confidence at flying over and around the rocky formations, her speed increased and her clearance decreased. After getting a sense of how far twenty meters looked and felt, she had little trouble maintaining the proper clearance.

"Status check," Ilika requested.

"Pilot is happy," Mati said, as she already knew she should respond first.

"Navigator good, recording flight," Sata said.

"Watch okay, nothing but a light wind."

"Engineer good. Green and yellow engines."

"Steward okay, all secure."

Mati, with a big smile on her face, turned the ship into a steep-walled canyon that penetrated deeply into the mountain range. She giggled out loud at the thrill of swishing by the vertical rock faces. Her display told her the walls were rapidly getting closer together, and suddenly the canyon made a sharp turn to the left. She pulled back on her flight control and spoke at the same time. "Thrusters, level two."

Boro had been gazing at his visual display. The sudden need to focus on his engine controls caused him a moment of dizziness, so he poked where he thought the right control should be.

A half-second later, an alarm sounded, Boro's console lit up with flashing lights, and Mati's flight control jerked right out of her hands. The ship suddenly performed several violent maneuvers that would have sent all six crew members flying if they weren't strapped in.

A moment later everything came to a dead stop high in the air above the mountain range. Five pairs of frightened eyes turned toward Ilika.

✷

"I am . . . so very . . . very sorry," Boro said between gasps where he sat in the sand, back at their landing site, with his captain and shipmates. While the others sipped on their cartons of chilled pinkfruit juice, Boro crushed his carton in his strong hand, then moaned with more guilt when it squirted all over Mati and himself.

Mati just smiled, gently took the carton out of his hand, and replaced it with her own hand. "You're not the only one who made a mistake, you know," she admitted.

"That's right," Ilika agreed. "I'm glad you can see yours too, Mati."

"I was having way too much fun. And . . . I guess . . . I treated Boro like a machine who could just do what I wanted instantly. I should have asked for that thruster change as soon as I entered the canyon."

"But I *should* have been able to do my job right when you needed me to!" Boro said, gasping for breath.

"Did you learn from it?" Ilika asked.

"Yeah! You taught us to keep our eyes moving, not stare at anything too long. I just . . . forgot. It seemed sort of . . . unimportant when you said it. I'm so sorry, Mati. I shouldn't be the engineer any more."

"You're in training, Boro. You will make mistakes, worse than this one.

Does anyone want me to replace Boro . . . with Toli maybe?"

Laughter and head-shaking circled the group.

"So . . ." Ilika began, "are you willing to continue learning, Boro?"

The stocky fifteen-year-old took several deep breaths as he made eye contact with his captain. "Y . . . yes."

Sata grinned and clapped, and others quickly joined in.

"Okay," Kibi said, "Boro feels about an inch tall, and I would too, in his shoes. But we all want to understand what Manessa did."

"Yeah," Mati almost whined. "Can Manessa be her own pilot? Am I . . . just for show?"

"No, Mati, not at all. Manessa knows her crew is in training, can spot *some* dangerous situations, and will *try* to bring the ship to a stable and safe place if the situation looks hopeless."

"You mean like when the stupid engineer shuts down all the engines?" Boro said with a cocky expression.

Ilika smiled. "Yes, like that. But the emergency maneuvers that Manessa will attempt at those times are not piloting. They are more like what Tera would do if she faced a wolf alone."

Mati nodded slowly.

"So . . . Manessa just . . . bolted?" Sata proposed.

"Yes, and there will be many times," Ilika continued, "when we are flying in tight quarters and will have to cancel Manessa's emergency responses entirely."

Mati took a deep breath. "I . . . I'm glad Manessa could save us today."

*

As they finished their lunch trays, Ilika got a hand-held knowledge pad and began writing on its screen in the language they all knew. His letters appeared on the large display above the steward's station.

	your kingdom	Nebador
citizens:	king, nobles	Services
partial citizens:	merchants	sapient beings
protected:	peasants	simple animals, trees, machines
used:	slaves, animals	small plants

"We've talked about this a little, but after our experience this morning with Manessa, who is sentient but not sapient, I want to make sure you understand how different Nebador is from your kingdom."

Sata grinned. “We’re gonna be up there with the king!”

“Don’t let it go to your heads,” Ilika began with a slight frown. “No one will be peeling your fruit for you.”

Kibi doubled over with laughter.

Ilika waited until everyone was quiet. “Consider a living tree in the forest, and you are tempted to pound in a nail to put up a rope.”

The silence stretched for a long moment, and then heads started shaking. “Protected,” Rini said.

“Good. Consider a donkey named Tera.”

“Also protected,” Mati said.

“Even a little better than that,” Ilika said. “We’ve already talked about creatures who can develop a soul. That is also the beginning of sapience, the beginning of wisdom.”

“So . . .” Boro said thoughtfully, “Tera would be . . . a partial citizen of Nebador?”

“Yes. She’s on the borderline, and obviously isn’t going to sit down and discuss philosophy while eating with a fork and spoon, but in Nebador, we respect her emerging sapience. She wouldn’t have been able to stay with Mati and face that wolf without it. We’ll study all this in more detail when we get to our first star station. Consider . . . a carrot you pull out of the ground.”

They all smiled, and Rini made a biting motion with his teeth.

“But we could also say thank you,” Mati said with a frown, “since the carrot is dying for us.”

Ilika smiled and nodded.

* * *

The illustration shows one cycle, forming a simple sine wave, of some form of electro-magnetic energy, such as light or radio. “Wave-lengths” are the only things we have found that are fixed, reliable, unchanging distances, so we use them today to define our units of distance measurement.

“. . . the length of the king’s shoe or the volume of his favorite drinking vessel” refers to the system of measurement still in use in the USA (feet, pints, etc.) The metric system, used by most of the world, is much easier to use, but was invented a little too early to be firmly based in physical reality.

Mati’s simulation of piloting with thrusters but no anti-mass engines would be like an airplane with a powerful propeller but no wings -- in other words, a helicopter. An aircraft that uses brute force to stay aloft can be very maneuverable, but is also very inefficient. A 2-person helicopter uses about twice the fuel as a 2-person fixed-wing airplane.

Boro learned the lesson every driver, pilot, and machine operator must learn: what is right in front is most important, but awareness of other directions, instruments, and controls must be maintained. The thing you forget about is the one most likely to get you.

When “cruise controls” first appeared on cars in the 1960s, many people thought they could set the controls and then get something from the back seat, or take a nap. People quickly learned, of course, that they provide some control of the accelerator, but not the steering wheel. Most professional drivers today never use them as they give an illusion of control, but without the intelligence and wisdom that only the driver can provide.

Ilika’s “ethics” chart has a column for a medieval society, and a column for an ideal society with values similar to those taught by most religions. How does your society fit into this chart?

Chapter 3: Attitude Flying

After several days of focused lessons, Ilika arranged for another training session.

"Take us up, Mati. Nice and easy, over the dunes at three hundred meters."

After a few moments, Mati calmly said, "Boro, please give me level two thrusters."

"I don't think so!" the engineer said in a firm voice. "You can't tell me what to do. You're not the captain."

"Oh . . . what's the use!" Mati said, whining. "No one ever listens to me . . ."

"Somebody do something!" Sata screamed.

"I'll save us!" Rini boomed, standing up. "I'll pilot the ship!" He strode to the pilot's station. "And if the engineer won't do his job, I'll do that too!"

"Do it quick!" Sata said hysterically.

Kibi yawned and leaned back in the steward's chair with her hands behind her head. "What's all the fuss about? None of this matters. Me and my passengers have plenty of ale to drink and we don't care what the rest of you clowns do."

"We're going to crash!" Sata yelled.

"Oh, shut-up," Boro said. "You're not the captain!"

"I give up . . ." Mati said. "You can be the pilot, Rini, or anyone else who wants to be. I don't care."

Kibi yawned again. "This is so pointless."

"Exercise over," Ilika said with a huge grin.

Laughter poured through the open hatch of the deep-space response ship where it sat in its usual place on the sand.

*

Around the oval table in the passenger area, the laughter and snickering lasted several more minutes before Ilika could begin a halfway-serious discussion.

"Manessa . . . would have to . . . take over . . . again . . ." Rini managed to say between chuckles.

"It was funny," Sata said, grinning, "but it also felt terrible to be so impulsive."

"Because you're normally so thoughtful," Boro said with admiration. "And I hated being . . . what was it called?"

"Anti-authority," Ilika replied.

"Yeah, that. My fingers were almost moving toward the engine controls even when I was refusing."

"Mati, you had a tough role," Ilika prompted.

"Yeah, being resigned to failure is sort of the opposite of being a real pilot. It felt like being a slave again."

The others nodded with understanding.

Ilika looked at his steward. "Nice touch with the ale, Kibi."

"Gave me a good excuse to feel invulnerable!"

Ilika laughed. "Rini, how did you like being over-confident?"

"It was sort of fun . . . until I looked down at Mati's console and saw all those symbols and controls . . ."

Mati grinned back at him.

"Okay," Ilika began, "same simulated flight, but give your role sheet to someone else . . ."

*

The last debriefing of the day, just before dinner, consisted of each student sharing which dangerous attitude he or she was most prone to have in real situations. Resignation to failure came up more often than any other, and considering their past lives as slaves, Ilika was not surprised. Sata leaned more toward over-confidence, and Ilika knew the next part of their training would be very good for her.

*

The following morning, an overcast sky and a fresh breeze greeted them, and they could see rain over the barren, treeless mountains to the east. Not a drop, however, landed on the dunes.

"Every day for the next six days, we'll do a simulated flight right after breakfast. At breakfast, you will all take a pill. Some of those pills will give you an altered state of consciousness that will be very obvious to you, and you will need to determine, along with your commander, if you can do your jobs in that state. Some pills will make you incapable of doing your jobs, but you won't realize it. However, other people will see it. And finally, a few pills do nothing."

The five crew members looked at each other and frowned.

"The altered states last about an hour. After debriefing and lunch, we can all go back to regular studies with no ill effects."

The students quickly learned that feeling sick to their stomachs did not entitle them to go off-duty. It merely caused Kibi to get them a bowl from the galley. If she was already having trouble, Ilika fetched the bowl.

Boro, with some experience under his belt in a real situation, instantly reported when he could not focus his eyes on his controls. Mati and Sata both had a little more trouble admitting they couldn't do their jobs because of vision problems.

Both Boro and Kibi, on different days, were slow to realize that the complete lack of any sound on the bridge wasn't because everyone was meditating. Incapable of hearing commands, they went off-duty.

Everyone knew something was wrong with Rini when they got old weather charts from some planet in another solar system. He, however, looked happy as a clam. Kibi had her head in a bowl, so Ilika guided Rini to the passenger area and strapped him in, with orders to stay.

On another day, everyone was wondering why Kibi was searching the passenger area with a wrinkled brow and a mission bracelet. They understood when she mimicked for them the snarling sound she was hearing. With Ilika's nod, she decided she could stay on-duty, but continued to glance behind herself often.

On the fourth day, Ilika finished his breakfast and sat down at the steward's station. "Kibi, instead of a pill, you have command. Same easy simulated flight, so just get some experience at spotting problems in your crew."

It was an altered state of consciousness for Kibi just to take the command chair for the first time. She needed to do very little because everyone had the steps of the simulation memorized. But when she noticed Sata sitting on the floor tapping at invisible controls on the back of her chair, Kibi doubled over with laughter.

Ilika smiled from the steward's station.

"Navigator, go off-duty and get some pinkfruit juice," Kibi finally managed to say.

"Why?" Sata asked, a puzzled look on her face.

At that, the rest of the bridge howled with laughter . . . except Rini who was busy hanging his head over a bowl.

Boro's most challenging hour came on the last day while Kibi was still in command. He went to make the power level changes that Mati requested, and discovered he had no feeling in his fingers.

Kibi came over and they discussed the problem. Since Boro could still control his muscles, and could see from colors and numbers when he had successfully touched the right symbols, they decided he could continue his work.

After the series of simulations was complete, and they had made great progress at their other lessons, from base eight mathematics to low-level altitude training, Ilika called for a day off. The cheering and clapping that greeted his announcement told him it was not a day too soon.

*

The three girls sat on the top of a dune watching the boys play tag among some bushes below. The sky was again clear, but the air had become cool and a stiff breeze picked up sand and pushed it over the slip-face of the dune.

"What's it like sharing a cabin with Ilika?" Mati asked with a subtle smile.

"Very sweet," Kibi said. "We don't always do anything, but he loves to comb my hair and just touch. Most nights he curls around me and I fall asleep."

Sata was grinning but didn't say anything.

"I guess . . . I love him . . . and nothing could make me want to leave."

Finally Sata couldn't hold in her secret any longer. "Boro and I are eating dinner together on the lower deck!"

Kibi smiled.

Mati snickered, then said, "We'll ask Ilika to start a video or something for the rest of us."

"Is Rini ever sweet these days?" Sata asked, looking at Mati.

"He smiles at me, but we've been so busy. I don't think anything's gonna happen until . . . you know . . . I get my knee fixed."

"Have you asked him to spend any time?" Kibi asked. "Rini's shy. He might need you to break the ice a little."

"You think so?" Mati asked with a thoughtful look.

Kibi and Sata both nodded.

* * *

Aviation pilots (and crash investigators) recognize five dangerous attitudes that can easily lead to an accident:

- Anti-authority: "Don't tell me what to do!"
- Impulsive: "Do something, anything, quickly!"
- Over-confident/Invulnerable: "It won't happen to me! I'm different!"
- Macho/Competitive: "I can do it! I'm better than him!"
- Resigned to failure: "What's the use? We're all going to die!"

All of these dangerous attitudes are SOCIAL processes, based on relations with other people. Cars, boats, aircraft, and starships all move, each in their own way, according to the laws of PHYSICS. Even though good relations and communication among the member of a crew is very important, it is a big mistake to think that any kind of social process will affect the laws of physics.

Altered states of consciousness can be caused by emotions, illnesses, and drugs. Just like in the story, some are easy for the affected person to see, others are not. Because of the 5 dangerous attitudes above, altered states of consciousness in a crew often go unreported. It takes a good leader or captain to create an environment in which his crew members feel safe reporting these things. All-male crews, as we usually have in our world, tend to allow some dangerous attitudes, and altered states of consciousness, to persist.

In our society, members of crews who work closely together are usually not allowed to have intimate relationships. By allowing such relationships, what level of maturity is the Nebador Transport Service requiring in its deep-space response ship crews?

Chapter 4: From the Heart

"Today we begin altitude training with slow, easy movement over the surface," Ilika said at breakfast.

Boro moaned, then forced out a smile.

"I've seen you master your body's reaction to altitude, day by day, lesson by lesson. Remember, hull excursions will be very rare. It may never feel wonderful. We just have to be able to do it in a pinch."

"I decided, on that first day, I was going to be okay with it," Boro declared. "I almost look forward to it now. Almost."

"Does everyone else feel ready for a little motion?"

The others nodded, some a bit slowly.

*

For this exercise, Manessa created five seats side by side at the front of the ship, a unique one for Mati in the middle. Boro and Kibi took the ends and let Sata and Rini surround their handicapped friend.

The ship had been moving slowly over the dunes at a hundred meters for several minutes when Rini noticed Kibi getting tense. With her jaw clenched, she remained silent.

Ilika, at the pilot's station, didn't see or hear any complaints, so he increased the altitude to two hundred meters.

Rini saw Kibi start to squirm a little, and heard her breathing become more rapid.

Ilika increased the altitude to three hundred meters.

Suddenly Kibi started screaming and fighting to get out of the safety bar. Finding it impossible to break by sheer strength, she began wiggling upward to extract her legs.

Rini started yelling to Ilika and trying to grab Kibi, but she was in a panic and didn't respond to his touch. Others soon noticed and joined in yelling.

Within seconds Ilika had the ship on the ground at a dead stop.

At that same moment, Kibi burst free and jumped down onto the sand. "I can't do this any more!" she yelled, staggering backward. "It feels terrible! I'm sorry! I need to feel the ground under my feet!" She started crying, turned, and ran into the dunes. "I just can't! I'm sorry . . ."

Ilika watched in shock from the open hatch as Kibi disappeared over a dune and the sound of her sobbing was lost upon the breeze.

✷

The other crew members gathered around their stricken captain at the bottom of the ramp, gazing in the direction Kibi had gone.

"Do you want us to help you find her?" Sata asked.

Silence lingered for a long moment.

"Finding her is not a problem," Ilika eventually said. "But I have to figure out what I did wrong . . . and if there is any way I can fix it."

Boro put his hand on his captain's shoulder. "Maybe . . . you didn't do anything wrong."

"That would be bad," Mati said, leaning on Sata. "That would mean only Kibi could fix it."

Ilika thought for another long moment. "Yeah."

✷

A very glum captain and partial crew accomplished little for the rest of the day. They picked at some food that Sata put on the table, then sat on the nearby dune tops and scanned the terrain for their friend as a cool breeze whispered across the silent desert.

Ilika clearly did not intend to follow Kibi, and the others slowly began to understand why as they shared thoughts and memories. They agreed that Kibi had been carefully holding in whatever was bugging her. No one could think of any hint Kibi had given that she was unhappy, other than her parting words as she disappeared into the dunes. These they quoted to Ilika whenever he asked, but little meaning could be found in them other than the obvious.

It feels terrible! I need to feel the ground under my feet!

Rini made dinner, and they ate knowing they needed nutrition, but no joy was shared, nor any of the usual excitement about evening videos and games.

Again they sat on the dunes until the sky and land darkened, then one by one crept into their cabins.

✷

The next morning, the remaining four crew members found their captain curled up in blankets in the sand outside the ship. They sat with him silently as he stretched and rubbed the grit out of his eyes. "My cabin just felt too empty last night," he explained.

After getting a little breakfast, they all sat together on a dune and scanned the desert.

"I wonder where she is . . ." Mati pondered aloud.

Rini pointed. "She's about a thousand meters in that direction."

They all looked at him.

"Well . . . I *am* the watch!"

Ilika smiled weakly. "I looked too."

After a long silence, Mati spoke. "Ilika, I have a question. If one of us started feeling the same thing Kibi felt . . . no one is that I know of, but just if . . . what should we do about it? I mean, what could we do to get over it, so we wouldn't wind up running away like Kibi did?"

Boro spoke first. "I realized something last night that might help."

Ilika nodded for Boro to share his thought.

"Kibi is . . . how do I say this . . . always full of feelings."

Everyone else nodded agreement.

"From what she's said, she used to be super-impulsive, like that one role in our attitude training."

Sata chuckled at the memory.

"Slavery taught her some self-control, of course. Whips are good at that. But now . . . I think she's letting her old ways come back. No one's . . . you know . . . whipping her."

Ilika laughed without humor. "Yeah. Feelings can be used as sources of information, or we can let them be our masters. I watched Kibi closely on our journey, just like I did with Toli and Buna. I thought she had it under control. Maybe I was wrong. But to Mati's question . . . if someone tells me they are having trouble with something, we can talk about it, break it down into tiny steps, think of little exercises we can do, all sorts of things. We're not in a hurry, and this isn't a race. We're all in it together."

"I think she'll come back," Sata said.

"Thirst and hunger will drive her back soon," Rini added. "She's not going toward the mountains where she could find water, maybe food."

Ilika nodded.

*

As the minutes of the day slowly passed, Ilika discovered he had an even bigger problem. He started overhearing comments from the others about professions they might want to follow back in the kingdom of their birth.

On a dune top in the late afternoon, after several deep breaths to fill himself with courage, Ilika said what he knew he had to say. "If you think Kibi's departure somehow ruins the crew, you are, of course, welcome to leave. I will be returning to the stars that are my home, with whoever has the courage to learn the lessons needed to be my crew. If Kibi — or any of you — can't handle it, can't learn to use your feelings as guides instead of masters, then you must like slavery more than you realize. In that case, you wouldn't like Satamia, or any other part of Nebador, where all members of the Services do their work with joy in their hearts because they choose to, not because any force, including their own emotions, makes them do it."

The four remaining students sat silently for a few minutes, then filtered away to walk in the dunes or poke around in the galley for dinner fixings.

*

The location where the Manessa Kwi had come to rest after the last training flight, and the surrounding dunes, were quiet as a graveyard that evening. No one seemed to want to talk to anyone else. Boro went out for a walk alone in the evening light. Mati sat down at her station and did an easy simulation. Sata took a long, hot bath and then sat on a dune as the sky darkened.

Rini was the only one who reassured Ilika with a smile that he wouldn't be returning to the stars alone.

The captain of the little golden ship again brought blankets out and curled up in the sand to sleep.

* * *

Humans are naturally born with a wide variety of personality temperaments. Those who tend to act impulsively on feelings are very good at some things, such as social leadership, but tend to be weak team members of a crew that must deal with non-social reality. It was not the fact that Kibi felt terrible on the moving ship that put her into this group, but the fact that she ran away.

Ilika explained that the members of the Nebador Services "do their work with joy in their hearts because they choose to." This is called "surplus motivation," and it happens when people like something enough to do it. The other kind, "deficit motivation," is when people act because they need to earn money, avoid punishment, or (like Kibi) are driven by their own emotions.

Chapter 5: Lizards or Bones

When dawn light crept into the sky the following morning, Kibi sat cross-legged on a dune overlooking the Manessa Kwi. As soon as she saw Ilika stir, she clenched her jaw, then stood and strode down the sand slope, stopping a few feet away from her captain and lover, and kneeling down in the sand.

Quickly shedding his blankets, Ilika knelt facing her, but did not lessen the distance she had left between them.

"I . . ." she began in a hoarse whisper, ". . . need some water."

Ilika looked toward the ship and saw Rini sitting at the top of the ramp witnessing the encounter. The lad hopped up and disappeared into the ship, and a few moments later emerged with a cup. Others came out behind him, and soon the entire crew was sitting in the sand facing their missing crew member.

Kibi sipped the water and made humble eye contact with all of them, one by one.

Sata grinned at her. "I'm so glad you're back, Kibi! Now we're a whole crew again!"

"Let's take this slowly," Ilika said firmly. "Kibi hasn't yet said why she's back . . . other than to get a cup of water."

They could all sense that Ilika was in a no-nonsense mood, and that Kibi wasn't going to get off lightly.

Everyone remained silent as Kibi finished her water and Boro handed her a carton of pinkfruit juice. She opened it and took a sip. "The desert is not nearly as much fun when you don't have a ship with water, food, and friends."

Rini chuckled at her honesty.

"I thought of heading west, finding that road, and looking for Buna and Misa, maybe working for my food. But I couldn't imagine what I'd tell them — I left my ship and crew, and my true love, because I panicked when the ship was moving?"

Boro grinned.

"I thought of going into the mountains, hiding my shame in one of those canyons. I know there's water up there. I guess I could eat lizards or something."

Mati smiled.

"For two days I talked to the sand and the scrubby bushes and the little hopping bugs. They all told me the same thing. Either grow up, Kibi, or leave your bones here for us."

Rini laughed dryly.

"I didn't feel quite ready to leave my bones. I'm here to ask you guys if maybe . . ." She paused to deal with the choking sensation in her throat. ". . . if maybe I could have another chance?"

⁕

At Ilika's insistence, after getting a good breakfast of stewed fruit, Kibi spent several hours going on walks with the other students, and listening to what each of them had to say.

Ilika knew what Kibi heard from all the others, because they told him while she was walking with another. Most of it had to do with feelings – what to do with them, and not do with them, if she had any intention of being a member of their crew.

When Kibi returned from a short walk with Mati, the older girl had tear stains on her face and looked ready to crawl into any available hole. As soon as Kibi left with Sata, the others gathered around their pilot.

"All I said was that whenever I look at her now, I think of Toli back in the forest."

Boro's and Rini's mouths opened with amazement at the courage of their handicapped pilot.

Ilika nodded. "That may be just what she needed to hear."

When they all finally gathered at the big oval table for lunch, Kibi looked very ashamed and thoughtful.

As Boro helped Sata serve the meal, the mood in the room was as fragile as glass. Everyone knew that nothing could happen, not even a base-eight math lesson, until they knew where Kibi stood.

"Um . . . I was wondering . . ." Kibi said in a slow, painful voice after eating part of her rice and fish casserole, ". . . if maybe there was time for a few more . . . altitude and motion training sessions . . ."

The other five immediately started clapping, and quickly swallowed whatever they were chewing.

"I think we can find some time . . ." Ilika said, smiling.

The other four nodded.

". . . but *you* have to pick our altitudes and speeds."

Kibi thought for a moment. "That's fair."

"And not until your nutrition is back to normal, say . . . tomorrow afternoon."

Kibi nodded and continued eating.

*

For the rest of that day, they watched videos that Ilika selected for their themes of overcoming personal problems. When they grew tired of sitting, they ran in the sand as Mati laughed from the top of the highest dune.

Back inside the ship, they gathered around the pilot's station to watch as Mati nimbly guided a ship or a creature through a simulated three-dimensional world. Kibi cringed every time Mati came close to some obstacle, but bit her tongue when she noticed how the pilot, instead of cringing, was using all her attention to avoid the obstacle.

That night Ilika made love to Kibi with all the passion in his heart, and saw a smile on her face for the first time since her return.

*

By the middle of the following afternoon, on the front edge of the Manessa Kwi at various low altitudes and speeds, Kibi was learning to breathe and relax, when her body would rather be screaming and running. Beside her, Rini took it upon himself, as the watch, to notice whenever she was tensing up or holding her breath. Each time, he would give her a friendly punch in the shoulder and flash her a smile.

Ilika was careful to check with everyone else between flights to make sure they, too, were okay. Boro was never going to love motion at altitude, but he was holding his own. Mati, Sata, and Rini had become completely comfortable on the outside of the ship.

"I'm doing okay, with Rini's help," Kibi said from her seat when Ilika came out to talk to them after a five-hundred-meter flight at the fastest speed they had yet experienced. "If I get comfortable with that, do I pass?"

"It's a good start," Ilika answered, "but you need to handle eight times that speed, at one hundred meters, which will make it feel like you're about to run into everything. It will be a serious test of your trust."

Kibi swallowed. "I want to try it."

"Now?"

After a pause, she nodded. "The sooner I try it, the sooner I'll know if I have to get used to eating lizards."

The other students laughed and Ilika couldn't help but smile. "The others may want to work up to that slowly."

"I'll . . . go alone," Kibi declared.

Rini looked at her. "I'll go."

Mati and Sata nodded.

Boro moaned.

*

"On planets a bit more advanced, little children love rides at this speed. Manessa has made different seats for you that will support your entire bodies under the acceleration you will feel, about twice that of normal gravity. I will take eight seconds to get up to speed, snake through the rocks south of here for a minute, then decelerate slowly. The goal is to NOT react to anything you see or feel. Be completely passive. Just breathe, and you will be okay."

Ilika made sure everyone was snug in their seats, then went inside and closed the hatch. While whispering a prayer for his brave students, he pushed the flight control forward and quickly accelerated. He threaded through the jumbled rocks, then decelerated over the salt flats on the west side of the desert. After bringing the ship to a stop, he dashed outside almost before Manessa could extend the ramp.

Running around to the front of the ship, he looked up at Kibi. To his amazement, she was smiling and a new light sparkled in her eyes.

"*That* was fun! Can we do it again?"

Ilika looked at Boro.

"I'm okay. It happened so quickly . . . I didn't have time to worry about it."

The other three were grinning with delight.

"Maybe I was going about this wrong," Ilika pondered. "After tasting the joy of fast flying, perhaps the slower stuff will seem easier."

"And I won't have to eat lizards!" Kibi declared with a grin.

✷

"So . . ." Rini began thoughtfully at dinner, ". . . you think that if we'd started at the highest speed, it would have been easier for Kibi and Boro?"

"Maybe. But there's something else that happened. Boro was handling the altitude and motion because he made the supreme personal decision, at the beginning of the training, that he was going to succeed. Mati made that decision a long time ago with Tera. For Rini and Sata, it just wasn't an issue. But I think . . . Kibi put off that decision."

Kibi's face was a study in guilt as everyone looked at her. "The little hopping sand bugs helped me with that. They reminded me I was free, and in the desert where I wanted to go. *So now what?* they asked me. *Dry up and die right here?* Truth is . . . I couldn't take even one step back toward the ship until I decided, with the huge sky and the countless grains of sand as my witnesses, that I was going to do it, I was going to sit on the outside of the ship and go as fast as Ilika wanted me to go."

"My teachers often told me," Ilika shared, "that half the job of learning anything is deciding to."

Mati nodded her agreement with wide eyes and a smile of understanding.

✷ ✷ ✷

The "little hopping bugs" are usually called sand fleas, and are common in most deserts.

Most deserts in the USA look somewhat like valleys, but are actually called "depressions" because they aren't created by water and erosion, as valleys are. The mountains surrounding them usually contain fresh water, but it can be difficult to find, as it often soaks into the ground before reaching the "floor" of the desert.

Why did Ilika make Kibi listen to each crew member, instead of just talking to her himself?

What meanings were attached to the memory of "Toli back in the forest" that made Kibi cry? Hint: *NEBADOR Book Two.*

If Mati, while piloting, had cringed (or made some other emotional expression) every time the task became difficult, how would that have affected her piloting?

By making love to Kibi, what was Ilika telling her?

In a medieval society, what is the fastest "ride" that most people ever experienced?

What experiences have most of us had that would prepare us for the high-speed, low-altitude training?

The "supreme decisions" that Mati and Boro made earlier, and Kibi finally made recently, do not come very often in life. They are difficult, life-changing, and usually full of unknown possibilities. Dedication to difficult training of some kind, as in this story, is one kind of supreme decision. Making a commitment to a partner/lover/mate is another. What other kinds of supreme decisions can you think of?

Chapter 6: Higher Challenges

Kibi and Sata returned to language studies in earnest, and everyone worked with Ilika to deepen their understanding of the many information and control options on their consoles. Rini, Sata, and Mati were starting to handle numbers directly in base eight, and Ilika worked with Kibi and Boro to help them along in the process. After one such lesson, when Ilika had departed to teach Sata some new navigation skills, the two slow math students remained on the dune in the thin winter sunlight.

Kibi looked toward the ship. "It's nice to have a buddy that's bad at everything I'm bad at."

Boro chuckled. "I wonder if other people who are slow at math also lose their lunch when flying."

"Hey! We're getting better!"

He nodded agreement. "Do you understand what Ilika was saying about numbers that are turned upside down?"

"Yeah, I think so," Kibi said, drawing in the sand. "It's impossible to accidentally read them upside down because all the digits, except zero, have a bar that points right, right?"

I L├ĿΓCFE

Boro smiled. "Yeah."

Kibi erased most of the digits. "Here's one two three."

L⊢ᒷ

"I'm not *that* dense," Boro said with his head cocked.

"I know! But here's the thing you were asking about. Look at it upside down."

They both scooted around to the other side of the sand inscription.

ㅋ⊣ㄱ

"How can you tell it's upside down?" Kibi asked.

"Okay, I see. Bars are pointed the wrong way."

"And the only time there are no bars, it's zero. Zero upside down is zero, so no problem!"

"Thanks."

They sat in friendly silence for a minute, gazing across the dunes.

"Sata isn't going to get jealous if you and I hang out a little, is she?"

"We've already talked about it, and she understands. Me and her are going on a walk in the dunes after dinner."

"Ilika's been a monster since I came back . . . a very delicious monster."

Boro chuckled. "You scared him. He loves you."

Kibi nodded and wore a dreamy smile. A few moments later, they both hopped up and headed back to the ship.

*

The five students sat on the dunes surrounding the landing site and watched as the ship rose a few meters and then hovered. Ilika appeared in the open hatch wearing a bright-green harsh environment suit and a vest with many pockets.

"First I connect my safety line. I know it doesn't seem important right now, but imagine doing this at eight thousand meters with a cold wind trying to blow you off the ship."

Mati shivered at the thought.

"Have to wear gloves. If you can do it with gloves, then it's easy without them."

Kibi looked worried, but took some deep breaths.

"Manessa will make steps and handholds wherever we need them." Ilika pushed his shoe against the hull and an indentation appeared. Then he reached ahead with his hand, tapped on the hull, and a depression formed with a bar through the middle, which he grabbed.

"Um . . . Ilika?" Mati began.

"Don't worry, Mati, you won't have to do this until your knee is fixed." She smiled.

"The goal of the exercise is to work your way to this point on the opposite side of the ship, then tap on the hull where Manessa has marked out a purple square. It will open, and you remove this practice device, put it into a vest pocket, and replace it with the one you brought."

"In the wind . . . at eight thousand meters," Boro said with a hint of disbelief in his voice.

"Without dropping either device," Ilika emphasized.

"How . . . um . . . fast will we be going?" Kibi asked.

"No one could do this with much wind or acceleration. The main challenges," Ilika explained as he worked his way back to the hatch, "will be ignoring the altitude, and dealing with the clumsiness of your gloves."

He disappeared inside, and a moment later the ship settled back onto the sand.

"Looks scary," Kibi said to no one in particular.

"Question is . . . what are you going to do with that fear?" Rini asked, looking at her askance.

Kibi shuddered for a moment and closed her eyes. "Feel it, let it remind me to be careful, and do my job . . . or go eat lizards."

The others burst out laughing.

✷

With everyone, including Kibi and Boro, doing well at their high-speed, low-altitude training, Ilika proposed they look at the world from eight thousand meters. It was, he explained, about thirteen thousand four hundred of their king's shoes in their old base ten number system.

"Everything will look very small from up there. Your main concern will be reduced air pressure."

"Hypoxia danger," Boro announced.

"Only if you stay a long time. Eight minutes to ascend, four minutes at the top, and eight minutes to come back down — you won't have any ill effects unless you are already sick. Anyone . . . already sick?"

"We're supposed to tell you that stuff!" Sata said, hands on her hips.

Ilika grinned and made eye contact with each of his students. "Just checking. You'll want your cloaks."

"Could we . . . use the seats that are all together the first time, just for moral support?" Rini asked.

Ilika saw Rini's eyes twitch in Kibi's direction for a fraction of a second. "Sure," the captain replied.

They soon had their cloaks, Manessa had taken on the appropriate shape, and they were snug in their seats.

Ilika made both the ascent and descent steady and smooth, without any noticeable acceleration forces. As always, he listened with the ship's external sensors, but heard only sounds of amazement.

*

They chatted like little birds when they arrived back on the sand, having glimpsed other lands to the east and south, and more snow-covered mountains to the north beyond those they already knew. Ilika watched and listened for any ill effects or traumatic emotions.

"Ilika," Kibi began, putting her arm around him, "that was too easy. If I know you, there's a twist coming up that will make us pee our pants."

An involuntary smirk appeared on his face.

"Tell us!" she asserted.

"Eventually, you get to make the ascent and the descent in eight seconds, instead of eight minutes."

* * *

The base eight numerals of Nebador are based on the binary (base two) representations of the same values. The horizontal bar on the bottom is the ones place, the bar in the middle is the twos place, and the bar on top is the fours place. The vertical bar with no horizontal bar is, of course, zero. For example "L" is (1 x 1) + (0 x 2) + (0 x 4) = 1, and "E" is (1 x 1) + (1 x 2) + (1 x 4) = 7. "Eight," the base, is written "LI" (we would write it "10" in our numerals).

As Ilika explained after he demonstrated a hull excursion, one of the main challenges would be to IGNORE the altitude (eventually "eight thousand meters" = 4096 meters = 13438 feet). The "exposure" (a mountaineering term) does not change the task, but it adds a huge psychological challenge. The other part of the challenge, working in a harsh environment suit and gloves, is important because the temptation to take off gloves, "just for a moment," leads to many accidents and deaths in "zero tolerance environments" (usually extreme cold).

Aircraft crews in the USA are allowed to fly for up to half an hour between 12,500 and 14,000 feet without a pressurized cabin or supplemental oxygen because our bodies only experience ill effects at those altitudes when we are there for longer times. The exception is, as Ilika explained, when someone is already sick.

Chapter 7: The Gathering

"Manessa's records about your planet say the tribes around here gather at every full moon for a marketplace, dancing, drinking, buying and selling slaves, weddings, and whatever else needs to be done. That's tomorrow. Shall we go peek at it, maybe pick up some local foods?"

Sata frowned. "I didn't know there were any people in this desert."

"Very few, mostly south and east of here, closer to the gathering place. It's supposedly sacred ground where no fighting is allowed."

"We take mission bracelets anyway," Kibi asserted.

"Of course. I'm putting Kibi in command of the mission so I'll have time to read the rest of the cultural information. We can fly most of the way, then arrive on foot."

The steward nodded. "We should wear our old tunics and boots, and take our cloaks."

Ilika went back to the knowledge pad he was reading.

*

That evening, as they savored a sticky dessert Rini made from cooked grains, honey, and flour, all the talk around the table was about the adventure that would begin early the following morning.

"It feels like we sort of know what we're doing now," Boro began, "and like we were just fumbling around before."

Ilika smiled. "You were. On our first flight, I had to remind you of every little thing, and you couldn't even read numbers yet."

Rini chuckled.

"It's good to have Kibi commanding again," Sata said, making eye contact with the steward.

Kibi blushed. "It's . . . a little embarrassing after . . . what I did."

"Now you know how I feel," Mati shared, "a crippled slave piloting a flying ship!"

Kibi smiled at her fellow crew member.

"Weaknesses overcome are strengths," Ilika explained. "If I wanted a perfect crew . . ."

"You wouldn't have gone to a slave market!" Boro jumped in.

"Or anywhere else on your planet. I have some notes about tomorrow."

They all fell silent and gave him their attention.

"The coins from your kingdom should work here, but don't be surprised if you see other coins too. The metal is important, not the stamping."

"We're ready with coppers and small silvers," Kibi said.

"I'll bring a few larger coins, just in case. There will be a language barrier – some of the people may speak your language, but probably not well. Talking louder does not help, and may offend people. Use basic signs. Point to something you are interested in, hold up a copper piece, and you will probably be shown what they want for it."

"I've assigned pairs already," Kibi announced. "You're with Mati, Ilika. Boro will have a rucksack."

"Good. No buying slaves or horses . . ."

The entire crew burst into laughter.

". . . and no getting drunk. This is not a safe, comfortable situation where we can let down our guard. I will be surprised if we get back to the ship before dealing with *something*."

They chuckled nervously, and looked thoughtful as they headed to their cabins to get some sleep.

*

A hint of light touched the desert sky as Mati carefully settled the Manessa Kwi onto a hidden rock shelf high in the mountains near the tribal gathering place. Ilika and Kibi examined the site with their bracelet lights, then returned to the ship.

Sata used controls she had recently studied to mark the location in Manessa's memory. Mati then lifted the ship back into the air.

Rini sent an infra-red view, showing heat sources in light colors, to all stations so they could see where people were camped and animals tethered. Kibi selected a vacant clump of dunes, and Mati cut her thrusters at five hundred meters, then lowered the ship using the silent anti-mass drive.

Already in their boots, they quickly slipped on cloaks. Boro grabbed a pack, and they filed out onto the sand like ghosts.

Sata used her bracelet to send the Manessa Kwi back to the rock shelf in the mountains.

The six visitors soon found themselves among other hooded figures in the dawn light, some just arriving, others carrying water or food toward animal troughs or tents. A few were talking, but not in a language any of the crew members knew.

People camped wherever they could find space, and groups arriving with horses or donkeys spread out in the sand. Following the new arrivals, Kibi and her followers soon discovered the main gathering area in a sheltered ravine. Huge boulders would provide shade in the summer, wind-break in the winter. Rocks marked a circular area of sand. Some important clans, and merchants of many kinds, had their tents nearby.

A donkey laden with baskets plodded along behind the group, so Kibi stepped off the path and the others followed. "Let's just mill around in pairs," she suggested, "see where things are, listen for anyone who speaks our language, watch for trouble. Meet back here mid-morning."

Ilika smiled at his second-in-command and walked slowly beside Mati toward the activity.

✷

"Kibi is so good at leading things," Mati said. "I hope she gets over her . . . bolting."

"Me too. She has plenty of challenges coming up . . . as we all do."

Mati chuckled. "What do you think we'll find here?"

"Maybe some food for the galley. Manessa's records didn't say what they eat. You never know when you'll find an interesting souvenir or a gift."

"I think . . . someone will get into trouble by breaking some taboo we don't know about . . . either Boro . . . or maybe Kibi. I feel safe with you, 'cause you've been to places like this."

"Yes, but every culture has it's own taboos."

"Something's cooking," Mati began, nose to the air, "some kind of bread. Over there."

"Shall we look, maybe taste?"

"Yeah!"

✷

When the six visitors regrouped, a thin sunlight was bathing the ravine, which by now was filled with the sounds of buying, selling, talking, and eating.

"I already picked up some nuts and dried fruits," Boro shared, hefting his rucksack, "because it looked like they'd run out."

"Kibi and I found some cheese," Rini added, handing the small wheel to Boro for packing.

"There's a trader here from our kingdom," Kibi said. "Brought a big horse piled with stuff, and people are buying him out. We talked for a moment, but he was busy."

Sata grinned and squirmed next to Boro. "Jewelry and things are at the far end of the ravine."

After Ilika and Mati shared the location of the bread they had sampled, Kibi set the next meeting time for early afternoon. As everyone took to the path, Boro lingered for a moment beside Ilika and spoke in a soft voice. "I'd like to get Sata something, but I don't think I have enough."

Ilika grinned and slipped him a great silver piece. "My turn with the rucksack," Ilika said aloud.

✷

As Boro and Sata threaded their way slowly among the tents and vendors, looking at the crafts, fabrics, spices, and foods, they started to smell a sweet smoke coming from many of the tents, and were soon smiling and laughing right along with the desert youth who went to and fro on errands or in play. Sata had, at first, been drawn to the jewelry, but now she took a keen interest in the fabrics, with strange printed or woven designs.

Having already done his share of the food shopping, Boro focused his attention on Sata, watching to see what she liked of the things for sale, sometimes slipping his arm around her as she stood looking over the wares. She smiled up at him and pointed to things that piqued her interest.

They bought fried bread and spicy bean dip for lunch, then found a rock on the side of the ravine where they could sit.

"I feel goofy, and like I haven't eaten in a week," Sata shared, then devoured half her lunch quickly.

Boro attacked a chunk of bread. "I think it's the smoke. It makes me hungry too."

"I was thinking . . ." Sata pondered once her mouth was free, "that I don't really want something just for myself, like jewelry, but something I can . . . you know . . . share with my . . . favorite boy." She looked at him with sparkling eyes, a mischievous smile, and bean dip on the corners of her mouth.

Boro was lost in her gaze for a long moment, but eventually found the presence of mind to say something. "Um . . . did you see anything special?"

"Yeah!" Sata replied eagerly, still looking into his eyes and grinning. "Those thin cloaks made of that fancy material with all the designs in it. We could get one for each of us, and wear them when we go on walks . . . or dates! But . . . I think they're expensive . . ."

Boro smiled. "We have enough."

*

During the afternoon, Ilika sat with Mati between short shopping trips, and they watched the people around them and discussed what they saw.

"I don't see any slaves . . ." Mati said with a half-smile.

"I think we're seeing them all the time, but they're treated much better than we're used to."

"I wonder why."

"I don't know. Maybe . . . just because there are fewer people, so slaves are harder to find."

"And . . ." Mati speculated, "it would be so easy to run away and hide in the rocks or dunes."

Ilika pointed. "Look! There's Rini dancing with those children!"

In the circular area at the middle of the gathering, about a dozen children, from barely walking to young adults, were prancing to the music of a piper, and Rini was quickly picking up the steps and the style of the dance. Kibi sat near, eating something.

Mati smiled with longing. "Will I be able to do that, Ilika?"

"Yes. We'll talk to the healers as soon as we get to Satamia Star Station. After the operation, you'll have a period of recovery as you slowly build your strength and learn to walk. A few months later, your injury will be nothing but a memory."

A far-away look lingered in Mati's eyes as she continued to watch Rini and the desert youth frolic and dance in the sand. But mostly Rini.

* * *

Ilika counseled his crew to avoid one of the most common mistakes tourists make: talking loudly to overcome a language barrier. It doesn't work, just makes people angry, and is one of the reasons that rich countries have such a bad reputation around the world. A humble, open attitude works much better.

Why did Ilika accept, without complaint, Kibi's decision to pair him with Mati?

Rini's infra-red view gave them the information they needed, to avoid landing the ship near any of the local people, because people and animals are usually warmer than the surrounding land. In what situation would an infra-red image not work to see people and animals?

Social drugs are much more common in cultures that don't operate dangerous machines. Sata and Boro were probably smelling marijuana or hashish, both from the hemp plant. In our culture, driving and operating other dangerous machines is so common that the only legal social drug is alcohol (which wears off quickly).

Chapter 8: An Unexpected Ceremony

When the group gathered in the late afternoon, Ilika announced that they had been invited to join the trader from the west for dinner in the large tent where the tribal leaders and other important people ate.

Boro and Sata, already feeling a bit like royalty in their new cloaks, grinned at each other. Ilika had to pass out more money so the others could purchase an article or two of new clothing for the occasion. Kibi and Rini dashed away, knowing they only had an hour to prepare for dinner.

*

Kibi found a robe of soft, dusty green material with brown trim that made her feel like Tima the elf. Rini bought a gray tunic with black trim, and a black leather belt. As they were leaving the clothing tent, a girl of about twelve years, who had been waiting outside, suddenly knelt in front of Rini and held up a little tray that contained a single small, fancy pastry.

She was slender, just entering the first flowering of youth, and Rini remembered her from the dancing circle earlier in the afternoon. Her dark gray tunic complimented her olive skin and black hair. He dug into his pouch and held up a copper piece to determine the price of the little treat.

She quickly shook her head and held the tray closer to Rini.

He looked into her sparkling brown eyes, then smiled back at her as he picked up the sweet.

She grinned happily, but waited.

Rini took a bite. The flavor of the honey and nuts, combined with the perfectly-baked shell, made him cringe with pleasure for a moment.

Her eyes grew wider, but still she waited.

Rini glanced at the remaining bite of pastry, then knelt down in the sand in front of the girl and offered her the other bite.

A huge smile flashed onto her face. She opened her mouth and closed her eyes.

Rini placed the little pastry on her tongue and watched as she blissfully chewed and swallowed the shared gift.

Kibi watched with a slight frown as Rini and the twelve-year-old girl stood up and faced each other. A moment later the girl dashed away, barely touching the ground as she went.

*

The sweet smoke was even thicker in the tent where the rich and important people were served dinner. The six crew members of the Manessa Kwi, and the bearded trader from the kingdom to the west, sat in a circle on rugs as slaves brought platters of fancy food that could be eaten with fingers.

"You wouldn't *believe* how much money I've made today!" the trader announced, pouring himself a drink from a fancy bottle of sweet liqueur. "They even bought my pack horse!"

"Any news from the capital city?" Boro asked, eating a piece of candied fruit. "Last time we were there, people were burning the religious orders."

The man laughed. "Two of them managed to get their gates shut, but not much of their wealth was left. The slave master bought the one near the city gate to expand his operation. That's the last time they go beast hunting for a while!"

The others around the circle laughed, but the trader didn't notice the knowing glances they exchanged.

Rini took a bite of some delicate pastry that Mati offered him, then put the rest in her mouth, just as he had done earlier with the desert girl. She smiled as she chewed.

"What brings you folks to the desert? I can tell the others are from my kingdom, Cobble Town in the capital by their education and bearing, but you're a foreigner, are you not?" the trader asked Ilika.

"Yes, I'm from another land. I have a ship, and these five are in training to be my crew." He took a bite of some sweet fruit he couldn't name.

"You're a long way from the port!"

"Just getting some training done. We depart for distant shores in a few weeks."

The five crew members grinned, noticing how Ilika kept everything within the trader's understanding.

"Do you come down here every full moon?" Kibi asked, nibbling a large briny olive.

"No. I come maybe four times a year. This moon more people come, and have more money to spend, than at any other time."

"How was the meat at Cattle Town when you came through?" Sata asked with a smirk.

"You know about that! It gets better toward winter, but the place still stinks. I buy what I need, eat bread and drink ale, and head on down the road. Then I have a good meal at the hamlet of Pos before tackling the steep trail down to the desert."

"Pos is nice," Kibi remembered aloud, dipping crisp bread into some sauce. "I had my last birthday party there."

Ilika noticed his students eyeing the liqueur, so he poured small amounts that wouldn't get them too tipsy. "What should we look forward to tonight?"

"Dancing and merrymaking start right after dinner," the trader explained, refilling his cup, "and go most of the night. I hear there's at least one wedding, the middle daughter of a rich man who has five daughters and is happy to see one of them off. Everyone sleeps all day tomorrow, heads home in the evening."

*

When the captain, crew, and trader finally left the eating tent, they were all stuffed with the delicious food and drink. Torches flickered all through the ravine, but especially around the ceremonial circle. Several young women, wearing little but flowing scarves, danced to the beat of drums and the melody of pipes.

Plenty of free space remained around the circle, so Ilika looked at his students. They all nodded. The group gathered between two torches at the edge of the circle, and Rini helped Mati onto a rock.

As they all got comfortable, the youth in the circle began a new dance, slow and sensual, to a tune plucked from a stringed instrument. Rini noticed a girl peek out through a tent flap on the other side of the ceremonial space, the same girl who had shared a pastry with him earlier that day. Then she disappeared back inside.

The dance ended and a large man on the edge of the circle clapped twice. The dancing youth quickly scattered, but the musicians began a new melody, both rhythmic and sensuous. The tent flap was opened by other girls, and the girl Rini had seen stepped through wearing a rich, shimmering blue gown with silver trim and gold accents. She took slow, measured steps and entered the ceremonial circle as the music played.

"Beautiful . . ." the trader whispered to himself.

Rini felt his heart beat faster, as she seemed to be looking directly at him. When she passed the middle of the circle, it became obvious that she was approaching the group. The music picked up its tempo as more people gathered to watch.

After several more measured steps, she stopped right on the edge of the circle and held out her arms toward Rini, still seated on the ground. Sweet, heady smoke came from many tents and filled the ravine with an otherworldly air.

Rini rose and took the girl's hands, and she made several careful steps backwards to guide him into the center of the circle. Many people clapped and cheered as the music changed again to the slow melody of deep-voiced pipes. The girl released Rini's hands and began a mysterious dance, slow enough that Rini could easily follow her movements. This brought a huge smile to her face, and the people around the circle clapped or pounded walking sticks on the ground in approval.

The dance lasted several long minutes, and Rini became completely engrossed in the movements of the girl, quickly learning the nuances of the dance.

Mati had a slight frown on her face. "I wish I could do that with him," she whispered to Ilika.

"Soon, Mati. Very soon."

"Amazing!" the trader from the west said. "I didn't realize . . ."

As Rini and the girl continued the slow dance, their movements now almost perfectly coordinated, other girls carried out four small tables and placed them in the circle, near the edge, at the four compass points. The girl guided the dance toward one of the tables.

Without quite ceasing the motion of the dance, she picked up a small cake and offered it to Rini. He took a bite, then offered the rest to her as he had done earlier in the day.

At another table, they did the same with a cup of some strong, sweet drink. The cheering and pounding of the spectators increased.

The third table held a large feather with which she pretended to tickle him under the arms, then handed the feather to him and he did the same to her as the crowd laughed and cheered.

"I had no idea it was him!" the trader said.

Ilika took on a puzzled expression, but conversation was difficult because of all the noise.

At the last table, the girl picked up a sharp knife and pricked her hand.

"Rini sure does love to dance!" Ilika said in the trader's ear.

Rini pricked his hand.

"That's not a dance!" the trader said loudly over the clapping and cheering. "They're just now completing their wedding ceremony!"

The girl reached out her hand toward Rini, and he did the same, a single drop of their blood coming together in the palms of their hands.

* * *

What clues were there in the first pastry-sharing between Rini and the desert girl that could have warned him that something unusual was taking place?

Most cultures expect anyone in them, even just visiting, to know the meanings of many symbols, from ritual actions to traffic signs. What symbols can you spot in the wedding ceremony that Rini (and his captain and friends) failed to notice in time?

Chapter 9: Wedding Bliss

As the cheering continued, Ilika looked around while trying to swallow the huge lump in his throat. Mati must have heard the merchant's words, as she had her head buried in Kibi's arms, sobbing deeply. Boro and Sata had looks of shock on their faces as the problem became clear.

Looking back toward the ceremonial circle, Ilika could see the girl trying to pull Rini toward her tent, but he was standing his ground and wore a frown of confusion. Ilika took a deep breath, stepped into the circle, and approached the couple. The cheering and clapping began to die down.

"Rini, did you intend to perform a wedding ceremony with this young lady?"

In the past, Ilika had seen Rini wear many expressions, including red-faced rage when the wolf threatened Mati and Tera. But Ilika had never before seen Rini white with fear.

Even as Ilika spoke, the girl kept trying to pull her beloved away.

"Uh . . . n-n-no . . ." Rini managed to stutter out. "We . . . were just . . . dancing and . . . playing . . . weren't we?"

A large and richly dressed man of obvious importance stepped into the circle, hands on his hips. He spoke loudly and clearly, and the crowd fell silent.

The merchant entered the circle and translated. "This is the girl's father. He demands to know why his newlywed daughter and her husband are being bothered on their wedding night, instead of running off to her tent to . . . um . . . take their pleasure."

Ilika took another deep breath. "This lad, my charge, thought he was just dancing and playing, as he did earlier with several of the youth. He had no idea this was a wedding ceremony."

The trader translated while the father and all the people listened.

The girl immediately burst into tears and ran into the arms of a woman on the edge of the circle. The woman held her sobbing daughter while looking daggers at Rini. The crowd began jeering and pounding sticks against the ground.

The father looked ready to chew nails, and with smoking eyes glared at Rini and spoke.

"He asks," the merchant translated, "if this . . . um . . . this pathetic wimp of a boy — his words, not mine — intends to fulfill his marriage vows . . . or not."

The people around the circle laughed and jeered.

"Rini," Ilika began, then paused to gather his thoughts. "Rini, regardless of what you knew or didn't know, you now must decide if you are willing to be married to this girl, and fulfill all the responsibilities that go with marriage."

Rini's eyes were wet and swirling with panic. He spoke with a broken voice. "Um . . . I can't . . . I already . . . belong to . . . Mati . . ."

Mati was still sobbing and shaking in Kibi's arms and didn't hear what was said.

The merchant translated for the father and his people.

An angry rumble ran through the spectators, and Ilika's right hand approached his bracelet.

Suddenly the girl's father raised a hand and the people quickly fell silent. He spoke loudly, slowly, and clearly. The crowd murmured approval.

"There is an old tradition that has not been used in many years," the trader said, translating. "A man that refuses to fulfill his wedding vows must give three years of service as a slave, one for hurting the girl, one for offending the mother, and one for offending the father."

Rini's head fell onto his chest and he started crying.

The father spoke again.

"The girl may yet take him to her bed if he now finds the courage to be a man," the trader said.

"I wish to offer a third option," Ilika announced loudly, and the trader translated.

The father spoke a word and cocked his head. The people remained silent.

"This lad is small and not a strong worker, but I have use for his skills. An old tradition in my country is that a gold piece may take the place of a year of service. I offer three gold pieces to replace the offense this lad has caused."

The merchant from the kingdom to the west again translated Ilika's words.

The father appeared thoughtful as he went to his wife and daughter and spoke in hushed tones. A disagreement of some kind passed between the parents, but Ilika and his students had to wait until the merchant spoke.

"The lad has three choices. Go to his marriage bed and be a good husband, be a slave for three years, or smash the wedding cup from which he and the girl drank and place three gold pieces in her hand."

Ilika had to shake Rini several times to get him to focus on the decision at hand. He repeated the terms, and added that the three gold pieces were in Ilika's pouch if he needed them.

It took Rini a minute to wipe his tears and focus his mind. "Which . . . do you think is best, Ilika?"

The captain of the Manessa Kwi thought for a moment. "The first or the third, as you choose. The second option, slavery, I will not allow."

Still white, Rini looked around. The girl was in her mother's arms, but had ceased crying and was looking at him. The wedding cup stood alone on the small table nearest the girl. Mati had also ceased crying and was peeking out from under Kibi's cloak, face tear-stained and hair tangled.

On shaking legs, Rini moved forward, picked up the ceramic cup, and knelt down at the first rock he came to on the edge of the circle. He glanced up at the girl, then back at Mati, and smashed the cup onto the rock, cutting himself in the process, but not feeling it.

The girl started crying again, but didn't hide her face or take her eyes off Rini.

Ilika found the only three gold coins in his pouch and went to Rini's side. When Rini slowly stood, shaking all over, he looked at his teacher with sad, wet eyes. Ilika held out the coins and Rini opened his bleeding hand.

In a fog of emotions, Rini somehow managed to take the last few steps toward the girl and her mother. The stern look on the woman's face nearly made him bolt. The girl, crying loudly with tears that had completely ruined her gown, held out her hand.

Rini placed the three blood-covered gold coins in her hand, then closed his eyes and let Ilika lead him away.

* * *

To solve the problem, did Ilika work within the local customs, or did he violate them?

What situation caused Ilika to consider violating the local customs (when he thought about using his bracelet)?

How did Rini make his decision?

In our world, citizens of powerful countries often expect their governments to intervene for them when they get into trouble in foreign countries. This sometimes happens if the person has wealth or power, but in theory, we are all subject to the laws of another country when visiting it, and if we go to prison there, it will be to THEIR prison, however good or bad their prisons might be.

Why didn't Rini feel it when he cut himself?

Was there any way Rini could have made everyone happy in that situation?

Chapter 10: Honeymoon

Ilika, Kibi, and Boro quickly led the others out of the ravine and into the darkness of the first cluster of dunes they could find, where Sata tapped the ship recall code into her bracelet. The Manessa Kwi was there in seconds, and back on the hidden rock ledge a minute later.

Rini and Mati collapsed into seats in the passenger area, not quite next to each other. Kibi got a towel for Rini's cut, and Sata stayed right beside Mati. Boro and Ilika weren't sure what to do, so they just found seats and tried to relax.

"Ilika . . ." Mati began in a very tentative voice, ". . . if I decided that I made a mistake . . . and I can't be on your crew . . . would you take me back to somewhere in my kingdom . . . somewhere I choose?"

Ilika took a slow breath to collect his thoughts. "Y . . . yes. But I think Manessa needs some engine maintenance that would force you to wait a few days."

"Yeah," Boro said with slight sparkle in his eyes, "three or four days."

Mati frowned but didn't withdraw. "And you'd take me . . . anywhere I wanted . . . even if it was . . . the meadow north of Lumber Town . . . just past Farmer Koto's house?"

The upper deck of the Manessa Kwi was suddenly filled with tense emotions and furtive glances.

"Yes, Mati, wherever you wanted to go."

"NO!" Rini screamed, suddenly jumping to his feet. "You CAN'T! I just hurt someone deeply, and wasted more of Ilika's money, because I chose YOU back at the swamp, and I love YOU!"

The silence that followed was filled with the smell of sweat and the sight of tear-stained faces. Mati slowly raised her head and looked at Rini. His face was filled with anxiety, and his hand started bleeding again.

The two ex-slaves just looked at each other for a long time, and no one else made a sound. Eventually Boro stood and whispered something in Rini's ear.

Rini suddenly looked foolish and embarrassed. "Why didn't I think of that?" He took several slow steps toward Mati, knelt down beside her, and with wet but sparkling eyes brought his head close to hers and placed a delicate kiss on her lips, the first he had ever given, the first she had ever received.

As the room filled with clapping and cheering, Kibi approached the couple and wrapped the towel around Rini's bleeding hand without interrupting the occasion.

"I love you too," Mati said when the clapping died down. Then she placed an equally delicate kiss on his lips.

"Actually, I think the engines are okay," Boro said, grinning at Ilika.

✷

After moving the Manessa Kwi back to their landing site in the dunes, Ilika discovered he had a new problem — how to get his watch and pilot to come to lessons and training sessions.

It wasn't that Rini and Mati were ready for the closeness of shared cabin and bed — they knew such things still lay out of reach somewhere in the future. If asked why, they probably would have pointed to Mati's knee.

But the deeper reason was clearly visible to at least Ilika and Kibi. Rini and Mati were two shy introverts, just learning to be together and share thoughts and feelings. They needed some time to find out what those first tender kisses meant.

They walked slowly into the dunes, Rini taking the place of Mati's crutch. The air was very still under an overcast cloud layer. Arriving at the top of a saddle between two sand dunes, they looked at each other.

"Would you like to sit here?" Rini asked.

"If you do . . ."

Rini laughed. "I know! We'll take turns making little choices."

"Okay!"

Rini helped Mati down onto the sand and they just held hands and gazed across the open desert in silence for a few minutes.

"Without my crutch, I'd die right here unless you helped me get back."

"The only reason I wouldn't help you is if I died right here with you."

With her head on Rini's shoulder, Mati smiled and closed her eyes to enjoy the warm glow she felt inside herself.

✷

"Now that we've studied a few cultural symbols," Ilika said from the head of the table under the large display screen, "let's see how many of these we can find in Rini's recent predicament."

"The breaking of bread together was obviously part of it," Boro said, "but I wonder if it had a special meaning because each one fed the other half of it . . ."

"Probably," Ilika agreed, "but the general meaning of bread-breaking is still the underlying idea."

Kibi searched her memory. "Peaceful coexistence and bonding . . ."

"That was the second time," Rini admitted. "The first time was just as me and Kibi were coming out of the clothing tent. The girl was waiting for me. It was the same kind of fancy pastry."

"And you shared it in the same way?" Ilika asked.

Rini nodded.

"My hunch is that you stumbled into a combination of two factors, Rini. First, the sharing of a single small pastry that could easily be eaten by one person alone. Second, the pastry may have been unique, perhaps specially made for just the purpose of a marriage proposal."

"So . . ." Kibi speculated, "if he had eaten the whole thing himself . . ."

"Or if it had just been plain bread . . ." Sata added.

"Then the girl may have seen it as rejection, or been unsure and attempted further communication."

"But I love sharing, and I love sweets . . ." Rini began.

The others laughed.

Mati didn't feel ready to take an active part in the discussion, but was paying close attention, and couldn't help but smile at Rini's admission.

"Since you eagerly shared *that* particular pastry," Ilika continued the thought, "the girl must have been absolutely sure you were hers for life, because that's how it's done in her culture."

Rini suddenly became sad at the painful memory of accidentally marrying one girl when he was already promised, at least in his own mind, to another.

*

"What did you mean about choosing me at the swamp?" Mati asked as she and Rini snuggled between some dunes, their hoods up and their backs to the cold breeze.

"Remember how Ilika had to ask me some questions about my written answers?"

"Yeah."

"I was . . . confused because I had feelings for . . . about three different girls. Ilika helped me to see . . . which of those feelings had any hope of . . . you know . . . ever being returned to me. That was when I chose you."

"You mean . . . you chose me to share a cabin with . . . when Boro and Sata decide they want to share one?"

Several thoughts and emotions passed across Rini's face before he could answer. "No. I mean yes, but not just that. I chose you to be the first and only girl I ever kiss."

Mati looked into Rini's sparkling eyes, then placed her lips on his, determined to do her very best to make him never regret that choice.

*

With big drops of rain pounding the sand outside, the captain and crew of the little response ship sat around the oval table in the passenger area. A bowl of nuts slowly worked its way around.

"Okay, we can see there are a million ways to get tangled up in the cultures we're visiting," Sata began, "but is there any way to know *for sure* what we should do . . . and not do?"

"Um . . . no. Just study, like we are doing, and practice, like when we went to the gathering. I've been studying this stuff for fifteen years, and I didn't see what was happening until it was too late."

"Will . . . the people who run the Transport Service . . . be mad at us?" Boro asked.

"As long as you're doing your best, and always learning, you're okay. If you make mistakes *on purpose*, or refuse to grow, then you can't fly starships."

Kibi smiled.

"I remember a certain crew member," Ilika continued, "back at the little lake near the capital city, who was *sure* that if the local people tried to drag us into their affairs, we wouldn't play along. Anyone remember who that was?"

Rini turned red and grinned. "Me."

"After accidentally marrying a desert girl, can you see how easy it is to do?"

Rini nodded vigorously.

"Think you'll be better prepared next time we interact with a local culture?"

Rini nodded again, then smiled at Mati.

"Overall, I'm very proud of Rini," Ilika went on. "He had options, and even though it was painful, he chose to untangle himself from the situation, and remain with the Nebador Transport Service . . . with Mati . . . and with us."

Kibi, Boro, and Sata all looked at Rini with smiling eyes.

* * *

Why was Mati thinking of returning to her kingdom?

What made her change her mind?

"Shy" and "introverted" are two different things, but Mati and Rini, to various degrees, were both. Shyness, or fear in social situations, was probably stronger in Mati, and introversion, finding comfort and meaning in inner thoughts and feelings, was probably stronger in Rini.

From Mati's dependence on her crutch, and both their experiences as slaves, they are both very aware of the possibility of death. How do you think this affected their relationship?

What 3 things made the pastry sharing a special ritual, instead of just a bite of food?

What was Mati's fear when she asked Rini to clarify what he meant by "choosing" her?

How is the criteria for being in the Transport Service (do your best and always learn) different from the criteria used by most employers in selecting workers? Hint: one is "social" in nature (relative to other people), and the other is not.

Chapter 11: Back to Work

After three days of recovery from the gathering of the desert tribes, Ilika looked over his training checklists. He asked Kibi and Sata to concentrate on the last few language lessons they would be doing by themselves. Several low-altitude flights were scheduled to help Boro and Kibi catch up with the others, and the entire crew returned to the high-altitude flights that challenged them in completely different ways.

✷

"I know it's almost lunchtime," Ilika began from the command chair as all five crew members sat at their stations after a simulated flight, "but there's one more thing we need to do. Boro is the only one who knows that the anti-mass drive is always used along with an artificial gravity generator."

Boro, guessing what was coming, couldn't help but snicker.

Ilika smiled. "Now it's time for you all to experience what it would feel like if that generator failed. Boro, anti-mass level one, and Mati, take us up to one meter relative altitude."

"But don't we need . . ." Boro tried to say.

"No. Manessa is ready."

Some of the others had worried looks as they felt the ship lift off the ground.

"Gravity off," Ilika ordered, and Boro complied with a mischievous grin.

Sounds of amazement, discomfort, and even a little fear, could be heard all over the bridge as everyone began floating out of their seats. Only Boro was silent.

"I can't reach my flight control!" Mati gasped with panic.

"It's okay, Mati," Ilika assured as both of them floated slowly up toward the ceiling. "Manessa expects us to lose control any time the gravity generator is down and we aren't using our inertia straps. This is zero gravity. It's harmless, but one of those things we have to get used to. I did it when your stomachs were empty for a very good reason."

"I don't care what is, or isn't, in my stomach," Sata grumbled, floating over the command chair. "I feel sick."

"I'm fine," Rini said, quickly discovering he could push off any handy surface to propel himself. He moved across the bridge toward Mati. "Shall we dance?" he asked, taking her hand.

Mati giggled.

Ilika could see that Boro was okay. "Kibi, how are you doing?"

"Queasy, but not too bad," she replied, slowly crossing the passenger area without touching anything. "It would be very hard to serve lunch like this."

"Almost impossible," Ilika confirmed. "You couldn't use any liquids or loose solids." A minute later he spoke several words in his language, and everyone slowly settled back toward the floor. Rini helped Mati get her legs under her, and Kibi climbed down off the big oval table.

"I'm the captain now," Sata said from where she had landed, sideways, in Ilika's chair, "and we're *not* doing that again today."

Ilika smiled. "Tomorrow."

*

That evening, the moon and stars came out in a crystal clear sky, so Ilika and Kibi grabbed their old bedrolls. Just past a clump of scraggly desert bushes, not six meters from the Manessa Kwi, they snuggled close against the cool night air.

"It's good to see Mati and Rini starting to talk . . . and kiss," Kibi said. "Do you think they'll be happy together?"

"I don't know. I'm a little surprised they got together so soon. I thought they'd keep their distance until Mati's knee operation."

"I guess Rini's mistake forced them to decide."

"Yeah. But it seems he had already decided. He just hadn't told her."

Kibi chuckled. "He really wanted to make everyone happy back at the gathering, but he couldn't."

"I see a strong romantic side in him," Ilika shared, "and I was worried he'd fall for the first girl who openly liked him. We would have lost both him and Mati."

"Turns out he's stronger than that."

"Yeah."

There was a long silence as the nearly-full moon peered down at them.

"I have an admission to make, Ilika."

He turned toward her and listened.

"I've heard that on ships — you know, of our world — only the captain gets to take a lady along. So all during our journey I felt special, maybe a little more important than the other students. When I bolted from the motion training, I was *so* ashamed. Now I'm glad it happened. I needed to get over thinking I was better than the others."

"Yep," was all Ilika said.

After a long silence, Kibi asked, "Why do only captains get to take ladies?

That's not fair. Everyone needs love."

"It's probably just a power thing. But it's true that many people get distracted when the opposite sex is around."

"So why is it okay in the Transport Service for all of us to have relationships?"

"At most jobs in the Nebador Services, even in the Transport Service, couples rarely work side-by-side. Deep-space response ships are different — we're small, self-contained, and have to be ready for long voyages. Therefore, we must be willing and able to keep our private and work lives separate."

"So . . . by passing those tests back at Doko's Inn, I was applying for the hardest job in the whole . . . universe?"

Ilika smiled. "Pretty close!"

Kibi laughed out loud before falling silent and watching a wisp of cloud move across the moon.

"You'll always tell me the truth, right?" she asked in a quiet voice.

"Or tell you honestly that I can't, and why."

After a few breaths, Kibi went on. "Is there a girl waiting for you up there in the stars somewhere?"

Ilika looked at her. "No, there is not. I . . . was hoping you'd be the girl who always waited for me, just as I want to always wait for you."

Kibi smiled in the moonlight as she snuggled close to her lover. "I'd like that."

✷

All five students got comfortable in their molded acceleration seats, equally spaced around the outer edge of the ship. Manessa created three safety bars across each.

Kibi smiled at the embarrassing memory of wiggling out of one safety bar, and wondered, just for a moment, if she could get past three.

"This is your final exterior high-altitude flight," Ilika announced as he walked around the ship in the sand.

Boro sighed with relief.

Ilika smiled. "Smooth acceleration to five gravities, and you'll be at eight thousand meters in only eight seconds. Remember, screaming is okay. One minute to sight-see, then eight seconds on the way down. Manessa is worthy of your trust, and will set you down gently. Everyone in good health?"

They all nodded.

"We'll be at zero gravity on the way down, won't we?" Rini asked.

"Zero and negative gravity, which just means you'll be pressed against your safety bars part of the time. Any other questions?"

After the mistakes, large and small, they had each made in recent weeks, from accidentally shutting down the flight engines, to accidentally marrying the wrong girl, none of the students felt they had any cause to complain. They knew they had to learn many things that would scare them silly at first, but they trusted their captain to only give them tasks they could, with proper effort, learn.

"Ready," came five different voices.

"Okay. Enjoy the ride."

✷

Ilika heard them scream, and he heard their cheers of pride when they completed both the ascent, and the far-more-frightening descent. He greeted them when they hopped out of their seats and smiled as they bounced up and down with joy at their success.

"That was the scariest thing I've ever done," Kibi declared with her arms around him. "But . . . you know . . . I was okay."

✷ ✷ ✷

Below Earth orbit, zero gravity can only be created for short periods of time by diving toward the Earth in "free fall." This can be done skydiving, from a high cliff into water, in an airplane, and in some amusement park rides. We do not have the ability to block (or create) gravity without using motion. In orbit, gravity is always zero because orbit is simply that path of falling toward a planet that never gets closer to (or farther away from) the planet, and instead goes around and around. Zero gravity is not dangerous to our bodies in the short term, but because we are used to having gravity always present, some people feel sick to their stomachs under zero gravity. In the long term, our muscles become weak under zero gravity because it is so difficult to exercise.

Most human organizations, past and present, do not allow close personal relationships between people who work closely together because, as Ilika explained, most people get distracted. What quality is the Nebador Transport Service requiring in its deep-space response ship crews by allowing them to have romantic relationships within the crew?

Kibi's fear is understandable. Many stories have been told about captains and officers of ships who have a lover in several different ports, who never know about each other.

The rapid descent from eight thousand meters was far more frightening than the ascent because the ground could be seen rushing toward them. Our instincts tell us we're going to crash.

Chapter 12: Getting Very Serious

"Sata and I finished language lesson twenty yesterday," Kibi reported at breakfast as they ate hot porridge, with fruit from the ship's original supplies that seemed almost fresh when soaked in water.

"Now the rest of you can begin." Ilika looked at his knowledge pad. "Kibi will be responsible for teaching Mati, Sata with Rini, and I with Boro. We'll do all the same lessons Kibi and Sata have already done, and between lessons we'll practice in those pairs."

As soon as breakfast trays were cleaned and put away, Kibi stepped to her console and raised the table, reorganized the seats, and started the first lesson on the large screen over her station.

When it was over, the two advanced language students smiled with pride, and felt very honored to be teachers. But as they strolled in the dunes with their students, they received dirty looks every time they accidentally used words from future lessons, and quickly learned how important it was to stick to the current lesson and be very patient with their friends.

✷

For the next two days, in between language lessons, Kibi, Boro, Rini, and Sata practiced the exterior hull exercise with harness, safety line, and parts vest, while Manessa sat quietly on the ground. Then Ilika asked if they were ready for the final exam.

"What's the final exam?" Boro asked.

"You've been there before," Ilika replied.

"Eight . . ." Sata began with a smirk.

". . . thousand . . ." Rini added calmly.

". . . meters," Boro finished with a sigh.

"How did you guess?" Ilika asked, smiling. "But this time you get to do the ascent and descent inside a nice, warm ship."

✷

By mid-afternoon, everything was ready.

Ilika had spent an hour with Mati going over the new piloting techniques she would be using, and another hour with the other four about the harsh-environment suit that did the same job as their cloaks, but was much less clumsy.

Rising in the lift, Rini grinned with embarrassment when the others saw him in the skin-tight vivid-green suit, face visor currently open.

Ilika came up next and said, “Stations.”

With much excitement and some nervousness, everyone dashed to their consoles.

“The anti-mass drive normally cancels most inertia, but lets a little through because it’s easier to pilot the ship when you can feel the motion.

“Today we’re doing three things at once — hull activity finals for most of you, Mati piloting rapid ascents and descents, and everyone getting a feel for different amounts of inertia, and how they affect your jobs.

“Rini, since you’re suited and ready for your hull work, you’re off-duty and I’m covering your station. Just take a seat in the passenger area for the ride up.”

Kibi slapped hands with her first passenger as he passed.

“We’ll start with the anti-mass drive canceling all inertia. In a sense, this one will be hardest for the pilot. Trust your instruments, Mati.”

She nodded.

“Preflight preparations, all stations,” Ilika commanded, stepping to the watch console. “Anti-mass and thrusters, level three. Transponder and flight recorder. Acceleration curve one, Mati.”

The captain strolled around the bridge to see how everyone was doing. Rini, in the front row of passenger seats, looked ready for anything.

“Mati, what’s your deceleration point?” Ilika asked.

“Um . . . oh, yeah, seven thousand six hundred.”

“Keep in mind — deceleration that fast would plaster us to the ceiling, and probably break several bones, if we could feel it.”

Boro swallowed hard.

“Engine status?”

“Anti-mass, level three, green, zero inertia. Thrusters, level three, green.”

“Steward and navigator, status?”

Kibi and Sata both declared they were ready.

“Pilot, overhead obstacles?”

“Weather clear, light to moderate wind at all altitudes, no birds on the screen.”

“Flight objective, straight up to eight thousand meters, as soon as you are ready, pilot.”

Mati looked over her controls and visual displays one more time. Her flight control was within reach, but she knew she didn’t need it. After one more slow breath, she touched the symbol that would engage the selected acceleration curve.

She felt nothing, but could see the dunes quickly shrink to tiny ripples, then the nearby mountains become small jumbles of rock. Mere seconds later, the altitude graph rapidly approached the deceleration point. She watched as Manessa followed the curve. The last hundred meters were quickly traversed, and the altitude display stopped at eight thousand. "We are there."

"Could I . . ." Boro said hesitantly, ". . . um . . . peek out the hatch. It's hard to believe we're up here 'cause I didn't feel anything."

Ilika smiled. "Steward, equalize pressure, then open the upper hatch. Engineer is off-station for a minute. Kibi is in command."

Kibi found the requested controls as Ilika went to the hatch and Boro followed.

"Yep. We're definitely up here again," Boro confirmed with wide eyes, then returned to his console.

"Ready, Rini?" Ilika asked.

The boy wearing bright-green, harness, and parts vest stood up and went to the hatch.

"What happens if you fall from up here?" Ilika asked.

"Die," Rini answered with a nonchalant tone.

Ilika opened a cabinet and handed the lad a safety line, which Rini inspected, as he had practiced.

"No time limit. It must be done with gloves."

Rini nodded, clipped on his safety line, closed his visor, and climbed out the hatch.

✷

"This is so wonderful!" they could all hear Rini say through the suit's intercom. "The sky is so huge and the world is so small. I can see a flock of birds going south, way down there at about two thousand meters."

"I see them on my obstacle display," Mati confirmed.

"Manessa is so sweet, making steps and handholds for me even way up here in the cold. I'm almost there — had to step over my safety line — it likes to go with the wind."

Ilika smiled from a personal memory.

"Old device is out," Rini reported, "and in a pocket. New one is . . . oops . . . got it. Yep, gloves are clumsy. New one is in. Close the little hatch now, please, Manessa. Thank you."

Several of those inside the ship chuckled. A long minute passed before they heard from Rini again.

"I guess I should come in now, but . . . it's so beautiful up here . . ."

Ilika returned to the open hatch, and soon Rini was back inside.

"Hatch closed, resume normal pressure. Prepare for descent, all stations."

✷

With Kibi in a bright green suit, and Ilika covering her station, the Manessa Kwi again made the ascent, but this time they could feel a small fraction of the true acceleration forces, just enough to give them a sense of motion.

Kibi completed the test slowly and carefully, remembering everything she had learned in practice, and recalling Rini's experiences with the safety line and gloves. Most importantly, she told herself as she crept across Manessa's hull, she had to complete the task with her mind, and save any feelings for later.

*

Bright green was not Boro's favorite color, but he smiled with only a little embarrassment when Sata grinned at him from her station. Then they both turned their attention to securing inertia straps.

Those still on-duty had a new challenge – making sure they could reach every corner of their consoles under two gravities of acceleration. The anti-mass drive canceled the rest.

Boro narrated every move he made while on the hull. He worked carefully and methodically, but didn't linger on the way in. Keeping his stomach relaxed and happy still required part of his attention.

Two gravities of deceleration on the way down caused arms to rise toward the ceiling when they needed to be on their consoles, and an assortment of colorful words, in the crew's native language, made Ilika smile.

*

Sata looked confident and happy as she sat in the passenger area and let her body melt into the supportive seat during the three-gravity ascent. The others were sorely challenged to move their hands on their consoles without accidentally touching the wrong control. Ilika assured them this was the highest acceleration they would ever be expected to endure while working.

The eleven-year-old navigator nimbly attached her safety line and climbed out the hatch, and Ilika returned to the bridge to listen to her progress.

"It's windy out here. Safety line is all over the place. Damn! Now it's around my legs. Manessa is wonderful, but the rope is like a snake. Ouch! It just whipped me. I'm almost there, but . . . shit! It's got me again."

Boro looked worried.

Mati glanced at Ilika, and thought she saw a suppressed smile.

"I'm at the little hatch. The damned safety line is around one of my legs twice, but I'm going to try to get the parts swapped before I deal with it. Hatch is open. Ouch! Old part is out . . . I can really see why Rini fumbled at this point. Okay, it's in a pocket.

"Eek! It's around my neck! I can't do anything! I'm going to take the bloody thing off even if it means I flunk the test, and when I get back inside I'm going to chop it up into little pieces! Ouch! It's like an angry snake!"

"Does she flunk if she takes the safety line off?" Kibi asked.

"Yes."

"Wait," Sata's voice continued. "I just thought of something. If it's okay, could Mati rotate the ship a half turn? *Please!*"

Mati looked at Ilika, and he quickly nodded. "Maneuvering thrusters," she requested.

Boro confirmed, and Mati quickly made the heading adjustment.

"Oh, wow, that is so much better. Thank you, Mati! I'm . . . getting . . . the pissing thing . . . off my neck. Whew! And off my legs. Yes! Now it's whipping at nothing on the other side of the ship. *Maybe* I can do my work now."

Everyone inside laughed to release their tension and fear.

"New part is out of its pocket . . . in place . . . and the little hatch is closed. I'm going to take a moment to breathe, if no one minds. The safety line is tugging at me slightly, but it's better than being constantly attacked."

"The wind must be stronger now," Boro speculated.

"A little," Rini confirmed.

"Okay, I'm coming in. Anybody have a mug of hot tea handy? I'm almost to the hatch."

Ilika helped his student inside, but when he started to pull in the safety line, she stopped him.

"It's mine, Ilika! I want the satisfaction of coiling up that slimy little monster. And I'll *think* about not chopping it to pieces while I drink my tea."

Ilika laughed at the completely serious expression on his navigator's face. "Let's descend first so everyone can shut-down and join you for tea."

"O . . . kay," Sata agreed with some reluctance as she hauled in the thin rope.

✷

As soon as they were back on the sand, Kibi lowered the table and dashed to the pantry to start tea. Sata got out of the harsh environment suit and everyone gathered at the table.

"Good work, all of you," the captain complimented. "The recordings of your hull excursion tests will be fun to review, especially Sata's."

Everyone howled.

"Sata demonstrated something I want you all to remember."

The students became very silent and attentive as they held their mugs.

"Except when it works against the mission, or creates an unacceptable danger, if you need it, you get it. We are here to support each other. At every moment of everything you do, all the resources of Manessa and your fellow crew members are yours for the asking."

✷ ✷ ✷

". . . fruit that seemed almost fresh when soaked in water," could be freeze-dried, a dehydration method that is usually only used for backpacking foods because of its high cost. Most camping gear stores have some for sale.

Teachers have long known that one of the best ways to help an advanced student gain mastery is to have them teach all their knowledge to a beginning student. This phase of their language lessons, therefore, was just as useful to Kibi and Sata as to the others.

The zero-inertia ascent and descent would be most like a video game, seeing the expected visuals, but feeling nothing.

When Kibi "equalized pressure," after the ascent to eight thousand meters, which way did air flow?

Two gravities of acceleration is about what you would feel in an amusement park ride that spins you on the inside of a cylinder, sometimes dropping the floor out from under your feet for extra excitement. Working our arms, hands, and fingers under 2g takes effort, but is not hard.

Why did Ilika wait for Sata to think of a solution to her problem, instead of just asking Mati to turn the ship? Since it was a test, was Sata being allowed to "cheat," in your opinion?

Chapter 13: New Horizons

The crew of the Manessa Kwi knew a change was coming when Ilika gave them an entire day of free time.

Boro and Sata hiked across the dunes to the nearest mountains, and found a narrow canyon to explore. Rini made both lunch and dinner for Mati, and they spent time outside during the day, and on the lower deck watching videos in the evening. Kibi walked alone, revisiting the places and thoughts of her panic attack. When she returned, she had a question for Ilika.

"When we start flying between the stars, how often will I be able to feel dirt, or sand, or rock, or something that doesn't move, under my feet?"

"Almost every day. But even planets move."

"I know, but I can't feel it, so it's okay."

"Even the smallest star stations feel completely solid. They have gardens and sandy play areas, and their movement is just orbital, like a planet."

Kibi smiled.

*

"We have done everything we can do here in this desert," Ilika announced at breakfast the following morning.

Excitement showed on all five faces, but the question they wanted to ask was too obvious to say aloud.

"To continue your training, the rest of you need to begin reading and speaking Manessa's language. Today I want Kibi to lead a review of your language lessons, and afterward, Sata will teach everyone how to access the planetary charts. Each of you may pick two places on the planet you'd like to visit, and I have a few on my list for training purposes. It will be a truly grand tour, and we won't always go the shortest possible route."

"Deepest ocean," Sata declared.

"Highest mountain," Rini added.

The others looked thoughtful as Ilika collected breakfast trays and Kibi prepared the room for a lesson.

*

By late afternoon, they were all at their stations, searching through the charts for the two magical places they would choose. Ilika helped when they only knew the location by description, such as Mati's wish to see the most beautiful hot springs. Kibi started a list on a knowledge pad so they wouldn't duplicate each other's selections.

Most of the students chose geological features of one sort or another, but Kibi had something else in mind. Her curiosity about the desert had been satisfied, so she looked at the charts until she found the symbol for cities. Knowing their ship could hover at any altitude with little chance of being seen, she picked two as far apart as possible.

After Ilika led an intense language review, everyone headed for baths and beds to dream about the mysterious places they would soon be visiting.

*

The following morning, when most of the students began using toilets and coming up the lift, the savory aroma of spiced potatoes greeted them as Kibi sliced the strong cheese from the desert gathering.

Ilika's first sentence of welcome to his crew of youth from a medieval kingdom contained several words from the star civilization of Nebador, but they had studied those words and hardly noticed. As he began to brief them about their first flight of the day, more new words were sprinkled into his sentences, especially relating to numbers and units of measurement. When he saw puzzled looks, he would repeat twice more — once in their native language, and again in his.

"Our first objective is to fly from here to a tiny island in the western ocean, location number one on Manessa's flight list. Your maximum altitude is one thousand meters above sea level. You have level one anti-mass and thrusters, but no inertia canceling."

As soon as they inhaled their breakfast, they gathered around Sata at the navigator's station. She displayed a chart that contained both their current location and the indicated island.

"Looks easy," Boro said. "We just need to go south, then west."

Suddenly Sata took on a troubled expression, and magnified part of the chart. "No, not so easy. The pass out of the desert southward is more than a thousand meters. Ilika's gonna make us work."

For the next hour they huddled around their navigator, looking for a way to get out of the desert within the given limitations. Ilika sat at the table, sipped tea, and worked on concocting even more devious puzzles.

"Flight plan ready," Sata finally announced.

Ilika looked at the convoluted course that went north, then east over a seven hundred meter pass, along a river to a far-northern ocean, through a narrow passage into the western ocean, and finally to the island. "Congratulations! Everyone ready?"

“Toilet break!” Mati and Sata both said at once.

*

When Mati made her first course change with full inertia, everyone swayed to the left, only held in their seats by inertia straps.

“Sorry!” she whined, red with embarrassment. “I’ll remember to bank next time.”

The rest of the crew mumbled forgiveness. Ilika just smiled and mentally checked off another item on Mati’s training list.

As soon as they slipped over the low pass and entered the large river valley, the scenery below became green with countless pine trees. As they continued to fly north, the trees became fewer and fewer, but many colors of green and yellow grasses still covered the land, along with a few stunted trees.

“This is tundra, typical of low-elevation land in sub-polar regions.”

“Why no trees?” Boro asked, gazing at his visual display, but remembering to glance at his engine status board occasionally.

“The ground only thaws very near the surface. Only a few feet down is permafrost. Trees can’t grow in ice.”

“There’s ice on the river already,” Mati observed.

Rini nodded. “I bet winter is long up here.”

“We should be able to see the northern ocean soon,” Sata said, watching their progress on her display.

“I see it,” Mati reported, “and it’s covered with thick fog.”

“Cloud top, Rini?” Ilika asked.

“Um . . . about one thousand seven hundred. Real-time topographics at your service, Mati.”

Mati touched her display selector until she had the projection she wanted, three-D with color-coded elevations. “Can’t go over them without breaking the rules, so I’m entering the cloud bank at four hundred. Nice, easy turn into the next leg.”

“Good control, Mati,” Ilika complimented. “Captain is off the bridge for a few minutes. Steward is in command.” He disappeared into the lift.

Kibi swallowed. “Er . . . um . . . status . . . reports?”

Everyone else was happy. Sata mentioned they were rapidly approaching the narrow passage to the western ocean. Kibi looked behind her, but Ilika was nowhere to be seen. “How wide is the passage, Sata?”

“Mmm . . . fifteen kilometers at the narrowest place.”

Kibi could feel beads of sweat forming all over her face and hands as they continued moving through the misty white clouds. “Mati, half-speed,” Kibi commanded with a shaking voice.

Mati started to roll her eyes, but caught herself and began slowing the ship.

Kibi heard Ilika come up and gleefully swiveled around. “You’re back in command, right?”

“No, not until I say I am.” He began to stroll around the bridge, looking over each person's shoulder for a moment.

Kibi tried to swallow the huge lump in her throat as she turned back to the bridge. "St . . . status reports."

"Passing through the straights now and entering open water," Mati reported. "Still at four hundred."

"On flight plan," Sata added.

"Fair weather ahead," Rini assured.

The white mist suddenly vanished from their visual displays and they could see deep blue water below, thin high clouds above.

Kibi let out a sigh of relief. "Resume full speed."

Ilika smiled at her.

*

On the long flight southward over the featureless ocean, the pilot was pushing forward on her flight control to get all possible speed from the level-one thrusters.

"Um . . . Ilika . . ." Boro began with a worried voice. "Thrusters just went red."

"What do you recommend, engineer?"

"Um . . . slow down?"

"What do you think of that, pilot?"

"I'd . . . like more speed. It's a long way."

"Let's go to level two, Mati. Boro's engines will be happier. Just remember inertia."

Boro took the thrusters up a notch. "Back to yellow," he said with a contented smile.

After being pushed into their seats for a minute as Mati accelerated, everyone was quiet as the little ship traveled effortlessly over the dark ocean.

"Big flock of birds ahead at our altitude!" Rini announced with a tone of urgency. "Moving east."

"I see them," Mati confirmed. "Going off flight plan to the west." Once she had made the course change, she glanced back at Ilika.

He looked happy.

* * *

Ilika's navigation problem was challenging because desert "depressions" can be completely ringed by high-elevation passes, unlike true "valleys" which always have a low-elevation river outlet.

"Fog" is just a cloud that happens to be touching the ground. Flying in a cloud is the most usual type of "IMC" (instrument meteorological condition). It is different from "IFR" flying (instrument flight rules), which is often done in perfectly good weather. IMC is real, and absolutely requires IFR flight.

What situation made Kibi so nervous during her first period of command during flight? What could she have done to reduce her nervousness? Hint:

Mati did it just before entering the cloud.

The crew's experience as Mati changed speeds shows the difference between velocity and acceleration. "Going fast" does not create acceleration forces (gravity and inertia). "Speeding up" does. Once Mati reached the new (higher) speed, the crew ceased to be pressed into their seats.

Mati's course change to avoid the flock of birds is a small example of something the crew will learn in much more depth in *NEBADOR Book Six*. Any piloting situation requires the crew to sometimes bend, even break, the rules. FAR (Federal Aviation Regulations in the USA) 91.3(b) states "In an in-flight emergency requiring immediate action, the pilot in command may deviate from any rule of this part to the extent required to meet that emergency." (Part 91 is all the General Operating and Flight Rules.) Breaking the rules "well" is one of the things that clearly separates adults from children.

Chapter 14: New Powers

"Normally, on a long flight leg like this, some of us could go off-duty. But with full inertia, that would be dangerous. Even my break to let Kibi get a little command experience was a risk. And now we have to decelerate with inertia. Give yourself about forty kilometers, Mati."

She nodded, and began carefully pulling back on her flight control.

"Our bodies are used to one gravity of acceleration downward, and they can handle two or three without discomfort. Our seats support us well for forward acceleration, but any other direction is a problem above one quarter gravity. In an emergency, we can flip the ship around so our seats cushion a rapid deceleration."

"Thirty kilometers," Sata announced.

Everyone felt their inertia straps holding them as Mati slowed the ship.

"The island is alive with birds!" Rini declared.

"Twenty kilometers," Sata said. "Chart on channel five."

"Full stop a kilometer from the island," Ilika commanded, "then go in dead slow. Kibi, landing site selection, without crushing any birds or nests."

Kibi nodded and began studying her display.

"Eight kilometers," Sata reported.

The small, rocky island had no trees or bushes, just a little grass where soil had collected in cracks and crevices. Thousands of sea birds called it home. As Mati hovered the ship nearby, the island most closely resembled an agitated bee hive.

"That flat place looks free of nests," Kibi noted. "Some birds are walking around, but I bet they'll move when we get close."

"I need a view straight down," Mati said.

Rini touched his controls. "Down view on channel four. Strong wind from the west."

"Look okay, Kibi?" Mati asked when she was directly over the proposed landing site.

"Um . . . there's a nest in that nook. Can you move back a little?"

Mati nudged her flight control until Kibi nodded, then extended struts and carefully lowered the ship. They could all feel a bump at the moment of contact. "Sorry."

Ilika nodded. "Manessa is changing shape to shed the wind. Kibi is out first to check for site dangers. We'll need boots and cloaks."

*

The island extended less than a hundred meters in all directions, and if the visitors wandered near any of the nesting areas, birds started whizzing by their heads in warning. Even so, they welcomed the wind in their faces and the smell of salty air, the cry of gulls and the view over the open ocean, seemingly endless in all directions.

Back inside, as Rini assembled a snack, Ilika spoke.

"You know about ions. You know they move very easily when in a plasma, like fire. Manessa's ion drive creates a region of frictionless flow around the hull. Combined with an aerodynamic shape, the ship can move through a fluid – air or water – at about a hundred times the speed that's possible with ordinary thrust."

"We could have made the trip here from the narrow passage in . . . seconds!" Sata said excitedly.

"That's right. Boro has studied his ion drive controls, but never used them. The open ocean is a good place to practice, but first you all must take to heart some life-or-death warnings."

Rini put the snack tray on the table, an assortment of crackers and other finger foods. Then he sat as everyone listened to their captain.

"The ion drive is NOT capable of slow acceleration. ANY inertia from it is deadly. It is ALWAYS used with zero inertia."

They all wore grave looks and slowly nodded.

"You CANNOT fly by visual references. By the time you see something and try to respond, it is far behind you, or you have crashed into it and died. You MUST have a known clear flight path in front of you to use the ion drive. That puts a new responsibility on the navigator to carefully examine all elevations the ship will pass over. Safe clearance, except in some dire emergency, is one thousand meters."

Frowning, Sata nodded her understanding.

"Of course, there are advantages. If you need to get away from something FAST, like an avalanche that's two seconds from burying you, the ion drive will do the trick. Manessa will even pick a course if you don't have time to set one, usually straight up."

Boro's mouth opened.

"We will start with a demonstration. We will fly toward another island, at an altitude one thousand meters higher than the peak of the island, and I want Mati to try to stop the moment she sees the island."

Mati's grin looked somewhat forced.

⁕

When they finished the snack and returned to their stations, Ilika went from person to person. Rini only needed to provide visual displays. Sata calculated the course to the target island. Boro double and triple-checked that the anti-mass drive was set for zero inertia, then hesitantly warmed up the ion drive with Ilika watching.

"Pilot, lock in an altitude of three thousand two hundred meters," Ilika commanded. "Verify that, navigator."

"Um . . . yes, two thousand two hundred plus one thousand."

"Steward, departure procedure."

Kibi looked over the landing site from her console and closed the hatch, then selected views of other parts of the interior. After personally checking the galley, she declared the ship ready.

Ilika noticed a worried look on Boro's face. "Report your concern, engineer."

"Shouldn't we . . . use inertia straps?"

"They wouldn't help. Without the anti-mass drive canceling all inertia, we'd just die, straps or no."

Boro swallowed and checked his controls again.

"Also, Manessa would yell at us if we even *talked* about using the ion drive without full inertia canceling."

"That's good," Boro said with relief.

"Pilot, take us up to the target altitude and hover."

No one could feel a thing as Mati lifted the ship and retracted the landing struts, but the little island and its many winged creatures quickly shrank on their visual displays. "Three thousand two hundred," Mati declared.

"Make the target bearing our heading and select your display."

Mati rotated the ship slightly and put the forward visual on her main screen.

"All stations, report readiness for ion drive."

The nervousness on the bridge was thick, but no one could think of anything else they needed to do.

"At your leisure, pilot."

Mati smiled. She could clearly remember a time, less than a year before, when nothing had ever been at her leisure. Now a deep-space response ship was under her fingertips, and her heart beat a little faster at the responsibility — and pleasure — of the situation. After a breath for courage, she touched the ion drive symbol.

The ocean below became a blur, and only the horizon and distant clouds remained in focus. A few seconds later, something gray flashed into view, and Mati jerked her hand off the ion drive control.

"Good work, Mati. You just piloted the Manessa Kwi across more than three thousand kilometers of ocean. Ion drive off, Boro. Let's see how far back the island is."

After blinking a few times, Mati turned the ship. Everyone could see the cone-shaped island sticking out of the water a ways behind them.

"We're almost thirty kilometers past the island," Sata reported, moving the image of a measuring scale on her display.

"Any questions about the possibility of using visual flight references with the ion drive?" Ilika asked the entire bridge.

"If we'd been at two thousand meters . . ." Rini began with wide eyes.

No one finished his sentence.

* * *

An acceleration force sideways would be like someone giving us a shove. When standing, we are top-heavy, so receiving a shove can knock us off balance. If we see the shove coming, we can spread our legs to form a wider base.

Why would Ilika ask his crew to not crush birds or nests? The answer is in *NEBADOR Book Three*, chapter 16.

Do you remember the meanings of "heading," "track," and "bearing" from *NEBADOR Book Two*? "Make the target bearing our heading" translates to "Point the ship the way we want to go."

"Visual flight references" (sometimes mistakenly called "VFR," but that means visual flight rules) is piloting by what you can see out the window. It is also called "pilotage."

Chapter 15: Boro's Volcano

"Why is it smoking?" Sata wondered aloud. "Does someone have a fire down there?"

"This is one of Boro's requests, a volcano. I picked an active one – I didn't think you'd be too impressed with a cold, dormant one that just looks like a mountain. Boro, you are in command to guide Mati on a complete tour of your volcano. This is new land rising out of the sea. No human being has ever set foot here, and probably none have even seen it . . . until now."

Boro's mouth was open. "Um . . . I thought it was going to be . . . something little . . . like the hot springs."

"Actually," Ilika said, "this is small as volcanoes go. They can be five or six thousand meters high. Come, sit in the command chair. I'll cover your station."

With a very unsure expression, Boro slowly rose from his seat. When he saw the proud look on Sata's face, he took a deep breath. "Um . . . Kibi got to just command from her station . . ."

"Kibi can see the entire bridge from her station, you can't."

Boro slowly seated himself.

"While Boro explores the volcano, Kibi will be looking for a safe landing site for lunch," Ilika announced.

"Um . . ." the engineer began with a scrunched face, "let's start at the top."

Mati turned to her console, and Ilika seated himself and looked over the control board at the engineer's station, then leaned back to relax.

*

The glowing orange lava fountain in the volcano's main crater made Boro very concerned about distance, until Rini reported that it was cooler than the fire the priests had built.

Sata shrieked when molten rock splattered onto the hull. The captain assured them that Manessa was okay.

Under Boro's hesitant command, Mati followed rivers of lava down the sides of the volcano as most crew members stared at their displays with open mouths. Kibi wore a frown, but wasn't looking at the lava. She went to Rini's station and asked about the outside air.

When Boro's tour finally reached the sea, they watched in awe as globs of molten rock plunged into the water and huge clouds of steam billowed up.

"Have you picked a landing site?" Boro finally asked, turning to Kibi.

"No. And I'm not going to. There are a few places we could perch with the hatch closed, but poisonous fumes are lurking everywhere. It's just *not* a picnic place."

Ilika smiled. "So, where should we have lunch, Kibi?"

"Well . . . if the engines and fuel are okay . . . I think we should just hover, somewhere upwind. We can open the hatch and watch the thing smoke and sputter while we eat."

Ilika touched some controls on the engineer's console. "We have enough fuel for the anti-mass drive, at level one, for about . . . eight years."

Kibi smiled.

Ilika nodded at Boro, still in the command chair.

"Mati," Boro said, "please pick us a nice lunch spot, somewhere upwind with a view."

Mati grinned and moved her flight control.

✷

With the hatch wide open and the salty smell of the ocean filling the ship, Sata served a tasty left-over stew made back in the desert.

"Kibi demonstrated something," Ilika began, "that I want you all to understand. To do your jobs well, you have to be willing to say *no*. You have to be willing to recognize when you can't safely function within the limitation you have been given. Then you and the commander can decide if the situation warrants a greater risk, like Kibi's idea of perching somewhere with the hatch closed, or something else entirely. Everyone see?"

Several heads nodded.

"But what if things are happening fast," Boro said, "and someone *needs* whatever you're supposed to do?"

"Then you do three things. You get them what they asked for as best you can, you point out the problem, and you prepare an alternative. Try it with your situation, Kibi."

"Um . . . there's a place we could land the ship down there, but there are poisonous fumes and we can't open the hatch, and I suggest we just hover."

"Good. Now you try it, Boro, with your overloaded thrusters from this morning."

"Okay . . . um . . . thrusters are still working, but they're red, and . . . um . . . I'm increasing to level two . . . or we could slow down."

"Excellent. Once you know your jobs well, it'll be easy."

✷

After lunch, while the others looked on, Sata concentrated on the ocean chart filling her display screen. Using the controls at her fingertips, she drew several different straight lines from their present position to the deepest ocean trench, their next destination. Each time she drew a line, Manessa displayed depth and clearance numbers. "Seems like there's always some little island or reef . . . wait a minute . . . it looks better up here at the north end of the trench . . . yes! More than four thousand meters deep."

"Good. Send Mati that heading. Stations."

Everyone scrambled.

"Preflight. Anti-mass one. Submarine topographics. Remember your underwater visual filters, Rini?"

"Yep!"

"Take us down to a depth of one thousand meters, pilot."

Mati was able to enter the water much more smoothly than on her first attempt, almost seven weeks before.

"Hull integrity check, steward."

"Yikes! Hull status is purple, not usable, totally broken!"

Without a word from anyone, Mati quickly had the ship back on the surface and several meters in the air. Ilika dashed up to Kibi's side. All the crew members stared at him with anxious eyes when, a moment later, he burst out laughing. "Manessa still has some lava stuck to the hull and doesn't like it."

Boro and Rini quickly joined the laughter, followed closely by Sata. Mati and Kibi just smiled.

"Extreme rotating shapes, Manessa," the captain requested of his sentient ship.

Mati watched as part of her console lit up with symbols she hadn't studied. They could all see chunks of rock falling past their visual displays.

When the process was complete, Kibi repeated the integrity check. "Hull status is blue-green . . . yellow. Thank you, Manessa."

"You are welcome, Kibi," Manessa said in the language of Nebador, in a pleasant voice that was neither male nor female, using words they had all studied.

Sata's mouth dropped open.

Mati spun around, eyes wide.

Rini grinned with happiness.

Kibi's eyes lit up. "That's the first time Manessa talked to me, except in lessons."

"As I'm sure you've all noticed," Ilika began, "I'm beginning to use the language of Nebador when I give commands."

Boro nodded vigorously. "We've noticed."

"You will soon be able to chat with your deep-space response ship to your heart's content."

* * *

By giving Kibi a problem (a safe landing site for lunch on the volcano) that has no answer, what is Ilika teaching her?

The method Ilika taught them of fulfilling a command that is not safe (preparing to follow the request, explaining the problem, and preparing an alternative) is almost beyond human ability because it requires both assertiveness and humility in the commander and the crew member. If you can learn to do this, you will be ready to tackle extremely hard and complex problems in a teamwork situation, but don't be surprised if other members of your team are not capable of it.

The Manessa Kwi, a sentient but not sapient deep-space response ship, challenges us to think about the meaning of the word "person." Some people will only grant that status to other human beings (and sometimes only if they are in the correct nation, race, or class). Other people grant personhood to higher animals (dogs, cats, horses, dolphins, etc.) Few would give it to a machine that has simple controls. When Manessa didn't "like" the lava on her hull, and spoke to the crew in a conversational situation, did she gain "personhood" in your eyes?

Chapter 16: Sata's Trench

The trip by ion drive through the water took longer than their previous flight by air, Ilika explained, because of the greater density, but none of the crew complained about fifteen seconds for one thousand six hundred kilometers of ocean.

"Ion drive off," the captain ordered. "Anti-mass one, thrusters three. Do you have good visual and topographic displays, pilot?"

Mati tapped at her selectors. "Yes. It looks like it gets dark down there."

"The water quickly blocks all the sunlight. You can pilot by your three-D, and then I'll show you the exterior lighting controls when we get to something interesting."

Mati sat quietly and took in the shape and direction of the huge canyon in the bottom of the ocean. Nearly a hundred kilometers wide at their current position, it tapered as it plunged into darkness. As soon as Ilika had received a status report from each station, he gave his pilot leave to enter the trench and proceed south.

The first thousand meters of depth, lit by the sun above, allowed them to peer into mysterious underwater fissures that cut into the sides of the main trench. Countless creatures clung to the rocks, some reaching out with tentacles, other with fronds that waved in the current. Schools of small shimmering fish, and occasional larger creatures, darted away as Manessa approached.

Soon the light from above dimmed, and Mati began to pilot by her instruments. "Two thousand meters."

"Bridge lighting to minimum, steward," Ilika requested, and Kibi touched her controls until the upper deck was almost dark, allowing them to better see their displays.

For the next few minutes, everyone was silent as the last hints of light faded and their visual displays became useless. The pilot continued to steer the ship downward into the trench. “Four thousand meters.”

They all listened to their hearts beat for another minute, while scanning their controls and displays.

“Ilika?” Sata called with a sharp voice that suddenly cut through the silence.

“Yes, Sata?”

The navigator swallowed a few times. “Oh, nothing,” she responded in a shaking voice, but didn’t turn around.

Mati glanced at her friend, could see a tear on her cheek, and noticed the tension in her clenched jaw. “You have to tell him, Sata. We can’t be a team unless we all do it together.”

By this time, Ilika was kneeling next to his navigator, who was starting to breathe in troubled gasps. He looked at her but waited.

“I . . . I don’t know what it is,” Sata burst out without looking at her captain. “I can’t . . . breathe! I feel like . . . I’m trapped . . . like I’m suffocating.”

“Kibi, internal air diagnostic,” Ilika commanded without taking his eyes off Sata.

“It’s . . . just fine.”

A moment later, Sata began gasping for air, while her eyes strained to see something on her visual display.

Ilika extended his hand. “Come on, navigator. Let’s take a break.”

After a moment of embarrassed reluctance, Sata allowed herself to be guided up to the passenger area, gasping and crying as she went.

“Boro, you’re off-duty too. Come sit with your friend.”

As soon as Sata and Boro were comfortable in two passenger seats, side by side, Ilika went to Kibi’s station and selected a video of wide-open outdoor scenes. Boro took Sata’s hand and held it tightly.

Ilika glanced at the engineer’s station, checked on his pilot who announced twelve thousand meters, then returned to the passenger area. Sata was breathing much easier, watching the video, and wiping at her tears. “I’m so sorry, Ilika. I don’t know what happened. It wasn’t anything I can put into words. It wasn’t fear or anything like that. It was just something my body did, and I can’t explain it.”

“That fits with what I’m seeing, Sata — some kind of reaction to . . . the darkness outside? The silence? I’d like to try something.”

Ilika returned to Kibi’s console and selected a lively piece of music with an interesting melody and a strong beat. Moments after it started, Sata was smiling and drying the last of her tears.

Kibi started moving to the beat in her chair. “Ilika, can I get up and dance?”

“*You’re* still on-duty,” he replied with a grin. “We can play when we find a landing site tonight. Where are we, pilot?”

“Holding position at the bottom of the trench, twenty thousand seven hundred meters down, waiting for you to show me how to turn on the lights.”

Ilika worked with Mati for a moment, and suddenly their visual displays revealed a bizarre scene of strange colorless plants, worm-like creatures, and inky jets squirting upward from the deep ocean floor. Noises of amazement came from all around the bridge.

"Nice," Ilika said. "Kibi, put this on the passenger screen and tell me how Sata takes it."

Kibi touched a symbol, then swiveled around. "She's still smiling!"

"These creatures have never experienced light, so they have no eyes. Photosynthesis plays no part in their life cycles, only the geothermal activity you see, which adds heat and minerals to the environment."

"I never thought something could be so beautiful and yet so strange," Rini commented.

Ilika smiled. "This is pretty ordinary compared to things we'll see on other planets. How are you doing, Sata?"

"I'm okay. It must have been the darkness."

"Hmm . . ." Ilika mused, looking around the bridge. "It's time for a little demo. Mati, I'd like you to go off-duty, take the navigators chair. Sata, you are in the command chair, and Boro is back on-duty."

Sata looked a little forlorn with tear stains on her face as she hesitantly took Ilika's chair. The song ended, so Kibi selected the next song on the list, equally good at uplifting the mood of the crew. Ilika sat down at the pilot's station.

"There's a knack to this that I haven't completely mastered," Ilika shared, "but the idea is to fly to the beat of the music. I know pilots who can make a ship dance. Engine check?"

"Anti-mass one, thrusters three, all yellow."

"Inertia straps, all stations. Full inertia, engineer."

For the next few minutes, with Manessa lighting up the bottom of the undersea trench, Ilika give his crew their first taste of artistic flying. He swooped the little ship among the rocks, strange translucent plants, and jets of black water with movements that matched the beats and phrases of the music. He glanced back at Sata often, who continued to look happy. Kibi swayed in her chair, anxious to let her feet move along with the dancing ship.

When the song ended, Ilika brought the ship to a halt on the bottom. "Twenty-four thousand meters, about as deep as this trench goes. What's the outside pressure, Rini?"

"Um . . . about two thousand times normal atmosphere."

"You okay hearing that, Sata?"

"Yeah. I trust you to tell us if Manessa can't handle something. I feel fine."

"Could someone go out there with a harsh environment suit?" Boro asked.

"No. This would take pressure suits, the red ones."

"My turn!" Mati said with a big grin, bouncing up and down in the navigator's seat.

✷

To another piece of lively music, the pilot guided the little ship out the southern end of the deep ocean trench. She knew her piloting wasn't as smooth and rhythmic as her captain's, but everyone clapped when the song ended and they headed for the surface.

With the sun approaching the western horizon, Sata navigated to a small uninhabited tropical island, and Kibi selected a pristine beach in a protected cove. Mati settled the ship carefully onto the sand, and a few minutes later everyone was outside, dancing as best they could to the music that poured through the open hatch, music that could not be composed, nor performed, on that planet for at least another thousand years.

✷ ✷ ✷

Sata's reaction to the ocean trench is on the border between a psychological (mental) reaction, and a physiological (body) reaction. No physical force was acting upon her (like reduced air pressure), but neither did it spring from emotions or beliefs. There exists a level in our minds that is very difficult to access, and is closely tied to the functioning of our bodies. This mental level can cause us to be incapable of doing certain things, or living in certain environments, and no amount of therapy (drug or cognitive) will help.

The ecosystem on the deep ocean floors was only discovered very recently, and has a completely different metabolic process than anywhere else on the planet. Instead of green plants making food from sunlight and minerals through photosynthesis, the ocean trench ecological niches rely on the heat from volcanic or tectonic activity. This process is called chemosynthesis.

The water pressure deep in the oceans makes it impossible to bring back living creatures. When brought to the surface, they immediately fall apart and die, just as we would in a vacuum.

Flying to music must be done with awareness of the limitations of the craft. When I am flying a Cessna 152, for example, I have to remember that it will not handle acrobatic maneuvers.

The extreme pressure in the deep oceans would require a suit primarily designed to deal with that pressure. Our "deep-sea diving suits" can only handle a fraction of that pressure. We can only visit the ocean trenches in small ships called bathyspheres or bathyscaphs. The crew's green harsh environment suits were for extreme temperatures, but normal pressure.

Chapter 17: Going Fishing

The following day was a well-earned rest for ship and crew. Ilika scheduled two language lessons, and spent some time with each of his students, but otherwise left lots of free time for everyone to run in the sand and lie in the sun. All day long, he overheard chatter about their experiences the day before, their growing wonder at their little ship's abilities, and their amazement that they were part of it all.

✷

"We made a plan," Sata said as she and Boro picked fruit on the edge of the tropical forest a short walk down the beach from the landing site. "I'm going to experiment with different things on my main display, and see if I can figure out what made me freak out. Ilika reminded me that I could have selected Mati's three-D topographic instead of staring at a dark screen. I felt so stupid."

Boro grinned. "I've been listening, and no one's bothered by what happened, 'cause you didn't bolt like Kibi did."

"Thanks. I don't think she'll ever bolt again."

"I think she knows it would be her last."

"Yeah. Are these long green things edible?" Sata asked.

"Uh huh. Kibi found a yellow one that had fallen off and ripened, and she tested it."

"Okay, I'll get this bunch if you'll carry back the pear-shaped things with the black seeds."

"Deal."

✷

With more language lessons under their belts, the captain of the Manessa

Kwi began to slip additional words of his language into routine conversations, and added to the list of words Manessa could use when speaking to them.

As they all sat around the table the next morning after breakfast, he passed out breathing masks. "The hardest part of underwater work is getting used to the mask. Our eyes don't work well in contact with water, and our lungs, of course, don't work at all."

Boro cocked his head and grinned.

"The masks take care of both problems, and also provide two-way communication with the ship."

"So . . . this would work if we went higher than eight thousand meters where the air gets really thin . . . or we had to stay up there longer," Boro speculated.

"Or in space where there's no air at all!" Sata added.

"Yes," Ilika confirmed, "although space requires a different suit."

"The orange ones," Kibi said from memory.

"Right. Today we use the blue suits. They don't keep the water out, but the little bit that gets in is quickly warmed by our bodies. The belt has adjustable mass so we can sink, float, or whatever we need to do. But we start by getting comfortable with the masks. You can do this part too, Mati."

Ilika put on his breathing mask and the others did likewise. They made faces at each other through the masks, which quickly fogged up when they laughed.

"It's instinctive to hold your breath when under water," Ilika explained through the intercom, "so you have to make yourselves breathe. Also, if you feel fear or anxiety, you might start breathing too fast. Sata has to really watch this in herself."

She nodded thoughtfully.

For the next hour, they prepared for their underwater adventure while getting used to the masks. Ilika taught them the bracelet code that would scare away any underwater beasties, then got into a blue suit while the others secured the landing site and the ship. Mati, still in her mask, piloted the ship to the middle of the cove and placed it on the bottom. Only about a meter of water covered the top of the ship.

With his five crew members watching, Ilika demonstrated the air lock on the lower deck. As soon as he was gone, they dashed up the lift to watch and listen at their stations.

"The bottom is sandy, and there's a slight current toward the open ocean," he said as he walked slowly around the ship through the water, "but nothing that requires a safety line. Since I'm in an environment that could have predators, you guys are watching my back."

Boro and Kibi both reassured him.

"I'm doing my work first. The practice hatch is open. The part is out. I'm pausing to check behind me . . . nothing in sight. Replacement part is in and hatch closed."

Those in the ship saw a shadow pass slowly over the sea bottom near their captain.

"Ilika!" Kibi nearly screamed. "Look above you!"

They could see him tilt his head back and reach for his bracelet at the same time. "Nothing above me. Might have been a cloud passing over the sun."

Rini selected a view straight up. "Yep, it was a cloud."

"Good. Now I'm adjusting my belt until I'm the same density as the water, so I can just swim around and get used to it. Even though I can still *see* the bottom, this would *feel* exactly the same if I had a deep trench under me."

Sata gritted her teeth for a moment, then made herself breathe slowly and evenly through the mask.

"I'm going to scare off this fish just for practice," Ilika announced. His students faintly heard the strange warbling sound made by the bracelet, and could see the little fish dart away.

"Um . . . Ilika, what about dinner?" Boro asked. "Do we have a net?"

Ilika chuckled. "Sorry, Boro, we do not. Maybe we can pick one up somewhere. I'm coming in. Kibi and Sata are next."

✷

The two girls waved to their friends as the airlock door closed and the chamber filled with water.

"How do you feel, Sata?" came Ilika's voice.

"I feel okay. I'm used to the mask, and everything's light and pretty out here. Kibi's standing watch, so I'm opening the practice hatch."

Sata's part replacement exercise was completed effortlessly, with several little fish watching. Then the girls changed places.

"I have the hatch open and the old part out," Kibi reported.

"Another shadow from above," Mati mentioned from her station without much concern.

"Kibi duck!" Sata yelled without warning as she stepped backwards, reached for her bracelet, and a moment later those in the ship heard a high-pitched sound.

Ilika tried desperately to see what was happening, but for a moment the view was clouded by stirred-up sand and mud. "Sata, report!" he yelled, ready to dash for the airlock.

"Wow. Hold on, I'm helping Kibi up."

"What was it?" Kibi asked as she collected herself.

"Damned big fish . . . with teeth!" Sata declared.

"It's gone belly-up," Kibi observed.

"I think I used the sleep code instead of the scare code," Sata admitted.

"How big?" Ilika asked.

"About . . . two meters," Kibi estimated. "And it's got a row of teeth you could plow a field with."

"Shark!" Boro declared. "Good eating."

"Can we keep it, Ilika?" Sata asked.

"I think . . . um . . . we have to. I forgot to mention it, but the sleep function is deadly to fish."

"Whoopee!" Boro cheered from his station. "Fresh fish for dinner!"

"I heard that," Sata said through the intercom. "We need a rope or something before it drifts away."

Ilika laughed and shooed Boro toward the lift to help the girls with their catch.

✷

The little ship had never before been used for the processing of freshly-caught fish, but in a pinch, it was up to the task. Ilika remembered a good supply of food preservation pouches, but neither he nor Kibi could find them. Eventually Rini, by lying on his belly, discovered them in the very back of the lowest cabinet, behind the sacks of dried beans.

Boro hoisted their catch onto the table, and everyone sat down with knives to dissect the aquatic beast. Kibi received bowls of cut-up shark meat to take to the galley where she carefully filled and sealed each pouch. Finally Ilika showed them how to select the proper type and amount of radiation in the oven to sterilize the pouches without cooking the contents.

Sata wrinkled her nose. "Our ship smells like a fish market!"

✷

Boro and Rini were soon ready to go. They stepped into the airlock and waved good-bye to Ilika and Kibi.

"This is fun!" Rini said through the intercom as he adjusted his belt and began to swim.

Boro preferred walking on the sandy bottom, but grinned as Rini twisted himself every which way and turned somersaults. "Okay, my turn," Boro finally said.

They traded places, and in his own way, much more slowly and carefully, Boro discovered the joy of moving in the water among several curious little fish.

Eventually Ilika cleared his throat. "Don't forget the parts exercise."

"Oh, yeah." Boro adjusted his belt so he would settle back to the bottom.

Rini approached the little practice hatch, glanced behind him to see that Boro was standing watch, and went to work. He was almost finished when Boro suddenly yelled, "Oh, no! Three or four of them!"

"No, Bor . . ." Ilika tried to say, but was cut off by the high-pitched sound of Boro's bracelet.

"I got one!" Boro declared with heart-pounding excitement.

"Don't try to get any more!" Ilika commanded.

"Why not?"

"Those aren't sharks," Ilika said firmly. "They're dolphins, sapient mammals, and must breathe air. Get the unconscious one into the airlock, quickly! I'll come out to help!"

Ilika dashed for the lift.

"I don't understand," Boro confessed. "It looks like a fish."

"I don't either," Kibi said from the ship. "Just drag it toward the airlock as fast as you can, and Ilika will meet you."

*

By the time Boro and Rini had the creature near the airlock, Ilika was already outside, breathing mask on but still wearing his clothes. He quickly maneuvered the gray mammal into the airlock and pulled himself in after, saying, "You two come in next cycle."

When Boro and Rini got inside and pulled off their breathing masks, Ilika had the creature on the floor of the lower deck and was carefully turning it onto its side while Kibi slipped blankets underneath. "Boro, help me. Rini, get a big bowl, cycle the airlock, and bring it in full of sea water."

Ilika and Boro worked together to turn the creature, then Ilika pushed firmly on its chest as water trickled out its mouth and blowhole. Then they turned it onto the other side and did the same. Finally Ilika slapped its chest hard several times, paused to watch and listen, then slapped again.

Nearing the end of hope, Ilika yelled, "Please breathe!" and slapped the animal's back one more time. Suddenly it sputtered and more water gushed from its blowhole, then it sucked air greedily.

"Hurray!" Mati and Sata cheered, standing by helplessly and not knowing what else to do.

"Let's turn her back over," Ilika said, and he and Boro worked together. "Rini, start sprinkling water onto her back. Manessa, talk to her." Ilika's last sentence was completely in the language of Nebador, but with a little thought, the others figured it out.

The ship began making rapid, high-pitched squawking sounds.

Boro's eyes opened wide with recognition. "I heard those sounds just before I used my bracelet!"

"That's their language," Ilika explained, stroking the creature and watching as it lay still, desperately sucking and blowing air.

"You mean . . . Manessa can speak their language . . . even though she can't speak ours?" Mati asked with surprise and a hint of jealousy.

"Yes. Their language is universal. Millions all over Nebador speak it. Yours is very local. Only seven or eight people, outside your planet, know it. I'm one of them."

Boro struggled with himself. "Um . . . I'm . . . I didn't know. I'm . . . sorry."

"It was an honest mistake, and partly mine for not telling you about them."

"So she's . . . sapient . . . like Tera?" Mati asked.

"Tera is barely sapient. Dolphins are highly intelligent. They're represented in the Nebador Services, and run Transport Service ships, just like you do. This young lady, of course, lives on a simple planet, and knows nothing of response ships, just like Pica and Farmer Keni."

"Can we . . . touch her?" Rini asked.

"Yes. They like touch, as long as they're wet with sea water. Mati and

Boro, please go up and move the ship to the edge of the cove — in about a meter of water."

The pilot and engineer headed for the lift, then returned to the lower deck when they had completed the task.

"I think our guest has recovered enough to return to the sea," Ilika announced.

"Um . . . Ilika . . ." Boro began hesitantly. "I'd like to say I'm sorry to her before she goes. Will Manessa translate for me?"

"Yes. Come sit where she can see you."

Boro seated himself on one side of the dolphin's head. "I'm very sorry. I thought you were a shark."

Ilika said something in his language that they couldn't follow, then Manessa uttered more squeaks and squawks.

The dolphin spoke for the first time since awakening.

"She says, please learn the difference," Manessa said in her pleasant voice with words Boro could follow.

✷

After releasing the dolphin back into the cove, the crew set to work preparing a dinner of fried shark, a tangy sauce created by Sata, vegetable stew by Rini, and fruit from the tropical forest.

Then Boro asked to fulfill the request made of him by the creature who had nearly died because of his mistake. Ilika selected several videos, and the entire crew soon knew the difference between the non-sapient denizens of the deep, and the intelligent mammals of the sea, some of whom could fly starships.

✷

The next day, with the shark bones out for the birds to pick, and the crew ready to say good-bye to the little island, Boro happened to glance through the open hatch. "The water's full of dolphins!"

"Shall we go swim with them?" Ilika proposed.

Everyone nodded.

Following Ilika's lead, they grabbed breathing masks and stripped down to their shorts. Mati smiled and came more slowly, knowing she would enjoy the warm sand.

For the next half-hour, the five humans swam and played with the pod of dolphins, sometimes reaching out to touch the slippery gray skin, at other times being shoved this way and that by strong snouts.

When the dolphins headed out to sea, the humans returned to the beach. Boro came last, and when he was standing in water just to his knees, he felt a nudge. Looking down, he saw the same female he had accidentally put to sleep. He sat down in the water and touched her.

"I'm glad you forgive me. I was so ashamed . . ."

Just then he felt a sharp pain, and the dolphin dashed away, then turned and danced on her tail while chattering. A moment later she slipped into the water and was gone from sight.

Boro sat in the water laughing deeply.
"What's so funny?" Mati asked from the beach.
He stood up, blood flowing down his leg. "She bit me."
Ilika started laughing. "She could have, just as easily, torn your leg off."
Boro smiled.

* * *

What tropical fruit is long and green, and only ripens to yellow off the tree? What is pear-shaped with black seeds?

The regular breathing that divers use, avoiding either holding their breath or breathing too fast (hyperventilating), is similar to breathing during meditation.

A shallow-water diving suit is called a "wet suit" because it doesn't attempt to keep out the water, but instead provides insulation from the cold of the water. The small amount of water that gets in, as Ilika explained, is quickly warmed by our bodies. Any suit that keeps all the water out (such as a "deep-sea diving suit") is very stiff and clumsy.

Many aspects of the crew's training, you might have noticed, involved dealing with the physical reality at hand, and avoiding any limitations placed upon us by our fears. No doubt Ilika compared swimming in a few meters of water, with swimming above an ocean trench, just for Sata's benefit.

For most of our history, anything that lived in the sea was called a "fish." There are stories about marine mammals doing very un-fish-like things (such as rescuing people), but only recently did we realize they are mammals, like us, with large brains, like us. The evidence, from both their bodies and fossil records, tells us they once lived on land, and at some point returned to the sea. Marine mammals include whales, dolphins, porpoises, seals, walruses, and manatees.

We cannot understand any of the sounds made by marine mammals, and many people would deny they have a language. That, of course, is an example of the point-of-view fallacy. We have noticed, however, that the sounds made by small dolphins are very similar to those made by huge whales, just higher-pitched. We have also discovered that these sounds can carry through the ocean for hundreds of miles.

Why were Boro and Ilika laughing after the dolphin bit Boro?

Chapter 18: Worse than Slavery

After showers in the entryway to rinse off the sticky salt, and a bandage on Boro's little bite, they pointed the Manessa Kwi toward their next destination.

"Back in your kingdom, I had the blessing of my superiors to let the ship be seen — and attacked — by the local people to help with your training. Here we will follow the more usual practice of observing a culture as discretely as we can. Manessa can become almost completely invisible by adjusting hull color to match the sky. Occasionally someone will see us, but not really know what they are looking at, and we will soon be gone. Kibi, you are in command."

Kibi's city spread out in a shallow river valley near the sea, on the east side of a continent, not far from the equator. As they approached over the water, a brown haze choked the air, filling the entire valley.

"Looks like there was a forest fire," Sata remarked.

"There are no forests nearby," Ilika informed them from the steward's station. "Switching to internal air."

"Let's start at three thousand meters just to get a look at the place," Kibi said from the command chair.

"Down to thrusters one," Mati requested. "I might need a high-resolution topographic."

"Thrusters one," Boro confirmed.

Rini touched two symbols on his console. "High-rez on channel four."

"How's this?" Mati asked, slowing the ship directly over the city.

Rini provided several down-angle views and everyone stared in amazement. Shabby wooden buildings teetered three or four stories high, and people clogged narrow winding streets everywhere. Smoke billowed from countless chimneys to darken the air. Nowhere could the crew of the Manessa Kwi see any wide avenues, any plazas or squares, or any section of the city that might be better off.

"Yuck!" Kibi blurted out from the command chair. "We aren't doing any shopping *here*!"

Ilika smiled.

"Give us a short tour, Mati," Kibi began, "just above the rooftops. You're taking care of camouflage, Ilika?"

"Manessa takes care of it automatically, unless we override," he assured.

The pilot lowered the ship and began to follow whatever street or drainage ditch caught her eye. Sometimes she had trouble telling the two apart. They repeatedly observed food taken by theft, if possible, open combat if necessary. Dogs fought over scraps, or attacked children. Balconies and flat roofs contained more people, sometimes just sitting or lying side by side, sometimes fighting, occasionally being intimate without caring who might be watching. Smoldering piles of trash in every street added to the smoke.

"I have some interesting notes about this city from Manessa's memory," Ilika announced. "There is no slavery here – these are all free people able to come and go as they please. Also, these people have such a high regard for human life that there is no war, and no killing, even of criminals. For the same reason, no one is allowed to use any method to avoid pregnancy."

Several troubled faces glanced at the captain, then turned back to their display screens.

Mati frowned deeply. "I'm sorry, but this is the most horrid place I can imagine. I'd rather be dead than live here."

"Actually," Ilika began, "in this culture you wouldn't be allowed to die. They keep everyone alive as long as possible, even if they are in pain and begging to die."

"That's not freedom!" Boro asserted. "I'd rather be a slave in our kingdom than a free person here."

Rini didn't have anything to add, but wore a sour expression as they continued to gaze at the dense urban scene below that contained nothing of color or beauty.

Kibi sighed. "Let's look at the rest of the valley. Maybe the farmers are better off."

Mati steered the ship westward and increased the altitude slightly.

"The river!" Sata yelled, pointing at her display. "It looks like . . . a sewer. Black goo . . . dead animals floating by . . . dead people . . . I feel sick."

Ilika grabbed a bowl from the galley, just in case she meant it.

Farmland came into view, but every field was ringed by little huts and campsites. Farmers with shovels and sticks tried to fend off the starving people, with little success.

"This can't last," Rini said, shaking his head. "They can't even grow food."

"It doesn't last," Ilika confirmed. "According to Manessa's records, the population collapses about every hundred years. If people won't control their reproduction, or limit their population through war, then the natural ecosystem will do it for them. Famine and disease sweep through the land and only a few survive. Then the cycle begins again."

"What is this crap about a high regard for human life?" Boro challenged. "These people aren't living, they're dying!"

Ilika nodded. "I agree. It's one of those simple ideas that leads to its opposite when it's used thoughtlessly."

"You mean . . . by trying to keep everyone alive," Mati began, still slowly moving the ship through the river valley, "they've accomplished nothing but disease and death?"

"Exactly. Observers come here often because it's such a clear-cut example of self-defeating social values."

"From Nebador?" Rini wondered aloud.

"Yes, and even farther away."

"This makes me remember what we were trying to do at Cattle Town," Kibi shared. "I'm not sure I'll be so interested in helping people solve their problems next time."

The captain smiled slightly. "Helping people is a lot trickier than it sounds, as we learned at Cattle Town."

"I've seen enough here," Kibi announced. "Anyone else want to stay longer?"

No one made a sound.

"Flight objective, captain?" Kibi asked without turning around.

"Find us a place to hover with a nice view. Our next task requires some briefing."

* * *

This chapter gives an excellent example of the difference between intelligence and wisdom. Only intelligence is needed to place a high value on human life. Wisdom is required to realize that such a value cannot be taken to extremes, or implemented on all levels of society, without serious problems.

One problem was discussed by the crew. If any creature will not limit its reproduction by choice, or thin its population through conflict, then nature will do the job instead with famine and disease. There are no other options. All ecosystems are limited, even for a species, like us, who can go everywhere on the planet. Infinite growth is not possible in a finite ecosystem. We humans of planet Earth have not yet come to terms with this reality.

But problems arise long before famine and disease limit a population. Since all living creatures need roughly the same things to live (land, water, air, sunshine, etc.), any effort to maximize the population of one species will minimize the populations of all others. Although we might be able to live on a diet of just a few plants, would we want a world with nothing but people and a few food plants (say, wheat and soy beans)? Other animals and non-food plants would not be allowed because they would take up space, or eat food, that could be used for more people. (Don't worry, it's not possible because such a simple ecosystem would be completely unstable.)

It is natural to place a higher value on your own species than another, and a higher value on a relative (by blood or marriage) than on a stranger. If we have the choice of saving a fellow human or a horse, we usually choose the human. If the choice is between brother and shopkeeper, brother usually wins. But this only works on the individual level. When we implement this idea on a societal level, such as by allowing the destruction of a forest so more houses can be built, we shrink the carrying capacity of the planet a little, and at the same time we raise our population a little.

Another problem, which we saw in the discussion about Kibi's city, is that a population never arrives gracefully at the carrying capacity of its environment, and stays there without going over. Instead, it "overshoots" the carrying capacity because all of the possible corrections (birth control, war, famine, disease) take time to get going. Having jumped up well over the environment's carrying capacity, the population will then "crash" quickly due to famine and disease, down to a fraction of the numbers that could have lived in the environment.

But also, in the process of overshooting, the environment is usually damaged, resulting in a lower carrying capacity than before. A human population, for example, that tries to recover from famine and disease, only to discover that the farmland is eroded and the water is polluted, will not be able to recover as quickly, nor reach the same population numbers (or quality of life) it had before.

Perhaps this is the ultimate test. We are a species with enough intelligence to "subdue the Earth." Will we find the wisdom to not destroy it?

Chapter 19: Ready for Trouble

Mati flew upriver until the ugly city was no longer visible, until the pathetic farms were far behind, until the river valley itself was lost from view. Only when she saw pristine forests and clean air all around did she turn to Kibi.

Kibi smiled and nodded.

"Position locked," Mati declared, touching the symbol that transferred the helm to Manessa for stability against the wind and any other forces that might come along.

"Captain has command," Kibi announced, then helped Mati up to the passenger area.

"An unbreakable rule on any ship," Ilika began as everyone settled around the table, "is that someone is on-duty whenever we're in flight. So I'm on-duty here at the steward's station."

"External air," Kibi whispered.

"Good idea," Ilika said and turned to the console for a moment. They all took deep breaths of the fresh, cool, pine-scented air that entered the ship.

"I am very happy with all the skill and trust I see developing in this crew every day. But the fact is, we are human, and we all have weaknesses. I have challenged you to keep growing and not get stuck, and you have all been willing to do that. That's your ticket into the Nebador Services — be human, but never stop growing.

"Neither is our ship infallible. Our next few destinations will be challenging because Manessa will simulate things breaking down. I want you to know ahead of time that all Transport Service ships are extremely reliable, and failures are very rare. We will usually go months, maybe even years, before something fails, and system redundancy makes it easy to handle most of those. During the next few days, they will happen quite often, sometimes several at a time."

Boro's face twisted into a frown. Rini looked ready for anything.

"These failures are contrived, but real. For example, if Manessa says we're running out of fuel, we aren't really out, but the flow *will* stop, and the engine using it *will* shut down. So you must treat each problem as if it's completely real. Only an override from me will cancel a simulated failure, and I won't, unless Death itself is knocking on the hatch."

Rini burst out laughing. "A high priest knocking on the hatch wouldn't be enough?"

Ilika smiled. "No. Any questions?"

"Um . . ." Kibi began, face scrunched as she formulated her thought. "How long will each failure last?"

"Until we don't *need* that part of the ship any more."

She nodded.

*

After a snack and more discussion about the upcoming drills, the passenger area was quickly cleaned and everyone went to their stations. The moment Mati sat down at the helm, a sudden jolt sent her a foot into the air, then back into her seat with a cry of pain. Even as she landed, she saw flashing symbols on her console. "Anti-mass is off and we're falling!"

Struggling to latch his inertia straps, Boro saw the flashing purple indicators on his engine control board.

"Thrusters!" Mati screamed, partly from the pain of her wrenched knee, partly from sheer panic.

Boro blinked away the water that had somehow gotten into his eyes and quickly punched at his thruster controls until he saw all sevens on his display. "You've got every thruster I can find!" Then another thought came to him and he reached for the ion drive controls, but a feeling in the pit of his stomach stopped him.

Fighting the pain in her knee, Mati wrestled with the flight control like a wild beast. At the same time, she saw the ground rushing toward them on her down-angle display. She felt the strong response of the thrusters, looked at her display again, and clenched her teeth.

Under a crushing three or four gravities of acceleration, Ilika worked from his knees to secure Mati's inertia straps, then pulled himself into the command chair.

"We're gonna make it!" Mati yelled as she watched their descent slow, and finally cease, just meters above the treetops, several whipping back and forth from the thrust.

"Oh crap!" Boro yelled. "We're almost out of thruster fuel!"

"Find some!" Ilika commanded, then quickly stepped to the engineer's station. "Next fuel choice?"

"Um . . . um . . . solid number three, through the oxidizer." Boro made the selections on his board. "Shit! Oxidizer's purple. Shit."

"Next choice?" Ilika coaxed.

"I don't know!"

"Open your fuel selection chart."

With shaking hands, Boro managed to get the chart onto his screen. "Um . . . solid four mixed with liquid one." Even as he spoke his hands moved. "Whew, mixer works."

"Mati, your thrusters will be rough for a moment as the fuel switches," Ilika informed.

"Okay. We're gaining altitude now," the pilot reported between shaking breaths.

Boro breathed a sigh of relief.

*

After the thrusters sputtered for a few moments, Mati eventually achieved a comfortable three thousand meters and managed something that resembled a hover.

"Looks like you're fighting sharks!" Sata observed with wide eyes.

"It's like riding a scared donkey," Mati admitted, "and right after tweaking my knee! Plenty of fuel, Boro?"

"Plenty right now, as long as Manessa doesn't hide the rest."

Nervous laughter came from several stations.

"Um, Rini," Sata began, staring at her chart display. "My position indicator's gone."

"That's because the ship's positioning system is purple, packed up and flew south. I just did a diagnostic, and it says it can't be fixed."

"What are we going to do? I can't tell where we are!" Sata said with desperation in her voice.

Ilika remained silent.

"Don't we know where we *were*?" Boro asked.

Sata glanced at Ilika with worried eyes. "Um, sort of. At least . . . before we lost anti-mass. We were somewhere over this forest . . ." She pointed at a large region on her chart.

"We're still over it," Mati said looking at her down-angle display.

"But *where*?" Sata asked with a note of panic.

"Can't we . . . take a compass reading," Boro suggested, "like we did in the big meadow near Farmer Koto's house?"

Sata's face lit up. "Ilika, would you make a compass on a knowledge pad?"

"Rini can give you a compass."

"That's right, I can! I can put a coordinate grid onto a visual!"

Sata turned to her console with excitement. "Give me a north view, Rini."

Several rounded hills made the horizon lumpy, but none of them were unique.

"Northwest."

Rini changed the view.

"Got one!" Sata said excitedly. "That mountain is either this one," she declared, creating a mark on her chart display, "or this one."

Everyone strained to see what Sata was doing.

"So I take the opposite compass direction," Sata continued, thinking aloud, "draw lines from these peaks to our forest . . . okay, we know we're on one of these lines. Give me a visual to the west."

More mountain peaks came into view.

"Oh, yes!" Sata nearly shouted. "There's no mistaking *that* mountain!" She drew another line. "So we're at one of these two places. Hmm. If we were at this point, we'd have a river right under us."

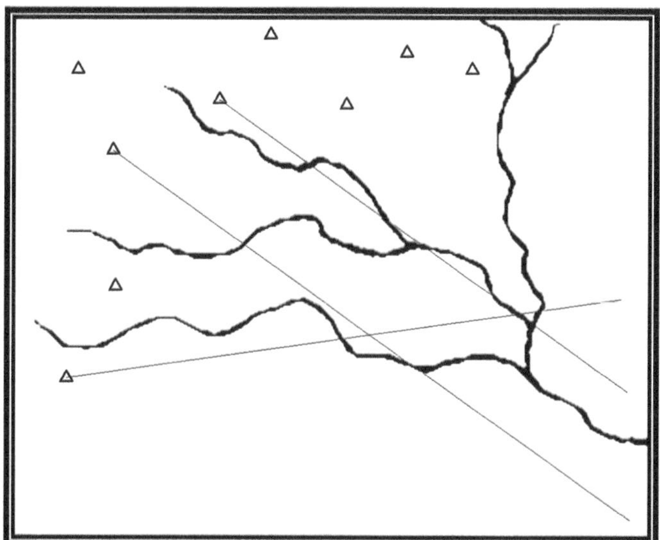

Everyone tapped their display selectors, then searched with their eyes.

"No river below," Rini reported.

Everyone else shook heads in agreement.

With a smile of pride, Sata drew a circle around their current position on the chart and deleted the other lines.

*

"Flight objective is location six on the list, thrusters only, impaired sensors, visual flight referencing to the highest mountain on the planet, twenty-one thousand meters above sea level. Rini has command."

Rini and Ilika changed places and secured their straps while Sata calculated the bearing and Mati turned the ship to make it their heading.

"Um . . . um . . . status, a-all stations," the freckled lad began with hesitation.

"Pilot has tamed her wild thrusters, but don't expect a smooth ride."

Rini chuckled and exchanged grins with the pilot.

"Navigator is going to track the flight, mountain by mountain, river by river."

"Watch has visual and magnetic sensors," Ilika reported, looking over the indicators, "but no positioning or topographics."

"Engineer reports thrusters all yellow, current fuel supply good, and I've whipped up another kind, just in case." He turned and grinned at Rini.

"Steward is having an easy day. I'd go take a nap if it wasn't for the inertia," Kibi said with a smile.

"What do we know about the weather?" Rini asked.

"Only what we can see," Ilika replied. "Some fog in the valleys, but flight above six thousand meters looks clear. The top of the mountain may be different."

"Distance to the mountain?" Rini asked.

"Um . . ." Sata said, working with her controls to move a scale on her chart, "three thousand seven hundred kilometers."

"That's going to take a while with thrusters," Mati announced with frustration.

"As soon as Mati finishes accelerating," Ilika began, "I'll show Kibi how to serve a meal under inertia flight conditions."

When Rini was sure everyone was ready, he asked Mati to begin accelerating. Soon they were streaking across the sky into the mountains.

Ilika and Kibi entered the galley, always keeping one hand on something solid.

* * *

Travel by water and air can never be made as "idiot proof" as travel by land because we cannot usually survive in water or air if our vehicles fail. A good airplane pilot is always looking for places to land, within gliding distance, in case of engine failure. A multi-engine aircraft pilot studies what his craft can and can't do "OEI" (one engine inoperative).

When our cars fail, we usually take them to a mechanic and get them fixed. Since there were no deep-space response ship garages on that planet, what is implied by making each simulated failure continue "until we don't need that part of the ship any more"?

Why was the first simulated failure (anti-mass drive) especially challenging for Mati as the pilot?

When Boro's fuel was suddenly threatened, be tried one alternative from memory, but Ilika had to coax him to look up a third option. An aircraft pilot (or other essential crew member) always keeps all necessary information within reach. When piloting a small airplane or helicopter, it's all in a small binder strapped to my leg.

After being reminded of the tools she had available, Sata took compass bearings to mountain peaks in two directions. One of the directions had two possibilities because the peaks looked similar. After selecting the peaks, Sata worked backwards. The unmistakable mountain peak (lower left), for example, was at a bearing of 260° (using our system). The opposite (or "reciprocal") would be 80°, so Sata drew a line in that direction from the peak. The crew saw no river directly under the ship. What was the ship's position?

The reciprocal of a compass bearing is the bearing plus or minus 180 modulus 360. It is the number directly opposite the bearing on the compass rose. The reciprocal of 50° is 230°. What is the reciprocal of 300°?

Boro got "ahead of his aircraft" by preparing another type of fuel. Any type of ship operation has long stretches with little to do, then suddenly moments of high-workload and stress. Whatever crew members can do ahead of time makes those stressful moments easier.

Chapter 20: Rini's Mountain

With finger food and beverage in a holder at her station, Mati was milking everything she could from her thrusters, until Boro pointed out that his status symbols were turning red. Ilika reminded Boro that they were out of danger and that one set should be held in reserve. Mati sighed and eased back on her flight control until the engineer smiled.

An hour later, they could all see a thick ring of clouds surrounding the highest mountain on the planet. But, Rini happily pointed out, the peak itself pierced the mist and was awash in brilliant sunshine.

"Manessa's records say there's a small landing site up there, but I've never been to it," Ilika informed them from the watch station.

Sata touched a symbol. "Chart's at maximum magnification."

"Can you see it, Kibi?" Rini asked from the command chair.

Kibi switched to the magnified chart. "It could be in that little cleft on the south side. I can't be sure 'til we get there."

With instrument flying impossible, Mati stayed well-clear of the thick clouds. "Hold on!" she warned as strong winds began to rattle their bones. Moving around to the south side of the mountain, she nudged the ship toward the peak.

A small cleft in the rocks, with a level floor, awaited them just a stone's throw from the top. "You want me to land a bucking donkey in *that*?" Mati asked.

"How wide is it, Sata?" Rini asked.

"About . . . six meters."

"How small can Manessa go, Ilika?"

"Two meters."

"What do you think, Mati?" Rini asked.

"Er . . . I'll try it . . . if it's okay with Ilika."

Ilika just smiled at his pilot.

"Um . . . Boro?" Mati began without turning. "Can you give me level seven up and down, and level two sideways?"

"Sure! Thrusters seven vertical, two lateral."

"Yeah, those words," Mati said, still concentrating on her flight control. "Mmm . . . that's better. Everybody ready for my donkey-in-a-barrel trick?"

Laughter rolled through the ship as several tight stomachs, including Mati's, loosened up a bit.

"Manessa is a little ball two meters across," Ilika announced. "I'll show you those controls soon, Mati."

Everyone remained silent as their pilot coaxed the bucking ship closer and closer to the mountain. The buffeting from the wind was the worst just a few meters from the mountain, but dropped to a calm breeze as Mati entered the cleft. She extended struts and set the little ship down without ever touching the surrounding rock.

"The Manessa Kwi is on top of the world!" Rini shouted with joy when Mati turned around and grinned at him.

✷

With a short and easy climb from the landing site to the top of the peak, the five who could undertake the journey got into harsh environment suits and grabbed breathing masks. Mati put on a breathing mask, determined to get all the practice she could in spite of her knee.

Kibi and Rini were ready to bound out the hatch, but Ilika stopped them and brought out a long safety line with attachment points every three meters, then put careful Boro in the lead.

With gloves now protecting their hands, they made their way up the icy rocks to the peak, a jumble of angular boulders bare to the sun and wind.

"We have arrived," Boro said for Mati's benefit. "The wind is fierce."

"Um . . . you guys have a problem," Mati informed through the intercom. "The clouds are rising. They're almost up to the ship."

"I think Ilika saw that coming," Rini began, "and that's why we're on a safety line."

"Great," Mati grumbled. "Now if you guys die, I'll have to pilot the ship all the way to Satamia Star Station by myself, right Ilika?"

The captain chuckled. "With Manessa's help."

"I guess I'd better pay attention during language lessons!"

"Yes," Ilika agreed, "but also, we'll try not to die."

Everyone fell silent. They could see the clouds rapidly rising to engulf the peak, and took the remaining few moments to enjoy the view. Other white peaks jutted above the clouds in every direction, all at lower elevations. In places, far away, they thought they could glimpse dark forests coating the lower flanks of the mountains. Southward, a hint of blue might be an ocean.

The mist quickly rose around them. Not like any fog they had ever seen, it shimmered with countless tiny ice crystals. Sata reached for Boro's hand, and Kibi reached out for both Ilika and Rini.

"We're in the cloud now, Mati," Ilika shared. "Sight-seeing is over and we'll be heading back."

Boro moaned. "I don't like this, Ilika. It's like . . . I can't even remember which direction I was just looking."

"I feel cold, even though I'm not," Sata reported.

"No one moves until I say so," Ilika said firmly.

"No problem," Kibi assured. "I'm shaking inside too much. Just don't ask me to let go of your hand. I can't see anything but your hand, and Rini's."

"Rini, how are you doing?" Ilika asked, unable to see the boy just a few meters away.

"I like this shimmery stuff. It almost feels like I'm floating in it. I'm okay."

"Kibi, I'm going to need my hand for climbing," Ilika asserted, "and so is Rini. What else do you have that feels solid and reliable?"

"Um . . . there's a rock under me, and some ice," she said with a trembling voice. "I guess . . . they're not going anywhere. The safety line was connected to you and Rini last time I could see."

Ilika tugged on the line.

"I felt that!"

Rini tugged from the other direction and chuckled.

"Okay! It's still connected."

"Boro, are you going to be okay bringing up the rear?" Ilika asked without any visual contact.

"I . . . um . . ." he began, but had to stop and breathe several times. "This is so unreal . . . my head's swimming . . . I feel so stupid!"

"Can you feel the rock under you?" Sata asked.

"Yeah."

"Do you have plenty of air to breathe?"

"Yeah."

"What else do you need?" Sata asked.

"Um . . . I guess . . . nothing . . . as long as someone else is leading."

"Rini is leading," Ilika announced. "It's his mountain. He has to get us back to the ship."

Everyone heard Rini chuckle again. Somehow the sound gave all of them a little extra courage.

"Anything I can do?" Mati asked from the ship.

"Just open the hatch when we get there," Ilika replied.

"Sounds easy enough."

"Everyone let go of hands," Ilika commanded, "and take a moment to feel the solid rocks under you, the good air to breathe, and the strong safety line between us."

He sensed Kibi's reluctance to let go.

"I've been remembering the way back," Rini shared, "and I don't think it will take long."

"Kibi, you ready?" Ilika asked.

"Ready," she said in a voice somewhere between panic and courage.

"Ready," Sata said, shivering.

"R . . . ready," Boro forced out.

✷

Once they began the return journey of about a hundred meters, everyone was too busy dealing with the rocks and ice to worry about the lack of visual clues. Ilika feared that Boro would drag his feet, but the engineer stayed right behind the navigator. Ilika could hear Kibi's shaking breath, though he could rarely see her in the icy mist.

When Rini finally said, "I see a golden ball that's too big to be a bird's egg," noises of relief flowed up and down the safety line.

A moment later the hatch opened, and each person slapped hands with their pilot where she sat at the steward's station wearing her breathing mask.

When the hatch closed and the ship repressurized, masks came off and long embraces were shared until everyone quit trembling.

Rini and Mati held hands, but neither was in distress. A kiss, however, seemed right.

✷ ✷ ✷

Why was Mati never bored when riding her donkey, but then, with only thrusters ("jet engines") available, she craved more speed?

All but the most extreme air turbulence and wind shear (rapid changes of wind direction) are merely inconvenient while flying, but become very dangerous when trying to land.

Disorientation in fog or darkness is a serious challenge for most people. Have you ever had to walk a short distance without useful vision? What feelings did you experience? Did you have any trouble getting to your destination?

Chapter 21: Demons

After the stress and disorientation of the walk back through the icy fog from the mountain's peak, a hearty stew brought contented looks all around the table.

"That was kind of like being in space, wasn't it?" Rini proposed.

"A little. In space you can see well, but it can have that feeling of not being connected to anything."

"We'll always have safety lines, won't we?" Boro asked.

"Either that," Ilika answered, "or you can use the little thrusters on the orange suits to move yourself wherever you need to go. Remember, in space you'll almost always be at zero gravity, right along with the ship."

Rini and Sata grinned with excitement at the idea. Boro and Kibi didn't look so sure.

"I have a video of mountain climbers scaling difficult peaks," Ilika announced. "Other than that, tonight is for relaxing. Tomorrow we'll stay here, do language lessons, and a little more station training."

"I want a hot bath!" Sata declared.

"I'm making snacks for the video!" Kibi added.

Mati grinned. "I'll help!"

*

Boro lay awake much of the night. He thought about the mountain climbers he had seen creeping up sheer rock faces. Often they dangled on ropes over huge cracks in the rock or ice. Sometimes they had to create steps or handholds, where none could be found, with loops of rope. But most often he remembered the scenes of tying knots or setting up tents in a fog or a blizzard.

The next day, after a hot breakfast and a language lesson, Boro got himself a bath and then approached Ilika, who was sitting at the big table working at a knowledge pad. "Where is everybody?"

"Somewhere around here. I saw Rini in the utility room."

"I was thinking that . . . um . . . I should go outside and get more practice in the fog."

"Good idea. Please use the airlock. You know what to take."

"Green suit, mask, and safety line."

Ilika nodded and went back to his training checklists.

When Boro stepped through the outer door of the airlock into the thick, icy fog, he found two safety lines already attached to the hull. "I thought I was going to be alone out here," he muttered.

"You're not the only one with demons to tame," Kibi's voice said.

"But we have some rules out here," Sata's voice added. "We're not sitting together, and we don't want much chatter."

"Yeah, it's sort of like a meditation session," Kibi explained. "Just you, your rock, and the wonderful terrible fog."

"Fair enough," Boro replied, clipping on his line and going off in a different direction.

About twenty minutes later the airlock opened again. Rini, in a harsh environment suit, holding a coiled safety line, saw the three other lines going off into the fog, and laughed deeply.

*

With Kibi and Sata at language lesson twenty-four, and the rest finishing lesson twelve, simple conversations in the language of Nebador began whenever two crew members worked together in the galley or elsewhere on the ship. They wouldn't last long before the less advanced student came to a concept they could not yet express, or the more advanced was forced to use words from lessons thirteen and above.

Sata and Rini, working together to make dinner at the end of the day, did their best to keep everything in the new language. They discovered by accident that if they spoke aloud what they wanted from a piece of galley equipment, touching the controls was unnecessary. Sometimes they also received unexpected commentary.

"Front stove element, level four," Sata requested.

"Front element is on level four, but that may be too hot, considering the thickness of the food," Manessa said.

After the two humans spent a moment looking at each other and holding in laughter, they conceded that Manessa was right and lowered the heat.

*

With a tasty dinner of stew and biscuits making them all feel lazy, most everyone went down to the lower deck or into bathtubs. Kibi did the dishes and put the left-overs in the refrigerator. When everything was clean and tidy, she looked around to make sure she was alone, then took a deep breath. "Manessa?"

"Yes, Kibi?"

"Can I talk to you?"

"Yes, at any time it doesn't interfere with ship operations."

"From anywhere in the ship?"

"Anywhere in or near the ship, or when wearing a breathing mask or mission bracelet, or when at a knowledge processor, except that in the cabins you must manually activate an audio link."

Kibi chuckled. "So you can't listen to me and Ilika in our cabin . . ."

"You have complete privacy in your cabins."

"Um . . . how old are you?"

"About one thousand times your age."

"Wow. Do you remember . . . when you were born?"

"I remember when I first awoke after being created, but I was not born in the same way you were."

"Do you have parents?"

"Yes. I will be able to visit them when we return to the stars. They are very beautiful and kind, and love to hear of my adventures."

"Is it true you're not a girl?"

"It is true."

"Do you . . . ever wish you were a girl?"

"No. I do not have the anatomical parts to be a girl."

A second later, Kibi laughed at herself. "It was . . . a silly question, I guess."

*

Sata got comfortable in her favorite bathtub, the one on the upper deck that was free more often. After filling it with the blue solvent as deep as it would go, she stretched out and felt every muscle in her body relax.

"Manessa, can you hear me?"

"Yes, Sata."

"If I talk to you about something, will you tell Ilika?"

"Only if it is important to ship operations."

"Are my feelings important to ship operations?"

"No, only your actions while on-duty."

Sata breathed a contented sigh and sank a little deeper into the blue liquid. "Sometimes I feel like . . . I'm crazy trying to be a response ship navigator . . . at eleven years old."

"Do you mean that there is some reaction in your brain that causes mental illness if you undertake this activity at your age?"

After a moment of thought, Sata chuckled out loud. "No. I meant 'crazy' as in 'stupid.'"

"So the reaction in your brain causes a reduction of intelligence?"

Sata laughed again. "I have to use words carefully with you!"

"I only know the common meanings of words. If you have a personal definition, or you are using an idiom derived from your language, you must tell me."

Sata thought for a moment. "I will say it differently. You've had many other crews working with you, right?"

"More than three hundred."

"Oh . . . okay. Have you ever had another crew member who was afraid of things, like I am? Dark ocean trenches, thick fog, even hot springs and steam vents?"

"I have had mammalian, avian, and reptilian crews. I cannot think of a single crew member, including a captain, I have ever worked with who did not harbor fears of certain environments that were challenging for them."

Sata smiled. "Thank you, Manessa."

* * *

Most people naturally avoid uncomfortable experiences. Practicing for any kind of emergency is uncomfortable. Although the information and supplies are easy to find, very few people (or families) practice fire drills, first aid, self defense, and other emergency skills. What do we learn about the ship's crew when we see them WILLINGLY go back out into the icy fog?

The Manessa Kwi was sentient but not sapient, intelligent and aware, but not wise. As Sata and Rini worked in the kitchen, they saw an example of this limitation. In this case, they agreed with the ship. If they had needed to heat the food more quickly, they might have left the stove on level four. Have you ever tried to use a machine that "believed" (through its programming) that it was doing the right thing, and absolutely "refused" to change?

Why do you think Kibi was interested in Manessa's gender? What challenges was Kibi facing that related to her own gender, and the assumptions her kingdom made about what young women could, and could not, do?

Why was Sata comforted when Manessa revealed that all previous crew members, including captains, had fears about certain environments?

Chapter 22: Mati's Waterfall

The captain of the Manessa Kwi chatted with his crew members at breakfast, with about half his words coming from the language of Nebador and the other half from a small medieval kingdom none of them had seen in almost two months. He noticed that they all seemed happier and more confident after their day of rest. Eventually he broached the subject of their next destination.

"The highest waterfall on the planet, requested by Mati, also happens to be one of the most beautiful, and it has a hidden secret."

Mati wiggled in her chair with excitement.

"Behind the falls is a limestone cave with growing calcite formations."

Blank looks met Ilika's glance.

"Okay, I'll put on a video as soon as we clean the table."

The rest of their porridge and tropical fruit vanished from their trays in seconds, and Boro dashed into the galley to do the dishes. Rini wiped the table and Kibi rearranged the room, leaving Ilika to select the video.

They were all soon seated and staring at the big display with round eyes and open mouths. Stalactites reached down from the ceiling to join stalagmites on the floor, stone draperies were sometimes thin enough to glow when lit from behind, and delicate mineral crusts ringed pools of crystal-clear water. Flying mammals occasionally filled the air, and blind lizards crept about in the silence.

"Let's see what works, shall we?" the captain ordered when the video ended.

The crew members were quickly at their stations going through preflight checks and diagnostics without further prompting.

"We have ship's position and topographics!" Rini announced excitedly.

"Anti-mass works!" Boro declared. "Oh, but thrusters are coming up purple . . . every one of them."

Mati turned around. "How can I fly without thrusters?"

"There's more bad news," Rini said glumly. "No visuals. Up, down, sideways, nothing."

"My refrigerator!" Kibi moaned, a wounded look on her face. "Manessa shut down my refrigerator!"

"Okay," Ilika said, trying not to laugh, "so we'll finish up left-overs for lunch, and Mati has to learn to fly with only the ion drive. What's the shortest duration ion burst you can use, Mati?"

"Um . . . one thousandth of a second."

"How far will that take you in this atmosphere?"

Mati searched for the graph Ilika had shown her several days before. "Here it is. Two hundred and forty meters."

"That, in a straight line, is your unit of movement."

"From right here on the mountain?"

"No. The ion drive causes enough air displacement to damage anything nearby that's solid. First use anti-mass to move us a thousand meters straight up. Navigator, location seven by ion drive, please."

Sata looked up the coordinates and then selected an appropriate chart. "That's halfway around the planet!"

"Transit time, navigator?"

Sata worked at her console in silence for a moment. "Four minutes, five seconds."

"Wow," Boro breathed.

"Clearance along the route?" Ilika asked.

"Aren't we starting a thousand meters higher than the *highest* mountain?" Sata asked, spinning around and giving her captain a smug look.

Ilika grinned. "Give Mati your bearing and exact time calculation. Ion warm-up, engineer."

"Anti-mass and ion drive are green."

"Um . . . Ilika?" Kibi began hesitantly. "Without visuals, I can't check the landing site."

"You'll have to do it yourself. All you need is a mask and gloves."

Kibi strode to the lift as Ilika began to go through status checks with everyone else. She returned a minute later and cleared her throat, holding up a coil of ice-covered safety line.

A guilty look appeared on Rini's face, the last one to come in on the previous day.

"I'll put it in the refrigerator," Kibi said with a twisted grin. "It'll help keep the food cold."

✷

The four-minute transit to a continent on the other side of the planet was spent watching Sata's chart move quickly by on their screens, and listening to a mellow song that Kibi selected. Once they were over an ocean and the chart was no longer interesting, they all poked at their diagnostic controls to see if the ship was ready to give them back any of the missing systems. No one reported any luck.

As soon as the ion drive disengaged, they all took a good look at the topographic map of the land far below.

"Hmm . . ." Sata began. "Highlands at two thousand meters, and the valley below us is less than half that."

"Trade places with me, Mati," Ilika said. "This is your waterfall."

The pilot grabbed her crutch and Ilika helped her into the command chair.

"Um . . . let's go down to two thousand one hundred and see what we can see, through the hatch I guess."

"If you don't mind, Mati, I'll just throw in a short zero-gravity session," Ilika said.

The acting commander grinned and grabbed her inertia straps. The others got the hint.

"Anti-mass seven, full inertia," Ilika requested.

"You've got it," Boro confirmed. "Anti-mass is yellow."

Ilika glanced around to make sure everyone was strapped in, then quickly pushed down on his flight control.

"Wee!" Rini shrieked.

"Ugh," came from the engineer's station.

Ilika watched his altimeter whiz past twenty thousand meters. "Prepare for vertical deceleration."

Sata swallowed several times, remembering a little too clearly what she had for breakfast. However, the three gravities that pushed her into her chair felt very comforting after the free-fall.

"Everyone okay?" Mati asked when the ship finally came to a stop.

"Boro said it well," Kibi replied. "Ugh."

Ilika could see that Sata was breathing and smiling.

"Is it cold out there, Rini?" Mati asked.

"No, very warm and wet."

"Can we . . . look, Ilika?"

"You're in command, Mati."

"Oh, yeah. Hatch half-open. Me, Boro, and Kibi will look, then the rest of you."

Below rocky highlands dotted with trees, a lush tropical valley spread before them, waterfalls cascading down the steep walls at many points.

Mati grinned, but said nothing for a long minute. The highest waterfall plunged over a cliff and fell straight down hundreds of meters, pounded against a rock outcropping, then dove another hundred meters into a large pool, kicking up clouds of spray and mist.

"Down another four hundred meters, please," Mati requested.

Ilika slowly lowered the ship.

Mati's face glowed as she stood gazing at the huge column of falling water. Boro and Kibi flanked her, each with a supportive arm around her back. The roar of the water filled the ship and mist collected on their faces. The pilot of the Manessa Kwi, currently in command, smiled like she had never smiled before.

✷

While Ilika, Sata, and Rini took a look through the open hatch, Boro ran his thruster diagnostics again and stared at the results. "Ilika, when you're done there, I want to talk to you."

The captain pried himself away from the beautiful sight and went to the engineer's station.

"This may not be a simulated failure. Look. The only way we could get these readings is if the intake filters were old and clogged."

"All of them at once? No, this is Manessa's doing, but our mischievous ship may have left us a way out."

"You mean . . . it's simulated, but if I replace them, the thrusters might work again?"

"It's worth a try. Mati, do you mind if Boro tries to fix the thrusters?"

"I don't mind. We certainly can't explore a cave with ion drive!"

Boro picked two helpers and led them down to the utility room. "Kibi, you can carry the new ones," Boro said, opening a cabinet and handing her a stack of replacement filters, "and Rini will receive the old ones as I pull them out."

They entered the engineering ring, where Kibi and Rini had only been once before. The anti-mass induction tubes that encircled the ship glowed violet, but few other devices were currently running. Boro stopped at the first thruster engine they came to and opened the intake filter cover.

He put his finger to his lips for a moment, then said, in the new language he was just learning, "Here's the old filter, Rini. Hand me a new one, Kibi." He handed the old filter to Rini. They could all see that it was pearly white and obviously not clogged. Then he took the same filter back from Rini and reinstalled it.

Both helpers grinned with delight at the game, but managed to hold their tongues. The same process was repeated at the other thruster engines.

As they exited the engineering ring, Boro put his finger to his lips one more time. Kibi returned the new filters to their cabinet.

Landing in his seat, Boro started another diagnostic. "Mati, you have thrusters!"

✷

"The cave is behind the lower falls, just above the pool," Ilika explained. "Going from one medium to another is a serious challenge for any pilot, Mati, as you know from entering the ocean. It's worse when one of the media is moving. I'll take us in, you stand right behind me and watch, then you can take us out when we're done cave exploring."

Mati rose with the help of her crutch and held onto the back of the pilot's chair. "I think I remember the basics."

"Good. You give the commands, and I'll add anything you miss."

"Okay. Um . . . um . . . thin vertical shape."

"Aerodynamic vertical profile set," Ilika acknowledged.

"Yeah, that. Um . . . ionize the hull."

"Remember that, Boro?"

"Yep. It even works!"

The others, intently watching and listening, chuckled.

"What's next, Mati?"

"Um . . . we need to see somehow, and we don't have visuals. High resolution topo, Rini."

A moment later a frustrated noise came from the watch station. "Purple."

Ilika glanced up at Mati. "Manessa's training program has struck again. What are we going to do, commander?"

Mati breathed a sigh. "If we weren't trying to go through a waterfall, we could just open the hatch and look!"

"I agree — not a good idea in a waterfall."

Mati noticed Sata squirming. "Got an idea, Sata?"

"The topo you want is in memory."

"Why didn't I think of that!" Rini muttered.

"How old?" Ilika asked.

"Um . . . about two years," the navigator replied.

"Acceptable risk, commander?" Ilika asked.

"Mmm . . . if we go slowly."

Ilika grinned. "I was planning on it."

✷

Mati watched closely as her captain carefully moved the little ship into the waterfall, anticipating the changing forces that were trying to shove them down into the pool. As soon as they passed the midpoint of the cascade, he went through the same process in reverse, tapering the anti-mass drive until they were clear of the pounding water.

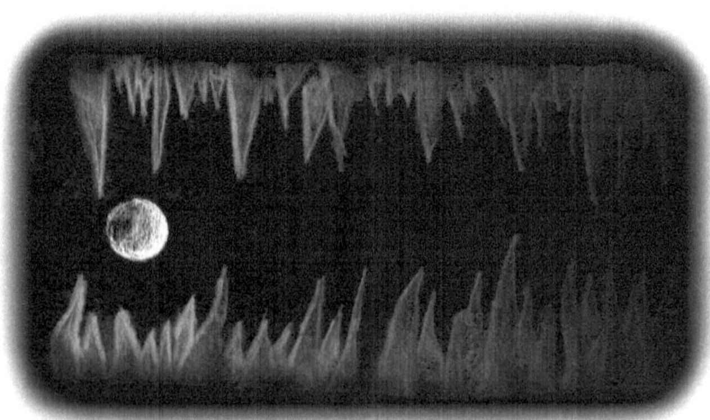

"We're not going to fly around in the cave by two-year-old topographic charts stored in memory because we have another option," Ilika announced. Seeing the puzzled look on Mati's face, he continued. "You already thought of it."

"Open the hatch and look out?"

"Sort of. Take a look at this hull configuration," he said, pointing to one of Manessa's possible shapes on the console display.

"A three meter ball with one seat at the top. Someone's gonna ride and tell us which way to go!"

"Yes. Rini is the watch, and I think this will also be good for Sata."

Sata swallowed, but wore a tiny smile.

"And the rest can enjoy the tour at the hatch, including you, Mati, until it's your turn to pilot."

"Hatch is open," Kibi said as the sound of the waterfall entered the ship.

"You will be responsible for the ship, Rini. I will do exactly what you say. And remember, there's one crew member who will *not* be protected by the ship's hull."

"Yeah, me!"

Rini was soon in harness and safety line, climbing out the hatch and making his way to the top of the ship where a molded seat awaited him. "It's loud and wet out here!" he yelled for Manessa's audio sensors. "Don't forget to turn on some lights for me!"

Ilika and Mati agreed on some engine adjustments, then Boro, Sata, and Kibi all went off-duty to enjoy the show at the hatch.

"Forward very slowly," Rini directed.

They began to move deeper into the cave, away from the waterfall. Those at the hatch could almost reach out and touch the rock walls.

"Stop. Down a little. No, not that far! Stop! Oh, yeah, you can't tell how far 'a little' is."

Ilika smiled as his student atop the ship began to realize which phrases would work, and which would create confusion. Those at the hatch chatted about a room full of prickly stalactites that opened up on the right side of the ship.

"Forward. Eight degrees left. Good."

"These are amazing," Boro commented. "We have to make Ilika teach us about them tonight."

"Stop. Up until I say stop. Yikes, stop! I forgot to look up and almost got speared by a pointy thing."

Ilika chuckled and cringed at the same time.

"Okay, forward."

"I wonder what that water tastes like," Mati mused, pointing at a blue pool that appeared to have hundreds of eggs at the bottom.

"Stop. Thirty degrees right and forward."

"Probably chalky," Boro guessed. "Everything's calcium carbonate."

"This is so beautiful!" Rini could be heard saying.

"Those drapery things almost look like bacon," Sata shared, pointing.

"Yikes . . ." Rini cried, but was cut off by a scraping sound. ". . . op!" A half second later a crashing sound filled the cavern.

Those at the hatch craned their necks to see what had happened. At the front of the ship, a large stalagmite had fallen forward across a group of delicate formations, breaking itself and the others into pieces.

"Oh, no!" Rini moaned in a sad voice. "I killed it. Can we put it back together?"

Ilika and the others would have laughed, but they could hear how deeply Rini was feeling his mistake.

"I'm sorry. I was looking all around and not paying attention. I shouldn't do this anymore."

With Kibi's help, Mati went up the entryway steps and looked at Ilika.

"It's your call, but I recommend Rini stay up there awhile to practice paying attention."

Mati smiled and nodded, returned to the hatch and leaned out. "You're on-duty up there until I say you're off-duty!" she yelled up to her friend.

"Okay," Rini said in a forlorn voice close to tears. "Do we have some glue or something?"

"It's just a rock, Rini!" Boro yelled out the hatch.

Rini managed to collect himself and carry out his task for the next quarter hour, but they could all hear the guilty tone in his voice. He did, however, pay close attention, and the Manessa Kwi didn't hit any more cave formations.

* * *

Stalactites, stalagmites, and other limestone cave formations are created over long periods of time by water that drips into the caves. The water begins as rain or snow, and as it soaks into the ground and passes through limestone rock, some of the stone is dissolved by the water. When that water enters the cave, some of the dissolved minerals are deposited on the ceiling or floor. It takes thousands to millions of years for cave formations to grow.

Rini and Mati were less affected by zero gravity (free fall), and other physical experiences that didn't cause pain or danger, because they were both intuitives. Intuitives pay less attention to physical reality and more to unseen patterns and meanings. Boro and Sata were both more "down to Earth" and so more affected by zero gravity. Kibi was a mixture of the two.

When reading about the intelligence of the deep-space response ship Manessa Kwi, it is easy to remember the HAL 9000 computer in *2001: A Space Odyssey*. In that story, mental illness was caused in the computer by placing it under conflicting political pressures. It's a uniquely human theme, based on the way the human mind (and therefore human society) is structured, and has no relationship to the Manessa Kwi.

Based on the evidence in this chapter, does Manessa have visual sensors inside the ship (as the HAL 9000 did)?

Giving voice commands to someone who can't see is a powerful exercise in mutual trust. If the person giving commands does a bad job, the person carrying them out has no way of knowing until disaster strikes. If the person carrying out the commands does not do so faithfully, then it doesn't matter how good the commands were. Again, disaster strikes.

Rini quickly realized that phrases like "a little" do no good. It is not its vagueness that is the problem. "Exactly half way" would be just as bad. The problem is that they are relative to the whole distance, which only the person giving commands can see.

Rini's last words before the accident were, "This is so beautiful!" What state of mind was he in?

Why would Ilika want Rini to practice paying attention when he was feeling something deeply?

In your opinion, was the stalagmite "just a rock" as Boro said, or was it something greater because of its beauty and the length of time it took to create?

Chapter 23: Mati's Problem

When they had explored deep into the cave and it was becoming too small for the ship with a watchman perched on top, Mati declared it was time to turn back and Boro yelled for Rini to come in. With an excited grin, the usual pilot took back her seat.

Sata climbed out the hatch as soon as Rini was back. "This is spooky," they could hear her say as soon as she reached the top of the ship.

"Kibi is in command," Ilika announced, "and Boro, you are at the hatch in case Sata needs you. I'll cover your station."

Boro smiled, then checked to see that another safety line was handy.

"Gosh . . . um . . . we need to turn around," Sata called from her perch.

"Ilika, are my thrusters and anti-mass in good shape?" Mati asked.

"Green and yellow."

Mati looked at Kibi, who nodded for the pilot to begin the return journey back toward the sunshine. She took the flight control and began to rotate the ship.

"Not that way! The other way!" Sata's voice came to them.

A slight frown crossed Kibi's face as Mati sighed and reversed the direction of rotation. The seconds ticked by with no word from the top of the ship.

"You're going around in circles!" Sata said sharply.

Mati turned to look at Kibi with a puzzled expression.

"Keep doing exactly what she says," Kibi ordered. "She'll figure it out . . . I hope."

Ilika was beginning to pay close attention to what was happening.

"Back the other way a little," Sata directed. "No! Just a little!"

"Grrrr," Mati intoned as she again brought the ship to a halt.

"Okay!" Sata yelled with a hint of panic in her voice. "Let's go! Let's get out of here!"

"Ilika," Kibi began, "I think the same thing might be happening to Sata that happened in the ocean trench."

"Could be. This is a pretty safe environment to let her work through it."

"I said forward!" Sata yelled, breathing fast.

"She did not," Mati mumbled. "But forward is what she'll get . . ."

"No! Not that far!"

Mati showed her teeth. "Grrrrrrr."

"Go back! Then down! No!"

With a sigh, Mati again brought the ship to a stop.

"Forget it and go forward!"

Mati complied.

"You passed it!" Sata nearly screamed.

Mati brought the ship to an abrupt halt and spun around, tears on her face for all to see, voice shaking. "Ilika said I should never pilot when something is making me do a bad job. Well, something is. I can't do this another second, I feel sick, and I don't want to hear Sata's voice ever again!"

With moisture forming in Kibi's own eyes, she said, "Lock your controls and go off-duty. You too, Rini."

Mati hit a symbol on her console much harder than necessary, then grabbed her crutch. Rini put his arm around her and pointed her toward the lift.

"What's going on down there?" came Sata's voice. "I said go up!"

✷

They didn't yell for Sata to come in. Boro clipped on a safety line and climbed up to get her. As soon as she was inside, Ilika could see she was frightened and gasping for air. Boro guided her to the table and Kibi brought pinkfruit juice and other snacks, then put on some music. Ilika went around the bridge making sure all systems were stable.

For the next hour, Sata nibbled and talked with Boro and sometimes Kibi or Ilika, slowly regaining her composure.

On the lower deck, Mati cried in Rini's arms for half an hour, then curled up on his bunk. When he was sure she was deeply asleep, he crept back up to the passenger area.

When not talking with Sata, Ilika grabbed a knowledge pad and read everything he could find about crew members having problems like this, and what he could do to help. Eventually, when the navigator and engineer were holding hands and watching a video, something funny that made them laugh, Ilika and Kibi slipped out and sat on the top of the ship together.

He surprised her by beginning their private meeting with a deep kiss.

"Mmm. What did I do to deserve that?" she asked with a coy smile.

"I can count on you . . . and I love you for it."

"Except when I run away to eat lizards."

"You didn't really eat any, did you?"

She smiled. "No, but they were starting to look tasty!"

"You got past that. I'm trying to figure out what we can do to get Sata past this."

"Anything in Manessa's memory?"

"Fear of darkness can be very hard to overcome."

"But Manessa is lighting up the cavern bright as day!"

"I know, but there must be something this has in common with the trench."

Kibi thought for a moment. "A huge weight above — water in the trench, rock here. I don't know much psych . . . ology, but I have an idea. It won't be easy for either of them, you know, one of those do-or-die things. I'll be the one to tell them, if you like it, since I was supposed to be in command until we got back outside."

"What's your idea?"

✷

"No way!" Mati screamed right in Kibi's face where they sat at a table on the lower deck. "She treated me like a slave! I can't do it. I *won't* do it!"

"It's that or . . . we can't use you on the crew. Either of you," Kibi responded, trying not to choke on the huge lump in her throat.

Rini, seated silently beside Mati, looked at Kibi with amazement.

At the large table on the upper deck, every word from below could be heard. Seated close beside Boro, Sata burst into tears.

After several minutes, she fell silent and wiped her face with a towel. "What do I do, Ilika?"

"You have to make one of those really hard decisions, like Kibi had to make about a month ago."

"My heart is screaming at me to go home and let my mother and father hug me and tell me everything's okay, and then . . . you know . . . wash tables or something. But I don't want to do that because I'd lose Boro!" She turned to him with a forlorn expression.

The large young man wore a soft, caring look, but said nothing as Sata searched his eyes for the answer to her dilemma. Not finding it, she started crying again and put her head onto his chest.

Soon she wiped her face once more and took some deep breaths. "I'll do it. I'll do anything you think will help me, here, in the deepest darkest trench, or anywhere else. But . . . how do I get Mati to agree?"

Ilika shrugged.

Sata looked at Boro. He too shrugged.

"I guess . . . I have to ask her . . . from my knees."

"Might work," Boro said. "She knows now that you guys are going to succeed or fail together."

Sata stood up, then saw that Boro and Ilika were making no effort to rise. "Yeah, I have to do this alone, don't I?"

Ilika reached over to the steward's console and touched a control. "Kibi and Rini, please come up."

A few moments later, Kibi appeared in the lift, then Rini. They quickly took in the situation of Sata standing alone, halfway to the lift, so they sat down at the table.

Sata's last few steps on the upper deck appeared painful, as if she was going to her own execution. Tears started streaming down her cheeks again as the lift took her out of sight.

"This is going to be one of the longest hours of my life," Ilika declared with deep feeling, "or however long it takes."

The others at the table nodded agreement.

*

The first hour brought little but the sounds of yelling, screaming, and crying from the lower deck. All of Mati's frustrations, from a lifetime of incapacity and slavery, were poured out for Sata to hear, even though the navigator had witnessed few of them and was the cause of none of them, save the very last.

The second hour was even more difficult for those on the upper deck because no sounds at all came from below. The captain and partial crew spoke in whispers, wondering if Mati and Sata had fallen asleep, or perhaps killed each other.

During the third hour, when those above were very quiet, they could hear soft voices coming from the lower deck. Then, as the end of that hour approached, little bits of laughter filtered up through the lift. For the first time since the trouble began, smiles came to those waiting. Boro and Rini started making dinner.

As the aroma of potato and onion soup began to waft its way throughout the ship, Mati appeared in the lift, hair snarled beyond recognition. Her face was red, tear-stained, and in one place, bleeding, but she wore a contented smile.

Sata appeared next, walking with a limp, but was also smiling.

After standing for a moment facing the rest of their friends and captain without speaking a word, Mati took Sata's hand and together they entered one of the toilet rooms.

Because of the importance of the situation, Kibi nodded when Boro asked to use some of their dwindling supply of foods and drinks from other worlds. As soon as the two girls emerged, slightly improved in appearance, Rini started shuttling trays to the table. Sata and Mati took seats side by side.

"This smells good!" Mati remarked.

"How did you know making us do stuff together was going to work?" Sata asked.

"I didn't," Kibi replied.

"But we didn't know what else to do," Ilika admitted. "You two declared your friendship the first day you were together. That friendship is now being tested. It looks like . . . well, you tell us."

"We . . . um . . . made a pact," Mati began. "We're going to do everything together, starting with what Sata . . . I mean what *we* messed up, and going on from there until Sata can go into deep, dark places without freaking, and I can pilot without getting mad."

"Tell them what you realized," Sata coaxed. "It's important."

"Um . . . it's not the first time I've been angry while piloting. It's just the first time I let it show. And I realized . . . this is embarrassing . . . I was mad at Tera many times too, even though I loved her."

"I've had some choice words for Manessa," Boro shared, "since the simulated failures started."

"Me too," Rini admitted.

"That's understandable," Ilika began. "Hopefully you can all forgive Manessa once the simulations are over."

"I think we all understand why we're doing them and why they're important, but they're frustrating," Kibi shared. "I was sort of just watching it all . . . until Manessa killed my refrigerator!"

Everyone else laughed and Kibi smiled.

*

After dinner, Ilika determined that Sata's limp was nothing permanent, but that she had a new respect for Mati's crutch. A little antiseptic ointment on Mati's cut was sufficient, as the bleeding had long before stopped. The two girls brushed each other's hair, and then declared themselves ready for duty.

"I want you to take turns giving directions to me," Ilika commanded, handing them a pair of safety lines. "Listen to each other and learn. If you do a good job, I'll stop and let you come in before we go through the waterfall." He let his last statement soak in for a moment before cracking a smile.

Both girls laughed heartily, then prepared to creep up to the watch nest on top of the Manessa Kwi.

"This'll be my first time on top of the ship!" Mati declared.

Ilika nodded. "You've seen it done, and we're not at eight thousand meters."

Mati chuckled. "Last I looked, we were at about one meter."

"Still are, exact same place."

She took a deep breath. "I'm ready."

Mati's ascent took some time, but with Sata's help, it proved nearly painless. By the time they arrived, Manessa had created an extra-wide seat that would hold them both.

Ilika took the helm while Boro and Rini stayed at the hatch.

"Should I start, or do you want to start?" Sata asked.

"Um . . . you can start."

"We need to go up a little. There's a big stalag-thingy just ahead."

Mati giggled at Sata's made-up word. "Ilika can't see, so saying 'a little' doesn't do any good."

"Oh, yeah. Up very slowly. How's that?"

"That works," Mati assured.

"Okay, stop," Sata directed. "Your turn."

"Slowly forward," Mati began.

*

About half an hour later, after much giggling and several lessons in clear communication, the two girls sat on top of the ship just a few meters from the roaring sheet of water that marked the end of the cave.

"I guess this is one way to take a bath," Mati mused aloud.

They both felt tugs on their safety lines and laughed. A few minutes later, they were back inside the ship and the hatch was closed.

"You up to taking the helm for the waterfall?" Ilika asked his pilot.

"I wouldn't miss it!" Mati declared. "As long as I get Sata by my side."

"Actually, for a couple of days, I want her right with you, watching over your shoulder, even taking the helm on some easy flight legs."

Sata grinned.

"I'll cover navigation during that time. I didn't know cross-training would start so soon, but you two, more than anyone else, need a good appreciation for what the other one does."

"I get to teach Mati how to juggle charts?" Sata asked with a grin.

"The basics."

The two friends quickly embraced each other.

"Status check for waterfall passage," Ilika ordered, and everyone went to their stations.

Mati, with Sata holding onto the back of her chair, was unable to take the ship through the torrent as smoothly as her captain, but Sata was impressed anyway, and quite in awe of how complicated the pilot's job was, now that she had a chance to watch.

The cave, with no visible daylight or noticeable temperature changes, had created a sense of timelessness, and the entire crew was surprised to emerge into the darkness of night. Above them, stars gleamed in a cloudless sky, and around them, the deep green jungle enshrouded its secrets.

With light provided by Manessa, they found a little clearing from which birds scattered into the air, then set the ship down. Ilika and Kibi made a quick check from the ramp for dangers.

Everyone knew which two crew members wanted hot baths that evening.

* * *

Would you have been able to pilot the ship, without any visual or topographic displays, using only the directions Sata gave? What do you think of Mati's refusal to continue piloting?

What leadership qualities did Kibi show during this crisis?

Most human groups that engage in teamwork operations, such as the military and corporations, normally isolate a person who cannot function on the team, and select a replacement. How did Ilika handle the situation differently than we usually would?

Kibi forced the two girls to solve the problem together. Why did that motivate them to come up with a solution? In what ways did it make that solution easier to achieve?

When Mati admitted she also had a problem (anger), how did that help the two girls form their problem-solving pact?

When Sata went up to the top of the ship again, what was different that helped her do a better job than the first time?

Ilika made an assumption about the way his crew members could learn to give directions when the pilot could not see. The method involves "trial and error" in which the one giving commands can see what happens when the directions are vague or relative to something the pilot can't see. It requires clear thinking, so it worked for Rini, but not for Sata because of her claustrophobia.

Chapter 24: Rini's Jungle

After Ilika and Kibi roused themselves late the following morning, they went up the lift to find the rest of the crew frowning at them.

"Manessa won't let us go outside," Rini grumbled.

"Says we need a captain's override to open the hatch," Sata added, her head cocked slightly askance. "It feels like we're . . . prisoners."

Kibi, not knowing anything about it, stepped back and looked at Ilika.

"Guilty," Ilika admitted. "Rini, you asked for a jungle," he continued as he got a cup of tea from the pot someone had made. "This is a jungle, and we might visit others. They are very beautiful, warm, wet, and have the greatest diversity of life of any ecosystem on this type of planet."

"That's . . . um . . . why we want to go outside and *see* it!" Mati asserted with an annoyed tone of voice.

Ilika smiled. "I'll give you some numbers." He sat down at the steward's console and selected something from Manessa's memory. "A typical jungle contains sixty species of dangerous mammals, including several carnivorous cats that can easily kill people, thirty types of aggressive birds, two hundred species of poisonous reptiles and amphibians, and twelve different carnivorous fish that will attack any animal in the water, including humans, and leave nothing but bones. Also, three thousand kinds of aggressive or poisonous insects, some of which move in swarms, and fifty-three thousand different microbial diseases to which we are vulnerable."

"Oh," Rini mumbled.

"Wait, I forgot to tell you about the seven hundred species of toxic plants. Many are poisonous to the touch, and some can shoot their poison a meter or more. I hope this also explains why I wouldn't let you go off the beach back at the tropical island."

"Thanks for locking the door," Boro said, eyes wide.

Ilika touched a control on the console, spoke a word, and the hatch opened. “The hatch is back to normal now that I’ve briefed you.”

They looked out to see huge insects buzzing about in the air, larger than any they had ever seen. Vines had already grown over the ship’s ramp, and a large snake was stretching toward the hull from a nearby tree. A growling sound somewhere in the distance caused Mati to shudder.

“We have to be smart and careful,” Ilika continued. “We are now the crew of a response ship, and we will be visiting many different worlds. You five grew up in a temperate climate. My childhood home was slightly warmer and drier, but not too different. Remember what happened to us when we went wandering around in the mountains of your kingdom?”

They all smiled at the memory of getting lost, running out of food, and nearly freezing to death in a mid-summer snowstorm.

“The desert is a simple eco-system in which you can easily see the few dangers. The mountaintop is devoid of life and the dangers are related to the weather.”

Suddenly a heavy rain started falling outside, reminding them of the waterfall.

“I’ve heard it can rain in a jungle so hard you can’t breathe,” Ilika shared.

Rini’s mouth opened. “Wow. We’re sorry.”

“No apologies necessary. I should have told you last night, but I didn’t think of it until we were all in our cabins. Fact is, we’re taking a chance just breathing the air because some of the microbial diseases are airborne. Manessa’s filters will catch most of it, and we’ll get checked for any health problems when we get to Satamia.”

Mati smiled at the prospect.

"So, let's get some breakfast, get our ship running as best we can, and take a tour of this beautiful and mysterious forest *without* getting poisoned or eaten."

✷

"Everything works!" Boro declared.

"Same here!" Rini added.

"Me too!" Sata echoed.

"Uh oh," Kibi moaned, ruining the excitement. "Manessa says we're out of water even though I *know* we have a tank and a half, and all the solvent filters are suddenly, mysteriously clogged, including, get this, the spares."

Ilika laughed.

"That means no hot baths!" Sata grumbled with mock despair.

"Oh, and there's more," Kibi continued. "The siphon controls have gone purple!"

"Manessa strikes again!" Boro said, laughing.

Ilika, still chuckling, led Kibi down to the utility room, and a minute later they returned with a couple of big jugs made of some soft, flexible material.

✷

With Rini in command, Sata watching Mati pilot, and Ilika covering navigation and watch, they spent the morning poking into groves of towering trees, shallow caves full of dripping ferns, and pools of emerald green water.

They had little trouble adapting to the new training situation, with Boro dipping jugs into pools while Mati hovered the ship and Rini swatted at huge flying bugs. Kibi took charge of filtering the water, then boiling it, while Ilika added a chemical to each toilet to keep down the odor.

Three different waterfalls reached out from the rocky cliff, allowing them to fly behind and peer at strange flowers and huge mushrooms that lived in a constant mist. They followed streams to places where the water disappeared into caves too small for the ship, then found the water gushing from rocky openings somewhere lower down the valley. When not sight-seeing, Mati hovered the ship beside trees while Kibi and Rini picked fruit.

Many times that morning, as Mati squeezed the ship into tight or dark places, Sata had to close her eyes for a moment as she relived the feelings that had overwhelmed her in the ocean trench and the cave. Whenever she could, Mati reached up with a free hand to touch her friend. That touch reminded Sata to breathe.

At lunch, Rini declared his curiosity satisfied, so they returned the Manessa Kwi to the clearing and spent the afternoon doing language lessons, watching videos about jungle creatures, and doing all their cooking and cleaning with small amounts of filtered, boiled water.

✷

Boro and Sata sat on the entryway steps after dinner watching insects the size of birds repeatedly try to penetrate the static energy field that protected the open hatch. None succeeded, but neither did they give up and leave. Boro took Sata's smaller hand in his and she leaned her head against his shoulder.

"It doesn't feel so cooped up in here when we have the hatch open," she shared.

"Yeah, as long as those vultures can't get in and suck us dry."

Sata chuckled. "Would they suck us dry, or poison us?"

Boro speculated, pointing. "The green ones with the sharp needles on their noses would just suck us dry, no pleases or thank-yous. The red ones that glow would poison us first, *then* suck us dry."

Sata laughed.

"I'm very glad you're feeling better, and you and Mati are friends again," Boro said tenderly.

"Kibi made it clear — we succeed or fail together. And if the pilot and navigator can't count on each other . . ."

"Yeah. Ship's in trouble."

"It's like . . . when I worked at the inn and I'd miss wiping a table, or break a dish, my mom would yell, but it wasn't any big deal. Now . . . people could die. There's no place on the bridge for a little girl."

Boro put his arm around her and held her close.

Sata smiled and closed her eyes.

* * *

Conditions in a tropical rain forest (a "jungle") are perfect for living things like those on planet Earth. Any wetter, drier, hotter, or colder, and the amount and diversity of life goes down. "Diversity" means the number of different species that are part of the ecosystem. The more diverse an ecosystem is, the more resilient it is to shocks and changes, because there are many different species doing the same "job" in the ecosystem.

Of course, being "perfect for life" also means a jungle is perfect for death. An ecosystem in balance (in other words, that continues from year to year) has to have just as much death and decay as there is birth and growth. That explains the many carnivorous (meat-eating) animals, and the countless diseases.

A creature is "part of an ecosystem" when it gets its food and water from the ecosystem, leaves its wastes (and upon death, its body) in the ecosystem, and reproduces within the ecosystem. Were the 6 humans in the Manessa Kwi part of that jungle ecosystem?

Kibi eliminated large organisms in the water by filtering (straining), then killed the rest with heat. We have no filter material that will remove all microbes from water. "Chlorine" (sodium hypochlorite) will kill most microbes, but not all.

A small area of special conditions, like the constant mist around a waterfall, is called an ecological "niche." It is still part of the larger ecosystem, but allows certain creatures to flourish that would have a harder time outside the niche.

Sata made the decision to get over her claustrophobia. Why is she still uncomfortable in dark or tight places?

By admitting that there's no place on the bridge of a ship for a little girl, what is Sata promising to Boro?

By sharing an intimate moment with Sata even when she is talking about her claustrophobia problem, what is Boro telling her?

Chapter 25: Flight Plan

"Preflight, diagnostics, and status reports," Ilika requested as soon as everyone had finished breakfast and personal needs.

"Everything's green on my console," Mati reported. "Me and Sata have been doing lots of talking late at night in our cabin, and I think it's helping me with my anger."

Ilika smiled. "Excellent!"

"It's also helping me with my fear of . . . um . . . growing up," Sata admitted, looking a little embarrassed. "All navigation systems are working."

Ilika made friendly eye contact with his young navigator.

"All sensors are green or yellow," Rini said happily, "and the weather map is coming out now."

Ilika glanced at the symbolic chart that appeared on the main bridge display. "Looks like good weather for flying."

"Thrusters, anti-mass, ion, anything you could want, all green," Boro declared, "and fuel reserves are back to normal."

"How's that bug bite you got yesterday?"

Boro scratched his arm for a moment. "It's not swollen any more, and I feel fine."

"Remember, there's no place for heroic silence on a response ship."

Boro nodded.

"Water and solvent are working again," Kibi announced, "but I'm keeping one jug of good water in a cabinet where you-know-who can't find it and say it doesn't exist."

Chuckles rippled through the bridge.

"We're down to about half the food we brought, but we have tons of fresh fruit. Vines are all over the struts and ramp, but Manessa says they're no problem. Otherwise, the landing site and interior are secure for departure."

"Everything's working," Ilika explained, "because we have completed all the failure drills for surface flight."

"Hurray!" the entire crew cheered.

Ilika smiled. "Boro wants to see one of the planet's poles. Your flight planning objective, Sata, is to place the Manessa Kwi on the surface of the land at the north axial pole. To make it more interesting, you may not fly higher than two thousand meters, or over or through any open salt water. Mati will be observing the entire navigation process, and I will be piloting. Boro is in command, in addition to his usual duties."

✷

Two hours later, a very frustrated crew began looking daggers at their captain every time he glanced over their shoulders to see how they were doing.

The process had begun at Sata's station, but once they realized they had a real pickle of a navigation problem to solve, Sata made hard copies and they moved to the big table in the passenger area. Mati, assigned to observe, had remained silent, but she often reached over and touched the navigator on the shoulder when Sata looked like she wanted to chew nails. They would share a smile and a few deep breaths, then Sata and her helpers would go back to the problem at hand.

The navigator had quickly determined that their destination was covered by a floating ice cap, and therefore setting the ship on land at that point required somehow getting under the ice. But, Rini pointed out, to slip under at the edge required going over at least a few meters of open salt water.

To complicate the problem, mountains or plateaus higher than two thousand meters spanned the entire continent, making it impossible to get from the tropics to the arctic within the rules.

When they finally pushed aside their papers to partake of a lunch that Ilika made, no one felt like talking, so the captain attempted to break the ice. "Mati, you've been quietly observing. Any insights that might help solve the problem?"

"I think they've been staring at charts too long. When I lean back and close my eyes, and imagine myself piloting the trip, I can easily see how to get around the altitude limitation."

"Will you *please* tell us?" Sata begged, showing her teeth as if she were ready to bite.

"Um . . . if Ilika says it's okay."

Before Ilika could answer, Kibi burst out laughing and everyone looked at her. "Somehow knowing that Mati could see it made it come to me. The beach!"

Mati grinned. "No mountain goes right to the edge of the ocean without a little bit of beach or rocks at the bottom. Even if it's a sheer cliff two thousand meters high, we just wait for low tide!"

Sata, Boro, and Rini all laughed at themselves.

"The other problem," Mati continued, "I haven't figured out. But as Rini realized, we can't get *under* the ice cap. So we have to go *through* it . . ."

Suddenly Boro sprang to his feet. "Sata, how thick is the ice at the pole?" he asked, sitting down at his station.

Sata, excited by the possibility of a breakthrough, dashed to her console and began searching through charts. "Here it is. Um . . . um . . . about four meters in the winter."

Except for Ilika and Mati, who were content with their lunch trays, everyone gathered around Boro.

"I haven't used this stuff yet, but Manessa's hull can absorb, reflect, or radiate just about any kind of energy. If we can find infra-red, and Manessa can radiate it, we can melt our way through the ice. Help me with these words, Kibi and Sata."

"That one's visible light," Sata quickly translated.

"Okay," Boro agreed, "I see the names of the colors now. This next one down . . ."

"That's it!" Kibi nearly yelled. "That word means *fast heat*."

"Okay, Manessa can radiate it, and the next two energy bands also. Problem solved!"

They returned to the table and presented their navigation plan, in concept, to the captain.

He smiled and congratulated them, but wanted a real, detailed flight plan, with as little time spent squeezing along narrow beaches as possible.

The rest was easy. After quickly finishing their lunches, Sata went to work at her station, taking suggestions from those gathered around when multiple routes were available.

Mati continued to silently observe from the command chair.

✷

Given the altitude limit, using the ion drive was not an option, but they would be passing over a continent they had never seen before, and didn't mind going slowly enough for sight-seeing. Jungles and winding rivers gradually became deserts as they flew northward. Ilika slowed the ship whenever anyone spotted something interesting, from smoking volcanoes to herds of grazing animals.

Mati was quite amazed by all the work Sata had to do. Even after the difficult flight planning, the navigator still had to feed charts to all stations, swapping them as the ship moved on, and sometimes changing the flight plan itself as they flew. She was often asked to look up information about their route, and could not have done so without her good language skills. At the same time, she was constantly verifying the ship's position by visual references, and looking ahead to see how Rini's weather reports might affect their flight.

Deserts became sagebrush prairies as they continued to move northward, but the altitude restriction soon forced them to descend into coastal river valleys. Ilika switched to a three-D topographic projection as rain clouds and fog made their visual displays useless. He would always leave the final decision to Boro whenever route choices emerged, or interesting sights begged to be explored.

Twice Boro okayed visits to waterfalls leaping from green mountainsides, but then, at the third waterfall, put his foot down and told Ilika to press on to the coast.

Towering trees pierced the fog and reached for the sky, like those on the western side of their own kingdom, as Ilika piloted the ship over a rocky coastline at the first place where the land quickly rose to more than two thousand meters. When the clouds parted, snow could be seen covering the higher elevations.

Kibi requested a hover when they passed near a village of people with houses and boats made of logs. Soon a mist creeping in from the sea made further observation impossible.

Ilika was again able to fly by visual references up a green river valley where herds of antlered creatures grazed, but they were soon in the clouds again after cresting a low pass back toward the ocean. At the next tight spot on the coast, he only managed to avoid breaking the rules by timing their dash along the beach between waves. Kibi laughed from her station.

Tall evergreen trees continued to cloak the mountains. At one point, attempting to slip over a pass at one thousand seven hundred and sixty meters, Ilika had to shrink the hull to its minimum size and squeeze between trees to avoid the two thousand meter limit. Mati chuckled from the command chair.

Soon they passed over glaciers of creeping ice, and all crew members were glued to their visual displays, with orders to Rini to not let any clouds get in the way. The slender lad smiled but didn't argue as they spent a quarter hour peering into crevasses and listening to the creeks and groans of the slowly moving ice.

Illka's last tight spot was a beach, more ice than rock or sand. After that, he easily followed the flight plan straight northward over the tundra toward the polar ice cap.

* * *

What could be the result if Boro's bug bite was infected, painful, or poisoned, and he didn't tell his commander?

By keeping a jug of water in a cabinet, what other situations, besides a simulated failure drill, was Kibi prepared for?

As the navigator, Sata was essentially "in command" of the flight planning process. What aspect of her personality made it hard for her to see the solution that Mati and Kibi saw?

The method of collecting information that Mati and Kibi are good at, and Sata not so good, is called "intuition." Boro is not normally intuitive. What statement by another crew member, an intuitive, allowed him to realize he had a tool that would help get through the polar ice cap?

Cross-training, as Mati and Sata were beginning to do by observing each other at work, is important so that a person's job can be covered if they are sick, injured, or absent. It also has another value that is almost as important. How will one crew member tend to react to another when a mistake is made if they think the other's job is simple and easy? How will they tend to react if they know how complex the other's job really is?

"Two thousand meters," in case you're checking, would be 2 x 512 x 3.28 = 3359 feet. Remember that "thousand" is 8 (not 10) to the third power.

The area they passed through with clouds, mist, waterfalls, tall trees, and people who made boats and houses from logs, was another kind of rain forest called a "temperate rain forest." Examples in our world are Norway, Scotland, Ireland, British Columbia, Washington, and Oregon.

How far from 2000 meters is 1760 meters? Base eight, of course.

Chapter 26: The North Pole

“Not very exciting,” Boro said, looking out the open hatch and surveying the twilight scene before him, a vast expanse of nearly flat ice that stretched to the horizon where it met the dim overcast sky.

“Has anyone ever been here before?” Sata asked.

“No one from this world,” Ilika began. “It’s hundreds of kilometers to the nearest land or open water, even in the summer.”

Kibi frowned. “I don’t see anything . . . alive.”

“Nothing to eat,” Rini observed, “except maybe in the ocean under the ice.”

“But the ice is too thick here for anything to get through,” Boro pointed out. “Except a response ship. Those bears we saw near the coast, fishing at holes in the ice, they’d starve here.”

“It’s very peaceful,” Mati shared, leaning on Rini. “I’d like to go for a short walk.”

“That would be good for all of us,” Ilika said. “We’ve been flying for hours, and we’ll soon be in the ship for several hours more.”

“But it’s so . . . dark,” Sata mumbled. “Couldn’t we wait for the sun to come up?”

The silence lengthened until Ilika spoke. “It’s the middle of winter. The sun doesn’t come up.”

“Oh . . . yeah,” the navigator said with embarrassment. “I remember that lesson now. And in the summer, it never sets!”

Boro put his arm around his trembling friend, knowing well she was experiencing more than cold.

*

After short walks in pairs over the nearly featureless ice, feeling naked in their wool pants, hooded cloaks, and leather boots, they gladly returned to the warmth of their little ship. Hot mint tea and lively dance music, provided by Kibi, thawed their spirits while Manessa thawed their bodies.

"Everyone ready for the last leg of the flight plan?" Ilika asked.

Sata made a tiny whimpering sound. "It's gonna be . . . dark down there . . . isn't it?"

"It's dark here," Rini pointed out.

"Manessa will light the way!" Boro proclaimed, smiling at Sata.

She nodded and sipped her tea, but didn't smile.

Ilika and Boro spent a few minutes at the engineer's station talking about the hull radiation controls, and everyone else prepared for departure. Kibi stepped outside for a few more breaths of the bitter crisp air, and Rini searched for aurora lights with his eyes and his sensors, but found none. Mati watched Sata drag herself to her station as if going to her own funeral.

"Okay," Boro began, still in command. "I guess Rini will be telling Ilika where the bottom of the ocean is, and Sata will keep us on the chart."

The watch and navigator reported their status.

"Kibi, why don't you do that hull thing, you know, diagnostic?" Boro requested.

"Already done, all green and yellow, internal air, ship secure for departure."

"Good. Um . . . anti-mass and thrusters are ready. Infra-red hull on your signal, pilot."

"Airborne," Ilika said as he lifted the ship from the ice. "Struts in, going to minimum profile, ready for infra-red hull radiation."

Mati watched Ilika as he smoothly made the transition to flight, then turned her attention back to Sata.

"Infra-red," Boro confirmed.

They all watched their displays as the ship settled back onto the ice, then slowly began to sink lower and lower. After about a minute, the smooth sides of the ice shaft became visible, its walls glowing blue in Manessa's external lights. As they continued to sink deeper, water soon covered their view, and before long they could see an ice crust quickly form on the surface of the water as it receded above them.

Mati noticed Sata gripping the arms of her chair fiercely, but waited.

"Two more meters of ice under us," Rini reported, watching one of his displays.

In the silence that followed, Mati could hear Sata's breathing, deeper and shakier than usual.

Ilika kept his eyes on the pilot's console. Suddenly the Manessa Kwi began to plunge downward into the inky depths of the mid-winter polar ocean. "We have punched a hole in the polar ice cap," Ilika declared. "Finished with infra-red hull."

With no nearby surfaces to reflect the ship's lights, their displays suddenly seemed pitch black.

"I . . . um . . . I wanna go home," Sata moaned loudly and burst into sobs.

Mati crossed the small space from the command chair by hopping on her good leg, then wrapped her arms around her friend from behind. "Well you can't, so you'd better start pounding on your display selector until you find something that makes you feel good, and then grow up and do your job, or I will personally *throw* you out the hatch and *chase* you all the way back to your parents' inn! If you fail, I fail, and that means you have to take care of a crippled girl for the rest of your life, and I'll remind you of it every day, with my crutch over your head if necessary!"

Ilika pretended not to hear, but jaws were slack at the other three stations.

Mati's voice was shaking and cracking, but even as she yelled at her friend, she continued to hold her tightly. "Go on, start selecting, or I'll kill you right where you sit even before we get the hatch open!"

Sata reached out with a shaking hand toward her display selector, now crying deeply but no longer gasping. She found dark visuals and a topographic too featureless to be interesting. Then on channel two, she discovered a video of a bright, sunny day in a gentle forest, tiny insects floating on the air and chipmunks scurrying about in the trees. A slight smile appeared on her face, and her crying became little more than sniffling.

"Thanks, Kibi," Mati said. "We could use a towel or two."

The steward soon appeared with the request.

"Now you have to do your job, navigator. And remember, I've been watching, so I know what your job is."

"Um . . . um . . . chart is still good. Um . . . updating the depth profile. Um . . . ship's position looks good, within eight meters of the North Pole, but I can't verify visually."

"No problem," Ilika assured, smiling, but keeping his eyes on his console.

Sata began wiping her face with a towel.

"You ready to take responsibility for yourself and get what you need?" Mati asked with a challenging tone, "or does Kibi have to pick you a video every day, maybe read you a bedtime story too?"

Sata took some deep breaths as she continued to watch the forest scene, which now included a doe and her fawn grazing. "I . . . um . . . I could never ask for anything back home."

"And not much was being asked of you, other than repetitive work," Ilika pointed out.

"Um . . . yeah . . . it was so boring I sometimes fell asleep doing dishes."

Mati chuckled. "Now you're a navigator. I've seen how complicated your job is. Which is it? Are you and me on or off this ship?"

There was a long pause as Sata watched the scene on her display and finished wiping her tears. "Kibi, would you show me how to select music and videos and stuff tonight?"

The steward smiled and nodded.

*

A few minutes later, Ilika extended landing struts and settled the Manessa Kwi onto the bottom of the polar ocean. Kibi and Sata made dinner while lively music played and outdoor videos, on every display, kept the navigator in good spirits.

But every half hour or so that evening, in between eating, watching videos, and playing games, Ilika called Sata onto the bridge. They spent a few minutes just looking at the actual underwater scenes around them with no audio or video distractions. Each time she would tense up and start gasping for breath, but he watched her gain more and more control over her reaction as the hours passed.

After a hot bath and a friendly pillow fight on the lower deck, Sata was in such a good mood that she forgot to ask Ilika to move the ship back to the surface before falling into a deep sleep in her bed.

* * *

Salt water freezes at lower temperatures than fresh water, so a floating ice cap is probably far below "freezing" (0°C = 32°F = 273°K).

Our own North Pole was possible visited by people and dogs in 1908 and/or 1909, but they could not prove it. It was seen from the air in 1926, submarine in 1959, and snowmobile in 1968.

Since the planet where the story takes place had 24-hour night in mid-winter and 24-hour day in mid-summer, it must have a rotational axis that is not at a right angle (90°) to the plane of the solar system (the "ecliptic"), just like our planet. Earth's axis is 67° from the ecliptic, so it is 23° "tilted" from "straight up and down." It is this tilt that gives us shorter days in the winter and longer days in the summer.

Although it varies from year to year, and has been thinner recently because of global warming, the 4-meter (13-foot) thickness of the polar ice in the story is similar to our own North Pole.

Infra-red radiation is what we call "radiant heat," and can be felt by placing your hand near any fire or dark, hot object. It is a broad band of electromagnetic radiation between microwave radiation and visible light.

When Sata experienced her claustrophobia again under the polar ice cap, why was Ilika careful to only look at his piloting displays and not say anything about it?

Almost by accident, Sata made the discovery that part of her problem was fear of asking for what she needed to deal with her problem. Have you ever had a problem, knew what you needed, but were afraid to ask for it?

It is true that in most human groups, there are negative consequences for admitting weakness and asking for what you need. How is Ilika's ship different in this way?

Ilika was “desensitizing” Sata to the ocean depths around them by having her take a short look once in a while. We can often take frightening things in small doses, and by slowly increasing our exposure, make progress toward mastering our fears.

Chapter 27: Learning by Watching

The next morning, Sata laughed when she realized the ship was still sitting on the bottom of the frigid, dark polar ocean. By that time, she already had a video of birds in flight on the main screen in the passenger area, and a mug of hot tea in hand.

"How did you sleep?" Ilika asked with a slight smile.

Sata laughed again, this time with a tone of resignation. "I think . . . I know what it means to be part of a team now. What happened to me . . . makes me remember Buna at the pool in the tunnels. You never abandoned her as long as she was willing to try *something*. I almost wish she could be with us now."

"Me too," Ilika agreed. "She worked hard to overcome her weaknesses."

Several others nodded as they sipped tea.

"I wonder if she's found Noni yet," Kibi pondered aloud.

"I think she'll look until she does," Boro began. "But if they do get together, they'll have to be careful and hide their relationship from the priests, won't they?"

"From everybody!" Kibi emphasized.

"Ilika . . ." Rini began thoughtfully from the galley, "in Nebador, can anyone have a close relationship with anyone else, no matter who or what they are?"

"Within the Nebador Services, yes."

Rini nodded.

"Only people," Ilika continued, "get it into their heads they can tell others what kinds of relationships are okay."

After a moment of thoughtful silence, Rini's eyes opened wide. "You mean . . . Nebador isn't run by people?"

"That's right."

Several crew members exchanged funny looks, but didn't know what else to say.

✷

Butterflies flitted about on one part of her display as Sata made sure everyone, especially her dear friend Mati, had the necessary charts at their fingertips.

After an ion-drive journey through the cold water from the north axial pole to the nearest continental shelf, Mati guided the little ship through shallow water looking for a hole in the ice. Marine mammals and wingless diving birds told them an opening was near, and with Ilika's approval, Mati nudged some floating blocks of ice farther apart so the ship could take to the air.

Sata picked a view of the winter sun, not far above the horizon, and put away her butterfly video. Then she turned her attention to clearance checking for another ion flight, this time through the atmosphere.

"Location eleven is near the equator," Ilika explained. "It's a city that Kibi requested, very different from the first."

"Good," the steward said, coming down to the bridge.

"Kibi is in command," Ilika announced, getting up. "We will be using ion level three, the fastest that can be used through air. Clearance is four thousand meters."

"We have a mountain range at almost seven thousand," Sata reported, studying her screen, "so we need thirteen thousand meters, Mati."

After Kibi got status reports from everyone, she swiveled to look at Ilika. "Could anyone see us at that speed?"

"We'd look just like a shooting star."

✷

Stone temples and wide avenues covered the top of a plateau that rose a thousand meters above a broad river valley teeming with farms and villages. Carts and people with baskets could be seen slowly ascending the four roads that connected the lowlands with the city above. Goods of all kinds went up, empty carts returned as the drivers reined back the animals and pulled constantly on the brake levers.

"Nothing like that other city," Rini observed as he selected several down-angle views and made them available to his shipmates. "I think I like this city better . . . but I'm not sure yet."

"It's clean," Sata noted, arranging all the external views side-by-side on her display. "Plenty of food, and not too many people."

Boro tapped at his controls. "Thrusters level one. Something's very different about this place, almost like . . . someone took paper and drew it neatly before it was built."

"Is that a group of slaves?" Kibi asked, peering intently at the large screen directly in front of the command chair.

Everyone saw where she was pointing, then looked more closely at their own displays.

"Could be," Mati said, leisurely moving her flight control. "But they aren't being put to work, just kept in a group."

As soon as Rini figured out which view they were talking about, he magnified the image.

"Thanks, Rini," Kibi said. "They're all young girls. One's being led away, but she's dragging her feet. Ilika, does Manessa know anything about this city?"

"Yes," he said from the steward's station. "I'm reading about it now, but I want you to learn all you can by observing."

Boro tapped at his display selector. "It looks like a parade or ritual. The girls are trying to get away, but the guards won't let them. I bet the one with the weird mask is a priest."

Rini increased the magnification. "The girls are all in fancy dresses and their hair is nice. They *can't* be slaves."

"If they're in fancy dresses, why are they trying to get away?" Sata wondered aloud.

Kibi squinted. "They're heading for that round building. Rini, would you magnify it?"

Sounds of shock and disgust came from all over the bridge as they gazed at the ugly open-mouthed demonic sculpture that formed one of the doorways to the temple. Even as they watched, a girl of about eight years, richly-robed and wearing flashy jewelry, was dragged through the open mouth into the building.

"I don't like this," Kibi said with feeling. "Mati, let's look at the other doors."

As the ship moved around the temple, the other three doors slowly came into view, each a different grotesque stone sculpture with the doorway going right through the figure's open mouth. Another group arrived, led by a priest, and one of the captive girls was forced through the doorway.

Boro cleared his throat. "I have a hunch I know what's going on . . . and we're not going to like it. Rini, can Manessa pick up sound at this distance?"

Rini looked at Ilika, and the captain stepped to the watch console to demonstrate some new controls.

"Mati," Rini began, "if you'll hold Manessa steady in sight of one of the doors . . ."

The pilot locked the ship's position with a good view of the nearest door.

The captain, from Satamia in Nebador, and his crew of five from a little kingdom far to the north on another continent, heard deep-throated words chanted by the priests as a girl was dragged inside, kicking and screaming. None of the words meant anything to any of them, but the chanting was cold and cruel, and the girl screamed with fear and anger.

When the chanting reached a climax, the girl screamed one last time, long and blood-curdling, and the sound echoed and faded away slowly, ending with a barely-heard thud.

*

Kibi and Mati both wiped at their eyes as they gathered around the big table to discuss what they had seen and heard. Boro wore a frown. Sata and Rini had far-away looks in their eyes. Ilika set a plate of crackers in the middle, and an empty bowl, just in case.

"Did you guess right, Boro?" Ilika asked to break the ice.

"Yeah. The girls are sacrifices."

"What good does *that* do?" Mati challenged.

After a long silence, Rini looked up. "I think . . . the four ugly things . . . are gods . . . and the priests are feeding them . . ." His gaze returned to the tabletop.

"I know what you're gonna say, Ilika," Kibi began, "but I want to rescue them so badly, I can taste it."

"So . . . you want to start a new religion to replace the one they have? Are you willing to stay and be the leader of that new religion?"

Kibi scowled. "Couldn't I just . . . give them a new revelation . . . you know, the voice of God speaking from the golden ball in the sky? I'd just tell them no more sacrifices."

"They'd have your revelation twisted to their own purposes in a week," Ilika predicted.

"And if you stayed," Rini speculated, "they'd find a way to make *you* their next sacrifice."

Kibi frowned.

Ilika nodded. "Sacrificing prophets is a long-standing tradition in most religions, especially when they try to make changes in the established ways."

"Damn!" Kibi breathed with frustration.

* * *

The value that Ilika shared, the freedom of "consenting adults" to enter into relationships, has been a goal of freedom-loving people all through history. We have made progress in that direction, but it is a constant struggle against people in both politics and religion who enjoy controlling others without good reason.

Can you imagine a civilization in which "people" aren't in charge?

On our planet, at the edge of the northern polar ice cap, the marine mammals are mostly seals, walruses, and bears. Our "wingless diving birds" are only found around the southern ice cap. What are they called?

7000 + 4000 = 13000?

Human and animal sacrifices are not part of most religions today, but they were once a common part of human culture. Our concept of deity (god and other spiritual persons) has changed slowly over the thousands of years of human pre-history and history. As our concept changed, so we changed the ways we relate to deity. The god(s) to whom human and animal sacrifices were made were thought of as cruel, vengeful, and angry. Some people still have that concept of deity today.

Chapter 28: The Lost City of the Atorura

The Manessa Kwi sat on a rock outcropping completely surrounded by jungle. Warm, humid air came through the open hatch as the crew lounged around the passenger area.

"Your next destination is the lost city of the Atorura tribe." After saying this, Ilika stepped into the galley and started pulling out ingredients for dinner.

The five crew members looked at each other. Kibi sat down at her station and opened the destination list that had always before included latitude and longitude in Manessa's planetary coordinate system. Destination number eleven was on the list, but said no more than Ilika had already told them. "Um . . . Ilika . . . we don't know where that is."

Ilika poured a measure of dried vegetables into the cooking pot. "You have to find it. Everything necessary to do so is available to you."

After a long silence, Boro sighed. "It's a puzzle."

"You're not fond of puzzles, are you?" Sata asked from where she swiveled in one of the passenger seats.

"No. I like knowing what I'm supposed to do and getting to work."

"Any time limit?" Rini asked from where he lay on the floor, hands behind his head, eyes sparkling.

"No," Ilika replied, stirring spices into the pot. "Manessa says it takes most crews several days to solve a puzzle like this."

Boro moaned.

"Manessa," Mati began, speaking to the air, "do you have any records of an Ato . . . rura tribe?"

"Atorura. A tribal nation of about seven thousand humans who currently inhabit one large and several small islands in the eastern ocean of this planet at coordinates . . ."

Sata dashed to her station and quickly had the correct chart on her screen. "Got it." Touching other controls, she centered and enlarged the group of islands and sent the chart to all stations.

"I'm putting it on the big screen back here," Kibi announced.

Rini sat up next to Mati's seat and gazed at the display. "Okay, there's a big village, three small ones, and several fishing camps. I don't see any lost city."

They studied the chart for the next quarter hour, occasionally asking Sata to enlarge a section of the main island, or one of the small outlying islands. As Ilika worked on his soup, a pleasant aroma began to fill the ship.

As time passed, Boro started making frustrated growling noises. "There is no lost city on *any* of these islands, no way, no how."

"If it was on the chart," Rini said with a subtle smile, "it wouldn't be lost."

Mati laughed and ruffled his hair.

Boro growled again.

"Manessa," Kibi began, "do your records about the Atorura tribe say anything about a lost city?"

"The Atorura have a legend about a city that was once their home. They no longer know its location."

"Do *you* know its location?" Sata asked, coming up from the bridge.

"No."

Silence settled over the entire crew as Ilika molded biscuits and spaced them evenly on a baking pan.

"We're stumped," Boro declared, chin in his hands.

"We've barely started!" Rini countered while Mati ran her fingers through his hair. "We just have to find out where they came from."

"Manessa," Mati began, "do you have any records about the Atorura from the past?"

"I have a large collection of oral traditions about their past migrations."

"We need to read them and look for clues," Kibi asserted.

Boro moaned.

"Boro . . ." Kibi began, a mischievous gleam in her eyes, "I'd like you to be our reader. Sata and I will help."

"Me? I'm not that good reading *our* language. I'm terrible at Manessa's!"

"I know," Kibi said.

Ilika kept his eyes on the soup he was stirring.

✷

"*I was . . . just a little . . . boy . . . when my father . . . guided our . . . boat . . . from island to island . . . always northward . . .*" Boro, with Sata at his side, slowly worked through one of the stories of the Atorura. The other three listened thoughtfully, searching for clues.

"*We thought we had . . . found a new . . . home, but the . . . fishing was poor so we . . . returned to the ocean way that went . . . northwest.*"

"Wait!" Rini begged. "Ocean way. What does *that* mean?"

"I don't know!" Boro responded with frustration.

"A 'way' on land is a road or trail," Sata began, "but that doesn't make any sense in the ocean."

"It feels like it's important," Kibi suggested. "Manessa, if a boat was left to drift on the ocean without sails or rudder, what would happen to it?"

"The boat would follow the ocean currents, unless caught by the breaking waves near an island."

Ilika wandered through and silently sat down at the watch station.

"Manessa," Mati asked hopefully, "do you have ocean current charts in your memory?"

"No."

Boro growled again.

*

The engineer struggled, with Sata's help, through several more stories, none of which included any clear locations or directions. Sometimes the "ocean way" went one way, sometimes another, but with rare exceptions, the Atorura followed it.

Suddenly Rini, massaging Mati's shoulders, burst out laughing.

"What?" Mati asked, swiveling around in the chair since her massage had stopped.

"We asked the wrong question! Manessa, do you have ocean current charts in memory?"

"No."

"Can you make them if we fly over the ocean?"

"Yes."

All five crew members looked at each other with big smiles. As evening light was rapidly fading from the sky outside, no one suggested they do anything that day, but they were all in silent agreement about their first task in the morning.

*

Mati locked the ship's position high in the sky directly above the current home of the Atorura tribe, a fairly large island in an otherwise nearly empty ocean. The horizon curved in every direction, giving the five crew members their first direct evidence that they lived on a round planet.

Rini, with Ilika at his side, began the ocean current mapping process, and Sata carefully matched the data with her charts as soon as each area was completed.

"Now this is more like it!" Boro proclaimed happily from the engineer's station. "We're *doing* something."

*

After settling the ship onto a small uninhabited island, little more than a sand spit with a few trees, they gathered around the big table and gazed at the new chart Sata just printed. It covered all the islands in that part of the eastern ocean, and little arrows revealed the surrounding ocean currents.

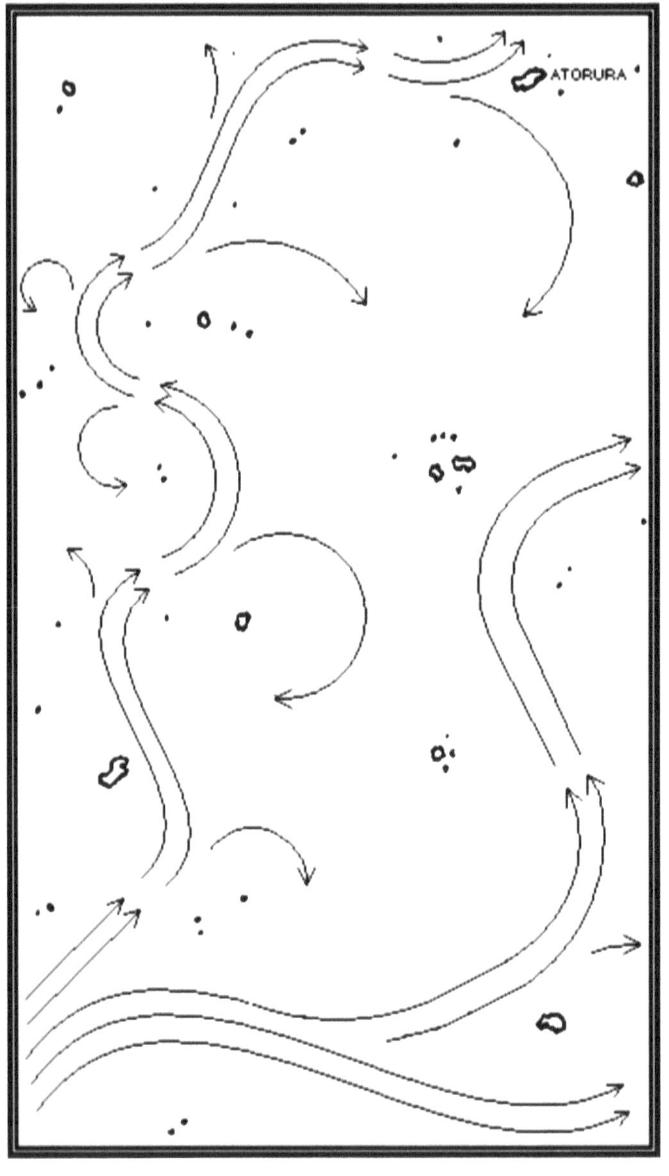
ATORURA

"I had no idea there were rivers in the ocean," Mati shared, standing on one leg so she could see.

"They definitely came from the south," Rini observed.

Boro growled. "This is the part I hate."

Rini glanced at Kibi, and she nodded just enough for him to see.

"Boro," Rini began, "would you draw the route the tribe probably took, working backwards along the little arrows?"

Boro moaned.

✷

With coaxing, Boro managed to complete his analysis of the ocean currents that eventually arrived at Atorura Island. The route snaked among many small islands, originating deep in the southern hemisphere as a branch of an even larger current.

"Okay, I get it," Boro began with a smirk. "You guys aren't going to let me avoid learning *anything* . . ."

They shook their heads.

"Sata and Mati had to sink or swim together," Rini reminded him. "Same goes for all five of us, together, if we really want to be Manessa's crew."

Boro sighed, but a tiny smile was starting to show. To cover his embarrassment, he looked at the chart again. "Okay. They followed this wiggly river in the ocean, except for a few times when they got cocky and found poor fishing."

"So they always came back to the current," Sata added, "from what we've read so far."

"And since they only moved their village one or two islands between father and son . . ." Rini began.

"Or mother and daughter . . ." Kibi added with a smile.

Rini grinned. "Yeah. So the journey took them a long time, maybe hundreds of years."

"Wow," Boro breathed softly, suddenly amazed by the complexity of the puzzle they were trying to solve.

"But we don't know," Mati began with a wrinkled brow, "where along this wiggly line their city was. We need to read more. I'd be glad to do some."

Boro took a deep breath. "Um . . . no thanks. I'm starting to catch up with you and Rini. I'll never read like Kibi or Sata, but it would be nice to not be, you know, dead last."

Kibi smiled, and Sata kissed him lightly on the cheek.

✷

"In the . . . old city, the . . . temple had many . . . seeing chairs so the . . . priests could watch the sun, the . . . moon, and the . . . stars."

Boro looked up from his knowledge pad. Everyone gave him blank looks.

"They saw many . . . creatures in the stars. The . . . Serpent and the . . . Clam were always . . . high in the sky. The . . . Eel and the . . . Pig were . . . shy, only showing themselves part of the time."

"Constellations," Rini suggested.

"But nothing useful . . ." Kibi proposed with a questioning look, glancing around the table.

No one responded, so Boro continued.

"The Great . . . Turtle would drink from the ocean each day, but her . . . feet stayed dry. When the people . . . left the city, the Great Turtle . . . dove under the water longer and longer."

When Boro paused again, Kibi frowned. "That sounds important . . . I think . . . maybe . . . sorta."

Rini closed his eyes. "If I was on an island, and I looked east or west, I'd see stars coming from or going into the ocean. But if I looked north or south, some stars would just skim the horizon."

"So . . ." Mati began thoughtfully, "if there was a constellation that looked like a turtle, and it just touched the horizon where they used to live . . ."

"And then they traveled north . . ." Sata added.

"And it started dipping below the horizon . . ." Boro recalled from his reading.

"They were looking south," Rini said firmly.

"Um . . . um . . . yeah," Mati confirmed, eyes closed as she tried to picture it.

Boro let out a long sigh and smiled.

✷

Sata was so good at locating planetary charts that she could do it with one hand while sipping tea and talking to Mati. Star charts were another matter.

Ilika knelt beside her as she learned how to select viewing location, direction, brightness of the stars, and many other factors. Grid lines could be based on planetary, solar system, or local universe references. Finally, the time could be the present, any point in the past, or far into the future. Rini and Mati stood near and paid close attention, while Kibi and Boro listened from their stations.

Once Sata was ready to manipulate the star-studded display, their problem became recognition. Manessa could not help to identify a constellation that had once reminded a long-dead tribal priest of a turtle. They all remembered the puzzle of the jar of flowers, so Kibi was made to sit in the command chair where she could see the large bridge display. The others got comfortable at their stations. Sata slowly changed the options for time of day, season of the year, and latitude from deep in the southern hemisphere, north to Atorura Island. They could hear Ilika making something in the galley.

During the next hour, Kibi found not one, but three possibilities. Rini found a fourth. With each discovery, Sata adjusted the star chart parameters so the turtle would just touch the horizon during the course of a day. She announced the latitude and displayed the proper planetary chart.

"Damn!" Boro cursed each time they discovered nothing but open ocean or tiny desert islands at the proper latitude.

When they ran out of turtles, the entire crew wandered slowly up to the passenger area, dragging their feet and looking at the floor. Although their minds were elsewhere, something spicy tickled their noses, and a sweet aroma brought smiles.

When he plopped into a seat, Boro noticed that the stars were still displayed over Kibi's station, so for lack of anything else to do, he stared at them.

Suddenly he saw something in the stars, but the moment he thought about it, the shape was gone and he couldn't find it again. "Sata . . . you can pick the brightness of the stars you display, right?"

"Yeah."

"Would you do me a favor and get rid of all those dim stars?"

"I suppose." Sata dragged herself back to her station. "How's that?"

"There's our four stupid turtles," Kibi commented, chin in her hands.

"Please, get rid of more stars," Boro begged, eyes intently fixed on the display screen. "I want just the very brightest."

"O . . . kay," Sata said half-heartedly as she poked at her controls.

Suddenly Boro was on his feet, dancing a clumsy victory jig. "Yes! I did it! Look! We forgot one word in the story." He grabbed a knowledge pad from the table and tapped at the controls to find the right page. "It said serpent, clam, eel, and pig. Then it said *great* turtle. Not little turtle, and not just plain old turtle. There's the *Great* Turtle!"

Everyone was standing around the table now, including Ilika, gazing up at Boro's discovery. Sata dashed back to her station, quickly had a latitude at which the Great Turtle touched the horizon, and a moment later replaced the stars with the planetary chart where the latitude crossed the ocean current. They could all see a fairly large island in the center of the chart, with lowlands for growing food, upland plateaus for building or grazing animals, and mountains to catch the rainfall.

"I had a hunch you were getting close," Ilika said with a smile, "so I made dessert and chilled a carton of tasty primola juice."

* * *

When the crew first discussed the puzzle, what personality difference could clearly be seen between Boro and Rini?

What aspect of leadership was Kibi performing when she asked Boro to read the Atorura records?

The ship gave the crew a good example of the difference between sentience/intelligence and sapience/wisdom. It answered the question about ocean current charts truthfully. The leap from that, to a way to create the charts, required the application of a "value" (a spiritual concept) by a sapient mind. What value did Rini apply?

Ocean currents are caused by many factors, primarily the rotation of the planet, the heating or cooling of the water at different latitudes, and the shape of the land. They are not completely stable, but change from season to season because of temperature, and also have multi-year cycles that we don't completely understand.

What attitude (or spiritual "value") did it take for Boro to accept the fact that his fellow shipmates were not going to let him get too far behind at any of the skills they needed? How common is that attitude in humans?

Parts of the ocean away from currents often have poor fishing because the ocean currents transport many living things and the nutrients they need for food. Large areas of still water tend to be relatively lifeless.

Small, low islands that are just sand and a few trees are called "desert islands" because they don't stick up high enough to catch any rainwater from the clouds, and so have no fresh (non-salty) drinking water. One of these may be the last resting place of Emelia Earhart.

Kibi's remark about mothers and daughters may actually be relevant to the Atorura culture. In our own history, there is a tendency for small, stable tribal societies, and sometimes federations of tribes, to be matriarchal (ruled mostly by women) and matrilineal (family lineage traced through mothers). The patriarchal and patrilineal society we have today can be traced back to ancient Greece, and before that, to migrating groups from central Asia.

Constellations are logical groupings of stars based on animals or other things they resemble. They are not reliable astronomical references because the constellations are all different sizes, and different people, in different cultures or at different times, will see different things in the stars.

At night, stars appear to "rise" and "set," just as the sun does during the day (and in the same direction), because of the rotation of the planet. We see this when looking east or west.

When the Atorura journeyed north, and began to see less and less of the Great Turtle constellation in their southern sky, what was blocking their view?

The controls Sata had available when selecting star charts are about the same as those in any good planetarium computer program, except that we only know the view from Earth, and local universe reference grids are not, of course, available.

What skill did Kibi (and Buna) show with the flower puzzle in *NEBADOR Book One* that caused her friends to select her for constellation-recognition duty?

As Boro discovered, not all the pattern-recognition abilities of our minds are under our conscious control. Sometimes they come when we least expect them (including during dream-filled sleep). Boro, although he glimpsed the pattern, was not used to listening to his intuition, so probably had a harder time "holding onto" the information than Kibi or Rini would have. How did he compensate for that weakness?

Chapter 29: The Old, the Hot, and the Cold

The ruins of the lost city of the Atorura tribe spread out on a plateau on the south side of the island, giving a view of the southern sky right down to the ocean. Stone blocks and simple statues lay at odd angles, with grass and bushes growing wherever they could. Few walls stood, and no roofs.

After setting the ship down on a level area that may have once been a plaza, the crew of the Manessa Kwi laced their boots, grabbed sun hats and mission bracelets, and crept about the ruins they had worked so hard to find.

"It seems like . . ." Rini began, struggling to express a thought as he balanced on a crumbling stone wall, "our old kingdom is the present . . . Nebador is the future . . . and places like this are the past."

"This place sure is the past for someone," Boro commented from the top of a stone block. "I don't think anyone's been here for . . . centuries!"

"I wonder why they left," Kibi pondered aloud from her knees, examining a bit of tile floor that was still intact.

"Maybe the rest of the stories Manessa has in memory will tell us," Mati suggested, slowly walking along beside Sata. "I want to finish reading them."

"Me too!"

"Yeah!"

Boro thought for a moment. "Me too, and I want to do at least half the reading."

Ilika, exploring some ruins off to one side of the plaza, smiled to himself, then took a good, hard look at what lay before him. "I think I found it."

"What?" Kibi asked, walking that way.

"The temple, where they observed the sun, moon, and stars."

As the others gathered, they gazed at the rubble and weed-choked circular space, slightly lower than the surrounding streets, with four stone towers in various stages of collapse.

"Kibi, would you see how those towers are aligned, please?"

"Um . . . if I can remember . . ." she mumbled as she opened the cover of her mission bracelet, tapped at the little keys, and slowly moved until she was lined up with two of the towers. "Yep . . . axial north and south."

"I thought so," Ilika said. "It was a simple astronomical observatory. I bet there are all sorts of interesting markings on the circular floor down there."

Boro looked at the rubble. "We could clean it out. None of those stones are very big."

"It's not ours, Boro. It belongs to this world, and someday the people of this world will discover the lost city of the Atorura tribe and learn many things from it. We are just visitors, here to carry out our mission and depart, changing things as little as possible."

"It's strange to think we're not part of this world anymore," Rini mused. "But I like the idea."

*

The mutiny was unanimous. Not one person, of the five Ilika had chosen for his crew, was willing to leave until the sun had set, the sky darkened, and they had seen the Great Turtle constellation with their own eyes.

Ilika chuckled and went up the ramp to make dinner.

After they had all gazed at the star-studded sky to their hearts' content, easily locating the Great Turtle and speculating about some of the other constellations, they finally returned to the ship.

But to Ilika's surprise, they completely ignored the food and drink on the table and gathered around Sata at her station. She entered star chart parameters, then stepped the hour forward until they were all laughing.

"We just learned something," Kibi announced with embarrassment as she sat down at the table.

"We couldn't figure out why the Great Turtle wasn't drinking," Mati explained.

"Sata knew," Boro added, smiling at her with pride.

"The Great Turtle will take its drink tomorrow about an hour before sunset," Sata revealed with a slight pout, "so we won't be able to see it."

"How long would we have to wait here for it to happen at night?" Ilika asked with a gleam in his eyes.

Rini squinted for a moment. "About half a year."

*

Eleven-year-old Sata, a medieval innkeeper's daughter, squirmed a little as she got comfortable in the command chair of the deep-space response ship. She was painfully aware of her ongoing battle with panic whenever they went anywhere dark and gloomy, especially if it included a great weight over her head. Luckily, both their current location, and their destination, were light and airy. She glanced at her friend Mati, unable to walk without a crutch. After swallowing a couple of times, Sata took a deep breath and forced herself to smile.

As her fellow crew members completed diagnostic and routine starting procedures, they turned to her for orders.

"Wow," she breathed as a shiver tingled along her spine. "Um . . . status reports?"

Everything was working and ready, and they knew the exact latitude and longitude of their destination. Boro was clearly happy with the situation.

A few minutes later, Mati announced their arrival. "The hottest desert in the world is a thousand meters below."

"Sata," the captain said from the navigator's chair, "you should work with Kibi to select a good landing site."

"What do you think, Kibi?"

"Hmm . . . you want dunes or salt flats?" the steward asked, glancing at view after view on her display.

"We've seen lots of dunes. Let's go for salt flats."

A minute later the pilot settled the ship onto a large expanse of crusty white minerals. As soon as Kibi opened the hatch, an oppressive heat invaded the ship even though the day was young.

Protected by sun hats, all six crept down the ramp, but no one showed any desire to go far.

"Does anyone live here?" Sata asked.

"Yes," Ilika replied, "but they stay close to the mountains where water can be found. They would rarely, if ever, come here."

"Since I'm steward," Kibi began, "I guess it's my job to say we can't stay long. Mati and Rini look wilted already."

"I'm not far behind," Sata declared, shading her eyes.

Ilika nodded. "This is an environment we can tolerate for a few minutes, but we have to quickly do whatever needs to be done, and keep an eye on each other. Any hotter and we'd just stay inside, or use radiation suits."

"Those are the white ones?" Boro asked, squinting at the shimmering horizon.

"Yes."

"I think we've done what we came to do," Kibi announced, seeing Mati limp toward the ramp. "You feel done, Sata?"

"Yeah. We can peek at other parts of this desert from a nice, cool ship."

A few minutes later, the Manessa Kwi hovered over a small oasis. Water bubbled out of the ground and was channeled to gardens and watering troughs. Brown-skinned people kept to the shade of the hundred or so trees as they tended their animals. Children ran out of thick mud houses, but quickly returned.

At the base of the nearby mountains, a boy and girl sat in the half-light of a cave entrance, shelling nuts. A handful of small goats occasionally poked their heads into the blistering sunlight, but quickly retreated. As Mati moved the ship up and over the barren mountains, Rini spotted the nut trees in a deep and shaded canyon.

When Sata declared she had seen enough of the hottest desert on the planet, she gladly returned to the navigation station and began nimbly selecting charts as Mati guided the ship southward.

"The next destination is across thirty-one thousand kilometers of open ocean," Sata announced as she sent the new flight plan to Mati.

Mati studied the plan as she took the Manessa Kwi up to five thousand meters with one hand. "I want ion drive three, Boro, unless Ilika wants me to go slower."

"Clearance check," Ilika ordered.

"Highest land, before we get to the coast, is seven hundred and thirty-two meters," Sata said.

"I'm ending the ion jump a hundred kilometers short of the far shore," Mati added. "We're at five thousand meters now."

"Ion three approved," Ilika said.

"Warming up," Boro reported. "Ion three, zero inertia, at your service."

After Ilika checked with Rini and Kibi, Mati sent the ship streaking toward the planet's south pole.

A three-hundred-meter wall of solid ice loomed above as Mati nudged the ship toward the coastline. Their visit to the North Pole had done nothing to prepare them for the spectacle before their eyes. As they watched, huge slabs of ice broke free of the frozen white cliffs and plunged, in slow motion, into the frigid blue water below. Huge waves of water and ice rushed toward them. Mati took the ship up a little higher.

"External audio, Rini," Ilika requested.

A moment later the ship was filled with an eerie groaning sound. Even as they watched and listened, a sudden loud crack made most of them jump. They saw, heard, and felt another massive chunk of ice slowly peel away from the glacier wall and plunge downward. Seconds later, it smashed into the floating ice with an explosion of sound and flying shards. They felt, more than heard, the resulting wave of black water and white ice that rushed beneath the ship.

"Hatch is half-open," Kibi announced.

The crew went off-duty two at a time to take a closer look at the fury of the glacier. Sata closed her eyes when a large column of ice came crashing down, but forced herself to open them before it hit the water.

"We are so lucky," Mati said at her side. "No one in our kingdom will ever see this."

"Or the hottest desert," Sata added.

"I don't know which one is scarier."

"This one, to me," Sata declared. "We'd be in trouble, either place, without a good ship."

"Yeah. I'm cold. You ready to go up?"

Sata put her arm around her friend and helped her to her station.

*

For the next two hours, the ship and its crew flew slowly over the ice continent, pausing to look at deep glacial crevasses, bare rocky peaks, and lakes of summer melt-water with nowhere to drain.

Swimming mammals and birds lined the coast where it came down to meet the water. Flying birds penetrated a few kilometers inland, pecking at clumps of wiry grass and building nests on the ground.

The ion drive brought them to the south axial pole where a blizzard was in progress. Mati landed by instruments, and each crew member braved a minute of fine ice crystals in the face at the half-open hatch.

After another quick flight, Mati and Kibi selected a level ice field near the south magnetic pole. The weather was clear, and the sun still up, but they all knew it had been a long day. Four of them left the bridge to make dinner and relax, while Ilika taught Rini how to scan for magnetic fields.

As they ate, they gazed at the large display over the steward's station, currently showing Rini's multi-colored fountain of magnetic field lines emerging from the nearby pole.

"Almost makes me dizzy," Boro shared.

"It's wonderful how Manessa can help us see things we usually can't," Mati began. "I use elevation color-coding all the time."

"That's even more important in space," Ilika explained. "Most of what's out there is invisible."

Rini smiled with anticipation, a far-away look in his eyes.

✷

After bowls of hot cereal the following morning, and half an hour of sliding around on the ice, they returned to the little ship to warm their hands and feet.

"Mati, you are in command," Ilika announced as he took the pilot's station. "I don't know if I selected *the* most beautiful hot springs on the planet, but the ones at location fourteen are pretty close, and easy to get into."

"After freezing my toes out there, hot water sounds very nice," Mati declared, leaning her crutch against the command chair.

Sata got the coordinates and started a flight plan. "I see why you put this after the ice continent, Ilika. It's on the other side of the planet from that desert."

"Overcast ceiling at two thousand meters most of the way," Rini reported. "Clear above five thousand."

"Landing site secure," Kibi added. "We need water soon."

"The mountains just beyond the hot springs should take care of that," Ilika said.

"You have anti-mass," Boro declared, "and the ion drive is green. We never seem to get low on fuel."

"It takes very little to poke around on the surface of a planet," Ilika explained. "When we start going into and out of orbit, we'll use more and have to plan carefully."

“Let’s stay below the clouds,” Mati said. “I want to see the swimming birds again.”

“Thrusters three, ion one,” Ilika requested.

Boro verified the acting pilot’s flight command.

Ilika took the ship up to a thousand meters, then headed for the coast. “There’s a small ice shelf on our way that should be teeming with birds and mammals. They’re called ‘penguins’ and ‘seals’ in some places, but I don’t think your language has words for them.”

A few minutes later, Ilika hovered while Rini sent views of the marine birds and mammals to all stations. Mati chuckled as the seals, barking happily, slid across the ice and dove into the water. Kibi smiled at the sight of a penguin carrying an egg between its legs as it waddled along.

Eventually Mati felt ready to say good-bye to the ice continent. Looking around the ship at her crewmates, they all nodded or smiled, so she gave the order to prepare for the ion jump. A few moments later everyone was ready, so she nodded to Ilika.

“Wait!” Rini yelled. “There’s someone down there!”

* * *

The chapter title is a word-play on the classic western “The Good, the Bad, and the Ugly.”

“Axial” north and south is what we would expect of the alignment of an observatory of a civilization that watched the sun, moon, and stars. Two points in the sky, one directly over each axial pole, do not appear to move as the stars make their daily journey across the night sky. In our sky, the star Polaris is very close to being directly over the north pole. It is the last star on the tail of the constellation Ursa Minor (Little Bear), or the last star on the handle of the “Little Dipper.”

“Magnetic” north and south, the other possibility, requires a delicate instrument that few early civilizations had (the compass), and it changes from year to year, making it a poor choice for building alignment.

What is the difference in attitude between (1) being from a planet and feeling free to dig things up, and (2) being visitors who want to change things as little as possible?

What did we learn about Rini by his reaction to being “not part of this world anymore”?

The crew could not see the Great Turtle “drink” (touch the ocean horizon) because, on any one day of the year, we can only see about half the sky. The other half is “up” during the day, so the sun prevents us from seeing the much-dimmer stars. It was just bad luck that on that particular day of the year, the Great Turtle "drank" during the day.

If the Great Turtle was a constellation in Earth's sky, and it "drank" at 4:00 pm, a month later it would "drink" at 2:00 pm, then 12:00 noon, etc., until 6 months later, it would finally "drink" at about 4:00 am and could be seen.

On Earth, the hottest deserts experience temperatures in the summer of about 60°C (140°F, 333°K).

Ilika judged the hottest desert, in summer, to be an environment they could only endure for "a few minutes" without special clothing. What other environments have they endured for "a few minutes" that would require special clothing for a longer stay? (In one of them, only Kibi went out briefly in regular clothing.)

The water at a desert oasis allows food and shade trees to grow, and a few people and animals to live. Such an ecological "niche" shows clearly the minimum requirements for a human habitation: soil, fresh water, and a tolerable temperature range.

An oasis where water "bubbles out of the ground" is the luckiest kind. Called an "artesian" well, it saves the labor of hauling or pumping the water out of a regular well.

When a glacier meets the sea, it is undermined at the bottom by the water until huge chunks fall from the slowly-creeping wall of ice. This is sometimes called "glacial calving."

On Earth, the south axial pole is on land covered by a thick polar glacier. The resulting elevation is 2835m (9301 feet), most of which is ice. It was first visited by people and dogs in 1911, then seen from the air in 1929. The temperature can plunge to about -80°C (-112°F, 193°K).

Making something visible that is usually invisible is the task of all instruments. Rini used the ship's sensors and displays to make the south magnetic pole visible. What instruments are found in most cars that make things visible that are hard or impossible to know otherwise?

Chapter 30: People Where None Should Be

Ilika quickly drew his finger back from the ion drive symbol, then locked the ship's position. "What do you see, Rini?"

"First I saw a pile of sticks way over on the far side of the ice shelf. When I magnified it, it turned out to be a wrecked ship. It's on channel four."

The others tapped at their display selectors.

"Then I saw a faint trail leading to the shore."

"I see it," Boro confirmed.

"Just as you were getting ready for the ion jump," Rini continued, "I followed the trail with my eyes to the shore and saw a pile of rocks that doesn't look natural. And I think I see smoke coming from it."

Everyone studied their visual displays.

"Survivors from a shipwreck?" Mati wondered aloud.

"They must be going back and forth to the ship for firewood," Boro proposed. "Nothing else down there will burn."

"Can we rescue them, Ilika?" Kibi asked, almost grinning from ear to ear at the prospect of her first real passengers.

"Maybe," Ilika replied. "Mati, you're back on duty as pilot. I need to work with Sata for a minute." He helped Mati switch seats.

"Ion drive off, thrusters one," Mati said. "I'm taking us closer for a better view."

Ilika stepped to the navigator's station. "Sata is going to be doing something completely new, and I want all of you to listen so you understand what's happening."

Sata looked up at her captain with much excitement and a tiny bit of fear.

"The rule we must follow, when thinking about interfering with another culture, is that we must do our best to communicate the situation to the leaders of the Transport Service. They are much older and wiser than any of us."

Rini cracked a tiny smile.

"It's happened several times since I came to your kingdom," Ilika continued. "The most important example was when I allowed our ship to be seen and attacked by the priests. I never would have done that without approval, since I could have easily hidden the ship somewhere off the trail."

"So you, and the Transport Service, *wanted* the ship to be attacked?" Mati asked with a frown.

"We wanted you all to be well-trained, and we knew no harm could come to Manessa. I did not anticipate what the religious orders would do, but the Transport Service did. Somehow, in ways I don't completely understand, it all fit into a series of events they knew would be good for your kingdom."

"I can see that," Rini said softly.

Mati nodded, but was still frowning slightly.

"So now I'll compose a description of what we see and want to do, and show Sata how to send it to the nearest star station. If they see anything wrong with our plan, they'll tell us."

"How long will it take them to decide?" Kibi asked with concern. "There are already several mounds near the little rock hut that could be graves. The survivors might not last much longer."

"When I propose something they don't like, I usually hear back in one or two seconds. I wait eight seconds just to be sure."

Kibi looked puzzled, but nodded.

*

Sata only needed to ask Ilika the meaning of two words in the message he composed. At his request, she sent it to all her shipmates so they could study the text. It was short and simple, as they knew nothing about the person or people in the rock hut. The only known fact was that they would soon die if not quickly rescued by the Manessa Kwi.

Sata's eyes were big as she stared at the reply that flashed onto her screen less than a second after sending the message, the first words she had ever read from somewhere out in the stars. *Rescue of the child is essential. Leave her in the care of the adult, and provide all possible material support. Melorania of Nebador.*

"Wow. I wasn't expecting that," Ilika shared with a look of surprise. "There's a child in that hut who is somehow very important to this world. Mati and Kibi, find us a place to set down that's nearby but not visible from the hut. I'd like to arrive on foot."

"Harsh environments suits?" Boro proposed.

"Mmm . . . no. I don't want to scare them. We'll have to make do with our stuff from your kingdom, just you and me, Boro. The rest of you . . . prepare to receive passengers."

*

Ilika and Boro put on every piece of wool clothing they could find, grabbed mission bracelets, and slipped out into the cold.

Kibi closed the hatch behind them, then headed for the storeroom beside the galley for blankets. “Sata, a big pot of soup. Mati, monitor the guys outside. Rini, weather watch and help Sata . . .”

*

The air was bitter cold, the rocks and ice slippery, and the clouds threatened to dump snow at any moment. Boro, with sparkling eyes and a half-smile of pride, walked beside his captain as they crested the shallow rise between the Manessa Kwi and their first real mission.

“The hut is in sight,” Ilika said into his mission bracelet. “No one outside. We can smell smoke.”

“Okay,” he heard Mati say. “Soup is on the stove.”

The rescuers continued down the gentle slope toward the simple rock hut, only big enough for about two people huddled close together. In the background, the small flat ice shelf stretched several hundred meters to dark open water, with the wrecked ship most of the way out.

A man in a heavy cloak suddenly crawled through a small opening in the side of the hut, stood, and gazed toward the ice shelf. Clutching his hood tightly closed with one gloved hand, he began walking toward the shipwreck.

“Hello!” Boro called in the language of Nebador.

The man ran back to the hut as quickly as possible, but his steps were slow and clumsy. He placed himself between the hut and the two figures who had appeared out of nowhere, put up his fists, and spoke strange words in a weak but threatening voice.

“I think . . . I’ve heard that language before,” Boro said softly to Ilika.

“I want you to remember, Boro, that our primary mission is to rescue the child. If this man doesn’t cooperate soon, we’ll have to be firm. Try *your* language.”

“Hello!” Boro called in the language of his kingdom. “Do you speak this language?”

The man suddenly relaxed and lowered his fists. “Little.”

“We have a ship and want to help you!” Boro said loudly and clearly.

The man looked toward the ocean, but seeing no ship, turned back and raised his fists again. “Not ship! You . . . demons!”

“He’s afraid, and the child could be dying,” Ilika said to Boro. “We’ll have to continue the introductions another time.” Ilika raised his left arm and tapped the sleep code into his mission bracelet.

Boro cringed as the man crumpled to the ground.

Ilika spoke into his bracelet. “Mati, bring the ship over, quickly. Tell Kibi to get into her cloak and boots.”

While Ilika spoke to Mati, Boro covered the distance to the unconscious man. “He’s breathing!”

“Good,” Ilika said, joining him. “Stay with him.”

At that moment, the Manessa Kwi appeared over the rocky hill and settled to the ground close to the hut. The hatch opened and Kibi dashed out.

“The child should be in the hut. Poke your head in and see what the situation is. I’ll be ready to pull you out at any sign of trouble. The man spoke your language a little, but the child may not."

Kibi nodded, got down on her knees, and pushed past the canvas flap into the hut. Ilika kept one hand on Kibi's cloak, one eye on the sleeping man, and listened carefully. He could also see Rini lacing his boots at the open hatch.

Kibi's muffled voice repeated soothing words of greeting and comfort, and occasionally Ilika caught a word or two in another voice. He did not understand the words, but guessed the child was female.

Kibi backed out and sat on the rocky ground. "She's about five, and I think I convinced her to come out. The fire in there is almost dead. By the smell, they've been here awhile."

A head of tangled brown hair suddenly poked through the little doorway. Kibi smiled from where she sat, and reached out her hand. The girl crawled out, clutching a small rag doll in one hand.

As soon as she saw the unconscious man, she ran to him and began talking and crying.

"He's okay, really," Boro assured. "He's just asleep."

The girl didn't respond to Boro's words, so he tilted his head onto his hands, closed his eyes, and began snoring loudly.

She quickly collected herself and laughed at Boro as she wiped her eyes with a sleeve that had not been clean for a long time.

* * *

What does the communication with "Melorania of Nebador" tell us about Melorania, or about Nebador?

The wooden ship was probably crushed by ice. Floating ice shelves are usually very thin and broken along the outer edge, so ships are tempted to penetrate for some distance to get closer to the land. If the ice begins to shift, or open passages freeze over, a wooden ship is easily crushed.

Why would the man, not seeing another sailing ship, assume Ilika and Boro were demons?

Kibi's soothing tone of voice, and Boro's sign language, was all the communication the crew had with the little girl at first. What other forms of communication work in a situation like that (when there is no shared language)?

Chapter 31: Important Stuff

By the time the man awoke, he was wrapped in a blanket and tilted back in a passenger seat. The hatch was closed, Kibi was slowly bringing up the temperature, and the aroma of hearty soup filled the ship.

The girl sat in another chair, playing with her doll but glancing at the man often. Boro sat across the table from them, keeping an eye on both. He and Ilika still wore mission bracelets.

The man looked around with frightened eyes but remained silent as Rini brought mugs of sweet, warm tea to the table. The girl drained her small cup quickly, but the man's shaking hands moved more slowly, and he sipped his tea cautiously.

Just then, Mati came up from the bridge using her crutch, took the seat next to the girl, and started drinking tea. The man relaxed and began drinking his tea in earnest.

Trays with soup, crisp bread, and stewed fruit came next, and the entire crew, by prior agreement, made light conversation with simple words in the language of their kingdom, and avoided talking about the ship or the Transport Service.

After all the crew members shared their names, the girl quickly revealed that she was Risan Gor. The man was much more hesitant, but eventually mumbled his name, Timod Gor.

*

After lunch, Boro and Kibi began their assigned task, and seemed comfortable speaking slowly in their native language using plenty of gestures. Timod Gor was reluctant to touch anything in the passenger's toilet and bathing room, but Risan Gor quickly mastered the bathtub controls and waited, arms crossed, for the two males to leave so she could bathe.

Over the course of the next few hours, Boro and Kibi managed to get both passengers into fresh robes while Rini ran their old clothes through the laundry machine.

When, with simple words and gestures, Boro invited Timod Gor to return to the hut for anything he wanted to retrieve, the man was quite confused. As soon as the hatch opened and he saw that his hut was just paces away, he became frightened, dashed outside, and began turning circles with his mouth open, trying to comprehend the situation of a ship, without sails or rudder, sitting upon the land.

Ilika was very proud of Boro for not laughing.

Risan Gor adapted more quickly, crawling into the hut and pushing out blankets, two small barrels, and a leather shoulder bag. Timod Gor quickly grabbed the bag, and the girl lovingly gathered the blankets into her arms, leaving Boro to bring the barrels, both nearly empty, one of salted pork, the other of hard crackers.

When Ilika and his crew began to prepare for departure, Timod Gor became very anxious, attempting to make himself understood with words they didn't know and urgent gestures. Soon he gave up and began pounding on the inside of the hull where he knew the hatch should be.

Boro opened the hatch and the man strode out, stood on the end of the ramp in his ragged socks, and motioned for the others to follow.

Boro, Ilika, and Kibi gathered on the ramp.

Timod Gor pointed toward the wrecked ship, struggled to remember a foreign word, then spoke with fire in his eyes.

"Gold!"

*

Fifteen seconds passed as Ilika considered the situation and made a decision.

Fifteen minutes passed as Ilika and Boro tried to coax Timod Gor back into the ship so they could go look for his gold.

Eventually they gave up as the man defiantly put on his boots and grabbed his cloak. He spoke firmly to Risan Gor and she parked herself in a seat, pouting and clutching her doll. Timod Gor bounded down the ramp, passed the hut without a glance, and strode onto the ice shelf toward the pile of broken timbers that had once been a proud sailing ship.

Ilika sighed as he closed the hatch. "Mati and Boro, move Manessa to the wrecked ship. Hover at one meter — the ice may be thin."

Timod Gor, only about half-way to the wreck, stopped in his tracks when the strange ship settled onto the ice next to his destination. He looked back toward the hut, then ahead again. Finally he resumed walking.

When he arrived, chest heaving as he breathed the cold air, Ilika, Boro, Kibi, and Risan Gor all sat on the ramp in boots and cloaks, while Rini and Sata watched from the open hatch.

Timod Gor looked at them for a moment, pointed at the wreck, and repeated the one relevant word he could communicate. "Gold!"

"Rini," Ilika began, "we need three harnesses and long safety lines."

Rini disappeared, and the equipment was delivered a minute later. Timod

Gor could hear the thin ice creaking and groaning as he walked. When he saw Ilika and Boro putting on harnesses, he huffed and walked to the ramp to do the same.

✷

While Kibi and Risan Gor watched from the ramp, the three in harnesses poked into every nook and cranny of the wrecked ship for an entire hour. They found many odds and ends and a little more food, but no gold.

Timod Gor, completely deflated from his earlier passion, removed his harness along with the others and entered the Manessa Kwi to warm up. His spirits improved when he received a hug and kind words from Risan Gor. A hearty stew completed the task of thawing all three treasure hunters.

Ilika checked on Mati at her station, practicing a piloting simulation but keeping an eye on the hovering ship. He saw Kibi bring up the freshly-washed blankets and some toys to keep their young passenger happy. Rini was helping Sata in the galley, so Ilika caught his eye and pointed at the watch station.

"I didn't think we'd find anything in the wooden ship," Ilika said softly in the language of Nebador. "Now let's do some *real* treasure hunting."

Rini smiled with delight and sat down at his station.

✷

A quarter hour later, Ilika had taught Rini how to scan for specific chemical elements or compounds. It didn't take long to verify that no gold, or any compound of it, was in or near the wrecked ship.

A large amount, however, was scattered on the ocean floor three hundred meters straight down. Rini grinned up at his captain, who put a finger to his lips.

"If . . . we find . . . gold . . ." Ilika began slowly and clearly, back at the table, in the only language he and Timod Gor shared.

Timod Gor held up a finger, then symbolically chopped it in half with his other hand while struggling to think of a word.

"Half?" Ilika suggested.

"Half! I . . . half. You . . . half."

Ilika held out his hand to seal the agreement. Timod Gor's grip nearly brought tears to Ilika's eyes

The man grinned.

As Ilika stood and carefully moved his bruised hand, he looked around. "We have an opportunity to do some treasure hunting," he said in the language of Nebador.

Rini was already smiling, and all the other crew members quickly joined.

"A little extra underwater practice would be good for some of you."

"I promise not to zap any dolphins," Boro assured.

"Hmm. You already have an assignment, Boro, an important one. I think . . . Rini and Sata will be going outside."

Suddenly, the smile fell from Sata's face. "Is it . . . really deep . . . and . . . dark all the time?"

"Just three hundred meters, and you'll have Manessa lighting your way."

"Red pressure suits," Rini declared.

Ilika nodded.

*

"The water will feel thick," Ilika explained as he checked their suits on the lower deck, "almost like you have to dig your way through it. Take your time, and don't try any acrobatics in these suits."

"They're too stiff for that," Rini admitted.

"One of you is always on watch. Manessa will shine a bright light on the gold. Bag a few handfuls and come in."

Ilika could see the fear in Sata's eyes as he closed the airlock door and started the cycle.

*

Sata listened to her heart pounding as she followed Rini through the blue water that rapidly became murky as their feet stirred the thin mud. Manessa gave them plenty of light, and a bright beam marked a place not far ahead. Pausing to look around, she saw nothing else, of any size, moving or still, living or dead, just empty blue water in all directions.

"I'm on watch," Rini offered.

Sata swallowed. "My heart's pounding like crazy."

"I think I can hear it. Tell it to slow down," Rini suggested calmly but seriously.

"I . . . never thought of that before. You mean . . . maybe I could just *tell* myself to get over this stupid fear?"

"You have to really want to, really mean it, or your body will know, and ignore you."

While thinking about it, Sata went down to her knees and began feeling in the mud where Manessa was shining the light. Under a coating of ooze, she found them, as large as the great gold pieces of her kingdom, and possibly thicker. She glimpsed the yellow metal in her gloved hand a moment before the mud swirled up all around her.

*

A sound filled her ears, a sound that made it impossible to think, impossible to do anything. She was supposed to be putting gold coins in the bag at her waist. How could she work with that stupid noise going on?

Suddenly she realized what the sound was. Someone in a pressure suit was crying . . . and it wasn't Rini.

"Stop it!" Sata screamed at herself with all the anger she had ever poured into anything.

The entire world was suddenly silent. Rini didn't say a word. No one in the ship spoke. And best of all, the crying had stopped.

Sata slowly became aware that she was okay, with air to breathe, her friend Rini kneeling in front of her, and a wonderful ship nearby giving them light. The mud she had stirred up finding the gold coins was starting to clear.

"I . . . think I got scared for a moment . . . but . . . I'm okay now."

"You want to watch while I dig?" Rini asked with concern.

"No. I still need to put some gold in my bag. You're on watch."

"Okay," Rini agreed, standing up.

"Good work, Sata," Ilika said from the ship.

Sata nodded, but didn't feel like saying anything yet. After several slow breaths, she plunged her hands back into the mud, knowing what would happen, and this time not caring.

As Rini stood watch, he saw the cloud of mud swirl up around Sata again. A few moments later, he stopped holding his breath when he realized the only sound coming from his shipmate was the sound of counting in base eight.

". . . four, five, six. Seven, eight, eleven, twelve . . ."

Rini smiled.

*

When Ilika greeted his two deep-sea divers at the airlock, he immediately knew that the Sata he had sent out to gather gold coins had not returned. The young woman who stood before him now was a different Sata, and a subtle smile of power and confidence told anyone who looked that she was in complete control of her life.

Once dressed, Sata and Rini grabbed their bags of gold and followed the captain up to the passenger area.

To Timod Gor's complete surprise, Ilika trusted him to count the gold coins at the large table while he spoke to his crew on the bridge in the language of Nebador.

"I think we are done here. Our guests have everything they want from the hut and the wrecked ship. Our next destination would be an excellent place to celebrate our treasure hunt, and other recent accomplishments." Ilika glanced at Sata, and she grinned back at him.

"Yeah!" everyone else agreed.

"Let's surprise our guests when we arrive. No visuals and zero inertia. Fly by instruments, Mati."

"Rini, I need real-time topographics . . ." Mati ordered, turning to her console.

"I just need to update the flight plan," Sata declared, sliding into her chair.

"Ion three, coming up!" Boro promised.

Ilika looked toward the table. Timod Gor, under the watchful eye of Risan Gor, was still counting coins.

* * *

The word "gold" is a good example of how languages from nearby countries often have similar words. Just east from England, the birthplace of the English language, several Germanic countries would easily recognize the word "gold" ("gold" in German, "goud" in Dutch, "guld" in Danish, etc.) A little farther away, in Latin-language speaking countries, they might be confused until you said "gold ore." Suddenly, eyes would light up ("or" in

French, “oro” in Spanish and Italian, “ouro” in Portuguese, etc.)

The gold from the wrecked ship was on the ocean floor because it is very dense (heavy for its size), and quickly moved downward as the ship was twisted and crushed by the ice. Other things made of metal would have done the same. Most of the wood of the ship’s structure, however, was lighter than water, and would continue to float even when the ship had been smashed into little pieces.

Why is Ilika making Sata do something uncomfortable?

Most people have no conscious control over several body functions, including heartbeat (pulse). Other body functions, like breathing, can be controlled by the body automatically (such as during sleep), but are also subject to conscious control. A few people have conscious control over body functions the rest of us don’t. They are usually disciplined meditators.

The human body seems to be capable of many things, when there is great need or deep feelings, that it can’t usually do. That’s why Rini warned Sata that she had to really mean it, when telling her heart to slow, or it would ignore her.

What emotion did Sata tap into that allowed her to stop feeling afraid of the dark, swirling mud?

Chapter 32: Where Hell Bubbles Up

The rugged, mountainous land was already deep in evening shadows when the Manessa Kwi carefully descended, by instruments, onto the small, level landing site.

Kibi already knew no large animals were about as she stepped through the hatch. Tall pine trees soared upward all around her. A ring of stones and logs, even a small pile of firewood, showed that others had camped here. The sound of bubbling and trickling water came through the trees, and she glimpsed the mineral formations of hot springs a short walk to the west. A hint of sulfur tickled her nose.

Activating the bright light of her mission bracelet, Kibi strolled the entire landing site and campfire area, seeing more geothermal activity in other directions, but no dangers. She returned to the ship where Ilika stood casually in the hatchway, keeping an eye on both her and their guests.

Just then, Timod Gor finished counting the gold coins. "Half!" he said firmly, gesturing at the two equal piles, each containing about twenty coins. One odd coin sat alone.

Ilika picked up the odd coin and handed it to Risan Gor. She smiled, as did Timod Gor.

*

Timod Gor walked about the landing site in a daze for several minutes, as the last thing he remembered seeing outside the hatch was the shipwreck on the ice shelf. His pride got the better of him when Boro began collecting firewood, and before the evening light completely faded, they brought in a good supply.

Ilika taught Rini and Sata the bracelet code that produced a beam of light so intense it quickly ignited dry pine needles. Kibi dug out a cooking pot designed for outdoor use, poured in a refrigerated container of left-over soup, and carried it to the fire.

"There must be a kingdom nearby, or maybe just a tribe," Boro speculated, "because of the campfire circle."

"Not for a thousand kilometers or more," Ilika replied. "This place is only known and used by visitors from Nebador. That little landing site on the highest mountain was another. They are sprinkled around the planet. Manessa can tell you about the others."

"Neba . . . dor?" Timod Gor asked with questioning eyes.

"Our . . . land," Boro explained slowly.

"Here?"

"No. Far away," Ilika said with a vague wave of his arm.

"I . . . home . . . walk," Timod Gor said firmly, pointing north. "Risan Gor home walk."

Ilika sighed. "If my guess about his home is correct," Ilika explained to his crew, "we're on the wrong continent."

"We could print a map of the world and show him," Sata suggested.

"Even better, I think Manessa has a simple map like the ones actually used by sailors today." Ilika turned to Timod Gor. "Come. I show map."

*

The rest of the crew, along with Risan Gor, lingered by the fire for another hour. When they finally started yawning and returned to the ship, they found Timod Gor at the table intently studying his new map, bag of gold at his elbow. Ilika had marked their current location, the southern edge of a large continent near the bottom of the map.

"Kibi and I will sleep up here," Ilika announced. "Boro, you're in charge of putting out the fire."

He nodded.

"Tomorrow we can play in hot water," the captain assured.

Sata grinned, then yawned.

✷

After breakfast, with hot springs of every temperature calling to them, all five crew members were ready to shed their clothes. Ilika, however, insisted they keep on their underwear in the hot springs because of their guests.

Even so, Timod Gor spoke sternly to Risan Gor, and she pouted, held her doll close, and found some sticks to play with. He made himself comfortable against a tree near the fire ring and pulled a book from his leather bag.

"Wee!" Sata shrieked as she jumped from a rock into the largest pool, pleasantly warm. Kibi, Boro, and Rini came after, while Ilika helped Mati into a smaller, warmer pool.

A few minutes later Risan Gor crept down the trail, stood for a minute with a questioning look, then shed her clothes and jumped in. Soon she was laughing and playing along with everyone else.

A quarter hour later, Timod Gor looked up from his reading and noticed that Risan Gor was nowhere to be seen. He barked a command, and she quickly dressed and dragged herself back to the campfire circle, where she sat glumly on a log.

Once he was deep into his book again, she crept away. She tried hard to keep from making any sound as she played in the wonderful water, but soon forgot all about Timod Gor and squealed with delight along with the others.

Twice more Timod Gor called the five-year-old girl back from her play, and twice more she returned to the hot pools as soon as she could slip away.

As noon approached, Timod Gor was no longer aware of anything but his reading, turning pages passionately and rocking back and fourth as he devoured the text. Both Ilika and Boro tried to get his attention to join them for lunch, but he didn't respond. They shrugged, and set a plate and cup within reach.

✷

After lunch, as the crew of the Manessa Kwi was getting ready to look for more pools, perhaps a little hotter, Timod Gor began to read aloud from his book. None of the crew members could understand a word. Risan Gor frowned and followed her new friends.

The girl cringed every time she heard Timod Gor's voice grow loud, but each time it was merely some dramatic line from his book. She quickly returned to the water play.

As mid-afternoon passed, Timod Gor arrived at the hot springs and began reading to them, loudly and passionately, often with a finger shaking or a fist clenched tightly. They tried to get his attention and explain that they didn't know his language, but he just glared at them before returning his eyes to the page. He no longer seemed to care what Risan Gor was doing, and looked at her with the same judgmental eyes.

After a while, they tried moving down the trail to a different pool, but he followed, reading as he walked.

Mati soon announced she was returning to the ship to do some piloting simulations. Others offered to come with her, but she begged them not to, unless they could guarantee the noise would not follow.

The venomous reading continued. The man's finger wagging was, as often as not, pointed in Risan Gor's direction. Now red-faced with shame, she climbed out of the pool and started crying.

After a few more minutes, during which no one enjoyed themselves and some had fingers in their ears, Risan Gor mumbled, "Toilet," and dashed toward the ship.

The heated words poured from Timod Gor for another minute, then abruptly stopped. Ilika and most of his crew watched the man's back recede down the trail, big smiles on their faces.

"Whew!" Boro breathed. "What was *that* all about?"

"I didn't understand a word," Ilika admitted. "But I'm glad it's over."

"It reminded me of . . . a priest trying to stir up the people," Kibi shared, "you know, sell them wood and oil to go burn some poor innocent monster."

Rini and Sata both howled with laughter.

"I think we should take the book away from him," Kibi suggested. "I'll put him to sleep, you hide the book, Ilika."

"Or use ion drive three to get him home *tonight*," Boro asserted, "before dinner, if possible."

Ilika sighed. "He hasn't yet shown me where he lives on the map. He just stared at it last night until I dimmed the lights."

"We could pick a place," Sata suggested with a mischievous grin, "like that little island with nothing but birds, and tell him that's where he's going unless he tells us."

Ilika suddenly raised a hand for silence. "Was Mati wearing a mission bracelet?"

"Um . . . no," Rini recalled.

"Damn!" Ilika cursed.

Just as he scrambled out of the pool, he saw the Manessa Kwi rise into the air and slowly move over the treetops toward the northeast, away from the landing site and the hot springs.

* * *

There is nothing high-tech about starting a fire with a bright beam of light, as any kid, who has played with a magnifying glass on a sunny day, knows.

Some of the many mysteries in our own history are the places, sprinkled all over the world, that seem to have something to do with aircraft or spacecraft, long before we had either one. Sometimes they are figures that can only be seen from the air, such as on the plain of Nazca in Peru. Sometimes they involve knowledge about the Earth that might have been gained from a high altitude, such as the Piri Reis map. Occasionally they are just primitive pictures of people with bubbles over their heads. Finally, the world contains many flat, level constructions that we can't explain. None of these things can be proven to have anything to do with aircraft or spacecraft, but neither can the possibility be disproven. They will probably remain mysteries.

In your opinion, which would have been more respectful of the passengers: to FORBID Risan Gor from playing in the water because of Timod Gor's wishes, to HELP her sneak away without Timod Gor's knowledge, or to remain neutral as they did?

What kind of book do you think Timod Gor was reading?

At the end of the chapter, when Ilika cursed, what mistake did he realize he had made?

Chapter 33: Saving the Manessa Kwi

The captain and most of the crew of the Manessa Kwi, in bare feet and underwear, watched from the landing site as their ship disappeared over a mountain ridge. Kibi and Sata appeared to be in shock. Boro frowned deeply. Rini's face was blank, but he clutched his stomach.

"How are we going to get Manessa back?" Sata asked with a deeply worried voice.

"A-and Mati," Rini managed to stutter out.

The captain, currently without a ship, took a slow breath, then let it out with a shaking sigh. "We'll get our ship and pilot back. We just have to be careful how we do it, so we don't put Mati in danger. It would be best for everyone, I think, if Mati herself found a way."

*

Mati spent the first hour of the flight holding back tears and trying to think of ways to make the ship move as slowly as possible. While she sat in the pilot's chair, feeling helpless one moment and angry the next, she rubbed her sore arm where he had wrenched it when he grabbed her. Occasionally she glanced at the blood-soaked shoulder of her tunic, but didn't dare touch it for fear it would start bleeding again.

Her mind raced as she remembered selecting the lowest power settings at the engineer's station. She had then nudged her flight control forward the smallest possible amount, and as soon as they were over the ocean, dropped down to a hundred meters so he would think they were going fast.

He sat at the table, gloating with a smile of self-satisfaction that reminded Mati of the high priest in front of the inn. His knife lay on the table within easy reach, the knife that must have been in his leather bag the whole time before he finally used it when he informed her, in few words, what she must do.

Mati turned her head slowly and glanced at the little mission bracelet cabinet by the entryway, but couldn't see any way to get to it. She tried to think of something else she could do. Things like screaming and crying came to mind easily. Constructive courses of action were harder to imagine.

Risan Gor sat in a chair at the big table, as far away from Timod Gor as possible, arms around her knees and tears on her face.

Just when Mati thought the situation could get no worse, it did. Timod Gor began to read aloud from his book.

✷

The five members of Manessa's crew who were stuck on the ground at the hot springs camp, once over their initial shock, took a good look at their resources.

Ilika, Kibi, and Boro wore mission bracelets. Ilika took a few minutes to teach the others how to send a universe distress call, but asked them to wait until other efforts to retrieve their ship had failed.

Rini located five towels draped on low tree branches, and Sata found Timod Gor's half-eaten lunch, already covered with ants.

Boro set to work gathering a pile of firewood. Kibi, Rini, and Sata went scouting for wild edibles.

Ilika sat down at the campfire circle and pondered Mati's probable situation, the resources available to her, and the chances of her applying those resources successfully against her hijacker, their guest and first passenger, Timod Gor.

✷

Mati got her first chance to arm herself when Timod Gor paused in his reading to use the toilet. She found the mission bracelet cabinet, however, to be completely empty. Marks and cracks showed where his big knife had pried it open.

Deep despair rose up inside her, like the many times she had been unable to run from an abusive master because of her handicap. Tears were close, but she held them in and went to the galley.

When Timod Gor emerged from the toilet room, he began raving at her, knife flashing in the air.

Mati reached down inside herself for courage. "If I don't eat, I'll die, and if I die, this ship isn't going anywhere, I promise you!"

Timod Gor relaxed, but kept a sharp eye on Mati, dashing her hopes of doing something with a kitchen knife. She got some crackers and returned to her station.

✷

Since Boro had no other way to vent his frustration, a huge stack of firewood grew rapidly. The others returned with towels full of berries and edible greens. The warm summer weather appeared willing to stick around, at least for the day.

Ilika finished learning everything he could from his mission bracelet. "Mati is moving northeast at little more than walking speed. It will take her weeks to get to Timod Gor's home, but I'm sure she knows that."

"You can just take control of the ship, can't you?" Rini asked.

"Yes, but I'm afraid Mati would get hurt if he thought she wasn't cooperating."

"Can't you talk to Mati, or have Manessa talk to her?" Boro wondered. "Maybe . . . give her ideas for, you know, helping him jump out the hatch?"

Ilika smiled. "I'm worried that if he heard another voice, he'd get violent. In fact, I've already switched Manessa to silent mode. However, I can put a written message on her screen, and I've been thinking about what to say."

"Tell her we're okay," Kibi said. "She might be worrying."

"Tell her . . . I love her," Rini added with deep feeling in his voice.

Ilika smiled and nodded.

"If she could just get a mission bracelet . . ." Boro mumbled under his breath with frustration.

"He might be watching her closely. I think her best chance is to learn which doors Manessa can lock. It's going to take me a while to explain what she needs to know."

"We'll go look for something more filling to eat," Kibi announced. "You want to come, Boro, or do you think we need more firewood?"

Boro glanced at the huge pile, growled, and followed the others away from the landing site. Ilika opened his bracelet and began tapping at the little keys.

*

Be calm. We are safe and well. Rini loves you. Manessa is in silent mode to avoid making him angry.

Mati was very glad she had worked hard at her language studies. Thinking was difficult with Timod Gor reading his stupid book, but during the next half hour, Mati learned that Manessa could lock the lift to the lower deck, as well as the door to the toilet room without a bathtub, which doubled as a detention cell. Even though the ship was in silent mode, it would still accept voice commands from her.

Suddenly Timod Gor stopped reading and began searching for something. Everything they had brought out of his rock hut was in plain sight, and his share of the gold sat in its little bag on the table. Mati frowned and felt like screaming at him, knife or no. Then she stopped herself and realized she was seeing something useful.

He searched the galley, the supply closet, the entryway, and the bridge, and in each place found nothing he wanted. But he was obviously afraid of the lift, even though he had seen it used several times. Mati smiled, remembering Ilika take their share of the gold down to the utility room.

After spending a few minutes pondering her new knowledge, she frowned. If gold was not enough to tempt him to use the lift, then getting him onto the lower deck appeared to be impossible.

Giving up on the lift, Mati considered the detention cell. Unfortunately, as far as she could remember, he always used the other toilet room, the one with a bathtub.

Suddenly Mati had an idea. Her freedom, as strange as it seemed, hinged on getting Risan Gor to take a long bath. She thought she might be able to do it, but her plan required one other thing.

As Timod Gor began searching the entryway for the second time, she headed for the galley to get started with her plan.

⁕

As the sun set and evening descended over the forest, the other five crew members of the Manessa Kwi sat around a small fire nibbling fresh berries and roasted starchy roots.

"We saw a deer," Boro shared, chin in his hands.

Ilika shriveled his nose. "Nothing smaller?"

"Beetles. Spiders."

"We'll get Manessa back before we need protein."

"How long are you going to give Mati before . . . doing something more drastic?" Kibi asked.

"About three more hours. Then I'll tell her to lock herself on the lower deck while I recall the ship."

"He might get angry and tear things up," Sata muttered.

"Yeah. I know."

⁕

Soon, Timod Gor gave up his search and returned to the table — and his book. Risan Gor put fingers in her ears.

Mati set three cartons of pinkfruit juice on the table. She sat down beside Risan Gor, tried to smile, and pretended to listen with interest.

Mati discovered that the man's reading, both before and after his fruitless search, had indeed worked up a thirst. He quickly drained his juice, so she calmly went to the galley to get him another carton.

An hour later, the man had read aloud twelve pages or more, and was on his third carton of juice.

Risan Gor never budged from her chair. Instead, she turned inward, whispered secrets to her doll, and rarely looked up.

Timod Gor had become used to Mati going to and from the galley, so the pilot of the Manessa Kwi began the next phase of her plan. Every time she hobbled near the little girl's chair, she paused and sniffed with a shriveled nose.

Half an hour and a dozen hints later, Mati sighed. Once or twice Risan Gor had looked up, but had not understood the message. Mati decided it was time to get tough.

After fetching another carton of chilled juice, Mati approached the table. She planted her crutch much too far to the side to support her, fell forward, and caught herself with her hands on the edge of the table. In the process, she squeezed the juice carton as hard as she could, and it sprayed all over Risan Gor.

⁕

After taking a walk with the others in the evening light to gather more berries, Ilika sat down and started transmitting the final plan to Mati's console.

Mati did not immediately respond, and Ilika had no way of knowing how quickly she would get back to her station.

✷

Mati was very glad her stumble didn't anger Timod Gor. He merely grinned, turned a few pages, and read a passage that Mati guessed had something to do with clumsy people.

Risan Gor, however, looked daggers at Mati, and dragged herself into the bathing room, sulking and muttering to her doll as she went.

Mati smiled politely at Timod Gor, got him another carton of juice, and sat down to listen to him read.

✷

Boro paced.

Sata started biting her fingernails.

Kibi poked at the fire.

Rini let silent tears roll down his cheeks.

Ilika wondered what he was going to do if Mati did not respond, very soon, to his last message.

✷

A quarter hour later, Timod Gor's juice carton was empty and Risan Gor was still in the bathing room, so Mati returned to the galley.

After finding one last carton of pinkfruit juice, she turned around, only to discover her captor was gone. Her eyes flashed to the entryway and the bridge, but he was nowhere to be seen.

A moment later, she clearly heard a powerful stream of liquid hitting the inside of a toilet. The door to the bathing room remained closed. She frowned for a second, then grinned. "MANESSA, LOCK THE DETENTION CELL!"

✷

Ilika was beginning to worry deeply, and dreaded the thought of recalling the ship without knowing Mati was safe. Suddenly, his bracelet chimed.

"Finally!" he gasped, opening the cover of his bracelet.

The others, huddled around the fire, looked at him.

Ilika saw words on the tiny display he had not expected. *No need. Be right there.*

Almost before he could read the words to his fellow crew members, the ship streaked into the nearly-dark sky from the northeast and quickly descended onto the landing area. The hatch opened and the ramp extended. A moment later, Mati appeared in the open hatch, leaning on her crutch and speaking in a brave but shaking voice. "I am no longer just the pilot. I am now the jailer, too!"

✷ ✷ ✷

What was Mati's state of mind right after the hijacking?

How might the hijacking have gone differently if Mati had freaked out instead of cooperating with Timod Gor?

What was Risan Gor probably feeling during that first hour of the hijacking?

When Mati went into the galley for the first time, she was using the power she possessed as the pilot. What might have happened if she had not found the courage to use her power, or if she had tried to use too much power?

There are many ways to vent frustration. Boro did something constructive, collecting firewood. What other methods have you seen people use?

To get control of the ship. Mati used trickery and manipulation. Was it justified?

Chapter 34: Learning from Mistakes

Rini was the first one up the ramp, wrapping his slender arms around the girl who had just been put to a test far greater than anything he had ever experienced.

Ilika, Kibi, and Boro slipped by them into the ship and saw the knife, book, and bag of gold on the table, along with six or seven empty cartons of pinkfruit juice. Next they spotted Risan Gor, wrapped in a bath towel, sitting on the floor just outside the door to the detention cell, poking a finger into the transparent static field covering the doorway, a mixture of sadness and fear on her five-year-old face.

Approaching, they could see Timod Gor trying to tear through the field with his fingers, his face twisted with anger.

Risan Gor looked up when the captain, steward, and engineer came close. "Timod Gor . . . bad?"

Ilika searched the cell with his eyes, seeing the usual towels and blankets, but nothing with which the man could do more harm. Kibi sat down beside Risan Gor and put an arm around the girl, who started crying softly.

Sata cleaned up the mess on the table, and Boro found the rest of the mission bracelets in Timod Gor's leather bag.

*

As midnight approached, Mati remained in Rini's arms with the rest of her friends close, sometimes talking, sometimes munching nervously on the snacks Kibi put on the table, sometimes just shivering. Everyone was impressed with the logic she used to get Timod Gor into the detention cell, and amazed at her courage.

Eventually she started yawning, so she said good-night to her captain and friends, and crept into her cabin along with Sata.

Ilika assured him it was not necessary, but Boro insisted on spending the rest of the night in a passenger chair, with a mission bracelet on his arm.

✷

"*The oppressed are not necessarily virtuous,*" Ilika quoted, searching his memory as he looked up at the tall pine trees bathed in morning light. "When I first heard that from one of my teachers, I didn't fully understand it. Now its meaning is crystal clear to me."

"But . . . Timod Gor wasn't a slave or anything like that," Sata pointed out.

"No, but we were lulled into trusting him more than we should, because we found him in a humble situation, caring for a little girl, stranded on an ice continent, both of them soon to die without our help."

"I should have had a bracelet on," Mati admitted, "just as if I was outside, alone."

"Yes, and I should not have allowed a passenger to get himself alone with a crew member," Ilika added, "bracelet or no."

"I think he just wants to go home," Rini said with sympathy. "He didn't understand that we were in the process of taking him there."

"Not so!" Mati burst out with more than a little anger. "He was looking for our share of the gold!"

Ilika let a moment of silence pass. Rini nodded acceptance of Mati's opinion, and she smiled at him.

"In either case," Ilika continued, "the language barrier we have with him, and which we will sometimes have with passengers in the future, doesn't make it okay to let down our guard like we did."

"Yeah," Boro agreed. "Me and Kibi are going to make sure it *never* happens again."

"It's mostly my fault," Kibi muttered with a glum look. "I'm the steward. It's my job to make sure my passengers don't . . . twist the pilot's arm and poke knives at her . . ."

Mati chuckled dryly.

". . . and as the steward," Kibi continued, "it bugs me to let Risan Gor go with him. Can't we . . . adopt her or something?"

"And Kora, Kit, Misa, and Kali too?" Ilika asked, eyebrows raised. "What about all the girls being sacrificed at that city in the tropics?"

"Okay," Kibi said, "I'll shut up."

"I've already talked about it with the star station," Ilika explained. "Risan Gor has a part to play in the future of this world, and even though we may not like him, Timod Gor is the best person available to raise her. And remember, all of you are starting to take on the values of Nebador and the Transport Service. How do Timod Gor's actions compare to the ways people usually treat each other on this planet?"

They all thought back to their lives in the kingdom of their birth, and remembered the other cultures they had observed on their planetary tour.

"He . . . fits right in," Rini admitted with a sad expression.

✷

Ilika adjusted the static field of the detention cell so he could slide the old-fashioned map of the world through. "Where?" Ilika asked, waving his arms with palms up.

The trapped man tried to claw at the place where the map had come through, but it had already returned to full strength. Ilika sat down on the floor and waited.

Kibi joined him with a towel over her shoulder. "The others are taking one last dip in the best pool."

Timod Gor looked at the map, then quickly jabbed at three different places.

"One," Ilika asserted, holding up a finger.

Timod Gor folded his arms on his chest.

Ilika sighed. "Okay. We'll take you both back to your hut by the ice shelf. You can have your salted meat and crackers, your book and your knife, and your blankets."

Kibi nodded her approval as they both stood up, but Timod Gor became very nervous and started speaking rapidly in his own language with a pleading tone.

"Where?" Ilika repeated.

With a shaking hand, the man pointed to a land in the northern hemisphere, not far from the kingdom where Ilika had found his crew.

✷

As soon as the other crew members and Risan Gor returned with laughter and wet hair, Ilika asked Sata to print a chart of the land Timod Gor had indicated. Kibi slid a lunch tray into the cell and Ilika gave him the new map.

"Where?"

Timod Gor stared in amazement at the detail of the map, but eventually saw things he recognized, and finally pointed at a village.

✷

As they prepared for their last flight with the two passengers aboard, Kibi found Mati outside leaning on her crutch and looking at the nearest hot pool.

"Hi, Mati."

"Hi, Kibi. I think . . . this is my favorite place in the world. The shack and corral was for a long time, but this is even better, far from any people. If I had to be stranded somewhere all alone, this would be it."

"Even after what happened here?"

"Yeah. That happened in the ship, and Timod Gor didn't even like it here, and never went in a pool. It's just ours. Unlike you, Kibi, I don't really like very many people. It feels good to have a place where no one but us can go."

Kibi nodded and put her arm around Mati, who leaned on her in silence for a minute.

✷

When Mati and Kibi entered through the hatch, Ilika was conferring with Sata at the navigation station and Boro was pacing in the passenger area, still wearing a bracelet.

Seeing that everyone was in and the hatch closed, Ilika took the command chair. "Flight stations and status reports."

Mati lowered herself into her chair. “Pilot has the flight plan. Looks easy compared to . . . last night.”

Everyone chuckled.

“Navigator is ready with local charts at our destination,” Sata assured.

“High cirrus clouds here,” Rini announced, “but lots of towering cumulus over the ocean. Weather map on channel four.”

Boro reluctantly sat down at his station. “All engines green. Anti-mass and thrusters are warm.”

“Landing site is secure,” Kibi reported as she glanced at a series of visual displays on her console. “I have two passengers, one happy in the front row with her doll, the other curled up in blankets in the detention cell, probably nursing his wounded ego.”

Ilika turned and grinned at Kibi for a moment. “Pilot has flight command for ascent,” he said, turning back around.

Mati gave them a fare-well tour of the hot springs area. Rini provided external views and Kibi put the forward view on the big screen so Risan Gor could watch.

Less than a minute later, Mati announced their arrival at eleven thousand meters.

“Clearance check from terrain and thunder clouds,” the captain ordered, and the navigator quickly verified both.

“Ion drive, level three,” the pilot requested.

*

Risan Gor didn’t understand a word any of them were saying. She knew Timod Gor thought they were demons, but she believed they were angels. They could fly, they played like children, they loved and cared for each other, and they didn’t hurt Timod Gor even when he was bad. Since they were angels, she and Timod Gor would soon be back home drinking warm milk by a cozy fire. She smiled and looked at the pretty clouds through the magic window that floated above the black-haired angel, but closed her eyes tightly when everything in the window went blurry.

* * *

We tend to naturally assume that anyone in an oppressive or dangerous situation is innocent, even virtuous. It is one of those “truisms,” so often true that we forget it might not be.

When Mati and Rini had a difference of opinion about Timod Gor’s motives, they could have gotten into an argument. Why didn’t they?

As Ilika pointed out, the language barrier contributed to letting down their guard. We naturally feel sympathy for someone who can’t communicate.

In your opinion, is it most useful to judge Timod Gor in relation to the values of his planet, the Nebador Transport Service, or some absolute standard?

Two answers are possible, one for how much to respect him in general, and one for how much freedom and trust to give him.

Do you think Ilika was bluffing when he threatened to take Timod Gor back to the rock hut on the ice continent? What would you do, in Ilika's place, if Timod Gor had refused to identify his home?

Mati expressed the point of view of introverts (about 30% of the population). They don't hate people. In fact, they tend to love and cherish others even more than extroverts because they focus their affections on a select few. The main difference is that introverts are drained of energy when they have to deal with large numbers of people, while extroverts are energized.

Timod Gor's "demons" and Risan Gor's "angels" are both conceptual boxes ("stereotypes") into which we put people when we don't know enough about their true natures. What other stereotypes do we use when trying to understand people?

Risan Gor thought the crew members were angels because "they could fly, they played like children, they loved and cared for each other, and they didn't hurt Timod Gor even when he was bad." What do you think of her reasons?

Chapter 35: Warm Milk by a Cozy Fire

The Manessa Kwi, currently the same color as the steel-gray winter sky, circled the valley where Timod Gor's village nestled under a blanket of snow. The still, cold air carried the sound of a farmer calling and whistling as he herded a group of cows through a gate. Risan Gor's face brightened as she gazed at the familiar countryside in the magic window.

Ilika stood beside Kibi at her station as Mati guided the ship slowly around the valley. "We have some parting business with our passengers. Somewhere . . . out of sight . . . but an easy walk to the village."

Kibi smiled as she continued to peer at her display. "How about . . . this little hill, clearing on top, easy trail down."

"Perfect."

*

Mati carefully lowered the ship among the leafless trees that covered most of the hill, letting Manessa test the frozen ground with struts before releasing the anti-mass drive. "Finished with engines."

"Boro is in command," Ilika announced. "You know what comes next."

Boro nodded and opened the mission bracelet cabinet.

Ilika and Kibi laced their boots and grabbed cloaks, then stepped outside. A thin crust of ice and snow covered the wiry grass, with occasional rocks and boulders scattered among the leafless trees.

"You've become close to Risan Gor, even learned a few words of her language," Ilika said as they slowly circled the clearing.

"And she's learned a few words of ours," Kibi added.

"Good. I have a very important task for you," Ilika continued, bringing a short metal tube from his cloak pocket. "Our share of the gold is inside, and I want you to communicate to Risan Gor that it is for her, but only in the future when Timod Gor is no longer taking care of her. When you are sure she understands, select a good hiding place, under a rock or an old log. Do your best to help her memorize the place."

"I . . . think I can do that."

*

Risan Gor grinned with pride as she tied her boots and pulled on her cloak, then took the hand of the angel Kibi as they walked together down the ramp.

Boro was very well prepared for his assigned task of getting Timod Gor off the ship without further mischief. Boro wanted to put the man to sleep and carry him out, but Ilika shook his head. Boro, however, promised that the slightest threatening move by Timod Gor would have the same result. Ilika nodded.

To give Kibi the time she needed, the rest of the crew relaxed in the passenger area or started making a stew.

Nearly an hour later, Kibi and the five-year-old girl returned, both smiling and snickering in cahoots over some deep secret. Kibi and Ilika exchanged nods, and everyone sat down for a quick meal. Boro slid a tray into the detention cell for Timod Gor.

*

The process of releasing the prisoner began with a silent drama enacted just outside the detention cell. With Timod Gor watching, Kibi handed Risan Gor the leather shoulder bag, the knife, the book, and finally the bag of gold that was Timod Gor's share. The girl put each item into the bag, then added her doll. She struggled for a moment to get the strap over her shoulder.

Rini came forward, kissed her on the cheek, and handed her the blankets that had been to the ice continent and back, now clean and rolled into a bundle.

Still blushing from Rini's kiss, Risan Gor shared hugs with all the other angels as Timod Gor watched silently from his cell.

Mati disappeared into the lift and Boro gestured for everyone to go to their places.

Kibi led Risan Gor to the hatch, opened it, and gave her one last hug. The girl descended the ramp and waited at the bottom.

"Manessa, open the detention cell," Ilika commanded in the language of Nebador. Then he gestured for Timod Gor to come out.

The man cautiously felt his way through the place where the static field had been, then warily glanced at Ilika at the rear of the ship, Rini and Sata in the galley, Boro near the steward's station, and finally Kibi on the bridge, all with their left arms raised and a finger of their right hand poised.

Once he arrived at the open hatch, he saw Risan Gor waiting for him at the bottom, mixed feelings on her face, heavy bag over her shoulder. He cautiously descended and took the shoulder bag she gladly surrendered.

He turned and looked back at the strange ship run by demons who didn't understand when he read from the Great Book. Three of them were in the opening, arms still raised.

Risan Gor said something about warm milk, so Timod Gor turned away from the demon ship, took her outstretched hand, and together they made their way to the trail that wound down the hill toward the village.

Ilika and Kibi watched from the ramp as their first passengers approached the woods. Risan Gor glanced once at the place where her gold coins were hidden, but said nothing and continued walking into the trees beside Timod Gor.

✷

Boro let out a huge sigh.

"I hope passengers aren't always that difficult," Kibi said, dropping into a seat at the big table.

"Rarely," Ilika assured them. "Our passengers will usually be members of the Nebador Services."

"Can I come up now?" they heard a faint voice call from the lower deck.

Sata giggled and went to the lift. "It's just us now! Hatch closed, no passengers!"

Mati appeared just as Rini put a plate of sweet biscuits on the table.

"We learned a bunch of things," Boro shared, "so I think it was worth it."

"*You* didn't get your arm wrenched and your shoulder pricked by a big knife!" Mati asserted as she took the seat next to the engineer and gave him a friendly poke.

Boro frowned with guilt. "You're right. Sorry."

✷ ✷ ✷

Why was Timod Gor's village covered by snow when the ship had just come from a pleasantly-warm forest where they could walk around in wet underwear without getting cold?

Why did Ilika give away their share of the gold?

When hiding something of value, in the woods, for possibly several years, what things make good markers that won't be moved by people or animals, and won't disappear over time? (You can assume no excavations, in that culture, by machines or explosives.)

What important information was given to Timod Gor as he watched Risan Gor receive their belongings?

What sort of logic was Timod Gor using when he labeled the crew as demons because (or at least party because) they didn't understand the words in his "Great Book"? Has this sort of logic ever played a part in human history?

Chapter 36: Orbit

The Manessa Kwi remained on the hilltop for the remainder of that day as the crew chatted about all the things that had happened since Rini spotted the shipwreck and the rock hut on the ice continent, and how they might do it differently next time.

When one or two of them would go for a stroll outside the ship, they would look at the trail that wound through the trees, half-expecting to see Risan Gor coming up, looking for her gold and trying to explain that Timod Gor had already spent his share.

Ilika remembered Kodi.

The following morning, after a filling breakfast of fried cakes topped with stewed fruit, Ilika could see in the faces of his crew that they were ready to move on, so he put their next task on the large display screen above Kibi's station.

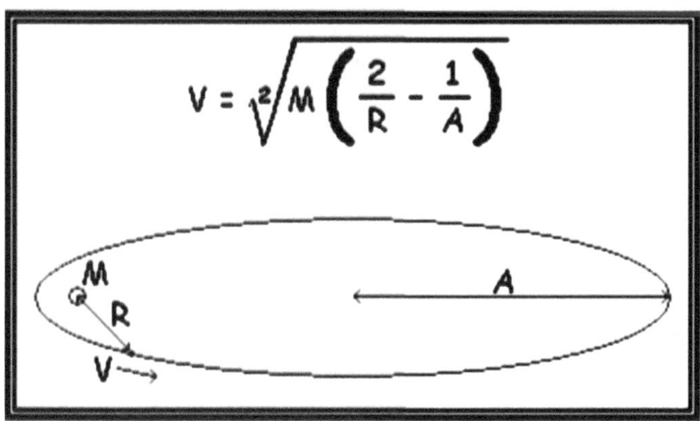

"You have completed your basic planetary flight training. You will learn new things every time we are on the surface of a world, from tiny asteroids to gas giants. As your language skills improve, I will give you advanced training materials and exercises. Eventually you will begin cross-training to learn the other stations during planetary flight.

"All that will come in time. Right now we are ready to leave the surface of this world. Our next stop is planetary orbit. It may sound strange, but when a ship is in orbit, it is constantly falling, but it is also the only place a ship in flight can rest without using any engines."

Frowns all around the table told Ilika that it did, indeed, sound strange.

"The formula on the screen gives us the most important information about orbit. During the next few days, you will come to know this formula well, and it will become your best friend. In space, it is life, more important than food and water."

He looked around the table. Every pair of eyes was glued to the screen.

"V is velocity, the speed of the ship. M is the mass of the planet you are orbiting. R is the radius, your current distance from the center of the planet. A is the semi-major axis of the ellipse of your orbit, in other words, half the long diameter of the ellipse. If your orbit is circular, R and A are the same."

He gave them a moment to absorb that much.

"In every group of students, there is always someone who thinks orbit isn't important. When I first learned about orbit, that someone was me."

"I was just thinking that," Boro admitted. "Can't we just use the anti-mass drive?"

Ilika suppressed his temptation to smile. "Usually we will. But imagine what would happen if we needed to go out onto the hull in a space suit. How far out does the anti-mass field extend?"

"Um . . . one meter."

"Correct. If a person is on the hull and accidentally gets more than one meter from the ship, he or she drops like a rock toward the nearest gravity mass, which might be a planet, and it might be the sun."

Boro swallowed.

"Look at the orbit formula. Is the mass of the orbiting ship a factor?"

"N . . . no?" Rini answered with an unsure expression.

"That's right. Everything orbits together, regardless of how big it is — the ship, the engineer out on a safety line, his tools, everything."

Boro nodded.

Sata's hand came up. "What's the little two in the big V-thingy?"

"Root, the opposite of power. Three to the second power is . . ."

"Nine . . . I mean eleven in base eight," Sata said.

"So the second root of eleven is three."

"Okay, that's easy."

Boro moaned under his breath.

✷

When Ilika announced an hour of free time, Sata made sure everyone understood the root operation. She had to spend most of the hour with Boro.

Rini was the first to realize that the bigger the planet, the faster the ship had to orbit. Ilika nodded, but also did a mini-lesson to make sure they knew the difference between size and mass, pointing out that some small, rocky planets had more mass than much larger gas giants, which could be lighter than water.

A little later, Sata lit up with a huge grin when she figured out that the ship would orbit at different speeds at different places in an elliptical orbit, faster when close to the planet, slower when farther away.

Ilika smiled, and asked her to explain her discovery to the others.

When everyone understood, both Mati and Kibi still wore slight frowns, but didn't know how to put their concerns into words. All Mati could say was, "We can't be just anywhere above the planet, can we?"

"No. We must be outside the atmosphere, or the friction would slow us down, cause our orbit to decay, and eventually we'd crash. On this planet, that's about a thousand kilometers from the surface."

"Wow," Boro breathed.

Ilika nodded. "The outer limit of usable orbit is different for each planet, as you must avoid the gravity of any moons, rings, or other planets."

*

The questions and insights continued during lunch, and Ilika let his students take the discussion wherever they wanted.

"Are there any . . . monsters in space?" Mati asked as she nervously pushed a dumpling around in her soup bowl.

"Oh, yes," Ilika replied, "but they are creatures of light and energy that Manessa knows well. Rini will learn how to find them. They are often very beautiful, like the aurora."

Mati took a deep breath, joined the others in smiles of anticipation, and spooned the dumpling into her mouth.

"It's dark out there, isn't it?" Sata asked with a shaking voice.

"In orbit, we'll get more daylight than we do on the planet . . ."

Sata relaxed a little.

". . . but in deep space between solar systems, it can be very dark."

She frowned.

"We'll jump over most of those dark, interstellar voids."

The navigator slowly brightened and glanced at Boro.

"Will I . . . get seasick?" Kibi asked with a slightly sour expression.

"I don't think so. Orbit and space flight are completely smooth, and it never feels like you're falling, even when looking down at a planet. But there is something I have to warn you about . . . especially you, Kibi."

Kibi looked at her captain and waited.

"When we depart for orbit, we will be taking a couple of weeks to visit several planets and a number of smaller objects. You will all get space suit time, but none of the worlds we will visit have breathable air. The next time we can open the hatch is at Satamia Star Station. It will be physically impossible to . . . um . . . run away."

Kibi gave Ilika a smile and a dirty look at the same time, then needed a moment to put her thought into words. "I . . . never thought I'd hear myself say this, but . . . sometimes not having choices is . . . okay."

Rini grinned at her and nodded.

*

The afternoon was devoted to getting Sata and Mati completely comfortable with the elliptical geometry of orbit, and the tools they had at their stations to perform the necessary calculations and navigation plots.

Sata learned she could just enter the parameters, and Manessa would draw the resulting orbit. Of more concern to Mati were the transitions from the surface to orbit, and from one orbit to another, which the ship could also calculate and draw.

Rini watched and listened for the entire afternoon. Kibi and Boro came and went, but also wanted to keep an eye on the landing site and start cooking dinner.

The navigator and pilot spent time learning about all the forces that could cause their orbit to decay, from the very thin atmosphere at those heights, to the magnetic field of the planet itself. "Remember, even though orbit is a place of rest, it is unstable by nature. If you speed up, but don't get the ship into a lower orbit, you'll spiral out into space. If you slow down, but don't get the ship into a higher orbit, you'll spiral in."

At first they were worried, but when Ilika showed them how Manessa could monitor the orbit and make tiny corrections automatically, they relaxed.

"Going into space is pretty complicated," Boro admitted with big round eyes from where he sat at his station, listening.

"Yes. It's one of the biggest tests a civilization goes through before . . . growing up. For you five, it will mark the end of your lives as simple people from a little kingdom, and the beginning of your adventures in the vast universe."

All five crew members took slow, deep breaths for courage.

* * *

There are many other things anyone who goes into space must learn about orbit, but the ship's velocity is probably the most important. When Ilika declared "it is life," he is echoing what fixed-wing airplane pilots learn about air speed, and what helicopter pilots learn about rotor speed.

The next time you do an orbit excursion (we call them "space walks"), remember that even though your tools will generally orbit with you, they will slowly wander away unless tied down somehow.

In our mathematics, the "2" is implied with the root operation when not specified.

Root operations of even powers (2, 4, 6, etc.) actually have two answers. The second root (also called the "square root") of 4 is 2 and -2. Only the positive answer is important for most situations.

Rini's realization that the bigger the planet, the faster the ship has to orbit, was because the Mass of the planet is being multiplied in the formula. If Mass goes up, Velocity goes up, and if Mass goes down . . .

Size or volume is the amount of space something take up. Mass is the total amount of matter present, and is related to weight. Mass / Volume = Density, a measure of how "tightly packed" the atomic particles are. If you take a certain volume of water, then freeze it, the mass remains the same, but the volume increases, which means the density does down. It will now float on liquid water.

In our solar system, Saturn is an example of a gas giant that's average density is less than water. That only happens because we are counting the entire volume of the "visible" Saturn, much of which is atmosphere.

Sata's realization that the ship would orbit faster when close to the planet, slower when farther away, was because Radius is a divisor in the formula. When we divide by a number, the greater the number, the smaller the result.

Mati was showing a different kind of intelligence when she realized they couldn't just orbit anywhere. She was using her natural "pilot's instincts."

What is a "monster"? Hint: the same creature would be a "monster" to a 3-month-old baby, and a "cute puppy-dog" to a 5-year-old child.

Sata was still aware of her claustrophobia. Even though she had made great progress at mastering it, deeply-rooted fears rarely go away completely.

What was it about that situation that made Kibi willing to risk motion sickness in space?

As Mati sensed, changes in orbit are tricky because they involve both the maneuvers to change altitude, and changes in velocity ("delta V").

In systems science, there are basically two kinds of feedback. (These two terms are mathematical in nature, and are completely unrelated to the use of the same terms in human social situations.) Negative feedback occurs when imperfections in the system lead to greater stability. Positive feedback occurs when imperfections lead to collapse of the system. Imperfections in the orbit of a ship, as Ilika explained, have positive feedback. The following number series illustrate both ideas:

Negative Feedback: 15, 5, 14, 6, 13, 7, 12, 8, 11, 9, 10, 10, 10, 10 . . .

Positive Feedback: 10, 10, 10, 11, 9, 12, 8, 13, 7, 14, 6, 15, 5, 17, 3, 20, 0 . . .

If going into orbit is “one of the biggest tests a civilizations goes through before growing up,” what might be other big tests for a civilization “growing up”?

Chapter 37: A New Tradition

After a hearty bean and vegetable stew for dinner, an evening with no lessons allowed everyone to mull over the many things they had learned that day. Games were brought out on the lower deck, and bathtubs saw almost constant use.

When the hour was getting late and Ilika was starting to feel sleepy, he went on a stroll around the landing site. A star-studded sky promised a bitter cold night. With his bracelet on a very low beam, he glanced at the hiding place of Risan Gor's gold, still untouched.

Returning to the ship and closing the hatch, he was a bit surprised to find his entire crew, at the big table in the passenger area, looking quite serious.

"We've been talking," Boro began. "We know you wanted to stay here for a little while to make sure our passengers didn't come back for the gold too soon. But we're all feeling that . . . going into orbit is really huge for us, like we're finally . . . leaving home. We don't want to do it from here. This place isn't special to us."

Ilika sat down with them and continued listening.

"We've realized," Rini took over, "that there's something we've done in two different places that we really love. We sit around in a hot spring and talk about stuff. Before we leave, we want to do it once more, just us six, no one else."

Ilika thought for a moment, then nodded. "I like that. It will become a tradition for us. There are hot springs on many planets, and often there's one with no people around, known only to the Transport Service."

Smiles and nods told him they were hoping that was the case.

*

After breakfast, everyone went out for one last walk around the top of the hill where Risan Gor's gold awaited the day she would need it. Cows mooed, farmers whistled and shouted, and the still winter air brought the sounds to the six deep-space response ship crew members who had no idea what this land was even called. Each whispered good-bye to their first passengers and returned to the spherical ship, knowing they had done what they came to do, and must now depart.

Ilika smiled with pride when a flight plan was created and all pre-flight preparations completed without a word from him.

After a leisurely flight across the western ocean at ion drive one, which took an entire two minutes, Kibi quickly located a pristine lake high in the mountains above the geothermal area on the southern continent. A few minutes later she announced that their tanks were full, and Manessa was very happy with the water after filtering it a bit.

Mati, this time smiling and taking her time, settled the ship onto the landing site. No evidence remained, in the ship or outside, that they had recently brought two passengers to this place, except for a broken mission bracelet cabinet and a noticeable lack of pinkfruit juice in the galley.

In their favorite pool, with pleasant summer weather continuing in the southern hemisphere, they looked at each other, knowing they were about to take a huge step in their lives. Ilika watched Sata for signs of home-sickness, but she seemed completely happy as she looked at her friends with affection and respect.

Ilika also noticed that everyone was wearing mission bracelets.

✷

Leaving a neat pile of firewood behind for the next Transport Service crew that needed it, the Manessa Kwi slowly rose into the air to one thousand meters, then streaked away into the western sky.

Without needing to even touch her flight control, Mati watched closely as the ship followed the elliptical curve that would end in a stable circular orbit around the planet.

Boro kept an eye on his fuel supplies, and could see a slight drop in solid number two. His eyes grew large when his display told him they were passing one hundred kilometers of altitude.

Rini grinned as he selected views of the shrinking world below and the darkening sky above, and added a color-coded image of the planet's magnetic field, just for fun.

Sata studied her chart, and saw that the moon was the only object in orbit. As they passed four hundred kilometers, she set the global chart of the planet to rotate automatically based on their position, and sent it to all stations, a subtle smile of pride turning up the corners of her mouth.

Kibi knew Manessa would never open the hatch in space, but just for peace of mind, she changed its status. After a slow breath and a moment to look deep inside herself, she smiled, very glad the ride into space was not upsetting her stomach.

Even though Ilika was very used to orbital insertion, he was experiencing a little bit of what his five crew members were feeling. As they passed one thousand kilometers of altitude, he remembered the day, nearly a year before, when he had entered the medieval walled city wondering where he was going to find a crew.

As he glanced around the bridge, he knew that both physical and emotional weaknesses remained, but also the strength and determination to keep chiseling away at those weaknesses until the universe was theirs to explore.

✷ ✷ ✷ ✷ ✷

Even though not everyone has hot springs handy, a similar traditions links us with just about every human being from the cave dwellers of 40,000 years ago to the present. Sitting around a campfire, discussing the events of the day just passed, and hopes for the following day, is an experience few people have missed. It is the essential "hearth," the heart of a home or community, and requires cooperation to gather and chop wood, kindle and tend the fire, and make food. Gazing into the flames puts us in a meditative state, perfect for listening to stories. It connects us with all our ancestors on an emotional level, and if we listen carefully to the cracking fire, we can almost hear the drums, songs, and voices of our ancestors.

Greetings, young people of planet Earth,

This grand, life-changing, soul-building adventure continues as the new crew of the deep-space response ship Manessa Kwi heads for interplanetary space. Will Satamia Star Station await them, just around the corner? Of course not. Those readers looking for *quick and easy* left the Nebador stories behind, probably several books ago. Those of you about to sink your minds into this book are made of sterner stuff.

Space separates the children from the grown-ups. Your age doesn't matter. If you are nine, and you are aiming your life toward standing on your own two feet and dealing with hard, cold reality, you are leaving childhood behind. One of the critiquers who helped make these stories possible started at age eight.

Interplanetary space is like the twenty feet of air that separates the bird nest, where the little birdies must first spread their wings, from the ground, where cats await their next meal. In interplanetary space, we will grow up or die.

But beware the temptation to gaze at the stars and planets too much. The first step into space starts on the ground, on the good fertile soil of planet Earth. We visited our moon in 1969 and the early 1970s, but have not been back, and have not done much else in space, because our "house" is not yet in order. We knew, in the 1970s, that energy and other resources would soon run short, and we decided, as a whole people and a whole planet, to ignore the warnings and do nothing.

The crew of the Manessa Kwi will see and understand many things as they journey outward from their original home to the stars. If you, young readers, have your eyes open, you will learn much from their journey, perhaps more than many people learn in a lifetime.

J. Z. Colby
2011

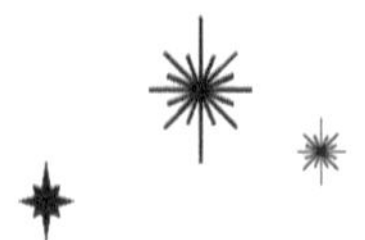

NEBADOR
Book Five
Back to the Stars

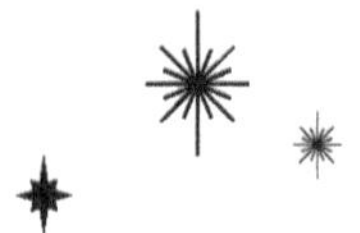

"The most beautiful and most profound emotion we can experience is the sensation of the mystical. It is the sower of all true science. He to whom this emotion is a stranger, who can no longer stand rapt in awe, is as good as dead."

— Albert Einstein

Chapter 1: Beauty Isn't Everything

Once again, Rini was embarrassed.

Earlier, during his low-orbit excursion, he was having so much fun playing with his suit thrusters, he accidentally induced a spin he couldn't correct. Mati smiled as she guided the Manessa Kwi into a matching spin so Rini could get into the airlock. Ilika gave him a mild lecture, but let it pass.

Rini's geo-stationary orbit excursion was worse. Since he wasn't paying attention to which way he was going, his suit thrusters quickly put him into a lower orbit, which rapidly began to decay. The Manessa Kwi came to his rescue, and Ilika made him do the excursion again.

But during his high-orbit excursion, Rini committed a crime he knew no one on the ship was going to easily forgive.

"Um . . . Sata? It's really beautiful out here with the world turning below and the stars above, but I just remembered something. A few minutes ago, my half-fuel alarm chimed and I forgot to start back."

"Oh, I see!" Sata said through the intercom with a taunting voice. "Actually, your half-fuel alarm was eleven minutes ago. Is that a problem, Rini?"

"Um . . . yeah. This is so embarrassing. I can't get back to the ship now. Manessa looks really small, and is getting smaller all the time."

Rini heard some giggling over the intercom, but didn't get an immediate response. He watched the ship continue to shrink with distance as he used his thrusters to slow his movement as much as possible.

Sata's voice came again. "Rini, we've discussed the situation, and since you've got enough air for about an hour, we're going to do a review of language lesson twenty-two. You don't mind, do you?"

Several voices in the background chuckled.

"Um . . . okay," Rini said with a sigh. "I guess I'll . . . be here."

The minutes passed slowly as Rini used the remainder of his thruster fuel.

He knew it wouldn't help, but doing something about his mistake brought some comfort. Finally his thrusters sputtered and died.

The silence was profound. He looked at the blue and green world below, but it no longer gave him pleasure. He looked at the stars above, but they now seemed dim and lifeless.

Tapping a code into his mission bracelet, he was informed he would be out of air in about half an hour. Helpless to do anything else about his situation, he began to recall scenes from his life. Moments of both joy and sorrow came to him, memories that had somehow touched him deeply.

Somewhat later, he tapped the code again. Twelve minutes of life left. He could see Mati's face clearly in his mind, her hair tangled like it usually was during their journey around the kingdom. He felt an intense desire to wrap his arms around her once more before he died.

Three minutes of air, and perhaps another minute after that as he suffocated inside his space suit. Tears formed and began to roll down his cheeks. Blinking them away, he made one last effort to see the ship, but found only blurry stars.

Forty seconds. His mind raced, struggling to find something to do with his remaining moments of consciousness. Fear crept all throughout his body, making his skin cold and tingly. His stomach churned and tightened.

Eight seconds. Suddenly he knew. "Mati! Nothing else in my life has ever mattered! I love you!"

"I love you too, Rini. So get yourself into the airlock so Boro can do his high-orbit excursion."

The tears in Rini's eyes blurred the golden sphere in front of him, with a dark opening close at hand. After one final alarm sounded in his ears, the air in his suit rapidly became stale. A suited arm reached out and pulled him into the airlock. He blinked away the tears and glimpsed his teacher and captain behind a face plate.

✷

After gasping and crying in Ilika's arms for several minutes, Rini slowly extracted himself from the space suit, trembling all the while. No one else came to talk to him on the lower deck. He didn't blame them. After stumbling into the toilet room to wash his face, he kept one hand on the wall as he rose in the lift.

All his shipmates were seated at the big oval table in the passenger area, sipping cups of fragrant tea. Looking at the floor, Rini shuffled forward and slipped into the empty seat beside Mati. Ilika took another seat.

"I really do love you, Rini," Mati said, "but you screwed up again."

"I . . . I know."

"When he's surrounded by beautiful things," Kibi began, "Rini loses track of time. It's not that big a deal, seems to me."

"He also loses track of directions," Boro said.

"And warning alarms," Sata added.

"And people who love him and are waiting for him to come back," Mati said with a tender frown.

Rini took a deep breath and looked up. “I’m sorry. I’ll do my excursions all over again. I’ll do better, I promise.”

Ilika had been sitting quietly, listening and wearing a subtle smile. “I think you finally heard us, Rini. There are several planets coming up. If you practice every chance you get, I think we can let Boro do his excursion, then move on.”

Rini took several slow, thoughtful breaths. “I will.”

“Fantastic!” Boro said, hopping up. “I’ll be in a suit in eight minutes!”

* * *

There are three kinds of simple (equatorial) orbit. Stationary orbit is at that one exact altitude (different for every planet) at which the orbiting object moves at the same speed as the rotating surface of the planet, so it always stays above the same point on the planet. Lower orbits require the object to move faster than the rotation of the planet, and higher orbits require the object to move slower.

There are many kinds of non-equatorial orbit, and orbit can also be in the opposite direction from the rotation of the planet, but none of these allow an object to remain above one point on the surface. On Earth, a stationary orbit has an altitude of about 35 786 km (22 240 miles).

Why did Ilika wait until the last possible moment to rescue Rini?

Why do you think no one came down to the lower deck to comfort Rini as he got out of his space suit?

What value is Rini learning that is necessary to be on any team?

Chapter 2: Leaving Home

With a tasty casserole of beans, rice, and vegetables on their trays, along with sticks of hard cheese and cups of sweet tea, the entire crew of the deep-space response ship Manessa Kwi gazed at the large display screen above the steward's station. For five of them, the world of their birth filled the screen and turned slowly as they watched.

After journeying the entire width and length of the small kingdom where he found his crew, Ilika was almost as attached to the place as they were. He recalled the many faces in the room full of slaves he had tested. He remembered Kodi and his sticky fingers, Miko's leap from boulder to boulder, and sweet Neti who was left to grieve and find a new partner. Toli had tried very hard toward the end of the journey, but was just not Transport Service material. Buna had chosen another path, and Ilika would always miss her.

"Our business here is done," he began. "This beautiful planet is the only place in the Sonmatia solar system with good air to breathe. The people who live here will not appreciate that fact for a thousand years or more, and will probably come close to destroying their atmosphere before they learn to take care of it."

"That's stupid," Kibi grumbled. "If anyone even *looks* funny at Manessa's air system, they'll have to get through me! I kind of like breathing."

Everyone around the table smiled or chuckled. They also knew their beloved steward wasn't joking.

Ilika grinned at his lover. "So . . . if everyone is ready to say good-bye to this little planet for a while . . ." He stopped and looked around the table.

Rini smiled, but still carried a measure of guilt about his recent orbit excursions. Boro nodded slowly, trying to hide his nervousness about warming up the ship's interplanetary engines for the first time. Mati sparkled with longing, knowing that only a few planets separated her from healers who could fix her knee. Sata, leaving parents and a brother behind at not quite twelve years of age, took a deep breath, planted her feet squarely on the floor, and grinned.

Ilika saw that Sata's grin was a bit forced, but after a moment, he continued. "Interplanetary space is scattered with countless wandering molecules, bits of rock and ice, and occasionally bigger things that Rini can detect and we will avoid. The ship uses a very slender shape, a repulsion field, and high levels of ion drive. You have all studied the necessary engines, controls, and instruments. Now it's time to use them.

"As you know, we measure interplanetary space in light-minutes. It's about eight light-minutes from here to the sun — an hour at one-eighth the speed of light, Manessa's cruising speed in space. I've started a new flight list. We're at navigation point one, and I've entered a proposed flight plan. See what you think of it."

Ilika collected empty trays and stepped into the galley.

*

As the captain of the Manessa Kwi did the dishes and started a pot of soup, he didn't have to look to see what his crew-in-training was doing. He had been through the process himself, and from words he overheard now and then, could clearly imagine their thoughts.

For a while, they huddled around Sata's navigation console. Then they moved to the engineer's station, where Boro slowly and carefully expressed his concern. Back at the large table, no less than three knowledge pads were in use, with Kibi routing their displays to the big screen when one of them had something to share. Ilika kept his eyes on his galley work.

More than an hour after starting, they spent a few minutes at Rini's watch station, then returned to the table.

Ilika could tell by the dead silence behind him that it was time to cover his soup pot. Rather unfriendly looks greeted him when he turned around, but he had expected as much. "So . . . what do you think?"

The others looked at Kibi.

"We don't like it one bit," the steward said in a firm voice.

Ilika held in his smile. "What's wrong with it?"

"There's nothing wrong with the trip from here to the sun," Mati explained.

"It's the part about hovering over the surface of the huge thing," Boro went on, his voice getting louder.

"At that distance, the gravity will be so great," Sata declared with despair, "that we'll need the anti-mass drive at level seven!"

"That will take all three anti-mass inducers," Boro explained, almost gasping for breath, "and leave us nothing extra for an emergency."

"What about orbit?" Ilika asked, trying to keep a straight face.

"Orbiting the sun at that distance would require one-quarter the speed of light!" Rini squeaked. "Manessa can't go that fast."

Ilika smiled. "You guys are good! We might take a risk like that in a dire emergency. We certainly won't any time we can avoid it. A good flight plan includes at least two paths to a safe destination. After a break, you can rewrite it so everyone's happy."

All five crew members sighed with relief. Kibi shooed Ilika out of the galley so she could find snacks.

*

After a few calculations, Boro was happy with the new hover altitude, giving him anti-mass power to spare. Rini, however, reminded them that if the anti-mass drive failed, they'd have to use space thrusters.

Mati frowned and grabbed a knowledge pad. "Thrusters only give me a thousand meters per second," she complained. "That's not escape velocity anywhere near the sun."

Ilika scrunched his face for a moment. "You're confusing velocity and acceleration, Mati. Manessa's thrusters can give you that much *change* in velocity, per second."

"Oh . . . yeah . . ." Mati mumbled with embarrassment as she tapped at the knowledge pad again. "Okay, I'm happy."

"But . . ." Sata began with a cringe, "wouldn't that much acceleration kill us?"

Mati frowned again and looked at Ilika.

"Yes," Ilika replied, "but Manessa wouldn't use maximum thrust with anyone on board. Look at emergency acceleration curve two."

Mati worked with the hand-held device, peering at its screen in silence for a moment. Kibi stepped to her station and sent Mati's display to the big screen so everyone could see.

"Okay, I get it," Mati said with a much happier voice. "It starts slow so we can get into inertia straps, or grab something, and backs off after eight seconds, but builds plenty of speed."

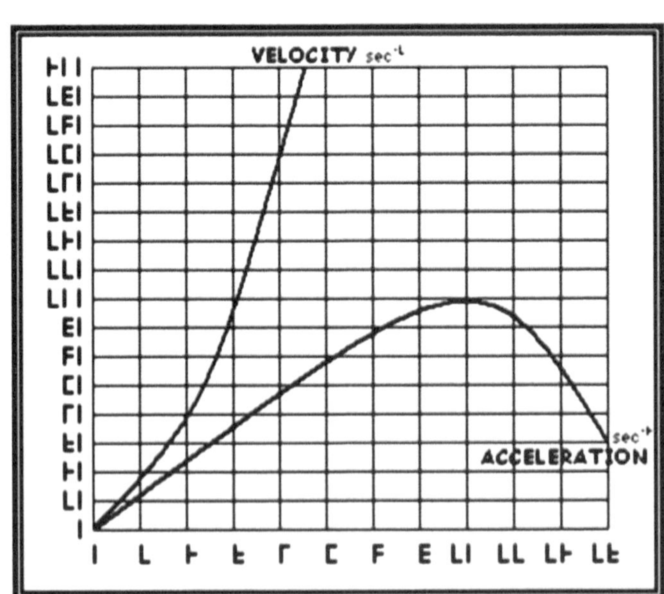

"Right. Your planet has a gravity of about twelve meters per second squared," Ilika explained. "This curve gently takes us to about six times that. We'd be moaning, but we'd live."

After Rini presented his chart of all objects along the way larger than a grain of sand, Ilika looked over the entire new flight plan, smiled, and said, "Stations."

Slipping into their console chairs, the crew began pre-flight checks while Ilika secured the soup pot. As soon as he took the command chair, he spoke. "We will no longer be working Mati to death on every flight. She will be on-duty at the beginning and end of each flight leg, and Manessa will remind her eight minutes before each navigation point so she has time to climb out of the bathtub, or wherever, and get to her station."

Mati grinned and gestured toward her crutch. "For me, make it twelve minutes. But I think I'll stay close this time. Leaving my station with the ship moving feels scary."

Ilika nodded. "Sata and Boro are also off-duty once we get moving, but Rini's job is critical."

The freckled lad smiled, turned back to his console, and started a solar wind chart.

"All stations, report flight-plan readiness," Ilika commanded.

"Pilot has the plan," Mati reported, "an elliptical course ending in a solar hover. Um . . . I want everyone in inertia straps."

"Good use of flight command, Mati," Ilika said. "Continue with reports."

"Manessa likes the plan," Sata announced. "Universe transponder on."

"Ion seven is green," Boro declared. "Full inertia canceling and repulsion field."

Rini touched another symbol on his console. "Flight path is clear, and I'll be watching it like a hawk."

Kibi finished looking over the inside of the ship from her console. "Ship is secured for flight."

✷

Evening light was fading as Noni leaned on her staff and looked up at the crystal clear winter sky. It would be a bitter cold night, and she envied her sheep their thick coats. Suddenly she saw a shooting star streak away toward the lingering sunset light in the west. She smiled and made a wish.

Just then Bo barked, signaling he needed help with a stray, so she pulled her old cloak tightly around her and went back to work.

✷ ✷ ✷

The speed of light (and all other frequencies of electro-magnetic energy) appears to be a universal constant. In a vacuum, it is about 300 000 km (186 000 miles) per second. Combining that with our standard units of time, we get units of distance that are well-suited for use in space.

The light-year is about 9 461 000 000 000 km (5 878 000 000 000 miles) and is handy for inter-stellar (between stars) distances. The nearest star to our sun (Proxima Centauri) is about 4.2 light-years away.

The light-hour is about 6 500 000 000 km (4 000 000 000 miles) and is useful for the long distances in a solar system, such as between the outer planets.

The light-minute is about 18 000 000 km (11 000 000 miles) and is handy for short inter-planetary (between planets) distances, such as between the inner planets. The orbits of Earth and Mars are about 4.35 light-minutes apart.

Since Nebador uses base eight, how many minutes are probably in their "hour" (instead of 60)?

Could any one of the crew members, working alone at his or her station, have analyzed the proposed flight plan?

"Escape velocity" is the relative speed an object needs to escape the gravity of any body in space without using additional thrust. On Earth, it is about 11 km/sec or 7 miles/sec.

Sometimes the illustrations show just what the characters are seeing, sometimes they are translated into the English language and Arabic numbers, and sometimes they are a mixture, depending on what is important in each illustration.

Speed (or velocity) is distance per time. Acceleration is CHANGE in speed per time, so its unit is distance per time per time, or distance per time squared. A constant speed does not cause any stress (gravitational force) upon our bodies. Only a CHANGE in speed (or direction).

"Speed" and "velocity" are not technically the same, but for most practical purposes, they are interchangeable.

The gravity we are used to on Earth is the same as an acceleration of about 10 meters (32 feet) per second squared. We call it one "g" or one "gravity." Amusement park rides let us experience 2 or 3 gravities. If our bodies are well-supported, we can tolerate 5-10 gravities for short times. If the acceleration is too much, or for too long, we will black out, and eventually be injured, then killed.

What was the shooting star shepherdess Noni saw? What is the most common type of shooting star?

Chapter 3: Solar System Primary

"Oh . . . my . . . god," Sata said under her breath as she stared with wide eyes. On her display, a huge loop of orange fire slowly arched up from the boiling yellow surface, almost reaching their current altitude.

"All crew members are on-duty in a situation like this," Ilika stated calmly.

Boro's mouth hung open as he gazed at the inferno below. "Y . . . yeah. Thrusters are all warmed-up, just in case."

Mati continued to stare at her fiery display. "The sun . . . is burning!"

"The . . . um . . . temperature and . . . um . . . radiation . . ." Rini whimpered in a thin voice.

"You feeling okay, Rini?" Kibi asked from her console.

"N . . . not really. Um . . . I promised I'd practice orbit excursions every chance I got . . ."

Kibi got a bowl from the galley and took it to the watch station with a motherly look of concern.

Ilika held in a smile. "Do you think a space suit could handle these radiation levels?"

Rini looked up the answer with sweating, shaking fingers, bowl in his lap. Soon he started breathing easier. "Whew! Not by a long shot!"

Ilika smiled, then tapped at the controls on the arm of his chair and a diagram appeared on the main bridge screen.

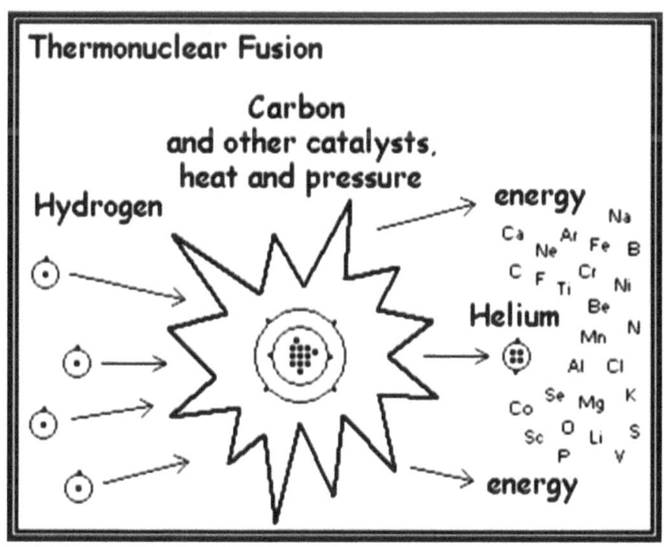

"Let's peek at what's happening down there. The chemical reactions you've studied involve the electrons around each atom. This is different. Here, great heat and pressure are forcing changes to the nucleus of the atom. There are several types of stars, but all of them burn hydrogen. Carbon is most often present as a catalyst, a helper that isn't changed by the process. Helium is created, a sprinkling of heavier elements, and a huge amount of energy."

As Ilika spoke, five pairs of eyes went back and forth from their visual displays to the diagram.

"The energy comes out as heat and light?" Boro asked.

"Every kind of energy you can imagine, Boro, and some particles too strange to classify. Rini, give us a full-spectrum graph."

Rini touched a small part of his display. "Channel four."

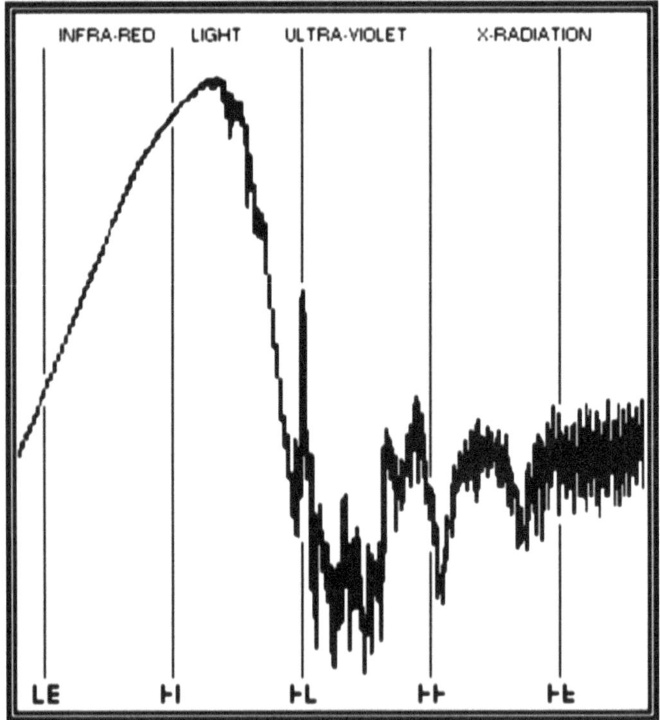

Ilika spoke in a calm voice as he went from station to station checking on his crew. "Even though visible light from the sun has the most energy, it's easy to deal with."

Rini chuckled nervously. "I just imagined Manessa wearing a sun hat!"

Ilika grinned. "See that sharp spike in ultra-violet? There's a layer in our space suits just to deal with it. But the x-rays are far worse, even though they have less energy, because they can penetrate so deeply. It's not the heat that keeps Rini from doing an excursion here, it's the x-rays."

The freckled lad smiled at his captain.

"Manessa's hull is the only part of this ship that can withstand all that radiation. As Boro knows, Manessa can't use atmospheric engines here, even though a fair amount of matter is present, because that would draw the hot solar material into the ship. Space thrusters use fuel very quickly, so we rarely use them. This is the best place to see what they'll do. Prepare for anti-mass failure drill."

Mati swallowed, then selected the emergency escape course and put it on her display.

Ilika stowed Rini's bowl in the galley, returned to the command chair, and pulled down his inertia straps. "Normally Manessa would begin the escape plan automatically if Boro shut down the anti-mass drive. I'm canceling Manessa's safeguards. We have to save ourselves."

"I'm ready," Mati declared. "All I have to do is touch one symbol."

"We're going to lurch straight up as the ship drops toward the sun," Ilika pointed out.

Mati nodded. "We've practiced that."

"Anti-mass off," the captain ordered.

None of the new crew members were prepared for the gut-wrenching sensation of the ship dropping out from under them. Sata and Rini both screamed with fright, and Kibi couldn't think of anything but the contents of her stomach. Mati cried out with pain as her bad knee hit the underside of her console, and tears filled her eyes as she tried desperately to see her emergency thruster control. Time seemed to stand still as she blinked and forced her hand down with all her strength.

Suddenly they were no longer falling, but the forward acceleration was almost worse. Boro began moaning loudly and couldn't stop. Kibi used all her strength to turn her head before losing her snack. Everyone else, including Ilika, howled as the space thrusters pushed them to six times normal gravity, then began to back off.

*

"Status reports," Ilika said when the acceleration finally stabilized at twice normal gravity.

"I . . . th-think . . . I pr-pressed it," Mati stuttered.

"You did," Ilika reassured. "Sata?"

"Um . . . don't know where we are."

"You work on that, and I'll come back to you. Boro?"

"Alive . . . I think. I can *see* the fuel level dropping."

"We'll switch engines soon. Rini?"

"Wow. Um . . . nothing on the flight path, until we get to that little planet without an atmosphere."

"Kibi?"

"This is embarrassing . . ."

"Report now, feel later," Ilika reminded her.

"I . . . um . . . have a mess to clean up. I'm just not sure where it is."

* * *

The basic explanation of thermonuclear fusion in the story is fairly complete. The process has been duplicated on Earth in small-scale experiments and in the hydrogen bomb, but has not proven useful as a power source, even though we have been trying for several decades.

Stars are the birthplaces of all the heavy elements that make life possible. Normal thermonuclear fusion creates many, but when a star explodes to form a supernova, an even greater variety of heavy elements are spread out for vast distances to someday become planets and everything on them. We are stardust.

The spectrum of solar radiation may not be completely accurate in the x-ray area because it is difficult for us to measure x-rays. Gamma rays and "cosmic rays," off the spectrum to the right, are even more difficult to detect and measure.

During the failure drill, the crew experienced negative gravity (downward acceleration), which is much more difficult for us, physically and mentally, than the same amount of upward or forward acceleration. They had practiced it a little in the desert in *Book Four*, but were still much less prepared than we would be since most of us have ridden amusement park rides.

Chapter 4: Orbital Velocity

When the ship finally quit accelerating, Boro looked at his thruster fuel gauge with a worried frown. "I hope that's all you need."

"We'll know in a minute," the pilot said as she and Sata studied the orbital entry diagram on their screens.

Sata entered another number and the diagram changed slightly. "According to Manessa, this should work. You just need to adjust speed and nail that entry point."

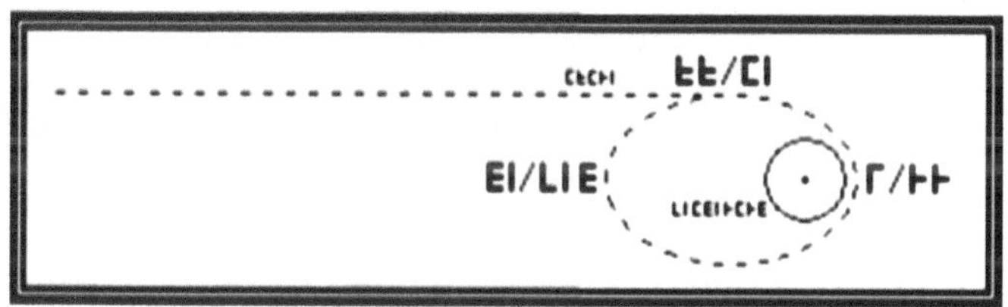

Mati glanced at her console. "Yeah, Boro, I need a little more. We're going too slow."

"Oh, okay. But you're doing the dishes next time I cook!"

Pilot and engineer exchanged grins.

For the next two hours, Ilika worked in the galley to finish the soup and make biscuits. Kibi got cleaning supplies from the lower deck and began the long process of washing all the passenger seats, the floor, and the walls. When Ilika pointed out a bit of the ceiling that also needed work, she burst into tears. He surrounded her with his arms, and they worked together to finish the job. The four other crew members stayed at their stations, or slipped quietly into the lift.

Finally Mati called everyone back and raised her flight control. "Inertia straps."

Ilika remained silent as he pulled down his straps, but as he turned to glance around the ship, Kibi noticed he was holding something in.

Mati remained focused on her work. "The speed matches our calculations perfectly. Just a slight course correction, and we'll slide right into an elliptical orbit around the first planet. Does it have a name, Ilika?"

"No, just Sonmatia One. No one on your world even knows it exists."

Mati continued working with her flight control. "Maybe we could name it. Course looks right. Check me, Sata."

"Um . . . looks good. Orbital entry in twenty-five seconds."

Everyone watched their displays as the Manessa Kwi approached the planet, a bright ball of rock floating in space with no water or atmosphere, and no visible surface features.

"Orbit in three . . . two . . . one . . ." Sata narrated.

Everyone watched the course diagram on their screens as the ship flew right past the planet with only a slight change in direction.

✷

Mati and Sata fussed and fumed over the orbit calculations for the next half hour, trying to figure out what went wrong.

Ilika let the others go off-duty, but otherwise remained silent. He stepped into the galley and added a few more spices to his soup.

Kibi joined him to help with trays. "You knew, didn't you?"

Ilika nodded so only she could see. "Two biscuits for each person."

Soon the pilot and navigator came to the table. "We give up," Sata moaned.

Ilika poured bowls of soup. Kibi added biscuits and dried fruit, then carried out the trays.

"Are you *sure* Manessa knows how to calculate orbits?" Mati asked with a slight pout.

"Yes . . ." Ilika said slowly.

"Mati . . ." Kibi began hesitantly, "I . . . don't know quite how to say this . . . and I don't know the math like you guys do . . . but as we passed the planet, it just *felt* like we were going way too fast."

Rini nodded agreement but kept his expression soft.

"But Manessa says the speed was just right!" Mati defended herself with a tone of despair.

"What speed did Manessa calculate for your orbit entry?" Ilika asked calmly as he sat down.

Sata craned her neck to see her display. "Fifty-three thousand five hundred and twenty."

"And what was our speed?"

"Fifty-three thousand five hundred and twenty!" Mati blurted out with frustration. "We've checked it over and over, even reviewed the flight log!"

Ilika took another spoonful of soup. "Relative to what reference point?"

Suddenly both pilot and navigator became deathly quiet. They looked around the table, then at each other. "Um . . ." Mati began in a tiny, sheepish voice, "based on our last navigation point . . . when we were . . . hovering over the sun."

"And what does a speed relative to that point have to do with orbiting Sonmatia One?" Ilika asked.

Sata swallowed. "Um . . . nothing?"

Ilika nodded. "Let's eat a good dinner, then Mati and Sata can put us into that elliptical orbit . . . and I bet it will be perfect this time!"

* * *

Do you remember the base eight numerals from *Book Four*? The number that looks like the word "LIE" is actually the number 107, which would be 71 in base ten. What is the value of the number that looks like "EI" in base eight and base ten?

Instead of making a joke about doing the dishes, what other reaction to Mati's fuel use could Boro have had? How would that reaction have affected their working relationship?

What method of gathering information were Kibi and Rini using when they guessed that the ship was going too fast for orbit around Sonmatia One?

On Earth, we assume that all distances and speeds are relative to the surface of the planet. We just don't need to think about the possibility of cities or mountains moving (except tiny amounts during earthquakes). In space, many of our earthly assumptions are no longer valid.

Chapter 5: Baked and Frozen

The two girls who worked at the front of the ship quickly finished their dinners and dashed to the bridge to recalculate the ship's relative speed. When they discovered it was four times too fast for any orbit around the first planet, they looked at each other with sad faces for a moment, then both started snickering.

Boro moaned when they began using his precious thruster fuel again, this time to loop back to the planet and slow down.

The orbit Mati achieved needed a few minor adjustments, but both the captain and the ship were soon happy.

"This little world has lost its rotation," Ilika explained as they all peered at their displays. "One side always faces the sun, so its surface is nearly molten. The other side is close to absolute zero, the temperature at which all electron activity stops. Neither situation allows an atmosphere to develop.

"Tomorrow we will learn how to do landings and excursions in these extreme environments. It's been a long day and we've experienced many things. Have a relaxing evening."

When Rini came up in the lift after a deep sleep, he found Ilika leaning back at the engineer's station and Kibi asleep in a passenger seat. "Didn't you . . . get any sleep?" he whispered to his captain.

"Yes. Kibi and I took turns."

"I'll make breakfast," Rini offered as Kibi began stretching.

Soon others arrived and Rini set out mugs of tea. As soon as everyone was at the table with hot cereal and honey, Ilika looked at the knowledge pad beside him.

"We have four kinds of excursions we can do here, two in the shadow of the planet, and two in the much smaller shadow of the ship. Rini and Mati, you are doing an orbital excursion together. Rini and Boro, you two will take some readings on the daytime surface. Rini and Kibi will look for the little creatures that live in the thin cusp between day and night. Finally, Rini and Sata will explore the dark, frozen night side."

Rini grinned.

"Rini is in command of each of these excursions. As we all know, he is practicing awareness of the situation. He is responsible for getting his companion, and himself, back to the ship, alive and well."

Everyone smiled at Rini.

"Here's the score," Ilika continued. "Eight seconds of exposure to the x-radiation from the sun at this distance, and you can forget having children."

Kibi looked glum.

"Twenty seconds, your hair will fall out and you won't be able to keep your food down . . . for months."

Mati frowned.

"Thirty seconds, you'll make it back to the ship, but quickly die."

Sata cringed.

"Forty seconds, your suit will be breached and you won't even get back inside."

Boro moaned.

"Rini, will you go down and get two space suits ready while we do the dishes? Mati will be down in a minute."

"Sure," Rini said, put his tray on the galley counter, and stepped into the lift.

As soon as he was gone, Ilika whispered further instructions to the other crew members.

*

Mati leaned on Rini until the outer airlock hatch opened. "I love excursions in orbit," she said through the intercom. "It's the only time my knee doesn't matter."

They both took a moment to hook their three-meter safety lines to the outside of the hull, then looked down at the little porch Manessa had created for them just outside the airlock.

"Nice," Rini said. "We can just stand here and look around at the stars and the beautiful little planet, without any danger of going outside Manessa's shadow."

Mati launched herself through the hatch. "Who needs a porch? We're weightless, remember?" She floated and slowly tumbled out to the end of her short safety line.

"Mati, I don't think that's such a good idea. They're just safety lines . . ."

"It's the only time I can forget I'm a cripple. And it's fun!"

Rini stood on the little porch, shuffling his feet and looking around. "Ilika just said these lines were about the right length. He didn't promise they'd keep us out of the x-rays . . ."

"I'll be careful, and if I feel any x-rays, I'll come in."

"But you can't feel . . ." Suddenly Rini stopped in mid-thought, seeing one of Mati's booted feet become brilliantly lit by the direct rays of the sun for a split second. He waited a heartbeat, then saw the same thing happen with one of her gloved hands. "Mati! On the porch! Now!"

Somewhat to his surprise, she said nothing, but immediately pulled on her safety line and a moment later was beside him on the porch, arms around him and a smile on her face. "Thank you, Rini."

✷

After Mati carefully brought the ship to a one-meter hover over the blazing daytime surface of the planet, Rini and Boro attached short safety lines and stepped out onto the little porch in the shadow of the ship. The slender lad had a complex instrument attached to the right arm of his suit, and the larger boy carried a sample container with several tools attached to the outside.

"Wow. I can feel the heat," Boro announced, shielding his face with a gloved hand.

Rini did the same. "Lucky for us, rocks don't re-radiate x-rays."

Boro raised his eyebrows. "They sure do a good job with infra-red! What shall we do first?"

"Um . . . instrument readings."

Both boys knelt down at the edge of the porch.

"We're still too high," Rini said. "Mati, can you take us down another half meter?"

"Sure," Mati replied from her station.

Boro shook his head with discomfort. "I'm starting to sweat, and my suit cooling system's doing all it can."

Rini thought for a moment. "Um . . . you move back from the edge while I get the readings, then you can get a sample."

Boro did what Rini commanded without hesitation. Rini didn't see his friend's slight smile.

Rini lowered the instrument's probe to the ground. "Ilika was right — it's so hot, it's almost liquid. I'm getting a bunch of weird numbers Ilika will have to explain. Okay, I'm done."

Rini moved back from the edge and Boro moved forward with the sample container.

Rini was leaning against the hatch, blinking to keep the sweat out of his eyes, when he saw Boro reach for a small loose rock with his gloved hand. "No! Stop!"

Boro jerked his hand back. "Oh, yeah, I forgot. I'm supposed to use the spoon." After detaching a sampling tool from the side of the container, he carefully scooped up the rock, placed it inside, closed the top, and replaced the tool.

Rini breathed again.

"All done!" Boro said in a happy voice.

*

Rini was the first member of the new crew to set foot on another world. Kibi came close behind.

The Manessa Kwi perched in the shadow of the planet, on the perpetual night side, but just barely. The intense solar wind streamed by less than a hundred meters over their heads. On the horizon, a short walk away, barren rocks blazed with light and heat. Even though no sound could be heard in the airless vacuum, both crew members felt a subtle vibration coming through the ground as the deadly solar wind slowly ate away the rocks, and anything else it touched.

"This is creepy," Kibi said with a shaking voice. "Let's go find those critters, make a painting, and get back to the ship."

"Photo . . . graph," Rini corrected, still struggling with the word himself. "We're safe as long as we stay out of the light."

"I suppose you're right. I never thought I'd say this, but I'd rather be in our ship than on *this* solid ground."

Rini chuckled as they began walking toward the glowing horizon, the home of the only living things on the planet.

A few minutes later, less than a kilometer from the blazing rocks, tiny flashes of blue light greeted them from the ground. "Don't step on them!" Rini shouted. "Ilika said they're sentient."

"I won't," she said, stooping down to look closely at one. "Wow, they're like little gems. No water, no carbon, just rocks and stardust." She opened the cover of her mission bracelet, made some adjustments, and took a picture.

Kibi stood up and gazed toward the bright horizon. "Looks like they get bigger closer to the light." She began walking slowly, avoiding the crystalline creatures on the ground. "I want to get a photograph of a big one."

Rini followed silently, watching where he placed his feet.

A little way ahead, Kibi stopped in front of a sparkling clump of blue crystals. "This is about as big as they get." She knelt down in a clear place and opened her mission bracelet again.

Rini looked all around at the crystal life forms, the glowing rocks on the horizon, and the solar wind streaming by not far over their heads. He smiled. When he looked back at Kibi, he saw blue crystals beginning to cling to the legs of her space suit. “Kibi! Run!”

She instantly jumped up and ran back toward the ship. The blue creatures on her legs quickly fell to the ground. Rini met her just outside the narrow habitat of the only living things on the planet.

“Thanks, Rini!”

*

Flying solely by instruments, Mati landed the little ship on a level place deep in the perpetual darkness of the planet. Only dim starlight suggested where the horizon might be, until the pilot activated external ship lights. Strange rock formations of all sizes, some taller than the ship, surrounded them in every direction.

“The rocks are built up over millions of years by frozen stardust,” Ilika explained. “They are very fragile, and may crumble if touched, but weigh very little.”

Rini and Sata were soon in space suits, ready to explore. As soon as they left the airlock, both activated their bracelet lights. Sata carried a sample container.

Rini was soon immersed in the mystery of the place, gazing open-mouthed at the eerie rock shapes all around, sometimes turning circles to look up at the star-studded sky above, occasionally even laughing out loud at the sheer wonder of being on another planet.

Sata felt the same joy and wonder, but remembered her task. About fifteen minutes into their exploration, she spotted what she wanted, a tiny stardust formation that would fit whole into her container. “I’m stopping for a sample, Rini.”

With some difficulty, he stayed within sight while she worked.

Sample container closed, Sata was back at his side, ready to follow wherever he led.

About half an hour later, Rini began to slow his pace. “Um . . . Sata, have you been paying attention to which way we were going?”

Sata took a few seconds to remember what she was supposed to say. "No. I got the sample. You're the leader."

Rini swallowed. "I just realized . . . we've been walking a long time."

"Yeah. Almost an hour."

"Ilika, can you hear me?" Rini asked over the intercom. "I . . . um . . . think we're lost."

He heard nothing but their own soft breathing.

"Mati? Boro? Kibi? Manessa?"

Again, only silence.

Sata cleared her throat. "I remember Ilika saying the stardust rocks might block our communications."

Rini was silent for a long moment, then spoke in a broken voice. "I'm . . . sorry. I'm not a very good leader. You can lead now . . ."

"No way!" Sata replied instantly. "I just came along for the sample."

Several more minutes passed as the two explorers stood among the eerie rock formations that all looked alike. Neither spoke. Rini stood slowly turning, looking this way and that. Sata stood calmly and patiently, not offering suggestions or encouragement.

Suddenly Rini began stomping around like a furious animal, sometimes growling with anger, at other times sobbing with guilt. Soon he bumped into a large formation and it came slowly crashing down, doing him no harm but knocking him to the ground.

Seeing he was okay, Sata said nothing.

His anger at himself spent, Rini began to pick himself up, and happened to shine his bracelet light onto the impression of his own boot in the stardust on the ground. A moment later he began laughing and couldn't stop, even while getting to his feet.

"I'm so stupid! We can just follow our tracks back to the ship! It's crumbly stardust the whole way! It may not be a perfectly straight line, but we'll get home."

Sata smiled. "I knew you could do it!"

*

When Rini and Sata returned, it was no simple meal of stew and bread that greeted them, but a feast from Manessa's original supplies. Rini started to tell what happened, but soon realized from everyone's expressions that they already knew.

"I think Rini has made great progress at situational awareness here on Sonmatia One," Ilika announced happily. "He has to keep practicing, of course, as we all must do. His biggest challenge will be when he is alone, with no one counting on him."

"The way I see it," Boro began, "when we're alone, we're *always* in command."

Mati sipped her tangy beverage. "And he has to learn that bringing himself home safely is just as important as leading others home."

Rini grinned and blushed. "Thank you, all of you, for helping me . . . um

. . . grow up."

"You've always been there for us!" Mati said with sparkling eyes and a smile.

Rini leaned toward her. "And I always will be." Then he leaned farther and kissed her.

She wrapped her arms around his neck and didn't let him get away for a long time.

* * *

The first planet of our solar system, Mercury, also has no rotation independent of the sun, so one side is always "day," the other side "night," and a thin ring of "twilight" cusp encircles the planet.

Different elements (only one kind of atom) and compounds (more than one kind of atom) change states (solid, liquid, gas, or plasma) at different temperatures, but they all share one temperature point: at absolute zero (0°K = -273.15°C = -459.67°F) all electron activity stops for all of them. At that temperature, they are more than "solid," they are completely inert (unable to interact chemically with anything else).

"Situational awareness" is a term used by pilots, but it applies to anyone in control of anything. It requires regular "scanning" (with the mind, if not the eyes) of all factors that could cause a problem. Since most dangers take some time to develop (or get to you), this gives you the time needed to deal with them before they do damage. For example, when driving a car, situational awareness includes road conditions, other traffic, weather, light, and the conditions of all vehicle systems.

The effects of exposure to a large dose of x-radiation, as described in the story, are similar to a large dose of any high-frequency radiation, such as a person might receive near a leaking nuclear power plant. Smaller doses can also be dangerous if they are received for longer periods of time.

Why would Mati's knee not cause her pain while doing an orbital excursion?

As Rini started to say, we can't feel high-frequency radiation like x-rays and gamma rays. Therefore, we have to use instruments and our intelligence to avoid over-exposure. Once we feel something during radiation exposure, we are sick and probably dying. This warning even applies to a simple sunburn (ultra-violet radiation).

Most matter that absorbs energy only re-radiates it in the infra-red (radiant heat) frequencies. The darker an object is colored, the more infra-red it will re-radiate. That's why iron (black) makes a good cooking surface.

The scene with Rini and Kibi in the planet's twilight cusp was depicted by artist Rachael Hedges for the book's cover.

The "solar wind" is not made of air, but charged plasma particles (electrons and protons). It emerges from the sun's photosphere and corona.

Why would the solar wind be more dangerous on the first planet than on the third planet? There are three reasons.

Why would Kibi propose they stop and make a painting? Did she bring a canvas, brushes, and paints?

Life "as we know it" could not live in that environment because there is no water. We do not yet know about life with other types of chemistry, but to assume they don't exist would demonstrate several fallacies (logic errors). Can you think of them?

What circumstances caused Rini to have a temper tantrum (perhaps the first in his life)?

Were the stardust formations really blocking communications?

Some of the worst enemies of situational awareness are altered states of consciousness, such as being tired or sleepy, feeling strong emotions, or the effects of some drugs (including alcohol). Rini's altered state of consciousness might be called "mystical euphoria," but it could be just as dangerous as any other altered state when moving through a challenging environment, and he had to learn to keep it in its place.

Do you have any "states of consciousness" that could be dangerous in an unfamiliar environment?

Chapter 6: The Sad Tale of Sonmatia Two

When Sata opened her sample container, the little stardust formation was nothing but a spoonful of sparkling gray powder on the bottom. Kibi and Boro insisted on an excursion to see the strange things up close and try to get a good one for a souvenir.

Ilika smiled, but said nothing. He had never walked on this planet, so he joined them.

Mati stuck out her lower lip for a moment, then grinned.

Ilika returned her grin, and put her in command.

*

Mati watched on the large bridge display from the commander's chair as Kibi, Boro, and Ilika wandered among the strange formations. She laughed when Boro touched one, then found himself standing in a pile of stardust.

Both the steward and the engineer brought back small formations. Furrowed brows and sad faces gazed into their sample containers, until Rini called them over to the watch station and explained the pressure difference between the near-vacuum of the planet and the atmosphere inside the ship.

Kibi looked thoughtful. "So . . . if we brought a little blue crystal creature into the ship . . ."

Ilika shook his head. "Same thing would happen as soon as you opened the container. This is their home, a strip of this planet just a few hundred meters wide, a little indirect warmth from the solar wind, and a pinch of stardust. Anything else and they'd die, as surely as we would die here without a ship or a space suit."

*

An hour later, Sata, Boro, and Ilika very carefully walked among the blue crystals, letting them cling to their legs for a moment before gently shaking them off.

Mati again watched from the ship, and silently counted the planets that lay between her and the healers of Satamia Star Station.

*

"We've learned many things from this little planet," the captain said after a hearty breakfast the next morning. "I'm glad Boro is feeling protective of his space thruster fuel. We won't use it often."

Boro smiled.

"I can see that Mati and Sata are anxious to calculate another orbit . . ."

Both girls nodded. "And get it right this time!" Sata said with a big grin.

"Good. The next planet we will visit, Sonmatia Two, is going to test us in very different ways because it contains the ruins — and even a few survivors — of a civilization that collapsed several hundred years ago. It's closer to the sun than your planet, and tends to overheat with any instability in the climate, just as your planet tends to cool off. Sonmatia Two is currently overheated because of the conscious choices of the people who lived there. They could have avoided the destruction of their civilization and the death of most of their population. They chose not to."

"That's stupid!" Mati spat out with a growl.

"They were much more intelligent than the people on your planet," Ilika pointed out.

Mati clamped her mouth shut.

"But they weren't smart enough. Every sapient race goes through this test, arranged by the overseers of the universe. Every planet full of people eventually discovers enough knowledge and power to change their climate. If they have also gained enough wisdom, they survive. If not, they die, or regress to a level that can survive on . . . whatever is left of their planet. It's like the little birdie that mother bird has to shove out of the nest, to fly or fall to the ground and be eaten."

A long silence followed.

"Um . . ." Kibi began, "those . . . overseers of the universe. Are they in . . . the Nebador Services?"

"No. We, in the Services, are just their helpers. None of us have the wisdom to manage a universe. Sonmatia Two is a perfect example, on a very small scale. The people who lived there were, as people go, quite wise. Now their world is a wasteland of corroded metal and poisonous fumes, with a few sickly mutated people surviving in deep tunnels, eating old food and a few mushrooms they grow, barely able to have children before they die."

Several crew members closed their eyes tightly and shuddered.

*

Mati and Sata planned the flight quietly and thoughtfully. They paid close attention to the orbital entry, wanting to get it perfect. Boro watched and asked a few questions. Rini worked alone at his station, then sent them a chart with a couple of asteroids to avoid. Kibi started a stew for lunch and dinner.

Boro smiled as he checked and warmed up the anti-mass and ion drives, both of which used very little fuel. After securing the ship, they floated up a thousand meters, then streaked off across the black sky on an elliptical course toward Sonmatia Two.

During the half-hour transit, they peered at maps of the planet, got a feel for the locations of gentle mountain ranges and shallow valleys, and were quite amazed at the number and size of the cities — all now ruins. As they approached the haze-enshrouded world, Mati instantly changed the ship's relative speed to match their calculations. "I *like* the anti-mass drive!" the pilot declared.

Sata double-checked everything and judged the ship ready to slide into a circular orbit.

"Finished with ion drive," Mati said to Boro as she concentrated on her three-dimensional flight plan.

"Ion drive off," Boro replied. "Maneuvering thrusters green."

Mati made a slight course correction. "That should do. Anti-mass to standby."

"Manessa is happy with the orbit," Sata announced.

Ilika turned to the watch station. "Anything up here with us, Rini?"

"Not this high. Several pieces of junk lower, all made of metal and in slowly decaying orbits."

"Update Manessa's satellite list, as we'll be going down later."

Rini went to work.

"Wow . . . um . . . Ilika . . . er . . . um . . ." Sata began, searching for words as she stared wide-eyed at her display.

"Report," Ilika said, "preferably with words."

"Um . . . the universe transponder . . . um . . . says there's another Nebador ship down there!"

Ilika stood up and stepped to the navigator's station. "Well, well. I'm not too surprised to see a life-monitor ship here. Also . . . you could use some practice at ship-to-ship communications."

"Me? Um . . . what do I say?"

The captain reached down and made a selection on Sata's main console. "Here's your outline. First, who you are calling, ship type and name. Second, who and where you are. Finally, what you want. For example, life-monitor Tirilana Kril, this is deep-space response Manessa Kwi in high orbit, request planetary information and practice at ship-to-ship communications. They'll know from the transponder that we're a crew-in-training."

"Um . . . okay . . . I'll try."

"Everyone, activate your station cameras so they can see us," Ilika instructed, then walked around to make sure each was ready. "Go ahead, Sata. Communications is primarily your job."

Sata touched the transmit control with trembling fingers. "Um . . . life-monitor Manessa Kwi . . . no, I mean Tiri . . . lana Kril . . . um . . . this is life-monitor . . . I mean deep-space response Manessa Kwi . . . um, what's next . . . oh, yeah, in high orbit . . . um . . . request ship-to-ship information . . . no, communications . . . sheesh!"

"You're doing fine," Ilika said from behind her with encouragement. "Keep going."

"And . . . um . . . planetary information. Whew!"

Suddenly Sata's display changed to a visual of her counterpart on the other ship. The ship's interior was much larger than the Manessa Kwi, and several other crew members could be seen working at consoles or tables.

"Greetings, Manessa Kwi! I am Drrrim-na, navigator of the Tirilana Kril, at your service, bok."

"Hello . . . um . . . I'm Sata. Um . . . everyone else say hello."

Each of the other crew members managed to say their names and add a smile or a little wave. Only Kibi kept her words untangled.

"Ilika Imni Zalara Sim, captain," he said, last of all.

Sata tried to collect her thoughts when Ilika looked back at her. "Um . . . what does a life-monitor ship do?"

"Bok. On this planet, the remnant of the sapient race is in a very dangerous transition. Their population is only about five hundred and falling, bok. They are running out of food, and are very hesitant to try new things, even though we often give them, bok, seeds and spores. They have an offer of relocation, but have not yet accepted."

"How many . . . um, people . . . work on a life-monitor ship?" Kibi asked from her station.

"Twenty, bok, with cabins for eight more visiting specialists or students. We are a mixed crew. I see that you are all, bok, what do you call yourselves? Monkey mammals?"

Hurt expressions came to Sata, Mati, and Boro. Kibi managed to hide her feelings. Rini just grinned.

"I am sorry, bok. I can see that I offended."

"It's okay," Ilika said. "They're still getting used to the variety of people in the Nebador Services."

"I have read about deep-space response ships," the other navigator said. "You have every kind of engine, and get to have mates on board, bok."

"Yes," the captain said as the other five blushed. "Are there any areas of the planet we should avoid?"

"Yes," Drrrim-na said, touching a control. "The inhabited areas are sensitive, bok. I will send you a chart."

Sata noticed the chart flash onto a small part of her display. "I have the chart."

"I must go now," Drrrim-na said. "I am cooking the next meal."

"Bye!"

"Thank you!"

"Bye!"

"I hope to talk with you again, perhaps meet you someday, Sata. Tirilana Kril closing, bok."

"That would be wonderful. Manessa Kwi . . . um . . . closing."

Everyone was silent for a moment as they absorbed the experience.

"Good work, Sata," Ilika said.

"Wow. I can't believe I just talked to another navigator, on another ship, and she's a bird!"

* * *

The pressure difference, which kept the crew from successfully collecting a stardust formation, is also the reason we can't bring creatures from deep in the ocean, to the surface, without killing them. The same thing would happen to us if we were placed, without a protective ship or space suit, on the surface of Jupiter.

Ilika explained that every sapient race goes through the "test" of gaining the knowledge and power to change their climate. This is a theological concept. In the Judeo-Christian scriptures, for example, God commands the people to "subdue the Earth." God does not say exactly why, perhaps so that we wouldn't have any hints and would have to figure out why for ourselves. The most obvious reason would be to see if we could do so successfully (sustainably). The people of Sonmatia Two failed that test.

Another theological concept is the question of whether or not we, mortal human beings, will ever have the wisdom to "manage a universe." There is a strong human tendency to think the answer will someday be "yes." Most science fiction stories follow this assumption, and indeed place us Earthlings at or near the top socially and politically. On the other hand, most religions say "no" and that only "spiritual" beings (gods, angels, etc.) can manage a universe. What do you think?

Sata's opening communication with another Nebador ship is modeled exactly on what a pilot has to say to another aircraft or a control tower when making radio contact. Her tangled words under that pressure were probably about what the author said the first time he had to talk to a control tower.

Many creatures add a sound to their speech that does not hold any important meaning other than to identify the type of speaker, and sometimes his or her mood. For the sapient bird on the other ship, that sound was "bok." The human crew of the Manessa Kwi was using such a sound also. Can you spot it?

Chapter 7: Watch Your Back

Mati made use of Rini's orbital junk chart as she carefully lowered the ship toward the planet. She took them near one of the metallic objects, almost as large as the Manessa Kwi, just to satisfy everyone's curiosity.

"It's a communications satellite," Ilika explained, "designed to receive audio or video signals from one place on the planet and send them back down to another place." He worked with Rini for a minute, and they detected a working energy source within the huge device, but no signals coming or going.

Mati continued the descent and soon entered the noxious yellow atmosphere. "Real-time surface topographics, Rini."

"Channel four."

"Synchronized map is on channel five," Sata added.

Mati arranged the new information on her display. "Atmospheric thrusters, level two."

"Warming . . . green," Boro reported.

"Kibi has command," Ilika said, standing up.

Kibi swallowed once, glanced at a few things on her console, then stepped down to the command chair. "You have that chart of the places we're not supposed to go, Mati?"

The pilot poked at her display selector. "No. I need that, Sata."

"I'm adding it to the map on channel five. There."

"Got it. Where to?"

Kibi thought for a moment. "I'm sure we all want to see a city. Other requests?"

"Any oceans or lakes?" Boro asked with a twisted grin.

"Not any more!" Rini replied. "It's so hot down there, all surface water is now just vapor mixed with the foul air."

"So this . . . sickly soup I'm flying through . . ." Mati began.

"Is a mixture of smoke and fog," Rini finished.

"Smoke from a million factories," Ilika explained. "By the time they realized the planet was overheating and they could never get the stuff back out of the atmosphere, it was too late."

The interior of the ship was quiet for a few minutes as Mati guided them toward a large ruined city. Ilika went from station to station, giving little reminders or pointing out new controls.

Their visual displays were useless until the Manessa Kwi was almost on the ground. Huge metal skeletons of crumbling buildings appeared in the putrid yellow mists, most of them towering over the ship.

Ilika went to the steward's station. "I suggest inertia straps."

Kibi nodded and everyone strapped themselves in.

Boro moaned as twisted metal seemed to reach out toward them when the yellow vapors parted for a moment. "Ugliest place I've ever seen. Makes Rumble Town look nice."

Mati guided the ship between crumbling towers, some partly collapsed, others leaning. Brownish fumes lurked at the base of one ruined building.

"Why did they make them so tall?" Rini wondered aloud. "Were they trying to touch the sky?"

Ilika was silent for a moment as he gazed at the statue of a sea creature in a bone-dry fountain. "I don't know, Rini. Most sapient races seem driven to crowd themselves close together, then compete violently for the scarce resources caused by the crowding."

Rini shrugged.

Mati took them through a large archway of bent metal and broken stone. Before they were all the way through, a loud thump filled the ship.

Rini looked up. "I th-think something hit the hull."

"Yes," Ilika said, working at the steward's console. "Many of these buildings were covered with stone, and now it's slowly falling off. No risk to the ship."

They gazed at their visual displays and saw piles of broken stone surrounding most of the buildings. At other places, broken glass glinted in the harsh yellow light. Where no rubble had piled up, the paving stones themselves jutted at odd angles.

"I suggest external audio, Kibi," Ilika said.

"Good idea."

Rini touched a control. "I don't hear a thing out there."

Mati guided the ship around a corner and they came face to face with the collapsed frame of a once-tall building.

"What was that?" Boro suddenly asked, looking up as if listening.

Everyone was silent as they strained to hear.

"I don't . . ." Sata began.

"Wait!" Kibi ordered, hand raised.

A few seconds later, a loud metallic creaking sound made them all shiver.

"I saw some metal move!" Rini yelled. "That building on the left!"

"Give us some distance, Mati," Kibi ordered with all the calmness she could muster while gripping the arms of her chair with white knuckles.

"It's coming down!" Rini shrieked at the same time that Sata yelled, Boro moaned, and they all heard a loud crashing sound. The entire metal frame of the tall building slowly collapsed onto itself, sending a huge cloud of brown dust outward in every direction.

Mati was still backing the ship away, and they appeared to be out of danger, when suddenly a loud clang was heard, the entire ship shuddered, and falling beams of rusty metal and chunks of broken stone came raining down, covering all the visual displays.

✷

Falling debris continued to pound the hull of the Manessa Kwi for the next half minute, becoming softer and softer as the layer thickened. Then silence filled the ship as the crew-in-training realized what had happened. Ilika could almost taste the fear as five pairs of wide eyes looked around the bridge.

After swallowing several times, Mati found the courage to speak first. "Um . . . I'm . . . sorry . . ." she said through tears.

Kibi shook her head to clear her thoughts. "Ilika, I imagine you want to take . . ."

"No. It's good for people to clean up their own messes, whenever possible."

She bared her teeth at her captain and lover for a moment, then took a deep breath. "Status reports, all stations."

Mati was wiping her eyes on her sleeve. "I'm the worst pilot in Nebador, and I want to go off-duty and clean toilets or something."

"Denied," Kibi said firmly. "And I still need a report."

"Um . . . I think I backed into a building, and it fell on us."

"I guessed that much," Kibi said as Rini started chuckling.

Mati cracked a tiny smile. "Um . . . I'm okay and we're . . . um . . . on the ground, I think."

"Sata?"

The navigator turned, eyes still wide. "I thought we were going to be crushed! Um . . . like Mati said, we're on the ground. The map on channel five shows our exact location."

"Boro?"

"I'm fine. Engines are all green."

Kibi nodded and smiled at the engineer, always solid and reliable in any emergency. "You can shut them down, do diagnostics or whatever they need."

Boro turned back to his console.

"Rini?"

"Um . . . visual sensors in all directions are blocked, air outside is full of dust but otherwise the same. Mati doesn't have to clean toilets when she goes off-duty. Instead, she gets a neck massage."

Mati turned and smiled.

Kibi swiveled around. "Ilika?"

"Hopefully you are all a step closer to believing me when I say that very little in the physical universe can harm our ship in any way."

* * *

A well-made communications satellite could remain in working order much longer than the civilization that built it, if not hit by an asteroid (space rock). Most of ours are solar powered and could continue to work during the day, even if the batteries failed and they could not work at night. Of course, if the planetary civilization failed, the communication satellite would have nothing to do.

Sonmatia Two was experiencing a pollution problem that we have never had to deal with. We have a working hydrological cycle (oceans, clouds, rain, rivers) that cleans our atmosphere almost constantly with rain and snow. If a planet gets too hot and loses its hydrological cycle, most pollution will simply stay in the air.

The word "smog" was made by combining "smoke" and "fog." It was first used to describe the air in London during the 19th century. The primary cooking and heating fuel at that time was coal.

What was Mati's mistake?

Chapter 8: Out of a Trap

After everyone shut down their consoles, Kibi served a simple lunch and Ilika clarified his last statement.

"It's us, the delicate little creatures inside the ship, who can be hurt. This was good for Mati. She hasn't made a serious piloting mistake in a while. Situational awareness is more important for her than anyone else. Luckily the building she knocked down was uninhabited, and of no value to anyone."

The pilot grinned shyly.

"But the fact that Manessa is unharmed, and we're merely shaken, doesn't change the fact that we're buried under a huge pile of twisted metal and rubble. We have to find a way out. Kibi is still in command, but I'm limiting your options. Space thrusters will do the trick, but there's another way."

Kibi ate her reheated stew in silence for a moment. "Manessa, have you ever before been buried?"

"Yes," the ship's pleasant voice responded. "Two hundred and thirty-one years ago I had an avian crew who liked being nice and warm, so they chose an active lava flow for a landing site. I complained, but they shut off automatic warnings, as Ilika sometimes does for training purposes. By morning, we were covered by solidified lava. It took the crew four days to figure out how to get free. They never again shut off automatic warnings."

"How did they get you out?"

"Ilika asked me not to tell you."

Kibi flashed her captain an expression so sour, he burst out laughing. Rini and Boro both joined him. Mati smiled, but was still nursing too many guilty feelings to join in the laughter. Sata's eyes showed some fear, but after a moment she too smiled.

Kibi sighed. "Ideas, anyone?"

"I don't think I dare use atmospheric thrusters," Boro said. "Too much dirt and junk piled all around the ship."

Ilika nodded. “That’s correct. They’d refuse to even warm up.”

“Anti-mass?” Rini proposed.

“That’s what I’m thinking,” Mati agreed. “I don’t know how much it’ll take, but hopefully by level seven . . .” She looked at Boro.

He nodded, and took another spoonful of stew.

⁕

The anti-mass drive at level one did nothing.

Level two caused a little bit of creaking and some dust to sift downward across their view screens.

Kibi ordered inertia straps before they tried level three. The ship quivered and shook, the metal above and around them groaned and creaked, but nothing moved.

As they tried level four, Rini started frowning and then doing something at his console. The ship moved up a small fraction of a meter, but could go no farther.

Once the screeching and thumping caused by level five ceased, Rini turned around. “We have a bigger problem.”

Kibi looked at him.

“The metal frame of that building was all connected together. It’s acting just like a net. The harder we push, the tighter it gets — I can tell from the pressure on Manessa’s hull.”

Kibi sighed. “So you mean . . . if we do get off the ground, we’re going to take the whole pissing thing with us — metal, stone, everything?”

Rini nodded with a sad expression.

Kibi turned and looked at Ilika. He was careful to keep his eyes on the steward’s console.

“Level six!” she said, turning back around. “We have to try.”

The ship bucked and lurched, the metal all around them screamed like a frightened animal, and countless chunks of rock pounded on the hull before Kibi finally let Mati stop. Then she looked at Rini.

“Pressure’s even greater. It’s wrapped around us like a spider web.”

“And we’re the damned fly,” she growled. “I don’t really expect it to work, but no harm in trying seven, I guess.”

Boro worked at his controls. “I’m bringing in more inertia canceling so we won’t be jelly on the floor if we suddenly break free.”

“Yeah, no jelly. Everyone ready?”

Sata’s eyes were larger than before, even though she had pretty pictures on three-quarters of her display. Mati looked determined, and still nursing guilt. Kibi nodded for her to begin their last and final hope.

The tortured metal screeched and screamed so loudly that Kibi yelled for Rini to turn off the audio. One visual display cleared for a moment, allowing them to see twenty or more beams stretch tightly across that part of the ship. It was soon covered again by dust and grit.

After nearly a minute, which felt more like an hour, Kibi screamed, “STOP!” and doubled over in the command chair, crying her eyes out.

*

Drawn faces sat around the large table nibbling on crackers without tasting them. Rini stood behind Mati, massaging her shoulders. Ilika tried to do the same for Kibi, but she just snapped at him.

Boro appeared unaffected. "I think we should all try to relax, maybe even get some sleep. We already know we can leave any time we want with space thrusters."

Kibi looked daggers at him. "That's easy for *you* to say. Some of us can *feel* in our bones that we're under a big pile of junk, even though we can't see it."

"Sorry," Boro mumbled.

Everyone remained silent for a minute. Mati had her eyes closed as Rini continued massaging her shoulders.

Ilika poked at a knowledge pad. "I think you need to teach Manessa how to dance."

Mati turned and glared at him. "How can a crippled slave teach a deep-space . . ." Their eyes met and suddenly her mouth opened.

"What?" Sata asked.

"What!" Kibi demanded.

"He's right," Mati said. "It's like a tangled ball of string. We've been using brute force. We have to untangle it, instead."

Rini smiled down at his dear friend.

"Boro!" Mati said in her flight-command voice, grabbing her crutch and standing up, "I want anti-mass one and maneuvering thrusters!"

Seconds later they were all at their stations. The pilot raised her flight control. "This could get a little bumpy. I want straps and seven-eighths inertia canceling."

Kibi nodded. "Whatever she wants, Boro."

"Warming up!"

Everyone pulled down their inertia straps.

"Anti-mass, maneuvering, seven-eighths canceling, all green."

Kibi looked around. "Sata?"

"Chart is still good, flight recorder on."

"Rini?"

"Sensors ready, as soon as there's something to see."

"Ilika?"

"The Manessa Kwi is ready for flight."

"Mati," the acting commander said, "you have flight command."

Mati started the process slowly, nudging the ship back and forth, getting a feel for how the metal web around her reacted.

"I'm getting seasick!" Sata moaned.

"Sorry," Mati said without looking at her friend. "I need to *feel* what the ship is doing."

Ilika delivered a bowl to Sata just as Mati began swinging the ship.

"Pressure is easing up on the hull!" Rini announced happily.

Kibi began to breath deeply.

"Boro," Mati began, "I don't want anti-mass, I want *more* mass. The way out is *under* this slimy thing."

"Can do. It's for underwater."

"Give me a little so I can see what it feels like."

Just then Sata gave up and lost her crackers.

"Sorry, Sata," the pilot said.

"It's okay, as long as I get to see the stars again."

The pilot concentrated for a few more seconds. "More mass, Boro."

"You've got it."

Ilika brought Sata a towel, holding onto things as he moved about the ship.

"Our cage is getting bigger!" Rini called out.

"I have an idea," Mati said. A moment later the ship began spinning slowly while still wobbling. Suddenly all the dirt and rock covering the visual sensors fell away.

"Whoopee!" Rini cheered.

Ilika grinned from the steward's station.

"Okay," Mati began, "I think we're getting somewhere. I want all maneuvering thrusters. Don't hold anything back, Boro."

"Okay, you've got the works."

"Let's see what happens if I take a swing at it right about . . . here."

The Manessa Kwi dove for a point in the tangle of metal where most of the beams were just hanging loosely. The impact make the ship quiver as beams gave up and bent away, or fell to the ground. Several more still blocked the way.

Mati didn't apply any more force, but began rocking and spinning the ship again, nudging at the remaining metal.

Without warning, Boro tucked his head between his knees and lost his last meal onto the floor. Rini was just a few moments behind.

"Sorry," both muttered.

Mati didn't let up her concentration. For another half minute, she tickled the few metal beams between the ship and freedom, then started the ship spinning. "Anti-mass one, Boro."

"Ready," he said, touching controls with one hand, holding a towel with the other.

As the Manessa Kwi began to float, Mati used all her maneuvering thrusters to slowly coax the spinning ship into the weakest point of the trap. The metal fingers slid around them on both sides until nothing stood between the little ship and the freedom of the debris-littered streets.

Kibi, Sata, Rini, and Boro all began cheering. Ilika grinned happily.

Mati paid absolutely no attention until she had the ship a hundred meters above the tallest metal ruins of the dead city.

* * *

A net, a Chinese finger trap, a tangled ball of string . . . none of these respond well to brute force because many of their parts are interconnected. A force that enlarges one part tends to shrink another part.

Why didn't Ilika or Kibi let people go off duty when they got sick?

Chapter 9: The Slow Way

"Is there anywhere ... nice ... on this planet?" Kibi asked from the command chair. "Somewhere we can relax?"

Sata began selecting charts. "The poles are a little cooler. No cities or people."

"Make a simple flight plan, Sata, to somewhere . . . anywhere."

The navigator soon passed the new flight plan to the pilot. "Your highest elevation is two thousand meters."

Mati took a slow, deep breath, then shivered for a moment. "Boro, ion three. Going up to six thousand."

Boro shook his head to clear the cobwebs before reaching for his console.

Ilika watched his crew deal with the lingering stress, and smiled to himself.

A few minutes later, with the yellow vapors much thinner at the south pole of the planet, Mati was able to use her visual display to lower the ship onto flat, rocky ground.

Rini selected atmospheric tests. "Sorry everyone, it's cooler, but we still can't breath it."

Kibi turned around and looked at Ilika. "NOW will you take back command of your ship? *Please?*"

Ilika smiled and nodded.

*

For the next hour, Kibi selected music and dreamily swayed in the space between her station and the galley, where Ilika worked. He often glanced at his beautiful lover and smiled.

Both Boro and Rini were on their hands and knees, under their consoles, with cleaning supplies.

Eventually Ilika brought cups of cold, sweet tea to the table. Kibi sat down with him.

He looked into her dark eyes. "I'm glad you're not . . . feeling any desire to open the hatch and run outside."

She frowned. “In that hot, yellow air? Actually . . .” She looked around to see who was on the upper deck. “I’ve been watching Mati. I think getting us out of that trap made her feel better about her mistake, but she’s really looking forward to Satamia Star Station. My knee almost hurts in sympathy when I see the longing on her face.”

“It’s been a heavy burden for her.”

“And I think Sata felt some of her old fear today.”

“A bunch,” Sata said, stepping out of the toilet room, drying her hair. “But I could see how bad Mati felt about what happened.” The navigator sat down beside her captain and reached for a cup of tea.

“I was really proud of both of you,” Ilika said.

“Both of . . . who?” Mati asked, appearing in the lift with wet hair.

“You and Sata,” Kibi informed.

Ilika looked into the sparkling eyes of his handicapped pilot. “You were both great.”

“I knew if I didn’t get us out of there, I’d feel like . . . like a crippled slave!”

Everyone at the table laughed.

“Today you were able to work out your feelings by getting us out of that little trap,” Ilika said. “At times in the future, you won’t be able to do that. You’ll just have to relax and let others help.”

“I know,” Mati said. “But it sure felt good to clean up my own mess!”

Boro and Rini both looked up from their cleaning work and smiled.

*

That evening, the five new crew members selected a video about ships in difficult situations, and how the crews overcame problems, and their own fears, to bring everyone safely home.

At first Ilika was surprised by their choice. Then he began to understand as he watched from the back of the passenger area and saw them beaming with pride any time a situation was similar to one they had experienced. He also observed them paying close attention when the danger was completely new to them.

*

After a good night’s sleep and a hearty breakfast, the crew of the Manessa Kwi looked at their captain to know the next phase of their journey.

Ilika took the last swallow of his beverage, then pulled a knowledge pad close. “We’ve already explored Sonmatia Three . . .”

Everyone chuckled.

“The journey from here to the fourth planet will be slow, with lots of time for lessons along the way.” He could see Mati frown slightly. “We will review a number of topics, bring Boro and Kibi up to speed on some mathematics, and study words and customs we’ll need at the star station.”

Mati’s frown changed to a grin.

“The next leg of our journey will mostly fall to Sata and Boro as navigator and engineer, although I want all of you to understand the basics after they work out the details.” He tapped at the knowledge pad, and a diagram appeared on the big screen.

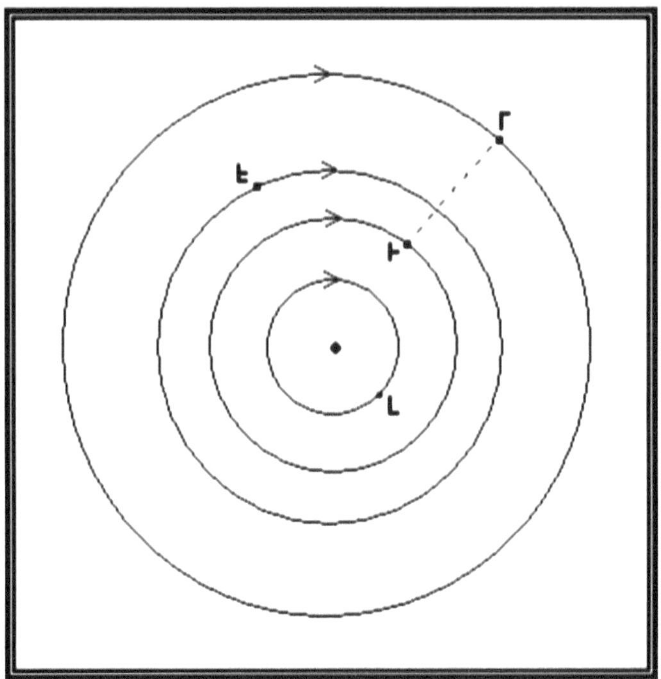

"Here are the current positions of the inner planets. Our location and our destination happen to be almost perfectly lined up. You might think that's a good thing. We'll see. Sata and Boro, you know how to use Manessa's orbit and transit simulation tools. Please calculate how much space thruster fuel we need for a direct route, orbit to orbit, no anti-mass, no ion drive."

Boro thought for a moment. "Depends on how fast you want to go."

"Start with minimum fuel usage."

Boro nodded. He and Sata headed toward her station, knowledge pads in hand.

*

Ilika began cooking in the galley, and the other crew members relaxed at the table. At first the sounds from the bridge were all calm and friendly. They heard Manessa's voice answering questions, and Sata or Boro chuckling with embarrassment.

As the first hour passed and the second began, the words and sounds from the front of the ship became more and more frustrated, sometimes almost angry. Kibi frowned as she fetched a game and sat down with Mati. Rini glanced at the bridge, didn't see any blood, so he stepped into the galley to help Ilika.

Near the end of the second hour, with the aroma of sweet biscuits filling the ship, those at the table became aware that no sound whatsoever was coming from the navigator's station. They looked and saw Boro and Sata standing side by side, holding hands and gazing at the display screen.

A few minutes later the navigator and engineer appeared at the table, looking happy but humble. Rini came out of the galley with a plate of sweet biscuits, and Ilika followed with cups of tea.

"I'm sure Ilika knew this was going to happen," Boro said with a half-suppressed grin.

"I'm not sure what you mean, Boro," the captain said, hiding his expression behind his cup.

"How did you put it, Sata?"

"There's no such thing as a straight line in space."

Ilika smiled. "Share with us what you learned."

Sata touched some keys on her knowledge pad. "Um, big screen, Kibi?"

The steward reached over to her console.

"Thanks."

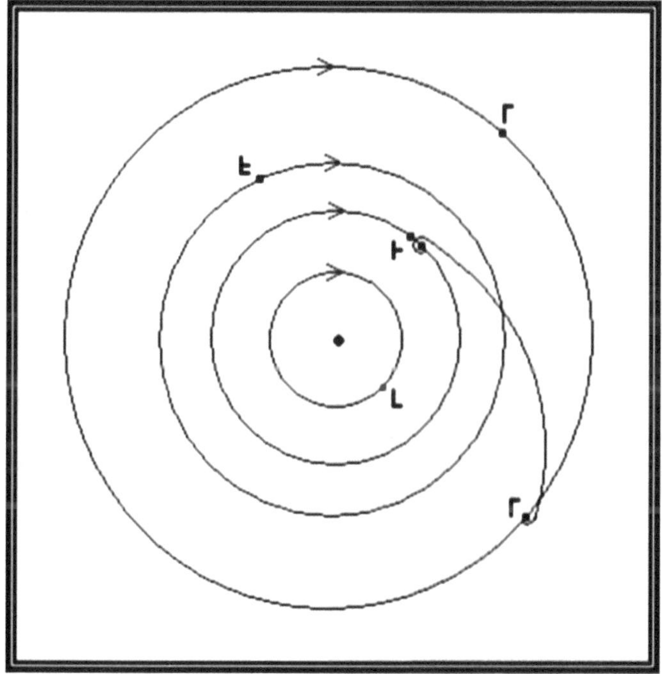

"First," Boro began, "Manessa reminded us that when we got free of this planet's gravity, it would be a little farther along in it's orbit of the sun. Okay, we could see that."

Sata nodded. "Then we tried to calculate flight path and time to that place where the fourth planet was supposed to be, and Manessa kept asking us why we would use that place as a navigation point."

Boro stepped in. "Manessa finally realized what was wrong when we said we wanted to go into orbit there. If a deep-space response ship could laugh, Manessa would have laughed."

Kibi chuckled, and everyone else was grinning.

Sata picked up the story. "Then Manessa explained that by the time we got there, the fourth planet wouldn't be there any more. In fact, by the time we could catch up with it, it would be almost a quarter of the way around the sun!"

"That means . . ." Rini started to say.

Sata put a finger to her lips.

"As Rini guessed," Boro continued, "that means that from here to the fourth planet, with minimum fuel burn, would take about half a year."

Mati turned white. "Half a year!"

"Don't worry," Ilika jumped in. "We won't be using that plan. It was just for learning purposes."

The pilot struggled to regain her composure.

"So . . ." Sata began again, "we learned that in space everything is always moving, nothing is as simple as we'd like it to be, and there's no such thing as a straight line."

"The funniest thing of all," Boro added, "is that Sonmatia Two will get to that part of the solar system way faster than we would!"

Ilika smiled and reached for a knowledge pad. "Well done, both of you, and thank you for sharing all your insights. Now let's see if we can whittle down that transit time. It just so happens that we have something handy that's a lot better than thruster fuel. We have a planet that's going our way."

Sata looked puzzled. "But if we just stayed on Sonmatia Two, we'd still have a big gap between the two orbits."

"I'm not thinking of this planet," Ilika replied. "I'm thinking of Sonmatia Three, your birthplace."

Expressions around the table varied from Rini's joy at anything that might be proposed, to Mati's dread at the slightest delay. No one, however, showed any sign of understanding what their captain could possibly be talking about.

Ilika sent another diagram to the big screen over the steward's station.

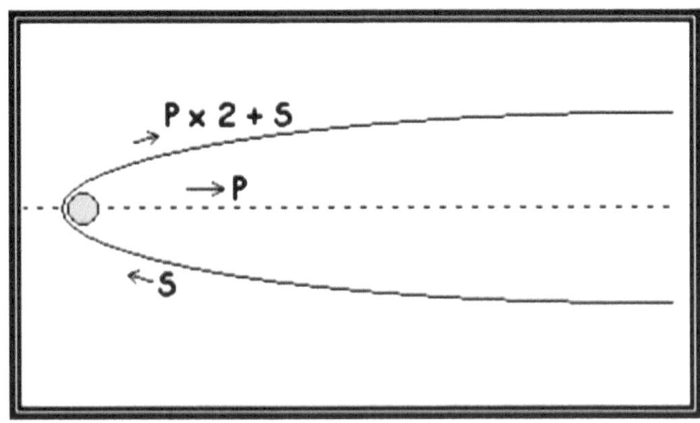

"If a ship, at speed S, swings around a planet orbiting the sun at speed P, the ship will add twice the speed of the planet to its own."

Boro sat with his mouth open. "Uh . . . that could really help."

Ilika nodded. "It's called planetary freeloading. All civilizations, who survive long enough to get into space, use it to get around their solar systems. By the way, how much fuel did your first plan use?"

Boro grabbed his knowledge pad. "Twelve point three kilograms, and that includes slowing down to enter orbit at Sonmatia Four."

"Use the same amount. With planetary freeloading off the third planet, you'll get a lot more speed."

Boro grinned at Sata, then they both drained their tea and headed for the bridge.

✷

When Kibi saw that Mati and Rini were happily engrossed in a game, and Ilika was tending something in the galley, she wandered down to the lower deck.

After tossing some dirty clothes into the laundry machine, she stood gazing around at all the cabinets in the utility room, each one labeled with its contents. She smiled, remembering the first time she had stared at the strange writing, the language of Nebador, unable to read a word.

Now she could read the language quite well, was familiar with the contents of most of the cabinets, and responsible for them all. She opened several and saw things that would need restocking at Satamia Star Station.

Another cabinet caught her eye, *Sample and Display Containers*. Inside, she found the sample containers they had already used, lined with the same material as Manessa's hull and able to hold just about anything without harm to the sample or crew. She smiled, seeing that Ilika had already placed the stardust grains, and the rock from the daylight side, in a clear display container. Suddenly her eyes lit up with a memory, and she dashed to her cabin.

Deep in her old canvas pack, not used since the day Buna, Misa, Neti, Toli, and Tera walked down the trail and out of her life, she found what she remembered, a pine cone from the world of her birth, almost completely intact.

With mounting strips from another cabinet, she soon had a dozen display containers attached to the wall of the lower deck, just below the large display screen where the crew sometimes watched videos. The first held the pine cone, the second their samples from Sonmatia One, and the rest were empty. As she stepped into the lift to rejoin her friends, she wondered what the others would eventually contain.

✷

"Amazing!" Boro said as he and Sata, glowing with pride, returned to the table less than an hour after going off to create a new flight plan using planetary freeloading. "I never would have guessed the best way to get somewhere was to go *backwards*."

Sata touched some controls on the steward's console and a new diagram appeared.

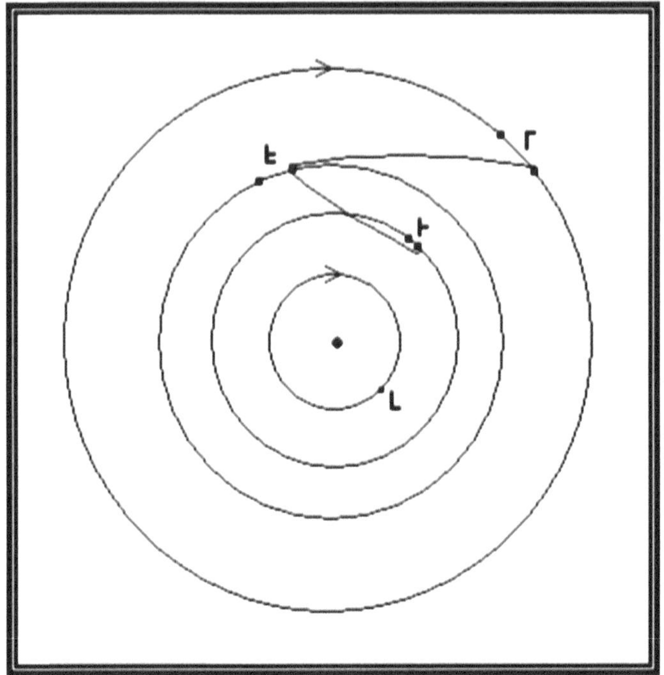

"Manessa says we should pass our planet at an altitude of fifty kilometers," the navigator explained. "That's almost close enough to pick berries in the mountains!"

Ilika smiled and nodded. "The closer you go, the more speed you pick up, as long as you don't get too much air friction."

"Or run into the mountains!" Mati added with wide eyes.

Everyone laughed, some a little nervously.

"So . . ." Ilika began after glancing at his handicapped pilot, "how long?"

"Just thirty days!" Boro answered, looking back and forth from captain to pilot. "That's . . . better . . . isn't it?"

Ilika watched as Mati took a deep breath, then cracked a little smile. "Yeah."

"Actually, we can do another trick," Ilika announced.

Mati's eyes widened with curiosity.

"Sata, your twelve point three kilograms of thruster fuel included both departure from this planet and orbit entry at the destination, right?"

"Of course. And most of it went to slowing down at Sonmatia Four."

"What would happen if you could use all of it for departure?"

"We could go *really* fast! But how? Are you going to let us use anti-mass at the fourth planet?"

"No. But that planet has an atmosphere. What happens if you go into orbit within an atmosphere?"

Both Sata and Boro were silent for half a minute, but the others could almost see the gears turning. A smile began to grow on Boro's face. "We'd . . . slow down from the friction."

"It's called atmospheric braking," Ilika explained. "Primitive space-faring civilizations rarely use it because it's so hard to build ships that can take the heat. Manessa's hull, as you know . . ."

"Can take just about anything!" Sata finished the thought.

Ilika smiled. "Manessa will show you how to calculate the braking orbits so you have just enough momentum left to get up to a stable orbit outside the atmosphere."

Boro and Sata looked at each other, grabbed knowledge pads, and headed for the navigator's station.

✷

As Mati descended in the lift, crutch under her arm, she wondered how much less than thirty days the flight would take with atmospheric braking. When she arrived alone on the lower deck, she reminded herself that even thirty, in base eight, was less than the thirty she used to know, a whole six days less.

She immediately spotted the new display containers on the wall under the large screen. Smiling, she gazed at the pine cone with fond memories, then entered her cabin.

After searching Buna's old rucksack and adding two dried maple seeds to the first display container, she looked at the third container, still empty. Suddenly a resolute expression came to her, and she hobbled toward the lift.

✷

A delicious savory aroma was coming from the galley when Boro and Sata plopped down at the big table and looked at Mati. "Eleven days!" they both said at once.

Mati grinned with thankfulness.

✷ ✷ ✷

All pilots and other flight crew members are trained to do their jobs under stress. The needs of the ship rarely wait for everyone to be rested with full bellies and empty bladders. Stressful situations usually pile up at certain times (take-off, navigation points, and landing) with long stretches of boredom in between. My airplane flight trainer liked to open all the doors and windows, and scream, during take-off.

Why was Mati pushing herself to be the best possible pilot she could be?

It is not literally true that there is no such thing as a straight line in space. However, the presence of gravity masses (stars, planets, etc.) cause space to act as if it is "warped" by those gravity masses. ("Warped" means misshapen, and has nothing to do with Star Trek's "warp drive.") Therefore, a straight line would be nearly useless, and a space navigator would most often deal with ellipses and parabolas.

Genuine laughter and other emotional expressions require self-reflection, and Manessa does not have that ability because she is not sapient. Most people have noticed how irritating computers are that are programmed to simulate some kind of emotion.

Why are the planets in a solar system always moving?

Planetary freeloading is also sometimes called "gravity assist," and has been used by our unmanned spacecraft several times. We barely made it to the Moon (1969-75) using thrust, and had to break the spacecrafts into six or seven parts to do it, leaving junk behind at every step. Thrust alone can get us no farther.

Why is "30" in base eight less than "30" in base ten?

Chapter 10: Presence of Mind and Memory

"Rini owes me an orbital excursion," Ilika said as they were finishing a tasty stew with a golden-brown biscuit crust.

Rini grinned. "I'm ready. I've been going over it in my head, remembering all the things I should have paid attention to . . . and didn't."

"Could you . . . um . . . do me a favor?" Mati asked with hesitation, looking at Rini.

"Anything," the freckled boy said with sparkling eyes. "After accidentally marrying the wrong girl . . ."

Mati turned bright red, and everyone else grinned.

"Actually . . ." she began, trying to find her voice, "it really is an excursion I want, back near a certain building that I . . . sort of . . . bumped into."

Ilika smiled with understanding. "Even though it's not the vacuum of space there, you can use the same suit, Rini, and then we'll go directly into orbit."

✷

When they reentered the dead city, Mati kept a sharp eye on all her visual displays, especially to the rear. She set the ship down lightly not far from the collapsed building that had entrapped them.

Rini stepped through the airlock with a sample container, kept an eye on the metal skeletons looming above, and only went a few meters before he found a little piece of corroded metal, a small shard of broken glass, and a chunk of flat, smooth building stone. He looked around one last time, thought he heard the groan of twisting metal, and quickly returned to the ship.

Mati had the Manessa Kwi above the ghostly towers even before Rini could cycle the airlock.

✷

Once they arrived in high orbit, everyone went down to the lower deck to see the new display.

"I know it's ugly stuff," Mati said, pointing at the collection of metal, glass, and stone from the dead city, "but it's part of our story, our new story, just us six, the crew of the Manessa Kwi."

The others nodded, then disappeared into their cabins for a few minutes. Soon the pine cone and maple seeds in the first container were joined by a feather, a small bone, a pretty rock, and a small dried mushroom.

✷

Rini floated through the airless void high above Sonmatia Two. This time, he had a plan. He set his bracelet to chime every minute. At each chime, he went down his checklist – air, thruster fuel, location, orientation, health status, mission status. It only took a few seconds, leaving him plenty of time for work or sightseeing.

On this occasion, he had no work to do. Ilika wanted him to practice presence of mind when he was most tempted to drift into an altered state of consciousness.

In one direction the sun blazed in a velvety black sky. The cloudy yellow planet turned slowly beneath him, causing him to wonder for a moment why he wasn't falling. Then he remembered that he was falling, just not straight down. He looked beyond the planet, and the stars seemed so close he could almost reach out and touch them.

Rini's minute-chime sounded, and his mind reluctantly returned from the stars. He took a few seconds to go through his checklist. "Sata, I'm down to five-eighths fuel, so I'm starting back."

"Great. I think Boro's making tea, and Manessa says a good orbital departure window is in about an hour."

Rini smiled and pointed himself back toward the little golden sphere orbiting not far away.

✷

Sata stayed at her station while Rini made his way back to the ship. She almost jumped when her communications display came to life with the image of the feathered navigator on the other ship. Sata smiled and touched a symbol.

"Hello, Sata, I noticed you were back in orbit, bok. Did you enjoy your visit to this sad little planet?"

"Hi, Drim-na. Well . . . we were in one of those old cities, and a building fell on us."

"Bok! Everyone okay?"

"Yeah, our pilot Mati is really good, and she got us out."

"Good. Our diplomats report that the people down here are looking at pictures of the planet we could relocate them to, bok, and are thinking about it."

"We're about to leave for Sonmatia Four, thrusters only."

"That will be slow and boring, bok."

"We have lots of things to study before we get to Satamia Star Station."

"The Tirilana Kril will be back there in a few days, bok, so maybe I will see you, and show you my favorite eating place."

Sata was silent for a moment. "That would be fun, Drim-na. You're the first friend I'm making who's not . . . on my ship. Rini's coming in the airlock, so I should get ready."

"Be well, Sata. Tirilana Kril closing, bok."

"Um . . . Manessa Kwi closing."

When the screen went dark, Sata turned around with a funny look on her face. "Ilika, what do Nebador birds eat?"

* * *

Why was Rini, in a space suit, able to hear the groan of twisting metal when he was out collecting souvenirs?

Rini is using a "personal checklist" that any pilot will recognize. One such checklist on my piloting knee board spells "ENROUTE" and lists Environment, Navigation, Radio, Obstacles, Up/down altitude, Time, and Eyes scanning. For a while during the 20th century, people dreamed of having a flying machine of some kind in every garage. We have let go of that dream, as it does not appear we can ever make piloting in a three-dimensional space easy and safe enough for most people.

While doing his orbit excursion, if Rini was falling, but not "straight down," what direction was he falling?

Why would it be natural for Rini to watch his fuel level in "eighths"?

How is the "relocation" that Drrrim-na talked about different from most "relocations" that have occurred in our history (such as when native Americans were "relocated" to reservations)?

By talking to another navigator who is a bird, and being offered to eat with that navigator at the star station, what prejudices might Sata be experiencing?

Chapter 11: Interplanetary Travel

"This kind of flight plan," Ilika explained from the command chair after everyone had completed basic pre-flight preparations, "is not possible manually. As Mati can see on her screen, all the timings are in thousandths of a second. Even so, Manessa will need to make further adjustments as we approach your home planet for freeloading, and the fourth planet for braking."

"So we just have to . . . trust Manessa?" Mati asked with a slightly worried look.

"Trust with knowledge. Sata and Boro have simulated the entire flight. With time, you'll be able to do that too, Mati. Manessa's contribution is the split-second timing, not the wisdom necessary to oversee the process. We're all on duty during the freeloading pass, and during braking orbits. Someone will be at or near the watch station for the next eleven days."

Rini sighed, but his eyes sparkled with a hint of pride.

"Orbital departure in four minutes," Sata announced.

"Even though you will not be handling the controls directly," Ilika continued, "you are still the pilot, Mati. You must approve each step before Manessa can carry it out. The first step is our orbital departure burn, then you have six days before the next step. But keep in mind that if you don't approve any part of the plan before its scheduled time, the entire plan is canceled."

"That would be terrible!" Boro complained.

"Remember, Boro, this is training. I'm going to do little things to force you and Sata to modify the plan at least once."

Boro moaned under his breath.

Sata rolled her eyes. "One minute."

Mati grinned, turned to her console, and approved the departure burn. "Up to three gravities of acceleration," she said, studying a graph on her screen. "We'll need inertia straps for a few minutes."

Everyone secured their straps.

"Watch station update?" Ilika requested.

"Nothing on the screen. Solar wind is on channel four, nothing unusual.

"Eight seconds," Sata said.

Remembering the space thruster burn that had saved them from falling into the sun, Boro, Sata, and Kibi gripped their chairs with white knuckles. As soon as the gentle departure burn was complete, they looked around sheepishly, hoping no one had noticed.

✷

For the next few hours, everyone got comfortable with the new routine. Sata disappeared into the galley, and Kibi sat down with Mati to start a list of videos they wanted to watch during the slow transit to Sonmatia Four. Boro went down to the lower deck, one of his strange tools with blinking lights in hand.

Rini found himself alone on the bridge, the only crew member on-duty, so he selected one of the advanced lessons about his station and got comfortable in his chair. Most of his screen, however, contained the displays and graphs he had to keep an eye on, everything from magnetic fields to wandering chunks of rock and ice.

Ilika had his nose in a knowledge pad, pondering all the things he had to teach his crew before they arrived at Satamia Star Station. He wore a slight smile, remembering his own interplanetary training at age eleven.

Kibi and Mati wandered the ship, getting ideas from everyone about videos. Boro was on his back in the engineering ring, adjusting a mysterious glowing machine, when he asked for a video about old sea-going ships, the kind they once imagined Ilika having. Sata was spicing and tasting her soup when she requested a video about the birds in the Nebador Services.

Back at the big table in the passenger area, Ilika transferred a list of about a dozen videos from his knowledge pad to Kibi's. She and Mati looked at each other with knowing smiles — they were all about star stations.

✷

The following morning, Ilika explained that a "day" on a ship in space was completely artificial, and always subject to change. If the crew felt plenty of energy, the steward could add a few hours. If they were exhausted from some trying mission, hours could just as easily be removed.

Kibi smiled for a moment, then took on a more serious look. "What do I do if some people have extra energy, but others are tired and want to go to bed?"

Ilika shrugged. "Life is full of tough choices. Of course, absolute Nebador time is the same everywhere in the local universe. Sometimes we'll have important things to do in the middle of our night."

Kibi yawned, but had a twinkle in her eyes.

After dishes were done, the captain began a series of advanced language lessons that focused on words needed at star stations. Every crew member received a list tailored to their jobs. Approach and docking terminology went to Sata and Mati. Rini and Boro learned the names of instruments and tools only available at a star station. Kibi received a short list about restocking supplies, and a much longer list related to passengers.

With plenty of breaks for meals, videos, and just plain fun, for the next two ship-days Ilika engaged each student in conversations when they least expected it, always emphasizing the new words they were supposed to know.

Rini noticed that something was bugging Kibi. Whenever she was not distracted by a tasty meal, an interesting video, or an intense lesson, she sat gazing at the walls and ceiling with a slight frown.

✷

With many new words at their fingertips, Ilika began to introduce them to the procedures and customs of star stations.

Rini would locate the artificial world, in its own orbit around a star. Sata would begin communicating with the station long before they could see it. Mati would use an assigned approach path to come to a complete stop near the station, then follow color-coded flight corridors both outside and inside. Manessa had simulations for each of them.

Boro, as always, was the crew member who would need to speak the least, but whose services would be absolutely essential. Kibi would have little to do until they arrived at the assigned space dock. At that point, Ilika assured her, she would wish for a twin sister.

Ilika shared one last thought. "As a deep-space response ship, we have an additional burden. We are the most maneuverable and flexible ship in space, so we have the lowest priority. If there is ever an overload, conflict, or emergency, we will be the ones to wait, move out of the way, or be called in to help."

Several crew members went off to try their simulations, and Boro entered the galley to work on the next meal. Ilika noticed Kibi staring at the main hatch for a long time.

✷

The following day, their fifth in space since leaving the second planet, everyone gathered for meals and videos, then went their separate ways for simulations and study. Ilika carefully watched all his crew members, looking for signs of cabin fever.

Boro seemed most happy spending time alone in the engineering ring, getting more familiar with all his engines. Ilika would occasionally wander through, and hear his student engineer asking the ship question after question about the pros and cons of the different fuels, or the difference between the electrical and magnetic fields of the anti-mass drive.

Sata liked to rerun the simulations of the freeloading pass and the braking orbits. She would try to guess what Ilika might do to make the trip to Sonmatia Four more challenging. None of her fellow crew members, nor the ship itself, cared to speculate.

Mati wasn't too concerned about the trip to Sonmatia Four, but her eyes sparkled every time she simulated the approach and docking at Satamia Star Station. She knew from the videos that student pilots could request automatic guidance through the color-coded maze, and if their piloting looked even a little dangerous, the station controller would require it. She intended to go from the outer system marker to space dock without giving them any reason to remember she was a student.

Rini discovered a new passion when he was on-duty at his station and not studying. While Sata's star charts were technical and not very pretty, Manessa also had countless pictures of planets, star clusters, nebulas, galaxies, and even stranger things Rini didn't yet understand. He would gaze at each one for a minute or more, and imagine himself flying among them like a creature of light who had no need of wings or a space suit.

Kibi dutifully studied her word lists and watched the videos that showed how busy a steward could be when passengers departed, supplies needed restocking, and new passengers came on board, sometimes all in just a few hours. She genuinely looked forward to those tasks, but right now she couldn't help but glance at the walls and ceiling every few minutes.

At one point late in the day, when Ilika was on the bridge talking to Mati, Kibi slipped away from her station, down the lift, and into the utility room. "Manessa, it seems to me the walls of the ship are getting closer, and the ceiling lower. I don't really understand all the stuff about dimensional shifting that lets the inside of the ship be a different size and shape from the outside, but is there any possibility the ship's getting smaller on the inside?"

"No, Kibi, the inside of the ship is always the exact same size and shape."

* * *

Working with a non-sapient ship like the Manessa Kwi is similar to working with a simple animal or machine. I can "trust" a wasp to be a wasp, to sting me if I bother its nest, to watch me if I'm between 1 and 6 feet away, and to ignore me otherwise. (Don't forget that each kind of wasp is different.) I cannot "trust" a wasp to do what I think it should do, or what I sweetly ask it to do. Working near wasps requires ME to be the one who understands them and adjusts my behavior. In a similar way, some of my computer applications have "bugs," and I have to "work around" them. Those computer bugs won't "heal" themselves with time, nor go away if I pound on the keyboard. One of the tasks of all sapient (understanding, self-reflective, soul-growing, wisdom-capable) creatures is to be the ones who truly *understand* and take into account the limitations of every object, machine, and simple creature they encounter.

Our minds and bodies are very used to a daily cycle of sleep and activities. This is especially true for us because we are one of many creatures who cannot defend themselves very well at night, so we like to find a safe "cave," or climb a tree, and wait for morning light. Large grazing animals like cattle can't use caves or trees, so they rarely sleep, and can defend themselves almost as well at night as during the day.

Scientists have used caves to see if we naturally stick with a 24-hour day when we have no way of knowing if it is day or night. The people in the experiment shifted to a 25-hour day. This implies that a day may have been longer in the past.

What would happen if Kibi abused the power she had, as steward, to set the length of their ship-day?

The same priority rules apply in aviation on Earth. The most flexible aircraft, helicopters, have lowest priority because they can most easily move out of the way, wait, or land just about anywhere. Blimps and balloons have first priority because they are the least flexible.

Why do you think Kibi experienced "cabin fever" but Sata did not?

Chapter 12: Knowledge

The following morning held an air of excitement, even though the approach adjustments for Sonmatia Three wouldn't happen until that evening. Rini and Sata made fried cakes with a sweet syrup on top, and Boro invited them all to see the video he chose.

The story began on an island that could have been Atorura. Brave men in hollowed-out logs dared to venture beyond the edge of the reef into the fury of the open ocean. Usually they returned to tell of other islands and good fishing waters, but sometimes they were never seen again.

Larger ships with a sail and a dozen or more rowers crept between mist-enshrouded islands seeking treasures and fertile lands. Those with crude compasses most often returned through the mists. Others left their broken hulls on the rocky beaches.

Huge wooden ships, driven by many sails, had crews of twenty or thirty, with two decks above the main deck, and three cargo decks below. A watchman, perched in a tiny basket on the tallest mast, scanned the horizon with a simple spy glass. Everyone smiled at Rini.

Enormous steel ships easily sliced through the waves as passengers lounged around swimming pools, or ate fine food in ornate dining rooms. Huge propellers churned the water as the engineer sat at a control panel with many lights and switches. Everyone looked at Boro, who instantly turned red.

*

"I want to be honest with you," Kibi said to Ilika as they sat side by side in the passenger area about mid-afternoon. Boro was in the galley, and everyone else was busy with simulations.

Ilika leaned forward and kissed her lightly. "I'm all ears."

Kibi grinned for a moment. "My fear of . . . you know, tight spaces . . . is eating at me. The ship seems to be getting smaller every day."

"And we're still more than three days from Sonmatia Four . . ."

"Yeah, I know. I just wish I could go outside, take a walk or something."

"You can."

Kibi frowned with disbelief. "Really? But I thought the ship was going fast . . ."

"It is. So are you. If you were going at different speeds, you'd be a lump of goo on the wall."

Kibi smiled.

"The only problem is, you can't really go on a walk, you'll have to crawl because the repulsion field is only a meter outside the hull."

"I'll take it! Maybe it'll help me relax."

"We won't do slow trips like this very often, but it's just part of the basics that everyone needs to learn."

Kibi nodded with a smile and strode to the lift.

✷

"You in your suit, Kibi?" Sata asked from her station.

"Yeah, just doing my checklist. Pressure, air, cooling, thruster fuel . . . even though I won't need it. Okay, I'm in the airlock."

"The weather's nice," Rini said from his console, "just a gentle solar breeze. Your limit for x-ray exposure is four hours, but we'll be getting ready for the approach adjustments before then."

"Don't worry," Kibi said through her suit intercom as she opened the outer hatch, "I'll be in much sooner. What happens if I touch the repulsion field?"

"You can't," Ilika said. "It'll repel you, feels about like the detention cell door."

Kibi remembered Timod Gor. "Safety line attached. See you guys in an hour or so."

✷

Rini kept half an eye on Kibi with his visual sensors as she crawled around the hull of the Manessa Kwi, currently a long cylinder tapered to a point at both ends. She rolled onto her back and looked up at the stars, then chuckled when she tried to touch the repulsion field, but couldn't.

Sata left the intercom open and went back to studying the navigation beacons around star stations.

Mati lowered herself into a seat at the big table and waved to Boro in the galley. "What're you making?"

"I'm trying that stew with biscuit crust, like Ilika made."

Suddenly an alarm sounded and Rini's console lit up with flashing red symbols. His eyes were wide as he quickly scanned his graphs. "X-ray spike! A huge solar flare! It's still rising!"

Boro dropped what he was doing and leapt out of the galley, saw that Ilika was not on the upper deck, and remembered that Kibi was outside. "Manessa, maneuvering thrusters! Mati, roll the ship! Get Kibi in the shadow!"

Boro grabbed Mati as she stood up and quickly walked her down to the pilot's station.

Sata took a deep breath. "Kibi, grab the hull and stay right where you are. We've got an x-ray spike and we're rotating you into the shadow of the ship."

"Okay," Kibi's voice said. "I don't see anything. Oh, yeah, I forgot – you can't see x-rays. I'm almost in the shadow . . . there, that's about right. Hey, it's dark over here!"

Everyone on the bridge laughed nervously.

Ilika appeared in the lift and Boro quickly filled him in.

"Good work, everyone."

"Oh, no!" Rini yelled.

"What?" Ilika demanded, stepping that way.

"Asteroid shower from deeper in the system, impact in twenty seconds."

"Anything big?"

"No, just the grains of dust and sand we don't track. The repulsion field will protect Kibi, won't it?"

Everyone on the bridge looked at Ilika with worried eyes.

"Yes." Ilika stepped to the command chair and touched a symbol. "Kibi, in a few seconds you're going to see . . ."

His words were cut off by her first scream, but many screams followed as each tiny asteroid impacted the ship's repulsion field with a bright flash of light.

"Kibi, you're in no danger, just hold on and try not to look at them!" Ilika couldn't tell if Kibi heard him, as her screams and deep sobs were nearly continuous. "Rini, how's the x-ray storm progressing?"

"Um . . . worse than before."

"Kibi! Can you hear me?" Ilika asked loudly and firmly.

In between shrieks and whimpers, ". . . yeah . . ." was faintly heard.

"Kibi, listen! I want you to follow your safety line to the airlock. We'll rotate the ship as you go to keep you in the shadow. Do you understand?"

Mati's fingers were poised on her flight control, and her eyes glued to the visual display of her friend cowering in terror as thousands of asteroids burst into light just above her.

". . . yeah . . . I'll try . . ." they finally heard their steward say in a tiny, frightened voice.

Several tense minutes passed with no sign of either storm letting up. Finally Mati reported that Kibi was making some progress, and she was rotating the ship to match.

"You're doing well, Kibi," Ilika said. "You're in no danger, so take your time."

Kibi, screaming less but still crying, managed to choke out, ". . . hard to see safety line . . . so dark . . . asteroids don't help much . . ."

"I know, but the x-ray level is still high. Just go by feel."

"She's almost there," Mati said.

"Boro, you're in command here," Ilika said and dashed for the lift.

✷

Tiny asteroids continued to sparkle when they hit the repulsion field as Kibi tumbled head first into the airlock, still crying. She screamed when she hit the floor, by which time Ilika had the outer door closed and the little room pressurizing. A moment later he was helping her remove the suit.

Drenched in sweat, she remained in his arms for several long minutes, crying with her eyes tightly closed, but still seeing clearly the countless flashes of light.

Slowly he guided her into the lift and up to the table, where Sata poured cups of tea. Rini remained on-duty at his station while everyone said comforting things to Kibi, and she slowly opened her eyes, ceased sobbing, and clutched her tea with shaking hands.

For the next half hour, while Kibi slowly collected herself, the others asked Ilika what they could have done differently.

Ilika reminded them that x-rays traveled at the speed of light, so prediction was not possible, and the tiny asteroids were not detectable until they were very close. He couldn't find any flaws in their response to the emergency.

Once the discussion was over, Kibi breathed a deep sigh. "I'd like to . . . get a bath and take a long nap."

Her fellow crew members smiled with understanding.

Ilika looked into her eyes. "Sorry, not right now."

She frowned.

"You saw something you've never seen before, and you were frightened. We understand. But you were in no danger, and no harm was done. So even though you have no important duties at the navigation point coming up, everyone needs to understand the process. And more importantly, I need to know, and your shipmates need to know, if you can recover from a little scare and do your job."

Kibi swallowed and slowly looked around. Boro nodded slightly, and a moment later Mati joined him. "Yes," came Rini's soft voice from the bridge. Finally Sata smiled at Kibi and nodded also.

With her eyes closed, Kibi took several slow, deep breaths. When she opened her eyes again, Ilika's smiling eyes looked back at her.

A tiny, nervous chuckle escaped her. "I . . . need to know that . . . too. Sata, how long before the approach adjustments?"

"About an hour, and Boro's gonna have dinner ready right after that."

Kibi looked into the eyes of her friends one more time. "Okay . . . I'm going back outside."

Rini focused on his display. "But both storms are still going, x-rays from one direction and asteroids from the other!"

"Good," Kibi said flatly. "You guys need to know if you have a steward . . . or if you should find a new one at Satamia Star Station."

Ilika looked at her. He would have been completely satisfied if she had simply stayed at her station and observed the approach adjustments. But he had seen that look before, and knew she was deeply determined to prove to herself, and everyone else, that a few measly asteroids were not going to stand in her way.

⁕

Kibi started by crawling a few meters from the airlock. By the flashes of light reflecting off Manessa's hull, she knew the asteroids were there, almost close enough to touch. But they couldn't get to her. "Good ship," she whispered.

"Thank you, Kibi," Manessa said.

Kibi chuckled, and while her courage lasted, she quickly rolled over and lay on her back, eyes closed. She could sense the flashes of light through her eyelids, and breathed through the feeling of panic that arose inside her.

After a few minutes, she felt completely relaxed, so she stretched out her arms as if to embrace the universe, but kept her eyes closed. *The last step, Kibi. They can't hurt you. Face them . . . or go home.*

She opened her eyes.

Breathe, Kibi. Breathe.

For the next quarter hour she struggled to keep her eyes open and her lungs working, slowly and steadily. Minute by minute the panic and tension became less, and the shaking in her body relaxed. The sparkling lights were not blinding, just completely outside her seventeen and a half years of worldly experience.

She thought of one more step she could take before going in. She reached up and tried to touch the flashes, knowing the repulsion field would keep girl and asteroids safely apart. After getting used to the tingly sensation, she began to feel a slight vibration every time an asteroid was repelled.

Kibi smiled, rolled back onto her knees, and crawled to the airlock.

⁕ ⁕ ⁕

Sea-going ships were our first attempt at traveling in a dangerous, 3-dimensional medium. Next came aircraft, with even more danger and 3-dimensional movement. All maritime and aviation traditions form the "roots" that space travelers will look back upon fondly, and learn from.

For most of the history of the human race, we never moved faster than we could run, went higher than a nearby hill or mountain, or saw lights other than the sun, moon, stars, campfires, and candles. Today, children get used to cars, roller coasters, airplanes, flashing city lights, and other sights and sounds outside natural human experience, at a fairly young age. When they reach adulthood, those experiences are no longer frightening.

Kibi and her fellow crew member did not grow up with these same experiences. That's why the movement of the ship was so difficult for them to get used to in *Book Four*, and why sparkling lights caused Kibi to panic. Most children today, who have seen a firework display or two, would have just laughed.

The process Kibi went through in this chapter is called “de-sensitizing.” It generally only works when the person is motivated and willing, and is best when they think of it themselves, as Kibi did. It involves taking the new experience in doses small enough to not trigger panic, and then slowly increasing the doses until the full experience can be tolerated, and the person can think and act freely.

Chapter 13: Planetary Approach

A new light showed in Kibi's eyes as she worked at her console, checking everything on the ship that was her responsibility, and at the same time listening to her captain.

"There are no mathematical solutions to the positions of the planets through time. We can make rough calculations, as Sata and Boro have done, but the universe is too complex for those calculations to remain good for very long. Rini, with Manessa's help, is about to find Sonmatia Three, compare it's position to where we thought it would be, and propose course adjustments for Mati's approval."

"No problem!" Rini announced. "It's right where it's supposed to be."

Kibi spotted the slight smile on Ilika's face as he turned to look at Rini. "Are you sure?" the captain asked. "Compare the numbers."

Rini worked silently for a moment. "Well . . . it's not *exactly* where it's supposed to be. It's off by . . . just forty kilometers."

"Not very far considering the planet is sixty thousand kilometers across . . ." Ilika began.

Mati's eyes snapped open wide. "There's no way I'd approve a freeloading pass at fifty kilometers altitude if we could be off by forty! We'd be smashing into mountains!"

"Everyone see Mati's point?"

Boro nodded. "And we can't just miss the mountains. We have to miss most of the air. We're trying to speed up, not slow down!"

"Exactly, Boro."

"Now I see why Mati has to approve each thing Manessa does," Kibi said with a serious frown. "I didn't get that before."

Ilika nodded. "Now the process moves to Sata. Take the new position of the planet, and have Manessa do the math."

"Will I be able to do this kind of fancy math someday?" she asked as she selected the right function on her console.

"Yes, but when you see how tedious it is, you'll be very glad Manessa can do it for you."

"Okay," Sata began, studying the results on her screen, "our wonderful ship wants to do a tiny little thruster burn."

Mati looked it over when it flashed onto her screen. "It's in three minutes. Hardly any inertia. Any reason not to?" the pilot asked as she swiveled around in a complete circle.

"Wait!" Kibi said suddenly. "There's something I should practice." She touched a symbol on her console. "All passengers," she began, her voice slightly amplified, "please be seated for a minor course correction. Inertia straps are not necessary."

The rest of the crew looked at her and smiled, then glanced at the fourteen empty seats behind her.

"Okay," Ilika said, "Mati will approve the burn, and Boro will provide the engines."

The engineer tapped at his large flow-control panel. "Warming up. It looks like Manessa saved enough to squeeze the adjustment into those twelve point three kilograms. Thrusters are green."

"Burn is approved," Mati said.

They waited in silence. Less than a minute later, they all felt a slight lurch.

"Shall we run the numbers again?" Ilika suggested.

Rini checked the planet's position. Sata requested another calculation, then turned around with a grin. "No adjustment needed!"

✷

Boro's pot pie was not perfect, but with excitement high, no one complained.

Even though six hours separated the approach adjustments from the freeloading pass, no one could sleep. Ilika might have been tempted to try, but question after question came at him about what they would see and feel as they swished by their home planet.

With a defiant glance at Ilika, Kibi went to her console and announced she was adding six hours to that ship-day.

Ilika laughed. "We'll be close to the equator, and might see some places we've been, but they'll flash by very quickly. Kibi has command," he said, and slipped into the galley.

✷

About an hour later, two exciting things happened. With Rini magnifying the image, they began to see the continents and oceans of their home world. Also, the aroma of sweet biscuits started to fill the ship.

Boro dragged himself away from his display and made tea. Kibi, still in the command chair, asked Rini and Sata to double-check the approach. Again, no adjustment was needed.

As the image of the blue planet with white clouds grew larger on their screens, they gazed in longing, remembering their journey on foot and donkeyback.

As the third hour passed, Kibi mumbled something about another approach check, then turned red with embarrassment and cancelled the request.

“It’s okay,” Ilika said, appearing behind her and massaging her shoulders. “You can ask for as many checks as you want. Manessa has to earn your trust, just as I once did.”

Kibi took a deep breath and made the request. Rini and Sata quickly announced that they were right on.

✷

During the hour before the scheduled freeloading pass, all five crew members were glued to their screens, searching for land shapes they recognized. Their own kingdom was hiding under a large cloud, far to the north of the flight path. From the command chair, Kibi gazed at the large display in front of her and spotted the tropical land where they had explored jungle, waterfall, and cave.

Sata smiled to herself, remembering her fear of deep, dark places. She reached over and touched Mati on the arm, a look of gratitude in her eyes.

Mati smiled.

As the white, blue, green, and brown planet began to completely fill their screens, Ilika sat down at the steward’s station. “Sata should be able to project our course around the planet now. That will give us another check on the calculations.”

Kibi looked at the navigator and nodded.

Sata quickly sent the course projection to all stations. “We’re only going about three-eights of the way around, then we head off into space again.”

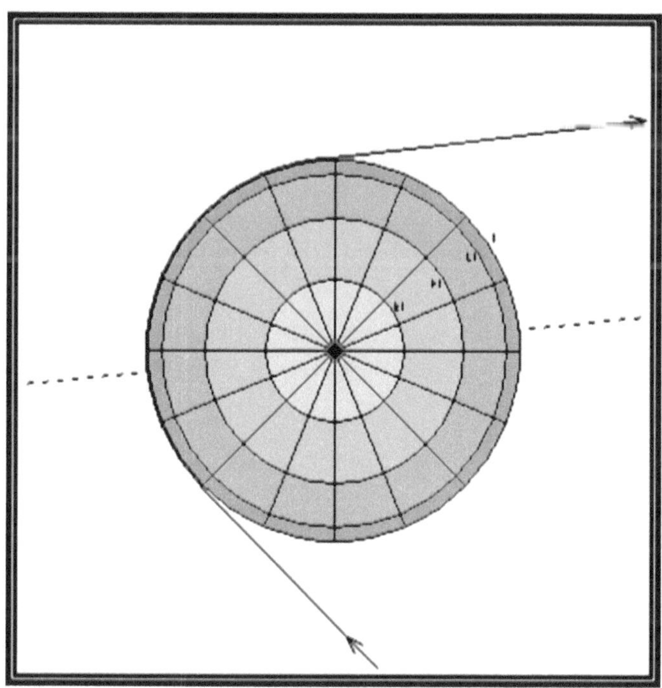

Boro stared at the projection. "That's . . . close! No wonder the course has to be exact."

"Freeloading in three minutes," Sata announced.

"Inertia straps," Mati said.

Kibi smiled, experiencing the joy of commanding crew members who knew what they were doing.

Ilika touched some controls on the steward's console, spoke a word softly, and all the display screens went blank.

* * *

People argue all the time about whether the universe is a huge machine, or something less predictable. One theory is that if we knew the positions and motions of every bit of matter and energy in the universe, we could reconstruct all past history, and accurately predict all future events. This theory does not leave any room for randomness or free will. In any case, we humans on Earth cannot predict the future positions of planets with a high degree of accuracy, and the author proposes that the Manessa Kwi and her crew could not either. Course corrections, for us mere mortals, in any task, are necessary.

Chapter 14: Flying Blind

"Did you do that, Ilika?" Rini asked after touching several symbols, none of which worked.

"Of course he did," Kibi said with a slightly irritated voice. "I'm in command. He can't resist the temptation when I'm in command."

"So . . . what are we doing?" Mati asked with concern. "I don't have visual, flight plan, projection . . . anything."

Sata tapped at her console, searching for any navigation functions that still worked. "The calculations were right on. The freeloading pass doesn't need any more course adjustments."

"Yeah," Boro added, "we should sail right through and pop out the other side. This is probably just practice at trusting Manessa."

Several faces turned to look at their captain, but his lips remained sealed and his kindly expression told them nothing.

"I think you're right, Boro," Sata said. "Nothing works at my station, but nothing *needs* to work. Ilika even encouraged us to double and triple-check the approach. It was perfect."

Kibi wore a frown, and her mouth shifted from side to side.

"The freeloading pass begins in about two minutes," Mati said, "and is going to happen unless we do something to stop it."

Kibi turned to Rini. "What do you think?"

With nothing on his console working, he swiveled around. "I don't know. I'm willing to try it."

Kibi nodded, then turned back to the front. "Mati?"

"Um . . . I'm uneasy, but I think Rini has good instincts. We do need to trust Manessa, and after that last adjustment, our altitude should be exactly fifty kilometers. The highest mountain is only twenty-one kilometers, and it's not on our flight path."

Kibi's face scrunched with worry as the other four crew members all looked at her. "Manessa?"

"Ilika asked me not to . . ."

"Okay, okay."

"One minute," Mati said.

"I think we should do it," Boro said softly.

Sata nodded. "Me too."

Rini nodded.

Mati squinted for a moment, then nodded also.

Kibi took two more deep breaths, then opened her mouth to say something, but no sound came out. A moment later she frowned again. "No. Every bone is my body is screaming at me." She turned and looked at Ilika. "If you want this ship to do that freeloading pass blind, you'll have to take back command, or put someone else in this chair. I can't. I won't."

Ilika smiled slightly. "You're still in command."

With her heart pounding, Kibi turned back around. "Mati, get us out of here!"

Mati wasted no time turning to her console and raising her flight control. "Boro, I need anti-mass and ion drive seven."

Boro swallowed once, then moved his fingers on his control board. "Warming up."

"Where's the moon?" Mati demanded with a tinge of fear in her voice.

Rini tapped at his console frantically for a moment, then threw up his hands. "It wasn't near our entry or exit flight path . . . but I don't remember where . . ."

"We'll go a different way," the pilot declared, saw that her engines were green, and pulled her flight control back and slightly to the right.

Seconds before the beginning of the freeloading pass, the Manessa Kwi suddenly gained altitude and streaked away to the north, out of the flat plane of the solar system where most of the planets and moons moved in their slow, steady orbits.

✷

"Kibi made the right call," Ilika said. His hands were the only ones not shaking as he held his mug of tea. "And I'm very proud of her for trusting her instincts and not giving in to the will of the majority."

Four faces around the table were riddled with guilt. "We're sorry, Kibi," Sata said.

Ilika continued. "There's no need to be sorry, Sata. Kibi asked for your honest opinions, and you gave them. That was the right thing to do, for Kibi, and for the rest of you. The commander needs honest opinions and uncensored options. Then, when she makes a decision, she needs skilled, coordinated action. You all did great. I have no complaints."

Everyone breathed easier as they sipped their tea.

"Very good call, Mati," Ilika went on, "taking the ship out of the plane of the solar system to avoid any chance of hitting the moon."

"Flying blind was the scariest thing I've ever done," the pilot responded. "Fighting off a timber wolf sounds easier — at least I can *see* it. All I could do was remember how the ship was angled the last time we had visual, and hope it was still the same!"

After a moment of silence, Boro worked up his courage. "So . . . doing a freeloading pass without sensors is . . . not a good idea?"

"Flying blind, with the slightest possibility of hitting anything within a light-minute, is way too dangerous."

Boro swallowed.

"There could be other ships," Ilika pointed out, "or artificial satellites, like around Sonmatia Two. But the biggest danger on a freeloading pass is the planet itself. This was on my list to teach you, but teaching is always better with an example."

"We'll remember!" Rini said with wide eyes while nodding.

*

After sensors were restored, Sata created a new flight plan. Mati looped the ship back to the final approach, then let Boro shut down the anti-mass and ion drives. Kibi had them check the course twice before they began the freeloading pass.

They watched the planet race by beneath them, trying to spot more places they knew. Rini thought he recognized the tallest mountain, but couldn't be sure. Mere minutes later, they were released from the planet's grip and flew off into space toward Sonmatia Four.

Sata looked sad for a few minutes, but none of the others gave it a second thought.

* * *

Kibi was a strongly intuitive person. Intuition isn't a perfect way of gathering information, but in this case, the usual methods were not available. Kibi also made important decisions with her heart, which is also far from perfect, but is sometimes necessary. Her mind, and her fellow crew members, were telling her one thing, and her "gut" was telling her something else. It was her nature to listen to her "gut."

Another important thing to notice is that the essential problem was physical: a small ship coming very close to a planet at high speed. Voting is a human social process. Even if everyone in the entire universe voted the same way, including Kibi and Ilika, the outcome of the vote could still be wrong.

Most of the planets and moons in our solar system (the only solar system we know much about) travel in orbits very close to a single flat "plane" called the "ecliptic." This causes our moon to sometimes come between us and the sun (an "eclipse"). The equator of the sun (which rotates just as most planets do) is also on the ecliptic.

A light-minute, you may recall, is about 18 million km or 11 million miles.

Why was Sata (but not the other crew members) sad after the freeloading pass?

Chapter 15: Slowing Down

After Ilika and Kibi said good-night and slipped into the lift, already kissing, Boro smiled to himself and swiveled in his chair. From the engineering station, he surveyed the entire bridge and passenger area, currently empty and silent.

Only a year before, he had been a slave in a little kingdom where people abused each other every chance they got. Now he was part of something else, something called Nebador that he didn't fully understand. He had seen many pictures of beautiful cities, gleaming star stations, sleek ships, and strange people. It had all come a step closer to reality when Sata chatted with another navigator, some kind of large bird. He cringed for a moment, remembering his first thought at the time, of plucking, gutting, and roasting the creature over a slow fire.

He turned to his console and selected some soft music as he pondered his new life. He felt a little confusion, and more than a little amazement. A few moments later, soft but strong hands began massaging his shoulders. He leaned his head back to look. "Hi, Sata. Couldn't sleep?"

She smiled. "Oh . . . I could, but I'd rather be with you."

After a slight flush of embarrassment, he swiveled around to face her. "Want to get a snack with me, sit in the passenger area?"

"Sure!"

Soon they had a plate with left-over biscuits, dried fruit, and cups of cold tea.

"This is only my second watch alone," he said. "I hope I remember what to do if Manessa starts screaming about an asteroid or something."

"You will, I know you. I think Ilika's gonna train me and Mati tomorrow. Then we'll all be doing it."

They nibbled in silence for a minute.

Sata cleared her throat. "Part of why I . . . um . . . came up here was because I couldn't quit . . . thinking about you."

Boro swallowed as he felt a wave of warm emotions flow through him.

She looked at him with dreamy eyes. "And . . . I want to make sure you know that I'm . . . ready to share a cabin with you . . . as soon as you want to . . ."

Boro's entire body suddenly became hot and sweaty, and he had to swallow several more times. He looked at Sata, and saw her sparkling eyes and happy smile, but his mouth was too dry to speak.

"Ilika tells me," she went on, "that in Nebador, girls ask boys just as often as boys ask girls."

She noticed his discomfort. "But . . . if you don't want to . . ."

"Um . . . no . . ." he stumbled, "it's not that. You're really . . . beautiful to me, and . . . um . . . I think about you too. It's just . . . you know . . . it's huge, and I want to . . . make sure it's just right, and . . . everyone feels good about it . . . you know. We have to think about Rini and Mati, and there's our training and work and everything . . ."

Sata grinned. "Mati and Rini aren't going to try anything until her knee is fixed, but I know they'd love to have some time to snuggle. And, you know, I wasn't asking you into my cabin while we're *on duty!*"

Boro chuckled nervously.

"Couldn't you just come over sometime so we could . . . play?" she asked with a smile of longing.

Boro's expression passed through several shades of smiles and two or three types of frowns as he sat wrestling with his emotions.

Sata slowly lost her smile, then looked down at her lap. "Okay, I get the message," she said as her voice started breaking. "I should have realized . . . why you've never even . . . kissed me." She started to get up.

Suddenly a strong hand grabbed her arm, and she froze.

"Please stay. I'm not as good as you at putting my feelings into words, but I still have . . . lots of feelings . . . and I want to be the only boy who ever . . . you know . . . touches you like that."

Sata settled herself back into the chair with a slight smile.

"And about kissing . . ." Boro continued, "I think I can fix that right now without any . . . complications."

Sata offered no resistance as she was pulled into Boro's strong arms. She felt the warmth of his lips on hers, timidly at first, then more firmly as he found his confidence.

It seemed like hours later when they finally parted and looked at each other shyly. Sata took a slow breath and smiled. "Yeah . . . slow is okay."

*

Somewhat to the crew's surprise, they received a complete trigonometry review the following day covering all the functions, along with the inverse functions that would give them the angle. With knowledge pads at their fingertips, they only had to remember which function to use for each problem. As Ilika clearly wanted them all to get it, Sata and Rini worked with

Boro and Kibi. Mati worked slowly and carefully, and Ilika was ready to assist, but she held her own.

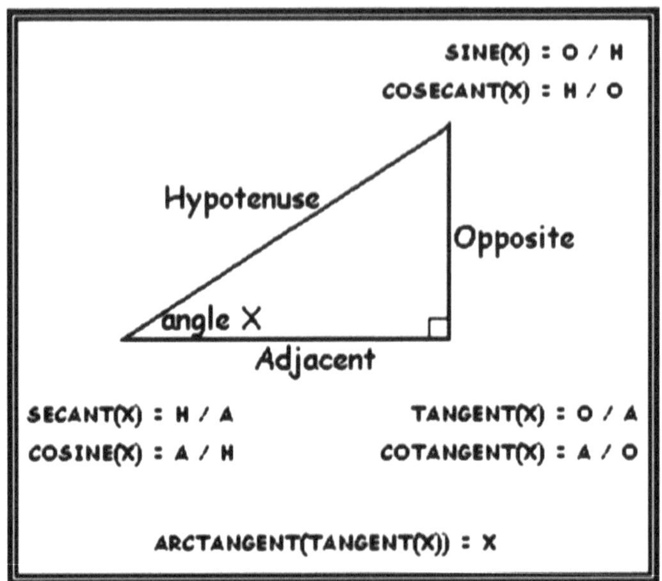

On the second day of their transit from Sonmatia Three to Four, they took turns presenting the new words they were studying. Sata and Mati could hardly stop giggling as they stood before the others, trying to explain star station approach procedures.

Boro, still a little clumsy with the language of Nebador, had trouble describing the new tools he was learning about, so he grabbed a knowledge pad and found pictures. Ilika, of course, made him do his best to describe them in words also.

Rini bubbled with excitement as he talked about the hundreds of instrument checks and calibrations the star station could do as soon as the ship was docked. Suddenly he stopped in mid-thought and looked at Ilika. "The star station . . . it's sentient too, with feelings and everything, right?"

Ilika smiled and nodded.

Kibi went through the entire passenger receiving process, using her shipmates as guinea pigs, and pretending they had never been on a deep-space response ship before. They were all soon tucked under soft blankets, in their reclined seats, with cold drinks at hand and a video on the big screen.

*

On the day they were scheduled to arrive at Sonmatia Four, Ilika emerged from a relaxing bath to find his entire crew at their stations, ready for approach adjustments an entire hour early. "Hmm. I need to find something for you guys to do. Let me think . . . we don't need to collect firewood or brush donkeys . . ."

Everyone laughed. A gleam of sadness crept into Mati's eyes.

After drying his hair and shooing Kibi away from her console, Ilika sent math and logic problems to all stations to pass the time. Finally, with the scheduled adjustments minutes away and his crew unable to concentrate on anything else, he gave in.

"You guys are tired of slow space flight, aren't you?"

Mati turned and nodded vigorously. "*Really* tired of it."

All the others agreed.

"Rini, any sign of Sonmatia Four?"

He smiled. "I've been watching it for an hour and a half! It's just a few kilometers from where it should be."

"Sata?"

"Approach adjustment calculated!"

"I should have known. Mati?"

"Burn approved, one minute."

"Boro?"

"Thrusters are green."

"Kibi?" Ilika asked, turning his head.

"The passengers are all seated," she said with a grin.

Ilika grinned back. "It is both happy and sad for a captain when he realizes his crew no longer needs him."

*

Three anxious hours later, as Sonmatia Four began to loom large on their screens, the crew gathered around the galley with worried faces. Ilika was busy making potato cakes. Kibi put into words what they were all thinking. "We need you, Ilika. We may have approach adjustments memorized, but we have no idea how to do atmospheric braking."

Ilika took a minute to secure the galley and wipe his hands. As soon as he took the command chair, his entire crew, back at their stations, looked happy again.

"The freeloading pass was too close to do without sensors, and this is far closer. Sata, what's our highest elevation on the equator?"

The navigator took a moment to enter the question at her console in the precise mathematical language that would allow the ship to search hundreds of charts in an instant. "Six thousand three hundred meters."

Ilika nodded. "If we tried to orbit at our current speed, what would our altitude be?"

Sata selected the proper function. "Eight thousand one hundred. Isn't that . . . too close?"

"No, it's just right. The atmosphere of this planet is thin, so we have to go as deep as we can. The safe lower limit is one thousand meters above terrain, but I've heard of ships going down to a hundred in an emergency."

"Whew," Boro breathed. "They'd almost scrape the hull!"

Mati peered at her display. "I'll have to do a slight adjustment to nail that eight thousand one hundred."

"Then, as we slow down," Ilika continued, "you'll raise the orbit, Mati. Sata will give you an orbital velocity graph. As soon as the line on the graph becomes flat, you'll know we're out of the atmosphere and in a stable orbit. Boro, Mati will need maneuvering thrusters and anti-mass on standby. Ready an alternate fuel for both."

Boro's eyes grew wide at the implied danger. "Engines warming," he said, turning to his console. "Alternate fuels . . . selected and ready."

✷

Mati's heart pounded as the little ship streaked toward the barren brown horizon of the fourth planet, lower and lower with each passing second. She watched the altitude constantly, ready to bring in the anti-mass drive if they went below eight thousand one hundred meters.

At first, the rocky surface appeared airless, but she soon glimpsed haze in the distance. "Eleven thousand four hundred and dropping." Barren mountains reminded her of those in the deserts of her own planet.

A thick reddish-brown cloud appeared on the horizon directly in front of them. "Dust storm," Ilika said. "Not a problem."

The ship, still moving at interplanetary speed, covered the distance in seconds. Mati frowned as they plunged into the brown haze, but gritted her teeth and kept her eyes on her display.

Sata's eyes snapped shut, and didn't open until the dust was far behind them.

"Eight thousand two hundred," the pilot said. A deep valley sliced the surface of the planet just before they streaked into the darkness of the night side.

"Trust your instruments," the captain reminded.

Mati smiled when she noticed the first bit of speed reduction. A glance at her altimeter showed eight thousand one hundred and five meters. She settled her hand on her flight control and nudged the ship up slightly to begin following the orbital velocity graph.

Back in the brilliant daylight, a cone-shaped mountain raced toward them.

"Volcano?" Boro wondered aloud.

"Yes, completely dormant now," Ilika said.

"That's the high point," Sata added, squinting at the sudden brightness.

"Eight thousand five hundred and climbing," Mati reported. "Another dust storm."

They streaked into and through the brown haze before Mati could finish speaking, then plunged back into darkness.

"Actually, same dust storm," Rini informed.

Sata swallowed. "Every time I see it coming, I worry there's a mountain hiding in it."

Mati glanced at her friend. "I'm watching the topographics. If there's *anything* hiding in it, I'll have us out of there in a heartbeat."

Ilika smiled as the volcano flew by beneath them again.

Sata breathed easier, but couldn't keep from closing her eyes on the next pass.

"Eleven thousand," Mati said as they punched another hole in the dust storm and entered the night-side once more.

* * *

Is something wrong with Sata for having sexual feelings at age 11? The fact is, the average age of puberty, for girls, in our world today, is 11-12. If that's the average, then some individuals enter puberty at 10, 9, 8, even 7, just as some do at 13, 14, 15, even 16.

What do we learn about the Nebador Transport Service when we see that the relationship between Sata and Boro is not being supervised or chaperoned by anyone?

An illustration summarizes the crew's trigonometry review.

Using atmospheric friction to slow a spacecraft creates a lot of heat, and the spacecraft looks about like a fireball. We've learned to use replaceable ceramic tiles, but our spacecraft require months of work after each use. A durable hull that can handle repeated atmospheric braking or re-entry is not yet within our ability.

Chapter 16: The Monuments of Zolko

Seven laps later, the Manessa Kwi had risen high above the dust storm and the volcano. The pilot announced they were almost in a stable circular orbit, but she wanted to go around once or twice more.

Rini reported nothing in orbit with them.

"If it's okay with all of you," Ilika began, "I think we are done with slow, old-fashioned space travel."

"Yay!" several crew members cheered at once. Mati grinned from ear to ear, while keeping an eye on their last climbing orbit.

"There's a small emergency shelter at the coordinates on your flight list, Sata. Please make Mati a flight plan. I'm going to give Kibi a tour while the rest of you solve a little puzzle."

Rini sparkled with curiosity.

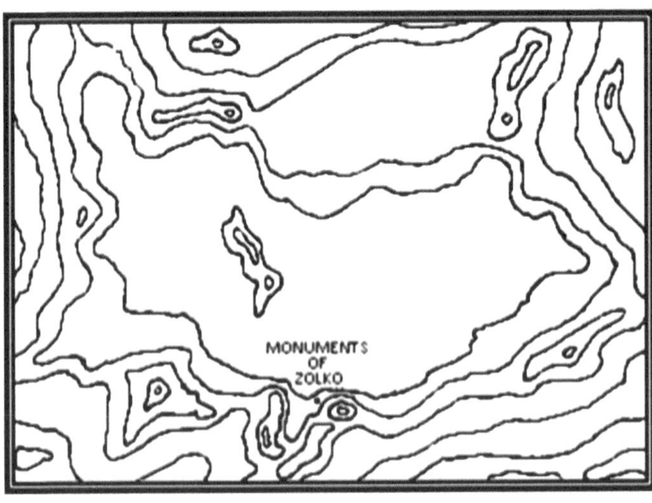

Sata studied a chart on her display. “It’s in some hills beside an old dried-up sea or lake. What’s a mon . . . u . . . ment?”

“Anything to remember someone or something important, usually made to last a long time.”

“Like a statue?” Mati asked, letting Manessa take over the orbit and swiveling around in her chair.

“Yes. A story took place here almost twenty thousand years ago, and it’s still told and retold all over Satamia. A plaque at the landing site will tell you about Zolko, the builder of the monuments, and you’ll learn the rest of the story as you solve the puzzle.”

Boro grinned, remembering the pride he felt after solving the puzzle of the Atorura tribe.

Sata picked a point on their orbital path and drew an elliptical curve from there to the destination. “You can de-orbit in about twenty seconds.”

Mati looked over the route when it appeared on her screen. “Boro, anti-mass two, ion three, please.”

*

Dozens of deeply-weathered stone monuments bristled all over the little valley surrounded on three sides by barren brown hills. The yellow and red stone columns were nearly devoid of features, but every once in a while, part of an ancient face would stare at them, or a few letters could be seen of a long-forgotten language.

Mati slowly piloted the ship among the pillars. Some appeared to be whole at twenty or thirty meters tall. Others were obviously broken, stone shards littering the ground.

The remaining side of the valley was just an ancient coastline that sloped down quickly into depths that once might have held sparkling water, but now contained only dust. A thin wind occasionally picked up the powdery dirt and spun it into ghostly funnels that lasted a minute or two.

Once they had looked at all the monuments and the ancient dry shore, Mati glanced at Ilika, and he nodded. She guided the ship toward a large stone platform in the center of the valley. Though rough from thousands of years of wind and sand, it was still almost perfectly flat on top, and large enough for several deep-space response ships. Obviously of about the same age as the monuments, two things upon it appeared much newer.

A small monument and plaque, of some smooth black material, perched on one side.

On the opposite side sat a brilliant-white dome, slightly larger than the ship.

"The plaque is part of your puzzle, so you can look at it after you drop us off. Mati, see the hatch on the right side of the shelter? It will mate with our airlock."

Hovering just a meter above the ancient stone, Mati guided the ship in that direction. Ilika stepped to the pilot's station and showed her several new controls. Mati lowered the struts and settled the ship when the diagram on her screen showed proper alignment. Touching another control, the shiny golden ship extended its hull and connected with the hatch of the emergency shelter.

"We now have a passageway from the ship to the shelter, so we don't have to mess with space suits. The rest of you can have a tour of the place after finishing the puzzle. Kibi, all we need are mission bracelets."

Ilika and Kibi quickly grabbed bracelets and disappeared into the lift.

Boro raised his eyebrows. "Why do I get the feeling this puzzle is going to make Atorura seem easy?"

✷

"What's going on, Ilika?" Kibi asked as soon as they stepped through the airlock tunnel into the domed shelter. A larger version of the ship's entryway surrounded them, with shelves for equipment and clothing, a shower, and soft light coming from the curved ceiling.

Ilika touched some controls on the wall and the hatch closed. "A number of things, most of them challenging, all very good for the crew."

"Where do you get these puzzles?"

"We've got millions of them, all over the universe, just waiting for students who need to sharpen their wits. Remember, Nebador is a huge college. As soon as you guys learn the basics, there's plenty of advanced training waiting for you ... and for me. You're familiar with all these emergency kits – they're the same as on Manessa, just larger."

Kibi looked over the kits and didn't see anything new. "But why don't I have to do the puzzle along with the others?"

"Oh, that. The head of the Transport Service has learned, from long experience, that new crews tend to get too dependant on their usual commanders at about this point in training. That's not good, so the training manual suggests they do a puzzle or two without us. They know everything they need to know, or, with Manessa's help, they can learn it."

"How long will they be gone?"

"This puzzle ... two or three days."

"Serious puzzle! What's this machine do?"

"Gas separator. It takes apart the thin atmosphere of this planet . . ."

✷

The remaining four members of the crew swiveled their station chairs and looked at each other.

"Who's in command?" Mati asked.

"While we were traveling," Rini said, "Boro was usually in charge after Kibi."

Sata smiled and nodded.

Boro turned slightly red. "But Mati has more experience than I do on the ship . . ."

The pilot squirmed. "That's just flight command, engines and straps and stuff. I always have to do that. We need someone who can organize this puzzle thing."

Boro looked around. The other three were grinning and looking at him. "Okay, but I'm handing it off if I get tired, or start screwing up." With an uncomfortable expression he took the command chair. "What do we know about this puzzle?"

"Nothing," Sata said flatly.

"The plaque on the little black monument is supposed to tell us something," Rini said.

Boro scrunched his face for a moment. "Mati, is the shelter hatch closed?"

"Um . . . yes."

"Okay, let's disconnect the airlock and go look at the plaque."

A minute later, the Manessa Kwi sat a meter from the little monument. Rini magnified the image. With a nod from Boro, he read.

"Satamia one-one-three-six, Sonmatia Four, marker four-seven. The Monuments of Zolko."

Boro frowned. "Is that all it says?"

"That's all we can read," Sata said, looking at her display, "but Manessa just received a transmission from the monument. It's the story of what happened here twenty thousand years ago!"

✷

King Zolko struggled to pull enough air into his lungs as he sat on his throne and looked over the shriveled fruit and hard bread on the silver platter close at hand. For a moment he bristled, then relaxed as he remembered the even-poorer food in the marketplace these days. Several councilors sat in lesser chairs, also struggling to breathe while keeping their gaze respectfully low. Servants stood, hands behind their backs, trying to hide their discomfort.

The great doors at the far end of the hall opened, and a well-dressed man strode in. For a moment, harsh sunlight entered, along with some reddish-brown dust. The door guards quickly closed the doors and tried to muffle their coughing.

"Councilor Ganlo!" the king said with both a friendly greeting and frustration. "Why is the air so thin today? Did you speak to the priests and scholars?"

Ganlo stopped the proper distance from the throne and bowed. "I did, Your Majesty, as many as I could find. Some have abandoned their duties and left the city. The priests have been praying day and night, they say, and the scholars have searched every book. No one knows what else can be done to appease the gods."

The king suddenly stood, his chin thrust forward. "The scholars have repeatedly stood before me and proclaimed that all important knowledge is in their books! I want all of you on the streets, searching for answers! I will not let this be the end of our great kingdom!"

The other councilors, most of them old men, started to rise.

"Sire, there is one other possibility," Ganlo said, head half-bowed.

"Speak!"

"There is a woman in the marketplace. She calls herself a prophet, but the priests deny it. She says we need not fear, that the gods will save our kingdom by taking a few to a new land flowing with nut milk and honey. She gathers people around her to listen, and children sit in her lap and are comforted."

The king stood thoughtfully, rubbing his chin. "How does she say the chosen few will be selected?"

"I do not know, Sire."

"Go! All of you! Sit at her feet and listen, and come back in three days with what you learn!"

✷

"Sounds like the atmosphere was getting thin twenty thousand years ago," Sata speculated.

Boro nodded. "I wonder what the puzzle is."

"It's probably like the story problem about Poki and his cows," Mati proposed with a furrowed brow. "We won't know until we hear the whole thing."

✷

The councilors of King Zolko listened to the prophet for two days, and when she was at table eating, or asleep, they questioned the priests and scholars further. Some of the councilors became convinced that the wrath of the gods could be appeased by great works. Others were not so optimistic, and tried to discover how the chosen few would be selected, as the king had ordered.

On the third day, Councilor Sarto crept away and sold all his property to hire a ship and many strong men. He believed the gods would look favorably on them if they found the most beautiful gemstone in the world and placed it in the temple. He carried books and maps from the great library, all telling him that such a gemstone could only be found across the sea, in the Desert of Bakka, somewhere along the eight degree line, for that was the number most sacred to the gods.

Also on the third day, Councilor Memna, the greatest politician in the kingdom and the king's official speaker, slipped away from the group to sell all her property and hire a ship. "I shall create a city in the wilderness, seventy-six kilometers west by northwest of here. All who love the gods may come, bring their children, and help make a society of peace and harmony. The gods will see our creation of love, smile upon us, and make the wind to blow and the rain to fall."

Word spread rapidly, and when she arrived at the dock to board the ship, hundreds of people were already assembled and ready to follow, in rowboats if necessary.

✷

"Yeah!" Boro cheered. "We've finally got some numbers we can use to find things! But there's something Ilika or Kibi usually did that we need to do."

Sata looked puzzled. "I don't think we know enough yet."

"Not enough to do the puzzle. But my stomach is telling me all I need to know about something else."

Rini grinned. "Lunchtime!" he said and dashed for the galley.

✷

On the evening of the third day, Ganlo and the few other remaining councilors entered the king's hall.

"Your Majesty, we are divided on how the gods might be appeased. Sarto seeks the most beautiful gemstone. Memna plans to create a city of peace and harmony. The priests, however, are convinced that only great monuments would be pleasing to the gods, monuments bearing the likeness of the high kings, such as yourself, and the high priests . . ."

"But I sent you to learn how the chosen few will be selected!"

"We were able to discover little, Sire. The prophet only babbles about children and their pure hearts. I don't think she knows."

The king questioned the other councilors. They were all in agreement with Ganlo, and could add little else. Silence prevailed in the great hall as the king rubbed his chin. Finally, he spoke. "So be it. Scribes!"

Two old men emerged from nearby rooms and sat down at writing desks.

"Let it be known that all men, and all women not with child, must report to the palace at sunrise every morning until suitable monuments have been raised to let the gods see the faces of all the high kings and high priests of the land."

"But Sire," Ganlo interrupted, "bringing that much stone from beyond the sea will take years."

The king took a breath of the thin air. "Then we shall not use new stone. We shall take down the buildings of the city, one by one. If necessary, only the foundation of the palace will be spared, a place for the gods to rest as they admire the beauty and grandeur of the Monuments of Zolko!"

✷

"Talk about full of himself!" Sata sputtered.

"About the same as kings and priests on our world," Rini observed.

Boro nodded. "I think . . . we're sitting on the foundation of the palace. It seems . . . somehow wrong to park our ship where the gods were supposed to rest."

Mati swiveled around. "Boro! Who do you think would have saved the children with pure hearts and taken them to a land of milk and honey?"

The bridge was completely silent for a long moment.

Rini swallowed before speaking. "Probably . . . the Nebador Transport Service."

* * *

In most organizations, it is not considered desirable for the "workers" to function without their "bosses." One reason is that most "workers" do not have the wisdom and experience to do so. What do we learn about Nebador when we see that the crew members are being trained to operate the ship without their usual commanders?

It may seem strange to us that everything was assumed, by King Zolko and his people, to be the will of the god(s). Today, even most religious people believe that weather and climate events are natural. We have to remember that before science began to unravel the mysteries of nature (starting in about the year 1400), almost everything that didn't have a clear human cause was assumed to be caused by divine intervention.

The story problem about Poki and his cows was in *Book Two*, chapter 35.

The number eight is sacred in one of our major religions, Buddhism. In the Judeo-Christian tradition, the numbers three and seven are sacred. The numbers four, five, and nine can also be found as sacred numbers in other religions.

In your opinion, was it okay for the Manessa Kwi to park on the stone foundation of the palace that was intended to be a resting-place for the gods?

Chapter 17: The City of Memna

Searching their memories for old measurement systems they thought they'd never use again, the partial crew managed to convert "west by northwest" into something Sata could use for a flight plan. The seventy-six kilometer trip took almost three seconds.

"I *love* ion drive!" the pilot declared.

Boro chuckled as he stepped to the engineer's console.

Mati raised her flight control. "Give me . . . anti-mass one and maneuvering thrusters."

"All green," Boro said, then returned to the command chair.

The City of Memna, on a level plain near the old shoreline, had no monuments or massive palace foundations. All that remained were small blocks of rough stone, piled no more than a meter high, that outlined former houses and a few larger buildings. As Mati lowered the ship from two thousand meters, they could see the circular layout of the ancient city, with an open plaza in the center, and avenues radiating out in eight directions.

"The number most sacred to their gods," Rini whispered.

Mati guided the ship slowly along the avenues and among the ruined buildings for several minutes. "It looks like . . . this city didn't grow, bit by bit, like the capital of our kingdom. It was planned and built all at once."

"I hope there's a Nebador marker somewhere . . ." Boro mumbled.

"It's in the middle," Sata said. "Manessa spotted it as soon as we arrived."

Boro nodded to Mati, and she guided the ship along one of the main avenues, then landed in a clear space near the black marker.

"Marker five-zero," Rini read. "The City of Memna."

✷

Councilor Memna worked side by side with her people, never asking them to do anything she wasn't willing to do. So it was that they worked with glad hearts, and within a year they all had houses and the new city was functioning well.

The air seemed to get no worse, and some even said it was a little better. The drought continued and the crops were poor, but they shared alike in what they had, and Memna made sure no one hoarded more than their share of anything. She dispensed justice as cases were brought to her, barely pausing in her work with stone chisel or garden hoe in hand. The people around her listened to her wise words as they worked, and knew in their hearts they had chosen the right path and their city would be pleasing to the gods.

"Why do you not take the best food and live a life of leisure, like King Zolko?" a young woman asked, pausing in her work to comfort her baby.

Memna smiled. "The gods are pleased when each citizen gives what she is able, and only takes what she needs. That is the essence of civilized life. King Zolko's way is the way of the animals in the jungle of Torku."

The girl smiled and returned to her work.

✷

Sata was grinning. "That is so wonderful! I wish our kingdom was like that. Could you imagine our king helping to rebuild the houses at Lumber Town, listening to petitions while he pounded nails?"

Boro howled with laughter. "No, I can't! I don't even think the soldiers will help. The people will do it all."

"I think . . . Nebador's sort of like that," Rini said with a smile and sparkling eyes, "like Memna's city."

Mati wore a slight frown. "I think you're partly right — about giving and taking. But I'm worried that in Memna's city, they did it for all the wrong reasons."

The others shrugged, and Rini continued reading.

✷

As the months of the second year began to pass, some of the people of the City of Memna became unhappy. Memna's judgments always favored social harmony, and whenever that goal was in conflict with the needs of an individual, the group won and the person lost.

Those who saw the city as a hive, whose purpose was to function as efficiently as possible, were happy. Artists and other sorts of free-thinkers did not feel the same.

Also, travelers occasionally arrived from the old capital city, now being quickly dismantled to create the monuments King Zolko had ordered. They hoped to find better air, less dust, and perhaps a little rain, but were disappointed. Memna tried to silence them and brand them as heretics, but the truth crept throughout the city like a disease.

Some people gathered in houses late in the evenings to carry on the traditions of their previous guilds and orders. One such order contained a couple of old masters and several young students, all dedicated to mental discipline and psychic abilities. After doing her share of the work of the city for more than a year and a half, Nosta, a young woman of the order, decided it was time to act. She knelt before her masters one evening.

"I believe the City of Memna is pleasing to many of the people, those who never have an original thought in their heads. I do not believe the gods are so small-minded. I have repaired a little boat that no one wanted, and I plan to depart tonight. I will find the fabled Arch on the Island of Glimpa, where I will sit in meditation until the gods receive my offering of mind and spirit, or until I die."

✷

"I thought so," Mati said. "If something is good just because it pleases the gods, that leaves you at the mercy of the priests to know what is good."

"Or . . ." Rini began, hands behind his head while looking up at the ceiling, "or other people acting as priests, like King Zolko, and Memna."

Mati nodded. "Nosta figured that out. She must have had good teachers."

Boro's face scrunched as he tried to follow the discussion. "So . . . by priests you mean people telling you what the gods think?"

Mati nodded.

"There's just a little more," Sata said.

✷

The masters and the other students of the order quickly gathered as much bread and dried fruit as they could find, and went down to the shore to see their brave friend off in the darkness. Nosta was never seen again by mortal eyes.

After that time, the air became thinner and thinner, and no more clouds appeared in the yellowing sky. The crops failed at both the Monuments of Zolko and the City of Memna. By the end of the second year, the people were dying and had forgotten all about the joys of peace and harmony. No one in either city claimed to know what might be pleasing to the gods.

✷

Boro growled. "But what's the puzzle?"

Sata swiveled in her chair and looked at him with sympathy.

"Maybe that's part of the puzzle," Rini suggested with a coy smile.

Boro growled again. “A puzzle in a puzzle. Let’s see if we can find that arch.”

Sata turned to her console and selected the chart. “Hmm. There’s only one group of hills that would have been an island when this was a sea. Must be Nosta’s island.”

“Glimpa,” Mati remembered.

“Thanks. It was big, about thirty-five kilometers from here, spanning the horizon from east to northeast. You don’t need a flight plan for that!”

“Nope. I’ll just use atmospheric thrusters, if Boro doesn’t mind,” the pilot said, placing one hand on her flight control.

Stepping to his console, Boro touched a symbol. “I think we can spare a few minutes.”

Mati lifted the Manessa Kwi a hundred meters into the thin atmosphere, then pointed the ship eastward over the empty, dry seabed, the same way young Nosta went, alone in her little rowboat, twenty thousand years before.

* * *

The City of Memna was run under an economic system we call “communism,” which advocates “from each according to his ability, to each according to his need.” It is an economic system, and should not be confused with the political systems attempted by the Soviet Union and China in the 20th century. Most recent experiments with communism were in the USA during the 19th century. It is most often attempted in a religious community setting, as it requires a level of discipline greater than people usually have on their own.

What “wrong reason” (in the motivations of the ancient people) did Mati spot when the crew was learning about the City of Memna?

Which is more comfortable for you: the social harmony of the “hive,” or the dis-harmony of “artists and free-thinkers”? Which did Nosta the apprentice prefer?

Why did travelers find the physical conditions (air, rain, etc.) no better at the City of Memna than at the Monuments of Zolko?

How was Nosta’s god-concept different from Memna’s?

Instead of Rini becoming defensive when Mati figured out something he had not, what did he do?

The sky was “yellowing” because a planet losing its atmosphere is also losing its hydrological cycle. Without rain or snow, the land becomes arid. Dust, therefore, becomes a major factor in whatever atmosphere is left, as it is today on Mars.

Chapter 18: The Fabled Arch of Glimpa

They could easily see the dark stain on the crumbling rocks where the ancient sea had lapped at the shores of the island. Mati took the ship a little higher and they began searching for an arch, or a twenty-thousand-year-old rowboat. No one held their breath about the rowboat.

About a quarter hour into the search, Boro grumbled. "There's probably a Nebador marker. Can't Manessa follow the transmission from it?"

"No," Rini said. "The markers don't start transmitting until the ship is near."

"Damn . . ." Boro whispered, and went back to staring at the visual on the large bridge display.

"You okay?" Sata asked, turning to look at him.

"Yeah. Just . . . learning patience."

"I know what we need!" she said, hopping up and dashing to the galley. Soon each person received a cup of cold tea in their drink holder. "We've been forgetting the things Kibi usually does."

"Bull's eye!" Boro suddenly shouted, bouncing up and down in the command chair and spilling his tea. "The Arch of Glimpa, or I'm a purple donkey!"

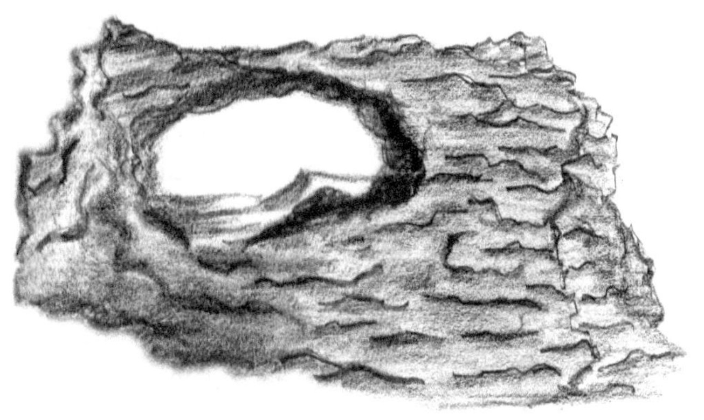

Mati grinned as the natural rock arch came into view, spanning fifty meters or more with stone of yellow, orange, and deep rusty red. She gained a little altitude and guided the ship in that direction.

"There's the Nebador marker!" Rini announced as they cleared a low ridge of boulders between the ancient coastline and the arch.

As Mati lowered the ship into the sandy open space near the little black monument, Boro frowned and looked askance at the huge rock arch that seemed to tower over them.

Sata noticed his worry. "We're uphill from it, and more than a hundred meters away. It's only about forty meters high, so it can't fall on us."

Boro relaxed, but his frown didn't completely disappear. "No closer!"

Mati nodded.

"Sonmatia Four, marker five-one," Sata read. "The Arch of Glimpa."

*

Day one. I rowed all night long. As the sun rose, my arms felt like lead, but I dared not stop or I would drift south. I entered a second-level walking meditation, but willed my arms to move instead of my feet. In a clear sky, the sun seemed bent on cooking me. Somehow, as the blessed evening finally arrived, I crawled onto the rocks at the south end of Glimpa.

Day four. The sun-blisters on my hands and arms are beginning to harden. The air is so thin, I drag myself along slowly, ever searching for the Arch. I found one spring with water, but many others are dry.

Day seven. The fabled Arch stretches itself before me, silent as a . . . tomb. My tomb, I guess. Whether the gods accept my humble gift or not, I know my mortal body is done. I shall never know the touch of a mate, nor bear a child. Perhaps, if my offering is accepted, the wind will blow again, the rain will fall, and my friend Kelsa will ask Regno to join with her, and they will have a daughter and name her Nosta.

Day eleven. At sunrise I sit on the Arch to salute the new day and summon courage and joy into my heart where dread and fear lurk in waiting. I can see smoke rising from the City of Memna, and in the exact opposite direction, somewhere in the Desert of Bakka, more smoke from the Mines of Sarto. By mid-morning I seek the shade beneath the Arch, and descend into the deepest levels of meditation. Slowly, without any act of will, I allow my spirit to rise up to Heaven.

Day fifteen. I am completely out of food. I am too weak to travel far, and the only things growing here are bitter and make me lose more than they give me. Even if I had the will to return to the boat, I know I would die on the way. No, I will finish what I started, here, at Glimpa's Arch. The act belongs to me, the consequence, pleasing or not, belongs to the gods.

Day seventeen. I can no longer climb the Arch to see the sunrise. My world has shrunk to the little strip of shade beneath the Arch as it moves from hour to hour.

Day twenty-one. Yesterday I sat in the most joyful awareness of the gods for half the day and all the night. The morning glow in the sky was like a gift to me, a little private celebration, for I no longer have the strength to follow the shade. After I write this, I will prop myself against the base of my beloved Arch, giving everything in my mind and heart and spirit to the gods. As the sun climbs into the sky, I will die.

My hand shakes and I can write no more.

* * *

"The act belongs to me, the consequence, pleasing or not, belongs to the gods." This is a theological idea found in most religions. What do you think of it?

Many plants are not actually poison, but they are "emetic," which means they make us vomit. When this happens, we lose not only what we just ate, but also anything else in our stomachs. This is what Nosta meant when she said, ". . . make me lose more than they give me." The same thing happens if we are thirsty and drink sea water. We will vomit, and actually be more dehydrated than before we drank the sea water.

Is there a person you know, or have heard of, who has given their life for something they believed?

How did Nosta die?

Chapter 19: The Sonmatia Four Puzzle

The bridge of the deep-space response ship was deathly quiet, save for a slight sniffling sound coming from the navigator's station. Tears ran silently down the pilot's face. Rini had his knees up in his chair and was hiding his face in his arms. In the command chair, Boro's unfocused eyes glistened with moisture.

A quarter hour later, Sata silently made her way to the galley and reheated some left-over soup. They gathered like zombies and poked at their bowls, but ate little.

"I think . . ." Mati finally said in barely more than a whisper, "I think it doesn't really matter what the puzzle is. We're here to . . . you know . . . feel what happened to these people, twenty thousand years ago."

A few minutes later, Rini collected his thoughts. "Yeah. We should do the puzzle, which is to learn everything we can about what happened, but the puzzle's not the important thing."

Boro nodded. "I think Nosta said something in her journal, near the end, that will let us find the Mines of Sarto."

"She said she saw smoke at Memna in one direction," Sata remembered, "and smoke at the mines exactly opposite. Calculating reciprocal compass directions is easy. The only problem is . . . I forgot to mark the city on my chart. I didn't think we'd be going back, or needing to know where it was."

"I can find it," Mati said, examining a spoonful of soup before slipping it into her mouth.

"Good," Boro began, "because I need to stretch my legs . . . in the City of Memna. Something about the place calls to me, and I think I would have liked it there. I want to walk the streets and see what the stones whisper to me. Rini, you're in command."

*

By following their flight path in reverse, Mati brought them to the old mainland shore within a few kilometers of the City of Memna, and a minute later lowered the ship near the Nebador marker.

After leaving through the airlock, Boro stood beside the marker as the Manessa Kwi retracted its landing struts and floated away.

"You guys have fun," Boro said through the intercom. "If you find the mines, look for something for our display containers."

"We will," Sata replied. "Remember to watch your air supply!"

"I've got two hours. I'll either find my ghosts by then, or get bored. Manessa will yell if I start turning blue."

"I *guarantee* we'll be back before then!"

"Thanks!" Boro waved one last time to the departing ship, then started walking down one of the streets where people worked and children played twenty thousand years before.

*

Rini looked very uncomfortable perched on the edge of the command chair on the trip back to the island. "I can almost *see* Nosta when I close my eyes, meditating under the Arch of Glimpa."

Mati turned her head slightly, a gleam of jealousy in her eyes for a second. "You want to walk around there?"

"Um . . . yeah."

Mati lowered the ship near the Nebador marker.

Sata went to work. "I marked the City of Memna on the chart when we dropped off Boro, and it matches his tracer molecule. All I have to do is draw a straight line, and we should be able to find the Mines of Sarto."

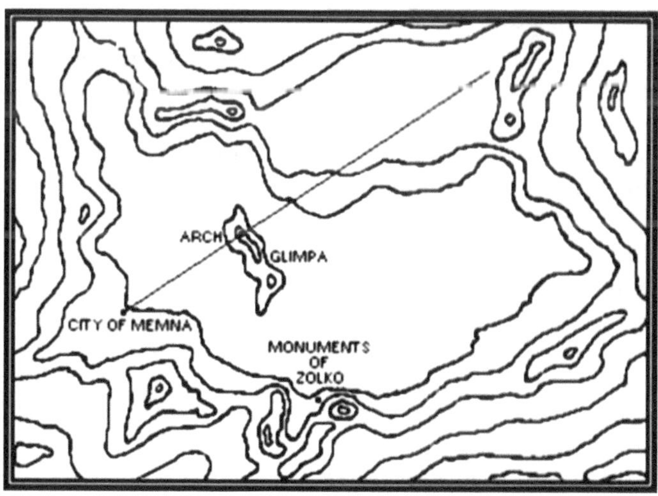

Rini hopped up. "I'll pay my respects to Nosta while you guys go find the most beautiful gemstone in the world! I guess . . . Sata, you want to be in command?"

"Um . . . sure. It doesn't really matter. Me and Mati are a team — we'll make decisions together."

Mati swiveled around and smiled. "This'll be fun, just two girls and our space ship!"

Rini smiled and stepped into the lift.

✷

As Rini walked down the sandy hill toward the Arch of Glimpa, a noticeable spring in his step even in a space suit, Mati prepared to lift the ship back into the air.

"We could just sit here awhile," Sata said from her station. "I have to do some trigonometry."

"I want to give Rini some space. He's got a thing for Nosta, and I don't want to come between them."

Sata glanced at her friend, but didn't say anything.

"Why trigonometry?" Mati asked as she piloted.

"We just had a review of all the trig functions. If that isn't a hint, I don't know what is!"

"I trust you. If you can't figure it out, I sure can't! I'll just pilot the ship wherever you tell me to go. I hope we can find it before we have to get Boro and Rini."

A minute later, Mati lowered the ship onto an ancient beach somewhere on the edge of the Desert of Bakka.

✷

Rini slowly climbed the surrounding rocks, then stepped carefully onto the rock arch, about three meters wide at that point. His bracelet chimed the four-minute reminder he had programmed. He paused to glance at his air supply, then looked around.

The yellow sky almost completely surrounded him, broken only by a small cloud of dust somewhere in the desert to the northeast. Directly overhead, the sky was nearly black. The sun hung in the west, over the City of Memna. Rini thought of Boro, opened his bracelet, and tapped at the tiny keys.

"Boro, this is Rini. Can you hear me?"

"Hi, Rini! Are you outside too?"

"Yeah. I'm on the arch. The girls are looking for the mines."

"Nosta really spoke to you, didn't she?"

"Yeah. I could see myself in her shoes. You find anything interesting?"

"The more I wander around, the more I can understand how deeply the people believed they were doing the right things to make their gods happy and reverse the climate change. I guess Zolko believed it too. And Sarto."

"And Nosta," Rini added.

"Yeah. I think they were all off the mark."

"Ilika can help us understand it when we get back. I'm almost to the middle of the arch, about two meters wide here. No cracks that worry me."

"I'm on the northern edge of the city. Just a large village, really. Nothing left but stone and dust, but every time I sit down, I can almost hear the people talking . . ."

✷

Sata cocked her head. "Manessa, how much air does Boro have left?"

"Assuming normal activity, one hour and seventeen minutes."

"Okay, let's see if I can figure this thing out," Sata said, moving her hands on the console. "Zolko to Memna was west by northwest, and I've got those points on the chart. Manessa, please playback the story of the Monuments of Zolko where it mentioned the Desert of Bakka."

"On the third day, Councilor Sarto crept away and sold all his property to hire a ship and many strong men. He believed the gods would look favorably on them if they found the most beautiful gemstone in the world and placed it in the temple. He carried books and maps from the great library, all telling him that such a gemstone could only be found across the sea, in the Desert of Bakka, somewhere along the eight degree line, for that was the number most sacred to the gods."

"Eight degrees . . . eight degrees . . . I hope it really was on the eight-degree line," Sata mumbled as she worked. "Okay, there it is! And we've got a nice, pretty triangle. I just have to figure out which trig function to use."

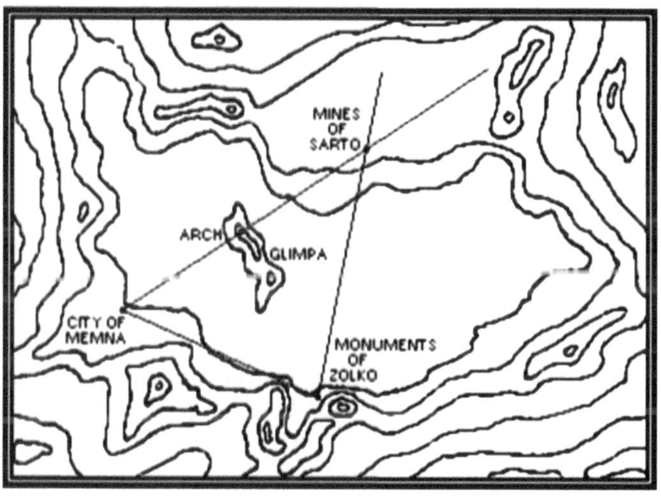

While Sata worked, Mati got her crutch and hobbled to the galley. As she slowly put together a snack for the two of them, she heard mumbled trigonometry functions, intermixed with curses, coming from the navigator's station. The words and other noises started out sounding a little annoyed, soon became frustrated, and eventually seethed with anger. Mati left the tray and hobbled down to the bridge.

Sata burst into tears when Mati put her free arm around her friend.

✷

"Rini, this is Boro."

"I'm under the arch now, probably about where Nosta died."

Boro was silent for a moment. "Any bones?"

"No, they would have turned to dust a long time ago. Any more ghosts there?"

"I think I found the place where they built the smoky fire. It's a pit in the middle of a small plaza. I scooped out some of the dust, and can see blackened sides, maybe even some charcoal."

"The smoke Nosta saw."

"Yeah. As things got worse and worse, I bet the people became frustrated and angry, so they burned stuff." Boro was silent for a long moment as he gathered his courage. "Rini?"

"Yeah?"

"I'm worried about something. I'm down to about half an hour of air. I was hoping I could let the girls finish what they were doing, but I'm starting to get a little scared."

"Want me to teach you how to change that half hour into an hour?"

"Could you?"

"First you have to let go of that fear — it will only make you breathe faster and waste air . . ."

*

"I've tried *everything!*" Sata nearly screamed, red-faced. "It's not sine or cosine, tangent doesn't work, and *forget* the reciprocal functions!"

"Secant or cosecant?" Mati asked in a timid voice.

"No! Nothing!"

"You're worried about Boro, aren't you?"

Sata burst into tears again. "He's down to . . . about a quarter hour of air . . . and I wanted to have some beautiful crystals to show him. And I wanted to show him . . . that I could be in command and not mess up!"

Mati wrapped her arms around her friend as best she could. Eventually, Sata relaxed and started wiping her tears on her sleeve.

Mati sat down at her own station. "Why don't you ask Manessa for help?"

Sata sniffled and pursed her lips in thought for a long moment. "I wanted to do it myself . . . but I guess I should. Manessa, please analyze the problem on my screen and tell me which trigonometry function to use."

"Ilika asked me not to tell you."

Sata didn't start crying again. Instead, she became beet-red and looked ready to explode. "Manessa! Who is in command of this ship?"

"You are, Sata. Rini transferred command to you before leaving the ship."

"Am I in *complete* command of this ship?"

"Yes, Sata."

"Then why won't you answer my question!"

"I will answer your question, if you wish. All you have to do is override Ilika's request."

Sata's mouth opened, but no sound came out.

Mati was trying very hard to hold in a snicker, but a little bit escaped.

"What?" Sata snapped.

"Manessa never said she wouldn't answer your question. It's happened to Kibi too. Manessa just said, 'Ilika asked,' not 'I can't' or 'I won't.' No one's ever tried overriding Ilika's request."

Sata was silent for a long moment, dumbfounded but thoughtful. Finally she took a deep breath. "Manessa, override any requests Ilika made about not helping with this problem."

"No trigonometry function works in this situation because it is not a trigonometry problem. The triangle on your screen is not a right triangle, nor are you attempting to find an unknown angle or length. It is a position problem defined by the intersection of two lines, and is best solved by creating two directional functions, one in which the direction to Boro's tracer equals the direction to Rini's tracer, and another in which the direction to Ilika's tracer equals the reciprocal of eight degrees. Then the pilot can use the functions, just as she would a navigation beacon, to adjust the flight path until both functions have a value of zero. We would then be right over the target. Altitude is not an issue because the target is, by definition, on the surface."

Sata remained silent for a moment, swallowing and breathing. Mati watched her friend, but said nothing.

"Boro should be out of air in eight minutes," the ship suddenly said.

Sata sat bolt-upright, moving her hands on her console, all hints of earlier emotions gone. "Boro, this is Sata! We're coming!"

Mati quickly raised her flight control.

"What's the hurry?" Boro asked through the intercom. "I've got forty minutes of air, several more stones to photograph, and a few more ghosts to talk to."

"Are you sure?" Sata asked with a wrinkled brow. "Manessa said you should be almost out."

"Rini taught me how to relax, turn down my suit temperature, and sort of meditate while I walk. I've almost doubled my suit time!"

"Um . . . okay. We're about to go find the Mines of Sarto. See you in half an hour or less!" She made another selection. "Rini? How much air do you have."

"More than an hour. I'm sitting under the arch, and sometimes I think I can almost feel Nosta's presence."

"Okay. See you in an hour or less."

Mati, following the conversations closely, let go of her flight control.

"Manessa," Sata began, "give me those directional functions again . . ."

✷ ✷ ✷

Reciprocal (opposite) compass directions, in our system, are calculated by adding or subtracting 180 (it doesn't matter which), then applying modulus 360. 70 + 180 = 250, modulus 360 = 250. 300 + 180 = 480, modulus 360 = 120.

In our compass system, what would be the reciprocal of 8 degrees?

Why was Boro especially interested in the City of Memna?

What qualities did Nosta have that caused Rini to relate to her?

Why was Sata so determined to find a trigonometry function that would allow her to solve the problem?

Chapter 20: The Mines of Sarto

Minutes later, Mati watched the two directional functions on her display as she guided the Manessa Kwi over the Desert of Bakka. Sometimes the indicator line of the Boro and Rini function would move slightly to the left or right, and she would correct the ship's course until the line was again centered. The line on the Ilika and Kibi function was still quite a ways off, but slowly approaching center.

"If we find it in the next few minutes," Sata thought aloud, "we'll have about a quarter hour for exploring."

"I think we'll be there soon," Mati said, "and ion drive can get us back to the City of Memna in seconds, although we might scare Rini as we pass."

Sata snickered. "You're a little miffed at him, aren't you?"

Mati was silent for a moment. "I guess it's a little silly to be jealous of someone who died twenty thousand years ago."

"Anyway, they probably weren't human."

Mati's eyes opened wide. "What were they?"

"I don't know. Manessa, what kind of creatures were the people who used to live here?"

"Ilika asked me not to . . ."

"Override."

"All of the sapient inhabitants of the places we have visited on this planet were reptilian bipeds."

Sata burst out laughing.

"No," Mati said, grinning and laughing, "I don't think I'll be jealous of long-dead lizards! We're getting close, and I'm taking us down to one hundred meters. Help me look for it."

Suddenly Sata received a transmission, and a symbol appeared on her chart. "No need. The Nebador marker just came to life, and it's off to the left a little."

*

"Marker five-two," Mati read. "The Mines of Sarto."

"No writings or recordings have been discovered that detail the lives of the people who worked these mines. Apparently all of the people who labored here were driven by an intense desire to find a gemstone worthy of offering to their gods. There is no evidence of slavery.

"Nor were there any class or status differences. Councilor Sarto appears to have worked right alongside the other miners, day after day, until the very end. Judging by the positions of bodies, tools, and gemstones, the following reconstruction of events seems most likely:

"Sarto and his followers decided on this location about half a year after crossing the sea. With shovels and blasting powder, they dug shafts into the bedrock until they found veins of crystals that angled deep into the planet. These they followed as far as they could, bringing every find to the surface to be cleaned and inspected.

"About a year into their work, they could go no deeper as carbon dioxide began to fill the lower tunnels. Many miners died from the bad air or sheer exhaustion. Sarto and a few hearty followers pressed on, taking turns working for just a few minutes each in the deep places.

"Those who could no longer work in the mines helped to clean and sort the crystals, each hoping to find the object of their quest. When nothing else could be done, they burned whatever they could find to send their prayers up to the gods.

"The day came when only Sarto and one other miner remained alive. The miner was large and strong, but his name is not known. He struggled up from one of the deep tunnels, placed a dirt-filled box at Sarto's feet, and died.

Mati paused to wipe her eyes. "You can finish. I can't see very well right now."

Sata waited until her friend was ready. "After honoring the fallen man with tools in his hands and gemstones over his eyes, Sarto was amazed to find, in the box of dirt, the most beautiful cluster of crystals he had ever seen. Alone, he lovingly cleaned the precious object. With his last bit of strength, Sarto placed it on a boulder for the gods to see, cried himself to sleep, and never woke up.

"The mine tunnels collapsed long ago. The boulder where Sarto placed the offering still sits forty meters east of this marker. The crystal cluster resides in the museum at Satamia Star Station, and the gods often come to admire it and remember Sarto and his people, just as they do the Monuments of Zolko, the City of Memna, and the Arch of Glimpa. Visitors may find souvenir crystals among the mine tailings north of this marker."

*

Boro had only twenty minutes of air, even with all the tricks Rini could teach him, so Mati and Sata agreed on a plan that would shave minutes off the last two things they wanted to do.

While Sata climbed into a space suit, Mati moved the ship to the boulder where the crystals had been offered up. About a meter high, it showed signs of braving dust and sand storms for at least twenty thousand years.

Sata opened the outer airlock door but didn't step outside. As soon as she had taken a photograph and glanced around, Mati moved the ship to the ancient piles of rock and dirt that had come from the mine. With sample container in hand, Sata was quickly on the ground.

"This'll be easy!" Sata announced after walking a few meters from the ship. "Crystals all over the place. I just have to pick out a nice one that'll fit in our containers . . . like this one!" She held up a small cluster of purple spikes for Mati to see.

"Looks perfect. Now let's go get our boys. It's been nice taking a break, but I'm starting to miss them."

Sata grabbed two more small crystals and added them to the sample container. "Me too."

* * *

The solution to Sata's navigation problem (using the locations of Boro's, Rini's, and Ilika's tracer molecules) would be similar to one method of radio navigation we use today called ADF/NDB (Automatic Direction Finder/Non-Directional Beacon). When the instrument is tuned to the proper radio frequency in our aircraft, a needle points to the radio source beacon, allowing the pilot to "home" to the beacon, or calculate the angle between the beacon and another heading or bearing.

The methods Rini taught Boro to extend his air supply all involve slowing the body's metabolism. What dangers might arise if Rini or Boro did this too much?

Why was Mati able to let go of her jealousy when she learned that Nosta wasn't human?

People argue endlessly whether our god(s) are just made up in our heads from wishful thinking, or really exist separate from our expectations. In the story of the ancient people of Sonmatia Four, which appears to be the case, and how do you know?

An illustration shows the boulder as it might have looked with the crystal cluster still on top.

Chapter 21: Picking Up the Puzzle Pieces

Mati took a deep breath. For the first time, she was about to move the ship a long distance with no one else on the bridge. Her heart beat faster as she gave the ship voice commands to warm up the ion drive.

Sata, by agreement, waited in the airlock in case anyone needed help getting into the ship.

"The City of Memna," Mati announced through the intercom a minute later as she extended landing struts. Long shadows reached out across the central plaza from the surrounding ruins as the sun approached the horizon.

Sata opened the outer door. "Boro? Are you nearby?"

"Sata, you in a suit? You gotta see this!"

Sata stepped outside to see Boro, not far from the Nebador marker, waving and pointing downward. She walked in his direction. "We can't forget Rini."

"He has about twenty minutes more than me, and I have at least eight, maybe twelve minutes. It's amazing how much air you save just by breathing through your nose."

She self-consciously closed her mouth and followed him down an old dusty stairway into the ground. He activated his bracelet light and she did the same.

"I found this just a little while ago."

Sata gazed around with wide eyes, taking in the faded mural paintings covering all four walls. Lizard-like people in ornate robes, sometimes with elaborate jewelry, stood or walked in ritual formation, carrying offerings of fruit, gemstones, or scrolls.

"They were reptiles," Boro said.

"Manessa told us, but we had no idea what they looked like."

The back wall, never touched by sunlight, was the least faded, and one figure stood foremost, reaching up with her offering of a large double-rolled scroll while searching the cloudless yellow sky with desperate eyes.

"Memna, probably," Boro whispered.

Sata nodded, then something caught her eye in one corner of the mural. She moved closer and aimed her light.

"I was hoping you'd see that," Boro said.

A small golden sphere perched on three legs, ramp extended and hatch open, and a reptilian in a blue robe stood at the top of the ramp, talking to a group of children who had gathered around.

✷

"Manessa says she has photographs of all the mural paintings," Mati said over the intercom, "including a bunch you haven't seen yet. Aren't you about out of air, Boro?"

"Yeah. I just got my four-minute alarm. We're coming."

The pilot made sure her engines were ready while Boro and Sata entered the airlock, then made quick-work of the journey back to the Arch of Glimpa.

Rini sat cross-legged on the arch, facing the sunset, as the Manessa Kwi settled onto the sand near the marker. He waved, and Mati's heart beat a little faster.

"Did you get Boro first?" he asked with concern, standing up.

"I'm right here!" Boro announced, touching the intercom symbol at his console. "Did you know they were reptiles?"

Rini was silent for a moment as he stopped dead in his tracks near one side of the arch, then burst out laughing. "I pictured Nosta having tangled black hair, like Kibi."

"Sorry, just scales and spikes," Mati said. "Aren't you almost out of air, or should we come back after dinner, maybe a video?"

Rini whimpered. "I'll make it to the airlock, but not by much. It takes a few minutes just to climb down from here."

Just then the sun sank below the horizon, and suddenly the land became pitch-dark.

"Uh oh," Rini said with a trembling voice.

"Thin atmosphere, no twilight," Boro explained.

"Rini, stay right where you are," Mati asserted, "that's an order." The ship's external lights came on and lit the area brilliantly. "Sata, you still in the airlock?"

"Yep!"

"Good. Boro, anti-mass one, maneuvering thrusters."

"Blue-green . . . green."

Mati carefully lifted the Manessa Kwi to the height of the arch.

"I just got my four-minute alarm!" Rini squeaked. "I guess I'm scared and breathing faster."

"That fear has to go . . ." Boro began in his deep voice.

Rini chuckled, remembering his own words. "Yes, master. It's harder when it's *your* air that's almost out!"

Boro smiled as Mati maneuvered to the top of the huge rock outcropping.

"Sata, I don't know how stable this rock is," Mati said, "so I'm just going to hover. Open the outer door, then tell me if I'm close enough."

"A meter lower . . . that's good. Rini's coming with his bracelet light . . . he's in Manessa's lights now . . . he's climbing in."

As soon as Rini was inside, Sata closed the outer door and pressurized the airlock. Rini opened his faceplate, and both he and Sata heard his one-minute air alarm. They both grinned and slapped hands before opening the inner door.

*

The four members of the crew who were not usually in command, but who had all experienced the responsibilities of command that day, agreed they needed some time to talk. By Manessa's external lights, Mati lowered the ship back onto the sand near the Nebador marker.

Sata, with Rini's help, quickly put together a hearty dinner of reheated left-overs from the refrigerator.

Boro transferred his photographs from bracelet to ship, then shared all his discoveries of strange symbols etched in stone, mural paintings, and pits where the people had once burned their belongings. With some embarrassment, he also talked about the voices he thought he heard in many of the ruins.

Rini had begun his stay on the Island of Glimpa thinking he was there to remember an apprentice wizard named Nosta, a girl about his age. He soon discovered she had friends, and the longer and deeper he meditated, the more presences he felt. He speculated that she was only the last of many who had come to the Arch for solitude and enlightenment.

Sata showed the boulder where Sarto had made his best and final offering, and described the mine tailings littered with beautiful crystals. She opened the sample container, and the shimmering pink and purple gems were passed around. Then she shared her deep embarrassment at trying to find the intersection of two lines using trigonometry.

Rini grinned with sparkling eyes. Boro's face twisted in thought.

In Mati's opinion, Sata had left out the most important lesson they learned. With a nod from Sata, she explained how any previous order from Ilika could be overridden by the commander.

"But we should only do that if we really need to," Boro said with a worried look.

"True," Rini agreed, "but I think Ilika *wants* us to know how."

Mati nodded. "It should be up to whoever's in command."

Boro thought for a moment. "That sounds right."

After talking for hours, the four crew members of the Manessa Kwi began yawning, and decided that Ilika and Kibi would find something to do without them for one night.

* * *

As Boro learned and shared with Sata, breathing through the nose slows our metabolism. It also conserves body moisture. Breathing through the mouth is only useful during extreme exertion, like running.

Why would gods, aliens, or the Nebador Transport Service, prefer to rescue children, instead of wise old adults, when a species was threatened with extinction?

There is little or no twilight on a planet with a thin atmosphere because twilight is caused by the air scattering the light that is still moving through it but otherwise destined to miss the planet.

In your opinion, is it cheating to override a previous commander's order, or a necessary part of ship operations?

Chapter 22: Farewell to Sonmatia Four

In the emergency shelter, Kibi pulled a warm robe closely around her and gazed at the display screen at the end of the table where six people could eat or work. On the screen, the rising sun lit up the tallest of the Monuments of Zolko, but the palace foundation was still in shadow.

Behind her, Ilika worked in a tiny galley sandwiched between shelves of supplies, racks of fuel canisters, and bunk beds.

"What smells so good?" Kibi asked, putting her bare feet up on the seat across from her.

"Eggs, mushrooms, and onions . . . cooked in a little bit of tasty nut oil."

"Yum! We'd better finish before the others get back, so we don't have to share!"

Ilika grinned, and carried two trays to the table.

*

The Manessa Kwi arrived about an hour later, rotated until the airlock aligned with the shelter's hatch, and settled onto its struts. Rini poked his head in. "Are we interrupting?"

The four from the ship received a complete tour of the emergency shelter. Ilika noticed Boro's eyes sparkling when the engineer saw the rack of fuel canisters. "Boro, we should get some liquid number five. Kibi will show you how to log it."

"Yeah! Space thruster fuel!"

"I've already picked out a case of pinkfruit juice," Kibi announced. "Just use this knowledge processor, open the shelter transaction list, and add a new record."

"How much does it cost?" Boro asked with a slight frown, remembering

Ilika didn't have much gold or silver left after Rini's marriage ceremony.

Ilika smiled. "Nebador doesn't use money. We keep different kinds for visiting planets like yours. There, I had to take metal coins. Sometimes it's seashells, sometimes just numbers stored in a machine."

Boro looked confused. Mati and Sata both shrugged.

"You'll learn more about that at Satamia Star Station. So . . . what did you learn on your adventure without Kibi and me?"

"Well . . ." Boro began with hesitation, "most of it we want to show you. But there is one thing . . . at first we weren't sure we should even tell you . . . but we decided to, and since Sata discovered it . . ."

All eyes turned to the navigator. She took a slow, deep breath. "We discovered . . . how to override . . . any commands you've given Manessa . . . that would keep her from helping us with something."

Kibi's eyes snapped open wide. "Teach me!"

Everyone else glanced at Ilika. He was trying to hold in a smile.

"I thought so!" Rini said. "He wanted us to know."

"It's a time-honored rule," Ilika began, "that a commander must have *complete* command to deal with unexpected situations, the ability to change any previous command or break any rule. Every emergency is different. No one can anticipate what will be needed. That is one reason Manessa, who is only sentient, must have a sapient crew."

Boro's mouth twisted back and forth for a moment. "But only in an emergency, right?"

"That's a little harsh," Ilika replied. "I think it would be better to say, only in need. Let's say we're doing a training flight, and I've restricted your engine power. The exercise may be hard, but you're learning things, and I'm watching for dangers. Then, during the exercise, I have to step into the toilet room, and while I'm in there, your flight conditions change. You have to be willing to override my previous limits because you know the current conditions, and sitting on the toilet, I don't."

Several cheesy grins greeted Ilika as he looked around at his crew members.

*

Ilika and Kibi took the front two seats in the passenger area.

Mati read the story of the Monuments of Zolko as she slowly moved the ship from pillar to pillar. Each ancient face gazed at them from the large screen over the steward's station, etched by dust and sand until the species could only be guessed, human or ursine, avian or reptile.

Boro read the story of the City of Memna, then continued with his own discoveries of charcoal pits, mural paintings, and whispering stones. The screen alternated between views of the city below and photographs selected by the engineer.

Rini told the story of Nosta and the Arch of Glimpa, while Mati slowly gave them a view from every angle. He described his own meditations on and under the Arch, and finished by telling of his rescue in the dark with one minute of air remaining.

Sata began with her embarrassing assumption that trigonometry could solve her navigation problem. Kibi admitted she would have made the same mistake. Ilika only smiled.

The navigator read the story of the Mines of Sarto while Mati hovered near the boulder and mine tailings, all that remained of a once proud and determined community. Sata finished by presenting the souvenir crystals.

"It's time for another display container!" Kibi asserted. "Do we have anything else from the fourth planet?"

Rini brought out a cup containing a handful of sand he had pocketed from beneath the Arch of Glimpa, about where Nosta had probably turned to dust twenty thousand years before.

*

Over soup and freshly-baked biscuits, Ilika looked around the table at his crew, more confidence showing in their eyes and bearing than ever before. He noticed that Kibi wore a thoughtful expression.

"If these Nebador markers are numbers forty-seven through fifty-two," she pondered, "there must be others all over the planet."

"There are," Ilika confirmed with a nod. "Several hundred. We could spend weeks studying the history of this planet, going from marker to marker, reading text and looking at pictures."

Mati looked up from her soup bowl with cold, flashing eyes.

"But we have important things ahead," Ilika said, smiling at his pilot, "and few of the markers make good puzzles, like these do. Want to take us out, Kibi?"

The steward of the Manessa Kwi grinned. "Flight objective?"

"Let's start with a stationary orbit."

Mati smiled. "Easy!"

"Then we'll put Sata and Boro to work figuring out how to get us to Sonmatia Five."

"No problem!" the engineer declared. "I've got fuel out my ears, *including* space-thruster!"

They quickly scraped their bowls, and Rini dashed for the galley to do the dishes.

*

"A stationary orbit . . ." Kibi pondered aloud from the command chair. "How high is that on this planet, Sata?"

The navigator began working at her console. "About a hundred thousand kilometers. Chart on channel five."

"Got it," Mati said.

"Rini, anything up there?" Kibi asked.

He looked over his displays. "Just two little moons. I'll add them to the chart."

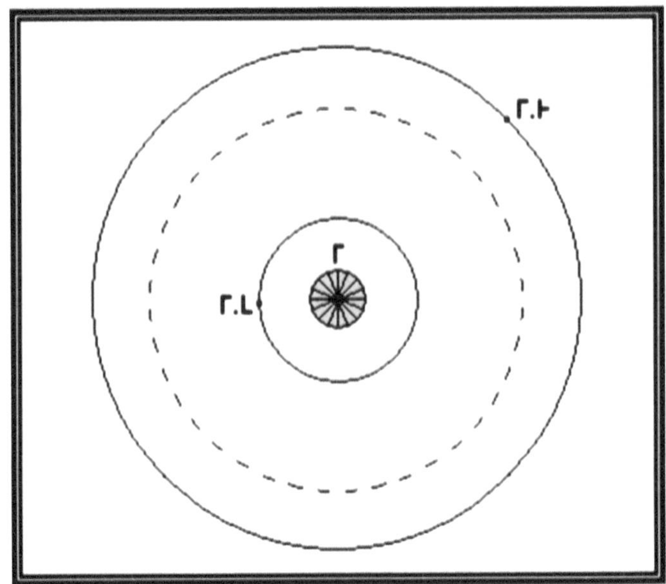

"Ilika!" Mati shrieked. "The orbit you want is *between* the two moons!"

The captain grinned from the steward's station. "Those orbits are more than a hundred thousand kilometers apart. Do you think you can squeeze Manessa in?"

Mati growled under her breath, leaned back in her chair, and stared at the graph. "I just don't want to get whacked by a big rock."

"Think in *three* dimensions, Mati. Remember, almost everything in the solar system is in one flat plane. You already made use of that, instinctively, back at Sonmatia Three."

Mati sat up straight and tapped at her display selector.

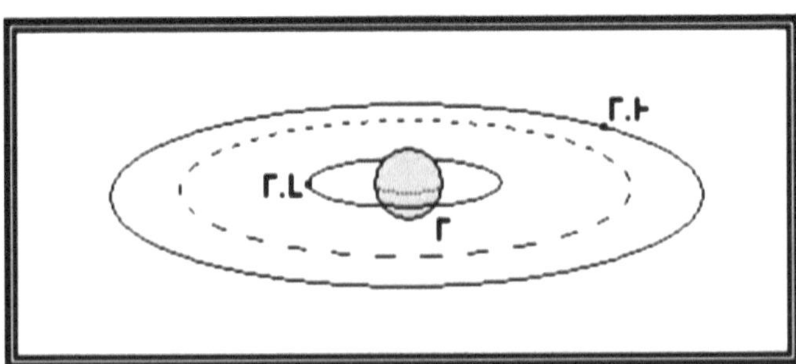

"Okay, I get it. Don't worry about the moons, just go over or under."

"Pay attention, Sata and Boro. You're going to need this technique to get us to Sonmatia Five."

Sata and Boro looked at each other.

"I need anti-mass and ion five," Mati said.

Kibi checked the status of all stations, and Rini produced a weather map showing a dust storm to the east. Mati slowly lifted the ship to a thousand meters, and with a nod from Kibi, the Manessa Kwi streaked away toward Sonmatia Four's north pole.

* * *

Ilika was able to cook eggs for himself and Kibi in the emergency shelter because eggs are very easy to dehydrate, powder, and store. You can buy them in many good camping supply stores. After adding a little water, they make reasonably good scrambled eggs. Mushrooms and onions, of course, can also be dried or freeze-dried. You will only have trouble if you insist on eggs over-easy.

What, in your opinion, is the purpose of money?

Can you think of a culture that used metal coins for money? Sea shells? Numbers stored in a machine?

In addition to overriding a previous commander's orders, any piloting situation (as we first noted in *Book Four*) could require the crew to bend, even break, the rules. FAR (Federal Aviation Regulations in the USA) 91.3(b) states "In an in-flight emergency requiring immediate action, the pilot in command may deviate from any rule . . . to the extent required to meet that emergency." Breaking the rules "well" is one of the things that clearly separates adults from children.

"Ursine" is the adjective that refers to the entire bear family of Ursidae. "Ursine" rhymes with "equine" (the horse family).

Two diagrams show the Sonmatia Four planetary system. Why did Mati have trouble thinking of a safe route into planetary orbit (the dashed line) when she was looking at the first diagram?

Chapter 23: Lots of Rocks

"Ilika!" Sata called from her station where she and Boro had been peering at solar system charts ever since they entered stationary orbit. "What's this nonsense about Sonmatia Five? There's nothing there but a bunch of rocks spread out in a wide band all along the planet's orbital path!"

Ilika looked up from the steward's console where he was working with Kibi. Rini stepped out of the galley to listen, and Mati looked up from her knowledge pad at the table.

"It was a nice little rock and ice planet once, I hear," the captain said, "about four billion years ago. Even had a bit of primitive life. Then it got too close to Sonmatia Six, the big gas giant. When gravity from another source interferes with the internal gravity of a planet, it usually falls apart."

"There are more than a million fragments," Boro noted, studying Sata's display. "You want to visit them all?"

Mati frowned from the table.

"One will do," Ilika said as he began tapping at Kibi's console. "Let's visit . . . five-three-three. It's a metallic core fragment."

Sata and Boro went back to work.

Mati looked happy again.

✷

"Ilika was serious about going over or under, instead of through," Sata explained as she stood at the end of the big table near the steward's station. She touched some symbols on a knowledge pad and their next flight plan appeared on the large display. "If we went straight along the plane of the solar system, we'd have to worm our way through thousands of rocks. If we go in from the north or south, there are only six or eight rocks between clear space and fragment five-three-three."

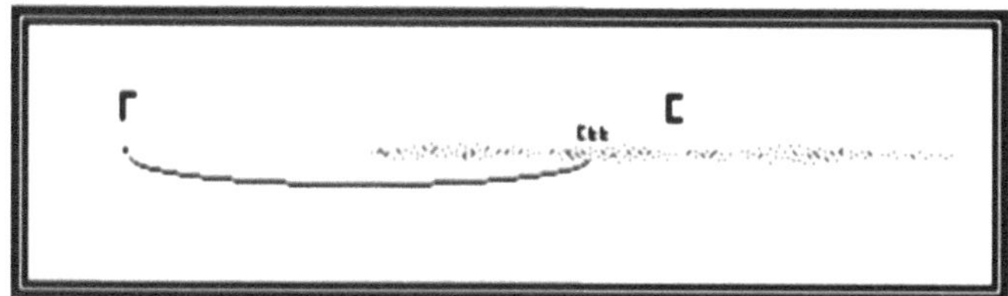

Mati gazed at the display. "Why did you pick going in from the bottom . . . I mean the south?"

"Ilika's idea. He wanted us to get used to the fact that over and under are exactly the same in space."

The pilot nodded.

Boro stood up, touched his knowledge pad, and a photograph appeared on the screen. "Five-three-three is a very irregular metal thing, two kilometers across, big pointy spikes sticking out all over it, gravity about one-thousandth of what we're used to. It's not just floating peacefully in space, it's tumbling. Ilika says if we can land on it, we can land on *anything*."

Nervous chuckles came from all around the table.

Ilika smiled. "It will require canceling Manessa's proximity responses, and good teamwork from watch, navigator, pilot, engineer, and steward. Are you up to it?"

Mati grinned and nodded, with Rini only a heartbeat behind. Sata and Boro joined a little more slowly.

Ilika looked at Kibi.

"This wouldn't be a good time to go back to the desert and eat lizards, would it?"

"No," Boro and Sata both said with stern looks. Ilika kept his mouth shut.

"Then . . . count me in!" she said, cocked her head, and smiled.

*

The departure from Sonmatia Four was completed with hardly a word from Ilika. Mati engaged her ion drive at its highest power level, and the Manessa Kwi followed an elliptical course that avoided the outer moon's orbit. The flight leg ended a little more than an hour later, after traversing almost fifteen light-minutes of interplanetary space, on the southern edge of Sonmatia Five's asteroid belt.

A black sky full of shimmering rocks greeted them, some large enough to reveal the crescent shape created by the harsh light from the sun, most so small they were no more than points of brilliance.

"I thought you said six or eight rocks in the way," Mati said as she touched symbols to transfer helm control to the ship.

"Er . . . um . . ." Boro mumbled from his station, gazing at his display while moving his hands to shut down the ion drive.

"I can explain," Ilika said from the command chair. "There are so many fragments in an asteroid belt, all the way down to dust particles, and all in constant motion, that it would be impossible to chart them all. We only attempt to keep track of those one-meter across and larger. There may be six or eight of those between us and fragment five-three-three, and millions of smaller fragments."

"We don't need engines for this," Boro began, "we need a shovel!"

The bridge erupted with laughter.

"There's one in the utility room," Kibi said, grinning from ear to ear.

Rini doubled over with laughter and almost fell out of his chair.

When everyone finally collected themselves, Ilika cleared his throat. "As you know, in space we have to avoid asteroids down to about a millimeter because they can be moving at very high speeds in relation to the ship. Here, there are too many to avoid, so we use a different solution. We go in slowly, with Manessa in her minimum profile, and the repulsion field at maximum . . ."

"Shape selected," Mati said, moving her hands on her console.

"Repulsion field three," Boro confirmed.

". . . and Rini will give us a real-time, color-coded, three-D view that will be much more useful than the sparkling visual scene before us."

Rini started making selections at his console.

"Sata will not plot an exact course," Ilika continued, "but instead will map out corridors that avoid the large fragments. Mati's job will be to fly the corridors, avoid rocks one-eighth of a meter and up whenever possible, and ignore everything smaller. We'll feel some reaction when we bump into things. Kibi may need a bowl."

The steward pouted silently for a moment, but when she saw that everyone else was too busy to notice, she sighed and stepped into the galley.

"Okay," Mati said, "I have the color-coded three-D, the big rocks on the chart are red, I avoid yellows, greens are little. What's the big purple thing?"

"That's our destination," Rini explained.

Ilika took a few minutes to help Sata plot the corridors, then went from station to station to see if everyone was ready. "Inertia straps," he commanded as he returned to his chair. "Maneuvering thrusters. Manessa, cancel all proximity responses."

Mati turned and looked at her captain. "No bolting allowed in that mess!"

"That's right. If in doubt, stop and be still. These rocks all orbit together, and rarely collide."

*

For the next quarter hour, the bridge was very quiet as Mati concentrated on guiding the little ship through the asteroids, following Sata's corridors to miss the worst. The pilot did her best to avoid the medium-size rocks, but was not always successful. None of the bumps caused Kibi to lose her lunch.

It was the sight of fragment five-three-three, slowly spinning and tumbling directly in front of the ship, that did the trick.

* * *

The navigation diagram is a cross-section of the asteroid belt Sonmatia Five. Where would this solar system's sun be in relation to this diagram?

We have theories about how the asteroid belt in our solar system formed, but no proof. Interference from the gravity of Jupiter is our main suspect. Whether Jupiter tore apart an existing planet, or just kept one from forming in the first place, is not known.

An asteroid field would be an extreme challenge for any pilot. A brilliantly-lit white rock could be blinding, and a dark rock in the shadow of another could be nearly invisible. That's why Mati used an image generated by the ship, with useful color codes, instead of a visual display.

Chapter 24: Hard Landing

Ilika declared a break so Kibi could clean up and everyone could munch on dry crackers. He promised a tasty meal once they landed.

"Manessa, general analysis of the motion of fragment five-three-three, please."

"An extreme negative pitch and a slight left yaw."

Several crew members frowned at the new words they were hearing.

"What's yaw?" Sata asked.

"Movement around the vertical axis," Ilika explained as he turned his head from side to side. He grabbed a knowledge pad, and a moment later a diagram appeared on the large screen. "Everyone needs to memorize these words."

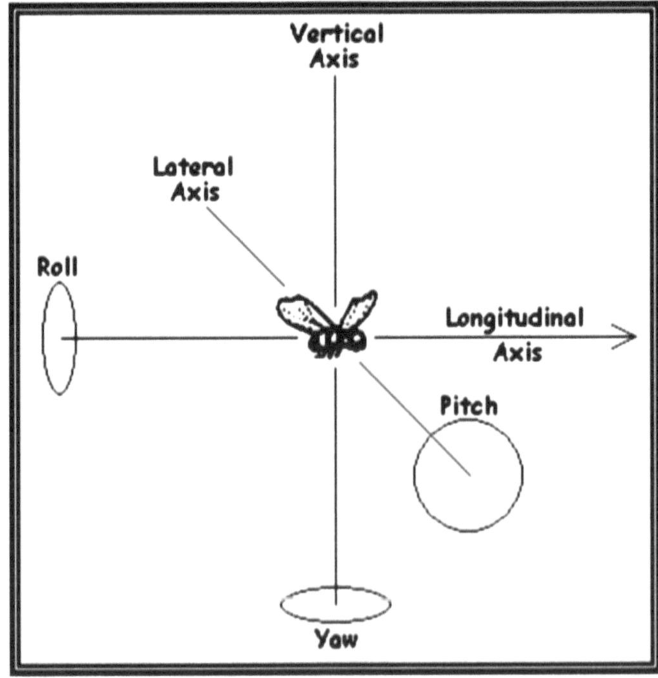

"Is that a bee?" Rini asked.

"We could use some of those," Kibi asserted, cracker in hand. "Honey's getting low."

Ilika smiled. "If I do forward somersaults, like this fragment is doing, that's called . . ." He looked around.

"A biscuit?" Kibi proposed with a goofy grin, her head cocked.

Ilika frowned at her lovingly.

Mati flashed Kibi a dirty look, studied the screen for a moment, then stuck out her arms, as if they were wings, and tucked her head down. "Pitching, around the lateral axis, one of the things I'm gonna do after I get my knee fixed."

Ilika grinned at his pilot.

A few more examples clarified the new words for everyone, with the possible exception of Kibi, who couldn't quit talking about food.

Boro passed her another cracker.

✷

"As I look at the huge thing turning out there," Mati began as she secured her inertia straps, "I know in my gut we'd crash if I tried to land the usual way."

Ilika nodded. "Your intuition is correct. Manessa, what is fragment five-three-three's nickname in the Transport Service?"

"The Meat Grinder," the ship said in its pleasant voice.

Boro made spooky noises. Sata looked at Mati with big, round eyes.

"We'd be the meat," Rini said through a shy smile.

Ilika turned to him. "Remember how to find a center of gravity?"

The slender lad started selecting functions on his console. "Um, um, um . . . reference grid . . . motion analysis. Yeah, got it."

"Send that to Sata," Ilika continued. "Now find the highest point on the fragment, Sata, add a hundred meters, and draw a solid sphere around ol' Meat Grinder. Then create a latitude and longitude grid, and place the north pole at the pitch axis."

"Yeah!" the navigator said as she worked. "Now it'll just look like a ball, and won't make us sick!"

"A ball with a monster inside," Kibi mumbled.

Ilika smiled to himself. "Rini, cancel all visual channels, but keep an occasional eye on reality for us . . . without getting sick."

Rini smiled. "I'll put it way down in the corner of my display."

"Anti-mass one and maneuvering thrusters?" the pilot proposed.

"Yes," the captain confirmed. "Both thruster sets, each one on a separate flight control."

Boro frowned with confusion for a moment, then shrugged. "All green."

"I've simulated that before," Mati said. "It's like patting my head and rubbing my belly!" She touched a symbol to raise a second flight control.

"It's not so hard," Ilika continued, "if you can take care of one at a time, and in this situation, we can. Start by moving Manessa right over the pitch axis at the north pole."

Everyone else watched their displays as the pilot concentrated for half a minute. "Here it is . . . but it's moving."

"That's the yaw — follow it," Ilika said.

The bridge was silent as Mati got comfortable with her task of following the axis of rotation as it slowly moved around the asteroid fragment. "Okay, flight control locked."

Ilika nodded. "Now there's only one motion left, that extreme pitch. Take your other flight control and cancel it."

Mati began by accidentally going the wrong way. After growling at herself, she slowly brought the ship into a matching spin.

"We have tamed the Meat Grinder!" the captain announced.

Clapping filled the bridge for a moment. Mati only grinned, as one hand hovered near each flight control in case they needed adjusting.

"Now we can switch back to visual, but first black out the background, Rini."

"Yeah, I was wondering about that. The more we matched the movement of the fragment, the more the stars and other rocks looked like they were spinning and swirling around. Visual on channel four."

They clapped and cheered again as they all beheld fragment five-three-three, seemingly still in space, against a black starless sky.

*

"Kibi, as steward, you have command for the landing," Ilika said.

She looked at her lover with a gleam in her eyes for a moment, then began studying the visual on her display. Although their destination appeared still in space, the many shadows cast by the metallic spikes were in constant motion, moving from side to side, stretching out to merge with the dark side, or shrinking to join the glare of the sunlit side.

For the next eight minutes, as the steward talked the pilot toward a level area deep down among the fragment's jumbled spikes, more and more details of its metallic structure came into view. Dark crystal shapes sparkled on nearly every surface.

Mati slowly reduced the power of her anti-mass drive, already at a low setting. When she arrived at zero and the ship was still descending very slowly, she chuckled.

Kibi smiled when she realized the landing site was not completely natural, but had been leveled to make room for a small ship.

As they descended past the last jumble of metallic crystals, Rini's eyes sparkled with curiosity when he noticed a dark cave opening.

Mati gave them a nice, soft landing without using any power from her engines.

* * *

The concepts of pitch, roll, and yaw are important to anyone who moves in a three-dimensional environment, including dancers and gymnasts. A car *normally* only does one of these (when turning a corner). Can you guess which one?

"The Meat Grinder" is a term of endearment used by spelunkers (cave explorers) to describe several caves the author has explored.

The landing they did on a tumbling asteroid is another example of a situation in which normal visual displays would work against a pilot. Rini's gravity analysis tools, Sata's sophisticated graphics, and Mati's two flight controls, are all things that would probably never be found on any craft built on Earth, but are not beyond our understanding.

Why was the landing, during which Kibi had command, still a challenge for her stomach?

Why was the landing very slow and smooth, even though Mati was not using any engines?

Chapter 25: The Meat Grinder

After looking around to see if anyone else was dying to learn the steward's job, Kibi sighed and dragged her feet to the lift, pulled on a space suit with a slight pout on her face, and stepped cautiously onto the metallic surface of fragment five-three-three. After several slow, deep breaths, the shaking in her legs finally relaxed.

The smooth landing site, not much bigger than the little ship, was surrounded by dark metal shapes, some low and easy to walk upon, others thrusting skyward with jagged points towering hundreds of meters above the ship.

Just then, Kibi happened to tilt her head back far enough to see the black sky. The countless points of light wheeling above quickly made her head spin, and a heartbeat later she fell over sideways.

To her surprise, she floated to the ground in slow motion and landed like a feather.

Those watching from the ship frowned with worry for a moment, until they heard through the intercom, "I'm not going to puke . . . I'm not going to puke . . ."

After Kibi slowly picked herself up, the first step she took away from the ship propelled her nearly four meters, ending at a jumble of metallic crystals just outside the landing area. "Uff!"

"You okay, Kibi?" Sata asked.

"Um . . . yeah. Just need a few more minutes to get used to the place. No one comes out until I say so."

Inside the ship, several eyebrows were raised at their steward's newfound strength of will.

✷

"It seems to be pretty safe since it's almost impossible to fall hard," Kibi reported. "Just don't look at the swirling sky unless you've got an iron stomach!"

Ilika smiled. "The micro-gravity does create one danger. It's possible to climb one of the spikes, then jump so high you'd achieve escape velocity and float off into space."

Boro frowned. "And because this thing is tumbling, the first asteroid you'd come to would smack you hard!"

"Fatally hard," Ilika added. "I think Rini might have been tempted to try that . . ."

"Not anymore!"

"Good," Mati said with a tender look in her eyes.

Rini grinned at her.

Ilika gave the couple a moment before speaking. "We'll explore our little Meat Grinder in pairs. Mati and Sata, Kibi and Boro, and I'll keep Rini from floating away."

Everyone laughed, then headed for the lower deck.

*

"I can walk!" Mati nearly screamed.

Ilika had insisted she leave her crutch behind in the ship. Now she knew why. It had taken a few steps to get used to the micro-gravity, but Mati soon discovered that the pressure on her right leg was below the pain threshold, and she could actually walk with both legs.

"This is so wonderful, Sata! I don't care about jumping and floating and stuff, I just wanna walk around the landing site, so if I die before I get to Satamia Star Station, I'll know what it's like."

The navigator smiled through her face plate, crouched down, and sprang upward. "Wee!" She ascended to about twenty meters, then floated down slowly.

Mati laughed, and kept on slowly walking.

Ilika, watching from a hundred meters up one of the metallic spikes, smiled.

"She's gonna have fun once her knee's fixed," Rini said from eight meters higher up. "You coming?"

Ilika bent at the knees, then sprang right over Rini, landing near the cave entrance.

Rini laughed, and bounded to join his captain.

With bracelet lights shining, they crept into the darkness, finding an irregular tunnel about three meters across slowly tapering as it pierced deeper into the asteroid. From all sides, crystals of many colors jutted into the passage, sometimes half a meter in length.

Rini looked all around. "So pretty! Can we take one for our display containers?"

"Crystals grow very slowly, taking thousands, maybe millions of years to get to this size. If every ship took one, they'd be gone already."

Rini frowned and nodded.

"But I see some broken pieces on the floor," Ilika continued, "that would go nicely in our containers."

Rini grinned and began to look around.

*

When Rini and Ilika returned to the landing site, Mati was still walking, almost skipping, while humming little tunes, mostly off-key. Sata was near, sometimes walking with her friend, sometimes jumping up to the top of the ship or one of the nearby jumbles.

Just then Boro and Kibi appeared over a rise.

Sata landed near Mati. "Didn't you guys go off in the other direction?"

Kibi snickered. "Yeah."

"We just walked around the world!" Boro announced proudly. "And I found a little piece of asteroid metal for the display containers."

Rini arrived and pulled out three small broken crystals: deep blue, fiery red, and bright purple.

"Fantastic!" Kibi said with a grin.

*

The three crystals seemed to glow when placed in the display container in front of the dark metal of the asteroid. Memories now peeked out of five containers, most of them natural objects, from stardust to feathers. Only the display for Sonmatia Two held objects made by hand.

At dinner, Kibi talked about her initial discomfort with the asteroid, and Ilika nodded his understanding. Then he invited her to climb to the highest point with him. Her eyes nearly smoked for a moment, then softened as she agreed.

Mati declared her intention to walk all the way around the asteroid, and Rini asked if he could come. Boro and Sata planned to peek in the cave, then climb the second-tallest metallic spike.

*

A few hours later, after the last pair came in the airlock, the entire ship was soon very quiet with six exhausted explorers collapsed on their beds.

Manessa lowered the temperature a bit as Kibi had programmed any time they were asleep, monitored all systems for anything unusual, and watched the stars turn overhead.

* * *

An asteroid would have "micro-gravity," much less than the one-sixth gravity our astronauts experienced on the moon (1969-1975). "Micro" is the Greek word for "small" and does not imply any exact amount, unless it is used with metric system units where it means one-millionth.

"Escape velocity" is the relative speed an object needs to escape the gravity of any body in space without using thrust. On Earth, it is about 11 km/sec or 7 miles/sec. If an asteroid had 1/5000 the gravity of the Earth, a person could literally walk (8 kph, 5 mph) into escape velocity. Luckily, the Meat Grinder had about 1/1000 the Earth's gravity, so it wasn't quite so dangerous.

The ethics of souvenir collecting is always relative to the number of visitor and the supply of souvenirs, and usually attempts to achieve sustainability. Which is more sustainable, and why: taking pine cones in a forest, or taking crystals in a cave?

Chapter 26: Gas Giants

The crew demanded another day at fragment five-three-three once stories were told of deeper caves and a metallic spike gentle enough for Mati to ascend. Both Kibi and Boro, at first unnerved by the constantly moving sky, spent extra time looking up, determined to conquer more personal demons. Mati and Rini looked up and shrugged.

On the third day, Kibi took command as they reversed the landing process, first floating up to a safe distance while watching the stationary asteroid below, then turning to see the inside of the solid sphere Sata created on their displays. Mati cancelled the pitch, then the yaw, and once again they beheld the stars, now behaving themselves.

Another quarter hour of bumping and nudging brought them to clear space. Sata plotted an elliptical flight plan with a course change at Sonmatia Six, Mati requested engines, and the Manessa Kwi streaked deeper into space at one-eighth the speed of light.

None of the five new crew members could keep their mouths closed as the huge gas giant filled their displays with mysterious bands of color — oranges, yellows, violets, even brilliant white with tinges of blue and green.

Rini tried to swallow. "We're not even very close yet . . ."

Suddenly a thin, straight band of rocks flashed across their view screens.

Boro nearly jumped out of his skin. "What was that?"

"Sata?" Ilika prompted.

She studied her chart for a moment. "Sonmatia Six has a little asteroid belt around it. We're still several light-seconds out, crossing into the northern hemisphere."

While monitoring their progress along the flight plan, Mati looked deep into wells and canyons among the multi-colored clouds, swirling so slowly the movement was difficult to see.

"Hard to believe we're still at ion seven," Boro commented, "but my board says we are."

"Mine too," Sata confirmed.

Kibi glanced at the empty passenger area behind her. "My passengers are on the edge of their seats!"

Ilika turned and grinned at her.

The bridge fell silent as the giant planet loomed larger and larger, slowly moving into the lower-left corner of their displays.

"The gravity is enormous," Rini reported. "Almost five hundred times our little world."

Boro looked worried, then relaxed. "I'm glad we're using anti-mass and ion drive!"

Silence lingered again as the gas giant grew slowly larger and lower on their screens.

"Nav point in twenty seconds," Sata announced.

Mati looked at the flight plan again, glanced at Ilika, and he nodded. "Course change approved," she said.

A few seconds later, the gigantic sixth planet moved quickly out of their forward view and the Manessa Kwi streaked into the darkness of space toward Sonmatia Seven.

✷

"Rini and Boro are right," Ilika began from the steward's station as a bowl of snacks worked its way around the table. "Without the anti-mass drive, we couldn't go anywhere near a gas giant, unless freeloading. The gravity is just too great. We *might* be able to achieve escape velocity using every bit of our remaining fuel . . . once."

"Is the seventh planet just as beautiful?" Kibi asked.

Rini nodded vigorously as Ilika tapped at the console, and the image of another ringed, multi-colored gas giant appeared on the big screen.

Mati beamed with excitement. "We get to land on that one?"

Ilika squinted for a moment. "Sort of. First we'll descend through thousands of kilometers of turbulent, poisonous atmosphere. Eventually it changes to a liquid at extremely low temperatures. Finally, it solidifies, but the solid surface is very unstable, constantly melting and refreezing. We can take a peek at it, but not really land. Far, far down, below an immense depth of ice, is a small rocky core, about the size of your planet."

Sata's eyes grew large. "Sounds dark . . . and spooky."

*

During the eight hour transit from Sonmatia Six to Seven, Ilika gave only one command. "Get some sleep, tomorrow's a big day. Sata has first watch."

After everyone else filtered away, Boro took a few steps toward the lift, then stopped himself and looked back at Sata. She seemed nervous as she selected pictures and videos to arrange on her display, alongside the star-studded blackness of space on her forward view. He smiled to himself, then went down to the bridge and started massaging her shoulders. "Want some company?"

She turned her head and grinned. "Yeah. I guess . . . I've got knots in my stomach. I'm not sure I'm gonna like gas giants."

Boro took the pilot's chair. "Because they're so big, or because they're way out here where it's almost dark?"

Sata twisted her face. "Not sure. Maybe I'll understand it better after we visit one."

Boro nodded. "Want to show me how to find charts?"

"Sure!"

*

Hours later, at the end of Kibi's watch, Ilika awoke in a passenger seat when others started coming up the lift and talking about breakfast.

Kibi looked over her console one more time before giving him a kiss on the cheek. "You're in command," she whispered, then stepped into the galley.

He stood up and stretched. "Manessa, flight plan status?"

"On flight plan, seven light-minutes to destination."

Most of the crew had already glanced at the little screens in their cabins, but seeing the ringed gas giant on the big screen was much more exciting. Soon everyone was sipping tea and staring with wide eyes.

"This one's more special," Rini suggested. "We get to touch it!"

"Have you checked the planet's temperature?" Boro asked, squinting.

Rini smiled. "I know. Only Manessa can touch something that cold."

Everyone quickly ate as the enormous planet, even more colorful than Sonmatia Six, grew larger and larger on their displays.

"We're out of flight plan," Mati reported from her station as soon as everyone gathered on the bridge.

"Bring us to a relative stop at the outer edge of the rings," the captain said. "I have to give you a few warnings before we go down."

Sata provided a chart and Mati kept an eye on the visual display. With the ship still weightless, she brought it to an instant stop within sight of the first rocks.

"We'll start with a fly-over of the planet's ring system," Ilika began. "You'll see gaps with almost no rocks because of the interaction of the planet's gravity and the sun's. Any rocks still in those gaps tend to be unstable and move in unpredictable ways without warning."

Mati blinked a few times, then nodded.

"The atmosphere is mostly hydrogen, so space thrusters might act strangely. There have been cases where a gas giant was large enough that a passing ship, using thrusters, ignited a chain reaction and the planet became a small sun."

Boro swallowed and looked a bit pale.

"This planet isn't big enough for that."

The engineer breathed again.

"The turbulence down there is worse than anything on your planet, but there's nothing to hit but the liquid surface, so we just cancel all inertia and enjoy the ride."

*

The little ship glided over the rings, just far enough for safety, near enough for excitement. No flight plan was used – Mati kept her hand on the flight control and her eyes moving from chart to visual to console.

Even without mass, the descent from the innermost ring felt like falling, as the intricate swirling surface of the planet's atmosphere grew closer every second. Kibi had to close her eyes part of the time.

"Mati, start slowing our descent," Ilika instructed.

She spoke without turning. "Um . . . ion two, Boro."

Boro confirmed the power reduction, and the visible surface of the planet ceased barreling toward them.

No one could feel a thing as the ship punched a small hole in a huge purple cloud. Their displays gradually became foggy, then slowly dimmed as they pierced deeper into the atmosphere.

"Ion one," the pilot requested.

Occasional shafts of brilliant sunlight penetrated deeply into the clouds, but soon the ship was once again surrounded by colorful mists growing darker and darker.

"This is creepy," Kibi muttered with a tinge of fear in her voice, "not knowing what's coming."

Mati smiled without letting Kibi see. "The chart on channel five shows our position and the liquid surface. It's no worse than flying in a thick fog back on our planet."

Kibi swallowed as she looked at the chart. "I'm glad *you're* the pilot!"

Mati smiled again and activated the ship's lights. "Ilika, I think we should float down from here."

"Good call, pilot."

"Finished with ion drive."

*

As the deep-space response ship, with its crew-in-training from a medieval world, approached the gaseous-liquid boundary of Sonmatia Seven, the pilot slowed their descent by requesting higher and higher power levels for the anti-mass drive. The navigator, with little to do, arranged pictures of butterflies and flowers on her display. The watch monitored his sensors and squirmed with excitement. The steward looked around at the walls and ceiling, took some deep breaths, and checked her internal views for anything loose. The engineer frowned when the pilot requested his highest anti-mass power level, and prepared an alternate fuel, just in case. The captain smiled.

As Mati watched the ship's position indicator approach the boundary, she brought in more and more of the power at her fingertips. Half-way through level seven, the ship's lights finally revealed the eerie churning surface of liquid hydrogen, with plenty of other elements adding color.

"I don't suppose the fishing's any good," Boro said with a smirk.

Ilika burst out laughing. "There are creatures in there, but you couldn't eat them, nor could they eat you, although they might try. Take us in, pilot. As with water, it's calmer below."

Mati lowered the ship into the strange, cold liquid. The ship's inertia canceling kept them from feeling the surface roughness, but the swaying motion on their view screens brought moans, and several fingers quickly poked at channel selectors to study the chart. Kibi now knew what clothes felt like in her laundry machine.

The turbulence soon faded as the gravity of the planet pulled them downward. The ship's lights became useless as the liquid hydrogen reflected most, and distorted the rest.

"All stations, report," Ilika requested.

"Pilot is good, though I don't have anything to steer by. And I don't want hydrogen-fish for dinner."

Boro chuckled.

"Up and down is all that matters," the captain assured. "Sata?"

"Um . . . I guess I'll never love dark places, will I?"

"Maybe not."

"Well . . . um . . . I'm okay, and the only useful chart is on channel five. The transponder is active, although the Tirilana Kril should be gone by now, so we might be alone in the solar system."

Ilika nodded. "Rini?"

"I'm . . . a little nervous. Visual is useless. Sonar shows chunks of ice that are getting larger as we go down. Channel four."

"Boro?"

"Engines are happy, but . . . I'm worried because we have to use so much anti-mass."

"Atmospheric thrusters will work here," the captain pointed out.

Boro scrunched his face in a moment of anger at himself, then laughed.

"Kibi?" the captain continued.

"Ship's getting smaller again, but as long as there's room to dance to a little music, I'll survive. Everything's secure."

Ilika turned and smiled at her.

"Bottom's coming up," Sata announced.

"Ice chunks are becoming ice boulders," Rini added.

"Slow our descent, Mati," Ilika commanded.

"Eight meters per second," she reported.

Ilika touched the selector on the arm of his chair. "Everyone switch to channel four."

Boro switched to Rini's sonar image of orange ice and clear yellow liquid. "Much better!"

"Four meters per second."

Suddenly a huge bubble appeared beneath the ship, white on the sonar image. The Manessa Kwi dropped like a rock into the gas pocket before anyone could respond. Hundreds of ice boulders began to plunge downward into the same void, pounding the top of the little ship and forcing it into a deep, dark crack in the planetary ice.

* * *

Gas giants seem to be about the same as the inner planets, with a small rocky core, but are cold enough to capture the vast amounts of hydrogen that are present during solar system formation. This bring up the question: why isn't Pluto a gas giant? It's irregular orbit may mean it has a very different, and much more recent, origin.

In our solar system, only Saturn was known to have rings until very recently. Now, with better telescopes and unmanned probes, it appears that all four of our gas giants have rings.

Mati's habit of keeping her eyes moving "from chart to visual to console" is an essential piloting skill. If you look at any one of those for too long, things might change in one of the others (but hopefully the chart stays the same). This is actually *more* critical when driving a car, as obstacles and other vehicles are much closer than when flying.

Sonar maps the external environment by using sound waves. It is used by submarines on Earth because light does not travel very far underwater. Radar, which maps using radio waves, also does not work underwater.

Chapter 27: Darkness

"Full anti-mass!" Ilika yelled.

By the time Mati moved her hand, the ship had plunged far down into the dark crack in the icy core of the planet. Boulders of frozen hydrogen rapidly filled the opening above, and the ship only quivered when the pilot pushed the anti-mass drive to its maximum power. "Oh, no, not again!" she wailed.

Ilika frowned. "This is different – and worse. Atmospheric engines, full power!"

Boro worked with shaking fingers. "Ready!"

"Inertia straps!" Ilika commanded. "Quickly, Mati."

Mati got her straps on, saw that everyone else was secure, and grabbed her flight control. The ship at first vibrated, then shook, and finally bucked and lurched, but went nowhere.

"Damn!" Ilika cursed, popping his straps and stepping to the engineer's station. "Anti-mass seven, thrusters seven," he muttered to himself, looking over Boro's settings. "Damn!"

"Continue thrust?" Mati asked, looking over her shoulder at her captain, a tinge of fear growing in her eyes.

"Yeah," he replied, stepping to her station. "Try rocking the ship, spinning, anything you can think of."

Mati tried every trick from Sonmatia Two, and a few she made up on the spot. Seconds ticked by. Sata, Rini, and Kibi barely breathed.

"Thrusters are going red!" Boro yelled.

"Any progress, Sata?" Ilika demanded.

"At first we were going up and down a fraction of a meter, but now . . . almost nothing."

"One thruster just went purple," Boro reported with despair.

"Cut thrusters," the captain commanded. "Ice is starting to choke them. How's the ice above, Rini?"

"It's starting to form between the boulders."

"Boro, space thrusters, all of them, full power."

The engineer looked at his captain, saw desperation in his eyes, and turned to his console. "You've got it all. At that level, we've got fuel for about . . . four minutes."

"Mati, go," Ilika said, taking his seat and strapping himself in. "Cut-off at two minutes, Boro."

Blue flames quickly ate away the ice around the bottom of the ship, and worked their way up the sides.

"One minute," Boro announced, fingers poised as he watched the clock.

The heat soon reached the top of the ship, and the Manessa Kwi slowly began to move upward.

"Maintain full anti-mass," Ilika ordered.

"I am," Mati muttered.

"Eight seconds to cut-off," Boro announced.

"Progress, Sata?"

"About three meters."

"Thrusters off."

Boro sighed. "Space thrusters off."

"Damn!" Ilika spat out.

*

In the silence that followed, Kibi knew she had to be more than a steward. She popped her inertia straps, stepped down to the bridge, and stood beside her captain.

Their eyes met and she could see moisture in his eyes. She suddenly knew, deep in her heart, that this was no test or training exercise.

"Rini," she began, "we need to know how thick the ice is above us."

He turned to his console and looked over the sonar options. "Ah!"

"Boro, how long can we keep the anti-mass drive running?" she asked.

"Months, but there's no point once the liquid under us solidifies again."

"It already has," Rini said, "and I just found out the ice above us is about a hundred and twenty meters thick, and now completely frozen to the walls of the crack."

Kibi took Ilika's hand. "With your permission, I think we should let Boro shut down the engines. We all need to rest and eat something before we can think."

Ilika scrunched his face several directions as the first tear rolled down his cheek. "Yeah. We gained three meters. We could gain another three with the other half of our space thruster fuel. No point."

"Engines off, Mati and Boro," Kibi commanded.

The ship fell silent, and no one said a word.

*

The mood, as the crew gathered at the large table in the passenger area, had only been experienced by this group once before. When the high priest and guards moved to arrest them outside Doko's Inn, about a year before, they knew it was no test. Every situation since had been an exercise of some sort, or a problem with a solution.

Rini wasn't smiling, but he had enough presence of mind to successfully make tea. The others received their cups with shaking hands.

"I'm in command for a while," Kibi said. "Nothing's getting any worse, so Rini and I are going to cook something. Everyone else, relax, especially Ilika and Mati."

Those not in the galley moped around while soup was reheated and crackers broken. They ate in silence, glancing at Ilika often to see if he had thought of anything.

Ilika finally broke the silence. "Kibi remains in command, but I'm going to work with Manessa to make sure I understand our situation fully. We should all get some sleep before we try anything else."

*

Ilika spent most of the next hour at the watch station, using every possible tool to peer into the strange ice on all sides of the ship. While he worked, most of the others wandered down to their cabins.

Next Ilika moved to the engineer's console, and after checking all the engines and fuel levels, he looked long at the star drive at the top of the display board. Even though he touched several symbols, it remained dark and silent.

After a few minutes at the navigator's console, he returned to the passenger area and took Kibi's hand. Last of all the crew members, they disappeared into their cabin.

She could tell by his eyes and his slumped shoulders that he had not yet found any reason to hope. Once the lights were out, she wrapped her arms around him and let him cry himself to sleep.

*

During the next fourteen hours, different crew members wandered up to the silent bridge at different times. They sat at their consoles, ran diagnostics, asked Manessa questions, then dragged themselves back to bed.

*

Sometime the following day, Ilika cooked a hearty breakfast. Rini appeared next, anxious to help with trays, but had to wait for the aromas to circulate throughout the ship before he had anyone to serve.

Everyone kept to light and happy topics during the meal. Once dishes were done, Ilika cleared his throat and sat back down at the table.

"You are not children. I'm not going to lie to you or sugarcoat the situation. We're in big trouble, and this is nothing contrived by me or Manessa. Sata, please activate the Nebador distress beacon."

With big, round eyes, Sata walked to her station, made the selection she had only simulated before, and returned to the table. "Manessa says only a tiny fraction of the signal is getting through the ice."

"Yes," Ilika confirmed. "That means another ship will have to be very close to hear us. We can't count on that happening, so we probably have to find our own way out."

"Can't we melt our way through," Boro asked, "like we did at the north pole of our planet?"

"We'll try, but I've done some calculations, and I'm worried. One piece of information we need, which I think you guys can figure out better than me, is how long we can live on the food and water we have, at absolute minimum usage."

Kibi tapped Boro, he grabbed a knowledge pad, and they went to work pawing through every cabinet in the galley.

Back at the table, Mati put into words what several people were wondering. "Did we . . . do anything wrong?"

"Not that I can see," Ilika answered. "And . . . as much as I wish I could take the blame . . ." He paused to take a deep breath. "Ships visit the liquid-solid boundary on gas giants all the time."

Kibi looked over the galley counter, then ducked back down to continue her counting and estimating.

"I've never heard of this happening," Ilika continued, "and neither has Manessa. It's just one of those rare geological events that can't be predicted."

After hearing those words, everyone breathed a little easier, but no one was ready to smile.

✷

"One month, max," Kibi announced. "That's using every scrap and every drop."

Ilika cringed. "Any way to stretch that?"

"Food . . . a little," Boro replied. "Water, no way. I know what people can get by on. We'll be dying in a month, dead in a month and a half, no matter how careful we are."

Ilika blinked a few times, then nodded. "We'll try melting our way out with Manessa's radiant hull. Sometimes simulations are wrong. Stations."

Happy to be trying something, anything, the crew was soon ready. Ilika worked with Rini for a few minutes, as precise measurements of the ship's movement were necessary. Boro and Mati had the simple task of making the hull glow with infra-red radiation, and applying all the anti-mass they could muster.

The experiment lasted half an hour. Rini reported three centimeters of movement. Ilika did a quick calculation. "It would take two and a half, maybe three months, to get up to the solid-liquid boundary. We don't have the food and water . . . or the fuel."

Sata burst into tears and ran off the bridge. Boro was half out of his seat before he stopped and looked at Ilika. The captain nodded. "Shut down your stations, everyone."

"Why was it so much easier on our planet?" Mati asked, standing up with the help of her crutch.

"That was barely-frozen water ice," Ilika explained. "This is far colder, and part of the massive core of the planet, which acts like a sink for any heat we apply."

Mati nodded and sniffed, then hobbled up to the table where Rini swiveled a chair for her, leaving Ilika alone on the bridge.

* * *

Although our bodies would be severely weakened and possibly suffer permanent harm, healthy people can live 2-4 weeks without food. But if we have no water, one week is about the limit.

Solid hydrogen ice is about 14°K (-259°C, -434°F) or colder. Water ice on Earth is quite hot by comparison (193°K or higher).

Chapter 28: Cold

For the next three days, the joyless crew moped around the ship, half-heartedly making simple meals, or just sitting with friends, holding hands and remembering past moments of happiness.

Ilika spent most of his time researching every possibility he could think of, and reading every account he could find of a ship in any similar situation. When his eyes would no longer focus, he spent more hours asking Manessa questions and doing simulations. When he could no longer think, he found Kibi, snuggled close, and listened to her thoughts and feelings.

✷

On the fourth day, Boro was poking at a bowl of barley and vegetables when he finally found his courage. "Ilika, I was a slave. I was hungry most of the time. I don't want to die of starvation . . . if there's any other way. I know some of the others feel the same."

Ilika looked at his engineer. "I understand." He looked around the table and saw nods from Mati, Rini, and Kibi. "Manessa can survive this . . . by hibernating . . . by lowering the internal temperature, conserving fuel, and occasionally sending a distress signal. It might be hundreds of years until that signal is received. Maybe thousands. Either way, she'll be okay. Unfortunately, we cannot use that same method to survive . . . at least, as mortals of flesh and blood."

Ilika could see tears on Mati's face, and remembered how close she was to getting her knee fixed.

"So . . ." Sata began between sniffles, "what would happen to us?"

"Once we all give our permission, of our own free will, Manessa will lower the temperature on the lower deck. Anyone who goes to sleep at that temperature will not wake up in this life. When everyone is asleep, she will do the same with the upper deck, and then patiently wait for rescue. Once that happens, our story will be told and all Transport Service crews will do their best to avoid the same fate."

Rini couldn't hold in his tears any longer. "It makes me feel cold just thinking about it." He left his uneaten meal and shuffled to the lift without looking at anyone.

*

Sometime in the hours that followed, everyone thought one of Manessa's engines had activated itself even with no one on the bridge. With nothing else to do, several of them followed the sound, and arrived together at the door to the engineering ring. Poking their heads in, they found Boro growling his anger and frustration to the engines, waving his arms and sometimes stomping around. They slipped away before he noticed.

*

After dragging herself aimlessly around the ship for most of a day, Kibi curled up in her own bed for the first time. With the exception of a couple of trips to the toilet room, which no one saw, she didn't show her face for the next two days.

*

Sometime the following day, Sata made a pot of soup, but rushed away before it was finished, hiding her face.

At the time, Mati was distracting herself with easy piloting simulations at her station, not even noticing the tears trickling down her cheeks. About an hour after her friend left the soup simmering, she wandered up to the galley, added some salt, and ate a bowl without tasting it.

*

Once Boro yelled himself hoarse and slept two nights in the engineering ring, he dragged his feet to his cabin where he found Rini staring at the knowledge processor on his desk.

Rini's eyes were red, but he was too dehydrated to cry. He gazed longingly at an endless stream of pictures — strange planets and moons, colorful nebulas, and gleaming star stations.

Boro put his arm around his friend and coaxed him up to the big table to drink cold soup.

*

Ilika went back and forth from researching any possible way out of their icy trap, to silently keeping an eye on each of his crew members.

Seeing Kibi in bed, usually not asleep but lying as if dead, tore at his heart almost more than he could stand. He left quickly each time, spoke his pain and anguish in the utility room to anyone who cared to listen, then returned to the upper deck to do more research or sleep in a passenger seat.

*

A day or so later, Mati wandered down to her cabin and found Sata under her desk wrapped in blankets. With some pain, she lowered herself to the floor, scooted in beside her friend, and they talked and cried together for hours before finally falling asleep.

* * *

All the early steps of the grieving process (denial, anger, bargaining, depression) can be seen in different crew members at different times, in different ways, and in a different order for each person. This is typical of real people. We do not all grieve in the same way, or on the same schedule.

What are they grieving about? Would this be possible for a creature who was not self-aware?

For each crew member, which step in the grieving process was most pronounced?

Chapter 29: Emptiness

Two weeks passed with the little ship trapped in the icy core of Sonmatia Seven.

The captain occasionally tried to get his crew together for a meal or a video, but most often they gave him blank stares, challenging him to give them a good reason. He could think of none, so he backed away with slumped shoulders and returned to nursing his shame.

*

At some point in time, days after Ilika had quit trying to boost morale on the ship, he was alone on the upper deck. He leaned back in the steward's chair and stared with sad eyes at the results of another failed simulation, another useless attempt to find a way out of the trap.

Suddenly Rini flew up the lift. "I've been so stupid! I've had a wonderful life, I got to see the aurora, fly in the air all over the world, and visit six other worlds! No one in my kingdom has *ever* been so lucky, not even the king! There's only one other thing I want to do. I want to make a video. Please teach me how."

Ilika blinked for a few moments, trying to get used to the sudden burst of life from one of his crew members. "Um . . . okay. Your station is as good as any . . ."

Rini smiled for the first time in many days as he got comfortable.

"Open the video editor and select New Project," Ilika began. "You have four visual channels, each with a sub-channel for filters and effects. Visuals can come from Manessa's memory, a bracelet, or the high-resolution camera in the excursion cabinet. You also have four audio channels . . ."

*

Ilika wasn't sure what was happening, but he decided to be as supportive as he could. While Rini learned to use the video editor, and often called out questions, Ilika began to clean the galley. He found messes nearly two weeks old, and spoiled food that should have been refrigerated.

As the hours passed and the galley once again looked usable, some of Ilika's guilt and shame melted from his shoulders. Rini continued to work happily on his video project, sometimes hopping up to grab a bracelet and record something, including, at one point, Ilika scrubbing the galley floor.

The lad's excitement was infectious, and Ilika decided to cook a nice meal, even if only he and Rini could enjoy it. The food stocks were getting thin, but he found flour and made a batch of biscuits. Once those were in the oven, he turned his attention to a tasty stew, using the last of their dried fish.

*

Several hours later, Boro appeared in the lift. "I'm done feeling sorry for my . . ." He froze and took in the unexpected aromas of fresh biscuits and fish stew, and the sight of Ilika with a bracelet recording Rini dancing in a clumsy free-form style to some lively music.

Boro waited, a smile growing on his face, while the song finished.

"Hi, Boro!" Rini greeted excitedly. "I'm making a video!"

"Wow. I didn't know we could do that."

"It's going to take me a few days, and I'll show it to everyone when it's done."

Boro cleared his throat. "I've got something I want to say." He stood at one end of the table as Ilika and Rini sat down.

"I . . . um . . . I've been thinking about how lots of my masters said I wasn't a . . . you know . . . a real man."

Ilika and Rini listened intently, sensing how hard this was for Boro.

"I guess I'm not sure what a real man is. Okay, I'm gentle and quiet, and I'm not very good with an axe. Whatever. I don't care about that stuff any more. I'm the engineer of a deep-space response ship, and I've been thinking real hard about what I should be able to do right now. I finally figured it out, and I want you guys to hear me say it."

Ilika and Rini both nodded slightly to show they were listening.

"I've had a good life, and I'm ready to be a man, my own kind of man. Manessa, you have my permission to begin hibernation as soon as everyone else is ready."

"Acknowledged," the ship said softly.

After a moment of respectful silence, Rini smiled. "I told her that too, but I said I wanted to finish my video first."

*

The three men of the crew sat around talking about what it meant to be a man. Boro shared what he knew from his culture, the ways he fit into the concept, and the ways he didn't. Rini admitted he didn't really relate to the concept much at all.

During a moment when no one was speaking, they started hearing voices from the lower deck.

"Can't you smell the biscuits?" Sata's voice asked. "Others must be getting over it too, and someone cooked!"

"I know," Mati's voice began. "I just don't want to do it looking like this. Tell them I'll be up soon."

The three males waited, and a minute later, Sata appeared in the lift, smiling. "Do I smell fresh biscuits?"

Boro smiled back at her.

Sata stopped part way to the table and stood firmly, with her feet somewhat apart, as if steadying herself on the deck of a sailing ship in rough seas. "Mati and I just spent three days . . . maybe it was four . . . dragging each other through every kind of grief and self-pity you can think of, and we both realized what we want to do . . . what we *need* to do with the rest of our lives. Manessa, this is Sata, your navigator.

"Greetings, Sata," came the ship's pleasant voice.

"I never thought standing on my own two feet, with a smile on my face, would be this hard. Of course, I didn't know I'd have to get ready to die. Manessa, you have my permission to hibernate, in about a week, after we've done the simulations I want to do, had one last feast together, and . . . done something else Mati wants to do."

"Acknowledged."

Sata let out a sigh and shivered. After a deep breath, her eyes fixed on Boro, and she began taking slow, measured steps toward him.

Wearing a slightly unsure smile, he stood up to face her.

"Boro, will you be the engineer of the Manessa Kwi for the next week while we travel all over Nebador with simulations? And at the end, after our last meal together, will you be there, with your arms around me, as the cold puts us to sleep?"

Boro took a slow breath. "Yes . . . to both questions."

Sata pulled him close, touched her lips to his, and they kissed long and deeply. Ilika and Rini slipped silently into the galley to work on the stew.

Boro suddenly felt he knew a lot more about being a man — his own kind of man.

✷

About an hour later, Mati appeared in the lift wearing her nicest tunic, the one from the desert gathering. Her long hair was nicely combed but not quite dry, and her eyes sparkled with a special light that had not been seen in weeks.

The four already on the upper deck fell silent and looked at her. Rini quit stirring the stew, came around the table, and stood facing her. His gleaming eyes met hers.

"I wanted to do this from my knees," Mati began, looking right at Rini. "I wanted to do it on Satamia Star Station, but I have to do it right here, because this is the only place I have, the only place I'll ever have."

The others, sensing the importance of the moment, gathered around. Sata was grinning from ear to ear.

"I'm still a cripple, Rini, but I've walked all the way around fragment five-three-three. That was one of the happiest moments of my life, and this is another."

Rini was turning several shades of red and squirming with embarrassment, but continued smiling.

"A desert girl once asked you to marry her, and even though there was a little confusion . . ."

Everyone chuckled.

". . . you found the courage to walk away . . . so you could be with me."

Rini nodded through his embarrassment.

"Now, here in the last place we can ever go, I finally found *my* courage. Ilika," she said, still looking at Rini, "you're a captain, and on our world, any captain can perform a wedding. I know we're not on our world any more, but we're still in Sonmatia, and there's no one else here except a few dying people on Sonmatia Two, so I think the rules of our world should apply."

Ilika grinned. "In the eyes of Nebador, you are married if you choose to be, and you can have anyone you want perform a ceremony."

Mati took a slow breath. "I don't have a special pastry to share with you, Rini. Maybe . . . we could use one of these fresh biscuits?"

Rini, still red with embarrassment and still smiling, grabbed a biscuit from the table and stepped close to his sweet friend Mati. No one else made a sound as the biscuit was broken, each of the slender youth offered their half to the other, then slowly chewed and swallowed what they had been given.

Just then Kibi rose in the lift. "Did I . . . miss anything?"

Boro and Sata burst into laughter. Rini and Mati didn't seem to notice the new arrival, and slipped their arms around each other. Ilika quickly strode to the lift, took Kibi by the hand, and pulled her into the room.

Unlike Mati, Kibi's eyes were red and her face crusty with dried tears. Her hair was completely tangled and matted, and her cheeks looked hollow. Ilika coaxed her along and gestured at different people as he narrated.

"Rini has decided to use the rest of his life to make a video, and he's been learning the video editor and collecting pictures. Of course, that might go slowly now, because Mati just asked him to marry her, and it appears he has accepted, so there will probably be a wedding ceremony sometime soon."

Rini nodded vigorously.

Kibi's mouth opened in amazement.

"Boro has made some decisions about what it means to be a man, and he and Sata have promised to go into hibernation together. But before that happens, Sata plans to navigate the ship all over Nebador using simulations."

Kibi tried to close her dry mouth and swallow, but couldn't manage it, so she just nodded. When she was sure Ilika had finished, she struggled to find her voice. "I . . . um . . . feel completely empty . . ."

Rini and Mati found seats side by side, and Sata stepped into the galley to get Kibi a cup of water.

After drinking deeply, she tried to collect her thoughts again. "For the first time in my life, it seems like I've felt every feeling and cried every tear, and there's nothing left inside me. This might sound funny, but . . . it almost feels good. For the first time, I'm not worrying about the next emotion that might . . . you know . . . slap me around. I've been to the bottom. There's nothing left. I'm completely empty and . . . um . . . when we've done everything everyone wants to do, I'll be ready to go to sleep in the cold."

"Acknowledged," Manessa said softly.

*

Ilika and Sata took a minute to get bowls of stew onto the table, and Boro promised to do the dishes.

Mati and Rini immediately began chatting and giggling about their upcoming wedding. Sata volunteered to cook the feast, and Boro thought of things he could use to decorate the ship. The engaged couple tossed out several possible dates, then settled on four days in the future.

Kibi remained quiet, her color and sparkle only returning very slowly as she ate. Eventually, when everyone else had fallen silent as they scraped their bowls, she let out a deep sigh and looked at Ilika. "I'm sorry I've been so . . . distant. It's part of the curse of being a feeling person, I guess. I thought I knew about every kind of emotion, and could handle them all, at least . . . after getting used to a moving ship."

Ilika smiled at her.

"The one I wasn't ready for . . ." she continued, ". . . and now I am . . . is dying."

"That's a hard one to practice!" Boro pointed out.

Kibi grinned shyly.

Ilika reached over and took her hand. "I don't think anyone's ever completely ready for that. But one of the things we can give each other, as fellow crew members, is the knowledge that if it must happen, we'll be together."

Rini and Mati both grinned.

Boro hopped up and collected the dirty dishes.

Kibi leaned her head on Ilika's shoulder, closed her eyes, and just listened to the sound of her own breath going in and out.

* * *

The final step in the grieving process is acceptance. Every person arrives at it on a different path, if they don't get stuck in one of the earlier steps. Luckily, no one on the ship stayed stuck.

In your culture, is "willing to die" part of being a "real man"?

If they are doomed to soon die, is there any value in Mati and Rini marrying?

Since emotions are, by definition, things that motivate us, what are we motivated to do when we feel the emotions caused by approaching death?

Chapter 30: Simulation

"What sort of simulation shall we start with?" the captain asked his crew, all of whom had just decided to die with their eyes open and their friends at their sides. "Manessa has memories from all over Nebador, and many places in deep space that are completely uninhabited and have not yet been assigned to a local universe."

"Somewhere pretty!" Rini suggested.

Mati frowned slightly. "Except . . . not Satamia Star Station. That would make me too sad."

"Me too," several others echoed.

"Hmm . . ." Ilika pondered as he stroked Kibi's matted hair. "Manessa, full simulation mode, Zekoria Comet Observation Platform. Stations, everyone."

This time, they didn't bolt to their consoles like excited children, but a subtle light of curiosity shone in their eyes, and perhaps a tiny bit of fear of the unknown.

While everyone else brought their stations to life and did their basic pre-flight checks, Sata searched for a chart of a place she had never seen or imagined. Her eyes opened wide as soon as she saw the large swaths of space colored red and marked *Extreme Navigation Hazard.*

Rini soon gave them simulated visual displays. "We're on a landing platform beside a supply dome on a tiny airless planet."

"Oh . . . wow . . . look at the sky!" Boro breathed.

They all tapped at their display selectors until they beheld a black sky streaked with twenty or more large, glowing comets, some plunging inward toward the system's primary star, others moving away. No matter which direction they moved, their shimmering tails pointed into deep space. Even as the crew watched, two of the comets silently collided, sending a spray of glowing ice in all directions.

"Let's get a closer look," Ilika began. "Departure pattern two."

Sata found the pre-defined flight plan in Manessa's memory. "Channel five."

Mati studied the plan. "It follows a band of space that's protected from the comets by the fifth planet, a small gas giant. Anti-mass one and ion five, please."

Just as Boro was announcing that the requested engines were ready, Kibi felt the hairs on the back of her neck tingle. She slowly turned her head to see what could have caused that sensation.

"Ilika . . . we have a passenger."

* * *

The crew's preparations for death marked the end of one phase of their lives, and the beginning of another. How can this be seen in their behavior in this chapter?

Chapter 31: The Passenger

Ilika quickly stood and looked. "Greetings, Melorania. You are a very welcome sight. Manessa, cancel simulation."

Kibi continued to stare with wide eyes. The lady in her passenger area smiled and sparkled like a happy girl-child, and at the same time radiated a subtle light of ancient and timeless wisdom. Her gown of many colors shimmered and flowed around her, obviously not made of any cloth. Kibi's eyes opened even wider, seeing that her guest was not sitting or standing, but instead just hovering effortlessly. Even as Kibi watched, the mysterious visitor floated closer and spoke.

"Hello, Kibi."

"Um . . . er . . . um . . . I know that voice."

"The last time I spoke to you, dawn light was barely in the sky, smoke swirled everywhere, and I had to take a simple form that was easy to see and follow."

Kibi suddenly grinned. "You saved Neti, Miko, and me from the fire!"

"Actually, I just saved you. You saved Neti and Miko."

By this time, the rest of the crew had gathered around Kibi's console. Except for Ilika, fear showed in every pair of eyes.

"I am well-pleased, Ilika," the passenger said, looking at the captain for the first time. "For monkey-mammals, they are certainly the best you could have found."

Sata remembered her navigator-friend using the same term, and shriveled her nose for a moment.

Ilika smiled. "Everyone, this is Melorania, head of the Nebador Transport Service. She was there when the fire drove us out of Lumber Town, she was near when we buried Miko . . ."

"And she responded to our question," Sata cut in, "when we found Risan Gor and her father."

The strange visitor nodded as her gown swirled around her. "Yes, Sata, and a hundred other times when everything in the Transport Service was going smoothly and no one needed me."

Rini chuckled.

"You may all sit," Melorania said. "We have much to discuss."

*

The simulation and its comets were completely forgotten as the passenger area was quickly rearranged into a circle of chairs. Kibi offered tea and left-over stew to her guest, and apologized for the lack of variety.

Melorania floated all the way around Kibi, her face twisted into a smirk that reminded them of Buna. "Kibi, do I look like I need tea or stew?"

Kibi lowered her eyes. "I'm sorry."

Melorania stopped to reach out and touch Kibi's face. "You need never cower before me, Kibi. Just keep learning, moment by moment, and you will be precious to me. You are prepared to die, are you not?"

Kibi couldn't keep herself from shaking. "I . . . I think so."

"Decide."

"Y . . . yes. I am."

Melorania brought her face close to Kibi's and looked deeply into her eyes. Kibi knew, in that moment, that her entire mind, heart, and soul were laid bare for the visitor to see. Time stood still.

When Melorania finally smiled, Kibi felt completely raw, as if every part of her being had been scraped and was in need of ointment and time to heal.

"You have a strong heart, Kibi, and even though you feel very empty right now, you will recover soon and find that many demons from your past have much less power over you."

Kibi's face twisted several directions and her eyes glistened with moisture as the mysterious visitor watched. Finally, a somewhat-forced smile appeared on Kibi's face, and she began to breathe easier.

*

Melorania became a blur as she spun around in the middle of the circle, then came to a stop looking right at Rini.

Lost for a moment in her child-like beauty, the lad grinned, then turned red as he realized she knew his every thought and feeling.

Melorania moved back a little. "Even though you claim to not understand what it means to be a man, I know lots of young ladies who would love to explore the subject with you."

Rini's eyes sparkled for a moment, then he chuckled. "I'm . . . taken."

"Yes you are. But are you ready to die with your fellow crew members and your ship?" she asked aloud.

"Yes," Rini began with confidence, "just as soon as I finish my . . ."

"I don't take conditions, Rini. Death can come at any moment, just as you might be needed at your watch station at any time of the day or night. Being in the Transport Service is not like a boy reluctantly doing his chores, or a slave dragging his feet to a work site."

Rini completely lost his smile, and tears were close. "I understand. Miko would have loved to say good-bye to Neti, but all he could do was whisper her name one last time."

"And what about you?"

"I . . . want to be there for Mati . . . and my ship . . . as long as I have breath. Then I'll willingly die if I must."

Melorania smiled and kissed Rini on the cheek.

*

The mysterious visitor swished around the inside of the circle and stopped right in front of the navigator. Sata nearly jumped out of her skin.

"Sata, when you asked to be tested by Ilika, I saw in you great potential, but I was worried about your age."

"I know. My mother had a little trouble letting go of me, and I got homesick a few times."

"You misunderstand me, Sata. I was worried that you might be too old."

Sata frowned with confusion.

"You are somewhat set in your ways. For example, you don't like being called a monkey-mammal."

Sata looked at her hands in her lap as they twitched against her will. "Um . . . we call ourselves people."

"The only problem is that 'people' now includes all the sapient races — insectoids, reptilians, avians, mammals, and others you know nothing about. And even among mammals, your species is just a small part of the incredible variety of sapient life in Nebador."

Sata took a deep breath. "I know that now. I talked to an avian navigator, and we were going to meet on Satamia Star Station, maybe . . . you know . . . be friends."

"Drrrim-na is sweet, and an excellent navigator. Are you prepared to let go of all the friends you have, and all the friends you might have made, and then die?"

Everyone else was so quiet that Sata's breathing and swallowing could be clearly heard during the next half minute. Eventually, she spoke in a tiny voice. "Y . . . yes."

"I know you are ready if Boro's arms are holding you tightly, and if it's a painless death, like a ship going into hibernation. What I really want to know is if — you know the saying by heart — if you are ready to stand on your own two feet . . ."

"With a smile on my face?"

Melorania nodded.

Sata glanced at Boro, then took another deep breath. "Without Boro, I'd probably cry like a baby. But I'll do my job for as long as I can, and then I'll die, alone if necessary. I . . . don't know if I can give you a smile."

The head of the Transport Service looked deeply into Sata's eyes, mind, and soul for a long minute, then nodded.

*

"Boro," Melorania called softly, turning to him slowly.

"Yes . . . what should I call you?"

She laughed. "The titles of respect in your language don't translate very well into the language of Nebador, do they?"

Boro shook his head.

"You may call me by my name."

"Melorania," he whispered.

"I really like the kind of man you have become, Boro."

He blushed.

"Too gentle for man's work, too clumsy for woman's work, but just right as a deep-space response ship engineer."

Boro grinned with embarrassment.

She came close and looked deeply into his soul. No one else made a sound. Boro soon started to tremble. His entire life seemed to parade before him in just a few seconds.

Melorania backed away. "You are often strong when others are weak. But will you be able to let go of your responsibilities when it is time to die, so you can be fully present in yourself, and fully experience the great mystery that lies beyond?"

Boro swallowed several times. "I . . . don't know. Not long ago, I wouldn't have even understood what you mean. After meditating at the monastery, and talking about death after Miko died, I think I understand a little."

"Perhaps . . ." she mused, "the last two weeks have helped with that understanding . . ."

"Oh, yes!" Boro declared.

"And maybe the next week will help also . . ."

Boro swallowed hard and nodded.

*

Melorania swirled around the room while looking into each of their eyes, and eventually stopped at Mati. "You have carried your burdens so bravely, precious one."

"I've never felt very brave."

"I know, but if you had seen the countless big strong men I've seen who were reduced to whimpering babies when they lost a leg or an arm, you'd understand what I mean."

Mati blinked several times, then nodded.

"Ilika guessed correctly that Kibi would not be ready for the Transport Service without her years in slavery. You would not be able to pilot this ship without your time as a crippled slave, and your long journey on donkeyback."

Mati glanced at Kibi, their eyes met for a moment, and tiny smiles were exchanged. Then Mati took a deep breath for courage and turned back to the mysterious visitor. A tiny bit of anger colored her words. "But I might have lived a little longer."

"No," Melorania corrected, shaking her head gently, "you would not have. You would be dead already."

"Oh . . ." Mati said with a thoughtful look as her eyes shifted back and forth nervously.

"So . . . are you ready?"

"You mean . . . to die?"

The visitor nodded.

Mati looked at Ilika, then at Sata, and finally at Rini. "So much of me just wants to cry, and let someone hold me and tell me everything's okay."

"That's natural. But right now it's your job, as pilot of the Manessa Kwi, to give me an honest answer to my question."

As Mati blinked, tears began streaming silently down her cheeks. "No conditions, right?"

"No conditions."

A long minute passed as Mati searched her heart for the courage to die. Tears continued to drench her best tunic. Suddenly she wiped her face on her sleeves, sat up straighter, and looked directly into the visitor's eyes. "Yes, I am ready to die."

The strange lady with a face of both beauty and wisdom smiled and nodded.

Mati cleared her throat. "Melorania, may I ask you a question?"

"Of course."

"I know we're going to die, but . . . you don't *mind* if Rini and I get married first . . . do you? I mean . . . if we have time . . ."

"Not at all, Mati! I love weddings! Being able to form a loving, working bond with another person is one of the things that separates the many barely-sapient creatures in the universe, from the few who might be called to universe service. I'll even come to your wedding, if you want me to, and if no one in the Transport Service is having a crisis that I have to go fix."

Mati grinned, and everyone else laughed.

*

Finally, the head of the Transport Service looked at Ilika. "You, I have already tested many times."

"And no doubt will again before I draw my last breath," Ilika said with wide, smiling eyes.

Melorania grinned. "Is that a dare?"

"No," Ilika said through his own grin. "Just a fact."

The rest of the crew tried to hold in their snickers and chuckles, but some slipped out.

* * *

Why did Melorania only rescue Kibi from the fire, not Neti and Miko?

Kibi and Melorania had different perspectives on Kibi's "emptiness." How would you describe each perspective?

Rini wanted to finish his video before he died. If you had only a year, what would you want to do before dying? A month? A week? A day? An hour? A minute?

Why was Melorania a little tougher on Sata than the others?

What title of respect might Boro have been considering, from his own language, that wouldn't translate into the language of Nebador?

What was it about Boro's personality that made Melorania emphasize the "letting go" aspect of dying?

How would Mati's experience as a "crippled slave" prepare her to pilot a starship?

How would Mati have probably died if she had not passed Ilika's tests?

Chapter 32: Melorania's Gift

Melorania of Nebador floated back to the center of the circle of chairs and turned slowly, looking at each of them as she spoke. "I must go. Others need me, and you all have preparations to make for a very important moment in your lives."

She then swirled around each member of the crew, leaving them feeling tingly and alive. Last of all she embraced Ilika and began fading from sight, her mouth still smiling like a sweet child, her eyes still sparkling with timeless wisdom. Then she was gone.

✷

The six crew members of the Manessa Kwi sat in the silence that lingered and looked at each other. Before anyone could think of anything to say, the ship began vibrating, then shaking, and loud cracking sounds came through the hull.

"Manessa!" Ilika shouted as he sprang to his feet and dashed for the bridge. "Emergency departure, all engines!"

After a half second to recover from his surprise, Boro grabbed Mati under her arms, pulled her out of her seat, and a few strides later, lowered her into the pilot's chair.

"Kibi, do what you can with the galley!" Ilika ordered. "Sata, flight recorder! Boro, be ready to cut the space thrusters as soon as the atmospheric engines are working!"

Everyone was in motion, finally realizing what was happening. The cracking and groaning sounds grew louder every second.

"Rini, color-coded sonar!" the captain continued. "I need to know what's solid and what's liquid, and I need it on the big screen!"

They all worked frantically with shaking fingers. Kibi stuffed dirty bowls and spoons into a cupboard and latched it. The ship began bucking and lurching, and she could barely keep her feet under her.

"Boro, inertia canceling, but fuel priority to the engines. Inertia straps, everyone!"

The Manessa Kwi was now jerking up and down violently. Kibi was knocked into a passenger seat before she finally reached her console and strapped herself in.

"We're moving up!" Sata shrieked with joy. "Four meters. Seven. Twelve.

"Boro, call engine status!" Ilika yelled over the scraping and bumping sounds from the hull.

"Space thrusters down to one minute of fuel. Atmo engines still purple. Wait! One of them is warming up . . . blue-green . . . green . . . yellow. Another one!"

"Cut space thrusters!" the captain ordered. "Rini, where's my sonar?"

Kibi looked and saw Rini desperately trying option after option on his console, none of which gave him the needed sonar image. She could see sweat pouring down his face, and his efforts to wipe his eyes on his sleeves only made his work harder. She popped her straps, grabbed the galley counter as the ship lurched again, and reached for a towel. A moment later she was on her knees beside Rini, holding his chair with one hand and wiping his face with the other. "You focus on your console, I'll keep your face dry."

A quick nod was all he could spare to express his gratitude as he struggled to clear his mind and find the right controls. "There it is! How did I miss it the first time?"

Kibi continued to care for her friend, knowing all their lives might depend on it.

"Sonar!" Rini cried as the image appeared on the big screen in front of Ilika.

The captain beheld freshly-cracked orange boulders of hydrogen ice swimming in yellow soup as the ship continued to push its way upward. The solid wall of the planet's core was still visible not many meters away. Crystals of ice tried to form between the floating boulders and the wall, and the ship was barely outrunning them.

"Ion drive status?" Ilika demanded.

"Green," Boro replied.

"Mati, get your flight control ready. You'll need a planetary chart."

"Coming," Sata promised.

Suddenly the icy walls of the crack in the core of the seventh planet came to an end, and everyone could see liquid hydrogen before them, with only a few small boulders floating about.

"Whoopee!" Boro cheered as he waved his arms while keeping an eye on his engine status board.

*

Rini soon quit sweating, but Kibi stayed with him, as he was now in danger of being unable to see because of tears of joy. Suddenly she realized that in the past it would have been *her* dealing with overwhelming emotions. Now, for some reason, her mind was clear and she was able to help someone else. It felt very good.

Ilika gazed at the sonar image in front of him. A few small hydrogen ice boulders floated about leisurely. "The rest should be easy. Anti-mass seven, Boro."

After several seconds, Ilika began wondering why his engineer hadn't verified his engine request. "Boro?"

"Um . . . sorry. I was just trying to figure out why all my anti-mass drives are purple. Diagnostics are fine. Everything looks like it should work."

Ilika was beside Boro a second later. "Manessa? Do you know anything about this?"

"Melorania asked me not to use the anti-mass engines, except for inertia canceling, until we arrive at Satamia Star Station."

Ilika frowned. "Manessa, over . . ."

"Wait, Ilika," Kibi said unexpectedly from where she knelt beside Rini.

He looked at her, his mouth still open to speak.

"I don't . . . really know what Melorania is," Kibi said as she struggled to put her thoughts into words, "but she's someone very important and . . . very powerful. She just looked into our hearts and she . . . you know . . . accepted us. No one's ever done that before . . . except you. We always try hard when you ask us to do things. Couldn't we . . . try it . . . before overriding?"

Ilika thought for a moment, then looked around the bridge. He saw a smile from Rini and little nods from the two girls at the front of the ship.

"I'm willing to try it," Boro said, "as long as we don't risk getting trapped in the ice again."

The captain thought for another few seconds, then smiled. "Okay, we have to figure out how to break free of the gravity of this gas giant with very little space thruster fuel. How much is left, Boro?"

"About a cup, maybe a cup and a half if I scrape the bottom," Boro said with a grin.

The captain looked at his engineer with stern eyes.

"Sorry," Boro mumbled.

"I understand, but I need a number."

Boro's fingers were already moving on his console. "At full power . . . forty seconds."

Ilika turned back to the big screen and sighed. "Melorania didn't make this easy. Guard that forty seconds with your life, Boro. Mati, begin pitching down. Bring us to thirty degrees relative to the planet's surface."

"We've got plenty of atmo thruster fuel . . ." Boro pointed out.

"Yes, and a very strong gravity well between the top of the atmosphere, where those thrusters will cease to work, and free space where the ion drive alone can get us out of here."

"Coming to thirty degree pitch," Mati announced.

"Time to liquid-gaseous boundary?" thc captain asked.

For a moment, everyone was silent.

"Oh, that's me," Sata said with a guilty voice as her hands started moving on her console.

Kibi gave Rini one last squeeze on the shoulder, left the towel for him, and returned to the galley. A minute later she had a cup of water in the drink holder at each console. "Sorry we're out of pinkfruit juice," she mumbled.

"Twenty-three minutes," Sata read from her console.

"Thanks," the captain said in a kindly tone, sipping his water. "Give me a planetary cross-section with ship's position. Continue monitoring sonar for obstacles. Pitch down to twenty degrees. Ion drive power level one. Recalculate time to boundary."

The four crew members who had just received commands all looked at each other like blinking owls as they figured out which of the tasks was theirs. Sata swallowed when she realized she had just received two orders at once.

From beside Ilika, Kibi started massaging his neck. He looked up with grateful eyes.

"Does this mean we're not going to die?" Mati asked without turning around after stabilizing the ship's pitch at twenty degrees.

Ilika was silent for a moment. "Ask me again in an hour."

*

"Two minutes to boundary," Sata announced.

"Mati," Ilika began from right beside her chair, "when we reach the boundary, Manessa will naturally gain speed and pitch up. We want the speed, but not the pitch. The moment we're clear of the liquid, bring us parallel to the surface. The tricky part is, there might be a wave or two in your face, and you need to make sure they don't scare you. Go right through them, get your pitch down, and stay as close to the surface as you can. Practice visualizing that before it happens."

Mati thought for a moment. "This is critical, isn't it?"

"Very."

"Maybe you should do it . . ."

Ilika took a breath for courage. "The problem is, Mati, that could be said about almost every piloting maneuver you've ever done and ever will do."

She gave her captain a long look, and saw respect and trust in his eyes.

Ilika returned to the command chair. "Full inertia canceling. Real-time topographic of the liquid-gaseous boundary. Pre-select hydrogen atmosphere filters for the forward view, maximum contrast. Ship's lights."

Boro, Rini, and Mati all confirmed, and Mati merged the topographic and the visual channels on her three-D display.

"One minute to boundary," Sata reported.

"I never thought I'd be so calm in a situation like this," Kibi said from her station as she secured her inertia straps. "I guess it was getting ready to die that did the trick."

Ilika flashed her a grin, then turned back to the bridge. "Magnify our current position on the big screen, Sata."

The small gold dot grew to a circle and rapidly approached the line where the yellow liquid ended and the white atmosphere began.

"Critical communications only," Ilika ordered. "Prepare to go to ion two, and select an alternate fuel."

Boro programmed the new fuel from memory, than began a diagnostic. When the indicator turned green, he smiled.

"Eight seconds," Sata announced.

Mati took the flight control in her hand and narrowed her eyes as she gazed at her display and waited to breach the surface.

✷

Even with full inertia canceling, they all felt the sudden transition from ocean to atmosphere. Kibi thought she heard dirty spoons rattling in the cupboard.

Mati was prepared for a wave or two in her face. Instead, her lights revealed a twisting tornado of liquid hydrogen, looming over the tiny ship and threatening to suck it into the dark, swirling clouds. Mati banked the ship so quickly that the entire visual scene turned sideways. "Ion two!" she yelled and pushed forward on her flight control.

A heartbeat later, the little deep-space response ship picked up speed and dashed away from the spinning funnel, streaking along less than a hundred meters above the eerie liquid hydrogen surface, just as fast as her engines could make her go.

✷

As soon as Mati had time to think, she rolled the ship so the surface of the ocean was once again beneath their feet.

"I don't think I could have done any better," Ilika admitted with a smile.

Kibi started clapping, and everyone else joined.

The pilot grinned without letting anyone see.

"Our next trick is all about speed," Ilika explained. "We need to gain as much as possible while deep in the atmosphere, but you'll need more clearance from the ocean the faster we go, Mati. I'd love to make one-hundredth light-speed before we lose the atmospheric engines, but we probably won't be that lucky. That's where Boro's forty seconds of space thruster fuel comes in."

"It's ready," the engineer assured.

"We need a vertical cross-section of the planet, Sata, so Mati can avoid the rings."

Sata wiped her brow and went to work.

"Other than that, it doesn't matter which way we go, as long as we get a few light-seconds away from Sonmatia Seven's gravity well. Then we party."

Laughter filled the ship, and hands started waving for toilet breaks. Ilika took the pilot's seat, and Kibi brought Mati her crutch from the passenger area. Then Kibi stepped into the galley, determined to do something about the dirty bowls and spoons.

✷ ✷ ✷

Why didn't Melorania tell the crew, before she left, that she was going to free them?

Just a reminder: the ship's "atmospheric engines" are what we would call "turbo thrust" or "jet" engines. They need something, like air, to work with, and so don't work in space.

Why, in your opinion, was Kibi's mind clear when she helped Rini?

Why was Kibi so deeply touched by a powerful person accepting her and her fellow crew members?

Which crew members got which orders when Ilika said, "Give me a planetary cross-section with ship's position. Continue monitoring sonar for obstacles. Pitch down to twenty degrees. Ion drive power level one. Recalculate time to boundary."?

Visualization is an important step in piloting. It allows the pilot to "practice" even before he or she is in the craft. It applies to difficult maneuvers, like Mati was about to do, and entire flight plans.

Mati's task, to quickly bring the ship parallel to the liquid surface, is similar to what an airplane pilot has to do in a "soft field take-off" in tall or wet grass, mud, or snow.

Which crew members got which orders when Ilika said, "Full inertia canceling. Real-time topographic of the liquid-gaseous boundary. Pre-select hydrogen atmosphere filters for the forward view, maximum contrast. Ship's lights."? How much longed would these commands have taken to give if Ilika had to think about, then say, who got each command?

What do you think of Kibi's guess that getting ready to die allowed her to be calm in that otherwise-tense situation?

Why would it be difficult to achieve a high speed in a thick atmosphere?

Chapter 33: Manessa's Secret

When everyone was back at their stations, Ilika looked around. "We'll be okay. Melorania has left us a challenge, but it would feel good to do this on our own."

Everyone nodded.

"When you're ready to die," Boro began, "having two feet under you again feels *very* good."

Sata flashed him a grin of understanding.

Ilika cleared his throat. "Pilot, do you have your chart and forward display?"

"Yes, Sir!" she replied, using a word from her native language.

Ilika smiled. "I'll give you thruster levels and altitudes, but take us higher if it feels too close. Remember, you always have flight command."

Mati nodded as she rearranged the images on her display.

"Ship's status?"

"We're still about a hundred meters above the hydrogen ocean," Mati reported, "skimming along at ion two. I've seen a couple of twisters in the distance, nothing on our flight path."

"Full inertia canceling," Boro said, "with higher levels of atmo engines at my fingertips. Forty seconds of space thrusters, warmed and ready."

"The galley is secure," Kibi informed. "I'm worried that everyone's gonna need food and rest soon."

Ilika nodded. "Thanks, Kibi. I agree, and seeing the stars again will help, whether we're free of the planet's gravity or not." He turned to the watch station.

"Oh, my turn," Rini chuckled. "Real-time topographics on channel four, and . . . I just figured out how to give Mati a long-range chart of those twister funnel thingies."

"Thanks!" Mati said, making room on her display.

"Flight recorder still active," Sata reported, "but I don't have any other useful charts unless we get into the rings or moons."

"I hope that doesn't happen," the captain said. "Pilot, one thousand meters, ion level three."

Mati was amazed at the sudden increase in speed, but felt high enough above the ocean for safety. The liquid hydrogen surface became a blur, so Mati concentrated on her topographic display. She noticed from her console that Manessa had changed into the double-ended needle shape she used for space travel.

"Four thousand meters, ion level four."

The pilot was suddenly grateful for the tornado map, and changed the ship's course slightly to avoid one.

"Pitch up to twelve degrees, obstacle check."

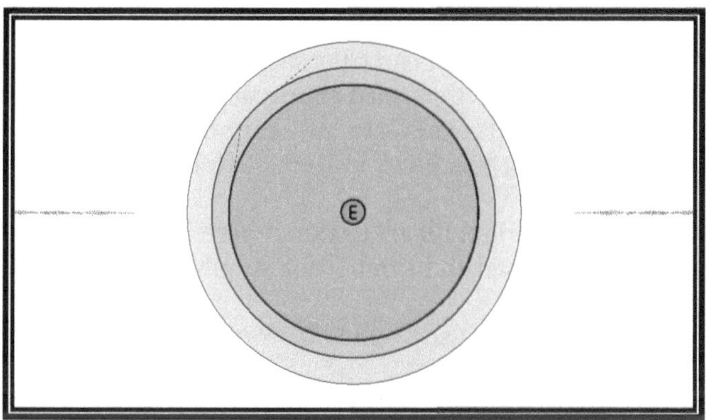

Mati focused on her planetary cross-section, and judged they would leave the atmosphere not far from the north pole. "No obstacles."

"Ion five. Ready space thrusters."

Mati gained all the speed she could, but her instruments and her gut both told her that the last increase made little difference.

"One atmo engine just went red!" Boro reported. "Another one!"

"That's okay," Ilika assured. "Just keep them from going purple by bringing them down, a level at a time, for as long as you can. Go to ion six, Mati."

"Stars!" Sata breathed as the last of the thick hydrogen clouds began to fade from her visual display.

Boro growled. "Atmospheric engines are dropping like flies, Ilika. I can't keep them going any longer. That's it. All purple."

"Ion seven! Space thrusters, full power!" the captain ordered.

Boro grinned as he touched the symbol for his most powerful, and most thirsty, engines.

"Now we're going somewhere!" Sata announced. "Escape velocity in thirty seconds!"

Everyone waited, hardly breathing. The captain glanced at each crew member while searching his memory for anything else they could do, any reserve of power his little ship possessed . . . other than the forbidden anti-mass drive.

"Five seconds to escape velocity," Sata reported.

Before she had finished speaking, the space thrusters sputtered and died.

"Damn!" came from the engineer's station.

Ilika quickly stood and stepped to the pilot's station. "Adjust your pitch, Mati, and bring us into a close orbit. Sorry, Kibi, we tried."

"I thought Melorania would give us a way," Kibi began, "but I guess I was wrong."

Manessa's gentle voice broke the silence that followed. "Boro, I believe you will find eight liters of space thruster fuel on supply line fifteen."

Boro frowned and looked at his control board. "Manessa, that's a spare line with nothing attached to it!"

"I know the fuel is there. You can trust me, or you can look for yourself."

Boro turned and exchanged puzzled expressions with his captain.

Ilika stepped close. "This is news to me. Your call, engineer."

After a deep breath, Boro's hand moved. "No harm in trying it, I guess. You ready, Mati?"

"Sure! You give me thrust, I'll get us out of here."

As soon as Boro touched the symbol for supply line fifteen, it lit up and the fuel began to flow.

"Hooray!" Mati cheered as she pulled back on her flight control. "I won't have to dodge rings and moons!"

* * *

What was it about getting ready to die that made Boro feel like he didn't have two feet under him?

The layers in the illustration, from the center outward, are: rocky core, hydrogen ice mantle, liquid hydrogen ocean, and thick mostly-hydrogen atmosphere. These layers may be typical for a gas giant. The only part we have ever seen is the surface of the atmosphere. All the rest are educated guesses.

In the middle of the illustration, what does the symbol "E" mean?

Chapter 34: Space At Last

It didn't take long for everyone to notice that the space thrusters were not running smoothly, but instead surging and sputtering almost constantly.

"Manessa," Ilika asked, still standing beside Boro, "how old is this fuel?"

"Two hundred and seventy-four years."

"Wow. And how did it come to be on supply line fifteen?"

"My engineer at the time, a very capable insectoid named Trrist'ku, put it there not long before she died. She said I might need it someday. I have not needed it . . . until today."

"Do you have any other secrets?" the captain prodded.

"By definition, if I told you, they wouldn't be secrets, so of course not."

The entire crew burst into laughter.

Kibi wagged a finger at her lover. "Us girls have to keep a *few* things to ourselves!"

After more laughter rolled around the bridge and finally died down, Manessa spoke again. "But Kibi, I'm not a girl."

Kibi grinned. "I know, Manessa, but you're one of us anyway."

"Thank you, Kibi."

"If anyone cares," a voice came from the pilot's station, "we are free of Sonmatia Seven's gravity, but I have no idea where we're going next."

*

Ilika didn't request a flight plan. He just made sure they were pointed into deep space, and asked Kibi to take first watch.

She arranged the necessary visuals and graphs on her display and lowered the table while everyone else came up from the bridge. Boro and Sata stepped into the galley.

Mati lowered herself into a seat with a deep sigh. "It looks like . . . we're gonna live . . . .right?"

"We'll die someday, somewhere, Mati," Ilika replied with a grin, "but not on Sonmatia Seven today."

Boro laughed deeply from the galley. "The last time we had a meal together, we thought we were *done!*"

Rini laughed nervously and looked at Mati beside him. She couldn't help but grin. When all the laughter faded, they continued to look into each other's eyes.

"Now . . ." she began, "I can get my knee fixed . . . and ask you again from my knees."

Everyone else remained silent.

"You don't have to ask again," Rini said softly with smiling eyes. "But you can if you want, just for fun."

Mati smiled, and continued looking into Rini's eyes. "Ilika, is a star station a good place for a wedding?"

"It's a great place. Satamia is small, with only a few thousand people, and most of them will come to your wedding if you want."

Mati's eyes grew large. "Even though they don't know us?"

"If you're in the Nebador Services, they know you've been through . . . experiences like we just went through. That's all they need to know."

✷

Sata and Boro quickly made sweet tea to warm nervous stomachs, then Boro got flour for biscuits while Sata started a pot of soup.

The three at the table, and Kibi at her station, chatted about everything that had happened in the last few hours. Boro and Sata jumped in whenever they remembered an important moment. With warm tea in hand and friendly eyes all around, they soon began to feel alive and safe again.

"Are we heading for Satamia Star Station now?" Kibi asked after looking over her console display.

Her question was answered by a long moment of silence.

"Um . . . we don't have to rush . . ." Mati began, peeking over her cup with courage in her eyes, ". . . if there are other things we should do first."

Ilika looked at her with surprise.

"I've made my peace with . . . the universe," she explained. "I'm ready to die whenever my time comes. I found the courage to ask Rini, and I have his answer. I can't think of any reason to rush. I want to savor every moment of my life, however long or short it is."

Ilika nodded. "There are two more gas giants . . ."

"Ilika!" Boro cut in after sliding biscuits into the oven. "We don't dare go anywhere *near* a gas giant with only a couple of liters of old space thruster fuel . . . unless we're gonna use anti-mass . . ."

"True," the captain said. "And they aren't much different from the ones we've seen up close — different colors because of different trace elements, but the same basic structure."

"And Manessa has oodles of pictures of them," Rini added from where he sat holding hands with Mati.

"There's also a small, rocky world far out in the solar system," Ilika went on. "The twelfth planet has no air, no sentient life, just crystals that grow slowly over millions of years."

Mati smiled with curiosity. "Much gravity?"

Ilika pulled a knowledge pad from the middle of the table and tapped at the keys. "More than fragment five-three-three, but I think you could walk there, maybe with a friend at your side."

The pilot grinned as the aroma of biscuits in the oven started to make their mouths water.

✷

After eating, the captain worked with Sata and Boro to see if they could get onto and off of Sonmatia Twelve without using the anti-mass drive.

Kibi listened from her station as she kept an eye on the ship, currently streaking farther and farther away from the Sonmatia sun. She noticed some surprised looks from both Boro and Sata as they huddled with Ilika to discuss the landing and take-off.

Eventually Sata turned around and announced that it could be done.

Kibi smiled, remembered the glow of happiness and wisdom on Melorania's face, and realized how much she wanted to be like that . . . maybe . . . a little bit . . . someday.

✷

Many hours later, Sata was alone on the bridge, sitting in the command chair with her knees up. Views of the stars, several graphs, and all the important status displays were arranged on the large screen in front of her.

"Manessa, please put my butterfly pictures around the edge of the main bridge display."

A dozen different creatures with delicate wings appeared.

Sata smiled. "Thanks. Now put out all the other lights."

The bridge and passenger area lights faded.

Sata's eyes became large as she gazed at the shimmering colors of the little creatures' wings. After a minute, her eyes were drawn to the visual displays of the stars. The forward view contained only stars, but the sun, much smaller than before, still glowed in the aft view.

For just a second, she thought she saw something in the stars she'd never noticed. She squinted and blinked, but all the bright graphs and butterflies made it hard to find whatever had caught her attention.

"Manessa, remove the butterflies, please."

They disappeared, but too many other distractions remained.

"Manessa, remove the radiation graphs and status displays, but tell me if anything happens that I should know about."

The other bright displays vanished.

Sata's mouth opened as she began to see colors and textures.

"Manessa, remove the aft view."

Suddenly the one remaining display, the forward visual of the stars, seemed to come alive and jump out at her. Reds, blues, and every color in between looked back at her from countless far-away stars, nebulas, and galaxies. The space in between was no longer empty, but revealed many different textures. In places it seemed thick with glowing mists. Elsewhere, it rippled and folded like a mysterious fabric. Sometimes it became thin, hinting at openings and passageways to . . . whatever might lie beyond.

"I never thought I'd see you sitting in the dark," Kibi's voice came from behind.

"Come see, Kibi! It's so . . . I don't know what to call it! I've missed so much by . . . always having lights on."

"Wow," Kibi breathed as she came down the steps and stood beside the command chair. "I never imagined . . ."

"Me neither!"

"Too bad Boro's not here to see this."

"He tried to stay up, but was yawning so much, I poked him until he went to bed."

Kibi chuckled. "And the darkness isn't bothering you?"

"I'm almost afraid to say it, but . . . not yet! I mean, I still like butterflies . . ."

Kibi smiled as she continued gazing at the textures and colors in the star field before her.

"What about you?" Sata asked. "Are the walls and ceilings closing in again?"

Kibi nodded. "Yeah, but it's okay now. They no longer have any power over me. After spending two weeks in the core of Sonmatia Seven . . ."

Sata began snickering, Kibi joined her, and they both turned to gaze once more at the mysterious universe into which they were flying as fast as their little ship could go.

✷ ✷ ✷

When Manessa said she had no more secrets, was her logic correct?

Living through difficult experiences together is one way that people form bonds. Knowing that someone lived through difficult experiences, even though you were not together, is another, although the bonds may not be as strong. What other ways of forming bonds can you think of?

What change do we see in Mati after getting away from Sonmatia Seven?

Why would Kibi have mixed feeling about her desire to be like Melorania?

Most of us have never seen the night sky without the "light pollution" of a nearby town or city. A clear sky, thick with stars, is a glorious sight when seen from deep in the wilderness. The view Sata and Kibi had was probably far better.

Why was it necessary for Sata to *turn off* other lights in order to see the stars well? Hint: what happens when you are in a dark room, or outside at night, and someone shines a flashlight in your eyes?

Talking about the walls and ceiling, Kibi says, "They no longer have any power over me." How is this like Sata's journey to "stand on her own two feet"? How is it different?

Chapter 35: A Strange Landing

Ilika emptied the last of the porridge grains into the cooking pot, and Kibi managed to find a little dried fruit in the back of a cupboard.

Others appeared one by one after getting baths and scrounging for clean clothes. For the first time in two weeks, Kibi announced she would start a load of laundry after breakfast.

While they ate, Rini displayed pictures of little Sonmatia Twelve on the screen over the steward's station, and shared what he knew between bites of porridge. They peered at frozen landscapes with a pitch-black sky even at mid-day. In places, vast level plains were covered by ice and snow. Elsewhere, jagged mountains stood like sharp teeth on the horizon. The ice, Rini explained, wasn't water ice, but frozen gasses that would be an atmosphere somewhere slightly warmer.

However, Rini didn't know the answer to the most burning question.

"Boro, would you brief everyone on the landing procedure?" Ilika asked as he began to collect dirty dishes.

Boro stood a little hesitantly, then drew himself up to his full height and took a deep breath. "This is going to be a little different than anything we've ever done. I've asked Manessa three times, and she swears it's okay."

Kibi, Mati, and Rini still looked clueless.

Boro continued. "Our problem is getting to the planet before we run out of food . . ."

Several people chuckled nervously.

". . . and then slowing down enough to land. We're saving the last of the old thruster fuel for take-off. There's no air, so we can't use atmospheric braking. We've got some tricks we'll use on approach to minimize the relative motion, like coming in from behind the planet in it's orbit. Luckily, parts of the surface are smooth, or this wouldn't be possible."

"What wouldn't be possible?" Kibi butted in, unable to contain herself any longer.

Boro grinned. "The final deceleration will be done with friction between the ship's hull and . . . um . . . the ground."

*

With twenty-two hours and several course adjustments before arrival at Sonmatia Twelve, those who had not already done so had plenty of time to ask Manessa for themselves.

Kibi asked from the utility room when she got the clean laundry.

Mati asked from a bathtub later that day.

Rini asked from the crawlway under the lower deck where he was pretending to inspect his sensors.

"The landing procedure will not harm me in any way," the ship assured each of them. "It is rarely done, as more elegant methods of landing are usually available, but it works. It is, of course, necessary to have complete inertia canceling."

"What would happen if something went wrong with inertia canceling?" each of them asked in slightly different words.

"All of the crew members would die . . ." Manessa began.

After a moment of reflection, Rini, Mati, and Kibi, at different times and places, each shrugged.

". . . and any cooking pot on the stove would spill," the ship added.

After rolling with laughter, which brought tears to all three crew members, they each went back to preparing for the strange approach and landing on the icy little planet.

*

Everyone managed to get a nap that day, but excitement was high, and Rini, Sata, and Mati all had duties at each course adjustment.

Repeatedly, during the hours of waiting, Ilika was asked if there was anywhere else in their home solar system they should explore. He soon realized what they were feeling. Satamia Star Station was far, far away, accessible only with the mysterious star drive, and they all knew it.

Boro settled the issue when the entire crew was at the table getting a snack before the last course adjustment. "If we explore anything else, it's gonna be on empty stomachs."

Several heads nodded slowly.

"Stations," Ilika ordered.

After checking all his sensors and sending displays and graphs to the other crew members, Rini quickly located the little planet. "It's hardly moved since the last time we checked."

"Because it's so far from the sun, right Ilika?" Boro asked.

"Right. Remember your orbit velocity equation? When orbital radius is large, velocity is low, and the other way around."

Boro made a selection on his console and looked at the equation and diagram for a moment, then nodded. "I can picture that."

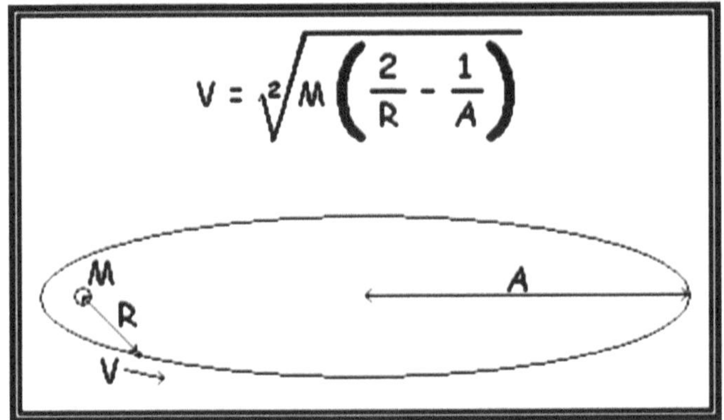

$$V = \sqrt[2]{M\left(\frac{2}{R} - \frac{1}{A}\right)}$$

"Sata?" Ilika inquired. "How do we look?"

"Just a tiny adjustment, and we should nail the . . . what do you call it? Landing? Belly-flop?"

Everyone laughed, releasing some of the tension in the air.

Ilika smiled. "Mati?"

"We just need a little puff from the maneuvering thrusters, Boro."

"All warmed up."

Mati approved the course adjustment, and Manessa did the work. Rini and Sata rechecked, and declared the course perfect. "Twenty minutes to . . . um . . . landing," Sata said with a somewhat-twisted smile.

✷

As they approached the small, airless world, Kibi appeared at Ilika's side. "It's about time I got some command practice, isn't it?"

He looked at her with surprise. "This is the first time you've asked to command a maneuver!"

"Yeah. And it'll be our first landing since you-know-where."

"The slave market?" Ilika asked with raised eyebrows.

"That was the you-know-*what*," Boro corrected without turning around.

Ilika laughed as he stood up.

As Kibi got comfortable and looked over the displays on the main bridge screen, Sata started squirming. A moment later she stood, and stepped beside Mati. "This landing doesn't need any great piloting skill, right?"

Mati looked up at her friend. "Just a little maneuvering as we make contact."

"Want to . . . let me try?"

After a moment of thought and a glance at Ilika, who nodded, Mati reached for her crutch. "I'll give flight commands and talk you through it."

Sata refreshed her memory of the basic piloting controls as Mati strapped herself into the navigator's chair. "Eleven minutes," Mati announced, "and the navigator's station is closed."

"We already have the only useful chart," Ilika said, putting on his inertia straps at the steward's station. "Make sure Manessa has the right shape,

Kibi."

"Oh, yeah. Manessa, round like a ball, please."

Sata chuckled. "That's called spherical."

"Yeah, that word," Kibi replied with a grin.

*

Boro ran every possible diagnostic on his inertia canceling system, each one several times, during the remaining few minutes. The little planet, gray on the sunlit side, black on the night side, began to fill their screens.

"Sata will need both maneuvering thrusters," Mati informed the engineer.

He announced them ready and in tip-top shape.

"See that light area just north of the equator?" Mati asked her friend in the pilot's chair. "That's the level plain we're aiming for. The flight plan will put us down near this end, and we'll have a hundred kilometers to slow down."

Sata magnified her flight plan display. "I have a three-degree glide slope right down to the ground."

Mati studied the same view on the navigator's display. "We just need to be ready for things too small to see on the chart."

Kibi took one last stroll around the bridge.

"Rini," she said from over his shoulder, "be ready to cancel the visual display as soon as Mati says."

He nodded.

"You see anything else we should worry about?"

"Looks like some rough ground on the edge of the level plain."

"I see it," Mati said.

Kibi moved on. "Sata, Mati has flight command, so if she speaks, you listen."

Sata nodded. "I may be ready to die, but that doesn't mean I *want* to!"

"No one talks during this landing, except Mati, unless it's *really* important," Kibi said to the entire bridge.

Ilika smiled and nodded.

Kibi stepped beside Boro. "Do we have a back-up plan?"

"Two of them. Old space thruster fuel, and the forbidden anti-mass drive."

Kibi thought for a moment. "Warm them both up. I'll decide which, if it comes to that."

"Two minutes," Mati announced.

*

The bridge was very quiet as they watched the dimly-lit planet grow larger and larger — no clouds, no weather, no air, just gray rocks and white ice. Soon jagged mountain peaks became visible as they swooped lower.

Sata followed the glide slope on her flight plan with white knuckles and tense muscles, determined to do a good job.

"Okay, here comes the fun part," Mati began. "We're going to come very close to that last row of pointy mountains. Forget the flight plan . . ." She reached up and canceled that part of the display. ". . . just follow my lead."

"Okay," Sata promised with a shaky voice.

"Nudge us a little higher, and aim for the largest gap between those peaks."

Sata worked with the flight control as sweat started forming on her brow.

"Good," Mati said. "Keep us up, don't let gravity get us yet."

The last of the jagged rocks swished by just a few hundred meters below the ship.

"Follow the curve of the land down, but not too closely until we pass those rough hills."

Kibi was concentrating on the visual display with her eyes, and Mati's words with her ears, when she suddenly saw a green light off to one side. It started flashing, as if trying to get her attention. "To the left! About twenty degrees! Now!"

Mati didn't see the green light, but she knew that tone in Kibi's voice, and gave Sata about half a second before yelling, "Do it!"

With sweat dripping into her eyes, Sata jerked the flight control and quickly banked the ship.

"Good," Mati continued more softly, "now steady your flight . . . come back right about four degrees . . . keep your altitude up just a little longer . . ."

Sata tried to blink away the stinging water in her eyes as the broken hills quickly passed beneath the ship.

"Okay, there's the ice," Mati pointed out. "Take us down, pilot!"

Sata wanted to smile, but was too close to tears to accomplish it. She tried to nudge the flight control downward, but her hand seemed unwilling to move.

"Don't be afraid of it. Either get us down, or I'll have Boro cut your maneuvering thrusters."

The engineer brought his hand close to his control board.

With a supreme effort of will, Sata jerked the flight control downward. A second later, the little ship hit the ground at a sharper angle than Mati would have liked, but in a pinch, it would do. "Visual off!" she ordered.

The entire crew saw the scene on their displays begin to tumble for no more than a second, but it was enough to bring moans and voices begging for bowls.

"Sorry," Ilika said as he gripped the arms of his chair tightly against the vibrations that were getting through. "No one moves until we come to a complete stop."

* * *

A planet far out in a solar system (like our Pluto), or in deep space, would receive too little sunlight to keep anything in liquid or gaseous form. Also, a small planet would have little internal heat (caused by internal pressure). Even the lightest element, hydrogen, would therefore be in a solid state, existing only as ice. Deep space is 3°K, and hydrogen freezes at 14°K.

In any equation of the form A = B / C, A varies directly with B, and inversely with C. In other words, as B goes up or down, so does A in the same direction, but as C goes up or down, A goes in the opposite direction. Notice the place in the orbit velocity equation of R, the orbital radius. Does V vary directly with R, or inversely?

If the "you-know-what" was the slave market, what was the "you-know-where"?

What combination of circumstances caused Kibi and Sata to both feel brave enough to do a different, more challenging, job?

Why did Boro run lots of diagnostics on the inertia canceling system?

A 3-degree glide slope is what most airplanes use. Helicopters use a 10-degree glide slope for a normal landing, but can use almost any angle.

What do you think of Kibi's command technique during the landing? How was it different from her previous attempts at command?

Sata's landing was very similar to what happens to inexperienced pilots: a tendency to lose altitude too soon, and then a fear of contacting the ground.

Chapter 36: The Littlest Planet

Soon after contact with the ground, Mati and Sata reached out and clasped hands. The bone-jarring vibrations seemed to go on forever.

All the crew members of the Manessa Kwi had learned to trust their faithful ship in many different situations, but as they slowly decelerated on the icy plains of the twelfth planet, they knew that not even Manessa had any control over what was happening. The situation felt strangely familiar to at least four of them.

Boro kept his stomach under control by sheer force of will. When he thought the vibrations might be lessening, he knew from his console they had only been rolling through the ice and snow for about two minutes. He was sure, however, that he would need at least two hours to recover.

Rini at his station, Kibi in the command chair, and Ilika at the steward's station, all managed to keep their teeth from rattling too much as the ship finally rolled to a stop, somewhere in the half-light of a frozen little planet far out in the solar system.

✷

After a deep sigh, Kibi remembered she was in command. "Um . . . status reports, everyone. Pilot?"

Sata hung her head. "I'm sorry, Kibi," she muttered. "I don't know why I . . . froze back there when you said turn. I think . . . I really like *navigating*."

Kibi smiled. "Will it be easier next time?"

Sata nodded as she made eye contact with the acting commander.

Mati, until that moment still and silent, grinned and touched the navigation console to get the ship's position, one of the few things she knew how to do at that station. "That was about like riding a donkey at a trot," she informed everyone as a small orange circle appeared on the planetary chart. "We rolled almost sixty kilometers."

"*You* sound okay," Kibi responded. "Boro?"

"Um . . . need to leave . . ." he said in a muffled voice.

Kibi saw that he had his hand over his mouth. "Go, go, go! Rini?"

While Boro dashed to the back of the passenger area, Rini made a selection on his console, then snickered. "Ready for visual?"

"I *suppose* . . ." the commander responded with suspicion.

The external view that flashed onto their displays revealed the surface of the planet on top, and a star-studded sky below.

Ilika, Kibi, and Mati burst out laughing. Sata managed to smile.

"You still have maneuvering thrusters, Sata?" Kibi inquired.

"Um . . . yes."

"Could you . . . you know . . . turn us over?"

"I . . . think so . . ."

Sata's first try caused the ship to spin completely around several times. Luckily, they felt nothing and only the external view tumbled.

Mati laughed. "We're on ice! Manessa, minimum power on the maneuvering thrusters."

Sata tried again, with much better control. After a few tries, she got the little ship almost upright. Mati pointed out the landing strut controls, and a moment later the Manessa Kwi rose out of the ice and snow and became perfectly level.

"You okay up there, Ilika?" Kibi asked, turning her head.

"I'm just sitting here feeling very proud of my ship and crew!"

*

With frayed nerves, everyone carefully checked the status of all systems, then shut down their consoles. Rini stepped into the galley to make tea.

"Welcome to Sonmatia Twelve," the captain said, taking a seat at the table. "The commander will brief us about that mysterious course change."

"Oh, that," Kibi said from the head of the table, brushing the concern away with her hand. "It was Melorania. Who else?"

Rini nodded knowingly from the galley.

"Any idea . . . why?" Mati inquired.

"No idea," Kibi admitted with a shrug. "Maybe she'll tell us someday."

Ilika laughed. "Don't hold your breath! She did things during my training that I *still* don't understand."

"Mysterious lady!" Boro concluded, returning from the toilet room.

After a moment of silence, Kibi took a deep breath. "The navigator will tell us about interesting things we can walk to."

Mati and Sata looked at each other, and Mati pointed at her friend.

"Um . . ." Sata began as she craned her neck to glance at the chart. "Just about nothing, but ice and snow, for a long way in every direction. Oh . . . except now there's a gouge in the ice about sixty kilometers long going back the way we came. That might be kind of interesting."

"Yeah!" Boro proclaimed with a big grin while others chuckled. "I wanna see that!"

When the laughter died down and cups of tea arrived, Ilika took on one of his serious looks. "Something you all have to understand."

They looked at him over their steaming mugs.

"It may look like ice and snow, but it's actually solid hydrogen and helium, and it's just as hard and sharp as any metal."

Rini pretended to pout for a second. "No snowball fights?"

"No," Ilika answered. "Extreme caution, every step."

"Can we . . . get a sample?" Kibi asked.

"It would probably explode as it warmed up, and soon be nothing more than a little bit of invisible gas."

She frowned.

"But the mountains look like they're made of rock . . ." Rini pointed out.

Ilika nodded. "And they're a long way from here. We might have to wait 'til we have all engines running."

Kibi looked forlorn. "I guess souvenir hunting would be a pretty poor excuse for overriding the head of the Transport Service."

Everyone else nodded and laughed, and Kibi cracked a tiny smile.

*

Ilika, as acting steward, led the first excursion through the airlock.

The tiny crystals they called "snow" crunched as Sata carefully placed her feet. Boro examined the larger crystals, sometime half a meter high, and found them tough and sharp, and determined to snag his space suit. All three soon retreated to the nearly-smooth avenue the ship had created as it rolled to a stop.

Sata looked around at the dimly-lit landscape and the starry sky. "About like our planet at night with a quarter-moon out."

Boro chuckled. "Except that it's early afternoon!"

Sata looked up at the sun, now just the brightest star in a black sky. "Our world is up there somewhere, right Ilika?"

"Very close to the sun, from this point of view."

"And yet . . ." A long pause followed as Sata continued to gaze in the direction of her home planet. "And yet, I'm safer here than I would be most places in my kingdom."

"And you could get to your parents' inn quicker from here," Boro added, "than you could from the monastery in the mountains."

"We could do it in seconds with the star drive," Ilika informed as they all began walking along the avenue, away from the Manessa Kwi.

"The star drive . . ." Boro pondered aloud. "That's next, isn't it?"

"Yes," Ilika replied. "This is the end of Sonmatia, not counting a few little asteroids and comets. Thousands of years from now, if your people take good care of their planet, they'll come this far. But try as they will, they can go no farther."

Boro nodded. "That seems like . . . enough. Why would anyone want more than one beautiful planet, and a few hotter and colder ones to explore?"

"I don't know, but they usually do want more."

"I can see that," Sata said as they walked along. "On our world, ship captains get all boastful when they find a new island with no one around to claim it. They talk like they're masters of the sea, but more often than not, they drag their ships home with broken masts and leaking hulls."

"And sometimes they never return," Boro added.

Sata nodded slowly.

They walked for another minute, then drifted to a halt.

"All looks the same," Boro observed, "and no sign of any rocks for a souvenir."

The others silently agreed, then began slowly crunching back toward the ship, a golden sphere gleaming in the dim light about half a kilometer away.

✷

After hearing Boro's report on the complete absence of souvenirs, Kibi, Rini, and Mati agreed it would be best to stay fairly near the ship.

They examined the snow and ice, wandered a hundred meters down the avenue, and gazed at the black daytime sky. Mati reported a little pain, but could walk if someone held her right hand. Rini was happy to be that person.

When they were just about to turn back, the eastern horizon began to glow.

"Looks like the moon is coming up," Mati said.

Rini frowned. "That's impossible!"

"Ilika?" Kibi called. "What's causing the horizon to glow? Anything we should worry about?"

"I'm looking into it. Rini's right, it's not a moon."

"I think we should . . ." Rini began.

At that moment, a bright, white ball appeared on the eastern horizon and quickly grew larger and higher in the sky.

"Comet!" Ilika yelled into the intercom. "Get under the ship, quickly!"

Rini started to stride toward the ship, but remembered too late he was holding Mati's hand. She spun and lost her balance, then instinctively leaned where her crutch should be. Rini's outstretched arm was not ready to catch her. He tried to hold on as she fell, but was pulled off balance. Mati slowly tumbled onto the ice and cried out in pain. A half second later, Rini landed on top of her, causing her to scream again.

"I'm so sorry, Mati, it's all my fault . . ." Rini began pouring out his guilt as they struggled to untangle themselves.

The bright ball of light was now almost directly over them, and had grown huge. A sparkling hazy glow seemed to spread from horizon to horizon in every direction.

Before Rini could make any sense of the situation, Kibi lifted him to his feet. "Under the ship! Run!"

"But it's my fault . . ."

"I can carry Mati, you can't!"

Rini couldn't make his legs move until he witnessed Kibi scoop up his precious friend and begin striding toward the ship. He ran along beside, his mind spinning with guilt and the desire to help. Before they had covered forty meters, tiny chunks of white ice and black rock started pelting the ground.

"Don't stop for anything!" Ilika commanded. "I'm rotating the ship so the airlock will be right in front of you!"

Suddenly something knocked Rini's legs out from under him, and he slid onto the ice, face first. He looked up to see Kibi's back getting smaller, and Manessa's airlock coming into view. A feeling of happiness filled him, knowing Mati would be okay.

A second later he was overwhelmed with anguish, realizing the grief she would go through if he died there on the ice.

He focused on the falling rocks, hitting the ground hard and often burying themselves deep in the ice. One of them had knocked him down. The next, he knew, would probably end his life. With all his might, he scrambled to his feet, ignored several flying shards of ice, and ran as fast as his legs would go.

✷

The airlock was too exposed, Kibi decided.

Mati screamed again as she was dropped onto the ice, then quickly dragged under the ship. A few seconds later, Rini dove under and skidded to a stop beside her.

Kibi breathed once to clear her mind. "Suit checks!"

Both Mati and Rini felt for their bracelets and tapped in the code.

"I'm . . . good . . ." Mati began with a shaking voice, still dealing with pain, ". . . as long as . . . I don't have to . . . bend my knee again."

Rini's heart throbbed in his throat. He had to blink away tears before he could remember Kibi's command. "My suit knows something hit it, but there's no breach. I'm so sorry, Mati . . ."

"It was an accident, forget about it! What hit you?"

"Rock, I guess. That's why I was a little behind."

The couple fell silent as they listened to Kibi and Ilika talking on the intercom. A moment later, the ship above them began to change shape, extending a wide brim over the airlock. Beyond, ice and rocks continued to fall from the sky, but seemed to come less often as the comet neared the western horizon.

"Rini," Kibi began as they all started wiggling out from under the ship, "would you like to take Mati in? I'll come after."

Kibi could see the gratitude in Rini's eyes, even through his face plate.

✷

Inside, Ilika quickly spotted the place where a rock or ice fragment had caught Rini in the leg. The suit was tagged purple for repair.

Rini continued to apologize to Mati several times each minute as they stowed the space suits. Kibi and Ilika kept their mouths shut.

The problem was solved when Mati stepped into the lift. Instead of making room for Rini as she usually did, she turned and blocked the entrance. "*You* stay down here until you quit feeling sorry for yourself." Then she rose out of sight, leaving Rini nursing his guilt, and Kibi trying very hard not to laugh.

*

"That was close!" Ilika began as Boro and Sata reheated left-over soup. "Comets don't often come that near a planet without . . . worse things happening."

Boro, in the galley, demonstrated an explosion with his hands. "Boom!"

Rini, now happily holding hands with Mati, chuckled.

"Everyone did well," the captain continued. "You were about one layer away from a suit breach, Rini. I noticed you hesitate when Kibi ordered you to run."

The freckled lad turned to his second-in-command with a slight cringe. "I'm sorry, Kibi. It was my guilty feelings . . ."

Kibi smiled. "I used to be the one who acted on feelings too often. I learned. You?"

Rini nodded. "I realized that if I died out there, Mati would go through even more pain . . ."

Mati looked him in the eyes. "And don't you forget it!"

Ilika smiled. "It's very natural to want to help after causing a problem. It's the honorable thing to do. But honor is a human value. Comets and other dangers don't know about our values. Next time your commander says run . . ."

Rini turned red as everyone looked at him. "I'll run, I promise!" he squeaked.

Everyone else clapped.

"Want to watch my back on a short excursion?" Boro asked the lad as he passed out bowls and spoons.

"Sure . . ." Rini agreed, "but why?"

"An hour ago there wasn't a souvenir in sight. Now they're all over the place!"

Rini smiled and nodded, and felt Mati squeeze his hand.

"First we all get some sleep," Ilika declared. "Tomorrow we say good-bye to this little planet . . . and the entire Sonmatia system."

All around the table, the eyes that looked up from their soup bowls sparkled with much excitement, and squinted with more than a little fear.

* * *

What experience had four of the crew members had that allowed them to relate to the ship (rolling to a stop with no control of any kind)?

Why would hydrogen ice explode if brought into the ship?

What makes Sata's kingdom less safe than a frozen, airless planet?

Beyond the planets, but still part of the solar system (because they orbit the sun) are many smaller object of rock or ice, collectively known as the Oort

Cloud. Some comets have long elliptical orbits that penetrate deep into this region.

We have visited, with the Pioneer and Voyager unmanned probes, all four of our gas giants, but not little Pluto. The probes are slowly leaving the solar system. The Voyager probes are still sending back some data, and are expected to do so until about 2025.

Whose responsibility was it to know the comet was coming?

A comet is a dirty snowball, constantly shedding material, and showing a long, glowing tail when it interacts with the charged particles of the solar wind. The tail always points away from the sun, regardless of which way the comet is moving.

Chapter 37: Final Departure

Ilika and Kibi were up early. Kibi, still in command, studied the planetary chart while Ilika scraped together all the grains he could find and made a thin mush. Alas, no sweetener or fruit was to be found in the nearly-bare cupboards of the little ship.

After getting a warm breakfast into their bellies, Boro and Rini easily found rocks from the comet. They brought back a fist-size lump for Kibi's display, and smaller ones for each crew member.

After souvenirs were stowed, Sata instinctively sat down at the navigator's station.

"Sorry, Sata," Kibi corrected. "I'm still in command, and you're still the pilot."

The innkeeper's daughter frowned. "But I stink at it!"

Kibi smiled. "Exactly."

Sata sighed and moved over. Mati, waiting nearby with her crutch, didn't say a word.

While everyone did their pre-flight checks, Kibi spoke. "Ilika promises me this will be easier than getting away from Sonmatia Seven."

The acting steward nodded. "And Boro's going to run that old thruster fuel through a couple of filters to clean it up."

"I am? Oh, yeah, I am." The engineer began working at his control board.

"It's easier, he tells me," Kibi went on, "because the gravity's a lot less, and we can use high levels of ion drive as soon as we're off the ground. We're going to look like . . ." She switched to her native language for a moment. ". . . like a bat out of the Underworld."

Everyone chuckled as they completed their preparations for flight.

"Straps, and inertia canceling," Kibi said, getting serious. "Flight recorder, universe transponder."

Mati had to get instructions from the real navigator.

"Equatorial and polar charts, real-time topographics," Kibi continued.
Mati and Rini provided the data while Sata arranged her display.
"Space thrusters, ready at full power. Ion drive, prepare for level five, ready for levels six and seven."
Boro touched several symbols, then smiled.
The commander of the Manessa Kwi, an ex-slave who used to have lice in her hair, listened as each of her crew members gave status reports.
"Have I forgotten anything, Ilika?" Kibi finally asked.
"Yeah. Preview the flight path with the pilot so she can begin to visualize it."
Kibi described what they were about to do, prompting Sata to add another graph to her display.
Finally Kibi took a deep breath. "I've got knots in my stomach."
"Welcome to the Transport Service," Ilika said from behind her.
She flashed him a grin that expressed several emotions, some professional and some personal, then turned back to the pilot. "You have flight command, Sata. Destination, deep space."
Sata breathed while looking over everything on her console and display. Finally, she couldn't think of anything else to do but activate the thrusters. She thought of Boro, at the next station over, and touched the symbol.

*

Slowly at first, then faster and faster, the icy plains of the twelfth planet moved lower in their visual displays.
"One hundred meters," Mati called.
"Come to a sixty degree pitch," Kibi ordered.
Sata moved her flight control and watched her vertical cross-section chart.
"Two hundred meters."
"Forty degrees."
Sata confirmed.
"Three hundred meters."
"Twenty degrees and ion five."
Sata made the course change and touched the ion drive symbol.
"Aha!" Rini exclaimed.
"What?" Kibi demanded.
"I found out why Melorania changed our course."
"Passing the south pole," Mati announced.
"Ion six," Kibi ordered.
"Escape velocity," Mati said.
"Ion seven."
"Nothing but deep space ahead."

*

Ilika took back command, and everyone gathered around the watch station.
"Manessa couldn't see it during landing because we were at a shallow angle, then rolling along the ground. But look what she spotted on take-off!"

The topographic on Rini's display showed the entire level plain where they had landed. About forty kilometers from the last range of jagged mountains, and right along the path they would have taken but for Kibi's course change, a deep meteor crater interrupted the smooth surface.

"It's not on the chart!" Sata declared with a tinge of guilt.

"Must be too recent," Ilika explained. "But now that Manessa's seen it, it's on the chart."

Sata, out of curiosity, stepped to her station and selected the equatorial chart. "Wow. It is. But how do we tell other ships?"

"Manessa already has. She's in contact with Nebador whenever we're in space."

"Will Melorania always watch our backs like that?" Kibi asked.

"No, very rarely," Ilika replied firmly. "I think she felt a little responsible for us this time because she's the reason we're flying without anti-mass."

"That's fair," Boro said, nodding.

* * *

Pre-visualizing the flight is even more important for a beginning pilot than an experienced one. Take-offs and landings are always "high workload" times for any pilot. This take-off, with one of their engines still not being used, was especially complicated.

What mistake did Rini make during take-off? (No one said anything about it in the story.)

What effect would it have on the crew if they thought Melorania was "watching their backs" all the time?

Chapter 38: The Star Drive

After a few hours of free time for everyone to get baths and otherwise relax, Ilika called them all back to the table. Rini stepped out of the galley were he had been putting the last few scraps into a small cooking pot.

Ilika looked around at his crew, all of them wondering what was next. "In some ways, you guys were handicapped because you'd never experienced air travel, never seen a space ship, and you knew nothing of ion propulsion and anti-mass drives."

They accepted their humble origins with nods and sheepish grins.

"In others ways, the fact that you're from a simple world with little energy and power, but what the wind and muscles can provide, means you can easily avoid a trap that people from advanced planets usually fall into."

"Power always goes to people's heads," Boro declared with a shrug.

Ilika nodded. "On most planets like yours, there are solid or liquid deposits of concentrated energy deep in the ground. As soon as people find them, they go crazy building cities, having babies, and making all kinds of machines to make life easy. It lasts for a century or two, then the energy starts running out."

"What do they do then?" Sata asked.

"It's often quite ugly. They've usually multiplied their population by eight or more. When the energy runs out, most of those people . . ." He paused to swallow the lump in his throat.

The other crew members nodded understanding.

"Those who are left are accustomed to very easy lives, and suddenly have to be farmers and laborers again, tilling the fields by hand, or at best, with animals."

Boro blinked several times. "I can't feel too sorry for them. Every gift has to run out someday. Anyone but a child knows that."

Ilika sighed. "Yes, but before that happens, they get some very strange ideas about the universe, and some very unhealthy attitudes. They start thinking they can have anything they want, go anywhere, just because they desire it."

Mati laughed out loud. "They should trying having a bad knee and a crutch! I get to go where Tera, Manessa, or Rini wants to take me, and that's about it."

Ilika nodded with understanding. "During their time of plentiful energy, they start dreaming of going to the stars. They invent countless ships, few of which can ever be built, and imagine engines that can take them wherever they want to go at the touch of a button."

Boro frowned and shook his head slowly. "I'm new at this space travel stuff, but even I know it doesn't work like that."

"After centuries of trying," Ilika continued, "if and only if they've saved some of the energy pockets on their planet, they learn how to carefully poke around their solar systems. But they still dream of the stars, and still imagine engines that can take them anywhere."

"You told us before that the end of the solar system is the limit," Kibi said, "but you never said why."

"The stars are far apart for a reason. Between the stars lie vast stretches of dark interstellar space. No ship made by mortal hands can cross those distances. No mortal mind or body can survive the journey. Manessa could do it, just as she could wait in the ice on Sonmatia Seven for thousands of years if necessary. But when she arrived at Satamia Star Station, the nearest outpost of Nebador, we would all be long dead."

The others nodded thoughtfully, remembering their recent preparations for exactly that.

"The universe is structured that way so that immature people will stay in their . . . what do you call it when a mother fences off part of the house for a child?"

"Play pen," Sata informed. "Mine was in the kitchen by the wood box."

Ilika smiled at his twelve-year-old navigator.

"So . . ." Boro pondered aloud. "This is where the star drive comes in, right?"

"Yes . . . the star drive. It is completely different from all the other engines. It uses no fuel, and has no moving parts. It does not *make* us go anywhere."

Puzzled looks greeted Ilika all around the table.

"People who are intoxicated with energy and power dream of flying to the stars as an act of will. Their make-believe ships and imaginary engines *make* them cross the vast distances between the stars, just because they want to.

"The real star drive, on the other hand, does the only thing that allows a flesh-and-blood person to make that journey. It *asks* the powers of the universe to move us from one place to another."

✷

Silence lingered as all his crew members tried to absorb what Ilika was saying.

"Does it ask . . . Melorania?" Kibi inquired with a very confused expression.

"No. The universe powers that the star drive contacts are far greater. But I assure you, if Melorania doesn't want us going somewhere, we'd have to get out and walk."

Nervous laughter circled the table. Several of them glanced at the large display over Kibi's station, currently showing stars in the vacuum of space.

Mati's face revealed a question forming. "Um . . . how does Manessa fit into all this?"

"The star drive is part of Manessa. She sends a complete description of where we are, where we need to go, and why. Since I'm a new captain, and you're a new crew, every star drive request will be checked carefully by Melorania. But as Sata found out back on your southern ice continent, she usually decides things very quickly. Later on, when we're all highly tested and deeply trusted, our requests will happen instantly, unless Melorania or someone else in charge thinks of a good reason to delay."

Boro took a slow, deep breath. "Wow. That really is . . . a different kind of engine."

"And that means," Rini began with a straight face, "we can't do stupid things with the star drive."

Ilika's eyes grew large. "I hope we never do stupid things with *any* of our engines!"

Mati snickered. "He means . . . you know . . . have fun."

Ilika smiled. "Having fun is okay, sometimes, even with the star drive."

Rini nodded and looked content.

✷

"So, jumping between solar systems with the star drive is gonna be easy!" Boro proclaimed. When the captain didn't immediately agree, the excitement drained from Boro's face. "Right . . . Ilika?"

They all looked at their captain and teacher. He appeared worried.

Kibi poked at him. "Spill."

Ilika took a deep breath. "To jump between the stars, Manessa . . . and all of us . . . must pass through a reality state where space . . . and time . . . don't exist." He looked around at his crew and saw mostly blank faces. Rini appeared curious, but clueless.

"That spaceless, timeless reality state has some rather . . . um . . . unpleasant effects on anyone who isn't . . . prepared."

Kibi swallowed. "What kind of . . . effects?"

"It . . . um . . . tends to make them go . . . insane."

"Oh," Sata said, her eyes shifting back and forth as if looking for a way out.

"But you guys are about as prepared as any new crew can be," Ilika continued. "You've practiced clearing your minds in meditation. That's the key to visiting non-spatial, non-temporal reality states. If you don't have expectations of finding space and time dimensions to relate to, you won't be bothered by the lack of them."

His crew started to breathe again.

"And you've had the extra preparation of preparing to die on Sonmatia Seven. That helps because the experience of star transit, if it can be compared to anything, is most similar to . . . you know . . . dying."

"So the sisters at the monastery," Rini began with sudden realization, "would be right at home with it!"

Ilika smiled. "They'd be better prepared than anyone else on Sonmatia Three."

"What would happen to the high priest?" Boro asked, squinting.

Ilika laughed and shook his head. "It wouldn't be pretty!"

"But what about passengers?" Kibi asked with concern. "Can I only have passengers who know how to meditate?"

"No. There are those in Nebador who have the power to shield others from the effects of the star drive. One of them will come along any time you have passengers who aren't Nebador Services people."

Kibi nodded, for the moment satisfied.

✷

"Actually, neither Manessa, nor any other ship, would ever cause anyone to go insane in star transit. The drive will simply not engage until everyone is prepared, or shielded."

"That's good!" Mati burst out. "I couldn't imagine Manessa hurting anyone on purpose."

"Thank you, Mati," the ship said.

"You're welcome, Manessa. So . . . when do we go? I think there's a healer I want to talk to at Satamia Star Station."

Everyone else chuckled.

Ilika looked around. "I need to spend about half an hour with each of you, going over your responsibilities before and after star transit. Most crews like to get their ship clean and tidy first, whenever they have time, because star transit is sort of like . . . well, dying and coming back to life. Also, we need to be well-nourished, but not have too much in our stomachs, especially the first time . . ."

"Yeah," Boro agreed, "if it's anything like *flying* the first time."

Kibi and Mati both nodded.

Ilika smiled. "So let's get Rini's soup finished, have our last meal in your home solar system . . ."

"And that's the last meal we're gonna get out of *these* cupboards!" Kibi declared.

"I'll help with the soup!" Sata volunteered.

"Everyone, tidy your cabins when you're free," Kibi requested, "and I'll do the common areas."

"Mati," Ilika began, standing up, "let's go down to your station and talk about piloting during star transit . . ."

* * *

The situation Ilika described when people on a planet discover "deposits of concentrated energy deep in the ground" is, of course, taken directly from the situation on Earth right now. It started in about the year 1700 with coal, increased greatly in about 1900 with crude oil, and was supplemented by uranium in about 1950. Today, we are just passing the peak of usage of all three because of dwindling reserves, pollution, or both.

Since any creature, animal or plant, always maximizes its population within the resources it has, it tends to "overshoot" the carrying capacity of its environment. The population soon crashes back to a point lower than it began, because the process tends to damage the environment. Before we discovered coal, oil, and uranium, the human population of the Earth was fairly stable at about 500 million (one half billion). Today it is passing 7 billion.

Our fantasy of exploring the universe at will is expressed most clearly, of course, in the Science Fiction genre, but glimpses of it can be seen in every other genre, and in every aspect of life.

The idea that the universe is purposefully designed, so that mortal races can only explore their home solar systems, is a theological concept, not a scientific concept. From this follows the notion that whoever decided this (deity, by whatever title or name) can also make exceptions. A thread of evidence and opinion, subtle and rarely talked-about, runs through our stories and histories that very occasionally an individual is chosen for direct service to deity. They tend to mysteriously "disappear" from human society, and so become lost in the statistics about people who are abducted and presumably murdered, but no remains are ever found.

The idea that a deeply-trusted servant of deity can exercise fantastic powers, seeming at will, but can only do so as long as they carefully follow certain rules (and never use the powers selfishly), is another theme that pops up all through history and literature.

What qualities of "space dimensions" are we used to that cause us to be disoriented in space when they are absent? Hint: we know many of these visually, some by touch/feel, and even some by sound.

What qualities of "time dimensions" are we used to that cause us to be disoriented in time when they are absent? Hint: we usually know these through rhythm, such as the timing of syllables in a spoken sentence, or the wing-beats of a bird.

What are the usual physiological (health) effects of disorientation in space or time?

Why would Ilika speculate that the high priest (in the capital city of the little kingdom on Sonmatia Three) would not do well in star transit?

Chapter 39: Star Transit

A special, tingly mood filled the Manessa Kwi for the next few hours as the crew learned what they needed to know, ate the very last of their food, and shared excited glances or touches as they passed each other, going from task to task. The cabins had not been so clean and tidy since the five new crew members moved into them, many months before and nearly six light-hours away in space.

Kibi and Rini gave the toilet rooms and the galley a good cleaning. Sata, at her station, glanced up with a guilty look, but had more study and preparation for star transit than anyone else.

Eventually everything was ready. Ilika went to the steward's console, raised the big table, and asked Manessa to arrange six seats in a close, inward-facing circle. "Soon this will be as easy as ion flight, and you'll be able to do it from your consoles without a second thought. But for your first time or two, holding hands really helps."

Everyone waited until Mati was comfortable, then Rini took one side and Sata the other. Boro seated himself beside Sata. Kibi looked over her console one last time, then she and Ilika took the last two seats. Hands found each other all around the circle, most a little sweatier than usual.

"Kibi," Ilika prompted.

She took a couple of slow breaths to focus on her task. "Manessa, secure all fluid systems. Switch all internal energy to standby. Lock hatches and the lift. Shut down my station and the big screen."

"Acknowledged," the deep-space response ship said.

The subtle background sounds of the ship suddenly ceased, leaving a profound silence. All of the passenger area and bridge lighting faded out, leaving only displays and instruments casting a soft glow.

"Rini," Ilika called.

He glanced at Mati with sparkling eyes for a second. "Manessa, shut down all sensors. Auto-restart on return to normal space and time."

"Acknowledged."

The watch station went completely dark.

"Sata."

"Manessa, feed ship's position and flight plan Satamia Five B to the star drive. Shut down navigation and communications."

"Acknowledged."

"Boro," the captain prompted.

"Manessa, lock all fuel lines and initialize the star drive."

"Acknowledged."

Boro's station became dark except for six tiny blue lights, high up on his control board, in an area he had never before used. Even as he glanced that way, they changed to blue-green, showing him the star drive was warming up and testing itself.

"Mati," Ilika began, "as always, the pilot has the honor, and responsibility, of making the final determination that we are ready for flight."

The handicapped pilot, who had hopes of not being handicapped much longer, looked around at her captain and fellow crew members. She didn't see anything in their eyes that worried her. "Manessa, shut down all remaining systems. Activate the star drive as soon as we're ready."

"Acknowledged."

The last displays and control symbols went dark. The only light now came from the six little indicators on the star drive at the engineer's station, all still blue-green.

✷

Rini felt Mati squeeze his hand as he closed his eyes.

Old memories, of a family who didn't understand him, fleeted across his mind for a few moments. Scenes from his years as a slave came and went. The painful moment, when Mati decided to stay with the goatherd, lingered, then the pleading face of a desert girl pulling him toward her tent.

Finally Rini cleared his mind and drifted into the timelessness of meditation.

One of the lights on the star drive changed to green.

✷

Kibi closed her eyes and reviewed many painful scenes from her childhood, always out-thinking her parents with ease, and always being punished for it. Her time in slavery passed in a blur, except for a sweet memory of Miko that lingered for a moment. She smiled slightly, accepting the part of her life that had made her strong.

The memory of seeing Ilika for the first time burned brightly in her mind, and the warm, almost hot feeling of wanting something with all her heart.

Realizing he was beside her now, holding her hand and sharing her bed, allowed her to relax into the comfort of the darkness around her.

The second light on the star drive changed color.

✷

Boro felt his heart throb from holding Sata's warm, sweaty hand, but let the feeling pass, knowing he could treat her to a nice meal or a gift at Satamia Star Station, and more of the deep kisses they had begun to share.

Memories of cattle, sometimes taller than he was, came and went. Painful scenes from slavery made him cringe, scenes of masters telling him he was good for nothing.

Eventually he relaxed, remembering his beautiful engine and fuel control board, and knowing that even now it was preparing to take them on a long journey. Thoughts fell away until only his breath remained, without measure in time or space.

Another light change to green.

*

Mati was so filled with the hope of getting her knee fixed that she couldn't relax. The faces of slave owners, soldiers, and a lonely goatherd peered at her, but had no power compared to the overwhelming dream she clung to with every fiber of her being.

Finally, she realized that as long as she held tightly to her hope of someday walking, running, and dancing, she would not be able to relax and clear her mind. Many long minutes passed as she wrestled against her deepest desire, its claws sunk deep into her heart. Sweat poured down her face and dripped onto her clothes.

Suddenly a memory came to her, a scene from the recent past in which she asked the most beautiful boy in the world to marry her, and he accepted. And he hadn't, she remembered, set any conditions, such as first getting her knee fixed. Her breathing slowed, a slight smile appeared on her wet face, and her mind cleared.

The fourth light on the star drive changed to green.

*

Sata's mind visited countless fond memories of mother, father, and brother. She could see every timber and board of the inn, and had personally scrubbed or swept most of them, except a few on the ceiling.

Then the anger returned from the day she overheard her parents talking about giving the inn to her brother, because girls just got married, they said. Slowly the anger faded and a smile grew on Sata's face as she remembered the navigation and communications console of the Manessa Kwi, just a few steps away, where she did a job her parents and brother could never understand.

Coming fully back to the present for a moment, she felt Boro's hand in hers, and her friend Mati's hand on the other side. She let her mind clear, and drifted into timelessness.

Another light changed color.

*

Ilika took his time relaxing.

Memories of his parents and sister were not overly painful, and far in the past. The faces of a few girls visited, girls who had liked him during his years of training. Zini appeared for a moment, then danced away into the crowd at some social event for the nobility of her medieval kingdom. Only one face lingered, a face of longing and desire, framed by lice-infested tangled black hair, first seen in the common room of Doko's Inn. She was the first girl to ever really love him, and she was beside him now, his second-in-command, his partner and companion for travel and service in the stars.

The captain of the Manessa Kwi took a slow breath and let his mind relax and go dark and quiet.

The last blue-green light changed to green.

✷

A moment later, all six green lights changed to yellow at once.

Manessa Kwi Habishu Glinta, deep-space response ship of Nebador, currently floating in the blackness of space on the outer edge of a little solar system called Sonmatia, began to shrink. Soon she was just a tiny speck of gold, barely visible in the dim light on the edge of deep space.

Then she was gone.

✷ ✷ ✷ ✷ ✷

A light-hour, you might recall, is about 6.5 billion km (4 billion miles).

All ship system must be shut down during star transit because they are physical systems, and so would not work in a spaceless and/or timeless reality state. Even the simplest device, such as a liquid flowing through a tube, can only function if space and time are as we know them. The idea of "flow" has no meaning without a "here" to start from, a "there" to go to, and some "time" to allow it to happen.

Each of the crew members, including Ilika, had emotional events or situations in their pasts that could have kept them from relaxing during star transit, thinking clearly when on duty, or otherwise doing their jobs and living their lives. Every time we are hurt physically or emotionally, we can heal, regain our strength, and become wiser, or we can fail to heal, and move closer to death or insanity. Will-power is certainly necessary, but there may also be an element of luck involved. That element of luck may or may not be divine intervention.

Greetings, young people of planet Earth,

We are all formed in the crucible of childhood.

"Slavery," in the sense of being "captive" by something that takes more than it gives, is often a part of our lives.

The "tests" begin early, even if just those boring days in school with countless multiple-choice questions to answer.

Some young people are called by a "journey" of growth, sometimes to get out of "slavery," sometimes in a very different direction.

The "selection" processes of our world can be very deceptive. Everyone wants to be a winner — but what are we winning, and is it worth it? The world will not tell us, for that would reveal its many games and scams. We must find out for ourselves.

"Training" is not so hard, *IF* we've had our eyes and ears open, with brain engaged, every minute since kindergarten. If not, we might have some catching up to do. A planet with tight resources and expensive energy will naturally have few people with comfortable lives, and many who are struggling to make ends meet. Training, at everything we can think of, is essential.

But occasionally, everyone needs to come home.

Does that mean we can just goof off? Since our parents are there, will they clean up our messes? Can we treat others however we want without getting slapped or bitten?

By stepping onto a star station, our beloved characters have left childhood far behind. They have, in some ways, even left adulthood behind. On a backward little planet like Sonmatia Three, being a grown-up just means staying alive until you die, and it doesn't matter who you step on.

On a star station of Nebador, it's not that simple.

Here on Earth, *we* must decide.

J. Z. Colby
2012

Greeting from the *Deep Learning Notes*,

You have probably noticed a progression of depth in the Nebador stories and their Deep Learning Notes.

In *Book One*, the characters were concerned with the basics of getting along, forming a working group, and learning to read and count. Those are things we all need to do to be anything more than . . . slaves.

Book Two, you will remember, added writing and calculation, basic chemistry, and a relationship lesson or two. For some, trigonometry was a headache. Others would rather do trig all day than what Mati went through right after that.

After learning to meditate, in *Book Three*, and wrestle with quantification theory, flying a little star ship seemed pretty easy — as long as no one was trying to burn it.

Book Four taught our characters the things any flight crew must learn, and some important lessons about people, even people in need. This is the basic work of anyone "standing on their own two feet."

Things got a bit more serious in *Book Five*. In space, there's always one more "person" on any excursion, most often seen in a black hooded cape, holding a scythe. He has much to teach us.

Suddenly, in *Book Six*, we are no longer alone and in the wilderness. A "million" lessons await us, from technical to spiritual, but none more important than the biggest question of all:

What's out there, and how do we fit in?

J. Z. Colby
2012

"It is not the purpose of the universe to get things done as quickly and efficiently as possible. That's a mortal preoccupation, especially strong in monkey mammals, but we all feel it to one degree or another . . ."

— Silmula Sorafax, in charge of the Great Transformation

NEBADOR
Book Six
STAR STATION

Chapter 1: Star Station Approach

Their minds floated joyfully in the darkness.

The timeless, spaceless nothingness of star transit did not allow the crew of the Manessa Kwi to think, or even to feel. But somehow, a seed of awareness remained.

Then something changed, and thoughts began to form. Silence. Darkness. Life. Breath. A faint glow seen through closed eyelids.

"Take your time coming back," a soft voice suggested. "You'll be disoriented, maybe dizzy."

That's my lover, Kibi thought, and a smile curled her lips, but she felt so strange that she decided to keep her eyes closed a bit longer.

"We are in the Satamia star system," Ilika's voice continued, "on course for atmospheric braking around Satamia Five."

Sata opened her eyes and blinked like an owl. "Ma . . . Mane . . . Manessa?"

"Yes, Sata?" the deep-space response ship replied in her pleasant voice.

"Nav . . . navigation status?"

"Four light-minutes to course adjustment at Satamia Five approach marker B. Relative velocity is point one seven light-speed."

Boro's eyes snapped open where he sat beside the navigator, still holding her hand. "I didn't know we could go that fast!"

"Normally we cannot," the ship explained. "The difference in universe motion between the two solar systems created the high velocity."

"Oh, okay. Engine status?"

"Repulsion field yellow. All other engines inactive. Anti-mass inoperative by request of Melorania, not yet overridden."

"Oh yeah, that."

Rini chuckled, squeezed the hand of the girl seated next to him, and stretched his arms toward the ceiling. "Manessa, sensor status?"

"Inter-planetary sensors active. All energy levels typical for this system. No objects on the flight path until approach marker B."

Beside Rini, Mati groped for her crutch. "Navigation markers! It'll be nice to pilot with some solid reference points."

"Okay," the captain said, standing up slowly and stretching, "let's take care of ourselves and be at stations in twenty minutes."

"There's a little dried peppermint," Kibi announced, "so I'll make tea!"

*

Mati got comfortable in the pilot's chair, touched a symbol, and her display glowed with the views and graphs she liked to have handy. Largest were the forward visual from Rini and the primary navigation chart from Sata. The red and purple gas giant Satamia Five, dead ahead, dominated both displays. Slightly to one side, a tiny white light pulsed with a regular pattern.

Also on her display, somewhat smaller but no less important, the engine list from Boro, and the internal ship summary from Kibi, gave Mati everything else she needed to know. "Since there's an approach marker for atmospheric braking, someone's had to do this before, right Ilika?"

"Yes. In a populated and well-traveled system like Satamia, there are navigation beacons for every type of ship and every kind of emergency. Back in your solar system, Sonmatia, we were in the wilderness. Here, things are more organized. Sata, would you teach the others about visual beacon identification?"

The navigator worked at her console for a moment and found the list she wanted. "Um . . . look at channel five."

The others tapped at their display selectors.

"All nav beacons transmit, just like the markers at Zolko and Memna on our fourth planet, so normally Manessa knows all about them. But if we just had visual, we could count the flashes."

"Three short and one long," Boro observed.

"Right. And there's only one beacon that flashes like that in the whole system."

"Satamia Five approach marker B!" Rini announced with a grin, reading his display.

"Okay," Mati interrupted, "we're almost there, so we need to do that course adjustment."

Everyone sat up straight and got serious. Rini touched several symbols. "Here's my fix, Sata."

The navigator made a selection. "Wow. We're almost one degree off!"

"That's pretty typical after star transit," the captain explained.

Mati peered at the numbers that flashed onto her screen. "All maneuvering thrusters, Boro. Inertia canceling."

"At least those still work. Green."

The pilot laughed nervously. "This will take about two minutes. How close can I come to the beacon, Ilika?"

"You can go right through it. It's not physically present."

Mati frowned for a moment, then shrugged.

The bridge was quiet as they watched the ship's heading slowly line up with the desired course. The correction was completed just moments before the little ship passed through the phantom navigation beacon, and continued its plunge into the gravity well of the swirling gas giant.

✷

Unlike the atmospheric braking around their own fourth planet, with its occasional dust storm, this one was done by instruments alone. By order of the pilot, a handicapped ex-slave from a medieval world, all visual displays were cancelled, lest her crew lose their peppermint tea, the last thing in their cupboards.

The deceleration from nearly one quarter light-speed took seven orbits through the thick and poisonous mists of the gas giant. Though smaller than the huge sixth planet of their home system, or the seventh where they had been trapped for two weeks preparing to die, Satamia Five hosted a completely different stew of elements, in addition to hydrogen, giving eerie shades of red, magenta, and purple.

The first three or four orbits went quickly. But as the pilot slowly increased the altitude, following graphs supplied by the medieval innkeeper's daughter in the navigator's chair, the process seemed to drag on and on.

The captain, a young man from a far-distant world he had not visited since childhood, noticed that some of his crew members were getting antsy. He was very proud of them for trying to stay within the engine restrictions set by Melorania, the head of the Transport Service. But with Satamia Star Station now so close they could almost see it, he knew their patience was being sorely tested.

"Boro," the captain declared, standing up, "you have command for the star station approach."

Kibi, the second-in-command, smiled from the steward's station, and had a hunch Boro would need a few pointers.

✷

Boro, a fifteen-year-old lad from a medieval cattle ranch, appeared both proud and nervous as he filled the command chair with his large, muscular frame. He had little to do but listen as the pilot and navigator worked together to complete the last few climbing orbits of Satamia Five.

Finally Sata turned and grinned at the boy in the command chair, the same boy she had just recently started kissing. "We're down to a thousand kilometers a second, but really can't go any slower, or it will take forever to get to the star station."

"Forever doesn't work with our food supply," Boro mumbled as he looked at the new chart that flashed onto the main screen directly in front of him.

Kibi chuckled from behind. "I *think* I can make one more pot of tea."

"The star station's only twelve light-seconds behind the gas giant," Sata continued, "in the same orbit. But that'll take us . . ." She worked at her console for a moment. ". . . about three hours."

Boro sighed. "I hope there's a pot of stew on the stove when we get there."

Ilika smiled from the engineer's station. "Even the smallest star stations have everything you could want . . . except red meat, of course."

"I could go for an apple," Boro declared. "Status reports?"

✷

After getting routine matters out of the way, the commander turned to his captain. "Ilika, how are we going to slow down at the star station? A thousand kilometers a second isn't a very friendly way to arrive."

"Good question, Boro. Maybe it's time to start talking to the star station."

Boro took a breath and wrinkled his brow. "Am I gonna be talking to a bird?"

Sata turned around and gave him a dirty look.

Ilika smiled. "You might be. Whoever's at docking control, I guarantee they'll know everything there is to know about getting safely in and out of the station."

"Um . . . okay. You do that, right, Sata?"

"Uh huh, as long as you're nice to whoever we talk to, even if it's a bird."

"It could also be an insect," Rini pointed out from the watch station with a gleam in his eyes.

Boro moaned, and didn't see the smiles on the other crew members' faces.

"Satamia docking control," Sata began, "this is the Manessa Kwi, eight light-seconds ahead of you in orbit. The commander has a question or two about our approach."

Boro moaned again.

A mammal with a snout and black nose, completely covered with brown fur, flashed onto the screen. "Greetings, beautiful monkey mammals of the Manessa Kwi! I see you are coming in very, very slowly. How can I help?"

"You're not a bird!" Boro observed with surprise.

"Not last time I checked my anatomy," the docking controller said, showing long, sharp teeth in the process.

"Sorry," Boro mumbled. "The only other person we've seen from Nebador was a bird."

The controller looked down at his console for a moment. "Oh, I see that you're a crew-in-training. What's this? Melorania made a note that you would probably be coming in slowly. Aren't her training challenges fun? Once it took me a week to get from one planet to another with nothing but maneuvering thrusters. Took *three* freeloading passes!"

Boro breathed easier and smiled. "Um . . . yeah, we're not supposed to use anti-mass. Actually, I'm the engineer. We did atmospheric braking around Satamia Five, but now we're wondering how to slow down the rest of the way."

"Well, we can handle that! I'll just send you the deceleration tractor . . . wait, what's this? I can't believe it! Only an hour ago, Melorania sent it to Satamia Two to help with something. She must really like you guys. Most new crews don't get *this* much tender loving care from the grand old lady of the Transport Service."

Boro chuckled, even as he absorbed the bad news. "It's probably because we're . . . monkey mammals."

"Could be. Your proper name is 'humans,' in case you don't know. We ursines can be a bit stubborn too. Anyway, back to our little problem. I'm not sure what else I can do on this end. Got any thruster fuel?"

"A little. We'll see if it's enough. Thanks."

"I'll stay on duty until you're safely in. For now, Satamia closing."

Boro sighed.

Sata smiled. "Manessa Kwi closing."

*

Ilika let most of the crew go off-duty. Boro sat down at his station, and with Ilika's help, transferred every drop of the old thruster fuel to a small holding tank, filtering and measuring it in the process. It came to twenty-three seconds at full-thrust.

Sata, the only one actually on duty, made some calculations at her console. "That'll get us down to about three hundred kilometers per second. Still way too fast for the maneuvering thrusters alone to stop us."

Everyone fell silent, Ilika wandered up to the big table to use a knowledge pad, and Boro began pacing.

"Found some dried parsley!" Kibi announced from the galley.

Her discovery brought smiles to all those within earshot, but no one grabbed a spoon.

"Stew on the stove," Boro mumbled to himself as he paced, "and we're gonna fly right on by unless we can slow down."

"When do we override Melorania," Sata asked from the front of the ship, "if we can't figure anything out?"

Ilika looked up. "Station approach marker A, which is one light-second out."

Sata looked at her chart and nodded.

"Wait a minute!" Boro suddenly boomed.

Everyone looked at him, including Mati and Rini who were just coming up the lift, arms around each other.

"Manessa," Boro began, "exactly what did Melorania say?"

"That we should not use the anti-mass drive until we arrived at Satamia Star Station."

Boro paced for a few more seconds, running his hands through his hair. Then he stopped dead in his tracks. "Manessa, exactly what does the word 'arrived' mean?"

"To achieve a destin . . ."

"No," Boro interrupted, "I mean *precisely* what does it mean, to a deep-space response ship, when coming to a star station? At exactly what point can you say you have arrived?"

"In that technical sense, a ship is considered to have arrived when it passes the inner navigation markers."

"Sata, how far . . ."

"I'm on it!" she declared, quickly switching charts. "The inner markers are exactly one kilometer from the station."

Boro began pacing again while rubbing his neck with both hands. "So . . . if we activated the anti-mass drive the instant we passed the inner markers, we wouldn't need to override Melorania's order. Right, Manessa?" he asked pointedly.

"Correct," the ship replied.

"But what about warming up the drives?" Kibi asked from the galley. "At three hundred kilometers a second . . . one three-hundredth of a second isn't enough time to do . . . anything!"

Boro lowered himself into the command chair, looked at the ceiling, and wrinkled his brow.

About half a minute later, his mouth snapped open. "Melorania said we shouldn't *use* anti-mass until we arrived, so it wouldn't matter if we *warmed it up* early. Right, Manessa?"

"Correct."

"And maybe *we* can't do that split-second timing," Sata said, "but Manessa can!"

Ilika was listening with interest.

"How precise?" Boro asked, still looking at Sata.

"Mati?" Sata passed the question up to the pilot at the table.

"Thousandth of a second."

"And in a thousandth of a second," Boro began with sparkling eyes, "we'd go less than half a kilometer, right?"

Sata grinned and nodded.

✷

Boro was clearly proud of himself, going from person to person to arrange every detail of the plan. Mati would do the deceleration thruster burn several minutes before arrival. Ilika, at the engineer's station, would warm up the anti-mass drive with time to spare in case anything went wrong and they had to override Melorania's order.

Judging by the expressions on Ilika's face, Kibi knew something was missing from the plan, and wondered if it had anything to do with Sata's wrinkled brow.

✷

As the last hour began, Kibi made more tea. She knew it wasn't providing much nutrition, but at least they wouldn't have to work on empty stomachs.

As she sipped her tea, the navigator looked at Boro with disappointment in her eyes. Kibi saw it, and was pretty sure everyone else did too . . . except Boro.

"I believe you have a job to do, Sata," the captain said over his cup of fragrant tea.

"I do?"

"Yes. You have something to report, and if you don't find your courage, the plan won't work."

Boro looked at Sata with surprise.

She took a deep breath and glared at Boro with smoldering eyes. "Are you *really* just going to go barreling in like a wild stallion without even *telling* the star station what we're doing?"

"Um . . . gosh . . . I thought it would be kinda fun to surprise them . . ."

The navigator rolled her eyes and slumped back in her chair.

"Sata," Ilika began, "why don't you explain to Boro the arrival procedures for a star station. You've studied them — he hasn't."

Sata breathed for a moment. "Sorry. I forgot you don't know this stuff. There are all kinds of ships going in and out all the time. You have to talk to the docking controller at the outer marker, there's a speed limit at the middle marker, and some ships have to let the controller guide them in past the inner marker. Big ships are sometimes parked outside the station. Inside the inner marker, people could be out in space suits!" When she finally finished speaking, she slumped into her chair, red-faced and breathing in gasps.

"Thank you, Sata," Ilika said calmly. "It's important for you to remember that you have an ability none of the other four have."

"I . . . I do?"

"Yes. You have the ability to trust, because you were raised in a working family where you could count on your mother, father, and brother to do their jobs and make good decisions about the inn."

Ilika looked around at the four ex-slaves. "The rest of you are used to assuming everyone in authority is against you, and cannot be trusted. I come from that background too, so I understand. You're learning to trust me, and slowly you will learn to trust everyone in the Nebador Services. The ursine controller you talked to is your brother now. You can trust him with your lives."

Boro took several breaths in the silence that lingered. "I . . . guess I should talk to the bear . . . I mean, the ursine controller."

Sata managed to force out a smile.

*

"Wow, that sounds exciting!" the image of the furry docking controller said from the main bridge display. "I bet the whole station will come out to watch. Let's see what the boss-lady thinks, she's over in the Rontilia system . . ." He hummed as he tapped at his console. "Okay, she approves, and apologizes for not being able to greet you, but she's helping with a stranded ship."

"I've plotted a course," Sata explained, "that will take us *past* the station, instead of into it, if something goes wrong."

"Excellent! I'll clear the way of ships when you pass the outer marker. Satamia closing."

"Thank you. Manessa Kwi . . . closing," Boro managed to say.

Once the screen went dark, Sata looked at him with returning fondness.

"Thanks for . . . making me . . . do it right," he muttered.

She smiled.

*

At Kibi's urging, Boro went over the plan in detail, twice, before they got to the first approach marker.

Mati asked the most questions, primarily of Manessa, as the pilot didn't want to approve a maneuver unless she was sure it was going to work. The braking thruster burn would be easy. Just thinking about the thousandth-of-a-second reaction time, needed to stop the ship just past the inner marker, made her stomach hurt.

Ilika smiled from the other end of the table and gave her a nod of confidence.

*

Finally Sata announced that outer approach marker A was at hand.

Boro called for stations, and ordered inertia straps, just in case.

The pilot peered at the deceleration graph, then made a decision. "Space thrusters, level five. It'll take a little longer than full power, but we've got the time."

"Good thinking," Ilika commented as he worked at the engineer's console. "Thrusters are green."

"Sata," the commander began, "Please tell the . . . controller that we're starting our approach."

Sata touched several symbols. "Satamia docking control, we are passing outer marker A, preparing to decelerate. The commander requests a pot of stew, preferably with fish."

Everyone on the ship chuckled, and the ursine controller roared with laughter as he tapped at his console.

Mati turned and looked at Boro.

The acting commander got quick status reports from Kibi and Rini, and glanced at Ilika to see if he was forgetting anything.

The captain nodded.

Boro took one more deep breath. "Slow us down, Mati. Use every drop."

*

The ship's inertia canceling kept the crew from feeling the deceleration that otherwise would have made them scream with pain. Sata listened for anything her dear friend and pilot needed, and called out the ship's speed.

"Seven hundred."

Rini watched for any ships or other obstacles.

"Six hundred."

Mati kept an eagle eye on their course with her three-D chart projection.

"Five hundred."

Ilika watched the thruster fuel get closer and closer to zero.

"Four hundred."

Kibi double-checked other parts of the ship from her console, and smiled at the thought of finally being able to fill her empty cupboards.

"Three hundred."

The thrusters began sputtering, and some of the jerks and lurches penetrated the inertia canceling. Boro felt his straps hold him tightly.

The space thrusters died.

"Two hundred fifty-three kilometers per second," the navigator reported. "Inner marker in . . . forty seconds."

Ilika's hands quickly went into action. "Anti-mass warming."

"Satamia Star Station ahead," Sata announced.

Everyone looked at their displays and beheld the glowing jewel in space, with countless facets gleaming from the yellow light of the Satamia primary sun, or the reds and purples of the nearby gas giant. It rapidly grew larger, and they seemed to be heading almost directly toward it.

"Anti-mass drive ready at level seven," the captain reported from the engineer's station. "All diagnostics good."

"The rest is up to Manessa," Boro declared with a trembling voice.

"Full stop, under ship's control, approved," Mati confirmed, still watching their course for any problems.

"Eight seconds," Sata announced.

The star station seemed to pick up speed and swoop toward them, making several of them gasp with fright. Suddenly it froze on the right edge of their forward view screens.

"Wow," Sata began, trying to catch her breath. "Relative speed . . . zero."

A heartbeat later, everyone on the little ship began clapping and cheering.

As soon as he could be heard, the captain spoke. "View to the right, please, Rini."

When the view angle changed, they could all see the gleaming crystal surfaces of the star station, seemingly just a stone's throw away. About half the facets of the giant jewel were clear, and hundreds of people, of all shapes and sizes, could be seen jumping up and down, swinging from the ceiling, leaping out of pools of water, or, if they had arms, waving them in greetings to the little deep-space response ship that had just passed another challenging test.

* * *

When we assume time and space as we usually experience them (as science does), the universe is mind-bogglingly huge and unfriendly. If we take a hint from what little we know about spiritual matters, and consider that there just might be persons (as most people believe) who can transcend time and space, then we gain a glimmer of hope about getting comfortable in our vast universe. Finally, if we recall that some cultures have spiritual practices that allow dedicated individuals to make some progress toward transcending time and space, then we begin to see the universe in a new light. These practices have shown us that life, even awareness, can exist in situations where thought is not desirable (or perhaps even possible).

Boro was surprised that the ship was going "point one seven light-speed." Manessa's usual speed is "one-eighth the speed of light." What would that be in decimal form, in base eight?

The crew was out of food, hadn't eaten in a while, and Kibi served unsweetened peppermint tea, a stimulant. Where were their bodies getting energy?

We get a glimpse of how Mati liked to arrange the graphics and information on her display. What factors might cause a different pilot to display things differently?

The visual-identification process for the approach marker is basically the same as used by our aircraft, ships at sea, and riverboats. Flashes of various timing and pattern, and sometimes color, identify the marker distinctly from all other markers in the area.

What does the fact that the navigation marker was "not physically present" tell us about Nebador?

Why might atmospheric braking around a gas giant cause the crew to "lose their peppermint tea" if they could see the forward visual?

The crew had been slowly learning the real primary colors. The colors cyan and magenta are little-known to us because, for most of our history, pigments in those colors have been rare or completely unavailable. Also, cyan is hard for us to see, whereas we elevate orange to a secondary color (it's really a tertiary) because we can see it so well. Do you know the difference between purple and magenta?

During atmospheric braking, why is Mati slowly increasing the altitude? What would happen if she didn't?

If you suddenly had to talk to "people" of another species to take care of necessary business, which of these would make you the most uncomfortable: other mammals, birds, reptiles, amphibians, fish, insects, or glowing balls of light?

In your opinion, was the deceleration tractor away from the station by accident, or on purpose?

Ursines are bears. Our constellation Ursa Major means the Great Bear. "Ursine" rhymes with "equine" (horse) and "feline" (cat). Just make sure your aren't pronouncing "feline" as "felion" which many people do, and is wrong.

What do we learn about the ethics of being a station docking controller when he declares he will "stay on duty until you're safely in"?

When Kibi figured they would have "one three-hundredth of a second" to stop, what math problem had she just done in her head?

How hard would it be for YOU to trust someone in authority, to whom you were speaking for the first time, who was an adult, and who also happened to be a talking bear?

Chapter 2: Docking Tunnel

"Kibi, would you take us in, please?" the captain asked.

"Whew!" Boro exclaimed and quickly hopped out of the command chair.

However, the captain didn't immediately let him retreat to the safety of the engineering station. He faced Boro and looked him squarely in the eyes. "Very good command, Boro. Thank you."

The fifteen-year-old blinked with embarrassment for a moment, then steadied his gaze and looked back at his captain. "Thanks. I guess . . . it was good for me."

Ilika smiled and let the younger man get to the comfort of his station.

Kibi was already on the bridge, chatting with Rini and Sata. The docking controller appeared on the main display. "That's one to make a story out of! I've already heard folks talking about Boro, the monkey-mammal engineer who out-smarted Melorania."

Boro cringed at his station, and busied himself checking fuel levels.

"So, who's in the hot seat for docking?" the ursine asked.

"Hi, I'm Kibi, steward and second-in-command."

"First, Kibi, I have to ask you for your honest and sound judgment, as commander of the ship. Do you need direct station control for docking? It's a maze in there."

Kibi looked at Mati, who returned the sternest frown ever seen on the handicapped girl's face. Then Kibi turned and looked at Ilika. He slowly shook his head.

"No, thank you," Kibi said firmly to the controller.

"Okay . . . you know the speed limits. Come to inner marker E and hold. I have a couple of ships waiting to get in."

"I need those speed limits," Mati urgently whispered as she located the marker on her chart.

Sata made a console selection and whispered back, "I'm adding them to the station chart."

Mati saw the area of space closest to the station take on a red tint. "Boro, anti-mass one, maneuvering thrusters."

✷

A minute later, Mati brought the ship to a stop beside the pulsing blue beacon floating in space. They arrived just in time to see a long, silver ship glide past and enter the dark, circular entrance to the star station. Half a minute later, a small round ship followed, with something gangly and irregular at the front.

"That looks like another deep-space response ship!" Sata announced with excitement, "but what's it carrying?"

Ilika looked up from the steward's console. "Planets who are just beginning to explore space often send little robot ships into the interstellar void. After they go dark and silent, we collect them and put them in a museum."

Rini peered at his display. "It's so . . . flimsy . . . compared to Nebador ships."

"Looks like a pile of sticks to me," Boro added.

"Manessa Kwi," the docking controller began, "follow the yellow path to sterilization and quarantine."

"What yellow path?" Mati whispered.

Sata made a selection. "This one!"

Lines in every color of the rainbow appeared on the pilot's three-D display, all going into the star station's docking tunnel. Mati took a moment to scan all her visual displays for other ships, then nudged Manessa forward.

Little breathing went on as the new crew approached the yawning dock entrance. Instead of a smooth circle, it appeared to be made of thick, woven strands, reminding the crew of vines or tree roots.

Sata touched a symbol, and Mati's chart was replaced by a plan of the docking tunnels. The colored lines continued into the depths of the star station, with one soon following a smaller tunnel to the left, and another entering a large docking area to the right.

"Wow, it *is* a maze," the pilot mumbled as she continued to follow the yellow line on her chart, deeper and deeper into the darkness.

✷

Just like the outside of the star station, most flat surfaces inside the docking tunnel seemed to be of crystal or glass, like the facets of a jewel. Between each surface, more roots or branches created an irregular matrix of rooms and spaces, some cozy for just a few small creatures, others roomy enough for hundreds.

"It's a . . . it's a big plant, right, Ilika?" Rini asked, looking at his captain.

Ilika smiled and nodded, but put his finger to his lips.

Many of the surfaces glowed with subtle colors. Others were crystal clear, and creatures of all sorts could be seen inside, going about their business or watching the passing ships.

Boro smiled when he noticed water behind some of the clear surfaces, and occasionally a sleek creature swimming by. The small scar on his leg ached for a moment.

Sata glimpsed three pink-faced monkeys hanging by their tails from branches, and realized the resemblance to humans was strong, even though she and her shipmates didn't have tails.

Mati concentrated on piloting and didn't speak a word. After several minutes and five turns, only three colored lines remained.

The small ship with the spidery wreckage was still in front of them when suddenly part of the wreckage broke loose and began to drift and tumble silently. "Look out!" Boro boomed, grabbing the sides of his chair.

Mati blinked once. "Docking control, you want me to get that?"

"Hmm. I'm not supposed to ask student pilots to handle unexpected things . . ."

"You didn't ask, I offered," Mati said firmly, and started to move the Manessa Kwi toward the drifting junk.

"Hey, I like you! Mati is your name?"

She nodded, but was concentrating again. "Manessa, you ready to grab that stuff?"

"Yes."

Kibi glanced back at Ilika, and the sparkle in his eyes told her he was completely happy.

Mati slowed the ship as they neared the debris, placing the Manessa Kwi right in its path. Rini and Boro cringed at the scraping sound that came through the hull as the metal from a distant world made contact.

"Grapple complete," the ship said.

"*Now* I see why Melorania likes you guys so much!" the ursine controller declared. "You're not afraid to jump in with both foot! I'm holding the traffic behind you until we get this junk squared away."

"Thank you," Sata said. "Where do you want it?"

"Follow the other ship onto the green path."

✷

A few minutes later, they waited while the first ship placed its armload of wreckage in a storage bay, then Mati did the same with the rest. A shy reptilian navigator appeared and thanked them with few words.

"It's important to remember," Ilika began as they retraced their flight back to the yellow line, "that just because some species aren't as social as mammals and birds, they are no less sapient. I've worked alongside reptiles, and they're some of the most reliable people in the Nebador Services."

Boro looked at the captain. "I'd like to meet them. And that bear, the controller."

At the junction, they had to wait for three ships to pass. First came a round golden ship about three times the size of their own. "That's a life-monitor, which you already know about," Ilika explained. "This is heavy cargo," he said as another long, silver vessel glided by. "Only a small part is habitable." Finally, a somewhat smaller ship with a shiny blue hull moved slowly past. "About a hundred passengers, plus the crew. Nice big galley, plenty of recreation space, and a little medical bay."

"Have you worked on all three kinds?" Kibi asked from the command chair.

"Yes, and that exact passenger ship, the Palantia Lisa. Two engineers, and I was the junior, at about thirteen, working under an ursine who knew engines better than I ever will."

Boro grinned.

Finally they could continue their journey along the yellow line. It soon took them a different way than the other ships.

"We're all alone in here," Sata said in a sad voice as they moved along slowly, deeper into the star station, with no other ships ahead or behind.

The ursine controller appeared. "You folks ready for sterilization?"

Ilika grinned. "I haven't told them about it yet. But they handled star transit . . ."

"Pfff. Then it'll be easy! Trust Manessa!"

As soon as the controller vanished from the screen, they rounded a corner and beheld a blue sheet of light, pulsing and crackling with energy, that completely filled the tunnel. Mati instinctively brought the ship to a dead stop.

Kibi swallowed. "Is that . . . sterilization?"

Sata looked at the station plan. "Y . . . yes."

"Am I supposed to go *through* that thing?" Mati asked with a troubled voice.

"Manessa?" Ilika prompted.

"I will take us through by feel," the ship explained, "as all sensors must be deactivated. When we emerge, my hull will be clean."

Mati and Sata looked at each other, then looked at Kibi.

Kibi took a deep breath. "Shut down all sensors, Rini."

Mati turned back to her console. "I'm approving ship control for sterilization."

"Inertia straps," Ilika said. "It can be a little bumpy, as Manessa will be going through blind."

✷

The crew grinned and giggled as their hair stood on end, their skin tingled, and the air smelled like thunder storms. A few small bumps and a minute later, the ship announced that hull cleaning was complete.

Rini was quick to restore sensors, and Mati gladly took her flight control back in hand.

The ursine appeared again. "That wasn't so bad, was it? I've assigned you to quarantine dock B-Three, up ahead on your right."

They moved slowly past two other response ships, both held in place by large, blue and purple docking fingers.

"This is it," Sata said as they approached the third docking berth, its fingers currently open and empty, like the petals of a flower.

"Your captain will explain docking and quarantine. Congratulations to you all! I have no complaints about your piloting, Mati. I understand there's a medical surgeon waiting to meet you."

Mati grinned as she eased the little ship into the docking berth with the alignment display she had already used at the Monuments of Zolko. As soon as they were in position, the blue and purple fingers closed around the ship.

"Manessa says the docking clamps are secure," Sata reported.

"I'm going off-duty now," the controller continued, "as my mate has a big, juicy fish she's been keeping warm, and I'm as hungry as a . . . a monkey mammal!"

Everyone chuckled and thanked the ursine docking controller.

Mati brought the power levels, on both anti-mass and maneuvering thrusters, to zero, waited a moment to make sure the ship stayed in place, and took a long, deep breath.

Suddenly it dawned on her that she had just piloted a starship from her home planet, where she was a crippled slave, through many tests and challenges, to a star station in another solar system. Her hands started shaking and tears threatened to come, but she kept breathing while she reached for her crutch and looked around at her beautiful ship and loyal friends, and especially at one very cute boy at the watch station, who was looking back at her with smiling eyes.

Then, as she stood up, she remembered one last thing she needed to do. "Boro, finished with engines."

* * *

What difference in command style (and perhaps experience) do we see between Boro, who started by sitting in the command chair, and Kibi, who started by chatting with other crew members?

Speed limits are a natural part of any congested traffic area. Aircraft have to deal with them in the airspaces near airports, just as cars do in cities. Would Mati have been able to successfully follow the docking procedures without a good navigator at her side?

Many people have wondered what will become of our Pioneer and Voyager space probes that are slowly leaving the solar system for interstellar space. They are not expected to get far before their energy systems fail completely. This story includes one possible fate.

What would have happened if Mati had yelled and grabbed the sides of her chair, as Boro did, when the wreckage broke free from the other ship? What did she do instead? What does this tell you about pilots?

Ilika mentions that mammals and birds tend to be more social than reptiles.

This appears to be true on Earth, and is usually assumed to be an effect of our longer childhoods. However, some of the most social creatures on our planet happen to be insects, who have very short childhoods.

In the hull sterilization process, “their hair stood on end,” which shows the presence of “static electricity” or isolated, non-flowing ion charges. “The air smelled like thunderstorms” shows the presence of ozone, 3 atoms of oxygen, which usually only occurs during electrical discharges.

The phrase “finished with engines” goes back to our steamship days. It took hours, and dozens of skilled people, to bring the huge boilers from cold to ready, so they were never shut down until the captain was absolutely sure they would not be needed again for days. It was often the last command given when coming to port, after the ship was completely secure at dock.

Chapter 3: Quarantine

"Can we eat now?" the engineer asked after shutting down his station and spinning around.

The captain didn't answer the question directly. "Boro, all empty fuel canisters go by the airlock. Kibi, I'll work with you on swapping out waste containers. Sata, collect all trash from the galley, and Rini from the toilet rooms. Mati just had a very intense hour, and is off-duty."

"I'm still shaking," she admitted.

They all heard a dull thud against the hull.

Ilika looked at Kibi. "You did it! You explored the entire Sonmatia solar system, then endured star transit, atmospheric braking, and star station docking, without ever panicking and opening the main hatch!"

She looked back with mischief in her eyes. "There were moments I was tempted to open it with my fingernails!"

Mati and Sata howled with laughter.

"I believe," Ilika continued, "if you check your console, you'll find a boarding tunnel in place and breathable atmosphere outside the hatch."

"Whoopee!" Kibi cheered as she stepped to her station. "Yep. Permission to air out the ship, captain?"

"Granted!"

*

They could see a walkway through the hatch, going straight as an arrow through a clear, circular boarding tunnel, but they had a quarter hour of work before they could begin the journey. After gathering trash bags and canisters near the hatches, Ilika had them pack a change of cloths and other personal things. Interior de-contamination took an entire day, he explained, about as long as they'd be in medical quarantine.

"Manessa," the captain said as he shouldered his bag, "you are in command. Make sure the cleaning crew does a good job."

"They always do, but I will monitor the process, even though I cannot technically be in command, as you know."

Ilika smiled. "Thank you for . . . all the countless ways you kept us alive since the last time I remembered to thank you. We will see you tomorrow."

"You are welcome, and I look forward to serving with all of you in the future."

*

The captain, four ex-slaves, and one innkeeper's daughter stood facing the hatch. They all bore rucksacks, save Mati. Rini's bag was heavier than the others.

"The cleaning, sterilizing, and quarantine is necessary because we just came from a primitive planet with all sorts of bugs and germs that might be harmless to us, but could infect others in the Nebador Services. Our time in quarantine will depend on what the healers find. Mati will probably begin chatting with the surgeon."

"Can we . . ." Boro began shyly, ". . . you know . . . buy some food somewhere?"

"There is no money here, Boro. Money is a way of rationing goods and services in a general society where some people would be lazy, or take more than they needed, if they could. People who do either of those are NOT members of the Nebador Services. This is a working civilization. We don't have time to be lazy."

"What . . . um . . . happens to someone who takes more than they need," Sata asked, "like maybe too much food?"

"If they can't grow out of it, they get a one-way trip home. I don't think any of you need to worry. Shall we go see what's cooking?"

Everyone nodded vigorously.

"Pilot and navigator, as you do in flight, would you lead the way?"

Sata held Mati's hand as they made their way down the steps, through the hatch, and slowly along the boarding tunnel. They could see in all directions, with crystal windows of the star station not far away, and thick roots and vines weaving it all together.

Boro and Rini came next. Boro's eyes were wide with wonder, but Rini wore a contented smile and looked like he was coming home.

Ilika and Kibi brought up the rear.

Soon the navigator and pilot stood at the end of the boarding tunnel and peered into a circular room, a bit larger than the main deck of the Manessa Kwi. About a dozen soft chairs and couches were scattered about. Around the edge, doorways with curtains, some open, led to little sleeping rooms. A double door on the opposite side was closed, and a large glass window, behind a strange machine, was currently dark.

The round table in the middle of the room, set with plates, cups, and serving dishes, drew their attention. From it came the aroma of hearty vegetable stew and baked fish.

Sata was about to dig in when she realized everyone else was slowly sipping pinkfruit juice. She remembered their warnings about eating too quickly after being hungry, turned to the engineer beside her, and looked into his warm eyes.

He smiled back and tapped his cup against hers when she held it up.

Kibi looked around the table with sparkling eyes. "What should we know about this place, Ilika?"

He set his cup down. "You have seen other sapient people in videos and on view screens. Now you must learn to walk among them, and get used to their speech. Most people here are far more intelligent than we are. Barely-sapient creatures, like Tera, do not roam about freely on a star station. There are four-legged people here, but they can think circles around you, I promise. We are just monkey mammals from backward little worlds. Remember that."

Everyone was quiet and thoughtful for a minute as they started eating their stew and fish.

"I know what Mati's doing here . . ." Sata began after taking the edge off her hunger.

The pilot smiled as she examined a strange vegetable on her fork.

"What will the rest of us be doing?"

"Ship maintenance, stocking supplies, getting to know the star station . . ."

Boro took another piece of fish. "Is this the center of Nebador?"

"Far from it. This is an outpost on the edge of the wilderness, like the little village of Nug in the mountains of your kingdom."

Rini chuckled. "But without the bones and flies!"

Ilika nodded. "While we're here, we'll get more comfortable with the notion that our lives are intertwined with beings much greater than us, like this star station."

"I know Manessa isn't sapient," Mati began, "but I think of her as smarter than me in most ways."

Ilika nodded. "There are also sapient beings here that make us look like children, but most of them are invisible unless they want to be seen."

"Like . . . Melorania?" Kibi posed.

Ilika nodded while chewing and swallowing. "We'll also get familiar with the Mission Assignment Room, where beings like Melorania are most often glimpsed. Mati will miss a few things, but she'll be doing something very important."

Mati nodded since her mouth wasn't currently free for speaking.

Suddenly Sata frowned, watching Boro take a third piece of fish. "Shouldn't we . . . stop eating soon, so they don't think we're taking too much?"

Ilika smiled. "No, Sata, I wasn't talking about having a hearty meal. Some people, when they have unlimited food, eat until their bodies blow up into blubbery masses of flesh they can barely move around with their own feet."

Everyone frowned at the thought. Boro breathed again, and dug into his delicious baked fish.

* * *

Why can't Manessa technically be in command?

Are there any hints in this chapter that Boro was hungry?

Ilika mentioned one of the differences between a "general society" and a "working civilization." We live in a general society. It has to find a place for everyone who is born, even if that means killing them or putting them in prison. A working civilization is more like a corporation: it doesn't have a place for everyone, and anyone it rejects simply goes back into the general society.

Why was everyone (but Sata) slowly sipping juice, at first, when they sat down to a meal? We know they were all very hungry.

How is Nebador, where "most people here are far more intelligent than we are," different than most places "out there" we have imagined in both science fiction and religion?

Why wouldn't Nebador welcome people without enough self-control to only eat what they needed?

Chapter 4: Healers

While the crew of the Manessa Kwi ate, the boarding tunnel closed and vanished. Manessa greeted old friends who arrived in space suits with cleaning and sterilization equipment. While they worked, they shared stories with the well-traveled deep-space response ship. The cleaning crew chuckled when they heard the adventures of the brand-new crew of monkey mammals, and promised the ship they wouldn't breathe a word after leaving.

✷

Ilika explained that the only other door out of the medical quarantine room was actually an airlock. The inner door opened to his pull, and a cart for their dirty dishes stood within, but the door beyond was sealed and locked.

Suddenly lights came on behind the large glass window, and the entire crew gathered to peer at the examining tables and medical equipment within. A man with gray hair, reading a knowledge pad, strolled into view.

Sata's eyes lit up. "He's like us!"

The man looked up. "Is my timing okay? Did you have a relaxing meal?"

When Ilika didn't immediately answer, Kibi smiled. "Yes, thank you. I'm Kibi, steward of the Manessa Kwi."

"Greetings, Kibi. I am Dakalio, general healer. You've been on two primitive planets with atmosphere, I see."

"Um . . . yeah," Sata confirmed. "Sonmatia Three and Four. I'm Sata, the navigator."

"Welcome to Satamia, all of you!"

The others introduced themselves.

"As you may know, I'm looking for parasites and microbes that are best kept on their home worlds. Step onto the scanner, one at a time."

Ilika went first to demonstrate. Parts of the machine moved around him and shined dancing beams of light at him in all directions. He stepped down, and the others quickly found the courage to step onto the medical scanner.

"Hmm . . . hmm . . ." the healer muttered as he looked at a display screen they couldn't see. "Not bad . . . that little thing will be easy . . . hmm . . . Boro, there are two of you."

The engineer's face took on a sour expression.

Sata grinned at her friend and cocked her head. "Pregnant?"

Boro turned red.

"Nothing so dramatic," the healer said, "just an intestinal parasite. It won't take long to get rid of, but I want to wait until you've absorbed your meal, as we'll have to empty you out."

Boro became, if anything, even redder.

"Kibi," the healer continued, "you have a virus I don't like, so I'll be giving you some pills."

"Okay."

"Um . . ." Mati began, struggling to find the right words. "Can you . . . um . . . fix my knee? I'll do anything . . . scrub all the floors on the star station, or anything else you want me to do . . ."

The healer sensed the depth of her feelings. "Mati, dear Mati, you are a starship pilot. You have already earned anything and everything we can do for you. But I'm sorry, Mati, I do not have that skill."

Mati's face fell and tears started running down her cheeks.

"But the healer with that ability is in the next room right now. She is very gentle and wise, and is one of the most skillful surgeons in all of Nebador. Would you like to meet her?"

Mati quickly wiped the tears onto her sleeves and collected herself. "A lady healer? That would be nice. We knew a lady healer in the city we came from."

"I'll see if she's free," Dakalio said, and left the room.

Mati breathed deeply as she waited. Rini held her hand, and Sata put an arm around her shoulders.

A minute later, a large, green, gangly insect almost three meters tall entered the room and stepped up to the window, towering over the crew of the Manessa Kwi. Feelers quivered in the air, and claw-like mandibles played around the creature's mouth. "Hello, Mati. I will be your surgeon."

Mati's face turned white, and the world around her went dark.

Rini and Sata caught her.

When Mati awoke, she saw the faces of her beloved Rini, her dear friend Sata, and her captain, all smiling at her. A moment later, Kibi joined them.

"Is the monster gone?"

Sata nodded. "Only problem is, my friend, that monster is the only surgeon around who can fix your knee."

Mati sighed, sat up, and accepted a cup of water from Rini. "I thought I was okay with people being all shapes and sizes. But . . . it was so *big!*"

"After we put you in bed," Rini said, "we chatted with the surgeon. She's really nice, and says you can have a friend with you the whole time. Her name's K'stimla. Did I say that right, Ilika?"

He nodded. "But *you* have to make the final decision, Mati, and tell surgeon K'stimla yourself, perhaps with a little apology thrown in."

Mati flopped back down and sighed. "Can I think about it?"

The captain nodded.

Mati looked at her friends. "Where's Boro?"

Sata chuckled. "He's in a toilet room, and will be in there for a couple of hours."

Mati sighed again. "I wish a couple of hours in a toilet room would solve my problem."

Her friends laughed.

✷

When Boro finally emerged, the rest of the crew was at the table eating.

The engineer held his hands almost a meter apart and said, "It was . . . oh, never mind."

The others howled with laughter, except Mati, who cracked a smile but otherwise continued brooding.

Sata suppressed her laughter enough to speak. "There's a fruit salad here for you, Boro."

"I have *never* felt so empty, even as a slave," he said, taking a seat and grabbing a spoon.

"But we never got fruit salads!" Kibi reminded him.

Boro nodded, but was already chewing something tasty.

"Healer Dakalio says we should be out of quarantine by tomorrow," Ilika announced.

"Another healer looked at the scans," Sata reported, "and found a little something in me, so I'm taking pills now too."

Boro looked at Mati as he ate, but could tell she hadn't yet made a decision.

✷ ✷ ✷

In the 19th and early 20th centuries, when many people began traveling across the oceans but dangerous diseases were still common, people often had to wait in quarantine for days, sometimes weeks, to see if they showed the symptoms of any diseases, before being released to move about freely at their destinations. In the late 20th century, that inconvenience was largely forgotten as antibiotics conquered most diseases. Today, our antibiotics are ceasing to be effective against some deadly diseases, and the need for quarantines for travelers may return.

Many people have trouble allowing a medical doctor to treat them who isn't their gender, race, or nationality. How would you feel about a surgeon who isn't even your species, and not even another mammal?

The intestinal parasite Boro had was probably from class Cestoda, usually called a "tapeworm."

Chapter 5: Different Paths

The following day, Dakalio scanned them all again. Three different healers peered at the results, then released the crew of the Manessa Kwi from quarantine.

Beyond the sealed door, each person, one at a time, unshouldered their rucksacks, shed their clothes, and entered a steamy shower room while their belongings went a different way to be sterilized. Mati's crutch was no exception, so Sata went with her friend through the shower.

On the far side, fresh clothes greeted them, and their packs soon emerged from a small door.

After dressing, each crew member stepped into the last waiting room and found places to sit on chairs or couches, some obviously designed for smaller or larger creatures.

Only one more door, of clear glass, separated the new arrivals from the interior of the star station, and they could see beings of all sorts walking, leaping, swinging, or flying along. Huge brown tree trunks soared upward, limbs and vines followed the edges of every crystal surface, and leaves spread out to catch the sunlight.

When all six had taken up their rucksacks or crutch, Ilika looked at his new crew, about to make the final step into a new civilization. Four faces showed excitement and eagerness to dash through the last door and into their new lives.

One face dripped with tears. "I can't do it Ilika. I can't go out there with you. I have to either find the courage to let the surgeon fix my knee . . . or go home."

Rini quickly declared his intention to stay with Mati, whichever road she took. The young couple got comfortable on a couch in the medical waiting room, snuggled close, and began whispering together.

Ilika swallowed several times, took a breath for courage, and led the others through the glass door. So it was that he stepped into the main hall of Satamia Star Station with only his steward at his side, and his navigator and engineer, holding hands, close behind.

A wide open area spread out before them, with balconies and landings rising four or five levels, all intertwined with rough-barked trunks and quivering leaves. A bright pool of water, off to one side, churned with creatures surfacing and climbing out, others jumping in, and some just floating while they chatted.

The foursome, three of whom gazed about with wide eyes, hadn't gone many steps when a large, sleek bird and a husky bear blocked their path. Both wore scant clothing, not much more than a vest with pockets for a few personal items.

"Bok. I was wondering if I could give my fellow navigator a tour of the station, and show her that eating place I mentioned."

Sata grinned and stepped forward. "Drim-na!"

"Drrrim-na," the avian corrected with a slight bow.

"Dr-r-r-im-na," Sata attempted.

The feathered navigator cackled.

Sata looked at her captain and saw that he was smiling. "No problem here, Sata. It looks like Boro is also getting an invitation."

The ursine docking controller bowed. "I have a mind to do some fishing, and wondered if Boro would like to join me. He'll get a tour also, of course."

"Real fish, out of a stream?" the engineer questioned with wide eyes.

"Real, live fish. Stream or deep-water. I don't yet know if you swim . . ."

"I do, and love it!"

Ilika tapped at his mission bracelet. "Manessa is out of quarantine and has been moved to dock C-Thirteen. That's our meeting place."

Sata and Boro both strolled away with their new friends, leaving Ilika and Kibi among hundreds of different creatures, some walking, some running on urgent business, and a few just hanging from tree branches by their tails.

* * *

Why would their packs and Mati's crutch have to be sterilized?

If you speak Spanish, you can probably roll your R's, as in "Drrrim-na." If you don't, you will probably have trouble with the name, just as Sata did.

If you are tempted to wonder how non-human animals could be speaking to the human crew, remember that even on Earth, there are birds who can speak our languages. Also, the language of Nebador is probably designed to be easy for everyone to learn, using only those phonemes (simple sounds) that all the intended speakers can make. On Earth, there is one language (Hawaiian) that, for unknown reasons, evolved with only 13 phonemes, when most of our languages use 40 or more. It is extremely easy to pronounce. But proper names, like "Drrrim-na," probably came from the person's native language, and so could be hard for some Nebador people to say.

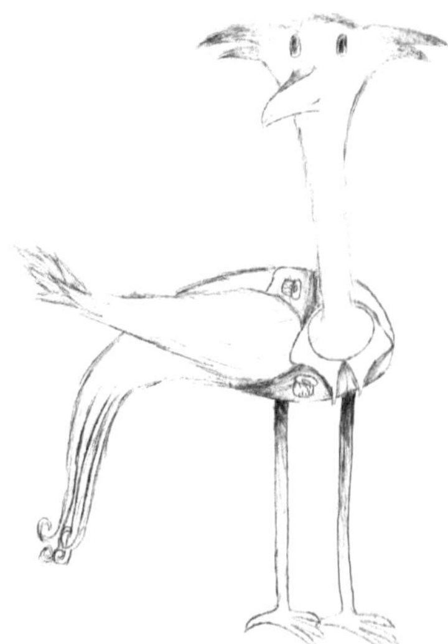

Chapter 6: Sata's Tour

Drrrim-na ambled slowly through halls, along walkways, and up ramps or stairs as her new friend and fellow navigator peered this way and that. Sometimes a wide path circled around a great tree trunk. At other times the way seemed made of stone, molded into steps and decorative shapes.

Creatures they passed made pleasant eye contact, but didn't bother the pair except when Drrrim-na stopped to chat with another avian, and a bit later a small, furry mammal approached them to ask directions.

When they were alone again, in a passageway under a canopy of huge leaves, Sata tried to put her question into words. "Um . . . it seems strange that no one is . . . you know . . . trying to sell us something, or steal from us, or tell us what to do . . ."

Drrrim-na clucked with humor. "That's all monkey mammal stuff! Remember, I know — I work on a life-monitor ship."

Sata thought about it as they walked on. "What . . . monkey mammal things . . . should I be careful not to do?"

The bird opened her eyes wider. "All of them, bok! I mean, the ones about messing with others, getting in their faces, that kind of stuff. Bok. It's not just you. I'd *love* to peck holes in these leaves, eat ursine babies for lunch, and let my bowels go whenever I'm flying. Not here, bok!"

Sata rolled with laughter when she imagined the huge mess, and the angry bears right on her friend's tail.

"Here's that eating place I told you about. Bok. Great view!"

Sata's mouth dropped as they stepped into the room and beheld the red and purple gas giant Satamia Five through several large, clear windows. Even twelve light-seconds away, it still loomed impressively large, and seemed to glow with its own light.

When Sata finally looked around, she realized that most everyone in the room was avian. She spotted Drrrim-na at a small table with two chairs, and self-consciously shuffled over.

"I think I'm the only per . . . monkey mammal . . . in this place."

"Bok. You might be the only monkey mammal on the station, except for your shipmates."

"There's a healer."

"That's good. It's always a little hard having a different kind of healer."

Sata described Mati's situation.

"Do you think she can do it, bok? The mantidae are the best surgeons. They've saved my life more than once."

"I think so. Rini's sticking with her." Suddenly Sata looked uncomfortable. "What is there to eat? I'm not sure you and I eat the same things . . ."

Drrrim-na cackled. "You didn't think I was going to feed you *worms*, did you, bok?"

Sata shrugged and cringed with guilt.

"This place is known for its seed cakes," the avian continued. "Sort of like a dense, nutty bread, bok, but much easier to chew. They come with fruit and tender, peckable leaves and flowers."

"I'll . . . try it."

"Bok."

*

The meal nestled in baskets with a handle, easy for the birds to carry to their tables. Remembering her years hauling food and drink from the kitchen to the common room, Sata was glad they served themselves at a counter, and would later clean their own table. She was amazed at how much she enjoyed the seed cakes, rivaling anything from Tori's bakery, except maybe fruit tarts.

She and her host chatted about the star station, then Sata shared her many adventures since they had first spoken. The avian listened intently to Sata's experience in the ice of Sonmatia Seven.

"Bok," the bird said slowly. "That is huge. I have never been tested like that, not sure I ever want to be, bok."

Sata smiled. "I'm certainly not looking forward to doing it again!"

Drrrim-na nodded agreement. "Bok!"

Just as they finished their meal, a noise of clucking and cackling came from the corridor outside, and about twenty avians crowded through the door.

"Bok!" the server at the counter yelled. "Need help!"

"Come on!" Drrrim-na said to Sata. "You have to learn how we do things around here."

Sata followed her friend. They quickly tossed their baskets into the washing room, and Drrrim-na pointed to a sink. Sata recognized the same dispensers they had on the ship, and washed her hands.

"Bok!" the server said with glee. "A monkey mammal can make baskets quickly!"

"I'll coach and carry, you assemble," Drrrim-na explained as she nudged Sata to a work table behind the counter. "Each basket gets a liner, seed cakes are in the warmer to your left, fruits and vegetables in the cooler on your right."

Sata opened doors until she found all the ingredients, spread them out on the table, and grabbed the first basket her friend placed before her.

"Two cakes, small bunch of jiba fruit . . . you remember what we had," the bird coached when she didn't have a basket in her beak.

"I think so. Just one flower, right?"

✷

Sata worked quickly, both hands moving at once, to assemble the twenty baskets of bird food. When she glanced up, she saw the group of avians patiently waiting for their lunch, and obviously enjoying the sight of a monkey mammal working in the kitchen. Sata grinned. "I've been doing this kind of work all my life!"

Just as she was finishing the last basket, Drrrim-na staggered over with a huge basket she could barely carry.

"Huh?" Sata questioned.

"Fanators!" her friend whispered after dropping the basket on the table.

Sata looked up. Behind the last few birds about Drrrim-na's size, two giant feathered creatures waited in line, almost scraping their heads on the ceiling.

Another huge basket landed on the assembly table. "*Eight* seed cakes, *big* bunches of fruit, lots of leaves and flowers, and *two* cartons of maka worms, bottom shelf in the cooler. Fanators always want their maka worms."

"I thought you didn't eat worms," Sata said jokingly as she worked.

"Maka worms are for dessert! I said I wouldn't feed them to *you* . . . unless, of course, you have an open mind . . ."

Sata twisted her face. "I'll think about it."

✷

When Sata completed the two large baskets, she looked up. The smaller birds were all seated, and only the two fanators remained at the counter.

"Greetings, skillful monkey mammal," one said.

"Hello. I hope you like your baskets."

"Thank you. You're new to Nebador, are you not?"

"Yes. I just arrived yesterday."

"Have you flown?"

"Well, yes," Sata said with a grin, "since I'm a deep-space response ship navigator."

"Excellent position. You'll get to see many of the mysteries of the universe. But I meant with us. I've been on a ship all day and need to stretch my wings after lunch. Would you like to come along?"

Sata swallowed. "Um . . . okay."

✷

The bird behind the counter thanked Drrrim-na and Sata for their help, then took over making baskets for the occasional guest or two who came in the door. The two navigators slipped out and peered over a railing. They could see several levels of the star station, and three or four thick branches of the great living tree that spread its leaves everywhere. Far below, small marine mammals played in a pool of deep water.

About a quarter hour later, the fanators joined them.

"I'm gonna find some still water to float in," the smaller female declared. "See you at the meeting!"

They clicked beaks together, then she hopped onto the railing, leapt into the air, and soon disappeared from sight.

Sata swallowed, and wondered what she had gotten herself into.

The male fanator stepped to a cabinet nearby. "There's supposed to be a harness . . . yes here it is." He slipped his head under a loop of shimmering fabric and the harness slid over his back easily. "I don't really like these, but it's better than getting feathers pulled out. If you like flying with us, there's a class you can take, and if you're really good, the harness is optional."

"You . . . um . . . carry people often?"

"Mostly on planets. It's a bit tight in here, but we'll make do. You coming along, little one?"

Drrrim-na nodded.

Sata smiled at her friend, looked back at the fanator, then blinked in surprise at the kinds of new friends she was making.

✷

The huge bird made sure Sata knew the two rules of flying with a fanator. Rule one, hold on or you'll fall and die. Rule two, no screaming or you might get *tossed* off.

Sata nodded that she understood, and placed her feet in the two lower loops of the harness. As soon as she had a good hold of the upper loops, the bird wasted no time hopping up to the railing, almost taking Sata's breath away in the process. Drrrim-na joined them on the railing.

A second later they were airborne, diving straight down.

Sata's mind screamed even though she managed to keep her mouth shut. A glimpse of her friend Drrrim-na, not far behind and looking very small compared to the fanator, gave her some comfort.

The giant bird soon spread it wings, flapped twice, and leveled out as it crossed the large open space in this part of the star station. Sata frowned when, seconds later, that open space came to an end.

The fanator clearly knew the station well, and banked sharply, entering a level passage that pierced a large block of rooms, taking them back toward the main hall. A few leisurely flaps kept them level and well clear of the furry and scaly creatures walking and hopping along the passageway.

They burst into the large main hall, causing Sata to gasp.

"Here's where we can really stretch!" the bird called.

Sata turned her head and glimpsed her smaller friend a hundred meters back, flapping with all her might.

Several powerful wing-beats brought them high up near the crystal roof of the hall, with nothing but stars beyond. Sata grinned, suddenly remembering that she was the navigator of a starship, and the universe was now her playground.

The fanator wheeled and swooped back across the open area, tucking his wings close when they passed a cluster of large leaves spread out in the sunshine. Sata giggled with delight.

Next the bird entered a narrow part of the hall, barely wider than his outstretched wings, and flapped several times to pick up speed. A solid wall of crystal, laced with branches and vines, blocked their way not far ahead. Sata closed her eyes.

The fanator suddenly tilted his wings back, beat the air twice, and they came to a dead stop in mid-air. Sata's eyes snapped open and her heart pounded in her chest.

The bird swiveled around in place, dove to pick up speed, then stretched his wings wide and they floated gracefully back across the main hall. The passenger couldn't help but shriek, "Weeeee!" A moment later, she added, "Oops, sorry."

"That was nothing," the bird replied, turning his head and glancing back with one sparkling eye.

Soon they entered another tunnel with no walkway below. Sata happened to look down. Several meters below stretched a clear, level sheet of glass, and she glimpsed a large rocky room with a number of lizard-like reptiles. The view was gone before she could make out anything else.

The fanator entered a smaller hall and banked several times, getting closer and closer to the floor each time. Finally he back-winged with powerful strokes above an empty place on the floor, and a heartbeat later landed on two feet without taking a single step.

Sata continued to hold the harness tightly.

"If you want more," the bird said, turning to look at his passenger, "you'll have to catch me later, as I have a meeting to attend in a few minutes."

Sata found her breath, and slowly loosened her grip. Half a minute later, she managed to step down to the floor, knees wobbling. "That was . . . wonderful!"

At that moment a furry monkey, smaller than Sata, ran up to the fanator, stretched out its arms, and the huge bird accepted its help slipping out of the harness. "Thank you, little one. Would you like to fly with me later today?"

"Yes, please!" it chittered, then dashed away with the harness.

Sata faced the huge bird, her heart still pounding. "If there is anything I can ever do for you . . ."

"You made my lunch," he said, eyes dancing playfully, "but I will keep your offer in mind for the future."

Sata grinned, and was suddenly moved to wrap her arms around the feathered creature.

He responded with a cooing sound.

She slowly let go and blushed with embarrassment.

Just then Drrrim-na landed nearby, quite out of breath.

* * *

We have the technology to make structures that "seem made of stone, molded into steps and decorative shapes." Can you name it? It was invented in Rome about 2000 years ago, lost doing the Dark Ages and Middle Ages, and re-discovered more recently. The Pantheon in Rome is probably the best example.

Sata noticed an absence of people "trying to sell us something, or steal from us, or tell us what to do." Drrrim-na added "messing with others, getting in their faces." Can you think of other common human behaviors that wouldn't fit in well in an advanced civilization composed of many different species?

The "seed cakes" Sata and Drrrim-na ate in the avian restaurant might sound strange, unless you remember that all of our "grains" are seeds (usually grass seeds), and so any kind of bread (muffins, cookies, pizza, etc.) could be described as "seed cakes."

What human tendencies, in our general society, make it difficult or impossible for a pair of "customers" to help out during a "rush" at a "restaurant"?

Based on stories, there may have been a time in Earth's past when birds existed who could carry human passengers. We may learn more about this in the future from fossil records.

What do the two "rules" of riding on fanator-back tell us about Nebador?

Chapter 7: Going Fishing

Boro glowed with pride as he walked beside the ursine docking controller. It dawned on him that the bear's swaggering gait was not too different from his own. "Um . . . that job you do . . . seems important . . ."

The larger animal chuckled. "Only if you want to get in and out of the station in one piece!"

Boro laughed as he continued to follow his host deeper into the maze of passageways and halls, passing thick tree trunks, doorways of all shapes and sizes, and ramps that went both up and down. "Um . . . I don't know your name . . ."

"Sorry. Ursines tend to be somewhat private about names and such. The part you can say, and that most people call me, is Glorm."

Boro tried the word with the same deep-throated intonation.

"Close enough."

"What do you . . . have to know to be a docking controller?" Boro asked as they descended a ramp.

"You have to be a pilot, and a navigator. Engineering and sensors don't hurt. Some command experience. And you absolutely *must* be able to juggle and dance."

Boro looked at the bear with a funny expression.

"I am deadly serious. A ship coming in with one of Melorania's little restrictions, like you had, is nothing compared to having two or three emergencies pile up in your face, and *you* have to figure out which one to deal with first, and what to do with the others who are screaming at you."

Boro was silent and thoughtful as they stepped onto another downward ramp. He was surprised to feel water on his feet.

Glorm laughed. "You're not used to the symbols, are you? Blue triangle back there. This is part of a whole maze of wet ramps, and you can go anywhere underwater, too."

"What if you . . . um . . . need to breathe?"

"Air pockets every eight meters. You'll see."

✷

A minute later they sat down beside a rushing stream. Water emerged from a dark tunnel on their left, and plunged into another tunnel just downstream. Roots stretched into the water on both banks, and large leaves blocked half the light that poured through a crystal window high above.

Boro frowned. "It isn't . . . natural — too smooth, no jagged rocks waiting to rip you open."

"Of course not. This isn't a planet. You'll get plenty of danger on your missions."

Boro laughed. "Had plenty on *my* planet!"

At that moment, a furry mammal about half the size of the bear, with webbed feet and a wide tail, emerged from the upstream tunnel. It grabbed a root and pulled itself onto the bank. "Glorm! Who's in the tower today?"

"M'sorpa, I think. This is Boro, response ship engineer, and fellow fisher."

The smaller mammal bowed. "Fish look good today, but I'm eating with my crew in an hour, so I resisted the temptation. Bye!"

"Don't shake until you're out of range!" the bear warned with a slight growl.

"I'll think about it!" the other said as he waddled up the ramp.

A moment later, they felt a few drops fly from above.

Glorm laughed. "He's fun. Works on a little ship that maintains navigation beacons. He and his mate are raising a cub right now, but he used to work on transport ships."

Boro was thoughtful for a minute. "It's hard to get used to all the animals talking, doing jobs, and being nice to each other. Where I come from, we would have just eaten your little friend for lunch."

The bear looked at Boro with intense eyes. "Just remember, there are planets where *monkey mammals* are eaten for lunch."

✷

After more chatter about the variety of planets that dotted space in the vast reaches of Nebador, Boro learned, to his delight, that none of the sapient species were fish, and amphibians were rare.

"I learned the difference between sharks and dolphins the hard way," he admitted, and went on to share his experience on the tropical island.

"You're lucky she only nipped you! Dolphins have serious teeth. You ready to go fishing?"

"Yeah, getting hungry. Do we use hooks, or nets?"

The ursine grinned. "No technology is allowed when fishing in the star station. We use our bare hands, and can only take what we eat."

Boro looked at the bear's claws, then at his own soft, pink hands and short nails. “I think . . . you’ll have better luck.”

“We’ll see. If I get one first, I’ll help a little if you want, but I’m sure you’d feel better if you got your own.”

Boro’s eyes glowed with a hunter’s passion. “Yeah!”

*

After hanging his vest on a peg by the ramp, the bear wadded into the water, then plopped down and let the current carry him. “Meet you at the first air pocket!” A moment later he disappeared into the far tunnel.

Boro breathed deeply for courage as he hung up his clothes. He stepped into the cool water, stood for a moment fighting the current, then sat down and let the water pull his feet out from under him. As soon as he entered the tunnel, most of the light faded and he was pulled down.

The current quickly slowed to a crawl as Boro blinked and looked around. Irregular but smooth rock walls seemed to glow with their own light. Behind him, air bubbles churned where the open stream plunged into deep water. Above him and ahead a few meters he could see the shiny surface of an air pocket, maybe two meters across, and a furry brown ursine treading water.

Boro felt with his feet, found the smooth bottom, and pushed off, aiming himself toward the life-giving air.

He broke the surface, saw a grab-bar within easy reach, and held on while catching his breath.

The ursine, also holding a bar, roared in welcome. “I had a hunch you’d be good in the water.”

“This is easy!” Boro declared. “Clean and clear, not too cold, plenty of air . . . what was that?” he asked with a start, looking down.

“Go down and see! Nothing dangerous in here.”

Boro let go and dipped down, then kicked back up to the air pocket.

“Fluke or fin?” the ursine asked. “If fluke, it might be your next mission specialist. If fin, it’s dumber than a cucumber, and fair game.”

“Fluke,” Boro said with a grin while chuckling.

“The best eating are the pink and silver fish, a meter long or more. They’re slowed by age, but are still strong. Much under a meter and they’re too young, and fast as lightning anyway.”

Boro nodded.

"Don't worry about getting lost," the ursine continued. "I'll keep track of you, and lead the way back to our clothes after we've bagged lunch."

"Thanks. Anything . . . with a fin . . . I shouldn't touch?"

"The blue and green ones taste like bird feathers . . ."

Boro made a face.

"Yellow is okay, and sometimes easier to catch."

Boro looked around. "I've never seen a lighted air pocket before, with fresh air coming through a grill."

"You've never been in a star station before! Ready?"

The deep-space response ship engineer took a deep breath. "Yeah!"

✷

For the next half hour, Boro experienced the joy of using every muscle in his body, in water of a perfect temperature, with air and rest whenever he needed it. His friend was always nearby, but seldom did they talk. Marine mammals swam by, or paused to chatter in their own language that carried well underwater.

Boro noticed all the types of fish Glorm had mentioned, some darting by almost too fast to see, others lumbering fearlessly, especially the blue and green ones. Boro looked at them askance, and decided he wasn't *that* hungry.

The yellow fish were fairly slow, and several times Boro came close to grabbing one, even though he wasn't really trying. But at an air pocket, Glorm held up his pink and silver catch, more than a meter long. Boro decided it was time to get serious.

At first he focused on the delicious ones, but they were lightning-fast. After a quarter hour of trying, Boro decided a nice, tasty yellow fish would be okay, especially since this was his first star station fishing trip.

After missing a couple, he had one cornered in a tight place, the fish was obviously confused, and Boro was about to grab it when something silver flashed across the corner of his vision. Instinctively he jabbed that way with his opposite fist, caught the large fish against the wall, and for a moment it drifted, stunned.

Before Boro had time to think, the pink and silver creature started wiggling again, trying to regain its wits. Boro grabbed and smashed the fish's head against the wall, as hard as he could, until he was sure it would remain still.

As soon as the passion of the kill was over, Boro's lungs screamed at him to breathe, and the only question was whether it would be air or water. He clutched the lifeless fish tightly under his arm, looked up, and pushed off the bottom toward the nearest shiny, lighted air pocket.

As Boro gasped air in and out, fighting off a light-headed feeling, Glorm surfaced. "What's that under your arm?" the ursine said with grinning teeth.

Boro smiled even as he continued gasping, and didn't attempt words.

After Boro rested and regained his breath, Glorm led them slowly from one air pocket to the next. At one point along the way, a clear wall allowed Boro to glimpse a shallow pool where several lizard-like reptiles waded, two large ones wrestling playfully, a smaller one polishing a piece of jewelry.

"What was that?" Boro asked at the next air pocket.

"Last of their kind, poor fellows. We're looking for a planet for them, but they're very picky."

Boro shrugged and continued following his friend until a strong current pulled at them. The next thing he knew, they emerged into the air and light of the open stream, grabbed roots, and pulled themselves onto the bank.

"Where can we cook these beauties?" Boro asked as he dressed.

"They're better raw . . ." Glorm asserted with head cocked.

Boro squinted for a moment. "I guess . . . compared to what our pilot has to find the courage to do . . . I should try it."

The bear laughed. "If she can't find her courage, she wouldn't last long in the Nebador Services!"

✷

For the next half hour, ursine and monkey mammal sat near the stream, each hunched over his catch, passing Glorm's folding knife back and forth as they worked strips of meat off the bones of their fish. Glorm brought out a clear, flexible bag for the innards and bones. Neither spoke much, but occasionally they both looked up. Their sparkling mammalian eyes met, sealing their new bond of friendship.

At the end of the meal, Boro had to agree — it was better raw.

✷ ✷ ✷

Glorm gave a clear example of how "juggling" is a necessary skill for a docking controller. How would "dancing" help?

If you were in Boro's shoes, how would you be affected knowing there were "planets where monkey mammals are eaten for lunch"?

A "fluke" is a horizontal tail, which only marine mammals (dolphins, whales, seals, walruses, etc.) have. The "fins" of fish (including sharks) are vertical.

Advanced civilizations are often imagined to be sedate, pacifistic, and vegetarian, in other words, a place that only a Buddhist over 50 could enjoy. In the descriptions of Nebador, the author has attempted to avoid that (in his opinion) mistake. One reason is that most of the highly-intelligent creatures on Earth, who presumably have the best chance of becoming sapient, are carnivorous. But the ones intelligent and mature enough to become citizens of Nebador would, of course, refrain from eating each other and similar creatures. But luckily "none of the sapient species were fish," so they were fair game!

Two carnivorous hunters, sitting together eating their catch, is an intensely civilizing experience because both could, just as easily, attempt to eat the other. Add to it the sharing of a knife (a weapon) without ever using it on each other, and you have the beginnings of a deep bond of trust. No meaningful relationship between two civilized creatures is possible without risk.

Chapter 8: Mission Assignment Room

Kibi watched closely as Ilika paused to talk to former shipmates, old friends, and a stranger or two. Among the furry mammals, large birds, a quiet reptile taller than herself, and an eight-legged spider that made Mati's surgeon look cuddly, Kibi observed a common ritual of greeting that included eye contact and slight bows. She saw very little smiling, hand shaking, or hugging, and started keeping mental notes on what gestures might be unique to her own kind.

Ilika directed them into an eating place where they could choose from a dozen different meals, from a big bowl of leaves and flowers, to strips of raw fish. Ilika selected a little of everything, and Kibi grabbed cups of juice.

The eating tables in the courtyard bustled with activity and overflowed with all kinds of creatures sitting or standing. The pair of humans looked around, then exchanged grins when they spotted a quiet deck beside a pool of water.

Just as they got comfortable on the deck, a large dolphin breached the surface clutching a fish between rows of sharp teeth. Ilika quickly held the tray higher as a wave of water drenched the entire deck.

Kibi looked at Ilika and saw that he was smiling, so she did the same. The dolphin, still upright in the water, tossed the fish into the air, caught and swallowed it, and settled back to the surface. "Zalara Sim!" it said in a high-pitched voice, laying its head onto the deck.

"Krish-ka!" Ilika replied in recognition. "I haven't seen you in over a year!"

"Been in Nebula Seven-Two-Seven for months. Very glad to be back eating fresh fish!"

"Zalara Sim?" Kibi questioned, looking at Ilika.

"The name of my planet, in the native language, and *some* scientists have very good memories. I was the navigator on a stellar observing ship for a while."

The dolphin laughed in a very human way. "You have a girl now?"

"Krish-ka, this is Kibi, steward of the Manessa Kwi."

The dolphin rolled its head back and forth, looking at each of them in turn. "She is much more than your steward."

Ilika sighed and smiled. "Dolphins can read emotions very well," he said to Kibi. "Yes, Krish-ka, she's my dear lover."

The dolphin brought its wet snout close to Kibi. With only a moment of hesitation, Kibi offered her open hand. The snout nuzzled her fingers, but its teeth remained hidden. "Is he a good lover?" the dolphin asked softly.

Kibi grinned and looked at Ilika. "Most of the time. Enough to . . . you know . . . make me want to keep him."

Krish-ka laughed and started to slide back into the water. "Be good, Zalara Sim! I must go teach some young ones the difference between a star and an asteroid. Bye!"

When the dolphin was gone, Kibi laughed. "Even *I* know that much!"

✷

After eating a dozen foods Kibi had never seen before, she took on a thoughtful expression. "I feel . . . perfectly safe here. I've never felt that way before . . . anywhere."

"Just remember," Ilika began, "Nebador star stations are about the only places in the universe where that's true. And don't forget, we're on-call. Danger is just a mission assignment away!"

Kibi laughed. "I don't know about you, but I'm sopping wet! Does that count as danger?"

Ilika grinned at her while shaking his head. "That's just the price of working side by side with other sapient creatures. Ready to see the mission assignment room?"

She nodded and rose to her feet.

✷

In fresh, dry clothes, Kibi entered the huge hollow sphere with her mouth open. Thick tree trunks curved around the sides, and ramps connected platforms at many points in the large open space. Soft lights of different colors illuminated all the platforms and other places where creatures of all sorts sat or stood, some talking, others working at consoles.

Mammals and arachnids constantly moved up and down the ramps. Birds floated through the air from platform to platform. Marine mammals and reptiles worked in or near pools at the bottom of the spherical room.

Kibi tilted her head back. Stars and planets shined through every crystal wall. "But . . . how can . . . aren't we . . ."

Ilika smiled. "Yes, we're still deep inside the star station. The walls are all display screens, most of them of stars and planets far from here, anywhere some problem needs attention."

Kibi's skin tingled as she began to see more than mammals, birds, reptiles, and big spiders. Barely-seen fuzzy balls of light, of different colors and sizes, moved casually from one platform to another, or streaked away faster than the eye could follow, sometimes right through solid walls.

One large orange glow, almost a meter across, hovered near a furry black ursine at a console. As the bear worked, he often turned his head to the fuzzy light, listened for a moment, then nodded and went back to work.

At a platform close to a crystal wall, three small blue lights danced around each other. A large bird changed the view angle and magnification of the star field with sweeps of his wings in the air. After a moment, the blue lights vanished and the bird stepped to a console.

"Ilika . . . with all these glowing orbs . . . I feel like I'm back at Lumber Town with Melorania . . ."

"You can see them? I had a hunch you might. How many colors?"

"Um . . . three . . . no, four."

"There are eleven or twelve different types of non-material beings here," Ilika said, his head tilted up as he scanned the room, "and we experience them as different colors. You'll see them all in time."

"Wow. But . . . what . . ."

"Not all creatures in the universe are flesh and blood, my friend. You've met Melorania. We'll work with her often, since she's head of the Transport Service, but there are many others who will be involved in our missions from time to time. The one in charge of Satamia Star Station is here right now. Can you spot him?"

After a few deep breaths to master her fear, Kibi searched the room with her eyes. She was tempted to point to the orange glow, but changed her mind. The little blues were always coming and going, like messengers. Finally she knew, and pointed to a beautiful forest-green light, moving slowly from place to place, as if observing.

Ilika grinned.

"Makes sense," Kibi declared, "because the whole station's a big tree!"

*

They strolled along the ramps and observed the work at display screens or control consoles. Often, hurried conferences took place among flesh and blood creatures, fuzzy balls of light, or both.

Kibi was starting to think everyone was ignoring Ilika and herself, when suddenly she knew she was being watched. She slowly turned and discovered the forest-green light floating in mid-air not far away, and even though it had no eyes or ears, she knew with certainty it was looking at her, and listening to both her words and her thoughts.

"H . . . hello . . ." she managed to stutter out.

Ilika noticed and observed, but didn't interfere.

The glowing green fuzziness did nothing, said nothing, but a moment later Kibi's mission bracelet chimed. She flipped open the cover and peered at the little display. "Kibi," she read aloud, "please move the Manessa Kwi from dock C-Thirteen to C-Fourteen. Kerloran of Satamia."

Kibi looked up, and the forest-green orb slowly moved away. The feeling of being watched faded as he departed.

"Move Manessa? Me?"

Ilika smiled. "I *think* your name is Kibi . . ."

"You'll help me, right?"

Before Ilika could answer, his mission bracelet chimed. "Nope. I have to go talk to someone."

Kibi looked forlorn. "Do I get Mati?"

"No way! She's got enough to deal with, and Rini with her."

"At least . . . Sata?"

Ilika tapped at his bracelet. "Sorry. She's in flight somewhere, and it's not on the Manessa Kwi."

Kibi sighed. "And I'm sure that if I tried to find Boro, he'd be busy too, right?"

Ilika tried to suppress a grin. "Probably. I'd better go."

"But . . . I don't even know where dock C-Thirteen is!"

"Ask someone!" Ilika called back as he headed for one of the doorways that led out of the Mission Assignment Room.

* * *

As Kibi observed, social rituals of greeting would have to be different based on the anatomy of the people involved. Smiling requires lips and teeth. Shaking hands requires . . . you guessed it. Hugging needs arms or wings. Bowing, a gesture of respect and submission, is one of the few things that could be done by just about any animal (at least, those with a head).

A common ritual of trust-building is offering a vulnerable part of the body within reach of the teeth or claws of the other person. Dogs and cats are doing this when they roll on their backs and show their bellies. Kibi did this with her hand near the dolphin's teeth.

There was a time, not very long ago, when people did NOT know the difference between a star and an asteroid. In fact, "asteroid" means "star-like."

Ilika and Kibi discussed how Nebador facilities are about the only completely safe places in the universe. (We'll skip, for now, why this is the case.) What rules, personnel, and institutions would NOT be necessary because of that?

Most people believe that the universe is populated by, and run by, non-material (or "spiritual") beings. However, most of these same people would not claim to recognize the scene in the Mission Assignment Room because we like to think our gods and angels look like us. In other words, we like "anthropomorphic" spiritual beings (not to be confused with "anthropogenic," or man-made). When they don't look like us, we usually refer to them as "false gods," "demons," "devils," or some other negative term. Ironically in most cases, these negative terms, while expressing our dislike, also accept the reality of the non-anthropomorphic spiritual beings.

Chapter 9: Heat

A minute passed before Kibi worked up the courage to ask directions. She didn't want to bother anyone who looked busy, so she waited for the first creature who appeared to be off-duty. It turned out to be a sleek, furry mammal that walked on all fours and had feline teeth that could have made quick work of a donkey or horse.

"Um . . . hello . . . um . . . do you have a moment?"

The animal's muscles rippled with strength as he sat on his haunches in front of Kibi, bringing his head level with hers. "Toran Takil, at your service, beautiful monkey mammal."

Kibi swallowed. "And . . . you are very . . . handsome. On my planet, mountain lions roam the land, and you remind me of them. But they are not sapient. At least . . . I don't think so . . ."

The powerful animal gazed into Kibi's eyes, and her rambling faded away. She felt nearly mesmerized, caught up in his penetrating glance. Her knees began to shake.

Seeing her mental state, he curled his lips slightly. "How can I help you?"

Kibi struggled to compose herself. "Um . . . I need to find dock C-Thirteen, and move a deep-space response ship. Do you . . . know where that is?"

The large animal yawned. "Sounds like one of Kerloran's little confidence-building assignments. You are new here, or I'm a kitten."

Kibi smiled nervously. "*Very* new here. I can't even find my own ship!"

"I am free, and would be happy to guide you."

*

They followed three corridors and four or five ramps, but Kibi was so focused on her guide that she paid little attention to the turns they made or the signs they passed. As she walked along beside the sleek, powerful animal, she felt an unusual warmth fill her body. Soon they arrived at a comfortable little room with soft seats and a clear boarding tunnel that bridged the short distance to the golden ship. An intense desire to impress Toran Takil welled up inside Kibi.

"Um . . . I'd be very honored if you'd . . . come with me."

The huge cat curled his lips, then stretched forward and licked Kibi's neck, sending chills all throughout her body. Somehow she managed to get through the boarding tunnel without stumbling over her own feet, and he followed closely.

Driven by some deep need to look as good as possible to the animal watching her from the passenger area, words came to Kibi's mind that she had heard others say, but had never spoken herself.

"Manessa, short-range sensors, please, and the docking tunnel chart. Warm up anti-mass one and maneuvering thrusters."

Several consoles came to life with the requested functions. The chart flashed onto the main bridge screen and the pilot's three-D display.

"Close hatch, hull diagnostic, retract boarding tunnel. Select docking controller channel."

"Greetings, Manessa Kwi," a raspy insect voice said as an image of stick-thin legs and compound eyes appeared at the navigator's station.

"Hello, I'm Kibi, and Kerloran asked me to move the ship to C-Fourteen. No station control needed."

"This must be the shortest trip I've ever approved!"

Kibi grinned.

"The docking tunnel is clear, and your destination is about forty meters to your right."

"Thank you, Satamia control. Manessa Kwi closing."

Kibi sat down at the pilot's station for the first time. She glanced back at Toran Takil, saw his sparkling animal eyes watching her intently from the passenger area, and touched the symbol she knew would raise the flight control. "Manessa, release docking clamps."

As soon as the blue and purple fingers let go, she nudged up the anti-mass drive until she could feel the ship floating, then eased the flight control forward. Adrenaline filled her veins, and her heart throbbed in her chest. She felt more confident and alive than she could ever remember feeling.

Glancing at all her view angles, Kibi found the docking tunnel completely empty. She cleared dock C-Thirteen, hoping her guest couldn't see her trembling.

Kibi grinned from ear to ear as they covered the forty meters to the next dock, and could feel the presence of the male cat every second of the journey. Finally she brought the ship to a stop, nudged it into the docking fingers, and breathed deeply when Manessa announced the ship secure.

"Manessa, shut down all systems and extend boarding tunnel."

Kibi was out of the pilot seat in a fraction of a second, and a heartbeat later stood before Toran Takil, breathing heavily but trying to look calm and confident.

"I am impressed," the cat said, and licked her on the neck again.

Kibi shivered and grinned with pleasure.

"Would you like to get some cold drinks with me, and I'll show you my favorite place in the station, a place few people know about, and fewer still ever go."

Kibi could think of no words to say, but nodded quickly and smiled.

*

As they followed ramps and corridors again, Kibi dug deep into her courage and placed her hand on the large feline's back. He didn't seem to mind, so she kept it there as they made their way through the station. From that moment on, she had no awareness of where she was, other than beside a beautiful and powerful animal who excited her more than anyone ever had.

At a low table somewhere among the leaves of the station tree, Kibi knelt on the soft floor close beside her new companion. She could feel his body heat, and sensing that he was comfortable with the closeness, she snuggled even closer.

The cold drink was probably delicious, but Kibi barely tasted it, and hardly noticed when they rose and wandered on.

Deep in seldom-used parts of the station, they followed narrow ramps and eventually arrived at a cozy patio among thick tree branches. A little fountain bubbled, and a dark doorway stood at the far end of the patio, but otherwise the area was empty and quiet.

Toran Takil sat on his haunches and looked at Kibi. She grinned and breathed rapidly. He stretched close, licked and nibbled her neck, and let her feel his teeth without breaking skin.

Kibi sighed and giggled as shivers of pleasure shot through her body.

"I am Toran Takil, citizen of Nebador," he began. "I stand and work beside the highest powers of the universe. I go where the bravest people fear to tread. I solve problems that planetary colleges and governments cannot even understand. Kings and presidents sit before me and ask my advice."

Kibi suddenly felt an icy chill replace her previous warmth.

The large feline continued in a softer voice. "If you want to play games with your heart, and other people's hearts, then you should return to your backward little planet as fast as you can. If you have any intention of becoming a citizen of Nebador, then you need to do some serious growing up, right now."

Kibi swallowed hard and tried to blink away tears, but felt too ashamed to wipe them.

"The next time I look into your eyes, Kibi, I want to find an equal, a citizen of Nebador, strong and true. Right now I see a silly little girl. Beyond this fountain is a doorway. Within are powerful teachers who can guide you on the journey from . . . where you are . . . to where you could be, if you are willing to do the hard work."

With those words, Toran Takil licked Kibi's neck one last time, then turned and walked away.

*

Kibi wrestled with her emotions for many minutes, knowing she was now the biggest fool in the entire universe. But somehow, she also guessed that Toran Takil would not tell a soul what she had done.

Eventually she managed to pull herself up straight. As she looked around the patio, she saw no sign of the big cat, and knew in her heart she would not see him again . . . at least, for a long time.

Kibi knelt down at the bubbling fountain and washed her face. When she looked up, she saw a little sign beside the door on the far side of the patio. Standing and going close, she read it.

Psychic Development.

She thought of Mati and her difficult decision. She wondered if Sata and her avian companion were becoming good friends. She tried to imagine Boro fishing with the bear. Finally, she thought of Ilika, and shame filled her mind and colored her face again.

After several deep breaths, she stepped through the doorway, not knowing what she would find within.

* * *

To what extent do you think the situation was Toran Takil's "fault" (error, mistake), and to what extent Kibi's "fault"?

What is the difference between "fault" and "responsibility"?

When the cat licked Kibi on the neck, what meaning did that probably have to him? (You may wish to take a moment to think about normal cat behavior.) What meaning did it appear to have to Kibi?

Did the situation in this chapter have a good purpose and outcome, or would it have been better avoided?

In general, in your opinion, is it better to avoid temptations, or to experience and overcome them?

The author has often been asked why he used the term "Psychic Development" instead of "Psychological Development." The reasons are many, all pointing in the same direction. "Psychological" has to do with the STUDY of the psyche (soul or mind). It implies a detached, academic approach to an intellectual understanding of something held at arm's length. "Psychic," on the other hand, while still essentially about the soul/mind, encompasses all the mental functions, including those that science has not been able to understand, sometimes not even acknowledge. It also implies a very direct, personal, hands-on process that someone studying "psychology" would not get. The Psychic Development program in Nebador would be most analogous to the training found in an elite monastic community, such as the legendary Shaolin Temple in Henan, China.

Chapter 10: The Surgeon

An hour after Ilika and the others left the medical waiting room, Mati and Rini were still entwined on a couch, whispering thoughts and feelings to each other. The gray-haired human healer entered the room.

"Hello, Mati."

She tried to smile.

"Hi, Healer Dakalio," Rini said.

"If you'd like, while you're thinking about your options, I could do detailed scans. That way, we'll know more, and you'll know more, before you have to make any decisions."

Mati's mouth shifted back and forth in thought. "Um . . . okay. You'll tell me everything you find?"

"Everything. I promise."

*

For the next three hours, Mati allowed the mysterious machines to hover over every part of her knees, legs, and feet. What she didn't allow was Rini leaving her side, except once when he was beginning to cross his legs and do a clumsy dance.

To her surprise, the healer had his scanners probe both her knees, not just the bad one.

"We have to have something to compare to. Your left knee has had a hard life, but it's a lot closer to normal than . . . you know."

Mati smiled up at the healer for the first time.

He smiled back. "I think K'stimla would want to work on your hips and ankles a bit, too. After all, you have two or three hundred good years ahead of you."

"Wait a minute!" Rini challenged with a frown. "Even after I change that into base ten, it's still a lot longer than we live!"

The healer smiled slightly. "Maybe on *your* planet, but this is Nebador.

It's not easy finding good people, so we keep them as long as we can. I'm two hundred and fifteen."

Rini and Mati looked at each other with open mouths.

✷

For the next hour, Healer Dakalio explained many things he could see in the medical scans, and promised that K'stimla would see even more.

A shadow came over Mati's face. "How am I going to find the courage to let a big, green insect be my surgeon?"

The healer's eyes gleamed. "The first step has already been arranged. The four of us are having dinner together."

Mati sighed. "I don't suppose she'll eat me."

The older man laughed. "Not unless you're a frog! She *loves* frogs' legs."

Rini nodded and his eyes sparkled. "We do too!"

Mati sighed again. "All I have to do is eat frogs' legs with a big bug who's my only hope of walking again. Being a slave was *so* much simpler."

Both Rini and the healer laughed deeply.

✷

Mati desperately wanted to avoid sitting next to the huge green insect, so she quickly hobbled to the chair between the other two human chairs. Then she realized that would put her directly across the table from the big bug, face to face. She sighed and carefully sat down.

When the mantid surgeon arrived, a few minutes late, she perched on the floor in the remaining empty space and exchanged friendly greetings with her fellow healer on one side. Rini, on the other side, quickly joined in the pleasant conversation.

Mati was glad everyone was ignoring her.

Soon a cart arrived, pushed by a reptile wearing a funny purple hat, which caused smiles and laughter among almost all of those present. Bowls of fresh leaves came first, with a variety of sauces and sprinkles to choose from.

Mati tried not to look, but couldn't contain her curiosity. The surgeon ate with her two front-most legs, but the finger-like mandibles around her mouth did most of the work.

Both Dakalio and Rini steered the conversation toward topics that would give Mati some sense of what would happen, if she had the surgery, without ever referring to Mati or her knee. Hearing that surgery was done underwater piqued Mati's curiosity. A big pot of steamed frogs was placed in the center of the table, and bowls of dipping sauces completed the main course.

Mati noticed that K'stimla preferred the sweet-tart sauce. At first Mati avoided it, only using the savory garlic sauce. But when she started on her second frog, she took a deep breath, tried the sweet-tart sauce, and immediately understood why the surgeon preferred it.

Rini shared stories from their travels that made Mati smile. Dakalio, without ever looking at Mati, recalled times when patients would almost rather die than let a monkey mammal provide medical care. He clarified that those patients had not been Nebador citizens.

Mati felt about an inch tall. She also felt completely left out of the companionship and good cheer encircling the table. She suddenly realized that if she refused the surgery and went home, Rini might go with her, but their relationship would probably be reduced to . . . something not much better than slavery.

"Um . . ." she managed to squeak, her eyes still on her plate, "I don't think I could let *any* healer work on me unless Rini was at my side the whole time."

Mati looked at Rini with a questioning smile. Rini grinned at Dakalio. Dakalio turned to K'stimla.

"Actually," K'stimla began, "I wouldn't attempt this procedure *without* Rini there, because he's going to be my assistant for the surgery."

Rini's eyes grew wide. "But . . . I don't know anything about . . ."

K'stimla's hundred or more insect eyes looked at the lad. "You know how to draw breath, pump blood, and regulate body temperature. A machine could do all that, but it cannot love Mati as you do." The surgeon then looked directly at Mati. "Can you place your life in this boy's hands?"

Mati labored for a moment to swallow the huge lump in her throat. "Um . . . um . . . yes."

* * *

Our lifespan, in a primitive, natural environment (such as "caveman" days) was about 25 years, but that was mostly due to predator attacks and accidents, not "old age." With agriculture for a greater food supply, villages and cities for greater safety, and basic medical care, we doubled that to about 50 years. In the 20th century, with plentiful energy and modern medicine, we have added another 25 to bring our lifespan to about 75 years.

We know that one major factor in aging is the radiation we receive from the sun and other sources. An advanced civilization, whose members rarely went "outside," might be able to add many years to their lifespan just by this one change. Other things they might do, both medically and spiritually, would be pure speculation.

Frogs' legs taste about the same as chicken, and are a common food in just about every culture on Earth, except a few that are so rich they can be picky about what they eat.

How was Mati's choice of dipping sauce symbolic of her changing attitude toward the surgeon?

Mati was looking for a way to accept the surgery, but wanted to retain some control, so she set a condition. By accepting the condition, and even going a step further and REQUIRING it, K'stimla created a situation Mati could hardly reject, since it had been her idea.

Chapter 11: Conference

Ilika entered the nearly-dark room with more than a little anxiety. He had been called upon to make many decisions during the previous year and a half of his life, ever since hiding the Manessa Kwi in the swamp near the capital city of a small medieval kingdom on Sonmatia Three.

He knelt and cleared his mind, knowing he had done what he had done, and could not now avoid the consequences of his actions . . . or inactions. After a few minutes, he felt a presence. The presence slowly took on the form of a fuzzy glowing mist, then the color of a ripe peach. Ilika smiled.

For the next few minutes, as silence continued to fill the room, Ilika opened his mind and let the presence experience everything the young captain had seen, heard, and felt.

Judge yourself, Ilika Imni, the presence said softly without words.

Ilika breathed slowly to center his thoughts. "It was a good mission that taught me more things than I can remember. I made mistakes, as you know, and will again, but hopefully not the same ones."

Ilika felt a moment of humor radiate from the presence. *Judge the five you brought back.*

"Rini is as close to perfect as I could want. The other four have weaknesses, and will probably make serious mistakes, but I believe they will be citizens of Nebador someday. I will do everything in my power to help them on that journey."

Mati needs to spend more time with other sapient creatures, the presence asserted, *and her surgery and recovery will begin that process. She and Rini will work best together, especially after the surgery.*

Ilika nodded.

Boro will always be loyal, but will need help and encouragement developing his mind.

"I was thinking of cross-training him into navigation soon."

Sata has greater lessons to learn. Be watching for them, but do not interfere unless you must for the safety of others.

Ilika nodded.

Your biggest problem is your steward.

"I . . . sense that."

Never ask what happened today. You do not want to know. But be comforted – she has stepped onto a path that may bring her to citizenship. It may take her away from you, at times, but you cannot deny her that path without destroying her.

Ilika swallowed, took a deep breath, and tried to smile.

Overall, I am pleased, Ilika Imni, the presence continued. *You have earned the companionship of Manessa Kwi Habishu Glinta, and the task of guiding your chosen five toward citizenship. Your ship and crew are now active on the Nebador Transport Service rolls.*

"I am honored," Ilika said as a flood of warm emotions filled his body and tears of joy threatened to spring from his eyes.

The presence embraced him for a moment, then faded away.

Ilika, still on his knees, let the good feelings of success linger as he felt the cool, sweet air of the star station flow in and out of his lungs. Suddenly his mission bracelet emitted it's emergency chime. He quickly looked at the little display.

Manessa Kwi – prepare for immediate departure.

* * *

Most people are uncomfortable with another being (of any kind) having complete access to our thoughts and feelings. That is because (the author believes) our life experiences have taught us that persons in power cannot be trusted to always treat us with kindness, logic, wisdom, and respect. Political leaders are, often enough, corrupt. Police, often enough, abuse their power. Judges are, often enough, biased. Those persons in power are all, of course, fellow mortal human beings.

A very few people, who have had direct experience with spiritual beings, and in this story the Nebador citizens like Ilika, can cultivate two different responses to "persons in power": one for most mortals, and another for those beings (mortal or spiritual) who have proven they will always exercise kindness, logic, wisdom, and respect.

Chapter 12: First Mission

Ilika's mind raced, and he quickly tapped at the tiny keys of his bracelet, marking Mati and Rini off-duty, and requesting location and status from the other three. Before getting any replies, he was on his feet, striding toward dock C-Fourteen.

"I'm about two minutes away," Sata's voice informed him. "Drrrim-na will guide me."

"Two or three minutes," Boro announced. "Glorm's asleep, but I found a big spider who knows the way."

"Less than a minute," Kibi said.

*

When Ilika jogged down the last ramp and could see the waiting room, Kibi was already there, stepping off a fanator.

"Thank you, sister," she said, embracing the huge bird. "Please tell Memsala I will redo that lesson as soon as I can."

"She knows," the bird said, turned and bowed toward Ilika, then walked up the ramp looking for a place to take off.

Kibi immediately grabbed Ilika and planted a passionate kiss on his lips.

"What did I do to deserve that?" he asked when she finally released him.

"Just . . . a tiny sample of what you're gonna get when we're alone in our cabin."

Ilika grinned just as Sata came striding down the ramp, with Boro close behind. They both turned and waved to the bird and spider who remained side by side at the top.

Ilika glowed with happiness for a moment, seeing his crew, except for those with a good excuse, all gathered and ready to work.

They stepped into the waiting room, but the boarding tunnel was blocked with a pallet of cargo that floated through slowly, followed by a small furry mammal with a wide tail.

"Ilika . . ." Boro began with concern, "we haven't restocked anything . . ."

"I know. I was planning to do that tomorrow. We'll have to . . . what would Drrrim-na say? Wing it?"

Sata chuckled as they slowly followed the cargo pallet into the ship. "I *doubt* Drim-na would say that!"

"Manessa," the beaver said as soon as he entered. "One pallet, and a seat for me, please."

The chairs in the passenger area rearranged themselves, leaving an open space in the middle. Kibi watched as the little mammal carefully positioned the pallet, then spoke to the ship again to anchor it to the floor. "All reasonable speed to Ubalora Four, Captain," he said after climbing onto the nearest seat.

"Pre-flight," Ilika ordered. "I'll cover sensors and helm. Kibi, I want you to get to know Rini's station whenever you can."

Kibi nodded as she stepped to the steward's console.

"No space thruster fuel," Boro reminded everyone with a worried tone. "Everything else will do for a short flight, I guess. Anti-mass and maneuvering thrusters ready."

"Docking tunnel, station departure, and Ubalora system charts on the board," Sata reported. "Controller on channel."

"Greetings again Manessa," the same insect said. "Nice to see you again, Kibi. Traffic is light, and you have first priority out."

Kibi grinned, and without a word from her captain, she closed the hatch, retracted the boarding tunnel, and released the docking clamps. She felt some desire to impress the little mammal behind her, but not nearly as much as she had felt earlier with the big, handsome . . . she stopped herself in mid-thought and remembered the huge trouble she had almost gotten into by letting herself fall for the first sexy male who looked into her eyes.

✷

The partial crew felt very comfortable with everything they had to do to leave Satamia Star Station. The discomfort began when the captain said, "Prepare for star transit."

Kibi, already studying the sensor options at the watch station, looked at her passenger. Without hesitation, he secured his inertia straps, relaxed, and closed his eyes. "Ship and passenger ready. No sensor warnings."

"Inner Ubalora entry chart is up," Sata said, then scrunched herself into a comfortable position.

"Star drive warming," Boro reported and closed his eyes.

If the passenger noticed the long delay before the star drive engaged, he didn't say a word.

✷

They popped back into space not far from the civilized planet Ubalora Three, and Ilika called for maximum ion drive to cover the five light-minutes to their destination, the fourth planet. During the half-hour flight, he gave his crew a sketch of the two sapient species, one mammalian and one avian, that shared the snowy little world.

The mammals were cave dwellers with thick fur, able to walk upright, but often preferring all fours to stay out of the wind. The birds ruled both the sky and the small seas when free of ice.

Sata looked thoughtful. "So . . . Ubalora Three has a civilization, and Four doesn't?"

"Right," Ilika began. "We only refer to sapient creatures as civilized when their society is willingly self-correcting. That means that any problem or imbalance that arises is fixed, and I mean really fixed – not ignored, not hidden, and not passed off to a future generation."

The beaver joined the conversation. "The avians have a complex society, but they love to lay eggs, so their population explodes, then crashes, based on the fish in the seas."

"What about the mammals?" Boro asked.

Ilika deferred to their passenger.

"More stable population, but they enjoy their tribal warfare. Thinkers and artists have very low status, along with women. Only warriors receive any honor."

Kibi frowned. "So what's Ubalora Three like?"

Ilika smiled. "Beautiful, every inch of it. They reserve large areas for different levels of social complexity. An entire continent is wilderness for those who want to live wild and free. And Ubalora Three welcomes the Nebador Services, and openly trades with us."

Sata smiled as she checked the ship's position on the chart. "Twelve minutes to destination. Our planet's a civilization, right Ilika?"

The long moment of silence that followed told Sata what she feared.

"No, not by our definition," he finally said. "My childhood planet isn't either."

After another moment of silence, the furry beaver looked at Ilika sternly. "Aren't you going to tell them?"

Ilika took a deep breath. "I guess I should."

Sata, Boro, and Kibi all looked at their captain.

"Every society *thinks* it's civilized. But by Nebador's definition, there are no human civilizations . . . um . . . anywhere in the universe."

Boro and Sata looked at each other, then both looked at Kibi.

"So . . ." Kibi began thoughtfully, "the *real* civilization on Ubalora Three . . . isn't human, isn't monkey mammal . . ."

"Right."

✷

The approach flight plan for Ubalora Four required them to stay high in the sky until right over a tiny, isolated valley deep in the most rugged mountains. After Ilika brought the ship to a stop eight thousand meters above the white peaks, Kibi poked at the watch console until she figured out how to get a down-angle view. Three domes, partly covered by snow, surrounded a small outdoor landing pad in a clearing among tall pine trees.

Ilika lowered the ship and selected a parking space.

"Welcome to Ubalora Four research station," the beaver said. "It is, believe it or not, the middle of summer."

Boro laughed nervously, gazing at his nearly-white display.

Their guest worked with his pallet of supplies. As soon as Kibi opened the hatch, the nearest door to the research station also opened. A mottled orange reptile emerged with another pallet, this one stacked with round canisters.

The beaver and lizard paused as they passed each other on the snow-covered landing pad.

"New monkey mammals," the furry one said. "Their first mission, I think."

"I know Ilika," the scaly one replied. "Stay warm!"

"Easier said than done in this place," the beaver grumbled in jest, then continued waddling into the heated research station.

*

Unlike the quiet beaver, the reptile greeted everyone with bows, flowery words, and a flashing tongue that tasted the air between them.

"Ilika! You got yourself a ship and a crew, I see!"

The young man and the lizard embraced.

"I will never forget our deep-space missions together," Ilika said when they parted and looked at each other. "Everyone, this is Sss'rol'ti, one of our beloved Quanasia, and my second-favorite steward in the Transport Service."

Kibi grinned.

"Don't let the scales and horns fool you," Ilika went on. "Under his charms, the wildest beast will soon be sipping pinkfruit juice and watching videos."

The talkative lizard greeted Kibi and Sata, then came to Boro. After kind words and a taste of the air, his eyes swirled. "You've been eating my favorite fish! Did you save me some?"

"Sorry," Boro admitted with a guilty frown. Then he looked into the lizard's deep, multi-colored eyes and relaxed. "Glorm showed me the under-water part of the station."

"Glorm the docking controller? He's fun! But as always, I'm chattering too much. I guess we should get these samples back before they spoil."

Ilika smiled and gave commands to prepare for the return trip.

Once they were in the air, Boro received a message on his console from the navigator. *Take me fishing tomorrow?*

He turned and looked at Sata. Their eyes met, they grinned at each other, and he nodded.

"Prepare for star transit," Ilika said from the helm.

*

The Manessa Kwi settled into Satamia Star Station dock D-Eleven. Sss'rol'ti chatted with the crew for another quarter hour, then floated his pallet of canisters down a ramp, humming a tune as he went.

Kibi looked at her console with surprise. "We've been awake almost a day and a half! It's almost breakfast time!"

Suddenly Boro yawned, and Sata couldn't stop herself from doing the same. "I don't need food," Boro announced through his yawn. "I need sleep!"

Ilika nodded. "Let's meet in eight hours and get this ship stocked."

"Yeah!" Boro agreed.

✷

Ilika could feel Kibi's intense emotions as they made their way, with arms around each other, down the lift and across the lower deck. For the next several hours, he almost thought he had a wild animal in his cabin.

When they were finally exhausted, Ilika lay half-asleep beside his lover. He didn't know what change had come over her, and he wasn't going to ask, but he knew for sure he was going to enjoy every minute of it.

Suddenly the knowledge processor on Kibi's desk chimed. She groped her way to consciousness and staggered across the cabin.

"I have to go to a class, and finish an intro lesson I started yesterday. It's something . . . important."

"That place where we ate has nutrition drinks you can grab on the way."

Kibi nodded and was about to dash out the door. She stopped herself and looked at Ilika, recent memories causing her eyes to sparkle. "Thank you."

Ilika smiled shyly.

✷ ✷ ✷

Nebador has a more specific definition of "civilization" than we do: willingly self-correcting . . . any problem or imbalance that arises is fixed . . . not ignored, not hidden, and not passed off to a future generation. In your opinion, does our "civilization" quality for Nebador's definition? If not, will it quality at some point in the future?

What happens to people on our world who want or need a lower level of social complexity than that which is currently common? What happens to people who want to live "wild and free"?

How do you think Sata, Boro, and Kibi felt when they learned their planet wasn't a civilization, and there were NO human civilizations in the universe? How would you feel if you learned that was the case in reality?

Why would the approach flight plan require them to stay high in the sky until right over the research station? Hint: it was in an isolated valley deep in the most rugged mountains.

Why was Kibi feeling so passionate? Hint: before the mission, she had just come from her first visit to the Psychic Development program.

Chapter 13: Decision

Mati dreamed of slave owners telling her she was useless, guards yelling at her to hurry up, and a young goatherd informing her that none of her skills mattered. All of them were *her* kind, monkey mammals, humans. She squirmed and thrashed until Rini wrapped his arms around her and held her tightly. Even though she was already drenched in sweat, somehow the extra body heat made her relax.

The dream changed. A large bird glanced at her with friendly, sparkling eyes. A bear roared and offered her a fish. A giant green insect opened its arms to embrace her. In the dream, Rini stood by, watching and waiting.

Mati awoke, swallowed to wet her parched throat, and felt Rini's arms around her. "You awake?" she whispered.

"Yeah."

"Do you think ... maybe ... we could have breakfast with Surgeon K'stimla?"

Rini smiled. "I think so."

✷

Bowls of small fruits, nuts, and wiggling grubs were delivered by a spider almost as tall as Mati. She chuckled when he sampled them before bowing. "Have to make sure they're fresh!" he explained, a berry in one claw and a grub in another, leaving six legs to stand on.

K'stimla soon arrived, and clearly enjoyed the grubs most. Rini and Mati stuck to the fruits and nuts.

"Ilika has told us many times that we always have to keep growing," Mati began, pushing berries and nuts around on her plate. "A dream reminded me that ... it's been monkey mammals who have treated me badly all my life. Even the wild animals on my planet have never been ... you know ... evil."

"Evil requires sapience," K'stimla replied between grubs. "If a creature isn't self-aware, it might be dangerous, but can't be evil."

Rini nodded thoughtfully, but remained silent.

"I guess . . . monkey mammals are the worst . . ." Mati admitted with a guilty look.

"Not at all!" the surgeon interrupted. "Every sapient race is capable of selfish, terrible evil, using and abusing others, even their own kind. My people have a tendency to make beautiful planets into dark, ugly, polluted places where machines rule with iron claws."

"Oh . . ."

"Being in the Nebador Services has *nothing* to do with the people we come from, and everything to do with who *we* are, as individuals. Very few humans, anywhere in the universe, could sit at table with me, and very few mantidae with you. But I can trust you to be my pilot, and you can, if you choose, trust me to be your surgeon."

The healer fell silent and dissected a piece of fruit with her mandibles.

Mati took a deep breath. "I . . . would like you . . . to be my surgeon . . . if you can forgive me for being so . . . thick-headed."

"I can."

Rini smiled and popped a grub into his mouth. It wasn't too bad, after it quit wiggling.

* * *

Mati's dream showed her journey from the simplistic (but erroneous) belief that species (race, nationality, etc.) matters, to the more mature realization that the inner qualities of each person are what matters.

"Evil requires sapience. If a creature isn't self-aware, it might be dangerous, but can't be evil." This idea stems from the definition of "evil," first explored in *Book One*: a wrong knowingly committed. Even in our human legal system (far from perfect), wrongs committed without awareness are much lesser crimes, or not crimes at all.

K'stimla explains that "Every sapient race is capable of selfish, terrible evil, using and abusing others, even their own kind." We do not know for sure yet, as we only know very much about one sapient race (ourselves), but the tendency to do great evil probably comes with sapience. We also, of course, do not know if any, some, most, or all sapient races eventually "grow up." The author hopes so.

The one thing we DO know is that individuals sometimes choose to "grow up" even when their species, in general, practices evil routinely. In this story, the Nebador Services are composed of a few of these individuals. K'stimla expresses this when she says, "Being in the Nebador Services has NOTHING to do with the people we come from, and EVERYTHING to do with who we are, as individuals."

Chapter 14: Stocking the Manessa Kwi

Ilika didn't want to start ordering supplies for the ship without his steward, so he had a leisurely mid-day meal with Boro and Sata, and showed them some new parts of the star station. They were just stepping out of the museum, after looking at the last crystal cluster Sarto found twenty thousand years before, when Kibi skidded to a stop in front of them. "Sorry I'm late."

"We didn't set an exact time," Ilika reassured. "If I need you on-duty, your bracelet will scream at you."

Kibi grinned as they headed for dock D-Eleven hand in hand.

✷

On the last ramp down to the docking area, Sata noticed Kibi touching and working sore muscles. "Did you hurt yourself?"

"No, just wrestling."

"With what?" Boro asked. "A mountain lion?"

A shadow passed over Kibi's face and she was silent for a long moment. Eventually she cracked a little smile. "Just a very strong reptile."

Ilika sensed that this was the area of Kibi's life to avoid asking about.

As soon as they stepped onto the ship, Boro grabbed a knowledge pad. "I know what *I* want!"

"Let me guess . . ." Kibi began with a smile. "Pinkfruit juice."

Boro grinned. "Pinkfruit juice for Manessa. In other words, liquid number five, space thruster fuel!"

"You could fill that little tank on supply line fifteen," Ilika suggested.

Boro nodded. "Manessa's secret fuel stash! Would you like that, Manessa?"

"It's not very useful empty."

The four humans laughed.

"Want to help me, Sata?" Kibi asked. "We need *everything*."

"Sure. I just need a roll of paper for the chart printer, and it's already on my list."

The two girls took knowledge pads into the galley, and Ilika went down the lift with Boro. The captain wanted to make sure his excited engineer didn't start stashing fuel canisters under the beds.

*

An hour later, with Ilika's help, Boro had a shopping list of fuel, a few other chemicals, and some power cells for the portable instruments.

When Ilika sat down with Kibi's shopping list, he immediately spotted a problem. "What are you going to feed avians, reptiles, and insects?"

Kibi grinned sheepishly. "Forgot about them."

Sata raised her hand. "I think I can make a list for the birds!"

"Go for it," the steward said, handing her a knowledge pad.

Ilika worked with Kibi, and they soon added preserved grubs and other things that Kibi had mistaken for cleaning supplies. The captain looked over the finished lists, marked them low-priority, and transmitted it all to the supply room. "It will be here in an hour or two. We can get stuff quicker in an emergency."

"That's all we have to do?" Sata asked with wide eyes. "All that stuff will just appear?"

"On a cargo pallet, in the waiting room. Then *we* have to put it away."

Just then Kibi's bracelet chimed. "Uh oh, class." She looked at Ilika with a guilty expression.

"Go. Sata and I can handle the food, and I'm sure Boro wants to personally stow each canister of fuel."

The engineer grinned and nodded.

Kibi slid her arms around Ilika's neck and kissed him tenderly. "I'll make it up to you."

"Yep," Ilika said. "You're in command of the next mission."

After a moment of thought, she licked him on the neck and dashed through the hatch.

*

Ilika, Sata, and Boro got a light meal at a quiet little place that served fruits and vegetables, then returned to the waiting room of dock D-Eleven. For some reason, the supplies were late, not arriving until just after Kibi returned from her class.

"That's weird," Boro mumbled. "It's like someone's watching us."

Ilika smiled. "Things like that happen all the time in Nebador."

The two girls looked at the huge stack of supplies. Not even Sata had ever seen so much food in one place. She and Kibi danced around the pallet, grinning from ear to ear, as Boro clapped for them and tapped one foot.

Ilika stood watching and smiling. The small ursine who had delivered the pallet just shook his head.

* * *

You probably know enough about Nebador now to guess why the pallet of supplies didn't arrive until Kibi got out of her class. If you were in that situation, would it be comforting, or would it be frightening, to know that events surrounding you were being manipulated for some purpose that you might not even understand?

Chapter 15: Evening on Satamia Star Station

A couple of hours later, every fuel rack on the Manessa Kwi was loaded to capacity, and the galley, storage closet, and utility room were bulging with food and other supplies. Boro and Kibi both looked very proud.

Ilika's bracelet chimed.

"Want to have dinner with us?" Rini's voice inquired. "We have wonderful news!"

Ilika looked at the others, and they all nodded.

The four wandered through the vast main hall of the star station, with its many levels of balconies, thick tree trunks, ramps, stairs, and pools. But they noticed a dramatic change. The light in the huge room was dim — the Satamia sun had recently slipped below floor level as the station slowly turned. Shafts of colored light occasionally flashed from devices on balcony rails, as if being tested. Some of the lights changed color, while others moved or flashed.

Most normal activity in the main hall seemed to have stopped, and those people who remained were busy cleaning or putting up decorations. Pallets of supplies floated out of tunnels and made their ways into the many kitchens on the edges of the big space. Cooks within were busy preparing food and drink, but didn't yet have any customers. A many-legged insect on a balcony tested his musical instrument, filling the hall with a flurry of pure tones for a moment.

Kibi stopped in her tracks, looked around, and grinned.

"What's . . . going on?" Sata asked.

"Evening. Party time. Don't worry, it won't get started for an hour or so, plenty of time for us to eat with Mati and Rini."

"But . . ." Boro began with a frown, "we came through at about the same time yesterday, and nothing like this was going on . . ."

"That was yesterday based on Manessa's clock, set to your planet's rotation and occasionally modified by Kibi. A day on the star station is about five times as long."

Kibi seemed lost in wonder, but somehow found her words. "Can we . . . go to it?"

"Of course, as long as we remember that this is Nebador, and the Mission Assignment Room, or your teachers, Kibi, can call at any time."

Kibi nodded, but her mind was elsewhere, up in the balconies with the colored lights, glittery streamers, and musical instruments.

Sata grabbed her hand and pulled her along to catch up with Ilika and Boro.

Rini and Mati knew nothing of the preparations in the main hall, and listened eagerly. The dinner cart arrived, and Mati proudly explained which dipping sauce was best with the steamed frogs. Bowls of vegetables and fruits rounded out the meal, and Rini even had a small cup of grubs. After eating a few, he passed the cup around, but it returned to him with the same number of grubs. He laughed.

"This is my last meal before . . . you know what," Mati announced, pulling a frog apart on her plate. "I don't get any breakfast, and K'stimla says the surgery will take most of the day."

"But she'll get nutrition right into her blood," Rini explained as he took some vegetables, "and I'll be with her the whole time. We already met the glowing purple guy . . . person . . . being . . . who will link our minds, and he said . . ."

"I thought it was a she," Mati asserted.

"Yeah, could be. She said part of the link would remain for the rest of our lives."

Mati smiled with pride. "He also mentioned that the link would be strong for several days, and that would help with my recovery."

"Are you each doing this of your own free will?" Ilika inquired.

The couple looked at each other and nodded.

Rini turned back to Ilika. "A really serious-looking spider came by to make sure we knew all the risks, and recorded our answers with his knowledge pad."

Everyone enjoyed their food in silence for a minute.

"You know," Mati began without quite looking at Rini, "*you* could go out and enjoy the party. I'm the one getting ready for surgery . . ."

Rini scraped the meat off a frog's leg with his teeth. "Nope. I go through that door when you do . . . on two feet, both of us. Wanna watch a video?"

Mati rolled her eyes, but was smiling with happiness.

When the four active members of Manessa's crew returned to the main hall, preparations for the party were just about complete. A group of reptiles played bits of music to test their instruments, and trays of drinks and snacks lined many tables.

Kibi turned circles in wonder, remembering the simple pipes and drums that played under torchlight back in her kingdom.

"Ilika!" a deep human voice called from somewhere above them.

Ilika looked up. "Sorrano!"

The others could see a man with long brown hair, wearing a shimmering orange robe, leaning over the railing of the first balcony level.

"Can you help? Some wonderful avians are trying, but making monkey-mammal food really does need hands."

"We'll be right up!"

As the others followed Ilika to the nearest ramp, Sata explained that this was how things were done in Nebador. She strode into the kitchen, found it similar to the one she already knew, and pointed to the hand-washing sink.

The birds were relieved and gladly made way for the crew of monkey mammals. A tall yellow-haired lady, in a shimmering blue robe and apron, bowed and thanked them.

"I'm Rossilia," she said, greeting the crew with a friendly smile and gesturing for them to gather around the assembly table. "I was hoping to make these little treats, until I learned there were hardly any humans on the station. Ilika, you've made these before."

"Years ago."

"A sheet of dried seaweed, a layer of sticky rice, then strips of veggies and fish. Roll them up and slice into single bites. Easy . . . if you have hands."

The crew went to work while Rossilia attempted to fix the ones made by the birds. "Each roll can be a little different."

While they worked, Sorrano sliced fish and chatted with Ilika. The three had worked on a ship together when Ilika was quite young. "I had a hunch you'd become a captain someday," Sorrano said. "You always liked seeing the bigger picture. I never got over being space-sick half the time, so I decided to stick to star and planet stations."

"He likes flying," Rossilia revealed, "but only by shuttle or fanator so he can see the ground."

"I've flown on a fanator!" Sata boasted. "I only screamed a little . . ." she continued more humbly.

Ilika looked at Kibi, busy holding in a smile.

"It's required for my training," she revealed, "and anything else I'm uncomfortable with."

"Oh!" Sorrano began, "you must be in the Psychic Development program!"

Kibi nodded. "What do you know about it?"

"Not much. I flunked out after a week. It's not required for citizenship, only if you want to walk and talk with Kerloran and such during the toughest missions."

Kibi swallowed.

"I'm just a supply clerk, power cell technician, and occasional cook," Sorrano continued. "I helped make up your pallet today. Your cupboards must have been bare – I thought I was stocking a transport ship!"

Kibi grinned and nodded as she took the last piece of fish.

"And he's a very good singer!" Rossilia added. "He's on the schedule tonight."

Ilika smiled as he sliced his last fish and vegetable roll. "That'll be a treat! I've always envied your rich, deep voice."

Sorrano brushed off the compliment with a jerk of his head as he cleaned up the pile of fish bones. "The party's about to begin. Let's get these goodies out there!"

As Kibi helped carry trays of food and drink to the serving tables, she fell in beside Ilika. "Have you done the Psychic Development training?"

He nodded. "It's required to be a captain."

In that moment, while carrying a tray of party food, Kibi became absolutely sure that she was going to go all the way through the program, and someday be Toran Takil's equal on all the hardest missions . . . *and* Ilika's faithful lover.

The music had just begun when Ilika and his partial crew descended to the main floor. On a landing above the largest pool, a spider worked a keyboard with most of his legs, while a lizard held an instrument that produced tonal sweeps. On another landing, a monkey with a long tail perched before a console that controlled a hundred dancing, flashing, changing lights, all coordinated to the music.

Several birds were already on the dance floor, hopping from foot to foot, or spreading wings upward and turning circles.

Kibi looked at Ilika. "I can just . . . go out there and dance?"

"That's the idea. Just don't step on anyone!"

As eager as she was, Kibi started slowly, watching those around her to see what they were doing, and being very careful where she put her feet. Deep down inside, she knew she was born to dance, but her only opportunity so far had been on the Manessa Kwi when off-duty. She was just figuring out how to move to the piece played by the spider and reptile when her bracelet chimed.

Sit, until I release you. Memsala.

Kibi's face fell and she stood motionless on the dance floor, fighting with her feelings. Ilika noticed, stopped dancing, and stood near. After more than a minute, she sighed and dragged herself to a couch in a dimly-lit area off to one side.

To her surprise, Ilika plopped down beside her.

"*You* don't have to stop dancing," she said with a hurt tone, wearing a pout. "*Your* bracelet didn't chime."

Ilika smiled. "I bet the message didn't say anything about eating, drinking, snuggling, or kissing!"

Kibi struggled with herself for a long moment. "Thanks."

"What are lovers for?"

They shared a long kiss while a quartet of furry apes began a new song with smooth horns and deep-toned strings.

"You ... um ... deserve to know about something," Kibi began with obvious difficulty once their lips parted.

Ilika nodded slightly and took her hands in his.

"I . . . almost made a huge mistake recently with . . . another male . . ."

"Oh, Toran Takil?"

Kibi's mouth opened in surprise, but she managed to nod slightly. "How did you know?"

"When you licked me on the neck, I guessed. That's sort of his trademark. And if you'd met him, but *hadn't* felt his magnetic qualities, you'd be about the only female, of any species, who could make that claim. Even some of the *males* . . ."

Kibi burst out snickering, and Ilika joined her. With that load of guilt off her chest, she felt much better. Still, she really wanted to dance, and kept twisting this way and that to see what the other dancers were doing.

Eventually she swiveled around to see what was behind her. She hadn't realized it until then, but the couch was not far from the medical center. Silhouetted behind the glass doors, she could see two small human figures holding hands, one leaning on a crutch.

Somehow, that helped her to relax.

Sata felt for Kibi, but knew it was Ilika's place to comfort her. She continued to hold hands with Boro, and even though she had never danced in her life, she felt drawn to the dance floor. As she watched the other dancers, she realized that few of them had any dancing skill. They were just prancing, hopping, or swaying to the music, each type of creature in a different way.

Occasionally someone with real skill would take to the floor, and others would give them room and watch. Most often it was a large bird with vivid green and blue feathers, or one of the reptiles that walked on two legs. The monkeys with tails could prance up a storm, but not very gracefully.

Sata tried to nudge Boro toward the dance floor, but became aware that he was trying to nudge her toward the food and drink. They both stopped and looked at each other with embarrassed smiles.

"How about . . ."

"Yeah, maybe . . ."

"Uh huh."

"You first?"

"No, you."

"Um, okay."

Sata guided Boro onto the edge of the dance floor, in a little-used area, far from any of the fancy dancers. She started moving her feet to the music. The only other dancers nearby, a pair of clumsy birds, continued hopping from one foot to the other while nuzzling each other with their beaks, and paid no attention to the new arrivals.

Boro tried shuffling his feet, but quickly became embarrassed. "I'm terrible . . ."

"Me too," Sata assured him. "Remember, we always have to keep learning."

Suddenly Boro remembered something Glorm said. To be a docking controller, you had to juggle and dance. Boro started moving his feet again, and thought he might have almost found the rhythm of the song just before it ended.

Sata offered her hand, and together they headed for the snack tables.

Boro realized with surprise that he was looking forward to the next song, and hoped he could get his feet moving to its beat.

With the help of a neck massage from Ilika, Kibi began to relax on the couch and accept the situation. "I guess . . . I was sort of all full of myself when I started dancing, thinking I was going to go out there and impress everyone. Now . . . watching the brightly-colored birds, and those fast-footed lizards . . . how do they always know our weaknesses?"

"Who?"

"You know, the people in charge, and my new teachers."

Ilika chuckled. "They can see right through us, my friend. It used to bug me too. Where I grew up, just like on your planet, no one knew or cared what anyone else was thinking or feeling."

As the entire main hall had become quiet, both Ilika and Kibi fell silent and looked around. All the dancers were finding places to sit, perch, or hang. The previous musicians put away their instruments, and a group of six rather large reptiles were setting up big drums on part of the dance floor.

"Oh, I know!" Ilika let slip.

"What?"

"You'll see. If he's gonna sing what I think he is, you'll see more than a thousand Nebador citizens nearly moved to tears. There are few songs that deeply touch all the different sapient species. If my hunch is right, this is one of them."

"Who!" Kibi demanded.

"Sorrano."

At that moment, the first drummer, the smallest of the six reptiles, began to beat a simple rhythm. Half a minute later, he was joined by another drummer, creating a richer sound, and soon a third added emphasis every fourth beat.

Birds and reptiles all around the dance floor sighed with anticipation.

The next drummer began a complex rhythm on several smaller drums, and the fifth drummer added a similar, but slightly different, rhythm that seemed to balance the first.

"There he is," Ilika whispered as a spotlight lit up a small landing about halfway between the main floor and the clear crystal ceiling. Sorrano stepped into the light, breathing slowly and deeply.

The last drummer finally added the deepest and loudest sound of all on a drum more than a meter across. The leaves of the great star station tree began to quiver, and the floor seemed alive with vibrations.

Suddenly the deepest drum stopped, its player silencing it instantly with his claws. At the same moment, Sorrano sang out in a deep, clear voice, creating an image of fire and flames in every listener's mind.

Five of the drums continued their simple or complex rhythms, and the largest resumed when Sorrano ended a verse. Kibi felt her heart beating in time to the drums, and wondered if everyone experienced the same thing.

A few of the most nimble dancers took to the floor, flailing wings or arms in wild expression to match the fury of the music.

The deep drum again ceased and Sorrano began a new verse, bending the theme into the fire of passion and love. Howls rose up. Arms, tails, and wings reached for companions, and the dances became slower and more sensuous.

The deep drum took over again, letting Sorrano breathe and recover. The other drums held their steady rhythm. The six drums were as masters, and every creature's heart was enslaved.

With a slightly softer voice, Sorrano altered the theme once more, pulling it to the fire of the mind, the search for truth and meaning, and the love of justice and wisdom. The dancers and listeners responded, the lighting changed colors, and the entire mood of the star station shifted.

Kibi's eyes sparkled and she grinned, letting the music take her emotions along on the journey.

Again the largest drum returned, and the deepest passions of the dancers resumed.

Suddenly all the drums but one fell silent, the dancers froze, and Sorrano sang of the subtle fire of the spirit. The entire room of more than a thousand sapient creatures was so enthralled, and so quiet, that Sorrano's voice filled the room, perhaps the entire station, with ease.

When he completed the last verse, he bowed, all the drums resumed, and nearly everyone jumped onto the dance floor.

Ilika felt Kibi start to spring, then catch herself. Instead, she wrapped her arms around him, the only thing she could do to express the deep emotions created inside her by the beautiful music of another of her kind, a simple monkey mammal.

Boro had no trouble finding the rhythm of the six drums as soon as Sorrano's song ended and Sata pulled him onto the dance floor. Once his feet were loosened up and moving on their own, he had time to look around at the other dancers. A green reptile caught his eye, moving slowly to the drumbeats, its strong and supple back curving this way and that like a snake.

Boro began to experiment with his own back, and found it not nearly as flexible and expressive as the reptile's long spine. But a thought came to him, and he added his arms, sometimes over his head, sometimes out in front, and discovered they gave him the extra length he needed to fully move to the music.

The only thing he still might wish for was a tail. No, he decided, he could do without that.

Sata didn't find much inspiration in the lizards dancing nearby, but could glimpse a trio of shimmering blue avians whose motions would have been beautiful even if their feathers were not. Her arms also began to move over her head, out to one side or the other, or in front as she ducked her head to mimic the graceful motions of the birds. She was not extending her spine, as Boro, but creating wings that reached for the crystal ceiling, or spread out as if to take flight.

Suddenly both Boro and Sata became embarrassed at the same moment. About a dozen other creatures had gathered around to watch the two graceful monkey mammals dance.

The reptilian drummers bowed and carried away their drums. The changing lights revealed a quartet — an ursine playing small drums, a green mantis with a complex stringed instrument, and two avians with keyboards. They began a slow, sensuous song that had most of the dancers swaying in twos or threes.

Kibi sat on her couch, swaying while holding hands with Ilika, completely lost in the flowing music as if carried along by warm water.

The song ended and dancers entered or left the floor. A lively tune began, carried by the keyboards and supported by the quick paws of the bear at his drums.

Kibi was completely happy, still sitting on the couch but moving her body to the rhythm and melody. Her bracelet chimed.

Last song. Dance with all your heart! Memsala.

Kibi looked at Ilika.

He grinned at her, hopped up, and motioned toward the dance floor.

She was quickly on her feet, pranced in place for a moment to loosen her muscles, then followed Ilika to a clear space.

As Kibi found the rhythm with her feet, and began to express the feelings of the music with her arms and hands, she realized something. At the beginning of the dance, she didn't know what it meant to dance with other Nebador people on a star station. Now she was beginning to understand.

She wondered how Memsala knew.

* * *

The usual human method of being in charge of a large organization is to attempt to mold it, using political, economic, or brute-force power, into the form we want it to take. Beings of greater wisdom would, the author believes, be more accepting of the natures of those who worked for them. The need for play seems to be greater the closer a creature is to sapience. The original artwork on the cover is a glimpse of the evening party on Satamia Star Station.

The dipping sauce for the frogs' legs is symbolic once again (see chapter 10). At this point in Mati's journey, what does it represent?

Rini's and Mati's different opinions on the gender of the glowing purple being could have been a point of friction in their relationship. What did they do with the issue instead?

Why was Mati happy that Rini refused to go to the party?

A sheet of dried seaweed, a layer of sticky rice, then strips of veggies and fish – what are they making?

If you had two people telling you about an educational program, one who had complete it and one who had dropped out, would it affect your decision that only one of them was your "kind"?

How was Kibi's "load of guilt" about Toran Takil changed when she learned that nearly every female, and some males, responded to him the same way?

Although it's a taboo subject in many cultures, sexual relationships across species have always existed, both with humans, and among many non-human animals. These relationships are non-fertile, by definition, because "species" are defined as those creatures who are similar enough to engage in successful reproduction together. The wolf and the dog, for example, can reproduce together. The cat and the dog cannot. Some creatures blur the species-line, such as the horse and the donkey, who can mate and give birth to a healthy animal, the mule, that is not, itself, capable of reproduction.

All humans currently alive on Earth are the same species, Homo sapiens, and are capable of reproduction together. Also, we know from the fossil records that human varieties who have died out as a distinct group, such as Neanderthal Man, were also the same species, did at least occasionally mate with other human varieties, and their traits are now part of our genetic heritage.

Why did it help Kibi to relax when she saw Rini and Mati in the medical center?

How did Glorm, the docking controller, help Boro learn to dance?

In your experience, is a teacher better or worse when they can "see right through you"? Are other qualities about the teacher important in how you might experience this?

Many of our musical and literary themes would probably not be moving to people of another species. What quality did the themes of Sorrano's song have that allowed them to touch everyone in the room?

Our arms are probably the most expressive parts of our bodies when dancing, and so much effort goes into learning to use them in most dance traditions. Anyone who has taken ballet lessons has spent long hours practicing "port du bras."

What two factors caused Memsala to release Kibi when she did?

Chapter 16: The Link

To Rini's eyes, Mati had been more relaxed as she prepared to die on Sonmatia Seven.

She clutched at her dear friend constantly as Healer Dakalio and two helpers, both ursine, carefully prepared her for surgery. They got her comfortable on a strange bed that sensed when its shape was not just right, and changed without a word from patient or healer. They connected her blood to something Rini guessed was half creature, half machine.

Breakfast arrived. Rini received a tray, and Mati could feel the sugars and proteins enter her bloodstream directly. She grinned up at the love of her life as he chewed fruits and nuts.

Mati's bed tilted up and the entire lower half of her body was immersed in a clear, warm liquid. Surgeon K'stimla arrived, and several more helpers. Bird, reptile, and spider all greeted Mati and explained what they would be doing.

After the surgeon and her helpers arranged all the tools they would need, there came a moment of silence. It reminded Rini of star transit. Into the silence came a fuzzy purple ball that seemed to float down from the ceiling, then slowly swirl around Mati.

She giggled. "It tickles!"

Rini smiled just as the purple being came to him. He had only experienced his mind and soul touched so deeply once before — by Melorania.

When the fuzzy ball finished with Rini, it placed itself directly between the two young humans, one hoping with all her heart to walk again, the other craving to prove his love.

The mantid surgeon touched Mati's hand with one of her claws. "In a moment, Mati, you will sense that your companion is with you, and he will remain with you while you sleep and we fix your knee. Don't be surprised if you have some strange dreams."

A moment later Mati began to sense Rini's presence, as if they were snuggled together by a campfire whispering secrets to each other. "That's okay," she mumbled in a slurred voice. "I've always had strange . . ."

*

Mati's mind slept, but her body quivered on the edge of terror.

Rini's outer senses dulled as the purple being of light linked his mind with the sleeping girl. He felt her awareness slip away, and sensed the nervous tension throughout her body.

"Find her breath," K'stimla instructed. "Take charge of it and breathe as one."

Rini sensed the last shreds of Mati's willpower fade away just as they began to breathe in unison. As a test, he held his breath for a moment, and Mati also stopped breathing. Then she took a big breath when he did.

"Good. Find her heartbeat. It's faster than yours right now."

Even as he listened for Mati's pulse, Rini was surprised to discover he could control his own — a little slower or faster — just by thinking about it. He guessed he shouldn't go too far in either direction. Suddenly he heard Mati's heart in his mind, racing faster than his own. He tried to slow it by sheer force of will, but nothing happened.

A subtle smile appeared on his face.

Rini speeded his heartbeat until it matched the pulse of the girl beside him — dangerously fast, it seemed to him. Soon their hearts beat in unison. He willed both hearts to slow. Mati's heart followed his for a moment, then slipped away and sped up. Three times Rini had to let his heart return to a faster rhythm, then slowly and gently coax his beloved's heart slower.

"As you can see, Rini, that's more difficult. There, that's a good pulse. Now for the hardest part of all. Mati may be asleep, but she's still tense, and that's causing high blood pressure. Caress and massage every part of her body until she relaxes."

Rini had massaged Mati's arms and shoulders many times, and sometimes even her back, but never from the inside. Now he willed himself to explore every part of her sleeping form, to coax every muscle to melt under his soothing mental touch. He smiled when he came to parts that were different than his. He frowned when he sensed the broken bones and misshapen muscles around her knee.

"Good. Take your time. Blood pressure is coming down. Don't forget her feet."

Rini smiled as he mentally massaged Mati's feet, one at a time. He was surprised to find bone and muscle damage in the ankle of her good leg. He cringed, suddenly realizing that Mati was probably in pain whenever she walked anywhere. Without opening his eyes, he told K'stimla.

"Yes, we know about that, Rini, and will fix it, along with minor damage in several other joints."

Rini was happy that all of Mati's wounds would be healed. He continued to work his way through her body, coaxing each part to relax, some muscles requiring three or four passes.

"Good, Rini. Breathing is okay. Heartbeat a little slower, please – yes, that's good. The surgery will now begin."

✷

For the next hour, Rini felt dull sensations as the surgeon cut into Mati's knee and began moving pieces around. He kept watch over breath, heartbeat, and muscle tension, but the fuzzy purple being would no longer let him focus his attention on Mati's bad knee, and he guessed why.

"This is going well, Rini, and I'm putting Healer G'sonk in charge of the bone reconstruction while I start on the left ankle."

Rini kept his eyes closed, but sensed the spider begin work.

"A little stronger heart rhythm, please, Rini."

He smiled shyly, realizing he had let Mati's pulse get too slow. He matched his heartbeat to hers and slowly strengthened both.

✷

After another hour, K'stimla put the reptile to work on Mati's ankle and came back around to observe the spider's work. She spoke with Healer Dakalio about blood sugar levels, then suddenly noticed the frown of concentration on Rini's face.

"What's wrong, Rini?"

At first Rini thought he could take care of Mati's slow pulse himself, as he had done earlier. Now he was beginning to worry. "I . . . I've tried three times, and her heartbeat keeps slipping too low," he said without opening his eyes or ceasing his effort.

K'stimla looked at some displays. "Try again."

Rini concentrated once more, slowing his own heart to match, then using all his willpower to bring Mati's back to a strong, steady rhythm. "It starts to follow me, then slips away."

The surgeon spoke with Dakalio again, and he adjusted the nutrients going into Mati's blood while watching the displays. "Not responding . . . getting weaker," he reported.

She checked the progress of the spider and the reptile, saw no problems with either surgery site that should be causing Mati distress, and looked at her displays again while her mandibles twitched with worry.

"Rini, I think you'll have to go into Mati's mind. Something is causing her distress, and I can't find it anywhere else. This is more dangerous . . ."

"I'll do anything you need me to do."

K'stimla smiled as only a mantis can. The purple being seemed to glow a little brighter as it deepened the link between the two humans.

✷

As Rini willed himself to enter the mind of the sleeping girl, he was amazed by all the activity. Voices whispered, talked, laughed, or shouted. He glimpsed scenes from dozens of places around their kingdom, and a few from more recent months in the Manessa Kwi, as if someone was holding up pages from a picture book. Some scenes he recognized, but many he did not. Although nearly overwhelmed by the sights and sounds, Rini focused on looking for something, anything, that would cause Mati's heart to slow.

For what seemed like hours, he explored, searching for anything that could be the cause, but finding only noise and fragmented memories.

✷

K'stimla quickly assigned the bird to care for Rini, and without his knowledge, monitors were connected to his hands and nutrition added directly to his blood.

"He is strong, bok," the avian healer announced after studying the displays, "but has a difficult task ahead."

K'stimla nodded.

✷

What seemed like days, maybe weeks later, Rini found something that made him nearly cry out with relief. A single nerve pulsed with the same rhythm as Mati's heart, down to about half the speed of his own. Wasting no time, Rini followed the nerve deeper and deeper into Mati's mind.

The voices and other noises became louder, the flashes of visual memory more frequent, and both seemed to be from earlier in Mati's life. The mental spaces Rini traveled were tighter now, and he sensed he was slowing down, as if trying to push through dense bushes in a forest. He clenched his teeth and forced his way through, still following the pulse of Mati's heartbeat, desperately looking for the reason it was too slow.

✷

K'stimla worked quickly but calmly, talking with her helpers, watching their work, and beginning the minor surgery needed to repair Mati's right hip. Two ursines fetched anything the surgeons needed, while Dakalio monitored blood, breath, and nutrition. The spider announced the completion of Mati's new knee cap, and the reptile carefully re-attached leg muscles to ligaments and ligaments to ankle bone.

✷

Rini was drenched in sweat and trembling from the effort of exploring Mati's mind when he finally cried out, "A dark place! Cold and creepy. Very tangled. The slow heartbeat is coming from there."

Memory voices assaulted him constantly, all yelling or screaming to hurry up or work harder. Flashes of whips and sticks made him cringe, and he felt the pain as if he was receiving the blows himself. Mentally, he held up his hands and arms, protecting himself and Mati as best he could. "I can't get in there, it's too tangled! But I have to! Mati can't live with that pain!"

K'stimla looked at the purple being of light and they talked silently in her mind. After a minute, she nodded.

Rini, the purple spirit said to his mind, *if I deepen the link enough for you to enter that place in your beloved, your minds will be linked for the rest of your lives, and you will never be free of each other's thoughts and feelings. A link that deep drives some creatures insane. Humans are especially prone.*

Rini swallowed. *And if you don't?*

It appears that she will not survive the surgery.

I could not live, knowing I let that happen. Mati and I live together or we die together.

The glowing purple being quickly brightened, and Rini discovered he now had the power to dive into the deepest, darkest part of Mati's mind.

✷

He soon came upon a tangled bundle of nerves, glowing with a faint light from deep inside, but blackened, battered, and broken on the outside. Mean voices and heartless images hurled themselves at it constantly, and with every blow, another tiny part turned dark blue, cold, and icy.

"I found it," he whispered.

The avian at his side heard and repeated for the other healers.

No more! Rini mentally screamed.

The hurtful memories paused, laughed, and resumed their attack.

Suddenly Rini realized he couldn't fight this enemy with anger. He knew what he had to do. He took several slow, deep breaths, smiled, and moved forward, wrapping himself completely around the vulnerable part of Mati's mind.

Now there are two of us! he warned the voices and the painful memories.

✷

"Pulse is coming up," Dakalio announced.

K'stimla studied the display. "How's Rini?"

"Smiling. Heartbeat slow but getting stronger, bok."

The head surgeon breathed a deep sigh of relief and continued reconstructing the layers of muscle and ligament in Mati's right knee.

✷ ✷ ✷

Few of us today have had the experience of placing our lives in other people's hands, or having others place their lives in our hands. It is not something people chose to do, just for fun. It can have a huge impact on how much we trust other people in the future, both in general, and that type of person specifically (healers, in Mati's case).

Surgeons today dream about machines that can regulate breathing, heartbeat, and muscle tension during surgery, but those things are under the control of the patient's mind, so we can only attempt to influence them with drugs.

Why do you think the purple being would not let Rini focus his attention on Mati's bad knee after surgery began?

"Traumatic" experiences (such as slavery) are capable of doing permanent damage to the human mind, even twisting it into insanity. It is also possible

for people to go through the same traumatic experiences without any damage at all. Most people fall somewhere in between these extremes, deeply affected, but able to recover enough to go on with life. We can do little but guess at the differences between people that cause this wide range of reactions. Some possibilities:
- Having the will-power to survive and recover.
- Going through the experience with another.
- Having a trusted support-person during the recovery time.
- Being old enough to have already developed strong self-confidence.
- Having a personality temperament that is not highly-dependent on others for validation.

When Rini wrapped himself around the vulnerable place in Mati's mind and declared "Now there are two of us," how was that similar to Ilika's offer to Buna in the water room near the end of *Book One*? How was it different?

Chapter 17: Sharing

Sata noticed the pride in Boro's posture and smile as he guided her down ramps toward the sound of rushing water.

"The blue triangle means we're entering one of the wet ramps. We can walk carefully, or just . . ."

Sata had the idea, so she plopped down in the shallow water and found the bottom smooth and slippery. Just then, a high-pitched voice called from higher up the ramp. "Look out!"

Sata turned her head and saw a gray dolphin barreling down the ramp toward her. She quickly pushed with her hands to get moving.

Boro jumped and landed with his legs wide apart.

Sata slid under and was picking up speed, but the marine mammal was a split second behind, wiggling to slow itself, but still going twice Sata's speed.

"Eeeeek!" it shrieked as it collided with the female monkey mammal who didn't know that wet ramps were for *sliding down*, not *sitting on*.

Boro turned and watched helplessly as Sata and the dolphin tumbled together the rest of the way down to the river, with legs, fluke, arms, and flippers all tangled up.

When they finally splashed into deeper water, Sata quickly grabbed a tree root and coughed out the water she had inhaled. The dolphin began churning the water with its tail to stay in one place while looking at Sata.

Boro arrived at the water's edge, but remained silent.

As soon as Sata recovered enough to realize what had happened, she poured out sincere apologies. "I'm so sorry. It's all my fault. I'm just a stupid . . ."

The dolphin opened its snout and started laughing.

Sata grew quiet.

"Are you hurt?" the marine mammal asked between rounds of laughter.

"Um . . . no."

"Me neither. Wanna do it again?"

Boro threw his head back and howled with laughter.

✷

Trekila Spimalo was a fresh-water ecology specialist who traveled all over Nebador, helping star stations and planets to understand and correct imbalances in their water. She sensed the bond between Boro and Sata, who sat close together at the water's edge. With a gleam in her eyes, she told them about her own handsome lover, currently on a deep-space mission.

"Are there . . . deep-space response ships full of water?" Sata asked with wide eyes.

"Only half-full. We have to breathe, just like you!"

Sata chuckled.

"And sometimes we need to bring along an avian or a reptile, and once in a while . . ." she paused for dramatic effect, "a silly monkey mammal!"

Boro and Sata both laughed.

"Farewell, new friends! I must go taste the fish, then get some water samples!" Trekila Spimalo danced on her tail, then turned and dove into the tunnel that led to the underwater world of Satamia Star Station.

✷

Sata snuggled close to Boro, and smiled when he put his arm around her. She looked up at him with sparkling eyes and a glowing smile. Boro felt his heart pounding as their heads moved together and they shared a tender kiss.

"Yeah . . . okay . . . so . . ." Sata began when they parted, as if grabbing something solid after feeling dizzy. "I think I just learned something."

"About kissing?"

"No!" she said with a friendly frown. "About what Nebador people do when accidents happen. They laugh. They forgive each other, have fun, and make new friends. Right?"

"Um . . . yeah. Way different from our planet."

"I know. But we have to learn how to do it. At least . . . all but Rini, who already knows how."

Boro chuckled. "I think Rini was born smiling."

"Mati's gonna need all the smiles he can give her, today and for many days to come."

Boro nodded thoughtfully.

"Okay. I'm getting hungry. How do we go fishing in this place since we don't have long rows of sharp teeth like Trekila?"

Boro grinned.

✷

Sata only hesitated a moment before following Boro into the water tunnel. He watched from below to make sure she was comfortable with the deep water. For the next hour, they swam from air pocket to air pocket, exploring the underwater world below for as long as each breath would allow.

Sata was almost as strong in the water as Boro, and he enjoyed teaching her the rules about catching fish. With the ursine docking controller Glorm,

Boro had made a new friend, another male, quiet and strong like Boro himself. Swimming with Sata, Boro had a different experience, admiring her graceful strength and female curves whenever he was in a position to take a good look.

For that first hour, the fish eluded them, so they discussed tactics at each air pocket. Sata clearly intended to stay as long as it took to catch a fish. Boro was reminded of the many times they had worked together on a navigation problem on the Manessa Kwi, which sometimes took hours, and he smiled with happiness that they could also share other areas of life. Maybe someday, he pondered, they could share . . .

Suddenly a huge surge of water burst into their air pocket, and both of them held their breath while the wave passed. As soon as they could see, they recognized Kibi as she reached for a grab-bar, her dark hair plastered to her head. They had, however, never before seen a turtle with a head the size of a man's, and a shell more than a meter long. The giant sea turtle nodded a greeting while treading water.

To their surprise, Kibi just breathed deeply, but didn't try to say much. "Only get . . . eight seconds. Psychic . . . Development. Bye!"

At that moment, her bracelet chimed, she took one last breath, then slipped down into the water. The turtle followed.

Boro blinked. "Wow. Some kind of *serious* training."

"She found out Ilika's done it," Sata said, "but she started even before she knew that. Something happened that made her want to, or need to, commit herself to it, but she won't say what."

"I wonder if we should do it."

"First . . . maybe we should see if Kibi survives."

Boro chuckled. "Ready to try our new plan?"

"Yeah!"

✷

The fish easily avoided Sata, waving her arms, by darting around a large rock. One of them didn't see Boro hiding in the dim light behind the rock. He proudly carried the yellow fish, three-quarters of a meter long, up to an air pocket.

"Hurray!" Sata cheered when she surfaced.

Boro made sure the fish was dead before stashing it on a ledge near the fresh air outlet.

After breathing deeply for a minute, they went down again. This time Sata crouched behind the rock and Boro herded the next school of fish that came by.

Boro struggled with himself back at the air pocket when he saw the pink and silver beauty Sata held up, easily a full meter long.

✷

Back at the river bank, Boro was even quieter than usual, and Sata could sense that her dear friend was challenged by the situation. "Knife?" she requested.

Without a word, he pulled if from a pocket of his dry clothes and handed it to her.

She eyed the meaty fish before her, judged the halfway point between gills and tail, and hacked the fish into two pieces.

"What are you . . ." Boro started to ask.

Sata handed him half the pink and silver fish, and the knife. "We worked together, so we share."

Boro looked at her for another moment, found his smile, and set to work cutting the yellow fish into two equal parts.

* * *

If the "accident" with Sata and the dolphin is embodied in the saying "When life hands you lemons, make lemonade," what, in Sata's situation, was the "sugar"?

Trekila Spimalo's specialty, fresh-water ecology, is sorely lacking in our human knowledge. For thousands of years, we have been changing the courses of streams and rivers, draining or creating lakes, and filling estuaries (shallow wet-lands). Even though we sometimes gain a little short-term profit from these projects, the results have never been good in the long run, and in many cases result in the complete "death" of the ecosystem. In the USA, for half a century after World War II, we poured vast amounts of money and energy into "straightening" rivers. We now know we were doing the worst possible thing, and have started to spend more money and energy to undo some of that damage.

Boro's and Sata's fishing technique was a good example of how much easier it is to gather food as a team, instead of as a lone individual. This fact led to the creation of tribes and larger communities. It is the same thing the wolf experienced in *Book Two*.

But, as Boro learned, living and working in a community (even of just two people) often requires pride to be set aside in favor of the benefits of sharing. The creature who cannot master his or her pride must remain alone.

Chapter 18: Memsala

Kibi sat on the soft floor of the dimly-lit room, toweling her hair dry. "That was fun! Exhausting, but fun."

"I'm glad you liked it," Memsala said from nearby. "What did you learn?"

"Um . . . lots of things. That swimming in warm water is really . . . more than fun . . . deeply satisfying. Where I come from, all the water is bitter cold, except little hot springs."

Memsala nodded her head, a barely-seen silhouette.

"And . . . I was amazed how little I needed to breathe. For a while I thought I was going to die, then the buzzing in my head went away, and eight seconds at each air pocket was plenty."

"What did you sense around you?"

"Fish!" Kibi chuckled. "Mostly avoiding me, of course. Some of the underwater plants tickled. I saw four or five dolphin types, two beavers, and one ursine. Oh, yeah, two monkey mammals. They're on my crew."

"You missed the most important thing . . . or didn't recognize it."

Kibi let the towel drape over her slender shoulders and searched her mind. "I . . . can't think of anything else."

"Did you taste the water?"

Kibi laughed. "More than I wanted to!"

Memsala made a deep sound that might have been a chuckle. "Did it all taste the same?"

Kibi concentrated on the question. "I think . . . wait. There was one place . . . near that jumble of rocks that aren't really rocks . . . I have a vague memory that the water seemed a little . . . off."

"Off?"

Kibi scrunched her face to try to remember. "Almost like . . . the smell of fear. Can you taste fear underwater?"

Memsala's shadow nodded. "A small marine mammal, newly arrived on the station, was lost and afraid, hiding in the rocks."

Kibi frowned with guilt. "I'm sorry! Is it okay now?"

"Yes. I sent a message, and a member of its crew came. How is it that you sensed the fear, in a place where there is rarely any fear, and didn't respond?"

Kibi hugged her knees and buried her face for a long moment. "I . . . I guess I was thinking about Mati. She was in surgery all day."

"How much of the time were you thinking about Mati?"

"I don't know, maybe . . . half the time."

"So, dwelling upon someone who was surrounded by all the care she needed, caused you to miss someone alone and in distress."

Kibi started crying silently.

"I know this moment is painful, my dear Kibi. To learn humility, we must be humiliated, over and over again. There's no shortcut."

Kibi tried to speak, but her throat had trouble forming the words. ". . . better . . . next time."

"Breathe and center."

Kibi tried to collect herself by sitting up straight and steadying her breath.

"Let me ask you a question. While you're on duty as steward, do you spend half your time and attention checking the levels in your water tanks?"

Kibi tried to laugh, but only a cough came out. "Impossible! I have about a hundred things I have to keep my eyes on."

"By choosing Psychic Development, you have set foot on the path to becoming, in a sense, a steward of Nebador. Now you have a million things to keep your eyes on, not to mention your ears, nose, tongue, and intuition."

Kibi wiped the tears from her face with the towel. "I . . . don't suppose . . . I get a checklist . . ."

Memsala made her deep laughing sound again. "No. You have left that level of simplicity behind. However, your mind is quite capable of scanning the universe around you for those things that need your attention. Ilika Imni does it. Toran Takil leads some of the most challenging missions that flesh and blood creatures can handle."

Kibi breathed slowly, holding back a nearly-dizzy feeling as she pondered the huge responsibilities she had taken on by stepping onto Ilika's ship, and then into the Psychic Development program at Satamia Star Station.

Memsala pulled her head back into her shell and slipped into the shallow pool beside her.

* * *

"To learn humility, we must be humiliated, over and over again. There's no shortcut." This is almost a direct quote from Mother Teresa of Calcutta. Normally, we tend to think "humility" is good, but "humiliation" is bad. Mother Teresa reminded us that you can't achieve the goal without going through the learning process. She began her religious life at age twelve.

Pilots learn to "scan" the airspace around them, their instruments, and the condition of their aircraft, constantly looking for anything that needs their attention. The earlier they notice, the more time they have to fix it. Most of you will not become pilots, but you will become drivers, which is the same thing. You will have the choice of learning to scan, with eyes, ears, nose, and mind, or becoming the kind of driver the rest of us hope will hurry along to your next accident, far away from us!

Checklists are nice when you have lots of time, and pilots use them for pre-flight inspections and start-up procedures. But once you are flying (or driving), checklists get in the way, and you just have to memorize and internalize the many thing you must watch for to arrive safely at your destination.

Chapter 19: Dreams

Even though no one had made an official plan, the entire crew of the Manessa Kwi gathered at the medical center when the dinner hour, ship's time, approached. Rini was ready for them, and delighted when Sata handed him a container of raw fish slices.

Mati was still asleep in a recovery room, half her body in a healing tank, and would remain asleep until the following day. Rini already had a pot of vegetables steaming in the little kitchen attached to their sleeping room, and soon located a baking pan as he chatted with his crewmates.

"It was the most intense day of my life!" he declared as he sprinkled salt and spices over the fish. "I fell dead asleep as soon as the surgery was over, and dreamed about spiders with slave whips, and goatherds that turned into mantidae!"

Everyone laughed.

"Sounds like you got some images from Mati," Ilika speculated. "Maybe the link hadn't yet faded."

Rini suddenly looked guilty, and everyone noticed. "Well . . . um . . . Mati had some trouble, and I had to go way deeper than we planned. It's . . ."

"Permanent," Ilika finished with large eyes.

Rini cringed and nodded.

Ilika took a slow breath. "I hope you two are still happy with each other, because it would be very difficult to ever be close to anyone else."

Rini smiled and nodded as he poked at the vegetables with a fork. "These are done."

Sata hopped up and held plates as Rini served.

"So, did everything else go okay?" Ilika asked.

"Yeah, when I woke up, about an hour ago, K'stimla said everything went just as she expected. She'll be making adjustments, but she knew that. Mati's sleeping and dreaming."

"I bet she's dreaming about surgeons with green mandibles!" Boro speculated with a grin.

"Nope," Rini declared. "I know exactly what she's dreaming about. The purple guy said this is normal for a deep link. When only one of us is asleep, they'll dream what the other one is doing. Mati's dreaming she's cooking veggies and fish!"

Ilika smiled and the others snickered.

". . . except that things get exaggerated and distorted in dreams, so she might be dreaming about steamed pine trees or baked whales!"

Kibi laughed deeply and passed a plate to Ilika.

Boro and Sata talked about their fishing trip, and with a reassuring girl's arm around his back, Boro admitted he had to nurse a wounded ego after catching the smaller fish. That gave Kibi the courage to mention the lost marine mammal she had sensed, but failed to help.

Ilika's eyes sparkled with pride as he listened to his crew members. He was just about to share his day when five bracelets chimed at once.

They all looked and saw the same message.

"Rini, you are on-duty," Ilika declared, "but let me know if any more surgeries are scheduled."

The slender lad nodded and started grabbing empty plates as soon as each person inhaled the last few bites.

"Kibi is in command, and is cross-training with Rini during non-critical times. Also, Sata with Boro. I'm your pilot."

They all drained their cups and headed for the door.

*

Rini, his hair brushed back and his face glowing with power and masculine charm, picked up an entire pallet of heavy boxes, and without effort, strode into the ship.

A chicken came next, clucking and tapping at a mission bracelet on her left wing as she guided the next pallet.

Boro flexed his huge arm muscles, showing them off to Sata, who swiveled her sexy hips in response. When he tried to lift a pallet, he grunted and strained, but it wouldn't move. He kept trying until Rini strode back out, grabbed it with one hand, grinned, and re-entered the ship.

Finally, taller than all the rest, Ilika came behind cracking a whip as beams of light flashed from his green eyes. "Work! Faster! Don't forget that the square root of the semi-major axis is equal to the velocity of the anti-mass drive at inner navigation marker C near the liquid-gaseous boundary on Sonmatia Seven!"

All four crew members saluted and scurried to their stations.

"You're in command, Kibi!" Ilika boomed. "I want to play games on my knowledge pad."

The chicken clucked loudly, hopped into the command chair, and laid an egg.

✷

Mati startled awake.

An avian healer wandered over from another part of the quiet, dimly-lit recovery room. "Bok. Hello, Mati."

"Did K'stimla . . . did I . . ."

"The surgery was completely successful, bok," the bird explained as she studied the blood chemistry display, "although there will probably be minor adjustments during the next few weeks. Our bodies sometimes do not heal the way we want them to, bok. How do you feel?"

"Weird dreams."

"Would you like a knowledge pad, bok, so you can record them?"

Mati thought for a moment. "No, not those dreams."

The avian chuckled as she tapped at the blood console. "A very deep link with your partner was necessary to overcome some stressful memories, bok. You and he will have some work getting used to that link. We will help, of course. Hungry, bok? Thirsty?"

"Um . . . no. Sleepy."

"Good. I'm increasing your sleep medication slightly."

"Okay. Good ni . . ."

✷

Several hours later, Rini soundlessly stepped into the recovery room. The avian met him and guided him into an office where they could talk.

"She woke up for a few minutes, bok, and reported strange dreams, probably because of the link."

"That's funny, it was a very uneventful mission — two pallets to a mining camp on an asteroid. The steward was in command, and we didn't have any problems at all."

"You know how dreams can be, bok."

✷ ✷ ✷

You can have fun, if you'd like, analyzing Mati's dream. What does it reveal about her deep-seated (probably completely unconscious) feelings toward Ilika, Kibi, Boro, and Sata?

Chapter 20: The Scrub Brush

Sometime the following day, after half an hour of guided meditation, then a lecture by one of the avians on the Psychic Development staff, Kibi received her next assignment.

She stepped out the door into the quiet patio with its bubbling fountain, remembered Toran Takil, and wondered if he had also endured humiliating assignments. Somehow, it was difficult to imagine the big cat, or Ilika, the captain of a ship, doing what she was about to do.

She looked at the scrub brush in her right hand and the bucket of blue solvent in her left, and sighed.

With heavy feet, she dragged herself along the paths, ramps, and stairs that eventually brought her to a balcony overlooking the main hall of the star station. The Satamia sun flooded the room with light, and the large leaves of the great station tree reached out to catch the rays. With a look on her face close to a pout, Kibi realized it would be many, many hours, nearly three days by her reckoning, before the next evening dance party.

Kibi leaned over the balcony and looked at the huge floor below. She judged it to be about the size of the entire marketplace in the capital city of her kingdom. Again she sighed.

Creatures of all sorts came and went, or lounged on couches, perches, or in pools. She noticed a group of four reptiles whose bracelets all chimed at once, and they hurried away. Kibi could only guess what their mission might be. She glanced at her own bracelet and wondered if it would save her from the task at hand. “Dream on, Kibi,” she mumbled to herself. “You’re probably off-duty until the floor’s spotless.”

Her mind wandered back to her parting words with Memsala.

The whole floor? But . . . where should I start?

Start . . . in the middle.

Kibi looked over the balcony railing again. The middle of the huge room was the busiest part, with people going every which way, pallets of stuff floating by every few moments, and avians taking off and landing.

Kibi sighed once more, then pointed her feet in the direction of a downward ramp.

*

As she stood in the exact middle of the great room, bucket and brush in hand, many things came to mind that seemed better than getting down on her hands and knees and scrubbing the floor. Slavery. Death. Lots of things.

People passed by going in all directions. Some moved quickly while reading bracelet displays or knowledge pads. Others were more relaxed, surveying the available eating places.

She knew she didn't have to do it. Sorrano had quit. Probably many others. She could just march back up to the Psychic Development room and tell Memsala . . .

Two voices came out of her memory, and listening, she put off making a decision.

First, she heard Ilika. *Kibi, you have command of the Manessa Kwi.*

It was not the words themselves that touched her heart, but rather the feeling deep inside herself every time she heard them. As a slave, nothing she did mattered much. If she died in the middle of a job, the owner would just get another slave to do the same job.

But the Manessa Kwi was a deep-space response ship, the fastest ship in the universe, ready to go into the farthest reaches of the unknown. She had been on the star station long enough to know that most citizens of Nebador looked up to the Transport Service crews, and the majority of those citizens, for one reason or another, did jobs that were simpler and easier.

Then she heard another voice from the recent past.

The next time I look into your eyes, Kibi, I want to find an equal, a citizen of Nebador, strong and true.

Deep inside herself, Kibi looked forward to that day. She wanted to look into Toran Takil's eyes again, and know in her heart that she had earned her Nebador citizenship, the stewardship of the Manessa Kwi, and Ilika's loving touch.

She wasn't aware of it, but a look of determination was forming on her face. Without further thought, she knelt down and started scrubbing.

*

Rini was giddy with excitement when Mati finally awoke, and K'stimla had to give him a stern look. "She still needs lots of rest, and with your new link, she can't get that unless you relax too."

Rini smiled and took several deep breaths.

Once Mati was lifted out of the healing tank, the surgeon and two assistants examined all the surgery sites. "The skin is healing quickly, bok," one healer said.

K'stimla looked at the reptile.

"True," he said, "but the muscles will knit much more slowly. Nutrition is now extremely important."

The surgeon nodded. "You two are in charge of that. Be firm with Rini."

Both assistants nodded, and Rini blushed.

✷

Kibi's moment of willful determination quickly wore off. She didn't dare look around, but knew everyone was staring at her. She kept scrubbing.

She could almost feel their glaring eyes, burning holes in her back. She could easily imagine their thoughts, gossiping about the stupid monkey mammal scrubbing the floor in the middle of the busiest room on the star station. Tears started coming, but she continued scrubbing.

She kept her eyes on the floor, but could almost feel feet and claws getting ready to kick her or rip her clothes, maybe even her skin. She started crying freely, and her tears mingled with the blue solvent, but she didn't dare look up. She scrubbed harder and faster, hoping beyond hope that she could finish before they killed her.

✷

Mati's special bed was floated into their little room and placed beside Rini's bed. A tray with a strange variety of fruits and vegetables arrived, and Rini began feeding his beloved friend, telling her about recent events while she chewed. Between bites she shared what little she remembered since they had last spoken, including images from her strange dreams.

They soon discovered that when one or both of them were eating, they didn't have to cease sharing thoughts and feelings, as their mouths and ears were no longer necessary.

✷

Kibi nearly jumped out of her skin when the claw-like feet of a large spider appeared next to her. She steeled herself to be laughed at, poked, and bitten.

The arachnid raised two of its legs, and Kibi flinched, but at the same moment she noticed something on its feet. The spider plunged both legs, and the small scrub brushes they held, into the solvent bucket, then began scrubbing the floor where Kibi's work left off.

She began laughing and crying at the same time.

✷

About an hour after they finished the tray, the young couple was still chatting, sometimes silently, sometimes aloud. The avian healer came in and announced it was time to let Mati get some sleep.

The young couple agreed, and Rini got comfortable with a knowledge pad, his place marked in a book about the evolution of stars.

Even though no more spoken words were heard, giggles or chuckles slipped out every few minutes, and Rini made little progress in his book.

✷

Kibi finally found the courage to look.

All around her, creatures of every kind were arriving with scrub brushes. More buckets of solvent appeared. Some of the helpers worked alone, but she also spotted entire crews of six or eight of the same kind. Soon the clean spots on the floor were merging with each other and connecting with Kibi's own small area.

Kibi stretched up from her knees and beheld several birds setting out purple marker cones, then moving them as the work progressed.

She dried her face on her sleeves and plunged her brush into the bucket.

✷

An hour later, Mati's thoughts became sluggish. *Okay, I really am getting sleepy, so you have to take a nap too, or go find something to do.*

He kissed her on the lips. *I'm gonna read a little, then maybe take a nap too. Good night!*

Mati mumbled something, then let sleep take her.

✷

From her knees, Kibi met the captain of a passenger transport ship, an avian whose entire crew of twenty was skillfully moving the marker cones so people and pallets could get by while the scrubbing work continued.

She thanked the captain with bird-like bows of her head as she dipped her brush again.

All around her, more and more teams of helpers appeared, set to work, and quickly had marker cones keeping people off their sections of wet floor. Kibi estimated it would all be done in another quarter hour.

The next time she glanced up, something strange caught her eye. Not far away, a lone scrub brush appeared to be moving all by itself. Kibi blinked several times, but still saw no one pushing it. Then, on a hunch, she let herself shift into a meditative state of mind.

Slowly, she began to perceive the forest-green glow that hovered over the scrub brush.

"Thank you, Kerloran," she said softly.

Kibi heard no words of response, but had the impression that someone hugged her gently, just for a moment.

✷

The steward of the deep-space response ship Manessa Kwi scrubbed until every part of the floor was clean. Then she wandered around the huge room, thanking all her helpers, exchanging bows and kind words, receiving names and offers of friendship. As she wandered, she picked up marker cones when sections of floor were dry, and stacked them in the storeroom the avian captain showed her.

When she finally arrived, alone with her scrub brush and empty bucket, back in the Psychic Development room, Memsala was with another student, so Kibi sat and meditated.

Perhaps an hour later, Kibi felt the presence of the old and wise giant sea turtle. She took some grounding breaths and opened her eyes.

"So, my dear Kibi, what did you learn?"

* * *

If you were in Kibi's shoes, would you have been able to do what your teacher asked by getting down on your knees and scrubbing the floor? What qualities in your teacher would increase the chances of you doing it? What would decrease the chances? What other relationships in your life would help you make the decision?

If you had a telepathic link with someone, the ways in which communication would be easier are pretty obvious. In what ways would communication be more difficult?

What are the sources of Kibi's initial fears about what would happen while she scrubbed the floor?

What qualities does a meditative state of mind have (that would allow Kibi to see Kerloran) that her state of mind did NOT have when she first started scrubbing?

Why, in your opinion, did Kerloran help scrub the floor?

What did Kibi learn by scrubbing the floor of Satamia Star Station's main hall?

Chapter 21: Juggling Lessons

A new day, ship-time, brought the four who slept on the Manessa Kwi to the breakfast table in good spirits. Nothing was planned for that day, and Kibi had a day off from her classes. She and Sata giggled and schemed together at the table, and soon dashed off to explore parts of the star station they had not yet seen.

After doing dishes, Ilika had his nose in a knowledge pad and mumbled something about advanced training for captains.

Boro felt a little lost.

He busied himself for a few minutes by cleaning up his cabin, then started a load of laundry. When he could think of nothing else on the ship that needed his attention, he wandered out to the dock's waiting room, and from there up a ramp to the nearest main corridor.

A shaft of golden light streamed in from a crystal window at the far end, lighting up the balcony above where several birds stretched their necks into the warm rays. Above them, near the ceiling, large green leaves dangled from a gnarly limb of the great station tree to catch the light.

Boro took a slow breath and smiled, relaxing in the good feeling of being a part of this wonderful place, even though he still didn't completely understand it. He was the engineer of a little ship, and knew he still had much to learn, but had been doing it long enough to know it was within his ability. Someone needed the Manessa Kwi, and other ships, to do the things they did, and they provided food and all the other necessities of life to him, his shipmates, and the many others who worked on the star station.

The larger purpose of it all was still unknown to him, and he wasn't sure it mattered. The kingdom where he was born and raised didn't seem to have a larger purpose. People lived as best they could, accomplished a few things during their lives, or didn't, and it mattered little one way or the other. Yet the question hovered in the back of Boro's mind, not fully formed, but never completely fading away.

Always keep learning and growing. Many times, someone on the crew had asked what they needed to do to become citizens of Ilika's civilization, and had received that answer. Boro rolled the idea around in his head as he stretched his arms toward the ceiling, enjoying the warm light of the Satamia sun. Then he remembered questions he had put to his new friend Glorm, a bear who could think, work, and swim circles around him, and one of Glorm's answers stuck in his mind.

Boro spotted a knowledge processor on the wall across the corridor. At that moment a cargo pallet floated by, lightly loaded so that it's operator, a large cat-like creature, sat on the pallet instead of walking behind. Boro smiled, waited for it to pass, then strode across.

He opened his mouth to speak his request to the device, but became embarrassed. Although it took some concentration, he managed to enter his question into the key pad.

Juggling lessons?

A list of classes flashed onto the screen. Some were clearly for other species. Most required previous training. Then Boro spotted the one he wanted. *Beginning, any species, new students any time.*

With the touch of a key, the knowledge processor displayed a map to the class location. Boro studied it for a minute, thanked the device out loud, and wandered along the corridor, looking for a ramp to the upper levels.

He didn't see the small, fuzzy blue light that hovered near the knowledge processor.

The little patio Boro found at his destination contained a small, bubbling fountain. Beyond, a simple doorway was marked with a sign that said *Juggling Lessons*. Boro smiled.

Inside, an aged, gray-haired monkey greeted Boro while keeping three balls in constant motion with his hands and tail.

Boro's eyes grew large. "Um . . . I don't think I can do *that*!"

"Of course not," the monkey replied. "If you could, you wouldn't need lessons. Are you willing to learn?"

Boro remembered his captain's words. "Y . . . yes."

Boro's new teacher immediately tossed him a ball, which Boro caught.

"Hot potato!" the monkey said. "Pretend that if you hold it for more than a second, it will burn you!"

Boro quickly tossed it up. "When do I get to try three?"

"When you're good with two."

"When do I get two?"

"When you're . . ." The elderly monkey stopped and grinned.

"Let me guess," Boro began as he continued to toss one ball up and catch it, "when I'm good with one."

"You're learning already!"

Boro grinned as he continued to toss and catch.

"Your first lesson is to walk about the star station while tossing, with complete awareness of everything, and complete attention to all your responsibilities."

Boro continued tossing. "Doesn't sound too hard."

The monkey smiled, bowed, and disappeared into an inner room, leaving Boro alone with his one juggling ball.

"Complete awareness of everything, and complete attention to all my responsibilities," Boro mumbled to himself as he tossed the ball up, first in the patio with its bubbling fountain, then as he slowly walked along pathways, ramps, and balconies.

He thought he was doing very well, until he stumbled into a bench on the side of a path. His leg throbbed painfully, but seeing that he wasn't bleeding, he picked up the ball and resumed tossing. As he slowly limped along, he mumbled to himself, "Complete awareness of everything . . . complete awareness . . ."

The small blue light came silently behind.

To Boro's surprise, no one laughed at him, or even asked what he was doing. The next hour of wandering about the star station saw three more minor accidents. The stair step, planter, and tree root seemed to suffer no damage. Boro judged that his feet and legs, although painful, would heal.

The faint blue light that witnessed each accident did not express an opinion.

As lunchtime approached, Boro started wondering if it was possible to eat and toss at the same time. There were certainly plenty of eating places where he could grab a cup or a plate with one hand. Since it was his first day of juggling, he decided to play it safe, and got a nutrition drink in a closed cup with a straw.

Even so, the new activity split his attention into three parts — walking, tossing, and drinking, and soon another bench sent cup and ball flying. Boro caught the cup, and after hopping on one foot for a minute while remembering some strong words from his native language, he retrieved the ball from where it had rolled.

A quarter hour later, with a liquid lunch in his belly and the pain in his legs dulled by time, Boro was leaving his cup at one of the dishwashing windows when a reptilian voice from within caught his attention. "Hey monkey mammal, we could use some help in here if you're not busy."

Boro looked into the dishwashing room and saw the reptile, a lanky mammal he didn't recognize, and two birds, all working together to process huge stacks of dirty plates, bowls, and cups. "Um . . . I'm supposed to keep tossing this ball . . ."

The reptile made a slight growling sound. "Sorry. I thought you were a Nebador person."

The fuzzy light above and behind Boro said nothing.

Boro became red with shame, and suddenly remembered Sata talking about making bird-food baskets. He looked at the little ball he continued to toss into the air every few seconds, and also remembered his juggling teacher's words. *Complete attention to all your responsibilities.*

After another second of thought, he pocketed the ball and pointed his feet toward the door to the dishwashing room.

Within half an hour, Boro had learned the routine, shared names with his fellow workers, and had an invitation to go tree climbing with the strange lanky mammal, also an engineer. Many plates, bowls, and cups left the room clean, but almost as many dirty ones replaced them. Boro was completely enjoying the work and the companionship when his mission bracelet chimed, startling him.

"Hi Boro, it's Glorm! I'm at work in the docking control room, and there are no students here for the next hour. Want to come watch, listen, and learn?"

Boro's face lit up, and he half-turned to take a step toward the door. Then he saw the sad look on the bird's face on one side, trying to hand him scraped plates, and the disappointment in the lanky mammal's eyes, waiting for the plates Boro was supposed to spray. He shuffled his feet for a moment, moaned under his breath, and finally set his jaw. "I wish I could, Glorm, but I'm in the middle of something, and people are counting on me."

The blue light near the ceiling glowed a little brighter.

"No problem. We'll find a time soon. Gotta go, ship coming in!"

Boro returned to his work, and the next time he glanced at his co-workers, he was greeted with smiling eyes and respectful nods.

Nearly an hour later, the dishwashers were finally catching up with the dirty dishes. Boro's bracelet chimed again.

After reading the message, he touched the key for audio. "Ilika, could Sata cover my station? I'm doing some work I'd like to finish."

Ilika didn't get a chance to reply. The reptile in charge of the dishwashing room had been looking over Boro's shoulder. "No, Boro. Your primary work *always* has priority over helping out here and there. Go, go, go! And thank you!"

Boro verified to his captain that he was two minutes away, hung up his apron, and bowed to his new friends.

The engineer of the Manessa Kwi dashed along the balcony and down a ramp. Just as he emerged into a corridor, he was startled by an avian bursting through a cluster of leaves. It back-winged desperately, but was too close to the wall. Boro cringed as the beautiful bird smashed helplessly into the vertical surface, slid to the floor, and lay twitching and gasping.

Boro glanced at his bracelet for a fraction of a second, gathered the injured avian into his arms, and began striding toward the medical center.

On the way, Boro's bracelet chimed twice more, but he made no attempt to answer.

The elusive glowing light hurried along behind.

Two hours later, the unlucky bird was still in surgery, but was expected to be okay. Mati was asleep, and Rini was beside her, reading. The Manessa Kwi was long gone, and Boro used a knowledge processor to learn that his ship and partial crew would be back in about three hours.

He wandered slowly through the station, wondering what to do in the meantime. The dishwashing room contained a completely different crew that wasn't in need of help.

After strolling up a ramp, he happened to feel the juggling ball in his pocket. After tossing it up a few times, he realized he wasn't in the mood. But he felt like talking to someone, so he continued on up to the little patio with its bubbling fountain.

As he waited on a couch just inside the door, he tossed the ball some more, just to stay in practice. Soon the gray-haired monkey appeared. "How was your first day of juggling?"

"Well . . ." Boro admitted, "I didn't get much practice. Other things kept coming up."

The simian's lips curled into a smile, and he appeared to be holding in laughter. "From what I heard, your entire day was *filled* with juggling practice!"

Boro looked into the monkey's sparkling eyes, and after a long moment, chuckled aloud at himself.

The fuzzy ball near the ceiling faded from sight.

* * *

For many people, "food and all the other necessities of life" (in other words, a living wage) is enough to receive in exchange for their work. Some people need a "larger purpose." What do you need to feel good about your work?

In your opinion, does the society in which you live have a larger purpose? At this point in your understanding of Nebador, do you think it has a larger purpose?

How is the requirement to "always keep learning and growing" different from the requirements for adult functioning in your society?

In general, humans on Earth learn and grow rapidly from birth to about 20, with raw intelligence peaking at about 15 (not to be confused with the accumulation of information and wisdom that continues much longer). Because of this 0-20 learning phase, it has been discovered that an examination of the culture when a person is 10 years old tells a great deal about the person, as that is the exact mid-point of the primary "absorbing" phase of human life.

Since no one reacted negatively to Kibi scrubbing the floor, nor Boro tossing a ball up and down, what does this tell us about how often people in Nebador get these little "assignments"?

"Simian" is the collective name for monkeys and apes. It does not include humans, but that is mostly because we like to think of ourselves as separate from monkeys and apes, and not so much because we are different.

What did Boro learn about juggling during his first day of juggling practice? At what point in the day did he "catch the ball" most perfectly, in your opinion?

Chapter 22: On Her Own Two Feet

Mati began another day in the medical center of Satamia Star Station with her usual routine.

Rini noticed the Satamia sun getting low, and knew a day on the star station, about five of their own, was coming to an end.

Mati's breakfast of strange foods, some of which she had never seen before, made her long for a bowl of simple porridge. Rini looked at her with smiling eyes when she tried to hide a slice of bitter fruit under the rim of her plate. She laughed out loud, remembering that she could never again hide *anything* from this freckled boy.

After finally eating – or choking down – everything on her tray, Mati spent an hour in the healing tank as a reptilian coaxed her through all the exercises designed to strengthen her muscles and joints. Rini sat in a chair beside the tank, wearing his usual contented half-smile, silently sharing her frustrations of trying to make muscles work that had not practiced in a very long time.

When they were nearly finished, the mantid surgeon K'stimla arrived, with the human healer Dakalio and two avians close behind. As Mati was lifted from the tank, the healers peered at displays and talked. After Mati was comfortable on an examining table, all the healers gathered around and used sensitive instruments to look deeply into Mati's knees, ankles, and hips.

Rini noticed the smile K'stimla formed with the mandibles around her mouth.

"Mati," the surgeon began, "it's time for you to walk out the door."

*

For the next quarter hour, Mati was nearly in a state of panic. K'stimla talked about the low-gravity pathways throughout the station that would allow her to start at one-eighth what she was used to, and slowly work up to normal. The young pilot hid her feelings well – from everyone but Rini.

He knew she was back on the slave auction block, feeling the emotions she had experienced there many times, fearing and dreading what was about to happen, holding onto her only possession, her precious crutch, for dear life.

Rini wrapped himself mentally around the fear and dread in Mati's mind, and said aloud, "We'll bring your crutch along, in case you want it."

After a moment, Mati wrinkled her face in thought and took several deep breaths. "Um . . . that would be pretty silly. You'll be at my side, right?"

He nodded.

✷

Even though they would be living in the medical center for another week, Mati insisted they clean and tidy up the sleeping room before going out. She refused to do less than half the work, so it went very slowly. Lunchtime arrived before they got anywhere.

Rini had never seen Mati take so long eating a meal, but he smiled. She savored the fish, sipped the chalky nut milk, and carefully nibbled the bitter fruit.

After lunch, Mati insisted they send their dirty laundry to be done. Rini smiled. Mati was suddenly very particular about what was dirty and what wasn't. She held onto furniture with one hand as she moved slowly around the room, sniffing and examining things.

Soon it was mid-afternoon.

Rini looked at Mati, and for perhaps the first time in his life, he wasn't smiling. "Want to ask for an early dinner?"

She turned red. "I'm sorry. I want to laugh and cry. I want to curl up in a little ball and just let you hold me."

"You can do all those things. Anything else?"

Mati went to the door of the little apartment and looked out. The bright yellow walkway started right at their door, curved through the inner waiting room, and continued through the doorway that led to the outer reception room and the main hall of Satamia Star Station. As she looked, a feline healer walked through the room on his way to another sleeping room, and when he came to the yellow path, floated right over with one slow step.

Rini appeared beside Mati. "That's your path to freedom, and someday Nebador citizenship."

Mati swallowed and listened to her racing heart.

✷

As they stood looking through the open door, an avian came by with dinner menus for those patients who had choices. As Mati's diet was completely pre-planned, she was puzzled when the bird stopped at their door.

"No dinner for you two tonight, since there's a *feast* waiting outside, bok!"

Mati frowned as the avian healer moved on.

Rini stood patiently at her side.

A minute later, she carefully stretched her right foot over the yellow walkway. It felt light as a feather. She let it touch the yellow surface, and felt no discomfort. To her surprise, neither did it feel like the healing tank, where the zero gravity did not allow her any control at all.

Rini held her right hand and waited.

She leaned forward, and without breathing, let the weight of her body move over her right leg, something she hadn't done since early childhood, and had no memory of doing.

Nothing happened. Her knee did not collapse under her, and no pain shot through her leg. She looked at Rini and grinned.

After that, a step onto her left leg was nothing.

The second step onto her right leg was taken very slowly and carefully, and the third with a little more courage.

Suddenly Mati looked at Rini with shock. He was holding her right hand, but had not taken any of her weight.

Since he knew exactly what she was thinking, he responded even before she spoke. "I'll be there if you need me, but so far, you don't need me."

Mati's mouth opened in surprise, and she looked back toward their room. They were three steps from the door. Suddenly she giggled. "I just walked!"

Rini smiled.

✷

As each step toward the door became a little less timid than the one before, Mati formed a thought. *It doesn't really count until I can do it at full gravity.*

Rini pondered the notion for a moment. *Does only the last leg of a flight plan count?*

Mati chuckled with embarrassment as the door in front of them opened, allowing them to see the main reception room of the medical center. A few other creatures were sitting or perching, talking softly among themselves or reading. The bright yellow path continued across the room and through clear glass doors into the star station's main hall.

"I haven't been through those doors yet, Rini. Why is it so scary? I can pilot a starship. Why can't I just walk out there?"

Rini shrugged.

Mati took several more slow steps, and was half way across the reception room when she focused on the activity outside. Strong ursines were moving furniture and planters around, musicians carried or wheeled their instruments, and monkeys swung from branches as they hung glittery streamers and shimmering lights.

A bird looked up from a knowledge pad. "Party time! Just my luck to break a wing. A big, kind monkey mammal brought me in. I think his name was Boron."

Mati sparkled. "You mean Boro! He's our engineer. Rini's the watch, and I'm the pilot."

"Oh! You're the . . . never mind." The avian quickly went back to reading, or at least pretending to.

"I think . . ." Rini began. "Never mind."

A split second later, Mati read his thought. "You think? No! Look, it's a mess out there — they're still setting up."

"You're right. Couldn't be."

Mati knew he was lying.

✷

As soon as the last door opened to Rini's touch, a musician plunged furry fingers into his keyboard and brilliant chords sprang forth that stirred the heart of every creature in the room. It was also a pre-arranged signal.

What seemed like the leisurely process of setting up for the star station's evening party, suddenly changed. Within seconds, as Mati and Rini slowly made their way along the low-gravity walkway, many hands and claws quickly cleared the middle of the room.

The path ended in a yellow circle, and Mati smiled when she recognized K'stimla on one side of the circle. Then she spotted Ilika not far away.

People of all shapes and sizes lined the yellow path, and suddenly arms and claws stretched toward her with plates and trays of finger foods and small cups. Mati giggled with embarrassment.

Now I see why we don't get any dinner! Rini said silently. *If we eat one tiny piece of each thing, we'll be stuffed!*

Mati laughed aloud.

The music continued as the couple moved slowly along, sampling the foods and sipping the drinks. Everything was delicious, with none of the bitter fruits or chalky nuts Mati had bravely consumed since her surgery.

As they neared the yellow circle at the end of the path, Mati could see most of the healers who had cared for her, and near Ilika stood Kibi, Sata, and Boro. But for some reason, a large space at the very end remained empty, even though people were crowded several deep everywhere else.

Suddenly the air in that space began to shimmer, the shimmering began to whirl, and the whirling took shape. A beautiful lady in swirling blue gowns looked at Mati with ancient youthful eyes.

"Melorania!" Mati breathed with a grin.

The music stopped on a final pleasing chord and the room fell silent.

"Mati, dear Mati. You have followed a long and difficult path to finally arrive here in the main hall of Satamia Star Station, and you have arrived on your own two feet!"

Cheering and clapping filled the room. Mati glimpsed Sata wearing an understanding grin.

When the room fell silent again, the head of the Transport Service continued. "Citizens of Nebador, I present to you, Mati of Sonmatia Three, the pilot of the Manessa Kwi, who began her training by riding a barely-sapient, often-stubborn creature called a donkey, who could have bucked or kicked Mati to her death at any moment if they didn't share a strong bond of love and loyalty."

The cheering resumed, and the musicians added a flurry of notes and chords.

Reminded of Tera, Mati couldn't hold back tears. Rini held her hand tightly in case her knees got wobbly.

Melorania spoke again. "And after she and her ship-mates handled everything I threw at them . . ."

Many voices laughed or moaned with understanding.

"... Mati went on to become the only pilot in the last twenty years to perform her first star station approach and docking *without* station control!"

Everyone cheered. Mati turned red and her knees started wobbling. Rini wrapped his arms around her.

Melorania became a swirling blur, enveloped Mati and Rini for a moment, then shot away into the upper balconies of the main hall.

Two ursines quickly carried a couch into the low-gravity circle, and Rini lowered his beloved onto the cushions. They sat close together and looked around with amazement. In every direction, and above on balconies and landings, creatures of all sorts continued their preparations for an evening of food, drink, music, and dancing, as the Satamia sun slipped out of sight for another day.

Mati craved to dance, but her muscles were far from ready. Even though she stayed in the one-eighth gravity yellow zone, moved her feet slowly and carefully, and Rini held her hands constantly, she was exhausted a few minutes into the party, and asleep on the couch before the first hour had passed. Everyone else was just getting warmed up.

Boro and Glorm carried the couch, sleeping pilot and all, back to the medical center. When she felt a soft blanket cover her, Mati awoke just long enough to make Rini promise he would return to the dance party so she could at least dream about it.

And dream she did. Sata grew feathers, and soon blended in with the blue and green birds, both in appearance and dance skill. Boro tossed a huge ball, easily a meter across, high into the air as he danced or nibbled snacks, sometimes bouncing it off the crystal ceiling of the main hall. Ilika and Kibi swung each other around until only a blur remained.

Every female in the star station approached Rini, who glowed with masculine charm. They begged him to dance with them, but he refused them all.

* * *

When we have been dependent on something (or someone) for a very long time, it almost becomes a part of us. Letting go of it, or even contemplating the possibility of no longer needing it, can be frightening. Kibi felt the same thing in *Book One* when she removed her slave's rags for the last time.

If you were in Rini's shoes, would you have had the patience to wait for Mati to work up the courage to walk out the door?

In what sense did Mati begin her pilot training by riding Tera in *Books Two* and *Three?*

How did Sata grow feathers? Where did Boro get a juggling ball a meter across? What can we tell, at the end of the chapter, about how Mati feels about Rini?

Chapter 23: Meeting

"Is anyone bored?" Ilika asked when his entire crew had settled at the large table on the upper deck of the Manessa Kwi.

Sata, still in a blue and green skin-tight dance suit that made her look like a nimble-footed avian, and feel completely naked, grinned and shook her head.

"You were impressive last evening," Ilika said with admiration, "and I saw some green birds watching and learning from your movements."

Sata shrugged and ducked in a very bird-like manner, then blushed as only a monkey mammal can.

Kibi looked at her knowledge pad and sighed. "I learn to trim the station tree later today, while dangling from the ceiling on a rope!"

"That was hard for me," Ilika admitted. "Makes orbit excursions seem easy."

Boro pulled a small ball from his pocket and tossed it up a few times. "From the fish and salad place in Orange Hall, third balcony, to the ship, without dropping it or running into anything!"

Ilika smiled. "Someday, you'll get to do it with raw . . . oh, never mind."

Boro's eyes grew large.

Rini turned his knowledge pad for Ilika to see — a diagram showed the layers of a red giant star, Nebador type two, stage three.

Ilika smiled. "I'm glad you're making good use of Mati's recovery time."

"I've been looking up at the stars all my life," the freckled lad said with a smile. "Now I get to really know them."

"I'm learning about stars too, whether I like it or not," Mati announced with a mixture of humor and irritation. Then she glanced at Rini, and the irritation melted. "It's okay, I just wish my muscles would heal faster. K'stimla says I can go to one-half gravity tomorrow, *if* she likes what she sees at my exam this afternoon."

Ilika smiled at his pilot.

"I have a question," Sata suddenly said with a wrinkled brow.

Ilika looked at her.

"There are so many things going on — dance lessons, getting to know the station, helping out, visiting Mati, mission bracelets chiming — sometimes I don't know what I'm supposed to do first!"

Boro cleared his throat. "I think I can help."

The captain looked at his engineer with a knowing smile.

"Emergencies come first," Boro declared from recent experience, "and if it's personal, where *you're* the one who has to do something, then that's the most important kind of all . . ."

*

Mati and Rini took the long way back to the medical center. At four different knowledge processors, they looked at the possible low-gravity pathways, then took turns picking the most interesting route.

The last path they chose, promising to return them to the main hall and the medical center, passed a small theater-like area where a number of creatures sat or perched while peering into a large window.

Rini was curious, so he stepped to the nearest knowledge processor and asked for a brief explanation. The one-way window looked into a large cavern-like room that simulated the home planet of a unique species of sapient reptiles. The planet was no longer livable, and the three hundred reptiles within were the only remaining members of their kind. Efforts were underway to find them a new home, but a suitable planet had not yet been found.

While Rini read, Mati stood at the back of the theater and gazed into the rocky desert environment visible through the one-way window. The reptiles wore no clothes, but jewelry shimmered on their necks, arms, and tails. They spoke to each other in deep-throated rumbles and hisses, often shared affection, and sometimes got into fights. Mati's heart went out to them, and she craved to somehow help them.

Rini stood at her side until her legs began to tremble with exhaustion. He held her hand tightly as they made their way back to the medical center along the low-gravity pathway.

The small, fuzzy blue glow that had been following them went a different way.

"I can tell by your blood chemistry that you really pushed yourself today, Mati," K'stimla said during the exam.

"Yeah, we went exploring, but I stayed on the orange path. Rini almost had to carry me the last hundred meters, but I made it!"

K'stimla's mandibles twitched. "If you tear something, we'll have to start all over."

Mati turned white. "I'm sorry."

"I'll let you go to one-half gravity tomorrow, but I want you to rest tonight, get lots of sleep, and take shorter walks tomorrow. No more than a hundred meters, then rest and eat something."

"Okay."

"I'll make sure," Rini promised from a chair nearby.

Mati flashed him a momentary frown, then smiled.

* * *

If you were in the Nebador Services, based at Satamia Star Station, what would you want to do with your free time?

How did Boro suddenly know so much about setting priorities during emergencies?

What experience has Mati had that made her "heart go out to" the homeless desert reptiles?

Why would Mati flash Rini a momentary frown after he promised to make sure she took shorter walks in the future?

Chapter 24: Dance Troop

Sata couldn't stop smiling.

She had just been offered membership in a dance troop. True, it was all students, but two were blue and green birds with natural skill, and one, her assigned dance partner, was an agile green reptile, one of the super-friendly Quanasia. She was glad her dance partner was a reptile, and even more glad that he was married. She didn't want Boro to get jealous.

After practicing some steps, and arm or wings movements to go with them, their teacher, a blue bird who could dance circles around any of them, shooed them out the door. "Do not stop dancing until you arrive at Violet Hall, but always with complete awareness of your environment, and complete attention to your responsibilities!"

Once outside, the eight of them practiced their steps in a circle around the little bubbling fountain for a minute. Faint music came from the troop leader's mission collar, just loud enough to stir the blood.

Sata looked back at the simple doorway, marked *Dance Lessons*, and knew she had found another home.

A moment of sadness washed over her, and she lost the dance step as she remembered the sand dunes in the desert, the monastery in the mountains, the hot spring terraces, and most of all, her parents' inn. All of those places were home. She focused her attention and found the rhythm again.

As her troop wound its way along paths and ramps away from the patio, Sata smiled. The Manessa Kwi was more than her new home. Since it was a ship, it would always be near, and she could go there for safety and companionship any time she needed. Her gentle but firm captain would be there, and her dear friend Mati, who would soon be walking, maybe even dancing.

They pranced along a corridor, and passed a small theater of benches and perches that clustered around a large window. Sata was curious, but couldn't learn anymore while dancing.

Sata thought of quiet Rini, and was glad he was staying at Mati's side. When Kibi's smiling face appeared for a moment in her mind, she felt a deep respect for the steward and second-in-command, and looked forward to learning that job someday.

Warm, almost hot feelings welled up when she thought of Boro, who was now learning the basics of navigation. It wasn't easy and natural for him, but neither was she comfortable working with the many engines on the lower deck of their ship.

Suddenly a group of children, two small ursines and a young monkey, came dashing toward the troop. The bird in the lead formed a tunnel with his partner, and Sata and her reptile partner did the same. The children laughed and chittered as they ducked through.

Soon the green reptile's mission bracelet chimed. He waved and pranced away. A little later, one of the birds' mission collars sounded, and he found a clear space and took flight. Sata paired up with a colorful bird, and spent the rest of the time learning from her bold wing movements.

Finally arriving in Violet Hall, the leader danced them right through the door of a little eating place, then silenced the music from his collar. They stood together, listening to their strong hearts and looking into each other's happy eyes, then turned and looked over the food and beverage options.

Having seen them dance in, the large spider at the counter had six cold, fruity drinks ready before they even asked.

✷

After sharing a meal and saying farewell to her dance troop, Sata felt drawn back to the little theater and its window. The people watching and taking notes before had left, but others had taken their places. Sata slipped into a free spot on a bench.

The window looked into a large open space with a sandy floor, rock walls, and at least a hundred reptiles scattered about. Some just talked in small groups. Others exchanged pieces of jewelry after shaking claws about some business deal.

Sata smiled when she saw a large green reptile strutting and speaking in melodic tones to a smaller blue one. For a while the smaller one acted uninterested, but eventually her eyes sparkled and she walked beside the larger one toward a cave.

A little later, a lone reptile climbed onto a rock and began grumbling in a loud voice. Others gathered to listen. Soon his audience was nodding and pushing in closer.

Sata focused all her attention on the reptile giving the speech. Even though she couldn't understand a word, she knew from his gestures he was talking about their living space, and his audience was rumbling with anger.

Just then Sata's mission bracelet chimed, and her attention returned to the halls and balconies of Satamia Star Station. Those around her continued to take notes while watching the drama within. Using the tiny keys on her bracelet, Sata confirmed her status, and rose from the bench with a thoughtful frown.

* * *

A highly-social reptile might be very rare, as the reptilian brain, as we know it, does not include the cerebrum, the outer-most layer of the mammalian brain, where (it appears) most social functions originate.

Where have we heard before the phrase "complete awareness of your environment, and complete attention to your responsibilities"?

How many places do you have that feel like "home"? They don't have to be residences in the literal sense. Tree houses, secret places in the woods, cozy campsites, special cabins or hotels, the guest bedroom at grandma's house . . . all these and many others can feel like "home."

Why do you think there would be children in a "working civilization"? (Most businesses and corporations do not allow them.) Since the members of the Nebador Services are carefully selected, what would happen to star station children when they grew up?

While Sata watched the homeless reptiles through the one-way window, she saw commerce, romance, and politics. Can you spot each of these?

Chapter 25: Observation Tunnel

Mati stepped out of the examining room at the medical center onto a normal, full-gravity floor, and stood on her own two feet, steady and confident. She was greeted by her five fellow crew members, six or seven healers, and a handful of other well-wishers, including Glorm the docking controller and Drrrim-na the navigator. They were all clapping or stomping, smiling or calling in gleeful voices.

Mati turned red. "It doesn't count," she muttered. "There's still a long list of things I can't do."

Sata noticed that her friend was holding in a grin. "Dance?" the navigator inquired.

Mati looked at the knowledge pad she carried. "In about . . . thirty days, real Satamia days."

Sata bounced up and down, clapping.

Mati sighed. "I can't do *that* for almost a year!"

*

The entire crew helped Mati and Rini move their things back to the ship, then partook of a relaxing meal on a balcony overlooking the star station's main hall. When their plates were empty, Ilika announced a training experience that would help them understand something they had all glimpsed in passing.

After opening a heavy door on one side of a little-used corridor, the captain led his crew along a winding, dimly-lit tunnel. The walls were sometimes smooth and solid, at other places like the insides of hollowed-out boulders, and transparent.

At one point, Boro stood still for a moment, watching a green female lizard feed grubs to her scaly infant. If the tender morsel wiggled, she dangled it within reach until the child's tongue shot out. If the grub was limp and lifeless, she tossed it aside.

Sata waited for Boro to catch up, but soon found herself watching four large, blue males playing some kind of game in a small cave. At times, it seemed like a game of chance as they tossed bones onto the sand. At other times, it became a game of strength when two, after roaring about a roll of the bones, grabbed each other and wrestled for a minute.

As Kibi watched a lanky male caress a plump female, she felt Ilika at her side. "Are they mates?" she asked in a soft voice, fearing to disturb the intimate scene so close at hand.

"Yes. She's carrying three girls and one boy, and the birth rate is so low right now, they'll be carefully protected, probably spoiled."

Kibi smiled for a moment, then frowned. "They know it's not a real planet. I can tell."

"Yes, they know. They're very intelligent and sensitive. That's one reason the birth rate is so low."

Rini looked at everything with curious eyes. "You're sure they can't see us, Ilika?"

"It just looks like rocks on the outside. Light and sound only passes one way."

Mati moved slowly, with Rini or Sata always near. She looked and listened at each observation point, and often wore a frown.

*

The crew members of the Manessa Kwi observed public meetings in large caverns, tense with disagreement. Hushed business transactions in dark corners sometimes ended with bows and other gestures of respect, more often with a fight. Intimate encounters between males and females occasionally resulted in mating, but usually just snapping and hissing.

"Why are we seeing all this?" Mati suddenly barked. "It seems like . . . it's none of our business!"

Rini squeezed her hand.

"Training," Ilika replied after considering Mati's question. "This is one of the things we do. These noble creatures would be extinct right now, but for the efforts of the Nebador Services, guided by much greater knowledge and wisdom. To help them find a new home, we have to understand them."

Ilika watched until Mati nodded, then continued to lead them along the tunnel.

The captain and crew witnessed several more glimpses of the public and private lives of the homeless reptiles. Their temporary lodgings were nothing but a simulated desert environment on a star station orbiting a star called Satamia. The reptiles had no knowledge of that star, except as a point of light, like any other, in the night sky they once knew.

The frown soon returned to Mati's face.

A small blue glow followed at a distance.

After half an hour of walking along the tunnel, Ilika could see that his crew was tired and hungry. He didn't linger at the last few observation points, and walked right past a closed door.

Mati, at the end of the line, paused to read the words on the door. *Caution: simulated environment beyond.*

Sata waited for her friend at the next bend in the tunnel.

Mati stood at the door, frozen, her brow wrinkled with indecision.

"Mati!" Sata called. "The others are almost at the exit door! What are you doing?"

Mati hesitated one more second, then pushed on the door in front of her. She heard a soft beep, and felt the door move slightly at her push, but her new leg muscles began screaming at her. "Sata, help me!"

The navigator glanced along the tunnel, and saw Boro disappearing through the exit door into the star station corridor beyond. She looked back at her pilot, still trying to open the door with its words of warning. After one more breath, and a few quick strides, she was beside her friend. The door responded to Sata's greater strength and opened a little.

"That's enough," Mati declared, seeing sand and small rocks on the ground beyond the door. She quickly kicked at the ground until a pebble bounced onto the door sill. "I just want to give them a chance."

Sata's heart throbbed as she watched Mati ease the door most of the way closed, but could see by the yellow symbol that it had not latched.

When Sata and Mati finally arrived at the exit door, Boro was holding it for them. "What took you guys so long?"

"Just taking one last look," Mati replied with a smile.

Sata didn't dare open her mouth. As she stepped into the corridor, not far from the observation window with its benches and perches, she wondered how long her heart would continue to throb loudly in her chest.

Rini turned and looked at Mati. *I don't know if that will do them any good, but I'll always be at your side, no matter what.*

Mati smiled at him.

The fuzzy blue light remained in the tunnel near the door to the simulated environment.

* * *

After major surgery, every patient gets a list of things they can't do for a while, sometimes a long while. Some activities may never again be possible, as damaged muscles and connective tissues that have healed are never as strong or flexible as the original, undamaged ones. Mati's long recovery time before jumping comes from the author's own experience: it was jumping (les changements) that stopped him from ballet dancing after an accident (while skating).

In our world, with rare exceptions, pets, zoo animals, refugees, hospital patients, and other dependent persons, get little or no privacy, and are often not allowed to have the relationships that would occur in a natural environment. What justifications might there be for this? To what extent might this be unjustified?

What experiences in Mati's life probably caused her to want to "give them a chance"?

What do we know about Sata's personality that caused her to help Mati, but then feel guilty about it?

Why do you think the small blue light didn't close the door, or get someone who could?

Chapter 26: The Guard

"Tar'gn'ja has discovered a Rip in the fabric of the universe."

"An anomaly? A dis-continuity? Can't be!"

"It is. And you knew it was coming, just as I did. The stars have been wrong for months."

"Yes. Water does not flow like it should."

"Directional instincts have been off."

"Few females are mating. They sense something's wrong."

"It's as if our world ended, and we didn't notice, when we moved out of the collapsed cavern and into this one."

"Tell us about the Rip, Shun'gsh'ta!"

"Tar'gn'ja says a huge boulder floats, and he can move it with one claw. He only peeked beyond for a moment, then became frightened. He mutters about small, glowing eyes in the dark that do not move, but sometimes change color."

"Spirits?"

"Demons?"

"Maybe both, I don't know!"

"We must activate the Guard."

"The Guard? It has not been used in our lifetime!"

"It must be used now. I am one, as are you."

"True, but in name only. We know nothing of the old skills. After we destroyed our enemies, one and all, there was no purpose to the old training."

"There is purpose now. We must find out where we are, and how we can return to the world we knew. This . . . tear in the fabric of the universe . . . may be our only chance."

"I am with you, although I wish my grandfather was here to lead, or at least advise us."

"So do I, my friend. So do I."

✷

"There are seven of us," Shun'gsh'ta declared as he looked over his fellow reptiles.

Five males and one stout female looked back, all wearing the jewelry of the Guard, long an honorary order without training or duties.

"I cannot tell you what we will find when we go through the Rip."

"Is it another dimension?"

"A time portal that will take us to the past or future?"

"The demon-filled Underworld?"

"I don't know!" Shun'gsh'ta snapped. "It is the unknown. Are you willing to go, knowing that if even one of us returns alive, with information that will lead us back to the world we knew, it will be worth the sacrifice?"

Silence filled the cave for a long moment. The female was the first to raise a claw. After that, none of the males dared show cowardice, and six claws were quickly held aloft.

"I am proud of you. I, too, tremble at the thought of stepping through the Rip. My scales rattle and my claws shake. But we all know that something is wrong, deeply wrong, with our world. We must find out what before all the females refuse to mate and we are doomed."

The others nodded.

"Because we know nothing about what lies beyond, we are all scouts. Explore for an hour at the most, always marking the way. Return to tell your tale. I can say no more."

The seven members of the Guard, with their hearts in their throats, crept to the mysterious boulder that opened into . . . they knew not what. The others gasped as Shun'gsh'ta easily swung it open to reveal a dark tunnel going in two directions. They stared at the strange symbols on the other side of the floating boulder, but only shrugged.

Finally, not knowing what else to do, four of them went to the left and three to the right, trembling as they paused at each nook that offered any cover or protection.

Small blue presences followed in both directions.

✷ ✷ ✷

If you and your community were transported into a simulated environment in which everything, at a glance, looked right, what signs might you notice that you were no longer on Earth? What signs might you miss? Some possibilities:

- The orbiting of our moon causes ocean tides.
- Water circles a drain clockwise in the southern hemisphere, counter-clockwise in the northern hemisphere.
- Many plants and animals, in their life cycles, respond to the seasons of the year, and without those seasonal cues, their life cycles are disrupted.
- In most places, the prevailing winds are primarily caused by the rotation of the Earth. In the middle latitudes where the author lives (around 45° north

latitude), the prevailing wind is from the west, for example.

There are many honorary orders, offices, and institutions in our world that once had purpose, and have been continued out of respect for tradition, but whose members no longer receive any meaningful training, nor have any serious responsibilities. For example, there is an official "Poet Laureate" in the USA. Have you listened to his or her poems recently? Have they been on TV, or recited at school?

If you and your friends found a "rip in the fabric of the universe," would you explore it for fun? Would you explore it if the world was in a dangerous situation (war, energy crisis, economic depression) and needed help? If you were the leader of the expedition, what would you advise your friends to look for, or avoid?

Why do you think the small blue lights didn't do anything to stop the escaping retiles?

Chapter 27: Refugees

"That looks good," the spider declared, dangling from his own thread. "Let's go lower," he directed as he played out more silk.

Kibi glanced down at the floor of Blue Hall, twenty meters or more below, then closed her eyes to steady her stomach and nerves. Soon she heard and felt wing beats very close.

"You okay, Kibi?" the large bird asked, hovering nearby.

She forced her eyes open. "Yeah. As good as a monkey mammal can ever be, high in a tree."

"Your ancestors lived in trees, swinging from branch to branch."

"That was when we had tails! You want this basket of trimmings?"

"Yes, please, unless you want to eat it for lunch. They're very tasty."

"No thanks," she replied, pressing the release symbol as soon has the bird had his beak on the handle. "Already tried them, at Drrrim-na's suggestion, don't know why you like them."

The bird made a laughing sound in his throat as he backed away, then tucked his wings to dive toward the floor far below.

Kibi looked down, saw the spider waiting for her four meters lower, and wrapped her fingers around the rope controls. As she slid down to the next tangle of leaves and vines that needed trimming, she noticed unusual activity below.

An orange reptile dashed on all fours across the hall, looked around, and quickly disappeared behind a trunk of the station tree.

Three small bears ran into the hall and turned circles, clearly looking for something.

Kibi looked at the spider. "Should we help them? It looked like one of the homeless reptiles, and I saw where it went."

The spider looked back with hundreds of eyes. "Do you *know* the reptile is dangerous, and the ursines are doing the right thing?"

"Um . . . no . . . I just thought . . . I don't know . . ."

"Because it was *one* reptile and *three* ursines?" the spider asked pointedly. "Majority rules?"

Kibi looked embarrassed. "Is that . . . one of those monkey-mammal bad habits?"

The spider nodded. "However, you're probably right, in this case." He scanned the room again. Two young monkeys had joined the small bears, and four little birds landed soon after and began talking with the other five. "It looks like the children are taking care of it. If we're needed, we'll be called. Let's trim this tree."

A bird arrived with a basket, Kibi clipped it to her line, and pulled a pruning tool from her vest.

*

Rini was spraying dirty dishes when a reptilian claw suddenly reached into the dishwashing room and grabbed a piece of food someone had left on a plate. Rini blinked in surprise, but his jaw dropped when a half-dozen young birds swooped into the room and swarmed around the fleeing reptile, who dove under a bench.

Still in his apron, Rini dashed out of the dishwashing room, ran to the bench, and jumped on top. "Stop it! He's alone and afraid!"

The birds settled onto the floor and ducked their heads in shame.

At that moment, a deep-green glow began to form nearby, took on more substance as seconds passed, and quickly became a green reptile with leaves twined around his head and neck.

Rini had never seen this exact shape before, but somehow knew who it was, and had a good idea why he was taking the form of a reptile. "Kerloran . . ." he whispered.

Thank you, Rini, the master of Satamia Star Station said directly to Rini's mind. *They are young, lacking in wisdom, and hopefully will remember what you just taught them. I will take this poor fellow back to a place he understands.*

Even before he finished communicating with Rini, the majestic green reptile gathered the trembling run-away into his arms and floated toward the simulated desert environment.

*

Boro and three fanators, with lots of help from others with time to spare, were coming to the end of scrubbing the blue-green floor of Cyan Hall, when a gray reptile burst from a corridor with three young ursines right on its tail.

Boro stood up to take in the situation, just as the bears succeeded in cornering the frightened lizard. He immediately saw the danger. "No! Be careful!"

Before anyone could heed his warning, a spiked tail flashed out, the bear children went flying, and blood splattered everywhere. Boro wasted no more time, ran and dove, and a second later had his strong arms and legs wrapped around the cornered creature. He felt his own skin pierced in several places by scales and horns, but nothing he couldn't handle.

Boro could hear the fanators helping the injured ursines, but could see nothing, and didn't dare allow the reptile to gain any distance and use its claws or tail.

The reptile tried to wiggle free, but had no success. After a long minute of effort, it began to relax.

Several minutes later, as Boro continued to hold the lizard tightly, he heard a voice in his mind. *You're very lucky that's a female. The males are much stronger. Thank you, Boro, I'm ready to take her back now.*

A green mist formed around them, and the reptile went completely limp. Boro, with some hesitation, released his grip. The mist-enshrouded lizard floated away, and Boro found himself sitting on the floor in a small pool of something red. A moment later, a large spider arrived and opened a medical kit.

✷

Sata and Mati sat nervously in the waiting room of the medical center, wondering why they had both been called in. They soon discovered why no one had time to talk to them.

A stream of injured creatures, of all kinds, began arriving — ursines and felines, avians and reptiles, monkeys and spiders. Both girls quickly noticed that most of the injured were children, but had no idea why.

A little later, four more stretchers came in the door. The first two held small bears with minor injuries. Both looked sad, but occasionally exchanged words with their attendants.

The third stretcher brought Mati and Sata to their feet. It came slowly, without urgency, a cloth covering the victim. From the shape, and an uncovered paw, they knew an ursine child was beyond help.

The next stretcher kept them on their feet.

Boro looked out from under a blanket, and when he saw them, quickly said, "I'm okay, just some little cuts and scrapes."

When all four stretchers had passed into the medical center, Mati and Sata tried to relax, but had no hope that anyone would have time to see them, or even tell them why they were there.

✷

Even before the stream of injured creatures were all treated, Ilika and Kibi received a call to a special meeting.

Melorania glowed a bright blue. *I hope you are comfortable enough with Nebador now, Kibi, that I don't need to bother with a material form.*

Kibi swallowed, then nodded.

Many people were tested by the situation that arose today. Of the young ones that Kerloran asked to help, most of them learned some valuable lessons, and they all dealt with the death of one of their fellows.

Feelings twisted Kibi's face for a long moment, but she eventually took several deep breaths. Ilika held her hand.

Rini and Boro helped, and even though they both responded well, they have much to learn about dealing with frightened, confused mortal creatures.

Ilika nodded.

After a few days of healing, we must take your pilot and your navigator from you for a time. I have high hopes that both will survive the project, and return to you stronger and wiser.

"I . . . hope so too," Ilika whispered.

Melorania faded and disappeared.

Kibi squeezed Ilika's hand. "What kind of . . . project . . . was she talking about?"

Ilika took a slow breath. "I'm . . . not sure."

* * *

Some, but not all, of our possible ancestors were tree-dwellers. Others lived in the forest, but primarily on the forest floor or in low branches. Still others roamed the grasslands where few large trees grew, but even a stout bush could be a life-saver when a meat-eating predator came by. Even those of us who are least comfortable in trees, and struggle to pull ourselves onto the first branches, can make some use of our primate ancestry, whereas to hoofed animals like deer and goats, trees are completely useless.

Why would a human have a greater tendency to consider numbers (as in "majority rules"), when evaluating a situation, than a spider?

What obvious information did Rini choose to NOT take into account when he protected the frightened reptile from the pursuing birds?

What could have happened if Boro had tried to hold the reptile at arm's length, instead of in a "bear hug"?

Why were Mati and Sata called to the medical center?

What do we learn about Melorania's nature when she doesn't "bother" to take on a material form when talking to Ilika and Kibi?

What kind of civilization would ask children to help with a dangerous situation that got one of them killed? Before you answer with a late-20th/early-21st century American/European value, it may be useful to stop and remember that in our human world, for most of our history, in most places, children were afforded no special protection, and the loss of a few here and there was of no concern to anyone but their parents.

Chapter 28: In Trouble

For the next day and a half, Satamia time, things seemed to return to normal. The many injured children, and a few adults, including Boro, were treated in the medical center and returned to their lives. The entire crew of the Manessa Kwi attended the memorial service for the young ursine who had not survived her encounter with a full-grown, cornered, frightened reptile.

✷

At the end of that long Satamia day, the evening party featured many excellent musicians, including a reptilian singer who chanted a lament for the deceased ursine that brought tears to many eyes, and other signs of sorrow to those without tears. But before it ended, the song changed into a spirited celebration of life that had nearly everyone dancing with joy.

Mati, of course, had to mostly watch, and she found she had lots of company. A transport ship from a far-away star system was in the station, a variety of creatures she had never before imagined. Most of the music and dancing was strange to the new arrivals, so they stayed on the edges of the main hall, and talked with whoever was available.

Mati learned they were students, and had come to observe something called the Great Transformation. She admitted she knew nothing about it, that she was just a simple response ship pilot.

To her surprise, the students' eyes opened wide and they begged her to tell them of her adventures. Soon she had twenty or more creatures gathered around her couch, about half of them floating in the air nearby. They listened intently as she recounted the time she accidentally backed into a ruined building that collapsed onto the ship, and how she eventually got it out.

Rini came and went, bringing his beloved what she mentally requested from the snack tables. Sata, Boro, Kibi, and Ilika stopped by less often, and smiled when they heard Mati tell of planets they had explored, places on her home world they had seen, and even locations visited on donkey-back.

Some of the students sensed the deep mind-link that she and Rini shared, and when Mati ran out of stories, they begged Rini to tell them how it came about. He was not as comfortable talking to other people as Mati, but satisfied their curiosity.

*

During the five days, ship time, between that evening party and the next, life for the crew of the Manessa Kwi seemed to return to normal.

Ilika and Kibi had several meetings they had to attend, and said little about what went on at those meetings, but were almost always on the ship for the minor missions that came up. Twice Kibi was deep into tasks assigned by the Psychic Development program, so Ilika marked her off-duty, and covered her station. Once, for the first time, Kibi commanded a short supply run without Ilika on the ship. She was very glad she had her pilot back on duty.

Boro finally got to spend time observing Glorm as he directed station traffic, and was amazed at the responsibilities of the job, but could almost see himself doing it someday. Almost.

Sata requested another fishing trip, and this time they invited Glorm, who got the biggest fish. Boro's and Sata's were so close that they declared it a tie.

Sata danced whenever she could, but spent almost no time with Mati during that station-day, except during missions.

Mati knew why.

What she had done in the observation tunnel of the simulated desert environment, and the events that followed, gnawed at her. She could now see that it may have damaged her friendship with Sata. She had asked her friend to help with something that had gotten one child killed and many others injured. It had not, as far as she could tell, done anyone any good. She remembered Rini predicting as much. She thanked the stars every day and every night that her actions had not caused any bad feelings with him. He seemed to accept her completely, even when she did stupid things.

Although no one seemed to openly blame her, she had a hunch, deep down inside, that it would someday come back to haunt her.

*

The next evening dance party began like any other. Decorations appeared, musicians and dancers warmed up, and food and drink came in from every kitchen.

But before the first song began, Melorania and Kerloran appeared, gathered form, and settled onto the floor in the middle of the main hall of Satamia Star Station. She wore a swirling blue gown that never completely ceased its motion, and he was covered with green scales and leaves.

More than a thousand Nebador citizens fell silent and looked at them with great respect. Most of those citizens sensed that something special was about to take place. The students from other star systems, seven transport-ships-full by this time, although still a bit timid, hovered in the air or slithered up walls so they could see.

When all was quiet, Kerloran spoke. "Mati and Sata, please come forward."

A moment of panic brought tears to Mati's eyes as she desperately looked around for her crutch. Rini sensed that if she found it, she would not use it to approach Kerloran, but instead to hobble away and hide in the deepest, darkest corner she could find.

Sata stood nearby, waiting for her friend to collect herself. She could feel her own body trembling, but had known this moment would come. She just wished it didn't have to be in front of everyone.

Eventually Mati remembered that her crutch was on the Manessa Kwi, under her bed. She looked down and saw her two good legs. Embarrassed chuckles began to mix with her tears.

Kerloran and Melorania waited patiently.

Mati and Sata looked at each other.

Sata knew, from the pathetic look on Mati's face, that Mati was deeply sorry for dragging her friend into this mess. Sata smiled slightly, and offered her hand to the friend whose fate had been intertwined with her own ever since they met.

Hand in hand, on shaking legs, they crossed the open floor toward the mysterious head of the Transport Service and the master of the star station. Both seemed to tower over the two girls.

"Most civilizations," Melorania began for all to hear, "would put you in prison for what you did, possibly execute you."

Two pairs of eyes dropped toward the floor. Four other response-ship crew members felt their hearts jump into their throats. Few others, anywhere in the star station hall, were breathing.

"But this is Nebador," Kerloran continued. "We do things a bit differently here."

Sata squeezed Mati's hand, and a tiny bit of hope entered both girls' hearts.

"We realized that we were being handed an opportunity that would be hard to arrange — perhaps even hard to imagine — if it had not happened as it did." He looked up and spoke to the entire room. "Yes, I assure you all, there is greater knowledge and wisdom elsewhere in the universe, and some things remain hidden, at least for a while, even from us."

A faint chuckling sound rippled through the star station.

"Mati and Sata," Melorania began, "you both acted out of love. Mati craves to share the freedom she now enjoys with all other creatures, and Sata has a deep need to prove herself to her fellow crew members, especially to Mati. You had the courage to put your necks on the line for a handful of homeless reptiles. Now I must ask you a very important question. Do you, or do you not, also have the courage to do what it takes to fully understand them, so you can help in the search for their new home, and possibly succeed where others have failed? In other words, do you have the courage to finish what you started?"

Mati and Sata tried to breathe, but it was not easy under the circumstances. Eventually they got some air into their lungs, but had to struggle for another long moment to swallow and clear their throats.

Mati knew in her heart she was more responsible for what happened than Sata. "It's . . ." She struggled to make her voice work. "It's . . . all my fault . . . and I want to take . . . the punishment for Sata. Someone died . . . because of me . . . and I don't deserve . . . to be a pilot . . . anymore."

Kerloran let the silence lengthen, then smiled. "You are very new here, my dear little monkey mammal. I will not attempt to teach you a lifetime of wisdom right here and now, as all these precious citizens want to dance and play."

More chuckles coursed through the huge room.

"But I will tell you three things very firmly."

Mati swallowed and tried to look at the majestic green master of Satamia Star Station, but the sight almost hurt her eyes.

"First of all, your friend Sata is responsible for herself, and you cannot take that away from her."

Sata cringed and nodded at the same time.

"Second, mortals do not get to decide what they deserve or don't deserve. You do not have that perspective, and you would not want that responsibility, believe me."

Mati swallowed and blinked, but could not think of anything worth saying.

"Third, death is not the tragedy you have come to assume. Nothing real and enduring was lost. In fact, much was gained, and much more may still be gained."

Melorania spoke next. "But you *do* have the responsibility to answer the question. Are you willing to do all it takes to understand the homeless creatures that we hold in the palms of our hands?"

"I . . ." Mati forced herself to begin. "I . . . have a hunch . . . that if I don't . . . I'm in big trouble."

"That's correct," Kerloran said firmly, leaving no doubt.

"Um . . . what would I . . . have to do?"

"I believe you would say something like, *walk in their shoes for a time.* They don't wear shoes, but the meaning applies."

"You mean . . . live with them? I don't think they like monkey mammals."

"You are right, they do not," Melorania replied, "especially after their recent experience."

Sata thought she heard Boro laugh somewhere behind her.

"But you would not live with them in the shape of humans," Melorania continued. "You would take *their* shape. That is the only way they would accept you enough to show you their true needs and desires."

Mati looked at Sata, still holding her hand.

"We have to," Sata whispered.

"I know," Mati whispered back.

Suddenly Rini was at Mati's side, looking up at Melorania and Kerloran, but he said nothing aloud.

"I see your concern," Kerloran said, looking at the freckled lad. "Yes, they will be females, and yes, they will be expected, by the other reptiles, to mate. If we accept your offer to accompany Mati, you must understand that you may have to fight off other males."

"I understand," Rini said for all to hear.

Suddenly Boro was beside Sata.

"Yes, Boro, you can go too," Melorania said with a smile.

Ilika and Kibi, near the back of the room, looked at each other with wide eyes.

* * *

What sort of creature would "float in the air" while listening to Mati's stories? What creatures on Earth can "slither up walls"?

When called before Melorania and Kerloran, what did Sata communicate to Mati by offering her hand?

Some people think the universe is a giant machine, and all future events can be predicted. Others say the universe contains random, unpredictable events. When Kerloran admitted that "some things remain hidden, at least for a while, even from us," which view of the universe is he implying?

When humans judge a "criminal," we usually dispense punishment, sometimes with a little rehabilitation or education thrown in. What are Melorania and Kerloran doing instead?

How do each of Kerloran's statements fit into your values, the laws of your society, or the teachings of your religion?

- First of all, your friend Sata is responsible for herself, and you cannot take that away from her.
- Second, mortals do not get to decide what they deserve or don't deserve. You do not have that perspective, and you would not want that responsibility, believe me.
- Third, death is not the tragedy you have come to assume. Nothing real and enduring was lost. In fact, much was gained, and much more may still be gained.

The idea of learning by taking the form of another creature has appeared in stories all through history, with some of the most well-known coming from the Arthurian tales of Merlin the magician.

When Rini and Boro offered to go with Mati and Sata, what effects might it have on their relationships?

Chapter 29: Briefing

Melorania and Kerloran soon shooed the four humans away so the party could begin. The four wandered into a secluded corner, found an unused couch, and huddled together to try to figure out what they had just gotten themselves into.

Kibi started to move in that direction, but Ilika grabbed her hand. "I think they need some time without us. This will be *their* mission, and you and I don't have a part to play, as far as I can see. If I'm wrong, someone will let us know."

Kibi was torn, but eventually nodded. A lively song began, and her feet started moving almost by themselves, so she grinned and pulled Ilika toward the dance floor.

*

"I am so sorry . . ." Mati began.

Rini gave her the sternest look he could muster. "Didn't you hear what they said? They are *glad* it happened. It gave them some . . . you know . . . volunteers . . . for something nobody else wanted to do."

"Yeah, but you and Boro will have to fight off a bunch of horny reptiles, with scales and claws, trying to get into Sata's and my pants! Except . . ." she continued thoughtfully, "we won't have pants . . ."

Boro laughed. "But *we* will have scales and claws, too!"

Sata nodded and smiled, and got the impression that Boro was looking forward to the experience.

*

By morning, they had the schedule.

For the next Satamia day, the four volunteers would be in meetings, briefings, classes, and training sessions almost constantly. They looked for times they could eat and sleep, and found only breaks for snacks or short naps.

Ilika and Kibi were only invited to the first meeting.

A large white feline leapt onto a table at the front of the conference room. "I am Silmula Sorafax. Although this is not something we do often, I have as much experience in these matters as any mortal in Satamia. I have been placed in charge of this mission, although you must understand that I will remain on the outside, and not join you for the Great Transformation."

Mati had heard that term somewhere before, just recently, but couldn't remember where.

"As you may guess from your schedules, the four of you are off-duty concerning your ship, and all other training and activities, until this mission is completed. Please note that, captain."

Ilika nodded.

Boro raised his hand. "We have the . . . pre-mission schedule . . . but we were wondering how long the . . . um . . . transformation will last."

The big cat was silent for a moment and seemed to almost smile. "As I understand it, a year would do you good."

The four fellow crew members in the front row, currently off-duty, swallowed hard.

"But since there is some urgency in figuring out where we can resettle those beautiful reptiles, and since good response-ship crews don't grow on trees, I'm thinking that about twenty days might do the trick."

Sata could almost see Boro doing the math in his head, then realizing, with wide eyes, how long twenty Satamia days would be.

"But the length will also depend on you four. This is not a vacation. You will be in there for a purpose, and to atone for what, as Melorania said, could easily be considered a crime."

Mati nodded, and mentally heard Rini's assurance that they would be together, no matter what.

*

After several hours of basic information, Ilika, Kibi, and a few others departed. The meal break was so short, it was served from a cart by a large furry ape whose nimble hands quickly assembled trays for each species.

The hundred or more students in the back of the room gathered into groups where they were comfortable, introduced themselves to each other, and chatted about the fascinating adventure they were witnessing.

Silmula Sorafax and about a dozen other advisors and teachers took a large table and talked as they ate. Even though the group included four reptiles, they could offer little insight into the situation that the large cat did not already know. Avians, ursines, a four-legged equine, and two humans completed the team.

Boro glanced at the two monkey mammals. "I wonder why we've never met them before."

Sata, holding his hand, shrugged. "Maybe they came in one of those ships that brought students. Come on, I have . . . something I want to say."

They grabbed a tray, saw that Mati and Rini were already huddled together, and picked a small table in a corner.

As soon as they sat down, Sata scooted her chair close to Boro, put her arms around his neck, and began the deepest, longest kiss he had ever received.

"Wow . . ." he began when she finally, reluctantly, let a little space come between them. "I guess I did . . . something right," he went on with a shy smile.

She grinned at him with smoldering eyes. "You certainly did! And I've been aching to get some time alone with you to tell you. I'd like to do *more* than tell you . . ."

Boro looked embarrassed. "Um . . . we've got less than a quarter hour, AND we have to inhale this food."

"It's very simple," she continued. "When you stepped up and agreed to go in there with me, I *knew* I was going to be yours, and only yours, whether we're reptiles, monkey mammals, or anything else . . ."

*

It seemed to Mati that a thousand different people had a million thoughts about the homeless reptiles, and she and her friends were going to have to sit through every minute of it.

Luckily, Silmula Sorafax was very skilled at breaking up the presentations, leaving time for questions, demonstrations, toilet breaks, snacks, and even little games and dances.

Even so, after about six hours, Mati was asleep on a couch, with Boro not far behind on another couch. The large white cat seemed to have anticipated this, and lessons and discussions continued as long as any two of the four humans were awake.

*

Rini awoke from a short nap to find Mati munching on fruit slices and nuts. She formed thoughts while chewing. *Hi. I saved you some.*

The slender boy sat up and yawned. *Did the equine ever quit talking about safety protocols? His deep voice put me right to sleep.*

Mati smiled. *Yeah. He became embarrassed when Boro and Sata both joined you in dreamland. But then Sata woke up, so we listened to a bird who's learned a bit of the reptiles' language.*

It's weird that none of the Nebador reptiles can speak it, Rini shared while eating.

They say it's mostly genetic. The homeless reptiles are born speaking it, and it's not like anything they've ever heard.

I was awake then. Did you hear that spider saying it's almost like some insect languages?

No, I missed that, Mati admitted. *I wonder how reptiles got an insect language . . .*

Maybe we'll find out.

After a long pause, Mati formed a new thought. *No matter what stupid things I do, you'll always be with me, won't you?*

Rini popped a few nuts into his mouth. *That's right. But . . . I'll be with you when you do smart things, too!*

Silmula Sorafax leapt onto a table and cleared her throat. "We're going to take some questions and comments from the students from other star systems . . ."

✷

Ilika and Kibi walked through the boarding tunnel hand in hand, then strolled around the Manessa Kwi, half-heartedly making sure everything was stocked and ready.

"I always like time alone with you," Ilika began as they descended in the lift, "but this wasn't exactly what I had in mind."

Kibi laughed nervously. "Do you think . . . they'll be okay?"

Ilika thought about her question as they entered the utility room. He touched a symbol and an access panel opened. "They have no idea what they've gotten themselves into, and all the briefing and training can hardly begin to prepare them for the experience of living in another creature's skin."

Kibi took a deep breath as she watched Ilika begin a diagnostic. "I gathered as much, since no one else is volunteering to go in their place, or even with them."

"Yeah," Ilika confirmed, closing the panel. "I've only done it with another mammal, of similar intelligence, and I'm not looking forward to the next time."

"What kind?"

"Equine. Beautiful creatures, but they live with more than their share of fear. Fear, as I'm sure you know by now, is the enemy of intelligence and wisdom. Horses have worked hard, on many different planets, to overcome that handicap."

Kibi nodded and opened her water filter cabinet. "So . . . the greater the difference in the creatures, the harder it is to live in their skin?"

"I'm not sure 'harder' is the right word. I'd say more like 'shocking.'"

"Oh," Kibi responded without voice. She finished looking over the supplies, and closed the cabinet. "So there's . . . real danger?"

Ilika's laugh was full of tension. "Oh, yeah! In addition to the claws and all that, there's the very real possibility of forgetting who you were, or just not wanting to come back. You have to *choose* to end the mission. Equine fear makes that very hard. There are things going on in this situation that will also make it a supreme decision for our friends."

Kibi swallowed, then took a deep breath to clear her head. "We won't be getting any missions while it's just you and me, will we?"

Before Ilika could answer, both their bracelets chimed.

* * *

What aspects of the situation would cause there to be no volunteers for what Mati and Sata had to do?

Where had Mati heard the term "Great Transformation"?

What is your opinion of Silmula Sorafax as a leader?

When living as another creature, what could make a person not want to end the mission and return to their previous form?

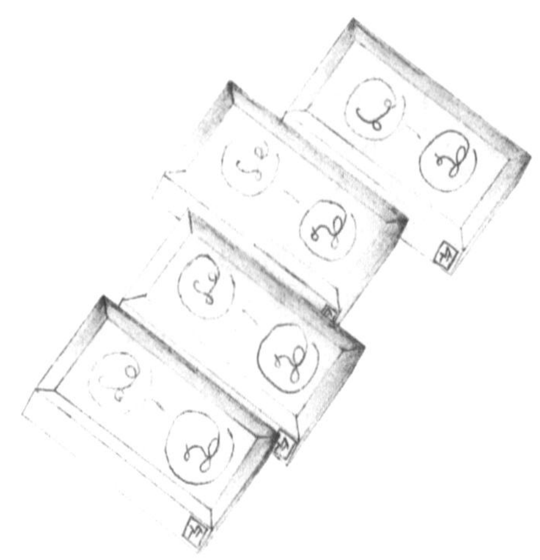

Chapter 30: The Great Transformation

As evening on Satamia Star Station approached once again, the main hall appeared far from ready for a party. Instead, four golden boxes sat alone in the middle of the hall, all about the size and shape of a wide coffin, and all glowing with an inner light.

Many creatures were at work, but not hanging decorations. The entire briefing team was present, under the firm leadership of the large white feline, Silmula Sorafax. They poured over checklists on knowledge pads, organized the visiting students into teams, and conferred with fuzzy, glowing orbs who came and went.

Eventually Kerloran whirled into the room and spun himself into a majestic green bird, larger even than a fanator. A moment later, Melorania appeared and became a wise old woman with sparkling youthful eyes. Silmula Sorafax approached them and the three spoke silently.

Mati, Sata, Boro, and Rini had not been back to the Manessa Kwi since the process began. They had occasionally, during the four days of lessons and briefings, been able to use a bathing room, but the crowded schedule had never allowed any leisure.

Kibi and Ilika had visited once or twice a day and shared their own process of learning to run the ship with a crew of only two. It was not easy, they emphasized, was never going to be easy, and they really looked forward to their friends returning to duty.

Now the captain and his steward stood off to the side of the main hall, trying to stay out of the way. A few minutes after Melorania and Kerloran materialized, Mati and Rini entered hand in hand. Behind them, Sata and Boro appeared.

Kibi looked into their faces and hearts. Mati might have been going to her own funeral, although Rini seemed content. A moment later, Rini looked deeply worried, and Mati suddenly became calm and ready for anything. Sata had tears on her face, but was smiling. Boro looked around warily, as if expecting wild, hungry wolves to be lurking, then stumbled over the corner of a bench and laughed at himself.

Kerloran, Melorania, and Silmula Sorafax turned and looked at the four monkey mammals. Everyone else in the huge room fell silent.

Kibi noticed all four of their moods shift once again.

"Mati of Sonmatia Three," Melorania began in a voice that everyone in the station, in every hall and room, could hear. "When you accepted Ilika Imni's offer to become the pilot of a deep-space response ship of the Nebador Transport Service, you jumped ahead of the people of your world, in some ways, by thousands of years. In other ways, they can never experience the marvels you have seen, and will continue to see, in the many long years ahead of you."

"But," Mati squeaked, tears suddenly springing from her eyes, "I have to . . ."

". . . experience transformation, Mati, and gain the wisdom that can only come with transformation, while most of the people of your little planet cower in fear of such changes."

Mati swallowed several times, wiped her tears on her sleeve, and nodded. Sata stood crying silently. Boro looked steeled for some dire fate, and Rini was not quite smiling.

"Have you decided, truly decided?" Kerloran asked.

Mati sniffled. "You'll take care of my . . . my body? I worked really hard to get two good knees."

Chuckles of sympathy rippled through the room. Kerloran nodded and Melorania smiled.

"Okay . . . then I guess . . . I'd better . . . do it."

"Sata?" Silmula Sorafax inquired.

"Um . . . yes," she said through tears. "I did a stupid thing, right along with my friend. It took me a long time to learn to stand on my own two feet, even though my knees were good, and I'm not going to stop now."

Mati cracked a tiny smile.

"Boro?" the large cat continued.

He nodded. "I wouldn't be worth my salt, as a man, if I didn't go with Sata."

"Rini?"

"I go where Mati goes, and some reptile is only going to mate with her over my dead body!"

More chuckles rippled through the crowd.

"As we have discussed, Rini," Silmula Sorafax began, "more than one reptile may try to arrange that."

"I know. They won't find it easy."

"Same here," Boro assured everyone.

✷

When nothing more remained to be said, the large white cat walked to the first golden box. "Mati, as you led the misguided effort to free the homeless reptiles, so you are now the leader, if anyone is, of this little team. Think of it as flight command."

Mati shuddered for a moment, then approached the glowing box. Silmula Sorafax touched a symbol and the box opened. The blue female reptile curled up within, deeply-asleep if even alive, appeared to be perfect, as if newly-made.

"She's . . . beautiful," Mati muttered.

"She is completely yours, and has no life of her own," the cat explained.

Mati knew what she had to do. It was one of the last lessons given by the briefing team, and they had made sure everyone was awake. She climbed into the box with the sleeping lizard, curled around it until she could feel its scales touching her body in many places, and tried to relax.

Silmula Sorafax touched another symbol and the box closed.

Sata climbed in with her green female, slightly larger than Mati's blue.

Rini curled around his gray male lizard and closed his eyes.

Boro's orange male had large muscles and sharp claws, and Boro was glad.

Unseen by those in the boxes, four glowing purple entities descended from somewhere near the ceiling of the main hall. One came to rest over each golden box, and spread wings of light completely around each container and its precious cargo.

The room remained silent as the minutes passed, and Kibi at first thought she was going to explode with anxiety. Then she glanced around, and saw that everyone else in the room, from Ilika to the floating creatures from a distant star system, were all meditating. After laughing at herself silently for a moment, she closed her eyes and began to slow her breathing.

✷

To Kibi, it seemed like hours later, but may have been mere minutes. The purple entities retracted their wings of light and drifted away into the upper balconies. Kerloran leapt into the air on giant wings, swept over the assembled Nebador citizens, and vanished into a corridor. Melorania began to swirl, became a blur, and disappeared. Only beings of flesh and blood remained in the huge room.

Silmula Sorafax stretched her long feline body, and stepped to Boro's box.

When it opened to her touch, an orange reptile slowly lifted his head, then looked down at the sleeping monkey mammal beside him in the box. After blinking and considering the situation for a long minute, he looked up, climbed out, and said something in throaty sounds and hisses that only one bird could understand, and then only a little.

A lanky gray lizard emerged from Rini's box, and scanned the room with a contented look.

Sata, in her new form, looked back and forth from the sleeping human in the box, to the large cat.

The blue female came out last, testing her legs to make sure all four knees worked.

"As you know," Silmula Sorafax began, addressing the four reptiles, "we can understand very little of your speech. If you succeed in your mission and return to us, you can tell us all you learned. If you do not return to us, that knowledge will be lost, and we may never find those noble creatures a suitable home."

✷

The four golden boxes, with their sleeping monkey mammals, were closed and floated into the medical center.

Ilika and Kibi spent a quarter hour with the four new reptiles, assuring them they would be missed, and promising that the Manessa Kwi would await their return. Drrrim-na, Glorm, Dakalio, and other friends came by. They could do little but wish their friends well. All those who visited looked at the four with great respect, and also a tinge of worry.

Finally, with preparations for the evening party going on all around them, Silmula Sorafax declared that it was time. The four reptiles took one last look around them at the decorations and musical instruments, shared clumsy embraces with Ilika and Kibi, and followed the white feline toward the simulated desert environment.

✷ ✷ ✷

Mati, Sata, Rini, and Boro experienced many emotions, some quite conflicting, as they prepared for the Great Transformation. What emotions would you feel if you were in their place?

What is the greatest "transformation" that causes most people to cower in fear?

The "technology" to achieve a Great Transformation, or anything similar, does not exist in our human world. We often like to fantasize that such technology will someday exist, and many science fiction stories have been written with that theme. However, the belief that we can do anything appears to be a fixture of human nature, while the actual ability to do anything, is not. One example is getting useful power from nuclear fusion. We once set our sights on this goal, half a century ago, and it is still completely out of reach. Advanced students may want to think about the "odor" given off by human dreams of god-like powers. Most notably today, this "odor" can be smelled when people predict unlimited economic growth in the future, even as our environment and resource base crumbles around us.

One-way communication is always difficult. Mati, Sata, Rini, and Boro, in their new reptilian forms, could still communicate will gestures and touches, and perhaps express some emotions with tone of voice. An even more difficult situation is when a person is in a coma, can hear but not respond in any way, and those who care must think of what to say, sometimes for weeks or months on end.

Chapter 31: Newcomers

The door that looked like a rock closed behind them.

It was far from the one Mati had left ajar days earlier, selected for its distance from the cavern of the homeless reptiles, designed to make anyone coming through it seem like they had just crossed the vast open desert.

Boro remembered well that they could not return to their lives in Satamia Star Station, and in the Nebador Transport Service, by going back through that door. But just to be sure, he used his new claws, quite long and sharp as claws went, to try to open the door. After a long effort, he gave up. "It's locked," he said with deep throaty sounds and hisses. "Like they said, the only way back is . . ."

"We know," Mati assured with a hiss. "It's strange *hearing* reptile sounds, and yet *understanding* them, just like you were talking our language."

"It's genetic," Rini recalled with a throaty gurgle. "This would be a lot harder otherwise."

"But that bird," Sata began with a wavering growl, "the one who knew the language a little, said there would be some idioms we wouldn't know."

"That's where the story about coming from far away will help us," Boro reminded them.

They all fell silent for a while, looking around at the rocks and sand.

The scales around Mati's eyes tightened. "I know they put me in command, but I don't think that'll look good here. Boro, I want you to be in command most of the time, unless I override something. Even then, I want you to *look* like you're in command."

Boro stood up on his hind legs and filled his chest with the dry air. Sata stood close beside him, letting her scales touch his.

Rini smiled without letting it show.

"We stay in pairs," Boro began, "as every male in this place — about a hundred of them — are looking for females willing to mate."

Mati nodded. "We're here for twenty Satamia days, not an hour more, and hopefully less if we discover what we're here to learn. Rini, will you keep track of that?"

"Sure. It's a hundred and forty simulated days in this place. I'll make marks on a rock somewhere," he promised, flexing the sharp nail of one finger.

Mati looked at Sata, who was rubbing up against Boro. "And don't forget what we *can't* do, with reptiles here, *or* each other, to have any chance of going home."

Sata collected herself and let some space come between her and the large orange male who was making her feel very affectionate.

✷

When the four new lizards arrived at the main cavern, they were immediately surrounded by about two hundred reptiles, mostly female, who immediately began showering the newcomers with questions.

Boro stood tall and silent, obviously in charge, while Mati, Rini, and Sata did most of the talking.

"We were in a small cavern across the desert when the ground started shaking," Mati began the story that had been suggested by the equine on the briefing team. "Many were killed when the cavern collapsed . . ."

"Ours did too!" many reptilian voices shared.

". . . and more of us died on the long desert crossing," Rini took up the story. "Our only hope was to find the great tribe our legends told us we once came from, long before we hatched."

"You have found it!" a very large male suddenly boomed, standing upright and towering over the females.

The four newcomers looked at him with respect, as they knew they must.

"But alas, we have little," he continued, dropping back to all fours. "The stars are wrong here, the water does not flow right, and most females are so upset, they never go into heat. We discovered a Rip in the fabric of the universe, but our scouts returned trembling with fear and muttering about sights and sounds that made no sense. The Rip will no longer open. We are a dying people. You are welcome to die here with us, perhaps distract us with stories from your cavern."

As Boro listened to the heart-felt words of the cavern's leader, he became aware that two young males were edging close to Sata, sniffing and reaching toward her. He took a deep breath, felt the muscles in his spiked tail respond to his will, and slapped the ground right in front of the two males, sending them scurrying backwards. "She's mine. Don't get any ideas."

An older male sniffed the air. "She's in heat. You'd better mate with her, or someone else will."

Boro growled, but the older male just shrugged and walked away.

The females quickly surrounded the new arrivals. "Come into the cavern!" an older female, wearing several pieces of jewelry, invited. "We just collected grubs. Not as tasty as the ones in our old cavern, but they'll fill an empty belly!"

Mati walked beside Sata and spoke in a soft voice. "*Why* are you in heat?"

"I don't know! I just got this reptile body an hour ago, remember?"

Mati sighed and continued following the other reptiles toward the cavern entrance.

* * *

Humans, when considering mating, are influenced by the natural cycles of our bodies, but also have a large degree of free choice. Many animals have little or no free choice in the matter, and their natural cycles are irresistible. Why would mating make it difficult for Mati, Sata, Rini, and Boro to decide to go back to their previous lives?

Chapter 32: Getting Comfortable in New Shoes

Kibi greeted the three avians and two small mammals who came through the boarding tunnel, but frowned when one bird stepped into the galley and began opening cupboards, and another hopped into the steward's chair.

Ilika, working on a flight plan at navigation, caught her eye and motioned toward the watch station. "They know we're short-handed. Try to ignore your human territorial instincts. That bird in your chair has more flight experience than you and me put together. The watch station is where I need your skills today, and probably at navigation too."

Kibi swallowed and began activating external sensors. "Why am I more worried about Sata than I am about Mati?"

"Anything we should tell Silmula Sorafax?"

"Nothing I can put my finger on, just my over-active intuition."

"That intuition of yours is one of the most important strengths of Manessa's crew."

Kibi smiled. "Am I still second-in-command?"

"Oh, yes. And the avian up there will respect that. Also, you can, and should, monitor what he does from here. Think of it like this — with just you and me on the crew, you are too valuable to use your time as steward when Nebador citizens can easily take care of themselves."

Kibi smiled, and felt her territorial instincts melt away. She placed a copy of the steward's status list in the corner of the watch station display, and noticed that the bird in her chair had almost completed his checklist. "Hey, you're good!"

"Glad to be of service, bok."

A moment later, Kibi squinted at her display. "Ilika, why are there four thousand seven hundred and fifty people on the passenger list? Manessa isn't as big as a star station, you know."

The captain chuckled, but shrugged.

One of the small mammals looked up from a knowledge pad. "They're non-material. It's a specialized type that can't go outside a gravity field. They're checking in with Manessa as they arrive, but are invisible to us."

Kibi glanced at the acting steward.

"All but eight are here, bok," he began. "There, the last group just checked in."

"Close hatch, retract boarding tunnel," Ilika commanded from the pilot's chair. "Kibi, I need you at navigation for the first leg of the flight plan . . ."

*

The main cavern of the homeless reptiles seemed almost perfect, with a sandy floor, many smaller alcoves and caves for storage or privacy, and rock balconies that overlooked the large public space. On one of these, the cavern leader ate grubs while surveying his tribe with sad eyes.

Water, apparently from higher in the mountains, gushed from a crack in the ceiling of a side-cave, then collected in a pool big enough for swimming. It flowed into a smaller pool, then disappeared, along with any waste, into another crack. The residents of the cavern had no idea where it went after that.

The surviving reptiles had found this new home almost immediately after a violent storm and earthquake collapsed the cavern they had inhabited for countless generations. It had seemed so close to their old territory that they wondered why they hadn't found it before, and could make no sense of the riddle. Their vague memories of that terrible time contained blanks they couldn't fill, gaps in their recollection that must have been, they presumed, caused by the fear and chaos of that frightening day.

Mati, Rini, Sata, and Boro were served wiggling insect larva, slimy fungus, and spiny cactus fruit. Their new bodies rejoiced at the sight and aroma of the fresh food, but their human minds were much less thrilled.

Rini noticed his friends hesitating. "This is all there is to eat," he mumbled softly, "and all there's gonna be."

Boro grumbled a little, then noticed Sata swallowing a grub. Her eyes lit up with pleasure, and she quickly grabbed another. He cautiously tried one. To his new reptile tongue, it was quite delicious. Noticing other reptiles watching, he puffed himself up. "Better than the grubs in our cavern! If you had even better in *your* cavern, I'm sorry our ancestors left!"

The watchers seemed delighted that their new guests were happy. They strutted with pride at the memory of their beloved old cavern.

* * *

In what kinds of situations are "territorial instincts" useful, maybe even necessary? In what situations are they NOT useful, maybe even dangerous?

Why was the new cavern "almost perfect" in its arrangement? Where did the water go after flowing through the two pools? Why did the new cavern seem so close to the old one? Why did the reptiles have poor memories of the day their old cavern collapsed and they found the new one?

Our minds can have a great effect on our ability to eat certain foods. Young children, and other very immature persons, can literally starve to death if preferred foods are not available. One sign of maturity is the ability to eat for nutrition, when necessary, instead of pleasure. Could you eat Brussels sprouts, every meal, every day, if you had nothing else? Slugs and snails? Raw eggs?

Chapter 33: Temptations

Nightfall soon came to the simulated desert environment, and the newcomers were shown to a small sleeping cave with a sandy floor, vacant because so few babies were hatching.

They curled up in the sand. Boro tried to leave some space between himself and Sata, but no matter how he placed himself, she quickly wiggled closer until their bodies were in contact. "Are you sure you want to tempt fate?" he asked softly.

"Yes," she replied without hesitation.

He sighed, put his arm around her, and wrestled with his own feelings for more than an hour, before finally drifting off to sleep.

*

Three times during the night, Boro's instincts woke him to find young males lurking near the entrance to the sleeping cave. He growled and they scurried away. Each time, Sata lifted her head, looked at him with sparkling reptilian eyes, then curled up beside him again, closer than before.

During that short night, strange dreams haunted all four newcomers. The half-remembered images seemed completely out of place for a desert reptile species. Shades of green colored everything, mists and dripping water formed a constant background, and all manner of living creatures lurked in every shadow.

*

Morning brought females with invitations to join food-collecting parties or mushroom-tending teams. Mati quickly indicated, by example, that they should fit right in and do their part. The other females assured Boro and Rini that their girls would be safe, and they could join the males playing Bones or brewing *shmur*.

Without an override from Mati, Boro decided to stand his ground. "Our cavern was not so fortunate, and the males could only . . . brew *shmur* and . . . play Bones when other work was done."

Sata's reptilian eyes sparkled with pride, and she brushed against Boro lovingly.

Mati remained silent, so Boro continued assertively. "I will be on the gathering team, to carry heavy loads and protect . . . anyone who needs protecting . . . from anything."

"And I can learn to tend mushrooms," Rini said calmly. For Mati's mind only, he added, *If I remember the lessons correctly, you'll probably go into heat sometime while we're here.*

Mati's eyes snapped open wide and she swallowed.

The other females giggled among themselves about the males who insisted on helping to gather food.

✷

Silmula Sorafax sat alone in the observation tunnel, watching Mati and Rini sprinkle water from a hollow gourd onto the reptiles' fungus garden. Three other females worked with them, talking with throaty sounds as they worked. Mati and Rini only spoke when responding to one of the females. When interacting with each other, they remained silent, but their glances often revealed something about their secret conversations.

The large white feline enjoyed trying to guess. Just then, someone licked her neck, and she knew by his scent who it was. She purred and turned to greet Toran Takil. "I am the luckiest cat in the universe to have a handsome male like you!"

He purred. "I'm just as lucky! How's your project?"

"They're just getting settled," she said, turning back to the observation window. "Days in there pass very quickly, six to our one. I don't think Mati and her crewmates have any idea how to find the information they need."

"Do you?"

"Of course not! Kerloran never makes things *that* easy! And with Melorania involved, it's *bound* to be a nearly unsolvable puzzle!"

Toran Takil sat on his haunches close beside the female cat and looked into the mushroom cave. "I almost wish Kibi was in there. It would be good for her. You're not mad at me for leading her on for a few minutes?"

"As I understand it, you led her on just long enough to get her to Psychic Development. And I *completely* understand her reaction to your presence. I experience it daily, you know."

The male cat growled lovingly. "But you get much more than she did . . ."

She licked his mouth. "That's right, and I plan to continue getting . . ."

Just then a large bird came waddling along the tunnel and the cats ceased their intimate conversation.

"Boro just had to fight off *another* male, bok, who was trying to get close to Sata. This time a little blood was spilled."

Silmula Sorafax chuckled in her feline way. "That's good for him, but not really a test. It's Rini who will be tested when Mati goes into heat."

The bird thought back to the day the process began. "But he was the first to step up and volunteer to go in . . ."

"Only because he's mentally quicker, and realized what would happen if he didn't," the white cat added.

The bird nodded. "It's going to be a strong crew, isn't it?"

"I think so, after they fully understand Nebador and work off some rough edges." She turned and looked at her lover.

"I was worried about Mati right after the escape, but now my gut tells me Sata has the biggest test coming up. But I agree about Rini, too."

At that moment, Toran Takil's mission bracelet chimed. "They want me at Mission Assignment."

"I'll come along. I want to talk to the ursine in charge of the planet search."

The two cats bowed to the large bird, who stayed to observe the fungus gardening.

✷

"WHY are you keeping all the males away from this perfectly ripe and beautiful female, but not mating with her *yourself?*" the cavern leader asked as he held Boro's gaze with his penetrating eyes. "If you'd just *mate* with her, her scent would quit driving the others crazy!"

Boro stood his ground. "Because, where I come from, we don't *force* females to mate! And she says she's not ready."

Sata rubbed up against Boro. "Well . . . actually . . ." She stopped herself and took a deep breath. "Yeah. He's right. I'm not ready."

The leader rolled his reptilian eyes and walked away, muttering, "It's your blood . . ."

Soon they were alone. "I'm sorry," Sata began with a shaking voice. "It's just . . . my whole body is screaming at me, day and night, and it's becoming harder and harder to ignore."

Boro wrapped his arms and claws around her. "I just want us to be able to go home . . ."

"Me too. I'll do my best to ignore it."

"And I'll keep fighting off other males, but . . ." He held her at arm's length and looked into her eyes. ". . . if you work against me, I'll quit trying."

Sata swallowed hard and slowly nodded.

✷ ✷ ✷

Sexual temptations are a serious test for anyone. They are often the root cause of abuses of power by government and religious officials. Some religions have tried to deal with the temptation by completely forbidding sexuality, with mixed results.

What forces or actions made it harder for Boro and Sata to avoid mating? What forces or actions made it easier?

What qualities can we observe in the relationship between Silmula Sorafax and Toran Takil?

Chapter 34: Grubs and Bones

After dreaming of dripping ferns and roaring streams leaping under and over slimy tree roots, the four newcomers awoke on their fourth day in the simulated desert environment.

With a tasty breakfast of fresh grubs and cactus fruit in his belly, Boro again hoisted up the big grub basket, allowing six females to concentrate on collecting, instead of carrying.

The team of more than thirty reptiles followed a carefully-planned route through the small, rocky caves that riddled one entire mountainside not far from the cavern. The winding route visited only the insect nests that hadn't been harvested in many days. The reptiles crept along quietly, knowing from experience going back countless generations that the insects would fly away with the fewest grubs if the gatherers arrived silently and worked quickly.

Claws were inserted into the nests of dried mud, slicing with precision where the scaly hunters knew the largest grubs could be found. The insects quickly went into action, about half attacking the lizards, the other half flying away with their wiggling young as quickly as possible.

Boro and Sata had flinched the first time several thousand angry flying creatures began hammering them, but quickly noticed that all the other reptiles completely ignored it. The reason was soon clear – the insects simply had no way to penetrate the lizard's scaly hides.

Today, Boro was again increasing the harvest by cupping his claws for those females working on nests near the ceiling, saving them from jumping down with each load of grubs. Sata noticed, and quickly started helping with the highest nests.

On the way back to the cavern, the females told stories of grubs their grandmothers collected that were twice this size. They even muttered half-remembered tales about grubs so big that one would make an entire meal.

The younger females shook their heads in disbelief.

*

Kibi's eyes were wide as the little ship approached Rontilia Star Station, much smaller than Satamia, yet glowing like a bright diamond in space.

With an effort of will, she tore her eyes away from the visual display and made the selection Ilika requested at the navigation console. With another part of her mind, she continued to monitor the watch station, often with voice commands to Manessa, occasionally just by reaching over.

The small docking tunnel only had berths for two response ships and one transport, all currently empty.

"Ssssss," came the voice of the docking controller. "Berth one pleassse, captain. It'sss very quiet inssside. Half the ssstation isss at Sssatamia for the Great Transssformation. I wishsh I could go, but sssomeone mussst run the ssstation."

Kibi smiled as she slipped back to the watch console. "Docking visuals on channel four. Any news about our naughty crew members?"

"Sssata now undersssstands how powerful her body'sss urgesss can be, and Boro hasss been injured ssseveral timesss. Many obsssserverssss ththink Sssata isss on the verge of mating withth . . . whoever isss handy."

Kibi swallowed, and remembered her body's reaction to Toran Takil. The silver and gold docking fingers wrapped themselves around the ship, and a boarding tunnel made contact with the hull.

"Bok. Welcome to Rontilia," the acting steward announced. "I know the Great Transformation will be challenging for your friends, bok, but understanding the lives of simple creatures is very important. Bok."

*

Many more nights passed as Mati and her friends dreamed about warm rain and huge insects of all sorts. During those nights, Sata became more and more affectionate. Even though she didn't do anything to directly invite him, or any other male, to mate with her, her indirect signals were becoming all but impossible to ignore, both for Boro, and a hundred other male lizards.

He cared very much about her, but he also wanted to go home and be the engineer of a deep-space response ship again, and perhaps something more challenging someday, like a star station docking controller.

As evening came to the simulated desert environment once more, Boro made a decision. *He* had had enough. *He* was going home. If Sata couldn't resist the temptation to mate with a reptile, it wasn't going to be him.

He approached a group of males about his age who were laughing and joking as they gathered the necessary ingredients from a storage cave. "I haven't played Bones and brewed *shmur* in a long time. You guys have room for one more?"

They welcomed him with slaps on the back that nearly drew blood.

Boro had to think fast that evening, as the rules to the game of Bones had not been known to the briefing team. *Shmur* contained several mysterious ingredients, one of which came from a different, much smaller, mushroom garden. Boro pretended that the rules and the ingredients had changed a little over the generations at his old cavern, so he humbled himself to learn theirs.

Soon a large hollow gourd bubbled with a frothy brew that went right to Boro's head when he took a drink. The other males laughed, drank deeply, and spent several minutes arm-wrestling.

Eventually Boro learned to play Bones.

It was not the loser of a round that had to fight the others, as Boro had assumed, but the winner. It was considered an honor, and the *shmur* made all the players feel invulnerable, but at the same time, rather slow and clumsy. Serious injury, therefore, was almost impossible, given their tough reptilian hides.

Boro had to reach inside himself for instincts he had never before let out. His large size allowed him to hold his own, but it was the fifth round before he started feeling some actual joy at the prospect of winning a throw of the Bones.

During a pause to drink more *shmur*, one of the other males casually said, "It's almost midnight. That girl you were protecting — she's probably mated by now."

Boro tensed up for a moment, ready to run and do his duty as Sata's protector. Then his *shmur*-clouded mind remembered the situation. "I protected her as long as I could. It's her problem now."

The others laughed heartily.

"When you asked to join us for Bones," one male said, "I almost offered to stay behind and . . . you know . . . try my luck!"

Boro laughed deeply and reached for the *shmur*.

* * *

Boro, by breaking tradition and helping with the grub collecting, is showing a level of intelligence and adaptability that the reptiles don't seem to normally possess. The struggle between "tradition" and "change" has always been present in our human societies, with tradition dominant at some times and places, change at others. Tradition seems to dominate in older, larger, more complex societies. Change seems to work best when no one is watching and judging, as in a sparsely-populated "frontier" setting. Which do you prefer? Which, in your opinion, is more dominant right now in your location?

In you opinion, did Boro abandon his promises and responsibilities to Sata?

Chapter 35: Failure

"I'm not in heat any more!" Sata announced with pride when Boro staggered into the cavern the following morning.

Boro's head felt like it had been run over by a transport ship, or maybe the star station itself. He had to struggle to understand what she was saying, and the implications of it. "Um . . . I bet that's a relief. Who was the lucky guy?"

Sata frowned. "Boro! I didn't *mate* with anyone! When I realized you were gone, I knew I had to stand on my own two feet. And besides, Mati's in heat now, so Rini's very busy protecting *her*."

When Sata's words finally penetrated his groggy brain, Boro threw his head back and laughed deeply.

"So with Rini busy," Sata continued, "I *really* had to think fast. I approached a group of older females. They let me sleep with them, and told me about some herbs. They made me a potion that tasted like it was straight from the Underworld, but it worked! Only problem is, it won't work on Mati until she's been in heat for at least a week."

At that moment, their attention was drawn to a commotion just outside one of the cavern entrances. When they arrived, others were already crowded around, three or four deep, trying to see.

"The little blue female is actually *helping* the skinny gray keep others away," they heard a tall male say. "I'd love to get my claws around *that* feisty girl."

Boro stretched up on his hind legs to see. Rini was bleeding in several places. He and Mati, side by side with their backs to a rock wall, were putting up a good fight. The large brown male, however, was not taking *no* for an answer.

Boro took one more breath, then muscled his way through the crowd, finally leaping into the fray beside Rini.

The brown male stopped in his tracks.

"What's wrong?" Boro roared. "Don't like a fair fight?"

The large brown reptile stood with his chest heaving, trying to catch his breath, and deal with his lusty feelings for the little blue female.

Boro glimpsed Sata appear at his side.

"What is *wrong* with you people?" the brown finally gasped out. "It's one thing that our females are too upset to go into heat. But you idiots won't even mate when you *are* in heat, and you have your pick of all the males! You don't like the ones who came with you, you've had offers from the largest, the strongest, and the fastest, and you refuse *everyone*. The population has dropped by seven just since you arrived. Don't you see what's going to happen if *someone* doesn't mate?"

"Don't *you* see that we're not *from* here?" Sata suddenly blurted out, breathing almost as hard as the brown male. "And we're not from some little cavern across the desert, we're from Satamia Star Station – what you call the Rip in the universe – and we are your *only* hope of finding a new home!"

After Sata fell silent, grains of sand could be heard sifting down through the rocks of the simulated desert environment.

Mati wasn't sure whether to laugh or cry, so she just rolled her eyes.

Rini smiled and started licking his cuts.

Boro stood his ground, but didn't have to do any fighting. The brown male stomped away, and the crowd silently dispersed, most of them wearing frowns.

✷

Rontilia Star Station's only large space, Silver Hall, gleamed with shiny crystal and bright metal. No great tree wound through the station, but small trees and bushes added color in many little gardens and big planters. One balcony overlooked the large silver floor.

So few people, of any species, were to be found in the station, that Ilika and Kibi had to fix their own lunch at one of the three eating places. Just as they picked up their trays, an ursine bustled in carrying a large carton.

"Sorry, had to run down to the storeroom, and couldn't resist stopping at a knowledge processor to see how the Great Transformation was going. Did you find everything you needed?"

The pair of monkey mammals smiled and nodded, then wandered away to pick a table.

"Are we the only ones not following Mati's and Sata's every move?" Kibi asked with amusement.

Ilika laughed. "Melorania knew we'd just worry if we didn't keep busy."

"At least now we can catch up on news . . ."

"Actually, no. While you were getting stuff out of the refrigerator, my bracelet chimed. We have an urgent cargo run."

Kibi chuckled and started eating faster.

When they slipped their trays into the dishwashing room, no one was working within, but they noticed a lone reptile, wearing an apron, glued to a nearby knowledge processor.

Ilika smiled when they discovered the supply room completely unattended.

"What do we do?" Kibi asked. "You said the cargo run was urgent."

"This isn't hard," Ilika replied, grabbing an empty pallet and a knowledge pad.

Kibi looked with wide eyes down the long rows of shelves. "There must be a thousand different things in here!"

"Probably more like twenty or thirty thousand," Ilika said. After touching some symbols on the knowledge pad, the pallet began to float slightly above the floor. "Your first piloting lesson," he said, handing the pad to Kibi.

She chuckled as she got used to the controls while the pallet bumped into nearby shelves, but soon had it moving down the first aisle.

As they began loading cartons and canisters onto the pallet, they heard someone else come in and prepare another pallet. Soon a large fanator was coming down the aisle behind them, lifting cartons with his beak through the loop at the top of each item.

Kibi hadn't really thought about it before, but could now see that every package had half a dozen ways to lift it. "There's so much to learn in Nebador."

"Little things and big things, bok," the huge bird said after placing a carton on his pallet. "It's your kind in the Great Transformation. How are you taking the bad news?"

Kibi swallowed and felt her entire body become tense.

Ilika glanced at her and chose his words carefully. "We've been very busy, and haven't had a chance to follow the news."

"The observers are saying it looks like a complete failure," the fanator revealed with a sad voice. "Bok."

Ilika could see the tears on Kibi face, and feel the huge knot in his own stomach.

"Bok. I'm sorry," the bird began. "I didn't realize you were emotionally involved . . ."

"They're our friends," Kibi whispered through her swollen throat.

The fanator came close and wrapped his large wings around the pair of grieving monkey mammals.

Kibi began crying freely.

"Don't give up hope," Ilika whispered. "Strange things can happen during Great Transformations . . ."

*

Silmula Sorafax trembled slightly as she waited in a small chamber near the Mission Assignment Room. It was unusual to wait so long for a conference with Kerloran, especially when he himself had requested the conference.

But the white cat knew a lot was happening in the star station. Dozens of visiting students were grumbling about all the things going wrong with the Great Transformation. Most members of the briefing team were asking for new assignments in the deepest, darkest corners of the star station, or even, if possible, off-station.

As the leader of the mission, Silmula Sorafax knew she could not hide from her responsibilities, and what now appeared to be her failure. She was a fully-trained graduate of the Psychic Development program, and about twenty other specialized programs, so she had no temptation to even try to avoid facing . . . whatever judgment was about to descend upon her.

Kerloran appeared suddenly, as if in haste, a green swirling cloud that filled most of the little room.

The cat nearly jumped out of her skin, then instinctively licked her paws and hung her head while purring.

The master of Satamia Star Station smiled to himself.

I . . . I was so ashamed, she began, *when Boro left Sata alone, still in heat, to fend for herself. I have made a list of training points that need to be emphasized in the future if any monkey mammal . . .*

Boro went off to play games and get drunk, the towering non-material presence said flatly.

The big cat flopped onto her belly with shame, and was about to cover her head with her paws, but stopped herself. *Yes, I was so tempted to open an access door, jump in there, and give him a good slap. I'm not sure I would have kept my claws retracted!*

You believe he should have stayed at Sata's side no matter what . . .

Silmula Sorafax rolled onto her back and presented her soft belly. *He promised to, and the need for them to support each other was stressed many times during the briefing. I don't think Rini ever left Mati's side . . .*

And then Sata broke one of the most important rules of the Great Transformation.

I have been going over the records of the briefing, the cat responded, sitting up on her haunches and hanging her head again, *and I cannot see how she missed the importance of non-disclosure, but I take complete responsibility for the failure of the mission, and plan to . . .*

Relax, little one, Kerloran said in a soothing tone, shrinking down to a small green ball.

Silmula Sorafax looked up into the swirling presence, and sensed a depth of intelligence and wisdom she could not even begin to understand.

The green ball continued to speak to the cat's mind. *The visiting students will need to see the entire process unfold, but you, as leader of the mission, do not have that luxury. Know that Boro's decision to cease protecting Sata was the best thing for both of them, and for the mission. Know also that Sata's disclosure was the only possible path to the success of the mission. Ponder these things. Hold your head up and do not grovel. You work for me, and I am well-pleased with your work. In you I place my trust.*

The green presence faded and was gone, leaving Silmula Sorafax blinking, trembling, and knowing she had a lot to learn.

* * *

After seeing the outcome of Boro leaving Sata alone, what is your opinion of what he did the night before?

Why did Sata reveal their true nature?

What public events in our culture cause as much interest as the Great

Transformation caused in Nebador?

When Silmula Sorafax met with Kerloran, what submissive behaviors did she show? Which of those are unique to felines?

What was Kerloran telling Silmula Sorafax about “following the rules”?

Chapter 36: Shunned

The four crew members of the Manessa Kwi, currently in reptile form, walked from the scene of the last fight, and Sata's strange disclosure, toward their sleeping cave near the main cavern.

Mati smiled at a young lizard who had been friendly when they tended mushrooms together, but received only a brief icy stare.

Boro waved to one of his *shmur*-drinking buddies, but the other male hissed and walked away.

Sata greeted an older female who had helped make the potion the evening before, but the female turned away and began talking with someone else about grubs.

Once in their sleeping cave, they huddled close and spoke softly.

"I . . . I blew it, didn't I?" Sata asked with a trembling voice. "First I was in heat, and came very close to mating with . . . anyone. Then I told the one thing I wasn't supposed to tell, ever."

"I . . . don't know," Rini replied.

Mati smiled with sympathy.

Boro was tempted to confirm Sata's suspicion that she had made huge mistakes, but decided to remain silent.

After a long pause, Mati said, "Actually, I don't care. If they can't handle the truth, that's their problem. I just wanna go home, so we either have to figure out why they don't like any of the desert planets they've been offered, or just survive another . . ." She looked at Rini.

"Fifty-six days."

Mati rolled her eyes again. "With me and Sata going in and out of heat, and Boro and Rini bleeding half the time, trying to protect us, I'm not sure we're gonna make it."

"But we never have *time* to figure out what kind of home they want!" Sata blurted out with frustration. "Now, because of my stupid mistake, they won't even *talk* to us."

The other three were silent for a long moment, but eventually had to nod agreement.

✷

The grub collecting teams departed without the newcomers, mushroom gardens were tended as usual, and cactus fruit was gathered and cleaned as it had been every day since long before any of the reptiles could remember.

Rini worked up the courage to humbly approach the food storage caves, but found several large males guarding them, and was chased all the way back to the group's sleeping cave.

The four outcasts talked quietly or dozed for the rest of the day. Sata carried her shame like a great weight, until late in the afternoon when Mati hissed at her. "The only way they would have accepted us, in the long run, is if you and me both mated, laid eggs, and hatched out lots of little lizards."

"She's right," a young reptilian voice came from above them.

They all looked up. A half-grown orange female perched on a rock shelf near the ceiling. As soon as she had their attention, she tossed down a dried gourd with a hinged lid.

Boro caught it, looked inside, and discovered lots of wiggling grubs.

"It's not a feast, but it's all I could get without making them suspicious."

"Thank you!" Mati said softly.

"Most of the people are scared and just want you to go away. Some, mostly males, want to kill you, or at least . . . you know . . . two of you. A few people . . . very few . . . mostly my friends . . . want to talk to you about this . . . star thing . . . and how you could help us."

"The ones who want to kill us . . ." Boro began, "how soon do you think they'll . . ."

"Probably tonight. There's a little tunnel up here that leads to the outside, but only three of you will fit."

Boro nodded with understanding.

"I have to go tend mushrooms. There are insect caves higher on the mountain where the grown-ups never go. The grubs are small, but they'll keep you alive." She turned and vanished into the rocks.

Boro passed out the precious gift of grubs as they all pondered the situation.

✷

Crouching between rocks at the entrance to their sleeping cave, Rini kept an eye on the cavern as nearly three hundred reptiles gathered for their evening meal. The mood was tense, he reported, with whispering and grumbling among the males, and repeated glances in their direction.

While Rini kept watch, Mati and Sata tried the little tunnel near the ceiling. Sata scraped herself a little, but could get through.

After they returned, Boro stuck his head in, then sighed. "I'll have to fight my way through the cavern. Right after they eat, they get a big drink of water, and are slow . . ."

"We know," the other three assured him.

Boro chuckled. "This feels good now that we know what we're doing, and have a plan."

Mati nodded. "We'll wait at the big boulder near the insect caves. Remember, you won't be protecting anyone, so just get away as fast as you can."

Boro blinked. "If I can catch them off-guard, I might get through without a scratch."

With all the details of the escape plan set, they fell silent. Rini reported that the meal was drawing to a close, and some were heading down to the water cave. A few young males crept near the sleeping cave, still attracted by Mati's scent, but older males warned them away.

Suddenly Rini frowned. "Not all the large males were at the evening meal . . ."

* * *

Shunning is a time-honored method of expressing social displeasure. In its simplest form, all those who are "in" pretend the one who is "out" doesn't exist. The goal is usually to make the shunned person change their ways and re-join the group. In a more extreme situation, the goal is to make the shunned person so uncomfortable they leave. In a modern society where violence is illegal, it is often the only method a group can use to get rid of an undesirable person, so the practice has a long history in most religions. In a more primitive environment where dangers lurk just outside the boundaries of the community, shunning can be a death sentence unless the shunned person is very self-reliant. *The Clan of the Cave Bear* by Jean Auel contains an excellent example.

Being "half-grown" seems to be a point in life that allows more insight and flexibility of thought than at any other time. The author receives his most honest feedback from people in the 8-12 age range. Enough of them (especially girls) are out of "childhood," but are not yet fully enmeshed in the loyalties and concerns of adulthood.

When Rini noticed that there were fewer large males at dinner than usual, what was he fearing?

Chapter 37: Escape

"Go, now, but be careful and silent!" Boro asserted in a whisper. "I think there's a trap somewhere, so I'm taking a round-about way."

Mati nodded and poked Sata, then motioned for Rini to follow her up to the escape tunnel.

Sata barely managed to hold her tongue as she squeezed herself through the rocks once more.

Mati followed Rini up to the tunnel near the ceiling. She looked back and saw Boro walk casually out of the sleeping cave. Instead of aiming for the nearest cavern entrance, he headed for the water cave. Mati smiled, turned, and wiggled through the rocks.

*

Boro's heart pounded in his chest as he did his best to look like just another lizard going down for a drink after eating his fill of grubs. Evening was at hand, and the passageway would soon be nearly dark. No one seemed to recognize him.

He drank little as he wanted to remain quick on his feet. As he pretended to drink, his mind raced, trying to decide which cavern entrance was least likely to be a trap.

He remained undecided on the way back to the cavern, but then stepped into enough light to be recognized.

"Hey, everyone! There's the freak!" a large male boomed.

The clearest path of escape was a small side entrance, so Boro judged it his best bet, perhaps his only bet. Most of the males, and some of the females, began calling loudly for blood. Boro started running as fast as his reptilian legs would go.

*

"Your friend will NOT get out unharmed," the half-grown female lizard informed them as the three outcasts crouched behind a boulder where twelve young lizards had awaited them, all wanting to know more about stars.

Mati set her jaw, looked into Rini's eyes in the fading light, then into Sata's. "We have to leave soon anyway, so we'll do it side-by-side with Boro."

Rini nodded.

Sata hesitated, whined a little, then collected herself with a deep breath and nodded also.

"We're coming too!" the young female declared.

Her friends all nodded vigorously.

Mati frowned.

"Don't give us that grown-up look! If we have to take risks to learn about the stars, then we'll do it."

Mati looked at the young reptile faces around them. Some were still children. The leader and a few others were old enough to mate, but barely.

Rini looked at Mati. "Whoever's going, we have to go now," he said aloud. "Boro would be here by now if he'd gotten out safely."

Just outside the minor cavern entrance, in the half-light of evening, Boro didn't see the first spiked tail swing toward him, but he felt it pierce his body deeply as pain shot from his inner-most organs, outward to every scale of his thick hide.

Remember, Boro, you'll be home soon, Kerloran whispered to Boro's mind.

Somehow, Boro found the courage to take a few more steps, only to feel another tail spike pierce his side.

Against his will, Boro fell onto the sand, and suddenly, all around him, a commotion of screaming and hissing erupted, forming a complete circle close around him. He glimpsed a green female he knew, just out of heat but still very beautiful. A blue female and a small gray male both moved too quickly for any of the big males to hit. But for some reason, many young reptile voices were also snapping and hissing, and occasionally yelling something about stars. Then everything went dark.

⁕

For a minute that seemed to last an hour, tails swung, teeth snapped, and claws ripped at anything they could find. Soon, no one was sure exactly who they were fighting. The enemy was anyone within reach.

In the fury of the fight, the large brown male, who had proudly sunk his spikes into the outcast's belly, didn't notice when his tail caught a female child and sent her flying against a rock with a bone-breaking crunch.

"ENOUGH!" the leader of the cavern boomed in his loudest, deepest voice, standing tall on a nearby boulder.

With some reluctance, especially from the large males, the two sides parted, one into a ring completely surrounding the other. For a long moment, everything was still and silent.

Then the small gray male from the inner group walked boldly toward the outer ring. He looked so weak and harmless, walking alone, that the large males laughed and parted for him. They fell silent with shame when he collected the broken body of the little female and carried her back to the inner circle.

Her friends gathered around, threw back their heads, and screamed their grief to the first few stars of the gathering night, and anyone else who cared to listen.

The grown-ups in the outer ring, who had bravely protected their culture from the freaks who claimed to come from the dreaded Rip in the universe, slowly filtered away to eat cactus fruit or brew *shmur*.

⁕ ⁕ ⁕

The word "freak" is one of many words we use to mean "unacceptably different." It has no fixed meaning, because we are all different in one way or another. Differences that are okay today might be seen as freakish tomorrow, and today's "freaks" can become tomorrow's "interesting characters," just depending on the swings of social opinion, usually driven by our media and leaders. This seems to be a constant part of human nature, but is less so during good times, more so during wars, famines, and other bad times.

Just so you know, in your own heart, without telling anyone else: would you have been in the group who "protected their culture from the freaks," or in the group who risked their lives for a chance to learn about stars?

After the fight, why would most of the adults go off to eat cactus fruit or brew shmur?

Chapter 38: The Mission

Having nothing else to work with, Sata and Mati clamped their claws over Boro's deep wounds, but had little success stopping the bleeding. Sata's eyes swirled with fear and grief, and she tried to say something, but couldn't make words come out.

Boro raised his head a little. "I . . . didn't do a very good job . . . getting to the meeting place . . ."

"Don't worry about it," Mati assured her friend. "None of us are very good reptiles, and this whole thing is all my fault . . ." she said, breaking into shaking sobs.

Rini left the dead female child with her friends, wrapped his mind around Mati's, and took over trying to stop Boro's bleeding.

"I . . . don't want to . . . stay here," Boro muttered between gasps. "Help me . . . get to the . . . insect caves."

As Boro struggled to stand, Rini and Sata took his weight as best they could, each keeping one claw on the worst wounds, those inflicted by tail spikes.

Mati, Rini spoke to her silently, *you'll have to carry the child. They're afraid to touch her.*

Mati blinked to clear her mind, gathered the lifeless child into her arms, and with eleven young reptiles trailing behind, followed Boro and his helpers across the sand in the twilight.

✷

Tapping into his deepest reserves of determination, when Boro arrived at the nearly-dark mountainside riddled with small caves, he didn't crawl into one of them as his friends had expected, but instead started climbing.

Rini and Sata had kept the blood loss to a small trickle until then, but when Boro started climbing, they were hard pressed to stay at his side, much less keep the bleeding under control. As he climbed, the rocks under his feet quickly turned red.

With a roar of relief, he came to the first of the small caves, much higher up, that were not used for grub harvesting. The first entrance was too small for him, so he reached down inside himself for one more burst of strength, somehow found it, and staggered to the next cave, nearly collapsing into the opening. After several long minutes of effort, with his friends powerless to help, Boro managed to drag himself inside so others could enter and again try to tend his wounds.

Feeling the need to keep a watch, Mati remained outside as the eleven young reptiles entered silently.

He's breathing easier, Rini reported to Mati from inside the small cave, *but is very weak, barely conscious most of the time, and won't be going another step in this reptile body*.

Mati was about to tell Rini that all was well outside, when she spotted the shadowy silhouette of an adult reptile creeping up the rocks toward their hiding place.

*

Rini, inside the cave doing everything he could to stop Boro's bleeding and make him comfortable, immediately knew what Mati saw. He whispered the situation to Sata and the eleven young lizards. The eleven quickly scampered out and lined up on both sides of Mati to look down and see who was coming.

The shadowy figure continued to advance, hopping from rock to rock on the mountainside. When it got to a certain point, about a stone's throw away, all eleven youth hissed in unison. Mati added her reptilian voice to the chorus.

When the warning faded away, a lone female voice floated up to them. "I just want to talk. There are others who also want you to help us, but they are afraid to come. May I approach? Please?"

The young ones looked at Mati.

"Yes!" she hissed in a no-nonsense voice full of warning.

The adult female, with her heart in her throat, slowly climbed the rocks until she perched just one boulder below the line of watchers. The swirling anger in their eyes told her they were quite willing to tear her apart.

"I am a member of the Guard," she began timidly, "and have been through the Rip in the universe, although I understood little of what I saw. I was cornered and had to fight, but a strong mammal grabbed me and held me, without hurting me, until the fight drained out of me. I knew, as he held me, that I could never understand that place, and I had best go home. The next thing I knew, I was home."

Mati smiled to herself, knowing who she was talking about. In the cave, Rini smiled also.

"Please, we are a simple people, and our pride keeps us from understanding many things, but we shudder at the thought of seeing the last egg hatch, the last female fail to go into heat because of the fear in her heart, the last male grow old without finding a mate. Please, if you can, help us to find our home . . ."

Mati became choked with emotion as she listened to the female lizard. She had to swallow several times before she could speak. "As my friend revealed earlier today, we came here to do just that. We have eaten grubs and cactus fruit with you, tended mushrooms, and raided insect nests. We have asked questions, and listened to every story you could tell us about your people, your old home, and what makes you happy. But . . . I have to admit . . . we have completely failed. Many new homes have been offered to your people, and in each you shrivel and die, even faster than here in this . . . small temporary home. We have no idea why. I am sorry."

"But . . ." the lone female whined with desperation, "have you not dreamed of our home, as we do every night? You slept in the same cavern with us. Did you not glimpse, in your sleep, what we see all the time? We do not know what to call it . . ."

The female stopped talking. Suddenly the blue female's mouth hung open, the slender gray male behind her bounced with excitement, and the green female poked her head through the cave entrance.

"Yes!" Mati said as soon as she found her voice.

"That explains it!" Rini added from behind.

Mati turned to Sata, who still wore a puzzled look. "They aren't desert reptiles!"

Sata smiled with realization. "Of course! I've been dreaming about jungles ever since we arrived!"

"Jun . . . gles?" the female of the Guard tried to say, not recognizing the word.

Mati turned back to the visitor. "My friend was just doing her best to say a word from our language. Jungles are very wet, warm, and green."

"Yes! *That's* our home!"

* * *

What leadership qualities do we see in Mati when Boro finally finds a cave?

What qualities do dreams have that made it hard for Mati, Sata, Rini, and

Boro to realize they were seeing the solution to the mission every night?

Even without the dreams, what can be seen by any observer that suggests the lizards probably weren't desert reptiles?

Chapter 39: Success

Although no one witnessed it, Kerloran smiled.

All over Satamia Star Station, groups of students, come to witness the Great Transformation, bounced, flapped, or swung from tree branches with excitement. Birds hugged reptiles, ursines embraced equines, cats rolled and laughed with monkeys as the tension and gloom was suddenly lifted.

The briefing team emerged from the conference room where they had been hiding.

Silmula Sorafax sat on the third balcony overlooking the main hall, her eyes sparkling with new knowledge and wisdom about how the mysterious universe worked.

✷

At an asteroid mining camp, Ilika and Kibi were helping to load canisters onto pallets. The strong ursine could carry four at a time. Ilika managed two. Kibi cradled one in her arms and called it good.

A large spider came bustling out of the control room, mandibles twitching and eight feet tapping on the floor with excitement. He stood right in Kibi's path.

Knowing something was up, Kibi set down her canister.

With gleams in his dozens of eyes, the spider shoved a knowledge pad into Kibi's hands.

After reading the first few words, Kibi's face lit up with a huge smile. She started bouncing and nearly hit the ceiling in the quarter-gravity cargo room.

As soon as she landed, Ilika was quickly at her side, reading over her shoulder. He looked up at the spider. "Are we the last ones in Satamia to find out?"

The spider's mandibles twitched again. "Probably."

✷

On one of the four golden boxes in the medical center of Satamia Star

Station, a symbol changed from yellow to green, and the top slowly opened. Healer Dakalio walked over and reminded Boro to move very slowly, as his body had not had any exercise for several Satamia days.

Boro felt for the bleeding holes in his belly and side, and was delighted to not find them.

When the young engineer felt ready, the older healer helped him to slowly sit up, then carefully stand. Boro held onto things as he made his way into a shower, then slipped on clean clothes. By then, he was ready to stand on his own.

He grabbed a nutrition drink on his way through the main hall, but was soon at his destination — a certain observation window in the dimly-lit tunnel that wound through the simulated desert environment.

Mammals, birds, large insects, and many others he couldn't name — all gathered around to watch the drama within — quickly recognized him and made a space.

* * *

Some religions have imagined future worlds in which "birds hugged reptiles, ursines embraced equines, cats rolled and laughed with monkeys," and other utopian images. Their mistake, in the author's opinion, is that they imagine this happening on Earth, with the people and animals that currently exist on Earth. The Nebador stories do not propose that this is possible. (Indeed, it is a common theme in most religions, including Christianity, that the "path" to "Heaven" is "narrow" and so, by implication, hard to find and difficult to follow.)

Advanced students: What "new knowledge and wisdom" do you think Silmula Sorafax was contemplating as she pondered the completion of the Great Transformation?

Chapter 40: The Hard Part

Rini soon returned to the cave to check on Boro. When he found no signs of life in his friend, Mati instantly knew. Sata, the eleven young reptiles, and the female of the Guard, all followed Mati into the cave and gathered around to pay their respects.

Rini could see Sata trembling with grief, so he put his arm around her. "Remember, he's home, probably sucking on a nutrition drink while watching us from an observation window."

Sata cracked a tiny smile, but her eyes still swirled with emotions.

Mati lifted the lifeless female child, from where she lay in one corner, and placed her close beside Boro.

"I'm sorry," the female of the Guard began. "It was stupid for the thick-headed males . . . and some females . . . to attack you. You were just trying to help us."

Mati swallowed and found her voice. "Same thing would have happened where we were born. Our teacher did nothing but help people, so they tried to kill him and burn our ship."

"What's a . . . ship?"

Mati smiled. "Long story."

The leader of the group of youth cleared her throat. "If you're done with adult talk, can I ask a question?"

Rini looked at the girl.

After stammering with embarrassment for a long moment, she finally collected herself. "Um . . . now that you know about our dreams, can you help us find that place again?"

Rini looked at Mati during a moment of silence, then he spoke. "Your planet . . . your old cavern . . . was probably once like your dreams — wet and warm, with plants and huge insects everywhere. Then it slowly changed into a desert. You survived by learning to live in caves, eat smaller grubs, pick cactus fruit instead of jungle fruit, and water mushrooms that used to grow by themselves . . ."

"Wow . . ." the female of the Guard began. "We have no memory of that, except in our dreams."

"That entire . . . world . . . no longer exists. It was burnt to a crisp when your star . . . your sun . . . became very large. That happened soon after you were brought to this . . . new cavern. You are inside a star station where thousands of people live and work, all around you, and many of them have been working hard to find you a new home, a real home to call your own."

"Will they find one?" the half-grown female asked bluntly. She and all her friends looked at Rini intently.

Rini smiled and looked at Mati. She smiled back. "I think we know of one you'll like," he said.

✷

Ilika and Kibi were soon back in Satamia Star Station. Their patience was sorely tested as reptiles and ursines slowly unloaded the cargo from the asteroid mine. The moment the last pallet cleared the boarding tunnel, the captain and steward dashed to the simulated desert environment.

Ilika and Boro embraced, then parted and looked at each other. Ilika could see a new light of confidence in Boro's eyes, a light born of passing through the Great Transformation.

Kibi greeted Silmula Sorafax with a bow and a friendly touch.

The big cat experienced a moment of jealousy, but had plenty of practice dealing with other females, of many species, who had felt the magnetic qualities of her beloved Toran Takil. She returned Kibi's gentle touch.

"What's happening?" Ilika asked, nodding toward the observation window.

Boro took a deep breath. "They're all standing around my carcass, talking about something. I don't understand a word of it anymore, but the bird over there is getting the gist of it. They're from a jungle, not a desert. I vaguely remember the dreams."

Ilika looked where Boro had gestured, and could see a large bird, his face nearly pressed against the window, muttering into a knowledge pad. Others followed on their own pads.

The captain of the Manessa Kwi turned to the big cat in charge of the mission. "Now that we know what to look for, we'd be happy to help find the reptiles' new planet . . ."

Silmula Sorafax licked a paw. "I'm sure Kerloran and Melorania will expect you to."

✷

"We must leave you now," Mati announced after everything had been said that anyone could think of to say.

"Will you . . . see if that . . . jungle . . . is still available?" the female of the Guard asked.

"Someone might already be doing it. Our people are watching over us constantly, day and night."

"How will you leave? The Rip in the universe will no longer open."

Mati looked at Rini and he answered. "We came in through another Rip, but can't leave that way. We need . . . a high cliff where we can . . . fly."

The female of the Guard opened her eyes wide, but eventually nodded. "There is one near here. Morning light will allow us to find it."

Boro and the little female were left alone in the silence of death. Out under the simulated stars, the living curled up together in a sandy hollow not far away. Mati, Rini, Sata, and the female of the Guard took turns keeping watch. The rest dreamed of dripping ferns, mushrooms springing from the wet forest floor, and big, juicy grubs.

✷

"I had it easy," Boro said as he worked his way through a hearty meal with his captain and steward on the second balcony of Violet Hall. "I was fatally wounded. I can't imagine how hard it's gonna be for the others."

Kibi nodded and smiled weakly. "That's one of the final tests in Psychic Development. I wonder what kind of creature I'll get to be . . ."

"Whatever you'd learn the most from," Ilika guessed.

"In other words, whatever would be hardest," Kibi decoded with a smirk.

Ilika smiled.

✷

When everyone was awake, the three visitors and one adult followed the eleven youth to some nearby caves where the grubs were small but tasty. After a light breakfast, they followed the female of the Guard to a cliff that overlooked a sheer drop of more than a hundred meters.

The adult female and the eleven youth stepped back from the edge to give the three visitors some space.

Mati looked at Sata, then at Rini. "I'm in command of this mission, right?"

"Right," Rini said firmly.

"Right," Sata whispered after a pause.

"Okay," Mati began. "Rini, I have an assignment for you. You already know what it is, but I need to say it out loud so Sata will know. You will be in the middle. You will hold our claws tightly and take us over the edge with you. Can you do that?"

"Yes," Rini said aloud, "but you both must be willing to step to the edge and take my claws. I won't go until you're both with me. We all go or we all stay."

"Fair enough," Mati responded. "You okay with that, Sata?"

"Um . . . yes," she said with a slight whine.

Rini stepped to the edge, facing outward, and stretched out both arms. He knew what he had to do, and it did not involve leaving any extra time for thought, worry, or fear. The instant he felt Mati's claw touch his on one side, and Sata's on the other side, he grabbed both by the wrists and launched all three of them into the air.

✷

Eleven youth and one adult reptile stepped to the edge of the cliff and looked down.

"They . . . didn't fly," the half-grown female said with sadness.

"No," the female of the Guard agreed. "I don't think they intended to. I think they just said that so we wouldn't worry."

They all stood in respectful silence for a long minute. Eventually one of the young males said what many were thinking. "I wonder how long it will take the star-people to find us a . . . jungle."

"Probably many days," the female of the Guard replied.

"We're going to stay on the mountain and wait," the leader of the eleven said, "eat small grubs and lick morning dew. You are welcome to wait with us."

"Thank you," she said. "That would be nice."

✷ ✷ ✷

After the female lizard apologized for her people killing Boro, Mati admitted that the same thing would have happened where she was born. How do you think the people of 21st century Earth would have handled the same situation?

How hard would it be for you and your friends to accept an explanation like Rini gave, considering that you had witnessed almost none of it? How hard do you think it would be for most adults?

Now that you know how the Great Transformation had to end, for each of them to be able to return to their former lives, can you see how difficult (perhaps impossible) it would have been to make that decision if they had mated while in reptile form?

Chapter 41: Debriefing

In the medical center of Satamia Star Station, three golden boxes opened at the same time.

The avian healer on duty squawked as Ilika, Kibi, and Boro came running in the door.

As soon as Sata blinked enough to focus her eyes, she saw Boro grinning down at her while catching his breath. She smiled and breathed a sigh of relief.

Mati was greeted by Kibi, and Rini by Ilika.

The bird ran around, trying to explain to three monkey mammals at once what they needed to know about recovering from the Great Transformation.

None of them were paying much attention.

✷

After showers, clean clothes, and nutrition drinks for the new arrivals, six mission bracelets chimed at once.

The large audience hall was packed with visiting students, the entire briefing team, and many friends and observers. Melorania, in the form of a beautiful lady with swirling blue gown, and Silmula Sorafax, whose sleek white fur seemed to sparkle, stood side-by-side at the front.

When the crew of the Manessa Kwi finally squeezed themselves into the room, a few pokes from Ilika were necessary to get the four honored guests moving down the aisle.

Boro, Sata, Mati, and Rini approached the head of the Transport Service and the large cat. The room fell silent.

"Boro and Rini," Melorania began, "you both willingly experienced the Great Transformation to support and protect your beloved girls. You did well, and neither I, nor Kerloran, have any complaint about the decisions you made. Some observers had negative judgments at some points in your journey, but they are pondering and learning from the process, now that it has completely unfolded. You two may sit and listen."

Boro and Rini smiled at each other with mixed pride and embarrassment. Seeing no empty seats or benches, they settled onto the soft floor.

Melorania looked at the navigator of the Manessa Kwi. "Sata, you were tempted by primal instincts, experienced deep emotional challenges, and remained true to yourself, your friends, and Nebador."

Sata smiled.

"And you violated THE most important rule of the Great Transformation, a rule that must have been repeated a hundred times during your days of preparation."

Sata's chin fell onto her chest and tears filled her eyes.

"Good Work."

It took Sata a long minute to recover, wipe her tears, and look up to see the smile on Melorania's face. Chuckles rippled through the audience.

"Rules are necessary for intelligent people, but as we approach wisdom, they must often be broken. This is especially hard for avians . . ."

Many feathered heads in the room ducked with embarrassment.

". . . and monkey mammals."

All six crew members of the Manessa Kwi, and the three or four other humans in the room, cringed.

"You, Sata," Melorania continued, "performed a great service by giving an excellent example, which just about everyone in Satamia was watching, of a situation in which a rule needed breaking. Most importantly, you did it *knowing* the rule. People who break rules without awareness are just simple mortals stumbling through life. We love them, but they cannot work in the Nebador Services."

Everyone in the room was thoughtful during a long silence.

"To break a rule with wisdom, you must first know the rule, and be willing to follow it most of the time. But, I'll admit that for a little while during your Great Transformation, we, who can see far into the past and future, could see no path to the success of your mission. You, Sata, changed that. Suddenly, when you broke that rule, new possibilities sprang into existence. A group of reptiles who had been powerless . . ."

"The young ones!" Sata interrupted.

"Yes, those born since coming to the star station. You created the moment, and they seized it. The rest of the story . . . you know."

Sata took several deep breaths to settle the many emotions she was feeling.

"But don't let it go to your head," Melorania warned. "Breaking the rules, with knowledge and wisdom, will serve you well as a starship navigator, as long as you do it carefully, knowing that every one of those rules was written with blood."

Sata looked puzzled.

"Every rule was written because they usually, in most situations, give the best chance of people coming back *alive* from their missions."

Sata nodded with understanding.

"You may sit, Sata."

*

"Mati of Sonmatia Three, crippled slave, Tera's first companion, starship pilot, Rini's beloved."

Mati was suddenly filled with amazement at all the things she had already been and done in her short life. She tried to look up, but Melorania's face was almost too bright to endure.

"You were the leader of the mission, and partly for that reason, you worked hard to avoid some of the feelings and experiences that Sata endured and learned from."

Mati cringed, and tears threatened to come.

"Kerloran is of the opinion that it would be very good for you to live an entire lifetime with the reptiles, including mating and raising little scaly children."

Rini quickly rose and stood close beside Mati, taking her hand in his.

Melorania smiled. "I agree with Kerloran completely. But I told him that you also have many things to learn as a deep-space response ship pilot, and good pilots, especially good monkey-mammal pilots, are very rare, and always will be."

Mati tried to collect herself, and Rini relaxed a little, but didn't leave Mati's side.

"Kerloran agreed, and offered as an alternative that you, Mati, begin Psychic Development training, which will include another Great Transformation as part of your final tests, although a shorter one."

Rini started to open his mouth.

"And I assured him," Melorania said before the freckled lad could speak, "that I would not allow Rini to begin *his* training until you, Mati, had completed yours."

Rini closed his mouth.

"Kerloran was satisfied with that. He apologizes for not being here, but is doing something very important right now."

*

Mati and Rini embraced, and a moment later Boro and Sata stood and did the same, a little more slowly.

"Citizens of Nebador," Melorania called out in a loud, clear voice, "I give you the full crew of the Manessa Kwi, all monkey mammals again, all able to walk, and all back on active duty!"

Claws and wings nudged Ilika and Kibi until they went up to join in the joyous moment, as everyone in the room stood, flapped, cheered, screeched, or howled.

✷

With another Satamia day nearing its end, most of the creatures soon began to filter out of the large audience hall, their minds turning to decorations, food, drink, and music. Ilika and Kibi knelt down and chatted with the large white cat about helping with the planet search.

"Melorania . . ." Mati began when finally, many minutes later, no one was talking to the head of the Transport Service. "I want you to know that the eleven young reptiles who helped us, and one adult female, are probably outcasts now . . ." She stopped when she saw the knowing smile on Melorania's face.

"Come, all of you, I want to show you something."

Melorania floated out of the audience hall, along a corridor, and onto a balcony. The six humans, one large cat, and a few others, all ran along behind. Eventually they came to a balcony railing that looked down into Yellow Hall.

The hall was nearly empty, as many citizens were already at work in the main hall to prepare for the evening party, but a group of reptiles stayed close together as a much larger lizard, bright green with leaves twined around his head and arms, led them along.

"Kerloran . . ." Rini whispered.

"It's . . . it's . . ." Sata began excitedly, almost bouncing up and down.

"It's our friends!" Mati declared. "Can we go down and talk to them?"

Melorania looked askance at Mati, but remained silent.

Mati looked at Rini and Sata, both of whom were holding in laughter. Then she realized the problem, rolled her eyes, and laughed at herself. "They wouldn't recognize us!"

"Worse than that," Rini began, "we couldn't understand a word of each other's languages."

Mati sighed and turned back to the balcony railing to watch as Kerloran gestured toward a huge branch of the great station tree and spoke with reptilian throaty sounds. Most of the lizards turned circles with amazement at everything they saw.

"There's one too many," Rini said. "An adult male."

"They're going to be re-settled separately from the rest of the cavern," Melorania explained, "and the adult female selected a mate. He's not one of those who tried to kill you."

"That's good!" Boro said with relief.

They watched in silence as Kerloran and the thirteen reptiles entered a corridor and disappeared from sight.

"I wonder how they'll remember the star station . . ." Rini pondered aloud.

"They'll probably start a new religion about it," Melorania speculated. "That's what most creatures do after glimpsing Nebador. It'll be a mixture of what they saw and learned, and their own stories and myths."

"Their gods will be you and Kerloran, I bet," Boro said.

"No, they haven't met me, and Kerloran is just pretending to be another reptile so he can talk to them and be their guide." Then Melorania grinned. "If I had to guess, I'd say their new religion will probably have *four* gods."

Mati's eyes suddenly opened wide with wonder and embarrassment.

Somewhat to Kibi's surprise, her friends who had just experienced the Great Transformation were quiet and thoughtful at the evening party. Some of the visiting students from far-away star systems also lingered on the edges, not used to the melodies and rhythms of Satamia. Others plunged into the merry-making, ready to try moving their tentacles to anything with a good beat.

Boro and Sata, hand in hand, wandered among the snack tables, not sure what they wanted. Eventually some wiggling insect grubs caught their eyes. They looked at each other, popped grubs into their mouths, and then stopped chewing as sour looks came to both their faces at once.

"They were a lot better when we were reptiles," Boro admitted as he bravely swallowed what he had already chewed.

Sata nodded. "Shall we . . . go find some fruit?"

"Yeah!"

Although Mati's knees could now handle a little careful dancing, she and Rini seemed happiest when snuggling close together on a small couch. Thoughts and secrets passed between them that no ears could catch.

If we had stayed reptiles, I would have missed the music, Rini shared.

I think the reptiles — at least the little group that's here now — will soon have music, Mati responded. *They're up on the fourth balcony with Kerloran, listening and watching. How could anyone hear the music of Nebador and not want to make their own music?*

Rini nodded, then noticed his two shipmates at the snack tables. *I think Boro and Sata are ready to . . . you know . . . hold each other.*

Mati followed Rini's eyes. Their friends had plates of food, but had stopped to share a long kiss. *I think Boro had to make promises about that, for Sata to avoid mating with anyone who wanted her, on about the first day of the Great Transformation.*

Rini chuckled.

Kibi and Ilika were enjoying a circle dance with a half-dozen large avians when four of the birds' mission collars chimed. The four danced their way toward a corridor. The two monkey mammals and two remaining birds tightened the circle and picked up the lively beat of the song.

When the piece ended with a flurry of notes from a spider's keyboard, the captain and steward bowed to the two avians and wandered over to the food and drink tables.

Kibi selected a cold, fruity beverage and took a long pull to wet her throat. "When we first arrived, I thought I'd never get used to all the different kinds of people. Now the usual Satamia types seem pretty mild compared to the strange creatures from far away."

Ilika looked at his lover and grinned. "You haven't seen *anything* yet!"

* * *

"Rules are necessary for intelligent people, but as we approach wisdom, we learn they must often be broken." If this makes sense to you, then you are most likely on the path to learning wisdom.

"People who break rules without awareness are just simple mortals stumbling through life. We love them, but they cannot work in the Nebador Services." Advanced students: Does this shed light on how the situation in the first note for chapter 39 might be possible?

Young people (for whom these stories are primarily written) have a unique contribution during times of great change: they can think more flexibly than adults, take greater risks, and form new relationships more easily. At certain point in our history, changes come so hard and fast that adults can be overwhelmed. At these times, young adults and older children can make the difference between survival and extinction. There are signs that one of those points in history might be approaching.

“Every one of those rules was written with blood” was a saying of my favorite FAA pilot examiner. He meant that for every rule in the 2-inch thick Federal Aviation Regulations book, there’s a wrecked airplane, and one or more graves, somewhere.

If your resume isn’t quite as long as Mati’s yet, have no fear. If you learn all you can from everything you do, opportunities for experience will present themselves. At times (like with “crippled slave”) you will not like the opportunities, but those that cannot be avoided will always teach you something if you have your eyes and ears open.

Why would Melorania not want Rini to do Psychic Development training until Mati had completed hers?

Our religions are formed from a mixture of revelation and evolution, in other words, a mixture of what the universe gives us (or lets us glimpse), and what we add to it from our own cultures. This can be seen in the differences between Theravada Buddhism and Mahayana Buddhism. Theravada, to this day, is relatively simple and “plain.” Mahayana, however, moved into Tibet, and incorporated the colorful culture and the pre-existing Bon religion. Another example is the Book of Revelation in the Christian Bible. In itself, it is believed to be a vision of heavenly and future things. Our commentaries and interpretations of it, if collected in one place, would fill a large library.

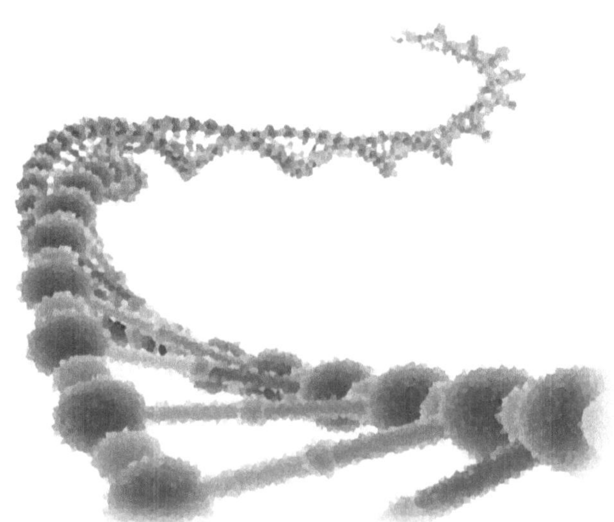

Chapter 42: The Search

Finding a jungle home for their reptilian friends wasn't quite as easy as Mati had imagined. She thought they could just be loaded into a transport ship and delivered to a jungle on her home planet.

Instead, she and her shipmates were invited to observe a much more complex process. Scientists began huddling around knowledge processors and combing through the hundreds of planets in Satamia with a tropical rain forest — a jungle. Twisted molecules glowed on big screens as the biochemical signatures of the planets were compared with that of the homeless reptiles. Simulations allowed the molecules to interact. Many Nebador citizens of flesh and blood discussed the results with each other and with the mysterious beings of color and light who came and went. Eventually, after nearly two Satamia days of work, many planets were eliminated, including, to Mati's disappointment, her own Sonmatia Three.

Silmula Sorafax explained that on those planets, the reptiles simply couldn't eat anything. Every insect grub, every mushroom, and every piece of fruit would be, at best, empty fiber without nutrition, and at worst, poison.

The specialists turned their attention to the hundred or so planets that had, in theory, a biochemical design that would allow the homeless reptiles to become part of the ecosystem.

Mati, Sata, Rini, and Boro were encouraged to recall any further details about their reptilian dreams. Birds listened, ursines took notes, and fuzzy balls of light observed.

Boro became very frustrated. Nothing was happening that he could sink his teeth into. "Watch, listen, and learn," Silmula Sorafax coaxed. Boro tried, but it wasn't easy. He even started to wish for a simple cargo run, but the Manessa Kwi remained at dock, while every other crew on the station, it seemed, was busy.

Finally, to Boro's relief, after another Satamia day of work by the scientists, the lists came out. The Manessa Kwi and Drrrim-na's life-monitor ship, the Tirilana Kril, were going to work.

✷

Four biochemists — reptile, arachnid, fanator, and ursine — each with an assistant, gave Kibi eight passengers to look after. They set to work with knowledge pads at Manessa's big table, long before the crew had the ship ready.

Kibi felt a little nervous at first, but the guests soon proved they could take care of themselves and stay out of the way. Seeing that Ilika was on the bridge, working with Sata on a flight plan that would take them to twenty different worlds, Kibi relaxed and strode through the hatch to get the supplies she needed.

She slapped hands with Boro in the waiting room as he guided a pallet of fuel canisters toward the boarding tunnel.

Mati and Rini emerged from the medical center, the pilot wearing an especially big smile. *Did you see how short my no-no list is getting? I'm so happy!*

I bet Boro and Sata will take us swimming after we get the lizards re-settled.

Yeah! Let's head for the ship. I need to review docking tunnel rules. It's been a while.

And I have to replace a sensor crystal before we go. It should be on the pallet with Boro's fuel.

✷

Finally, about two hours later, the steward declared the ship stocked and ready, the navigator sent the flight plan to the pilot, and the docking controller cleared them for departure. The Tirilana Kril, with six scientists, their assistants, and thirty worlds to visit, would soon follow.

Ilika smiled with pride when all his crew members quickly relaxed and cleared their minds for the first star transit.

✷

The crew of the Manessa Kwi settled into a routine that lasted an entire Satamia day. Ilika rotated station assignments, with Kibi sometimes covering watch, Boro taking navigation on easy flight legs, and Sata piloting during non-critical maneuvers. Ilika would cover one or two stations, and send a couple of crew members below for sleep, baths, or play, as they needed.

At each planet, after locating a tropical rain forest, the huge bird and her assistant took wing with plenty of sample bags, the lizard and bear explored on foot, if safe, and the spider crept into dark places, returning with bags of mushrooms and grubs.

When walking around was not safe, Kibi extended a small porch and the scientists picked fruit from trees and vines while Manessa hovered.

Every sample bag was carefully labeled and placed into temperature-controlled boxes in the rear of the passenger area.

As soon as each specialist's task was completed on a planet, they would curl up in a passenger seat for a nap before arriving at the next planet.

The five crew members from a medieval world paid close attention to how real Nebador citizens did their work on a real mission. They all knew that little cargo runs were easy, but they guessed that someday their missions would be much more challenging.

*

When the ship arrived back at the star station, the scientists and their helpers guided the pallet of sample boxes toward the laboratory, and Silmula Sorafax greeted the crew with a serious look in her eyes. "I have to talk to you about the next step, so you will all . . . be prepared for what might happen."

They followed the cat to a small conference room.

"Eight years ago, the sapient reptiles' population was two thousand one hundred and forty-three, and very slowly, year by year, dropping by two or three — hardly enough for them to notice — as the climate grew hotter and drier.

"When their star began to experience rapid shifts in mass and gravity, all of the planets of the system were affected. As tremors and earthquakes caused their caverns to collapse, most of the reptiles died. When our ships arrived, less than a day later, only one group of three hundred and twenty-five could be found, wandering in the desert, dazed, confused, and hungry. We put them to sleep, brought them into our ships, and collected every plant and animal we could find that might be important to their survival.

"When Mati took pity on them and left an access door open . . ."

The pilot closed her eyes for a moment, took a deep breath, and wondered what she had been thinking.

". . . the lizards' population was down to two hundred and seventy-five, mostly because the birth rate is nearly zero. Four of you understand why, even better than I do. Today the population stands at two hundred and forty-seven. At this rate, they will be unable to function as a society in a year or two, and completely extinct in less than a decade."

Sata made a slight whimpering sound, and Boro put his arm around her.

"With the help of what you learned in the Great Transformation, our scientists began using every possible tool to find our friends a new home. Many planets, as you know, were removed from the list because we could predict the biochemical reactions. Now, with the instrument readings and samples you and the Tirilana Kril brought back, we will be able to eliminate many more planets. That work will begin immediately, and proceed as quickly as possible.

"But I must prepare you for the final phase of the search, for it will probably cause you some grief. Not all biochemical problems can be detected in the laboratory. Before a planet is selected, we will have to offer its possible foods to your reptile friends. They will be able to eliminate some by taste and smell, of course, but not all. Some of the reptiles will probably get sick, and we will care for them as best we can. A few may die."

Boro's hand shot into the air. "I think you should offer stuff to the big group first, you know, the thick-headed adults."

Silmula Sorafax cracked a slight smile.

✷

The scientists on the two ships had been able to eliminate almost half the possible planets from their instrument readings and observations in the field. Once the samples were analyzed in the laboratory at Satamia Star Station, another fifteen worlds dropped away. Eleven remained.

The females of the simulated desert environment chatted happily as they gathered cactus fruit. An egg had hatched that morning, bringing new hope for the future to their hearts. One cactus they came to bore a strange fruit they had not seen before. An elder female sniffed it, found it sweet, and took a bite. She moaned in pain as her stomach twisted and she vomited the fruit, and everything else she had eaten that morning, back onto the sand.

Eight planets remained.

A large male looked at the gourd full of grubs he was handed, big and juicy, but a slightly different color than usual. He found them quite delicious so he ate them all, got a drink, and curled up for a nap. His strange dreams faded into a darkness from which he never awoke.

The list shrank to seven planets.

A new mushroom appeared in the supply cave, right next to those for *shmur*, and of a similar color. A young male, newly arrived at manhood and looking for a mate, grabbed a claw-full of mushrooms and the other ingredients he needed. An hour later, he and his friends began drinking the heady brew and rolling the bones. But unlike the usual evening laughter and harmless wrestling, they were all soon fighting to the death and had to be separated and restrained by older males.

Another planet was crossed off.

✷

The following day, simulated desert environment time, Boro and Sata joined a scientist at an observation window. Two half-grown lizards sniffed at some fruit they didn't recognize.

Sata frowned. "Even though they're not in the group of kids who visited the star station, I hope they don't get sick."

Suddenly both reptilian youth turned around, backed up, and peed all over the new fruit, then walked away.

Boro and Sata rolled with laughter, and the bird taking notes honked and flapped his wings.

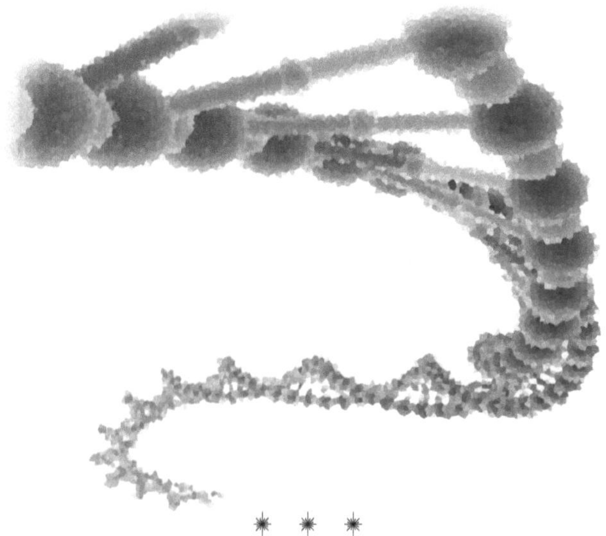

* * *

As far as we know from observation through light and radio telescopes, the entire universe is composed of the same stuff we have here on our planet and in our sun:
- 82 elements that have stable forms, and their isotopes.
- a few heaver elements that do not have stable forms.
- electromagnetic energy that ranges from very low frequency radio waves to very high frequency "cosmic rays" (and includes, in the middle, visible light).
- a handful of mysterious energy particles, such as neutrinos, that we know little about.

But when it comes to the composition and structure of living things, we have only one sample: life on Earth. Life here uses 30-40 of the stable elements, but the vast bulk of it is Oxygen, Carbon, Hydrogen, Nitrogen, Calcium, Phosphorous, Potassium, Sulfur, and Sodium.

The "trace" elements that seem to be necessary for most living things, in small amounts, are Magnesium, Copper, Zinc, Selenium, Molybdenum, Fluorine, Chlorine, Iodine, Manganese, Cobalt, Iron, Lithium, Silicon, Vanadium, Arsenic, Bromine, Chromium, and Tungsten.

A few other elements may only be necessary for life in extremely small amounts, or only for certain species. These include Aluminum, Strontium, Bromine, Gold, Silver, Lead, Cadmium, Tin, Germanium, and Boron.

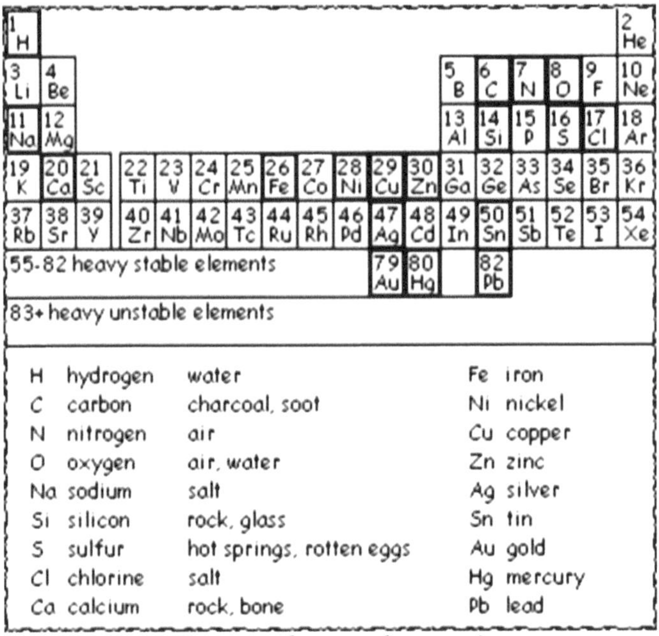

1 H																	2 He
3 Li	4 Be											5 B	6 C	7 N	8 O	9 F	10 Ne
11 Na	12 Mg											13 Al	14 Si	15 P	16 S	17 Cl	18 Ar
19 K	20 Ca	21 Sc	22 Ti	23 V	24 Cr	25 Mn	26 Fe	27 Co	28 Ni	29 Cu	30 Zn	31 Ga	32 Ge	33 As	34 Se	35 Br	36 Kr
37 Rb	38 Sr	39 Y	40 Zr	41 Nb	42 Mo	43 Tc	44 Ru	45 Rh	46 Pd	47 Ag	48 Cd	49 In	50 Sn	51 Sb	52 Te	53 I	54 Xe
55-82 heavy stable elements										79 Au	80 Hg		82 Pb				
83+ heavy unstable elements																	

H	hydrogen	water	Fe	iron
C	carbon	charcoal, soot	Ni	nickel
N	nitrogen	air	Cu	copper
O	oxygen	air, water	Zn	zinc
Na	sodium	salt	Ag	silver
Si	silicon	rock, glass	Sn	tin
S	sulfur	hot springs, rotten eggs	Au	gold
Cl	chlorine	salt	Hg	mercury
Ca	calcium	rock, bone	Pb	lead

(from *Book Two*, chapter 7)

We often call life on Earth "carbon-based" because Carbon is the most common element in life that is not common in non-living things. Oxygen is the most abundant element in living things, but it is also abundant everywhere else, such as in the atmosphere.

We have a fossil of a bacteria-like microbe that we believe came from the planet Mars, but no other information about life on other planets yet. This leaves open the possibility that life elsewhere may have a different chemistry than on Earth.

The essential structure of life on Earth is based on sugars (glucose, sucrose, lactose, etc.), amino acids (in proteins and enzymes), and ribonucleic acid (RNA, DNA, and similar long-chain molecules that can encode genetic information). We know so little about how this arrangement came to be that arguing about "evolution" and "creation" reveals a great deal about our egos, and very little about the origins of our biochemistry.

Chapter 43: Re-settlement

The fruits, grubs, and mushrooms of only three planets were offered to the eleven youth and two adults of the special group. Unlike the main group, these thirteen knew what was happening.

Kerloran, in his bright-green lizard form, divided them into four groups, three reptiles at each of the three trays of food, the other two receiving the grubs and cactus fruit from their original home.

They knew the same foods had already been consumed, with no ill effects, by the main group. They looked at each other, sensed the importance of the moment, and started eating.

*

The scientists and specialists took another Satamia day to make sure no biochemical surprises lurked in the complex molecules of lizards, insect grubs, jungle fruits, or rain forest mushrooms. Even on the three planets that looked best, there were many things the reptiles could not eat. The scientists just had to be sure there were many things they *could* eat.

The Great Transformation briefing team, the crew of the Manessa Kwi, and the crew of the Palantia Lisa, a large passenger transport ship, were all summoned to a conference room. Visiting students squeezed in wherever they could.

With neither Kerloran nor Melorania present, Silmula Sorafax trembled inside, knowing the huge responsibility she bore. After a slow, deep breath, she leapt onto a table at the front of the room. Everyone fell silent.

“Our beloved Kerloran is very pleased with the course of events that have brought us to this point . . . as am I.”

The room erupted with cheering and clapping, then respectful silence returned.

“Our reptilian charges, whom we know much better now after the mischief of a certain monkey-mammal pilot . . .”

Mati grinned with embarrassment as others chuckled or honked.

"... will be re-settled on all three of the planets that can sustain them. On one, a sapient equine race lives in the temperate zone, and they will someday interact. On another, a global avian race is already highly sapient. The reptiles will grow in their shadow, and hopefully someday learn wisdom from them."

Many heads nodded and sounds of approval rippled through the room.

"The planet with no sapient life will be given to the small group who befriended our dear monkey mammals, and have seen a star station. They will, most likely, become the dominant form of life on the planet, and we will watch over them closely as they grow."

The room broke into cheering again as wings flapped and feet stomped.

"Captain Kam'rrral-ta?"

A large bird stood.

"Two hundred and thirty-one sleeping reptiles, and their meager belongings, will be delivered to the Palantia Lisa later today. Please prepare your ship. You will have two destinations, and a Local Universe Guardian will accompany you to protect your passengers from the effects of star transit."

The captain nodded and reached for the knowledge pad at her side.

"Captain Imni?"

Ilika stood.

"You have the honor — or problem, I'm not sure which — of transporting two adults and eleven youth, with their eyes wide open and their claws *itching* to touch everything."

The room filled with laughter and Ilika smiled. "I think we can handle it."

"Just remember," the large cat warned, "even the children have tail spikes."

Boro grinned knowingly.

✷

Kibi was relieved when Kerloran stepped into the Manessa Kwi with the thirteen passengers following behind. She knew that if anyone could keep them in line, he could.

But she quickly frowned when one of the youngest reptiles hopped into the steward's chair and began pounding on her console. She glanced at Kerloran, but he only returned her glance with smiling eyes.

She sighed, tapped the sleep code into her bracelet, and gathered the limp lizard child into her arms. "Please translate for me, Kerloran. If anyone wants to be *awake* during the journey to your new home, you will sit in your seats *calmly*, unless you are using the toilet."

The master of Satamia Star Station nodded his approval, then repeated the gist of Kibi's warning in sounds the passengers could understand.

They settled a little, but still wiggled with excitement. Then Kibi brought out her secret weapon.

As soon as the video of jungle sights and sounds began on the large screen over the steward's station, all twelve reptiles who were still awake, from the youngest to the two adults, sat completely still and stared. Somehow, their dreams were playing before their very eyes.

Kerloran smiled, and Kibi went through the passenger area securing inertia straps, even though the flight was expected to be completely smooth.

*

With all his crew members at their primary stations, Ilika hardly had to say a word.

"Flight plan is on channel five. Satamia Control, Manessa Kwi at dock C-Eleven requests station departure."

"Manessa Kwi, you are cleared on the orange path to inner marker B."

"I need anti-mass one and maneuvering thrusters, please."

"All engines green. Plenty of fuel."

"Hatch closed, boarding tunnel away, ship and passengers secured for flight."

"Sensors active. No unusual energy signatures. Visuals on channel four."

As the crew fell silent and Mati piloted the ship through the docking tunnel, she had a moment of fright. Something was missing — something that had always been near, leaning on the console beside her, ready whenever she needed it.

It's in your cabin. I could go get it for you if you want . . . Rini silently offered.

Mati, still guiding the ship along the orange line, took some deep breaths to settle her nerves. *That would be pretty silly.*

The freckled young man at the watch station smiled.

A quarter hour later, Kerloran protected all thirteen reptiles from the effects of star transit. None of them noticed the twenty-second nap they took while gazing at dripping leaves, buzzing insects, and sprouting mushrooms.

The crew of the Manessa Kwi had to take care of themselves.

*

Once back in space and time, Kerloran asked Kibi to switch to a view of the planet they were approaching.

Most of the young reptiles gasped and hissed.

"This is what a world looks like," Kerloran began in the reptilian tongue. "You will not see it again, from a distance, for many long ages. It has everything you need, but it is also very much alone. We place it in your hands, as there are no other creatures here who can grow in knowledge and power, as you can. You will make many mistakes. They are yours to make, and yours to fix. We will watch over you, but not help you solve the problems you create.

"Someday, if your children of many hatchings become noble and wise, they will visit star stations again, walk and talk with us, and help with the work of the universe. Until then, you must follow your hearts."

Kerloran, however, would not allow the passengers to see the ship's planetary approach. Kibi switched the big screen back to the jungle video, but happened to glance at her console just as the surface zoomed toward them. Suddenly the view froze as Mati stopped the ship at four thousand meters. Kibi swallowed and remembered how frightening that had once seemed, not so very long ago.

"Finished with ion drive," the pilot said calmly. "Maneuvering thrusters, please."

A few minutes later, the Manessa Kwi settled into a small clearing in the jungle. Mists lurked about in the trees, birds called to each other in curious voices, and a small waterfall splashed into a crystal-clear pool. Two dark cave entrances stood nearby.

As soon a Kibi opened the hatch and extended the ramp, Kerloran strode out and the thirteen passengers followed. They looked around with wide eyes and open mouths, anxious to explore, reluctant to leave the safety of the ship.

The crew watched from the top of the ramp.

"Although you do not really need them anymore," the tall, bright-green lizard declared with throaty sounds, "we knew you would find comfort in caves. But unlike the dry, dusty, desert caves of your recent memories, these caves already contain other creatures, some of whom may not want to share."

Eyes swirled with determination, mouths snapped, and spiked tails swung back and forth to show Kerloran they were up to the challenge.

"I will remain here for seven days, so that you may share, if you wish, your stories as you begin to explore your new home."

After speaking those words, the master of Satamia Star Station curled up at the foot of the ramp as if to take a nap.

*

For the remainder of that day, the youngest reptiles hardly dared leave the clearing, until the two adults and the older youth returned with stories of tasty fruit and juicy grubs. But by nightfall, all thirteen were back to tell Kerloran their stories, ask questions, gaze up at the passing moons, and eventually sleep.

On the second day, the caves were carefully explored, and indeed many spiders and snakes already dwelled within. The spiders were shy and willing to share. The snakes retreated to smaller caves after learning their fangs could not penetrate lizard hides, and after feeling tail spikes that easily pierced snakeskin. The thirteen returned to the clearing, as evening fell, to tell Kerloran of their adventures and ask him questions about spiders and snakes.

During the third day, Kerloran saw his charges often, and heard of fruits that made them sick and mushrooms that made their heads spin. As evening gathered once again, only the children returned to the clearing to sleep near him.

The following day, with no real reptiles in sight, Ilika allowed the crew to stretch their legs and gather tropical fruit. About noon, Kerloran shooed them all back into the ship, and soon the reptiles appeared, telling of a cave with fingers of rock on the floor and ceiling, pools of delicious water, and dry nooks for sleeping. After another visit from his charges as the sun prepared to set, Kerloran slept alone that night.

The fifth day brought a few scattered visitors, sharing that the older youth had dared to climb high into trees where they found insect nests with huge, tasty grubs, and all the fruit they could ever want. But the evening was quiet, with only monkey mammals to keep Kerloran company.

Only two reptiles visited the clearing on the sixth day. The two adults announced shyly but proudly that soon eggs would be laid and babies hatched. After sharing their news, the pair returned to the edge of the jungle, but glanced back at the bright-green lizard of great power and wisdom who had brought them to their new home, and the mammals behind who did his bidding. Then they scampered away in search of grubs.

All during the seventh day, the tropical mists lurked through the trees, insects buzzed, and birds called. No one came to tell him stories or ask him questions, so Kerloran rested.

* * *

When the foods of 3 planets were finally offered to the special group of mostly-young reptiles, they were divided into 4 groups because any experiment needs a "control" group, a group that does not experience anything different from normal, to have something to compare the other groups to.

How might the results of the "experiment" be changed because they "knew what was happening"? If this is a weakness in the "experiment," why do you think Kerloran told them?

How could 3 + 3 + 3 + 2 = 13?

What qualities did Silmula Sorafax have that allowed her to lead the final meeting before the re-settlement (without Kerloran or Melorania present)?

The "temperate zone" is the band of latitudes, both north and south of the equator, between the wet and warm tropics, and the boreal forests and tundras that approach the artic regions. The continental USA and most of Europe lie in the temperate zone, and in the southern hemisphere, Argentina, South Africa, and Australia.

If you were one of the homeless reptiles, which would you prefer: sapient horses on another part of the planet, sapient birds everywhere, or the planet to yourselves?

Kibi's use of a jungle video to calm her passengers is based on an Earth tradition that began in the 1950s: one of the first nicknames for television was "electronic babysitter."

Can you tell which crew member is saying what as they begin the flight?

Do you have anything you would "freak out" without? Eye glasses? Medicine? Mobile phone? How long could you live without each thing?

We have many images on Earth, made by people from our distant past, that appear to be of things we shouldn't have been able to see or know about until much later. Some can only be seen from high above the ground. Others are of ships in the air, or people operating ships, or people wearing suits that we use today only in space or deep-sea diving. What purpose do you think these "anomalies" (things that don't fit) serve in our society? What do you think the lizards in the story will do with their memories of their new planet as seen from space?

Kerloran tells the reptiles that they will make many mistakes, and that those mistakes are theirs to make, and theirs to fix. Today, our problems are larger and more complex than ever before, and include a trembling economy, wars and other political conflicts, and climate changes that could overshadow all else. Many people believe science, God, or aliens will save us. What do you think?

Why did Kerloran not allow the lizards to see the planetary approach? What tends to happen to humans when they witness a rapid approach to a solid surface?

What myth (story to explain what we do not fully understand) do you think will be told (and someday written) by the reptiles about the first seven days on their new planet?

Chapter 44: Unfinished Business

When the crew of the Manessa Kwi arrived back at Satamia Star Station, most of the visiting students had departed, and the simulated desert environment was in the process of being cleaned. Silmula Sorafax, the briefing team, and the six humans gathered in a conference room and listened for hours as the specialists and the crew of the Palantia Lisa shared stories from the re-settlement of the other two groups.

When the others finally wandered away, the large white cat looked at the four monkey mammals who had lived, for several Satamia days, as sapient reptiles. “Even though it feels like this project is complete, it has just entered a new phase that will stretch on for thousands of years. Non-material beings will watch over the reptiles constantly, and several times a year, a ship will visit the three planets to see how they are doing. For the rest of our lives, I, and you four, will be part of that process. As long as you are all together on the Manessa Kwi, it will probably be the ship assigned to make those visits.”

“I must admit,” Boro began with a slight smile, “I’ll be curious to see – from a safe distance, of course – what kind of world they make for themselves.”

The large cat curled her lips and nodded. “And Mati now begins Psychic Development training.”

The pilot cringed slightly.

“Kibi can show you the way, but it is best, Kibi, to not attempt to describe the experience, as it is different for each person. Boro’s introductory class, for example, was disguised as juggling lessons, and Sata began the process by joining a dance troop.”

Boro’s mouth opened with surprise for a moment, then changed to a knowing smile. Sata just stared with wide, curious eyes.

“Perhaps both of you will someday choose to go through the whole program. I do not know. For now, farewell. I will see you in the station often, and occasionally on missions." The large cat brought her mouth to each of their necks and gave them a lick. She saved Kibi for last, and made it especially wet. Then she walked out of the room.

*

Life on Satamia Star Station began to settle down for the crew of the Manessa Kwi, as much as life can ever settle down for members of the Transport Service who are always on call for whatever universe work might arise.

Kibi returned to her training, and a day later, Mati stepped into the simple doorway beyond the little bubbling fountain. Sata returned to her dance troop with a new light in her eyes and more passion in her movements than ever before. Boro introduced Rini and Mati to the joys of swimming and fishing in the underwater world beneath the halls and balconies of the star station.

Ilika and Kibi worked with Melorania to plan the lessons and cross-training that each crew member needed, and the types of missions that would best build their knowledge and skills. They agreed that the little ship was ready to move beyond simple cargo runs, but the head of the Transport Service didn't yet say what she had in mind.

*

Two slender monkey mammals strolled, hand in hand, along the first balcony overlooking Green Hall. A chuckle would occasionally come from one or the other, even though no spoken words passed between them.

Suddenly Rini recognized the place he had been looking for. Leaves of the great station tree shielded a small bench from view, so he steered Mati toward it.

Mati knew something was up, but Rini carefully hid his intentions in a corner of his mind. She sat down and couldn't help but smile.

Rini didn't sit. Instead he went to his knees in front of her and pulled a small box from his pocket. He opened it to reveal a tiny pastry, good for two bites at the most.

Mati laughed deeply as she relived the bitter-sweet memory of watching Rini accidentally marry a desert girl.

He waited until she recovered from her laughter and dried her tears. *I once made a big mistake*, he began, *and I did my best to fix it. Back on Sonmatia Seven, you asked me to marry you, but then things got really busy.*

Mati grinned. *Really, really busy!*

If you're still interested, I think we can find the time now, he continued, offering her the pastry.

She took a bite, then placed the other half in Rini's mouth. *Let me think* . . . she pondered for him to hear, *I have to meditate with some bears this afternoon, then I'm helping to put up decorations for the party . . . yeah, I think we can squeeze it in.*

Rini chuckled, then joined Mati on the bench. *Only problem is, I don't know how they do it here.*

Mati pulled a knowledge pad from her pocket and touched a key. "Who do we talk to about getting married?"

A map appeared on the screen. *Blue Hall, balcony two,* she silently shared.

The pair hopped up and strode toward a ramp with purpose and determination in every step they took.

✷

The glowing purple ball of light listened to Mati and Rini describe their desire to be married. It overheard the unspoken thoughts that passed between them, and peered into their memories of childhood, slavery, test, journey, and selection. Finally, it scanned the universe records of their service on the Manessa Kwi, including the recent Great Transformation they endured together.

"I see the problem," the being of color and light said when the two monkey mammals had said all they could think of to say. "Because of the culture into which you were born, you conceive of marriage as something that someone else does *to* you — a priest, whatever that is. I'm sorry, but you are about as married as any two creatures can be. What you really want to know, it seems to me, is how you can *celebrate* your marriage, and share your happiness with the citizens of Nebador. Am I not correct?"

Rini and Mati looked at each other. Several thoughts passed between them before Mati spoke. "And . . . we want to know . . . that our marriage won't be a problem for anyone . . . and if it ever is . . . they'll tell us and . . . you know . . . help us fix it . . ."

"You can assume all that," the glowing purple light assured. "Your captain watches over you, as do your other teachers and trainers. Melorania and Kerloran, and others even greater, know what is in your hearts at all times."

After a long silence, Mati and Rini both nodded. "So . . . how can we . . . celebrate?" Rini asked.

"There's a very creative equine who's in charge of the party this evening. Let's go talk to him, shall we?"

✷

After a long day of excitement that included the successful completion of the reptile re-settlement mission, the Satamia sun once again began to set relative to the star station's main hall. Ilika and Kibi wandered up from the ship after checking the galley stocks. They didn't see any of their other crew members anywhere.

Kibi looked worried, but Ilika grabbed her and pulled her toward one of the kitchens that obviously needed help carrying food out to the tables. "They've earned our trust, and both relationships are deepening after their recent experiences. We can always find them with their bracelets if we really need them."

Kibi let out a long breath. "You're right. Mati said she'd be hanging decorations. I'm just so used to her hobbling along on a crutch . . ."

"I bet she'll be dancing tonight!"

Kibi smiled. "I will be, too!"

They helped birds and reptiles push carts and carry trays for half an hour, then found a bench where they could snuggle close together as brilliant music announced the star station's evening party. But for some reason, the dance floor remained closed, roped off by a blue cord. People gathered on couches, benches, and perches, or just floated on the surface of the large pool, hundreds of sparkling eyes wondering what surprise might be in store.

The first song ended, and an ursine drummer took up a slow, steady beat as a spotlight found a slender female monkey mammal riding on the back of a large golden equine. Horse and human approached the dance floor, and long legs easily stepped over the ribbon.

The human slid off the sleek golden fur, but instead of standing, crumpled to the ground. The audience gasped. A spider stepped forward and handed her an old, tattered crutch.

Kibi and Ilika looked at each other, both grinning.

The horse walked away, and with dramatic effort, the girl got to her feet and stood alone.

Suddenly another musician plunged furry fingers into his keyboard, just as a fanator swooped into the main hall and circled, a slender human boy riding. Huge wings beat the air and sent leaves fluttering and decorations swinging as the giant bird brought itself and its passenger to a halt just above the dance floor, then settled with strong webbed feet right in front of the girl and her crutch.

Kibi put her arm around Ilika as they continued to watch.

The boy stepped down clumsily, clearly not used to riding, and the audience chuckled. The fanator departed, and the boy bowed to the girl, who pretended to be embarrassed and shy.

Just then a large monkey mammal, wearing crude wool clothing, stepped onto the dance floor. He grabbed the girl and started pulling her away. A musician somewhere added tense, dramatic music.

The slender boy stood alone with sad, downcast eyes.

The girl suddenly lifted her crutch and started swinging at the large man. He cowered and backed away, and the girl ran into the boy's waiting arms.

The audience cheered and honked with happiness, but fell silent when another human girl, dressed in a flowing green gown, danced toward them with seductive movements. She hid her face with a long green scarf as she coyly took the boy's hand, causing him to forget, it seemed, all about the girl he had just embraced. In a trance, he joined in her sensuous dance and followed her.

The audience moaned and screeched with anger.

The music changed to a fast and anxious rhythm as the boy shook himself out of the trance, planted his feet, and crossed his arms.

The audience cheered and the seductive girl danced away, even as the boy returned to the girl's arms. They took hands and bowed in several directions to the many creatures around them.

When the room finally fell silent, the girl spoke. “I am Mati, a simple monkey mammal from a backward little world called Sonmatia Three. I am honored to be the pilot of the Manessa Kwi, and happy beyond words to tell all of you that I *love* this freckled boy, and will be his girl as long as I have life.”

The hundreds of Nebador citizens in the room roared and squawked with approval.

“I am Rini, same backward little planet.”

Chuckles rippled through the huge room.

“I was a slave, and now I am Manessa’s watch. I love this girl, and will be her boy as long as she will have me.”

The audience roared with approval, and on cue, the musicians began a slow, intimate song. The two slender youth began to dance, alone on the dance floor, together in the limelight. Their timid, clumsy movements brought smiles to many watchers, who waited silently outside the blue cord.

When the first dance ended, the pair of monkey mammals bowed, helpers quickly removed the cord, and dozens of creatures headed for the dance floor.

As thrilled as Mati was to be sharing her marriage with all the people of Satamia Star Station, her knee soon yelled at her to slow down and spend time on a cozy couch. Many creatures came by to congratulate the couple, and often they carried baskets or trays from the snack tables.

Silmula Sorafax and Toran Takil appeared about an hour later. They sat side by side on the floor in front of the couch, which placed their heads at the same level as Mati’s and Rini’s.

“You two are married, aren’t you?” Mati inquired.

“Yes,” the female cat said with glowing eyes. “And there are forms of marriage that go beyond mortal life, beyond what most people call marriage.”

“You two have such a bond,” Toran Takil began, “because of your mental link. We have another type that will, if we are strong and true, survive death.”

Rini and Mati sat silently, pondering what the large cats had just shared, and looking into their beautiful feline eyes. Mati looked mostly at Toran Takil, and could feel her heart beating faster and her skin becoming hot.

Boro appeared. “Sata’s in a circle dance with some reptiles. May I dance with my pilot?”

Mati quickly hopped up, glad for a reason to break the male cat’s spell.

Rini smiled, having easily seen and felt Mati’s reaction to Toran Takil. As soon as Boro and Mati were gone, he turned back to the cats. “I have a funny question.”

The cats' ears twitched as they looked at him.

"Why do I get the feeling that . . . Kerloran and Melorania knew, all along, that the homeless reptiles needed a jungle?"

Toran Takil looked at his mate with a sparkle in his eyes.

"Of course they did," the female cat answered. "It is not the purpose of the universe to get things done as quickly and efficiently as possible. That's a mortal preoccupation, especially strong in monkey mammals, but we all feel it to one degree or another. The purpose of the universe is experience and personal growth. If Melorania, Kerloran, and others like them, just did everything without helpers like us, none of the citizens of Nebador would get any training. Small minds with a little knowledge and power try to keep it to themselves. Real wisdom is for sharing."

Rini nodded thoughtfully.

Boro and Mati soon returned from the dance floor, and a moment later Sata appeared, nearly out of breath but smiling.

Toran Takil touched Silmula on the shoulder, and they bowed and slipped away.

A minute later, Ilika and Kibi wandered over, arms around each other.

Kibi looked at Mati and Rini. "You two have gotten us talking about marriage. We agree we're not as ready as you, but we're thinking about it."

Boro exchanged looks of understanding with his captain, and Sata grinned at Kibi.

Mati danced whenever the music moved her, but also listened to her new muscles and joints, and often found a couch where she could snuggle with her beloved Rini. More creatures wished them well in their marriage, and sometimes left invitations to eat or play together.

Kibi noticed the tenderness growing between Sata and Boro, and it made her even more determined to learn, along with everything else she was learning, how to be Ilika's faithful companion and lover.

Sata was on the dance floor almost constantly, with Boro, or anyone else who would dance with her. But her mind often recalled what Silmula Sorafax had said, that her dance training was just an introduction to something greater.

Boro could feel dreams and desires inside himself coming to the surface. As he watched Sata dance with some nimble-footed birds, he knew he was no longer too gentle for man's work or too clumsy for woman's work. By combining the two, he was just right.

Rini sensed he had become part of something bigger than anything he had ever imagined. Mati, the Manessa Kwi, and the homeless reptiles were all parts of it, but it stretched far out into the universe, farther than his mind could follow. He smiled, knowing he would just have to wait and see.

Ilika looked around at his solid engineer, his bright-eyed watch, his brave pilot, his young but rapidly growing navigator, and, longest of all, at his sweet steward. For perhaps the first time, he felt confident that they had all firmly planted their feet on the path to becoming citizens of Nebador.

After a few more songs, just as the crew of the Manessa Kwi was beginning to yawn and think about cozy beds in their cabins, all six mission bracelets chimed.

They looked at each other and laughed.

* * * * *

We humans of planet Earth have no experience with projects that can "stretch on for thousands of years." Rome can claim more than a thousand years of history from its founding to its fall (-753 to +476, not counting Byzantium), but that history was divided into three major periods (monarchy, republic, and empire). Most leaders had their own priorities, and often ignored, or completely undid, the accomplishments of previous leaders. Some of our most durable architecture survives the millennia, but rarely in a usable form; an exception is St. Peter's Basilica in Rome, with wooden trusses that have been under stress for more than a thousand years, but only because the building has received constant care and maintenance. Our most recent building spurt, during the 20th century, will probably not leave much of enduring value, as it was all built with the assumption that electricity would be cheap and plentiful. Any building over about 4 stories tall becomes uninhabitable without electricity for heating, cooling, ventilation, water pressure, and elevators.

A few of our stories survive the millennia. We still read and love Homer's

Iliad and *Odyssey*, written more than 2500 years ago. But much did not survive, such as the contents of the ancient library of Alexandria, Egypt. Medieval monks labored for centuries to copy fading manuscripts, and they saved much, but much more was lost between the Roman Empire (400s) and the Renaissance (1400s). Today, as we surf the internet, dead links often outnumber good ones, and we wonder what is being lost every day.

What qualities would a society need to have to realistically consider taking on projects that would "stretch on for thousands of years"?

It is calculated that we need to store the wastes from our nuclear power plants for about 25,000 years before they will be safe. What physical and organizational structures might make this possible?

Does it seem right that Nebador REQUIRES certain training programs and experiences for its people, and sometimes even disguises them as something else (like Boro's juggling lessons)? How is this different from slavery?

To some people, "marriage" is the forming of bonds and the making of commitments between two people. To others, it is a legal contract, and a ceremony in a church or temple with a priest of some kind. To most people, it is a combination of the two. Some people make the mistake of doing the legal contract and ceremony, but forget to build the personal bonds and commitments. Whether you once did in the past, or in the future hope to enter into such a relationship, what personal, legal, religious, or social elements do you think the event should have?

What differences can you see between those who "watch over" the people of Nebador (like Melorania and Kerloran), and those who "watch over" us in our society (bureaucrats, police, etc.)?

Who was the large monkey mammal wearing fuzzy material, and whom did he represent?

Who was the human girl wearing a flowing green gown, and whom did she represent? What meaning might the color green have in this situation?

The exchange of marriage vows parallels any social exchange, and sets it apart from all economic exchanges. If we both have cookies, I give one of mine to you, and you give one of yours to me, we both end up with the same economic value, and so the exchange was a waste of time economically. But socially we just established a deeper level of trust, and we might have started a friendship that will have great value to both of us in the future. In the case of marriage vows, I pledge life-long companionship and love to you, and you do the same to me. In your opinion, have we gained anything?

Advanced students: Although human religions vary widely in their concepts of "life after death," they have even less to tell us about "love after death." Assuming, for a moment, that marriage could survive death, several questions arise. How good would a marriage have to be to make the people in it WANT it to continue after death? Since "bread-winning" and "house-keeping" are probably not part of spirit life, what "job" would you want to have, and what "job" would you want your partner to have, in a spirit-life marriage? If a couple wanted their marriage to survive death, what should they do in their mortal-life marriage to prepare themselves?

Advanced students: "It is not the purpose of the universe to get things done as quickly and efficiently as possible. . . . The purpose of the universe is experience and personal growth." Which people and institutions in your society would agree with this idea? Which would disagree? Are the two purposes completely incompatible, or is there some overlap?

Advanced students: "If Melorania, Kerloran, and others like them, just did everything without helpers like us, none of the citizens of Nebador would get any training." This explains why deep-space response ships have a crew of six, while (using voice commands) they really only need a crew of one or two. What do you think would motivate powerful spiritual beings like Melorania and Kerloran to share universe work, instead of just doing it all themselves?

"Small minds with a little knowledge and power try to keep it to themselves. Real wisdom is for sharing." Have you met anyone who fits into the first category? The second category?

Why did Toran Takil "slip away" before Kibi returned to the couch?

For each of the six crew members of the Manessa Kwi (or just your favorite), what life-lessons have they recently learned? What life-lessons do you think they need to learn next?

Assuming their mission bracelets didn't chime during the dance party just for a simple cargo run, what kind of mission do you think they'll get?

Afterthoughts

As *Book Six: Star Station* is being published, *Book Seven: The Local Universe* has been written, *Book Eight: Witness* is about half-written, and *Book Nine* (not yet titled) has been "assigned." The Muse (or whatever you would like to call Her) is obviously not done with Nebador. And yet, this is a good time to pause. The essential Nebador story has been told, and most of the unanswered questions from the earlier books have been answered.

As I'm sure you know by now, this story isn't really science fiction. That genre has done the great service of hosting (and, in a sense, protecting) those stories that attempt to explore our place in the universe. Ideally, that would be the task of religion, but it isn't ready to take up that role yet. Perhaps it will be someday.

In the meantime, while waiting for *Book Seven* and beyond, the author invites all readers to dig deeper. The *Deep Learning Notes*, available both on the www.nebador.com internet site and in printed book form, are a good place to start.

But the most important "depth" can only be pursued in each of our lives, minute by minute, day by day. If the Nebador stories have anything to leave to the world, it's a glimpse of the difference between REALITY, and the many layers of assumptions and myths that most people live by. If, while reading these stories, you have experienced even a tiny peek beyond normal "monkey mammal" thinking, then you have set your feet on the path to "Nebador" (by whatever name).

Good journey to you!

J. Z. Colby
2012

About the Author

Born in the Mojave Desert, J. Z. Colby now lives and writes deep in a forest of the Pacific Northwest.

He has studied many subjects, formally and informally, including psychology, philosophy, education, and performing arts, but remains a generalist. His primary profession as a mental health counselor, specializing with families and young adults, gives him many stories of personal growth, and the motivation to develop his team of young critiquers and readers.

All his life, he has been drawn toward a broad understanding of human nature, especially those physical, emotional, mental, and spiritual situations in which our capacity to function seems to reach its limits. He finds fascinating those few individuals who can transcend the limits of our common human nature and the dictates of our cultures.

In his spare time, he flies helicopters and airplanes.

He may be contacted at the email address listed on the internet site www.nebador.com.

www.ingramcontent.com/pod-product-compliance
Lightning Source LLC
Chambersburg PA
CBHW030823310726
48980CB00006B/610/J

* 9 7 8 1 9 3 6 2 5 3 6 0 9 *